A
BLOODSMOOR
ROMANCE

OTHER BOOKS BY JOYCE CAROL OATES

NOVELS

Angel of Light
Bellefleur
Unholy Loves
Cybele
Son of the Morning
Childwold
The Assassins
Do With Me What You Will
Wonderland
them
Expensive People
A Garden of Earthly Delights
With Shuddering Fall

SHORT STORIES

A Sentimental Education
Night-Side
Crossing the Border
The Goddess and Other Women
Marriages and Infidelities
The Wheel of Love
Upon the Sweeping Flood
By the North Gate
The Hungry Ghosts
The Seduction
The Poisoned Kiss (Fernandes/Oates)

CRITICISM

Contraries
New Heaven, New Earth: The Visionary Experience in Literature
The Edge of Impossibility: Tragic Forms in Literature

PLAYS

Miracle Play
Three Plays

POEMS

Invisible Woman: New & Selected Poems 1970–1982
Women Whose Lives Are Food, Men Whose Lives Are Money
Anonymous Sins
Love and Its Derangements
Angel Fire
The Fabulous Beasts

ANTHOLOGIES

The Best American Short Stories 1979 (edited with Shannon Ravenel)
Scenes from American Life: Contemporary Short Fiction (editor)
Night Walks: A Bedside Companion

JOYCE CAROL OATES

A BLOODSMOOR ROMANCE

E. P. DUTTON, INC.   NEW YORK

Published in the United States by E. P. Dutton, Inc.,
2 Park Avenue, New York, N.Y. 10016

Library of Congress Cataloging in Publication Data

Oates, Joyce Carol
A Bloodsmoor romance.

I. Title.
PS3565.A8B5   1982   813'.54   82-2416
AACR2

ISBN: 0-525-24112-4

Published simultaneously in Canada by Clarke, Irwin & Company Limited,
Toronto and Vancouver

10 9 8 7 6 5 4 3 2 1
First Edition

For Elaine Showalter

Acknowledgments

Of the divers books consulted in the preparation of this definitive chronicle, some four stand out, as deserving of especial note; these being, *The Ladies' Wreath, A Magazine Devoted to Literature, Industry, and Religion*, Mrs. S. T. Martyn, ed. (New York, 1847); *The Wedding-Day Book*, arranged by Katharine Lee Bates (Boston, 1882); *The Sociology of Invention*, S. C. Gilfillan (Chicago, 1935); and *Psychical Research, Science, and Religion*, Stanley De Brath (London, 1925). Frequent quotations in this volume, particularly of verse, are liberally drawn from the excellent books assembled by Mrs. Martyn and Miss Bates, to whose literary labors, and bounties, I am very much in debt.

Oh the Earth was *made* for lovers, for damsel, and hopeless swain,
For sighing, and gentle whispering, and *unity* made of *twain.*
All things do go a-courting, in earth, or sea, or air,
God hath made nothing single but *thee* in His world so fair!
The *bride,* and then the *bridegroom,* the *two,* and then the *one,*
Adam, and Eve, his consort, the moon, and then the sun;
The life doth prove the precept, who obey shall happy be,
Who will not serve the sovereign, be hanged on fatal tree.
The high do seek the lowly, the great do seek the small,
None cannot find who *seeketh,* on this terrestrial ball;
The bee doth court the flower, the flower his suit receives,
And they make merry wedding, whose guests are hundred leaves;
The wind doth woo the branches, the branches they are won,
And the father fond demandeth the maiden for his son. . . .
The *worm* doth woo the mortal, death claims a living bride,
Night unto day is married, morn unto eventide;
Earth is a merry damsel, and *heaven* a knight so true,
And Earth is quite coquettish, and beseemeth in vain to sue. . . .
There's *Sarah,* and *Eliza,* and *Emeline* so fair,
And *Harriet,* and *Susan,* and she with *curling hair!*
Thine eyes are sadly blinded, but yet thou mayest see
Six true, and comely maidens sitting upon the tree;
Approach that tree with caution, then up it boldly climb,
And seize the one thou lovest, nor care for *space,* or *time!*
Then bear her to the greenwood, and build for her a bower,
And give her what she asketh, jewel, or bird, or flower—
And bring the fife, and trumpet, and beat upon the drum—
And bid the world Goodmorrow, and go to glory home!

—EMILY DICKINSON, 1850

Contents

I

The Outlaw Balloon

1

Our history of the remarkable Zinn family, to end upon the final bold stroke of midnight, December 31, 1899, begins some twenty years earlier, on that beauteous September afternoon, in the golden haze of autumn, 1879—ah, now so long past!—when, to the confus'd shame and horror of her loving family and the consternation of all of Bloodsmoor, Miss Deirdre Louisa Zinn, the adopted daughter of Mr. and Mrs. John Quincy Zinn, betook herself on an impetuous walk, with no companion, and was, by daylight, *abducted from the grounds belonging to the stately home of her grandparents, historic old Kiddemaster Hall.*

Well may you blink and draw back in alarm at that crude word, *abducted:* and yet, I fear, there is no other, to be employed with any honesty.

Indeed, as the authorized chronicler of the Zinn family, I should like very much to be more circumspect in this wise, in presenting, to the reader, so frightful and so lurid a state of affairs at the very outset; I should like, too, to shield the Zinns and the Kiddemasters from that exposure to the noisome world of talebearers, gossipmongers, well-intentioned fools, and journalists of every ilk, soon to plague them, in the midst of their grief. Yet there is no remedy: for *A Bloodsmoor Romance: A True History of the Zinns of the Bloodsmoor Valley,* must begin on this ignominious day, with the unlook'd-to disappearance of the youngest Miss Zinn, in plain view, I am bound to say, of her terrified sisters.

That the dark-haired and very pale-skinned Deirdre was to be borne away from her loving parents, and her devoted sisters, at the maidenly age of but sixteen, is surely tragic; that she was to be borne away, in such unwonted circumstances, *in an outlaw balloon of sinister black-*

3

silken hue, manned by an unidentified pilot, is so singular and so unprecedented in the annals of the Valley, or elsewhere, that one cannot entirely
condemn the gossipmongers for their cruel whisperings. An innocent
child, indeed—for what child, of good family, is *not* innocent?—yet,
withal, was there not something strange about this youngest Miss Zinn;
something willful, and truculent, and brooding, and *indelicate?* Was she
grateful to have been adopted by so illustrious a family? Was she devout
enough a Christian? Was she not rather furtive in her manner, and stubborn in the melancholy of her visage; and, tho' a member of the Zinn
family for some six years, a *daughter,* and a *sister,* much cherished by all,
was she not curiously *faithless?*

Thus, the gossipmongers: their ignorant prattle, I am happy to say,
rarely found its way back to the family itself, so sparing them additional
grief.

Ah, Deirdre, how many misfortunes are to follow from your initial
misfortune! How many tears must be spilt, and hearts rent; unseemly
passions inflamed; precipitant outbursts unleash'd, to work their evil
amongst the faultless! And all as a consequence of a willful young lady's
decision to absent herself from the company of her sisters, in something
approaching a *disheveled state of mind,* with no thought, and no concern,
for the feelings of others!

Indeed, I am bound to confess, here at the outset of my chronicle,
that a darksome wave of *revulsion* oft o'ercomes me, at the consideration
of all that must be endured, in future years, by the Zinns, and the elder
Kiddemasters as well, as a consequence of this unfortunate episode—
springing, as it were, out of the incorporeal air of Bloodsmoor: the warm,
luxuriant, dreamy, and golden-hazy air of an autumn day shading to dusk,
not long past teatime.

(It will not be objected, I hope, that, at this juncture, I hasten to inform
the reader that, though the Zinns are to suffer much tumultuous misfortune, and oft despair at the riddlesome nature of our life here on earth,
there are myriad blessings—nay, triumphs—in wait for them: for it is a
self-evident truth, as the much-loved poet, essayist, and distinguished
man of the cloth, the Reverend Cornelius Potter, has declared: *Through
the dismal face of Adversity, the sun of Our Lord's Benevolence ne'er ceases to shine.*
Nor has God forgotten His especial children, in even this most dismaying
of periods in the history of our glorious nation.)

The mysterious abduction was perpetrated not by night, not even in the
sombre-tentacl'd shadows of first dusk, but by daylight, and not many
hundreds of yards from the white-column'd splendor of Kiddemaster
Hall. The young lady, it seems, wandered off alone, down the pleasingly
gentle and picturesque slope of the grassy lawn, to the river below,

quitting the company of her four elder sisters, who were sitting in a graceful little gazebo, a short distance from the rear of the great house. (Perhaps you know the Bloodsmoor River, and are familiar with its wide, placid waters, and the eurythmical grace of its motion, as it snakes its way, with no undue haste, through southeastern Pennsylvania: that scenic, that noble river, rivaling the mighty Hudson in its lissome grandeur and in the craggy heights of its granite promontories!—peaceable now, and, indeed, a solace to the wearied eye, though, not many decades previous, the great river suffered much bloodshed on its banks in the tragic War Between the States—Gettysburg being close by; and in numerous earlier skirmishes, harking back to the 1770's and '80's, and, beyond, to divers Tory atrocities, and mutinies amidst the common soldiery, and, in the 1650's, to the cruelties of the greedy Dutch against the Scandinavian pioneers who had made some small valiant effort to settle our Valley.)

Tho' there was to be disclosed, afterward, that Deirdre Louisa's willful absenting of herself from her sisters' company may have been partly the result of some trifling, girlish discord amongst them, and tho' even the most censorious heart cannot fail to feel pity for the child's fate, nonetheless it should be recorded that Deirdre's behavior on this autumn day, subsequent to a luxuriant high tea at the Hall, was characteristically perverse and exhibited that frequent want of gentility, and ladylike decorum, that had long stimulated compassionate dismay in the Zinn and Kiddemaster families, and in certain of their kinfolk. "Prudence and John Quincy have perhaps o'erextended their Christian charity in so wantonly adopting an orphan of doubtful blood," Great-Aunt Edwina Kiddemaster oft observed over the years; for, as one of the elder matrons of the great family, and one whose alarm'd concern with the decline of morals and etiquette in the nation, subsequent to the War Between the States, did not stint from a courageous examination of her own family, she felt the need to speak frankly, no matter whose feathers (as she curtly expressed it) were ruffled. Other members of the family were less harsh, wishing to cast no blame on Mr. and Mrs. Zinn for the improvidence of the adoption, tho' they whispered of Deirdre that she "went her own way," or declared herself, by her habitual scowling melancholy, "a sadly troubl'd young lady"—perhaps even "haunted," *by they knew not what!*

Beauty being a dutiful concern of all the ladies, both of the *intrinsic* sort and the *cultivated*, it was generally believed—indeed, all the judgments were in, from family members, and from society itself—that, apart from poor Samantha, Deirdre was the most ill-featur'd of the Zinn girls: Samantha's lack of beauty being primarily one of puzzling *plainness*, whilst Deirdre's had much to do with her pale, leaden, lugubrious countenance, and the sinister *recalcitrance* with which her brightly-dark eyes beheld the world. "The child is no beauty," Grandmother Sarah Kiddemaster observed, with a delicate shudder, "yet I somehow fancy that she possesses beauty in secret, and is too grudging, or too shy, to reveal it to us." (A most peculiar notion, issuing from that sensible lady!)

Albeit that young Deirdre was, in legal nomenclature, and in all official records, adopted, it must not be thought that she was ever considered by her family to be but an outsider; nor was she made to feel different from the other girls save, perhaps, in certain rare and negligible episodes of impatience, on the part of one or two of her sisters. (In this wise, it should be recorded that the sisters felt themselves so frequently rebuffed in their efforts to befriend Deirdre that they naturally grew resentful, and, at times, somewhat irascible.) Indeed, it was a common observation, both throughout the Bloodsmoor Valley, and in Philadelphia, amongst families conversant with the situation, that Prudence and John Quincy Zinn clearly cherished their adopted daughter, as if she were of their own blood.

That the Zinns acted out of selfless Christian compassion in bringing this deprived child, at the age of nine or ten, into their harmonious household, the reader is free to infer, with no demurral from me; that they acted—alas, how innocently!—with some small measure of imprudence, the reader is invited to judge for himself.

Yet, I cannot help but think that, like Mr. Ralph Waldo Emerson, that great New England gentleman of Mr. Zinn's acquaintance, both Prudence and John Quincy would have rejected, with proud vehemence, any thought of behavior of an uncharitable, or small-spirit'd, nature. For did not Mr. Zinn, earlier in his life, oft recite, with benign smiling countenance, these instructive lines of Mr. Emerson's?

Tho' love repine, and reason chafe,
There came a voice without reply—
" 'Tis man's perdition to be safe,
When for the truth he ought to die."

If you have never glimpsed Kiddemaster Hall in its noble site above the Bloodsmoor River, some fifty miles to the east of its junction with the Christiana, I will swiftly limn it for you.

This historic house, widely acclaimed as one of the most majestic, yet most tasteful, examples in the region of that style known as Philadelphia Greek Revival, possessed, at the time of our chronicle, a grace, beauty, and wholesome elegance, rivaling that of Monticello; and far more harmonious, in its natural bucolic surroundings, than Rumford Hall, some miles distant, or the Ormonds' ostentatious Mt. Espérance but a few hours' drive away, or, indeed, the manor house of the family of Du Pont de Nemours, on the Brandywine.

The house glimmered white, on even the most gloomy of December days, possessing ten serene columns in the Doric style supporting an immense triangular portico; eight high, stately, perfectly proportion'd windows faced front; there was a graceful tho' large dome, in the shape of a pentagon; there were gently banked roofs, covered in slate; and numerous handsome chimneys; and serpentine walls; and countless minor ornamental touches of a restrained nature. (Indeed, Kiddemaster Hall exemplified, throughout, that classical dignity, and quiet opulence, mawkishly but vainly imitated in the pretentious baronial palaces and "English" mansions erected in the Seventies by war profiteers, and that contemptible new breed, the "government contractor"—and even by the wealthier of those gentlemen who, tho' calling themselves *retailers*, were but common *shopkeepers;* a race of indefatigable vulgarians, and opportunists, who could not have traced their *American blood* past the turn of the century!)

Tho', on its twenty-five hundred acres of land, Kiddemaster Hall possessed a charmingly rural aspect, it was yet no more than a few hours' drive by carriage from Philadelphia; and even closer to Wilmington, Delaware, across the Bloodsmoor River. From these cities, and from divers parts of the countryside, the guests of the Kiddemasters had journeyed, upon that portentous day with which our history begins: the occasion being a formal high tea, in honor of the engagement of the eldest Zinn daughter, Constance Philippa, to the Baron Adolf von Mainz, of Germany, and more recently of Philadelphia; and, in addition, to quietly honor the presence of three distinguished gentlemen, from the American Philosophical Society, who had journeyed down from Boston to make the acquaintance of John Quincy Zinn. (Mr. Zinn, I should explain, had, by 1879, acquired a considerable reputation as an inventor, and thinker, of rare originality; though his real fame lies in the future when the Congress of the United States, and President McKinley himself, took an especial interest in his career, and had much to do with bestowing upon him numerous grants and honoraria to aid in his research. On the day of his youngest daughter's abduction, Mr. Zinn was but fifty-two years old, and had labored at his oft-thankless vocation of *invention* since early boyhood.)

Ah, might that unfortunate day have been averted!—might Deirdre have been ill, or somehow indisposed, that her mother would have commanded her to remain at home abed!—and so much grief would have been prevented. But, alas, nothing of the kind transpired; and though Deirdre oft cast a sickly, peevish, and, as it were, *green-hued* countenance upon the world, she was as healthsome as any of her sisters, not excluding the overly robust Constance Philippa, who frequently dismayed the elder ladies with her declared pleasure in *walking*—not in the company of her fiancé, nor even in the company of her sisters, but *alone.*

There were upward of one hundred guests at Kiddemaster Hall, and some thirty or more servants to attend them, dressed in the subdued, and scrupulously proper, attire favored by the Kiddemasters for their help, over many generations—indeed, harking back to Federalist times. (The men wore livery, and highly polished black leather shoes; the women, modest black cotton-and-flannel dresses, with stiff-starched white aprons, and caps, and, despite the heat of the afternoon, heavy lisle stockings.) As the guests convened, what a joyous medley of voices ensued!—and how gratifying to the eye, the ladies' dresses, many-skirted, frothy, and airy, and as varied in their hues, as the beauteous autumn flowers that bloomed in the myriad beds! I cannot but think it by Our Lord's mercy, that the tea was over, and all the guests departed, when Miss Deirdre Zinn was carried away by her abductor: for think what an unspeakable humiliation *that* would have been, if these distinguished gentlemen and ladies had stared down from the terrace, to the hellish scene below!

Amidst the guests, however, no one was more pleasing to the eye, or excited more comment, than the five Zinn daughters of local fame. As we advance more intimately upon the sisters, we will not shrink from taking note of countless small imperfections, and some major faults; so it is well to remember that, observed and judged from a distance, as doubtless guests to Kiddemaster Hall were wont to do, *Constance Philippa*, and *Octavia*, and *Malvinia*, and *Samantha*, and even *Deirdre* did strike the eye as uncommonly attractive young ladies, though they lived in a society in which Beauty—whether of face, or form, or manner, or attire—was very much a requisite, for the female sex. It is true, Samantha was plain and pinched of countenance; and so undeveloped for her age, she might have been a child of twelve, or less: yet, presented in the midst of her sisters, and as gaily adorned as the prettiest, she, too, excited generally favorable comment, and was held to be "petite," and "fairylike," and "possessed of an elfin charm."

John Quincy Zinn's somewhat unique position in Bloodsmoor, as the father of five distinctly marriageable young ladies, might not have seemed an enviable one; less enviable still was his position as head of a household of limited financial resources—for John Quincy was, and oft was made to feel, but the *son-in-law* of the wealthy Godfrey Kiddemaster. Being of a private, and even hermetic, turn of mind, he shrank from frequent public appearances, yet, when he did appear, how admiringly all eyes were drawn to him, and to his striking family!—Mr. Zinn tall, wide-shouldered, and abash'dly handsome; Mrs. Zinn of Junoesque stature, formidably clad in lavender, with an immense lavender and cream-colored hat; and the daughters!—self-conscious, yet resplendent, in their finest Sunday clothes, radiant as walking candles, fully cognizant of admiring—nay, *examining*—eyes on all sides. "How they stare!" Octavia murmured to Malvinia, so excited, she had begun to breathe swiftly and shallowly, and could not constrain herself from grasping her sister's arm. "And is it we whom they stare at, so frankly?"—whereupon Malvinia laughingly murmured, in reply, "Nay, I think it is Father's five daughters; or Grandfather's five aspiring heiresses."

Upon that historic day, guests arrived at Kiddemaster Hall in vehicles of greatly varying species, ranging from the bronze coach of the house of Du Pont de Nemours, to the more tasteful, yet still splendid, coaches of the Whittons, and the Gilpins, and the Millers—these excellent old families of the Valley, and of Philadelphia, being intricately related by both blood and marriage to the Kiddemasters. And there were innumerable modest, yet, withal, entirely respectable, victorias and surreys owned by local residents. And the Baron von Mainz, that dashing figure! What commentary *he* stimulated, by choosing to ride out from Philadelphia, on horseback: on his wide-nostril'd black English Thoroughbred stallion, some seventeen hands high, with its deep-set, glaring, crafty eyes, that seemed, in playful manner, not unlike the Baron's own. "Your fiancé, and his handsome mount, are altogether striking," Malvinia whispered to Constance Philippa, behind her part-opened fan. "Alas, my dear, are you not gravely *intimidated* by both?" Whereupon the flush-cheek'd Constance Philippa lowered her gaze to the ground, and somewhat sullenly replied, "I am intimidated by no one, and nothing; and I must beg you to make no further unwelcome speculation on the nature of *my* feelings."

Mr. and Mrs. Zinn, and their five daughters, were fetched to the Hall from their home, a short distance away, by the Kiddemasters' own coach for, unfortunately, they could afford no carriage of their own, save a "country" surrey of distinctly outmoded style, which would hardly be appropriate for this important occasion; and so they were driven through the park, and up the quarter-mile gravel drive, to Mrs. Zinn's parents' home, in a vehicle of such tasteful splendor as to gratify Mrs. Zinn, even as it deeply embarrassed her husband. "I take no more account than you do, Mr. Zinn, of the vagaries and vanities of the material world," Prudence declared, "yet, upon certain emblematic occasions, I feel that it is not only apt, but obligatory, that we align ourselves with my father's house: that the coarse-minded gossipers of Bloodsmoor may be constrained, from speculation as to my father's *favoring,* or *disfavoring,* of any one of our daughters, or of you; or the entire Zinn family."

It was surely a touching indication of John Quincy's democratic temperament, and the simple, rural, and unadorn'd nature of his background, that he felt some small revulsion for the display of wealth the Kiddemaster brougham—with its glaring coppery finish, and its smart ebony trim, and its handsome fringed hammercloth—represented to the world; and, it may be, for his own reluctant acquiescence to it, in the interests of conjugal peace. (The elegant brougham, adorned with the Kiddemaster coat-of-arms on its sides—a demilion rampant, grasping an olive branch—was drawn by four high-stepping, and immaculately groomed, white geldings, with braided and beribboned manes and tails, and "treated" coats and hooves: the coats being whitened, and the hooves more emphatically blackened, by art, so that the noble steeds might offer a yet more dramatic appearance, when glimps'd in public, than they might have done otherwise. Thus John Quincy's father-in-law, the retired Chief Justice Godfrey Kiddemaster, indulged himself, in small ways, and harmless manifestations of pride: this desire for a striking *public appearance* being, perhaps, nothing more than an aspect of his Federalist heritage, for we must recall that President Washington himself similarly decreed that his horses be "treated," with an eye toward exciting admiration amongst the common folk. And I cannot think but that it was a considerable pleasure, for these personages, to gaze upon the Kiddemaster carriage as it passed, drawn by the beauteous horses, and swaying with luxuriant grace on its large C-springs—a properly attired Irish driver up front, and an attendant footman, in livery, perched high at the back, as rigidly perfect in posture as a statue.) "I fear we are a spectacle, being, after all, but *Zinns,*" John Quincy quietly observed, "yet I suppose the Kiddemasters must be indulged; and it is, in any case, but a temporary endurance."

Whereupon his vivacious daughter Malvinia could not resist observing, to anyone who cared to hear: "Alas, dear Father, that it *is* but temporary: and tomorrow, if we venture forth, we shall be obliged to be carried in our own humble surrey, that hardly requires the Zinn coat-of-arms, to be identified as ours."

It is necessary, I believe, for me to interrupt my narrative at this point—the Zinns not yet arrived at the tea, the sky a feckless china blue, the dread abduction many hours hence—in order to quickly sketch a portrait of Mr. John Quincy Zinn, that the reader may become more adequately cognizant of him, in terms of his great value, in the eyes of his daughters, and his slow-growing reputation, in the eyes of the world.

In this year of 1879, John Quincy's fame lay all before him, and he was not yet popularly known by the initials J.Q.Z., as he came to be, in the closing years of the century. Yet, withal, he enjoy'd a considerable respect amongst his fellow inventors, men of science, and philosophers: witness the presence of the gentlemen from the American Philosophical Society, who wished simply to meet with him on an informal basis, and converse with him with an eye toward promoting his candidacy, as a member of their austere organization. (In his old age, what honors will be offered! From the Royal Society of the British Empire, for instance; and from other international organizations, as well as those in the States, that had, for a time, withheld recognition from the modest-temper'd Mr. Zinn.)

A more respectful consideration of our subject, and his myriad achievements, will be offered elsewhere in this history: for I must limn, as clearly as possible, the biographical facts pertaining to this famous American, that his role—both *tragic,* and *triumphant*—will be adequately comprehended. Suffice it to say, for the present, that he rose from a humble rural background, in the mountains of southern Pennsylvania; that he enjoy'd a meteoric rise to prominence, in Philadelphia, in the 1850's, as a consequence of his advanced pedagogical methods, in a rural common school in Mouth-of-Lebanon, Pennsylvania; that he fell most passionately in love with Miss Prudence Kiddemaster, the daughter of the distinguished juror Godfrey Kiddemaster (then Chief Justice of the Supreme Court of the Commonwealth of Pennsylvania); that he assiduously courted her, until her virgin heart was won; that they were wed, and came to dwell here in Bloodsmoor, some twenty-three years before that autumn of 1879, with which this narrative begins.

On several acres of particularly scenic land, part wooded, and part meadow, belonging to the Kiddemaster estate, the devoted young couple established their residence, enjoying the occupancy of an *eight-sided domicile* of Mr. Zinn's own design, which Mrs. Zinn's munificent father financed. There, in that remarkable dwelling place—known locally as the Octagonal House, and, later, to be avidly written of, by journalists seeking to portray the complexity of Mr. Zinn's genius to their disparate readership—four healthsome, and angelic, infant girls were born; to which bountiful household there was, in 1873, added an additional child, the orphan'd Deirdre Bonner.

Whilst this happy family life blossomed, with very few incursions of ill-fortune, save some three or four miscarriages suffered by Mrs. Zinn, and the common run of illnesses, there was pursued, with marked singleness of purpose, and unswerving dedication, John Quincy Zinn's vocation of *invention,* which the modest gentleman was wont to call mere "tinkering." ("For only God *invents,"* Mr. Zinn quietly asserted.)

To those readers whose grasp of history is so deficient that the name John Quincy Zinn means very little to them, it will perhaps be of interest to learn that the distinguished inventor George Washington Gale Ferris believed Mr. Zinn to be "one of the most remarkable men of his acquaintance"; and that Mr. Hannibal Goodwin praised his "tireless, questing, resolutely *natural* mind." That brilliant, albeit somewhat eccentric, Swedish scientist John Ericsson, spoke privately of John Quincy Zinn as an "equal," as did Ralph Waldo Emerson, on at least one recorded occasion. (It was unfortunate indeed that Mr. Emerson, being of the *poetic,* and not the *mathematical,* genius, could not grasp, and consequently felt the necessity to disparage, certain of Mr. Zinn's most challenging projects—the experimentation with the *perpetual-motion machine,* for instance. Yet, in a much-priz'd letter of 1869, found in the inventor's workshop after his death, Mr. Emerson declared him-

self an "admirer" of Mr. Zinn, for the "very doggedness of his passion
for Truth.")

   *A naturally inspired teacher, as informed by Love as by Intellect—a near-
divine intelligence—an inventor of rustic, but original, genius—a Saint in his purity,
as in his zeal:* so John Quincy Zinn was praised, by divers gentlemen,
during his long and productive lifetime. Charles A. Dana lauded Mr.
Zinn, whom he had never met, as the single personage "hailing from that
Transcendentalist tribe, who had *contributed* something worthwhile to our
civilization." Mr. Samuel Clemens, an enthusiast of invention in general,
had naught but admiration for certain of Mr. Zinn's numerous "domestic" items—the automatic hair clippers, for instance, and the rotary toothbrush, the which an embarrassed John Quincy Zinn had no great pride
in, and would as soon have forgotten!—these "tinkerer's toys" being, in
his censorious eyes, quite contemptible, when set beside his more ambitious projects.

It was one of the first questions put to John Quincy Zinn, by the journalist
Adam Watkins, in 1887, as to why he had applied for so very few patents;
for was it not a common practice, on the part of his fellow inventors, to
file their applications with the United States Patent Office, on the slightest
pretext? Many of the inventors being sadly deluded, in their estimation
of their own originality and genius!

   Mr. Zinn's reply to this impertinent query was a simple one, yet not
lacking in dignity: "Perhaps, Mr. Watkins, I am somewhat less deluded
than my brethren."

   But the question continued to be asked, over the years, not only
by inquisitive strangers, but by those relatives and acquaintances who
might have been expected to sympathize with Mr. Zinn's Transcendentalist faith, which scorned the mercantile world, and sought to incorpo-
rate the Higher Law into the secular life. Alas, it was truly another, and
yet more impertinent question, that might have been worded thusly: *Why
are you so unlike other men?*

   There was much triumph in John Quincy Zinn's life; yet, withal, a
secret sorrow, in that, apart from a very few exemplary individuals, no
one understood him; and certain personages, even within his family, took
delight in misunderstanding him. What a pity it is, that he had not the
opportunity to commune more frequently with his equals—a pity, for
instance, that Bloodsmoor was not Concord, Massachusetts, where Mr.
Zinn might have dined with Mr. Emerson, Mr. Thoreau, and Mr. Alcott,
and where, surely, he would have been a central member of the Transcendentalist Club! A pity, too, that his sensitive nerves were so ill affected
by the uproar and clatter of large cities that he abhorred visits even to
Philadelphia (one of the more attractive cities, which Mr. Zinn had liked
well enough in his young bachelor days); and would never have dreamt

of journeying to New York, or Boston. It was his solemn belief that he "swam in the pulsing bloodstream of Nature, Man, and God" without leaving Bloodsmoor, or, indeed, without stepping outside his workshop door; and, in a jesting mood, he liked to say that his pet monkey, Pip, who routinely kept him company during the long workday, was all he required of intellectual companionship.

Yet I cannot restrain myself from observing, with all reverence for my subject, that John Quincy Zinn might have been less lonely, and less susceptible to bemused despair, had he cultivated the friendship of worthy persons and traveled with more ease. But, doubtless, it was as a consequence of his shattering experience in the War Between the States, in which he valiantly participated for the better part of three years, that, once safely home, he vowed to remain, and to work in blessèd solitude, for the remainder of his life.

But others failed to understand; and the rude question *Why?* was asked repeatedly.

Why did John Quincy Zinn, one of the most gifted inventors in our Great Age of Invention (now, alas, an epoch long past), reap so very modest a harvest from his lifelong labor? Why, save at the end of his career, when manufacturers vied for his contracts, did he display such lofty indifference to personal gain? Even as a young, brash, and ostensibly ambitious man, in his mid-twenties, he had declined to insist upon a satisfactory arrangement for the publication of his pedagogical study, *The Spirit of the Future in America,* of 1854; with the shocking result that the erstwhile reputable publishing house of A. T. Plumbe & Sons, of Philadelphia, was to reprint some twelve times in all, but pay to its acclaimed author only $300—the original flat fee for the assignment of all rights. And, though he protested himself a loving and devoted husband to his wife, and a no less loving and devoted father, it was very curious that he could not seem to pay his considerable debts to the Kiddemasters—both his father-in-law, Godfrey Kiddemaster, and Great-Aunt Edwina, of whom we shall speak shortly—let alone enjoy some private gain, of his own. Mrs. Zinn, who was to remain loyal to John Quincy for some forty-three years, oft declared, with sombre amusement, or droll resignation, or stoic calm, that she should not mourn the loss of so many patents, and so much abstract wealth, if Mr. Zinn's aptitude for providing for his family in other regards were more reliable; if there were not four—nay, *five*—young ladies, in the Octagonal House, who must be provided with dowries—the protracted munificence of her father being, she believed, near to exhausted. And, too, the maintenance of Mr. Zinn's modest laboratory-workshop, in a crude cabin built by his own hands, fell to Judge Kiddemaster as well, as an informal "partner" in the inventor's work.

"The question you are putting to me, Prudence," Mr. Zinn replied, with gentle dignity, albeit with a melancholy cast of his eye, "is simply thus: *Why are you not like other men?* And it is a question, I am sorry to say, that cannot be answered save by reference to one of our greatest Americans, Benjamin Franklin, who, as you know, might have become a millionaire many times over had he troubled to patent *his* inventions."

Tho' it may be Mrs. Zinn had heard this rejoinder before from her husband, she did not protest, but stood silent, her stern, handsome, rather strong-boned face slightly coloring; and her hands clasped together. Poor Prudence! For all her anxious displeasure with her husband, and his resolute idealism as to mercantile success, she was, finally, and to her credit, an *excellent wife,* who took her marital vows with utmost seriousness, and would more readily have surrendered her personal distinction as a Kiddemaster heiress than fail to love, honor, and obey her stalwart husband. Thus she stood wordless, her gaze meekly lowered, whilst, with closed eyes, and a fond stroking of his fair-hued beard, Mr. Zinn quoted these familiar words of Benjamin Franklin's: *"As we enjoy great advantages from the inventions of others, we should be glad of an opportunity to serve others by any invention of ours; and this we should do, freely and generously."*

It was to be widely, if quietly, deemed, after the abduction of Miss Deirdre Zinn, that had Mr. Zinn been patient enough to remain at Kiddemaster Hall with his womenfolk, in order to accompany them back home in the brougham, the tragedy would not have occurred: but, to his misfortune, the restive inventor, whose imagination, I believe, never truly left the domain of his workshop and his workbench, insisted upon leaving for the Octagonal House *on foot,* as soon as the last guests had departed. With Mrs. Zinn claiming the need to speak with her parents in private, and the girls grateful for another hour's stay at the great house, it was altogether reasonable that John Quincy Zinn might linger to converse with one of the family (for Great-Uncle Vaughan, who had some small interest in Mr. Zinn's "sun-furnace" experimentation, would have greatly enjoyed speaking with him at leisure), or simply to stroll about the wisteria garden, or contemplate the handsome fieldstone wishing well, in the company of his five pretty daughters. But, alas, his nerves had grown so strained, as a consequence of both the ordeal of the formal tea and the ordeal of being impertinently, if courteously, *interrogated* by the Boston visitors, that he felt himself aflame with the desire to escape.

Mr. Zinn had not been able to avoid, on this important occasion, fitting himself into so elaborately proper a costume, that his very flesh chafed in rebellion, and perspiration ran in unsightly rivulets down his forehead and cheeks!—presenting so uncomfortable, and so ill, a vision, it was no wonder that his wife and daughters felt embarrassment for him, and his Kiddemaster relatives stared at him in dismay'd alarm. Yet, how was it to be prevented? John Quincy Zinn towered over most of the guests, at six feet five inches of height; he was inordinately wide-shouldered, and possessed a stiff, rather rustic, dignity, in awkward combination with an intermittent boyish pleasure, which struck some observers as possibly too eager, and too indiscriminately friendly.

For the occasion of the Kiddemasters' tea, Mr. Zinn had been obliged, under pain of his wife's severe displeasure, to submit to a tailor's exasperatingly protracted services, over several weeks: an expenditure of time that greatly tormented him, in that he might have spent it far more profitably at his work, or even, as he sadly jested, in colloquy with Pip. His daughters protested that he looked so handsome, and so very noble, how could the new suit displease him? It was fashionable, it was stylish, it sported a "European" silhouette: narrow, tapering, black wool-and-flannel trousers, with the much-vaunted *smooth* fit, firmly secured by an rubberized strap under the foot; a black velvet coat with a pronounced *nipped-in* waist; a matching vest, of the same heavy velvet material; a white linen shirt so fiercely starched it had the texture of veneer, with a raised, and very stiff, collar, that cut cruelly into Mr. Zinn's neck; and a black satin cravat, so resolutely tight, it put the poor man in mind of a noose—not the most felicitous association, in these circumstances. Despite the unseasonable warmth of the day, Mr. Zinn had no choice but to wear his old top hat, which had served him at his wedding many years previous, but did not seem, in his eyes, too clearly outmoded, despite his daughter Malvinia's pique; and he had no choice but to jam on his hands a pair of white gloves that stank of camphor; and to jam on his large feet a pair of black leather shoes with pointed toes, that he secretly feared he had ruined some months previous, as a consequence of certain *waterproofing* experimentations he had been doing, on an improvised basis. (Mr. Zinn had methodically varnished the shoes, and then soaked them for five hours in a mixture of beeswax, turpentine, Burgandy pitch, and oil; with the dismaying result, they gave off a powerful *medicinal* odor, and might be embarrassing in close quarters, should his feet perspire. . . . Yet, he could not regret the experiment, for he believed he was very near to discovering the principle of *waterproofing*: and if he could then swallow his pride, and force himself to file an application at the Patent Office, he might then realize enough income to provide respectful dowries for his daughters; and to repay the debts he owed his in-laws. Had Mr. Zinn time for such commonplace matters, it would surely have been a matter of grave concern to him, that, as it was, Judge Kiddemaster was providing a modest dowry for Constance Philippa, that the Baron might not be acquiring her "for nothing," and the old man had crudely jested, just the other day, that he was grateful for Malvinia's exceptional beauty for, perhaps, in her case, no *bribe* would be necessary, to ensure a wedding.)

So far as John Quincy Zinn knew, the tea had gone well enough, and he had managed to endure any number of strained conversations with his daughter's fiancé, whose German accent made graceful communication difficult; and with the Boston gentlemen, who had revealed themselves, to Mr. Zinn's disappointment, as egregiously ignorant of the theoretical principles underlying electricity, odylic force, time-travel, perpetual motion, and the homely elevator, or dumbwaiter, with which Mr. Zinn was now experimenting; nor were they wholly enthusiastic about the possibility of auto-locomotives, both for the road and the air (the which Mr. Zinn could not keep from declaring would soon be "as commonplace as the horsedrawn carriage, and far more efficient"); and with his Kiddemaster, Gilpin, Whitton, Kale, and Miller in-laws, whom he found no easier to recall by name than he had upon first marrying into his wife's vast family. All these exchanges he had forced himself to undergo, with every outward expression of social pleasure, tho', it may be, an occasional grimace of pain, or involuntary sigh, or the distracting presence of the rivulets of perspiration on his face, gave some hint to his companions of the extreme distress he felt.

In any case, there was no guest at the tea more ecstatic with relief, when the festive event was concluding, and one might safely escape, than the father of the prospective bride: Mr. Zinn's revulsion being so extreme, he declared he must leave at once, on foot, and would not be able to wait to accompany his family, in the accursèd brougham. "And I shall go with you," Samantha declared, "for I am heartily sick of the Kiddemasters, and cannot wait to unpin my hat."

Whereupon Mrs. Zinn objected, for Samantha was wearing a many-skirted, heavy dress, in cotton and poplin, with a substantial fishtail train; and, if she had any pretension of being a lady, she would never wish to go tramping through the woods, but wait with her sisters, and sit quietly, and make no further fuss.

"Mother, I assure you, I *have* no pretensions," the haughty miss said, her pale, freckled face coloring warmly, "and, in any case, who would be watching? Father and I would take the river path; and I *would* carry my skirts all the way; and I could remain with him at the workshop, until it was time for supper."

Mrs. Zinn heard her out, and then said: "It is quite impossible, and you know it; you are not, after all, a child any longer. You might be seen from the river, if anyone chances to be boating—you might be seen by any of the servants—you *would* be seen by your father, and the sight would not be attractive. So you will remain here, and do your fancywork."

Thus it was that the Zinn girls remained behind, and Mr. Zinn impatiently departed, and the situation, at the time, appeared to be *altogether natural.*

("Of course you could not have known, my dear, you could not possibly have known," Mrs. Zinn was to say, afterward, when her shock at the disappearance of her youngest daughter had somewhat lightened, and both grief, and rage, contended for her heart, "but the shame of it!—the shame!—the humiliation! The papers have spread the story up and down the coast. Cousin Rowena assures me they talk of nothing else in Washington, there is a rumor the Baron will reconsider his alliance, and I cannot think—I cannot bear to think—of what is being said in Philadelphia. The wretched child! Kidnapped! Despoiled! *And she was not even our own!*")

2

O Father I dreamt that my sisters stood over my bed as I slept and though I was asleep I saw them clearly and heard their cruel whisperings and gigglings O and Father Malvinia drew out of her bodice a tiny silver scissors like the scissors in Mother's sewing basket but much, much brighter—Father please hear me out please do not smile and kiss my forehead and turn away O Father please hear how Malvinia leaned over my bed and snipped at my breast and I cried for her to stop and she paid no heed I was awake yet unable to move even my smallest fingers and toes even my eyelids Father Dearest do not deny me I begged for her to stop but she pierced my flesh she lifted the skin away she touched my heart O O O O Father my stepsisters hate me my sisters resent me they are jealous of your love for me they whisper together about me even Octavia who is the kindest O Father they stood over my bed I saw them clearly Malvinia touched my living heart with her cold fingers and Octavia did not protest Constance Philippa merely frowned and watched Samantha drew near to observe the working of my heart I cried for Malvinia to stop but she paid no heed she pays no heed Father she broke off a piece of my heart and ate it and Ah! but this is bitter! *she spat but the others drew near Octavia Constance Philippa Samantha they broke off pieces of my heart and ate* How bitter, how ugly, *they cried O but Father they did not heed my tears Father they hate me they resent the love you give me the little love you give me your stepdaughter the last of your children the orphan poor Deirdre poor bereaved ugly bitter Deirdre they laugh and jeer and mock* How bitter it is, her heart!—her heart! *they said* but she has nothing else to offer us *they stood over my bed Father they ate of my heart Father please do not deny me please do not pretend all is well O Father please hear me please save me I cannot bear this life otherwise*

3

Who is He, so swiftly flying?
His career no eye can see?
Who are They, in secret dying,
From their birth they cease to be?
TIME: Behold his pictur'd face!
MOMENTS: Can you count their race?
—MRS. F. L. SMITH

The outlaw balloon, manned by a pilot never to be identified, much less apprehended by the authorities and brought to justice, is all the while swiftly approaching historic Kiddemaster Hall: black, and silken, and conical of shape, of majestic tho' sinister proportions, and silent, save for the throaty hissing of its flame!—the while the five innocent Zinn daughters, prettily seated in the gazebo above the river, busy themselves with their divers fancywork.

Here is Constance Philippa in her handsome mauve-and-ivory dress, of stiff starched piqué; here is Octavia, in many hues of pink, her square-cut neckline covered in tulle, with yet more tulle at her elbows; and Malvinia, a vision, in white *mousseline-de-laine,* and ruffles of silky *blonde* lace, and pink velvet ribbons. (The innumerable layers of frothy white of Malvinia's dress seem hardly substance, they float so airily about her!) And Samantha somewhat plainer, in pale green; and Deirdre, in a dress of yellow satin-and-poplin, made over from a costume of Malvinia's, and very charming indeed. Ah, if only the mellifluous afternoon would not so

19

swiftly ebb, shading into dusk! If only the catastrophe might be prevented!

Alas, there will be no warning—and no evasion—of *Fate.*

"A melancholy sort of happiness," Malvinia observed with a sigh, and a
dreamy smile, "the aftermath of a particularly gladsome occasion."

"A happy sort of melancholy," Constance Philippa said, unsmiling, "if one is inclined to find such *gladsome* occasions *intolerable.*"

Constance Philippa was crocheting, with no excess of industry, or
concentration, a pretty pink smock for Cousin Rowena Kale's newborn
baby girl; Malvinia, delicately hiding a yawn, had just allowed her sizable
square of needlepoint to fall into her lap; Octavia was humming to herself, and working, with great contentment, and exactitude, on a patchwork child's panda, with the most mischievous black button-eyes; Samantha frowned over a towel meant to be elaborately cross-stitched in gay
orange yarn; and the sullen Deirdre was crocheting, with a perceptible
absence of spirit, a white antimacassar for the haircloth settee in Mrs.
Zinn's parlor.

"Why, Constance Philippa, what can you mean!" Octavia inquired
of her elder sister, her eyes opened wide with amazement. "You know
very well the tea was a magnificent event, and quite fitting, to mark the
end of our o'erlong summer. And you, in particular, should be grateful,"
she added, her lower lip trembling for a scant moment, "for you are now
betrothed: and naught but happiness awaits you."

Samantha glanced up at Octavia, and at Constance Philippa; and
seemed about to speak; then thought better of it, to her credit, and
resumed her somewhat clumsy work. Deirdre, however, remained with
her head bowed, and worked so mechanically at her crocheting, that the
hook flashed and winked most wickedly.

Malvinia sighed again, and made a very desultory effort to take up
her needlepoint. "I have come to believe," she said, "that *melancholy* and
happiness are inextricably joined: and that, were they separate, we should
soon find even happiness unspeakably dull!"

By this time, every one of the numerous guests had departed
Kiddemaster Hall: and what a confus'd merriment there had been, of
broughams, and victorias, and surreys, and prancing matched teams with
high-flung heads! And costumed footmen with countenances so proper,
they might have been painted; and bright-shining eyes, and tear-streaked
cheeks, amidst farewell embraces enjoyed by the ladies. All eyes had
dwelt upon Constance Philippa's fiancé, the redoubtable Baron von
Mainz, as he galloped off on his noble black steed; all eyes had followed
the bronze-hued coach of the house of Du Pont de Nemours, in which
Malvinia's "young man" Cheyney, and divers members of his family, had

departed for the Brandywine. Farewell, ah, farewell! For, indeed, the summery days are fast declining! The Whittons—the Kales—the Bayards —the Gilpins—the Woodruffs—Reverend and Mrs. Silas Hewett—Cousins Odille, and Hayden, and Steven, and Rowena, and Flora, and Basil —Mr. and Mrs. Martineau, and their lovely daughter Delphine—the Broomes—the Millers—the Rhinelanders—Mr. Lucius Rumford, of stately Rumford Hall—Professors Jameson, Newbold, and Lyndon, of the American Philosophical Society—and Mr. Zinn, hurrying away on foot, tugging nervously at his collar and carrying his regal top hat crushed beneath his arm. Farewell! For nothing at Kiddemaster Hall will ever be quite the same again.

For some minutes the sisters bent assiduously to their work; and then Malvinia said in a languid voice: "Father spoke well this afternoon, I believe. He is so eloquent!—and so charming, when his color is high, and his eyes glisten. His views on the future of the nation—the inevitability of progress, the *evolution* of perfection—were most persuasive. Yet, did you note that wizened little Professor Newbold? I thought he looked somewhat skeptical."

"Skeptical?" Samantha asked, startled. "Why, what do you mean?"

"Perhaps it was Professor Jameson," Malvinia said carelessly. "I cannot keep the old gentlemen straight, there are so many; and they are always *staring* at one!" She adjusted the luxuriant tulle veil that dropped from the brim of her hat, and picked up her needlepoint; but showed very little inclination to apply herself to her work. "A pity, though, that, as the tea commenced, and the terrace grew o'ercrowded, Father grew so warm; and his birthmark so pronounced."

"I did not think the birthmark so very pronounced," Octavia said, taking up her sandalwood fan, and staring at Malvinia with an expression of startl'd perplexity. "Indeed, it seemed to me that Father was unusually handsome this afternoon."

"Oh, yes—yes—yes, of course," Malvinia said hurriedly. "I did not mean that he was *not* handsome; please do not misunderstand!"

Plump, frowning Octavia began to fan herself, as she had been taught, in slow decorous movements. It may well have been that, as a consequence of numerous tidbits, consumed at the tea, she was rather uncomfortably warm, in her sturdy whalebone corset, with its innumerable metal eyelets and crossed lacing. She sighed, and said: "Ah, but the hot shortcake was delicious! Did you think so, Samantha? Deirdre? How very quiet you two are! But you *did* enjoy the afternoon, I hope?"

Samantha murmured a near-inaudible assent, without glancing up from her work; but Deirdre, her pale face pinched and stubborn, made no reply at all.

"Your sister has asked you a question, Deirdre," Malvinia said sharply. "Though neither Mother nor Father is here and, I suppose, you need *not* o'erexert yourself, so far as courtesy is concerned, you might at least have replied, and not sit there as if you were deaf!"

"The hot shortcake—the strawberry jam—the new China tea off Uncle Vaughan's ships—" Octavia chattered nervously. "And, yes, the exquisite fresh honey! You *did* have something to eat, Deirdre, I hope? Otherwise you will be feeling very faint."

"Thank you," Deirdre whispered. "It is kind of you to be solicitous of me; but, I assure you, I am altogether well."

So saying, the youngest Miss Zinn lapsed into a stony silence and, staring fixedly at the crocheting in her lap, resumed her rapid mechanical work, as if she were indeed alone. I cannot think it a reasonable observation, that startling commentary of Grandmother Sarah Kiddemaster, as to this young lady's possessing a sort of *secret beauty;* for, if you were to closely observe the narrowed and downturned eyes, in which naught but a froward spirit glowed, and if you were to gaze all unjudging upon the high pale forehead, marred by the untidy widow's peak, you would have very little hope that this child might one day blossom into a beauty, to be placed beside our legendary Bloodsmoor beauties. For, harking back to Dutch and Colonial times, this fertile Valley was famed for its lovely young women, of aristocratic family; and a fair number of them were Kiddemasters, as I hardly need add.

It may have been to forestall some reiterated criticism, by Malvinia, of their youngest sister's behavior, both at the present time and at the tea (when, it seems, she had spent an inordinate amount of time hiding in a corner, and was too tongue-tied even to converse with her cousins Basil and Steven), that Octavia said warmly: "Yes, it did seem to me, that Father was particularly handsome, and eloquent, this afternoon. I felt my heart begin to beat hard, when he spoke of the future—of the next century—and his eyes shone—and his beard looked so fine, and bold—and his voice did not quaver—" She paused, fanning herself, now more hurriedly. "The professors from Boston *will* elect him to their Society, will they not? For it would be so cruel now—after so much anticipation, and talk—"

"I cannot think that they would *not,*" Samantha said.

"No," said Constance Philippa at once, "I cannot think that either; for Grandfather, you know, would be most grieved."

"He would be most furious," Malvinia said idly, again fussing with her dotted tulle veil, the which she was obliged to wear, even in the late afternoon, that her flawless complexion might not be rudely touched by the sun. "Indeed, since his retirement from the Court, he is likely to be thrown into a fury at any time. How unhappy Father will be, if—!"

Samantha sighed in exasperation, for her orange yarn had become badly snarled; and it was always a source of uneasiness to her, that

Malvinia, or any of her sisters, should take it upon themselves to discuss Mr. Zinn. She said: "Mother is quite certain that the election will be successful, for, I believe, Mr. Bayard thus informed her, tho' the matter is of course confidential: and not to be chattered about, in every treetop and from out every window, as Pip would do."

Whereupon, for no clear reason, unless, of course, to forestall some small contretemps, Constance Philippa gave her pink fancywork a vigorous shake, and said suddenly: "Miss Delphine Martineau behaved disgracefully this afternoon—she flirted with all the men—not excluding Octavia's widower, Mr. Rumford—or my fiancé—or Grandfather himself —or that insufferable Mr. Ormond, who reminds me so forcibly of a barnyard hog! I hope you all took notice?"

"You are most unfair to Delphine!" Malvinia cried. (For, indeed, she and the vivacious Miss Martineau were very close friends.) "She does not *flirt*, any more than I do: but simply converses with any of the gentlemen, no matter their age, who approach her. Yes, Constance Philippa, you *are* unfair, and I cannot think it very generous of you," she continued, warmly. "As if Delphine should give a snap of her fingers for—well, for any of the men you mention!—any more than *I* should—"

"You are insulting Constance Philippa, and me," Octavia said gently. "I beg you to reconsider your rash words."

"I will not hear Delphine slandered," Malvinia said archly, "nor do I wish to reconsider anything I have said. If Constance Philippa speaks out of rank jealousy, or vile wicked envy, she should be more direct, and not hide behind cruel scatter'd shots!"

In reply, the flush-faced elder sister flung her crocheting down upon the floorboards of the gazebo; and for a long terrible moment no one spoke. (Indeed, it was well for the sisters, that no servant hovered near; and that the great house was a sufficient distance away, that none of their elders might chance to spy upon them.) To her credit, Constance Philippa held her tongue, as she had been instructed to do, in such flurried circumstances, when the blood pulses too strenuously through the veins, and the sturdy bone undergarments give every impression of growing yet tighter. The eldest Miss Zinn was, as the reader might infer, a strangely troubled young lady, and not at all grateful, it seems, for her engagement to the Baron, nor made so ecstatically happy at the prospect of being a wife to him, as she should have been. She breathed with enforced calm, and paused yet further, and finally spoke: "Yet there was no cause, Malvinia, to insult Octavia and me—to boast that you would not give a snap of your fingers for my fiancé, and Octavia's suitor! Indeed, that is most cruel. For, after all, I have not yet heard that the banns have been announced for you and the dashing young Cheyney."

Malvinia prepared a capricious retort; then, thinking better of it, began to hum rather loudly, a mannerism that could be counted on to annoy Constance Philippa; then, thinking better of *that* (for this lovely if impetuous child did have a warm heart), she turned suddenly to Octavia, and said: "But I did not mean to insult you! Of all things, dear Octavia, I did not mean *that*. Mr. Rumford is a fine, upstanding, and altogether considerable gentleman, of whom, I believe, Uncle Vaughan thinks highly; and Aunt Edwina has, I believe, never said a censorious word, in my hearing at least. And we know that Mother respects him."

Octavia, smiling sadly, applied herself to the patchwork toy in her lap, and did not reply for some strained moments. She then said, without raising her tremulous brown gaze to Malvinia's: "I fear, Malvinia, that all this chatter of Mr. Rumford—and Rumford Hall—and this and that—is, at best, premature. And may even be," she said in a quavering voice, "finally quite irrelevant."

"Octavia!" Malvinia breathed. "What are you saying?"

"Octavia—is it so?" Constance Philippa asked.

Bravely the young woman said: "I fear—I fear he may be, after all, interested in someone else: and Mother's fancies, and, I am ashamed to say, my own, may be quite insubstantial."

"Someone else!—ah, he does not dare!—not after things have so advanced, and he and Grandfather had, I thought, come to some sort of agreement with each other," Malvinia said heatedly. "Of course, I do not *know* that any such conversation took place, but Mr. Rumford has *behaved* in so conspicuous a way. . . . Who might the other girl be?"

"Perhaps it is Delphine," Constance Philippa said dryly. "No, more likely Felicity Broome, with her gossamer veil. Only fancy, she pretended to be chilled, and faint-headed, in *this* heat!"

"I do not know the identity of the other girl," Octavia said. "It is naught but a rumor, out of Philadelphia. Indeed, it was Felicity who whispered it in my ear with, I thought, an expression of such gleeful cruelty, I felt my heart pierced; and wanted nothing more than to be carried back home, to my bedchamber, and my bed."

"Octavia, I am certain you are mistaken," Constance Philippa said, with some attempt at chastisement, "for, you must remember, Mr. Rumford is a deeply religious man, and the recent death of his wife—but some six or seven years ago, I believe?—must weigh very heavily upon him. It is common knowledge that he was ordained a Lutheran minister; his nature is hardly lightsome and fickle."

"That is true, I suppose," Octavia said slowly. "Mr. Rumford *is* uncommonly deep."

"The fact that he remains in mourning for his wife," Malvinia said, "can only be encouraging to you, for it suggests the gravity with which he contemplates the sacred bonds of matrimony! Indeed, Octavia, I should hardly be despondent, if I were you—and, in any case, it is quite impossible, to read a gentleman's heart."

"Impossible, indeed!" Octavia observed, with a small stoic laugh.

In such wise the sisters idly spoke, the while they did their fancywork and the languid afternoon waned; and no disturbance announced itself more stridently than a nearby raven, or a cicada, or an o'erimpetuous bullfrog down at the river.

It was then, in a stealthy motion, that Deirdre drew forth the locket she wore on a gold chain around her neck, to open it, and to stare intently at the faded daguerreotypes inside: an action that could not fail to offend her sisters. (For the daguerreotypes were of her *natural parents,* who had died some six years previous, in the dread typhoid epidemic of 1873. It was believed that Deirdre's mother had given her the locket, shortly before her death, with instructions *never to remove it,* lest something unfortunate happen: so the stubborn child, in the very bosom of her new family, made a show of opening the locket upward of a dozen times daily, to gaze upon the old pictures with an expression of sickly yearning.)

In order to deflect attention from Deirdre's rude gesture, Samantha said nervously: "Do you think there might be some difficulty? I mean, with Mother, and her private interview with Grandfather, in the Hall? For if Grandfather is not sympathetic this time—"

"Samantha," Octavia scolded, "you are speaking out of turn: for we are hardly meant to know our mother's private business."

"We are not *meant* to know," Samantha said, blushing, "but, in fact, we cannot escape having a very good idea of what it might be. And if Grandfather is adamant, and refuses to continue his support, what will poor Father do? You know, he is so *very* close to discovering the principle of the perpetual-motion machine!"

"Indeed, is he?" Malvinia asked, now peeking out from her veil at the sky, that she might judge whether the sun's rays were still injurious. "This is the device, I believe, which is to run forever?—and require no rewinding?"

"A device to run forever!" Constance Philippa murmured. "How very strange."

"Strange," said Samantha, "and miraculous. Indeed, there will be nothing like it under the sun: and *our father* will have invented it."

"Invented it," Octavia said firmly, "*and* patented it. For, this time, Mother will hear of nothing else."

"A perpetual-motion machine is one that runs—*perpetually?*" Constance Philippa asked, knitting her brows. "I find that concept most remarkable. Indeed, I find it most distressing. Are you certain, Samantha, that you have understood Father correctly?"

"I work by his side in the laboratory, when he will allow me," Samantha said boldly. "And, I assure you, it is precisely as I have said."

Poor Constance Philippa held herself so stiffly, with so pained an expression, one might have wondered whether the strong admixture of

chloride of lime and powdered salicylic acid, which, some hours ago, she
had applied beneath her arms, for purposes of daintiness, had begun to
sting; or whether, like the others, she felt the continued strain of *not*
looking at her youngest sister. (Who, whilst the others conversed, held
herself in distinct opposition, being seated somewhat to the side, and
brooding, still, to no useful purpose, over the old locket.)

"Father is so very close to grasping it! So very close to consummation," Samantha said warmly. "What a pity it would be, and what a
tragedy, for our nation, if he should not be allowed to continue; and for
mere financial reasons."

"Yet Grandfather, I have been told, is greatly displeased," Malvinia said slowly, "with what he calls Father's *perversity:* a word that rather
puzzles me, since it is so rarely used."

"And Great-Aunt Edwina is said to be skeptical," Constance Philippa said.

Octavia gave her patchwork toy a vigorous shake, and said: "It is
wrong of you, Malvinia, and Constance Philippa, to discuss our elders like
that, out of their presence. It makes me distinctly uneasy."

"You are right, of course," Malvinia said, "and yet, how I wish
we Zinns were not poor! That is our problem, at bottom; there is the
origin of all our unhappiness. Four dowries—I mean *five*— Four grown
girls—that is, *five:* or do I truly mean four, since our beloved Constance
Philippa is, after all, betrothed to her Baron? Alas, it is all so troublesome!"

Doubtless there is some error, in ascribing to past events, certain
logical interpretations that come to mind only after time's ineluctable
passage; nevertheless, it may have been this rash speech of Malvinia's
that, entering the heart of the youngest of the Zinn sisters like a blade,
did some mischief there, with the immediate consequence that Deirdre
raised a startl'd and incautious gaze to Malvinia's blithe countenance; and
a near-inaudible gasp was heard, tho' issuing from which of the sisters,
I cannot say.

Whereupon poor Octavia, all ablush, murmured: "Malvinia! You
forget yourself."

Yet Malvinia continued, briefly meeting Deirdre's childlike gray
gaze (in which simple *hurt* had not yet begun to be o'ercome by *reproach*):
"Yes, I have thought long upon the subject, and have come to the conclusion that the origin of our unhappiness—for we *are* unhappy, tho' we are
Zinns!—lies in our impoverishment. For, only consider," the bold young
lady said, lowering her voice, and now leaning toward those three sisters
whom, it is to be supposed, she considered her *true* sisters, "only consider, how, almost alone in Bloodsmoor, amidst so many excellent families, we are forced to a fortnightly wash!—with the shameful result,

that all the households know the exact limits of the Zinns' changes of clothing."

Constance Philippa sighed loudly, and fanned her warm face with her fancywork, having mislaid, or forgotten, her fan, and said: "Malvinia, I cannot tolerate this subject any further, from you: and you know that Mother has forbidden it."

Octavia's plump cheeks now resembled lovely cream-hued peonies, upon whose petals a scarlet blush had just begun to bloom, for this warm-hearted young lady was most distressed, both that the outlaw topic was introduced, and that Deirdre had been injured—albeit quite innocently, and, as it were, only in passing. Thus she said in a flurried voice: "It is an unspeakable subject, to bring up at this time, and in this wondrous place, after the Kiddemasters' great generosity to us!—a magnificent tea in honor of Constance Philippa, and, too, in honor of Father, that his candidacy to the Society is being considered so seriously. Nay, it is an impossible subject: we will not hear of it!"

"The Gilpins and the Martineaus and the Ormonds, and many another household, do their linen each quarter-year," Malvinia said boldly, "and it is hardly a secret, that the Broomes, tho' once poor, have, as a consequence of the railroads, I believe, enough wealth, and enough good linen, to do but a half-year wash: or so it is whisper'd. And the Whittons, and the Millers, and the house of Du Pont de Nemours, and—"

"Hush, Malvinia!" Octavia said. Her moist startl'd eyes were turned upward to the great house, not one hundred yards away; and then to poor Deirdre, who continued to sit, stiffened, and blankly staring, at the floorboards of the gazebo, her crochet hook now stilled in her hands. "Hush, hush, we will not hear of it, how you would injure Father if he knew, and how you injure *us*, with your cruel utterances! Nay, hush, we will not hear!"

"*Four* Zinn sisters, and, indeed, the talk of the Valley, as 'twas: and then *five*," Malvinia said, most impulsively, "which is of course a credit to Mother and Father, and not to be questioned, or ridiculed. Nay, I will *not* hush, I *will* speak, there is no stranger near, not anyone who might pretend to be surprised, by anything that is said. Indeed—"

Constance Philippa, now tugging with unconscious force, and vexation, at the fashionably tight sleeves of her piqué dress, interrupted forcibly to say: "You are correct, Malvinia; and yet you are improper. And so—do as Octavia and I, your elder sisters, say, and *pray be still.*"

There then ensured some moments of ill-natured silence, during which, naught was to be heard, save the distant lowing of a cow; and the melodic queries of the bright-feather'd creatures in the stately elms nearby. Octavia broke the quiet with nervous chatter, the which was greeted with relief, tho', perhaps, scant attention: "The blackberry tea as well—I thought quite successful—and the fresh honey, from Uncle Rhinelander's hives—and—and—I must say, Constance Philippa, I do not truly think Delphine Martineau is to be censored for her gaiety and high spirits for she *is* so winsome, and quite pure of heart, I am sure. And the gentlemen from Boston—Professor Lyndon in particular—and Father's eloquence—and the great promise of the *perpetual-motion machine* . . . Perhaps, Samantha, we might beg of you, a helpful description of that amazing device?"

"Nay, I will make no serious attempt, for you are all distracted, and Mother will shortly be summoning us. The machine upon which Father has been working since last spring is, properly speaking, the *new machine*, for he felt of a sudden obliged to scrap virtually everything he had done beforehand—a heartrending decision, yet, I must believe, a necessary one. Alas, poor Father!" Samantha said fiercely; "how very hard he labors, and yet the ignorant world presumes to judge him!" She paused for a moment to calm herself, and then continued: "The new machine is designed with a copper pendulum involving not the swinging motion, with which you are familiar in household clocks, but a part-rotation, clockwise 180 degrees *precisely,* and then counterclockwise, 180 degrees *precisely.* So far as I comprehend the source of energy, it derives from the coordination of *magnetic fields, gravitational tides* (exerted by both the sun and the moon simultaneously), and *odylic force;* and the great difficulty at present is, how to release, yet inhibit, the energy thus summoned, that it will not rush into the mechanism with such force that the mechanism is destroyed—nor will it flow haplessly into the air. To this end, Father has been experimenting with magnets of various dimensions, and strips of lead, and putty, and silk threads, that the magnetic field may be more closely controlled. We are greatly anxious," the young lady said, in an abruptly lowered voice, and with a covert gaze around her, "that no spy from Menlo Park discover this latest experimentation: for you know that it would destroy Father utterly, not only the theft of another of his discoveries, but the theft of *this,* his greatest work—nay, when it is brought to fruition, it will be one of the greatest works of all time. Thus, if Father spoke at times circumspectly with the Boston professors, it was with the sad knowledge weighing upon his heart, that, for all their evident sincerity, and scientific objectivity, they might be spies in Mr. Edison's employ—or innocent dupes in his web. Alas, who can know!" Samantha concluded, with so profound a sigh, it might have issued from a woman twice her age.

Malvinia then inquired, in a somewhat subdued voice, as if she felt a modicum of regret for her rude words: "Yet work is progressing, I assume? And when does Father predict the mechanism will be perfected?"

"Father does not predict such things," Samantha said, crinkling her brow in startl'd disapprobation, at her sister's ignorance. "You know him very poorly, if you imagine his thoughts stray onto such notions!"

"Not in time for Constance Philippa's wedding?" Octavia inquired, with wistful regret. "Nay, I suppose not: it is ignorant of me, to ask."

"Not in time for Constance Philippa's wedding!" Malvinia exclaimed, in such alarm, she allowed her sunshade to fall to the floor. "Why, that cannot be possible, surely that cannot be possible, for the wedding is set for over a twelve-month from now! Surely, Samantha, you do not know everything, and may be mistaken in this issue?"

"Indeed, I may well be mistaken," Samantha said, with unlook'd-for humility, "yet, pray do not make these inquiries of anyone else: not of Mother, and, of course, not of Father."

"Then Grandfather must pay for Constance Philippa's wedding, and many another expense, and perhaps Octavia, too, will become engaged, and what of me, what will be my fate, ah, how wretched! *I shall not think along these degrading lines,*" Malvinia continued hotly, "not that they are *forbidden,* but that they are *degrading.* Nay, I shall not think—yet—yet—"

Several of the sisters exclaimed at once this young lady's name: and it might have been observed, how visibly poor Deirdre shrank back, out of apprehension, that, in Malvinia's outburst, she might again figure. Whereupon, with admirable alacrity, and poise, Constance Philippa turned to Samantha and inquired: "Not *months,* then, until the new mechanism is perfected; but—perhaps—"

"Years," Samantha lowly intoned.

Again there was a strained silence, the which was broken by Samantha's postscript, in a somewhat more casual voice: "Of course, as I have said, I may well be mistaken."

"In any case," Octavia murmured, "it is not anyone's fault—it cannot be anyone's fault—I scarce know, of what we are speaking, save that it is no one's fault and, surely, not to be laid at the feet of anyone *here,* amongst *us.*"

"Of whom, pray, are you speaking?" Malvinia inquired, with a show of startl'd incredulity. "Your words are most ill-considered."

"I mean only—I mean—it was my intention—alas, why does my tongue trip over every other word today!—and I am so very, very warm —and quite unhappy— Indeed, Malvinia," Octavia said, in a tremulous, hushed voice, "I believe it altogether unnecessary, for you to speculate aloud, and to vex yourself, with the possibility of *my* engagement. Please do not concern yourself with that eventuality again, Malvinia. You are *cruel,* in pretending to be *kind.*"

"I was not aware," Samantha said, "that Malvinia *pretended* to be kind. Did I, perhaps, misunderstand a word or two, in the course of the past several minutes?"

"How very odd a thing to say!" Malvinia exclaimed. "Are you in alliance against me? You and *she,* sharing a bedchamber, and a bed—" (This reference being in regard to the fact that Samantha and Deirdre enjoy'd, in the Octagonal House, a common room.) "Nay—it is most unfair."

The impetuous Samantha then said: *"You* are most unfair, Malvinia! If we are poor—and I do not say that we are—it is surely not Deirdre's fault—nor is it Father's—and, in any case, one would have to be uncommonly ignorant, not to know that poverty is but a relative state: for there are innumerable families, in Bloodsmoor alone, beside whom we are quite wealthy, indeed!"

Malvinia snapped open her fan, and fanned herself energetically, and said: "You need not sermonize *me,* Miss! You are very much mistaken, to attempt to sermonize *me!"*

"Dear sisters, please," Octavia pleaded, *"please* do not quarrel, on this wonderful day. We all know that poverty, and wealth, and any *secular condition,* are of very little significance, set beside Our Heavenly Father's abiding love for us; and the love of our dear Father and Mother, here on earth and—"

"I believe I will go home," Samantha boldly said, groping about for her mislaid gloves. "Octavia, you may make my excuses to Mother; simply tell her that I became faint, and hurried away home."

"That is impossible," Octavia cried. "You will *not* go anywhere on foot, unaccompanied, and in your new dress—alas, what would happen to your beautiful train alone! Nay, Constance Philippa and I cannot allow it."

"I shall do what I please," Samantha said. Her small pale face was aglow with feeling, and her green eyes fairly flashed; yet, once she had caught up her gloves, and squeezed them on her hands, she did not rise from her chair, but remained sitting—as if a great weight suddenly pressed upon her.

"Fancy such a notion!" Malvinia marveled, staring the while at her sister, and continuing to fan her face. "To talk wildly of hurrying away home, through the woods, no doubt, trotting like a horse! Why, it would be amusing, if it were not repulsive: I am only grateful that all our guests, and our dear cousins, have departed."

"Why cannot I go home by myself," Samantha said, in a vexed voice, "for surely it is not dangerous? And I promise to carry my skirts, and train; and I will not—alas, I *cannot*—run."

Octavia shook her head so earnestly, her plump cheeks quivered. "But it is dangerous, Samantha. Alas, indeed it is."

"Dangerous in what sense?" Samantha asked. "I do not under-

stand you. Deer there may be, in Grandfather's park; and smaller creatures like rabbits, woodchucks, raccoons, and opossum; yet I am reasonably certain that there are no *bears* any longer, and have not been any for
many years—"

"Hold your tongue, Samantha," Constance Philippa commanded.
"You are very young, and very silly; and know not whereof you speak."

"Indeed, yes," Octavia said sternly. "There is danger in the woods,
and even along the riverbank path, and you are not to walk unescorted,
and the subject is closed."

"Why don't we *all* walk together, then," the willful child persisted,
"arm in arm, as we did when we were little!"

"Impossible," Constance Philippa said, "and there's an end of it."

"Impossible," Octavia said, lowering her voice, "for we should still
be in danger."

"Impossible," Malvinia could not resist, "for, now, there are too
many of us Zinn sisters, to comfortably navigate *any path.*"

Again there was a startl'd silence, and an intake of breath; and this
time Deirdre roused herself to speak, with a toss of her head, and a
perceptible trembling of her lower lip. "I did not—" the overwrought girl
said, "I did not—I assure you, *I did not ask to be born.*"

This outburst struck the sisters as so piteous, and so lacking in any
vestige of dignity, that, all ablush, they scarce knew how to reply: nor even
where it might be most tactful to turn their eyes: toward one another; or
at the fancywork in their laps; or up toward Kiddemaster Hall, with the
hope that Mrs. Zinn, or one of the servants, might now be summoning
them.

I did not ask to be born—the desperate words repeated in a hoarse
whisper, or in an echo, issuing out of the very air itself!

Thus another strained silence o'erswept the sisters, whilst, her
small bosom heaving, Deirdre boldly stared at them, each in turn, as if
daring them to reply; or even to meet her gaze fully. But Constance
Philippa became, of a sudden, deeply absorbed in her pink yarn, which
had gotten tangled—and Octavia closed her tear-brimming eyes, and
clasped her small plump hands together, as if silently communing with
her God—and Malvinia, flush-cheeked, her blue eyes bright with feeling,
turned all her attention to her silken parasol, the carved ivory handle of
which, just the day before, kindly Mr. Zinn had attempted to clean with
a powerful chemical solution of his own formula—and Samantha gave the
linen towel in her lap a nervous shake, and, with unusual zeal, again took
up the embroidery needle, and spoke not a word.

Indeed, for some minutes, naught was heard upon the great sloping lawn save the rapturous songs of birds; and the quaint cry of the
cicada; and a faint breeze rustling the reeds and ornamental sere grasses,
that grew close about the gazebo, and the old stone wishing well, and the

picturesque river path: tho', it may be, an ear of especial keenness, might have detected, from afar, an indistinct, tremulous murmur very much like thunder!

Thus the minutes passed, and, after a great deal of pained silence, during which, as you can imagine, none of the sisters wished to confront Deirdre's ill-mannered gaze, Malvinia delicately cleared her throat, and dabbed at her nose with a lace-trimmed handkerchief, and inquired of Samantha, with as much propriety as if they were two Philadelphia dowagers at a tea: "Dear Samantha, please excuse me, for I freely confess my ignorance!—but I neglected earlier to inquire, as to the *purpose* of Father's perpetual-motion machine?"

Samantha looked up from her elaborate cross-stitching, and a smile illuminated that oft-peevish countenance, as, grandly, she spoke these words: "Its purpose, Malvinia, is nothing more, and nothing less, than *to run forever.*"

It was at this precise moment, the sisters afterward testified, that Deirdre, of a sudden, having given no warning, rose to her feet and allowed the unfinished antimacassar to fall to the floor.

The sisters stared; Octavia may have spoken Deirdre's name; yet, in the confusion of the moment, nothing was clear, save that the impetuous young lady made her way out of the gazebo, and down the little steps to the lawn, with not a backward glance, or so much as a murmured apology, for the unseemliness of her exit, or for having brushed her skirts and heavy train so rudely against Constance Philippa that her hat was dislodged!

In amaz'd alarm the four sisters stared after the fifth, as, with bold resolute step, she made her way down the grassy slope to the riverbank, *choosing not to walk on the gravel path,* her head held high, and the many ribbons of her yellow dress aflutter. She had left behind her gloves, and her fan, and her sunshade; and it would have been clear at once, to any eye, that her hat was no longer set correctly on her head, but had shifted some degrees to the side.

"Why," Malvinia breathed, pressing a hand against her straining bosom, "why, the vulgar creature is *near-trotting!*"

4

I slept, and dreamed that life was Beauty;
I woke, and found that life was Duty.
Was thy dream then a shadowy lie?
Toil on, sad heart, courageously,
And thou shalt find thy dream to be
A noonday light and truth to thee.

Thus, the noble words of Mrs. Ellen Sturgis Hooper, penned not long before her tragic death, at the age of thirty-six.

Beauty there is, in this Bloodsmoor chronicle; but *Duty* as well—*Duty*, I am bound to say, at the fore.

Therefore, whilst the sisters stare at Deirdre's retreating back, I shall force myself to illumine them, as clearly, and as briefly, as possible. (Alas, *force* is not inappropriate here, for, knowing well the prospects that lie ahead, for each of the sisters, I suffer to recall their fresh young faces, upon that September afternoon of 1879!—and wish only that it were given me, as chronicler of this history, some measure of *omnipotence,* that I might guide their destinies in happier directions.)

Nevertheless, I shall begin, turning my attentions first to *Constance Philippa.*

Amidst the charming Zinn girls, and their numerous female cousins, it was, perhaps, the eldest Miss Zinn who was most striking: as a consequence of her unusual height, which she carried with reluctant grace; and her mercurial manner, which wavered between outright truculence, and a sudden childlike warmth; and the Grecian cast of her features

33

—stubborn, noble, haughty, chaste—which would have done honor to a bust of antiquity, executed in white Italian marble.

At the advanced age of twenty-two, Constance Philippa was possessed of a surprisingly narrow, and angular, physical self, with nether limbs both long and sinewy, having very little agreeable plumpness to them, nor felicity of proportion. Her profile was hard, and regal, and had about it at times a somewhat predatory air, as a consequence of her long patrician nose; her forehead was high, showing the strength of bone, that gave to Mr. Zinn, as well, an appearance of dignity, and calm authority.

Her hair was very dark, lacking in natural wave, and lustre; but of so pleasing a thickness, it required but a single switch, looped about the crown of the head. Her eyes too were dark—dark, and bright, and intelligent, and restive, and given to that frequent expression of irony, which so distressed her family, and did little credit to Constance Philippa herself. When she made the effort, her voice possessed the melodiousness of any young lady's voice; at other times, unfortunately, it was low, and graceless, and dry, and droll, and stirred some apprehension in her sisters, particularly in Octavia, as to whether, in fact, *it was always Constance Philippa who spoke!*—and not, upon occasion, a stranger.

Many years ago, when Mr. Zinn was away at war, and sending heartfelt letters home to his family from Antietam, and Chancellorsville, and Gettysburg, and Richmond, it was Constance Philippa (then but a very small miss, indeed) who most wanted to be at his side: and to be, in fact, a *soldier,* bearing arms against the "nasty Rebs!" During these sad years, which seemed all the more protracted, as so much sorrow, and apprehension, and unspeakable pain were involved, Mrs. Zinn made every effort to keep her little girls as merry as possible; and to prevent them from dwelling o'er much upon the fact that their belovèd father was absent and risking his precious life, that the Union should not be dissolved. Of course the little girls and their mother prayed together, on their knees, at least thrice daily; but, in the evenings, they greatly enjoyed themselves, gathered around the piano, singing Mother Goose songs, whilst Mrs. Zinn played, with as much spirit as she could summon forth. How warm, how merry, how delightful, these evenings in the parlor, so very long ago! Yet, even upon these frolicksome occasions, Constance Philippa exhibited a curious want of propriety, in her choice of song: her oft-requested favorite being not "Sweet Lavender," or "The Fairy Ship," or the e'erpopular "Hey Diddle Diddle," or the lively "Yankee Doodle" and "Looby-Loo," but, I am sorry to say, the cruel "A Fox Went Out" —soundly disliked by the other little girls, who declared that it was *nasty,* and, as sung by Constance Philippa, too *loud* for their ears.

Yet Constance Philippa would beg Mrs. Zinn to play it, and she would get her way, and, standing straight and tall as a little miss of seven or eight might manage, she fairly shouted the words, her dark eyes aglow—

A Fox went out on a starlight night
And he pray'd to the moon to give him some light
For he'd many miles to go that night
Before he could reach his den O!

He came at last to a farmer's yard
Where the ducks and geese declared it hard,
That their sleep should be broken and their rest be marr'd
By a visit from Mr. Fox O!

Mr. Fox takes the poor gray goose by the sleeve, and, despite the valiant efforts of Old Mother Slipper Sloppers and her husband John, the goose is hauled away to Fox's den, to seven little foxes, eight, nine, ten, who devour her without fuss or ceremony, whilst Constance Philippa's sisters clapped their hands over their ears; and Octavia in particular thought the song very, very wicked, all the more so in that the quaint illustration showed Mr. Fox seizing Madame Goose who rather resembled Grandmother Kiddemaster in her morning cap! "A *very* wicked song," Octavia cried, "for why did not Baby Jesus intervene?"

A decade later, and more, the eldest Miss Zinn, now an affianced young lady, oft found herself humming this old and near-forgotten nursery song beneath her breath, to her own surprise, and with some embarrassment. *He took the gray goose by the sleeve,/ Quoth he "Madame Goose, now, by your leave,/ I'll take you away without reprieve,/ And carry you off to my den O!"*—these uncouth words, adjoined to a most unseemly boisterous rhythm, running through her mind in the very presence of her fiancé, or in the midst of a formal dinner party, or a tea, or a reception at one or another stately Bloodsmoor home, with such percussive force that she oft lost track of the conversation about her, and sat in unnatural stillness. *He sat him down with his hungry wife;/ They did very well without fork or knife;/ They ne'er ate a better goose in all their life,/ And the little ones picked the bones O!*

It cannot be said that Constance Philippa was very well acquainted with her fiancé, the Baron Adolf von Mainz, to whom she had first been introduced but the previous December, at the resplendent Christmas ball given annually by the Kiddemasters of Wilmington: nor, I suppose, can it be said that the reticent young lady felt, as yet, any o'erwhelming sentiment pertaining to her fiancé, and to the impending matrimonial state. That, however, she would in time come to love the Baron, and have every wish to bear his sons, she did not doubt, partly as a consequence of Mrs. Zinn's enthusiasm and encouragement, and partly as a consequence of her frequent readings in the field of romance—such novels as *The Bride of Llewellyn, Blanche of the Brandywine, Phantom Wedding,* and many another: the which promised many blessings, though difficult of interpretation, springing from the marital state.

The Baron was of indeterminate age, and gave off a commingl'd scent of tobacco, red meat, and something very dark and very moist; he was not uncommonly tall of stature (being, in fact, some negligible inches shorter than Constance Philippa); nor above the ordinary, in terms of conventional handsomeness, and personal charm. The pronounced nature of his Germanic accent, coupled with an intrinsic shyness, on the part of Constance Philippa, made casual intercourse betwixt them somewhat difficult, yet, as their meetings were always in company, or closely attended by one or more chaperons, this was by no means a serious impediment to their romance: and, indeed, oft struck Constance Philippa as felicitous, in that she doubted she had anything to say to him, or he to her, at this early stage in their acquaintance.

The quality in him which most impressed Mrs. Zinn and the Kiddemasters, was less his social manner than his ancestral name, the which, it was said, was *nine hundred years old,* and very well known in Central Europe. The quality in him which, alas, most impressed Constance Philippa had naught to do with his name, or his probable fortune, or his personal charm, but with his *sportsmanship,* of which she actually knew very little, though she had upon several occasions seen him mounted on his stallion Lucifer, and once with his falcon Adonis on his wrist: both the stallion and the falcon being such sleek, magnificent, beauteous creatures, Constance Philippa's breath was near snatched away, in utter awe! —though, being by nature and training a perfectly comported young lady, she took care to give no sign.

The approaching wedding necessitated some intimate discussions, betwixt Mrs. Zinn and Constance Philippa, as to the phenomenon of *conjugal love,* and *woman's ministration,* and *wifely duty;* and it was with considerable warmth that the elder woman insisted that Constance Philippa lay aside all her hesitations, for, in time, she would surely come to "love" the Baron, with a love befitting their circumstances. Upon one occasion, however, Constance Philippa, her countenance ablush, inquired of Mrs. Zinn as to *her* early acquaintance with Mr. Zinn: "Was it the case, Mother, that your feeling for Father *grew* with the passage of time?—or was it, from the first, a considerable one?" Mrs. Zinn stared at her daughter with amaz'd displeasure, that the girl should be so bold, and Constance Philippa felt compelled to continue, albeit with pronounced nervousness. "I mean, Mother, one does get the impression, from things one has heard, amongst your family, and elsewhere, that the courtship betwixt you and Father was exceedingly romantic—or, at any rate, not characterized by excessive formality—which is to say—I mean—there have been allusions in my hearing—as to—as to—"

But here the fiercely blushing young lady lost her courage, and her words trailed off into shamed silence; and Mrs. Zinn drew herself up to her full height, so that she might stare her impertinent daughter in the eye, and, in a ringing voice, speak in this wise: "That Mr. Zinn and I were agreeably impress'd with each other, upon the occasion of our first meeting, in my godfather Dr. Bayard's home, is hardly to be denied, since, of course, the first meeting did precipitate a second; and the second, a third. But beyond that, my dear daughter, you have not the privilege to speculate; for I cannot but think it unwholesome, as well as unseemly, for you to concern yourself o'ermuch with such matters," whereupon the chasten'd young woman murmured her apologies, and withdrew.

(There is *mystery* hidden in my parents' lives, and, doubtless, *romance* as well, Constance Philippa bethought herself, and yet, how straining to the imagination, to envision!—for they are, now, so very settled in their lives; and so very proper.)

Constance Philippa's much-heralded engagement to the Baron was the result of a series of negotiations presided over not by Mr. Zinn (who, necessarily immersed in his work, possessed neither the time, nor the spirit, to oversee his daughters' matrimonial prospects), but by Grandfather Kiddemaster, aided by one or two legal advisors, and, of course, Mrs. Zinn, who applied herself to this task with all the more zeal, in that it had been long-awaited, and, for a time, despaired of—for Constance Philippa had reached an advanced age before a worthy suitor stepped forth: and how many anxious hours had been passed, by Mrs. Zinn, in secret shamed worry, that her Kiddemaster cousins should be marrying off *their* daughters with such ease, and opulent ceremony, whilst the Zinns of Bloodsmoor had yet to celebrate a wedding!

Now it had come about, however; and all was well; or would shortly be well, when the contractual agreement was settled, and the Baron's demands met, and the date firmly fixed. From time to time Mr. Zinn amiably inquired as to the proceedings, and was met by a blank startl'd expression on his daughter's face, followed by a severe blush, and an immediate warm response from his wife: "My dear John, all is moving ahead with agreeable alacrity, and you should not trouble yourself, any more than Constance Philippa should trouble herself, with vexing details."

"So long as the young persons are happy, and the Baron is conscious of his good fortune, in such wise as Tennyson discerned," Mr. Zinn benignly observed, pausing, and drawing breath, that he might recite, with near-shut eyes and an expression, directed toward Constance Philippa, of such abstracted love, that the poor girl blushed all the more fiercely!—these lyric words, of the great Poet Laureate:

> Indeed I know
> Of no more subtle master under Heaven
> Than is the maiden passion for a maid,

Not only to keep down the base in man,
But teach high thought, and amiable words,
And courtliness, and the desire of Fame,
And love of Truth, and *all that makes a man.*

Whilst in secret, the unhappy daughter suffered these curious—nay, maddening—words to tumble through her brain, as if they possessed a volition of their own, and an energy, proportionate to Mr. Zinn's: *The little ones picked the bones O! The bones O! The bones O! And the little ones picked the bones O!*

5

Alas, to be gifted with the semblance of *omniscience,* in thus recording the history of the Zinn family, yet not with *omnipotence!*—for though I can foresee the numerous vicissitudes of fortune, and the several tragedies, that lie ahead for Constance Philippa and her sisters, I cannot of course guide their destinies: this chronicle being a faithful recording of events long past, and not a mere fictional fancy, in which, at will, the author directs the fate of this personage, and now that, in accordance with some whimsical scheme.

Thus, I am filled with an unspeakable sorrow, to carry in my heart the knowledge that Constance Philippa will indeed be a *bride*—yet not, to the griev'd consternation of her family, a *wife.*

It was well for her peace of mind, however, and that of her sisters, that, as she sat in the stately gazebo, gazing with disapprobation after Deirdre's departing figure, Constance Philippa knew nothing of this; and, indeed, the surprise of Deirdre's ill-mannered exit so occupied her thoughts, that she had quite forgotten the Baron, and was caught up in her sisters' divers commentaries on the incident: whether it was to be adjudged an *insult* to them, or naught but another manifestation of Deirdre's *uncouth nature;* whether it warranted reporting to Mrs. Zinn, or had best remain unmentioned.

In the midst of this murmurous disputation Constance Philippa said, in a voice suddenly brusque with impatience: "Let her go, she is not one of us! *A cringing dog does invite the boot.*"

"You are cruel," Octavia cried, in her excited alarm, rising to her feet with such unwise alacrity, that, for a long moment, she felt quite faint:

for her numerous hair switches, and her large festooned hat, and her many-skirted dress, and innumerable petticoats, and, most constraining of all, her corset, had acted in some unfortunate wise, in conjunction with the hot shortcake, apricot-cream trifles, shaved beef, Virginia ham, and other dainties of the tea, as to induce sensations of giddiness and dyspepsia in the o'erheated young lady: the which she managed to subdue, for her sense of injustice was such that she could not allow her sisters to malign poor Deirdre. "You are cruel—you are unfair—you are not *sisterly*," she pronounced, "and, I am bound to say, you are not *Christian*, to speak thusly."

"And *you*, dear Octavia, are but o'erwrought," Malvinia archly said, "as a consequence of a surfeit of Mr. Rumford, and other captivating gentlemen, at this afternoon's festivity."

"There is no need for further insult," Octavia exclaimed, fanning herself hurriedly, as, alas, her plump affronted heart beat so very hard, she felt still the danger of faintness. "You have wronged poor Deirdre, and I believe I shall go to her: for it is very, very wicked of you to allude to her unfortunate background, and to suggest that she is less loved than the others of us."

" 'Less loved'?" queried Constance Philippa, with an expression of amused scorn. "*I* should not have said that she was loved at all, should you, Malvinia?—and see no reason for all this fuss."

Whereupon Constance Philippa and Malvinia succumbed to lightsome laughter, the while purse-lipped Samantha looked resolutely away, working on her cross-stitching, and making a pretense of hearing none of this, though Octavia was prick'd close to tears: "Nay, it is *truly* unchristian of you, to utter such wicked thoughts! I fear Our Lord has heard you, and is most surprised and displeased, the more so in that you are not commonfolk, but Zinns."

Yet, alas, the wanton sisters did not curtail their mirth, still less did they offer any sign of chagrin or apology!—so that Octavia was moved to further exclaim: "I pray Mother will send for us presently, that we may be safely escorted to our own home: for, I fear, something unlook'd-to may transpire, before this day is done."

Whereupon frolicksome Malvinia opened her lovely blue eyes wide, in a pretense of anticipation: "Something 'unlook'd-to,' Octavia? Why, are you not teasing?—are you not being cruel? I cannot recall an 'unlook'd-to' event in recent memory, in our placid Bloodsmoor!"

And, to their shame, both Constance Philippa and Samantha joined in her gay careless laughter, the which surely was heard by the weeping Deirdre; and, I am bound to say, by Our Lord Himself.

My preference for Miss Octavia Theodora Zinn, the most sweetly acquiescent of the sisters, will be, I believe, given further validity, by that comely young lady's eventual fate, so far as marital experience is concerned: tho' it is not to be denied that she will suffer, and suffer greatly, before her piety, diligence, generosity of spirit, and intrinsic Christian demeanor are suitably rewarded.

Octavia was now twenty-one years of age, and had, from perhaps the tender age of ten, been lovingly called "the little lady," and ofttimes "the little woman," by both her family and the household staff: as a consequence of the precocity of her figure, and its agreeable plumpness, and her own maturity of manner. (Indeed, Octavia had blossomed so prematurely, in terms of her *feminine attributes,* that Great-Aunt Edwina, the unrivaled arbiter of such matters within the family, had found it necessary to decree—with not a little alarm, and some natural repugnance—that the child, then but ten years of age, must be fitted at once for a *full-figure corset:* it being something of a scandal to allow the little girl to appear, even in the nursery, with her flesh unbound and "aquiver," as Great-Aunt Edwina put it, "in every direction.") That her manner was unfailingly mature, and wondrously magnanimous, should not have greatly surprised, I am bound to say, seeing that Octavia was, after all, a Kiddemaster by blood; yet such were the displays of ill-temper by Constance Philippa, and wanton capriciousness by Malvinia, and, at times, a most unnatural *ratiocinative preoccupation,* on the part of little Samantha, that the second-eldest bloomed the more admirably, and exhibited all those traits and virtues the world is wont to term *gracious,* and *genteel,* and those of a *born lady.*

Indeed, as Mrs. Zinn had every reason to modestly pronounce, to her wide circle of female acquaintances, Octavia had oft been called, even as a young girl, "the little mother" as well, in consequence of her loving concern for children younger than herself, and the tremulous intensity of her feeling. She wept as readily over others' mishaps as over her own; her warm brown eyes were all aglow, when she was allowed into the presence of an infant; she loved to fuss over very small children, kissing and fondling them, and begging to be allowed to hold them. (The innocent little miss quite shocked Mrs. Zinn and several of her lady visitors one afternoon when, in a shy yet firm voice, she announced that she was most eager to acquire an *adorable babe* of her own, once she was tall enough, and strong enough, to safely carry it!)

Upon one fearsome occasion, when she was but six years of age, Octavia had managed to save two-year-old Samantha from drowning in the old stone wishing well behind Kiddemaster Hall: that precociously inquisitive, and naughty, child having crawled over the rim of the well, to "determine, to her satisfaction, how deep the water might be." (Though this quaint and rough-hewn well, with its handsome fieldstone, and sturdy oak, was agreeable enough, to the casual eye, its interior was, withal, somewhat sinister: the waters being very deep, and altogether

devoid of light, and unhappily odoriferous.) The unreliable Irish girl in
charge of the children had, to her shame, fallen asleep, thus allowing the
restless Samantha to make her way directly to the well, with that instinct
for dangerous mischief that would, with the passage of time, frequently
declare itself in the red-haired little miss; and, with no thought whatsoever of her own safety, Octavia had dashed forward to seize her baby
sister, and to save her, the while screaming for aid. Thus "the little
mother" prevented a tragedy from occurring, and was so innocent of
heart, and so devoid of vanity, that she but fiercely blushed at the professed gratitude of all, and pronounced that "Lord Jesus had taken
Samantha in His arms—and not Octavia!"

Upon another upsetting occasion, some years later, Octavia was
the sole girl to remain composed when Constance Philippa cut her face
whilst playing in one of the apple trees behind the Octagonal House—
a grotesque, and, it hardly needs to be said, forbidden activity, quite
inappropriate for a young female. Constance Philippa was then *eleven years
of age,* and, though fully clothed, in skirts, petticoats, cotton stockings,
morning cap, and even a tulle veil, to protect her fresh complexion
against the sun's coarse rays, she had wantonly decided to *climb a tree,* as
she had witnessed the servants' sons do, back in the woods, as much for
the unlikely sport of it, as for purposes of shocking, and titillating, her
small audience, consisting that day of little Miss Delphine Martineau, and
little Cousin Rowena, as well as her own sisters. (Alas, this bold action
prognosticates great sorrow, and not a little scandal, to come—the which
will be, I am gravely sorry to say, well borne out, by Constance Philippa's
behavior, in the darksome years that lie ahead.) I am not certain as to the
accident's precise details, but, within minutes, after the headstrong young
miss had climbed but ten or twelve feet above the ground, she lost her
footing, and slipped, and fell, scraping her tender hands, and badly
ripping her bodice, and, most alarming of all, so cutting her jaw, that
blood sprang forth, and copiously flowed.

Well may the sensitive reader recoil, in alarm, pity, and disgust;
and, doubtless, as I am bound to confess I do, experience some momentary *faintness,* at the mere pictur'd notion, of a young girl of good family
falling through the air, shrieking for help, and so badly injuring her
delicate face, that a great quantity of blood freely flowed, for all to see!
Indeed, three of the witnesses—Malvinia, Delphine, and Rowena—were
so terrified at the spectacle, and so sickened by the outpouring of blood,
that, within seconds, they sank to the ground in swoons; and Constance
Philippa herself, her bravado being quite fled, went a hideous chalk-
white, and, lying piteously upon the ground, began to weep, and to
whimper with fear, as a much younger child might have done. Nonetheless, amidst all this confusion, the ten-year-old Octavia summoned forth
enough strength of character, and maturity of spirit, to o'ercome her

natural revulsion, and to rush to the hapless child's side, there to stanch the flow of blood first with her apron, and then with her pretty new beribboned morning cap, the while embracing her sister, to comfort her, and to steady her; and murmuring these astonishing words: "Dear Constance Philippa, do not despair! Jesus is with us—Jesus helps me hold you—He will stop the dreadful bleeding, and make you well!—for He loves you, dear sister, and will not *inordinately* punish you, for all that you have displeased Him, in disobeying Father's and Mother's wishes!"—words which, no doubt, had their desired effect, in calming the frightened girl.

And there were numerous other instances, in which "the little mother" exhibited her warm heart, and canny sensibility, with the general consequence that she was the best-loved of the sisters, within the family, and amongst the many servants, at the Octagonal House and the great Hall.

Constance Philippa was, as we have seen, a sternly handsome young lady; Malvinia was known throughout the Bloodsmoor Valley, and in Philadelphia, as an *angelic* beauty; whereas Octavia was deemed but pretty—tho' *very* pretty—with her brown eyes, and somewhat snubbed nose, and soft plump cheeks, and warm smile. I am not certain of her height, but believe it to have been no more than five feet two inches, some seven inches below that of her elder sister's. Her complexion was fresh, tho' oft heated, and rather too pink, or flushed, for Mrs. Zinn's taste; her figure was ample, quite lacking in that angularity that characterized Constance Philippa's, yet, I am sorry to say, possessing very little of that pleasing harmoniousness of proportion, which characterized Malvinia's, and gave her the air of a veritable goddess. (Poor Octavia! I hope I am not injuring her, by confiding in the reader that, try as she would, with the rigorous aid of the servant girls, she could never cinch in her waist below *twenty-four* inches. Whereas Constance Philippa's waist was but *twenty-one* inches; and Malvinia's a lightsome *nineteen*. It is unfair to bring in a comparison with Samantha and Deirdre, who were both unusually petite, and might have given the impression, to the hurried eye, of being mere girl-children of eleven or twelve; unfair, too, to mention, save in passing, that Octavia's white-haired grandmother, Mrs. Sarah Kiddemaster, still possessed, at her advanced age, the legendary waist of her youth—a much-envied *seventeen!*)

Like all young ladies who had attained the age of nineteen or twenty, with no definite prospects of marriage, Octavia was oft distracted by thoughts of an anxious nature, for she felt it quite pitiable, that her elder sister was at last engaged, and the beauteous Malvinia might have her pick of attractive suitors, whilst she, for all her good nature, and good works, and resolutely cheerful Christian demeanor, was in danger of being unchosen. If she thought perhaps too frequently of the widower

Lucius Rumford, of stately old Rumford Hall, it was not, I should hasten to say, as a consequence of any indelicate inward motion of hers, so far as inclination, or appetite, might be concerned: the predilection had exclusively to do with her eager desire to be wed, and to please her family, and her Maker. "Alas, dear Mother! If I should be left behind, if I should grow an old maid, and *live*, and *die*, without the blessing of a gentleman's love!" Thus Octavia wept in the privacy of Mrs. Zinn's dressing room; and was stoutly encouraged by Mrs. Zinn, who embraced her, and said: "Dear Octavia, that cannot happen, and it shall not: not while I draw breath, and Grandfather Kiddemaster befriends us, and there is justice on this earth."

It was with brave optimism, however, that Octavia prepared her hope chest, as the years passed, for, like any young lady of her station, she would require twelve dozen of everything, and considerable quantities of silver, crystal, and china. She alone of the Zinn girls applied herself with great zeal to those excellent books written by Miss Edwina Kiddemaster—*The Young Lady's Friend: A Compendium of Correct Forms* (1864); *The Laws of Etiquette; Or, Short Rules & Reflections for Proper Conduct in Society* (1867); *A Guide to Proper Christian Behavior Amongst Young Persons* (1870); *The Christian House & Home* (1874); *A Manual of Etiquette for All Times & All Ages* (1877), and others, of similar import. (For Great-Aunt Edwina, despite her native modesty as a Bloodsmoor Kiddemaster, had attained some eminence in the world of letters, about which I shall have occasion to speak, at a later time.) Octavia also busied herself with close readings of the more crucial articles in *The Ladies' Wreath, Godey's Lady's Book, Youth's Companion, Harper's Bazaar,* and *Peterson's Ladies' National Magazine,* that all facets of life's complexities might be known to her: with the result that Constance Philippa upon more than one occasion swallowed her pride, to ask of Octavia what must be done, if, at a formal dinner party, she was o'ercome by internal gastric distress; or, as a houseguest, she might find herself confronted with those noxious vermin known popularly as *bedbugs*. Since the dramatic appearance of the Baron von Mainz in Constance Philippa's life, that young lady appealed to Octavia for all manner of advice, the which poor Octavia did not hesitate to supply, though her heart was pained, and secret tears welled in her eyes.

Constance Philippa had, some years ago, strongly sued for her own private bedchamber, on the second floor of the Octagonal House; but Octavia shared a cozy, and very prettily appointed, bedchamber with Malvinia, who was wondrously affectionate when the sisters were alone together, and loved nothing better than to confide her secrets to Octavia, and ask advice of divers kinds. (I hope it will not offend the reader, to learn that Malvinia, whilst still a very young and innocent girl, had all unwittingly attracted the attentions of certain gentlemen: these attentions being, to her giddy mind, both flattering and disconcerting, *for she did not comprehend their grave import.*) There were rain-lash'd nights when the sisters would cuddle in their canopied "sleigh" bed, beneath their warm blankets and goosedown quilt, whispering together, and giggling, and, upon occasion, dissolving into heartfelt tears; and, upon more than one tempestuous night, the mercurial Malvinia cried herself to sleep in "the little mother's" accommodating arms. (For Malvinia "adored" her suitor Cheyney Du Pont de Nemours, and "dearly craved" to be wed: and yet, at the very same time, the fickle young lady declared she "wanted never to marry" because she "couldn't abide the thought of a *mustach'd kiss*"!)

Samantha, too, oft appealed to Octavia, in private, despite her proudly stated lack of interest in "female" matters, and her pose of independence within the household. The Octagonal House being modestly compact, rather than o'erlarge, it was the case that Samantha and Deirdre shared a bedchamber: and, I am sorry to say, the experience was a somewhat uneven one, on Samantha's part, though she refrained from outright complaint to her mother. (For Deirdre's behavior was, alas, willful and unpredictable, and had been so, since the first day she was brought to the Octagonal House, as an orphan badly in need of the love of a Christian family. If, upon the morn, she was melancholy of spirit, and leaden of brow, she was sure to be o'erly gay by noon; and sullen by teatime; and irritable by bedtime; and insomniac by night—fearful, or restive, or susceptible to childish fits of giggling, or inexplicable spasms of tears. She was insincere whilst giving every impression of being utterly faithful, to the words she spoke; she was ill-mannered when no adult was near, and then mockingly gracious; she could not, the sisters complained amongst themselves, be *trusted* as to her occasional displays of affection, and of sisterly solicitude. For several years, commencing in 1875, when Deirdre was twelve, the Octagonal House and, in particular, the bedchamber shared by Deirdre and Samantha, was visited by fearsome and ne'er-explained *ghost phenomena,* consisting of bodiless voices, knocks, raps, and other intrusions, and during this tumultuous time the unhappy child also suffered an intensification of those troublesome dreams she routinely endured: the which, as the reader may infer, placed a considerable burden upon poor Samantha, who, chastised for complaining against Deirdre by Mrs. Zinn, sought solace with Octavia. "Alas, I fear that I cannot *love* her!—that I cannot succeed in *liking,* or even in *enduring* her!" —thus Samantha wept angry tears, to be answered by Octavia's warm embrace, and these heartfelt words: "Nay, but in time you will come to love her: if you are patient, and diligent, and pray to Lord Jesus, for the aid He so freely offers us, in combating our sinful natures.")

Abandoning her own bedchamber, and her adopted sister, Samantha spent many an hour in the company of Octavia and Malvinia, and oft secreted herself in their congenial room, when no one was near. There, she greedily read books from Mr. Zinn's library, with an emphasis less on the Transcendental utterings Mr. Zinn so prized, than on the books and periodicals Mr. Zinn had accumulated, pertaining to scientific discoveries through the ages, and inventions. The girls' educations being irresolute, and subject to some controversy within the family, it was the case that Mr. Zinn assigned "themes" and "problems" to them, for their perusal, and Samantha naturally excelled in such matters, and minded not at all sharing her findings with the others.

Upon one tearful occasion, when it looked as if Samantha would be barred from assisting Mr. Zinn at his work (for Great-Aunt Edwina thought it peculiar, and decidedly indelicate, that, after Samantha's coming-out in Bloodsmoor and Philadelphia society, on the day of her eighteenth birthday, she should continue to spend so many hours in the laboratory in the woods "like a common apprentice-boy"), Octavia soothed the distraught Samantha, and kissed her fever'd brow, and counseled her to do nothing rash—the weeping girl having said she scarcely knew what desperate things: that she would "make a heap of Great-Aunt's execrable books beneath her window, and burn them all in one great bonfire," that she would "run off, in boy's attire, to Mr. Edison's workshop, and beg to be taken in," that she would "throw herself into the ravine—and plunge, if God so willed it, into Hell itself."

Shocking words, to be uttered by a young lady of high station, and considerable intelligence! Yet, such was Octavia's magnanimity of character, she allowed the unseemly outburst to run its course, and advised her sister, with shrewd prescience, that, if she but held her tongue, and did not protest, their aunt would shortly forget; and, Mrs. Zinn rarely being in agreement with Great-Aunt Edwina, she would not care to enforce the elder lady's injunction, so that, within a few weeks, Samantha might all unobtrusively return to her father's side, *with no one the wiser.*

When this counsel emerged as faultless, and Samantha did return to the workshop, and to the much-lov'd company of her father and Pip, away off in the woods, it was a joyful sight to see how Samantha embraced the wise Octavia, and declared, with passionate affection, that Octavia had "saved her life," and that she would be "forever indebted to her."

Octavia laughed, and kissed Samantha's brow, and allowed that it was but a small thing, for one sister to demonstrate loving concern for another.

Thus Octavia was greatly cherished by her three *natural* sisters; but, it gives me pain to say, not by her *adopted* sister.

From the very first, when, brought to the Octagonal House at the age of ten, Deirdre had exhibited a considerable mournfulness of spirit, it was Octavia's intrinsic response to lavish affection upon her: the which was crudely rejected, as the orphan shrank from both embraces and kisses, and grew sullen at the slightest provocation. It was only after a considerable passage of time that she made some pretense of returning Octavia's affection, and then she was so little consistent, that Octavia frequently turned away in tears, quite rebuffed, and bewildered, and querying of herself, how she had *done wrong*.

"Nay, pay no attention to Deirdre," Malvinia whispered, stroking and soothing the weeping Octavia, not many weeks before the very day of the abduction, "for, tho' Mother and Father will have it otherwise, the little hussy is *not* one of us!—and will, if we are fortunate, one day grasp this unalterable fact, and shrink away of her own volition, and save us all great sorrow."

"That is cruel," Octavia feebly objected, "that is not in the spirit of the Zinns, Malvinia—"

"It is, then, in the spirit of *Malvinia*," that forthright young miss proclaimed, "and that will have to suffice, for all."

Thus Octavia struggled to o'ercome her natural repugnance for the orphan, and, with grim resolution, to continue to return *good* for *evil*, the while years passed, and the sisters grew out of careless childhood, and began to take their places in society: the situation being, at the time of the abduction, that Deirdre alone had yet to make her *début*, the other sisters having successfully come out, in both Bloodsmoor and Philadelphia, under the generous sponsorship of the Kiddemasters. As she matured, Deirdre was less demonstrably ill-natured; yet it could not be argued that she exhibited much warmth for anyone save Mr. Zinn, whom, in any case, all the sisters adored.

But a fortnight previous to the September afternoon, on which our history begins, Octavia had been standing, lost in reverie, at the top of the staircase, in the Octagonal House, so distracted by the troubled thoughts that assailed her, as to her probable spinsterhood, that she failed to hear footsteps behind her, and turned with a startl'd gasp, to see the mournful-countenanced Deirdre, who, showing no agitation herself, calmly reached out to take Octavia's hands in her own, as if to comfort her. That this spontaneous gesture betwixt the sisters, issuing with unprecedented compassion from Deirdre, was most remarkable, and quite astonished Octavia, I hardly need state; and it was all the more disconcerting, in that, for a long moment, the younger sister gazed with a queer avidity into Octavia's eyes, her own being somewhat o'erlarge, and possessing no color in themselves, save perhaps an unnatural silvery-gray, the pupil inordinately dilated. Octavia summoned forth all the strength of which she was capable, to resist snatching her plump warm hands from out the grasp of her sister, whose hands were chill and clammy, and so thin, as to suggest a skeleton's: as she afterward confided in Malvinia, it was all she could do, to refrain from crying aloud, in sheer, thoughtless fright.

After some awkward moments, during which the pale Deirdre

continued to gaze into Octavia's eyes, and to squeeze her unresisting hands, the younger sister ventured, in her low, whispery voice, this decidedly peculiar statement: that she had comprehended, of a sudden, the worry that so darkly abided in Octavia's heart, and "felt compelled" to hurry to her, to comfort her with the wisdom that, much great suffering being in store for her, in the years to come, it would be well for her, and surely practical, to *rejoice* now, and to leave *sorrow* for later.

"A cruel—nay, a hideous—comfort!" Octavia proclaimed, afterward, to the sympathetic Malvinia; "and the malevolent chill of the creature's hands! Though I suppose she meant well; and acted out of a compulsion of generosity, unskill'd in her."

"Generosity!" Malvinia laughed, with infinite scorn. "Nay, I should term it the reverse; and only pray that she should not undertake such a pretense with *me,* and seek to squeeze *my* hands!"

6

Since memory's birth, no year but took
Something the heart held dear;
Each page of life on which we look,
Is blotted with a tear.
—MRS. S. T. MARTYN

Alas, impetuous Malvinia!—"The Rose of the Kiddemaster Garden," as all of Bloodsmoor was wont to call her, to the silent dismay of her less comely sisters—for it was a *careless attitude* of her own, pertaining to Deirdre, that helped precipitate the tragic mischance to come.

Bitter is this ironical fact; yet is it not profound, and instructive, as well?—partaking of that *cosmic scope* of the tragic, that so guided the hands of the ancient tragedians, as to temper their rude heathen energies with genius, and to provide us with immortal portraits of self-delusion, and self-ruin: the principle being that, unbeknownst to the protagonist, his actions, and his very attitude, necessitate his calamitous fall.

Yet, I submit, nothing could have seemed more innocent, and more sisterly, than Malvinia's behavior on the morn of the abduction: the which, rudely spurned by Deirdre, must have had much to do with the mocking words we have recently heard uttered, in the Kiddemaster gazebo.

For, taking pity on her adopted sister's plainness, and the particular misfortune of her hair style, the beauteous Malvinia had offered to make repairs—with what consequences, we shall see.

Much admired, and, indeed, much envied, Miss Malvinia Zinn was a young lady of lithe and aristocratic height, always fastidiously groomed, and attired in impeccable taste, within the financial limitations set by her father's modest income. She possessed a graceful carriage, with sloping shoulders, and slender arms, and perfectly proportion'd hands; her waist required very little forcible cinching, to be marvelously slim; her foot was agreeably small, though she oft succumbed to some small gesture of vanity, in insisting to the cobbler that her shoes were a perfect fit, when in fact they were tight, and caused her some secret agony, the more so when she danced.

Her rich dark hair was voluptuously threaded with lightsome shades of brown, and auburn, and red; and there were some stray hairs of a mysterious hue of silver, or silver-blond. Her eyes were of that regal blue of the flower known as Greek Valerian—a bountiful cluster of which, in fact, the adoring Cheyney Du Pont de Nemours had surreptitiously pressed upon her, not many days previous to the tea. These eyes sparkled, and glowed, and were capable of darkening, with the onset of tempestuous ill-humor; they were almond-shaped, wondrously bright, with fine thick lashes; oft dancing; covert, and sly, and teasing; childlike in innocence; angelic; and then, alas!—of a sudden, narrowed, and flashing, and demonic; yet no less captivating, as her numerous admirers would attest.

Her neck was long and slender, of that graceful beauty associated with the swan; her ears, somewhat elongated, possessed an exquisite shell-like translucence. An almost imperceptible widow's peak, the which faintly adumbrated that of her noble grandfather, Judge Kiddemaster, gave to her lovely face a heart-shaped poignancy that many gentlemen (not excluding her own dear father) found remarkable, and infinitely pleasurable to gaze upon. Yet, withal, and unbeknownst to her, Malvinia Zinn, like many individuals of extreme beauty, possessed an aura of something *uncanny*—less definite, and less distracting, than that of Deirdre; but tangible nonetheless. In all her girlish, and therefore innocent, labors, to make herself the more beautiful, and the more fascinating, to society, the young woman had no clear understanding of how fascinating —nay, how disturbing—she was in truth.

"Am I pretty?" she had demanded, as a very young child, of a nursemaid, or tutor, or one of her sisters, or Mrs. Zinn, or, upon occasion, Mr. Zinn himself. "Am I pretty enough? Shall I be beautiful when I grow up?"—the while peering into the glass, and sighing, and crinkling her smooth little forehead in an expression of doubt.

"You are pretty now," she would be told, with a kiss, "and you shall be even prettier, when you grow up."

"But shall I be *pretty enough*? Shall I be *beautiful enough*?" Thus the charming little miss refused to be placated.

At the age of twenty, Malvinia, like most of her circle, talked and worried ceaselessly about her complexion, the which was subjected to methodical treatments with such creams, oils, and washes, as Esprit de Cédrat, Sirop de Boubie, Bouquet de Victoria, honey amber, and Micheaux's Freckle Wash; and protected from the fearsome rays of the sun, by gauzelike veils of a therapeutic thickness, and wide-brimmed hats, and silken sunshades, required in all but the most gloomy weather. Such cautions did not invariably produce dewy-moist and luminous skin, it hardly needs to be said, but Malvinia's was indeed flawless; and her high-boned cheeks were touched with the most subtle of rosy blushes, by natural art. (Alas, in later years, to her shame, Malvinia would more and more employ *cosmetics,* including even lipstick, rouge, and black mascara, that she might succeed in counterfeiting that very naturalness of beauty, so confidently, and proudly, hers, in youth.)

Even in the cradle, Malvinia was her father's favorite; though that gentleman, possessed of absolute good sense, did his best to disguise the fact, in order not to upset the other girls. Yet Malvinia surprised all by being the brightest, or, at any rate, the most clever, of the sisters, during those sporadic periods when Mr. Zinn, impatient with tutors, governesses, and formal school, undertook to educate his daughters himself, in the schoolroom-nursery of the Octagonal House. (For Mr. Zinn, as I believe I have mentioned, enjoyed an early and very successful career as an educator, of radical principles, before his marriage to Prudence, and his embarkment upon a career of invention.)

Throughout his life, John Quincy Zinn attested to the belief that the child's soul, pristine and unblemish'd, is a fathomless reservoir of wisdom; and that the skillful teacher is one who, rather than imposing knowledge from *without,* seeks instead to draw—by artful persuasion, by "Socratic" interrogation, or any wholesome means—this very wisdom from *within.* Thus the little Zinn girls took instruction simply by answering questions put to them, as methodically and patiently as possible, by their devoted father, making an effort to *deduce,* or even to *remember,* truths which resided intrinsically within them: and it was Malvinia, mercurial, bright, indefatigable in her father's presence, who shone above the others, though one might have thought both Constance Philippa and Samantha superior to her, in intelligence.

(Let us picture Malvinia at the age of seven, sitting pert, erect, and unfidgeting, at the little hickory desk with the spool-turned legs, which Mr. Zinn himself had lovingly fashioned, in his spare time: let us picture her with small hands clasped eagerly in her apron'd lap, and wide blue eyes solemnly fixed upon her father's handsome countenance, as, *for long as an hour at a time,* he conscientiously interrogated her, in such wise:

MR. ZINN: Do you think, Malvinia, there is *one* Soul, or *many?*

MALVINIA: One, Father.

MR. ZINN: And why is that, Malvinia?

MALVINIA: Because the *one* that came first would then make the *other ones*—it would be the strongest of all—it would be the *Father.*

MR. ZINN: And how would you characterize this Soul, Malvinia?

MALVINIA: It would be like—like a Poppa—it would love the little souls—it would take care of them.

MR. ZINN: And would they take care of one another?

MALVINIA: Yes—because they are all sisters and brothers.

MR. ZINN: Very good, my dear!—very good indeed. And now tell me, where does the Soul reside?

MALVINIA: Where—where you can't see it.

MR. ZINN: But where is that, Malvinia?

MALVINIA: Oh—far away, I think. Back behind the mountains. Where the sun comes from.

MR. ZINN: And is the Soul anywhere else?

MALVINIA: Yes—it is everywhere, I think—it must be everywhere—like rain when it rains—like snow in the winter.

MR. ZINN: And how do you know that with certainty, dear child?

MALVINIA: Because—because we are all made by it—sisters and brothers of the same Father.

MR. ZINN: Is the Great Soul *inside* you, Malvinia, or *outside?*

MALVINIA: It is inside, I think—and outside too.

MR. ZINN: How can you discover it inside?

MALVINIA: By closing my eyes.

MR. ZINN: Very good, dear! And how can you discover it outside?

MALVINIA: By loving my sisters, and my father and mother, and Grandmother and Grandfather Kiddemaster, and Great-Aunt Edwina, and Great-Uncle Vaughan, and all my cousins, and—and all of the world! —for the Soul resides in all, and I am only good, when, by loving *them,* I love *it.*)

It is to be remarked that, long before her infamous *career* was begun, and long, indeed, before it was even dreamt of, in the solitary recesses of her heart, Miss Malvinia Zinn was a consummate actress, albeit of an altogether innocent type: most happily herself, and consequently possessed of a radiant beauty, when she had the occasion to perform for others— as if preening, with childlike vanity, before a mirror.

Thus "The Rose of the Kiddemaster Garden" had no need, like poor Octavia, to pore over Aunt Edwina's numerous manuals, or to peruse, with knitted brow, the new issue of *Godey's Lady's Book,* in order to be sufficiently charming, to the opposite sex: she knew by instinct how to give her numerous admirers the very same rapt attention, which never lacked, at the moment, in sincerity, that she had, in the nursery, given her dear father.

Accomplished as she was in every social, and public, respect, I am bound to confess that Malvinia's famed vivacity, and above all the bountifulness of her lovely smile, did not invariably extend themselves to those closest to her—to her sisters, in truth. Ofttimes unprovok'd quarrels arose, betwixt Malvinia and Constance Philippa: for the eldest Zinn daughter declared herself exasperated, and resolutely *uncharmed,* by Malvinia's queenly manner, and could not resist challenging her, on certain of her remarks. Infrequent indeed were quarrels betwixt Malvinia and Octavia, but this might have been because the latter was so tirelessly generous, and so forgiving of all trespass, that Malvinia had no cause for annoyance: many were the times Octavia took great pains to dress Malvinia's hair in a particularly demanding style, adjudged to be beyond the skills of the Zinns' single lady's maid; many were the times Malvinia declared herself *desperate,* and but *partly clad,* if she could not borrow for an afternoon, or an evening, or a weekend, some pretty accessory of her sister's—she so passionately coveted a lovely East Indian shawl of fine twilled goat's wool, a gift to Octavia from Grandmother Kiddemaster, and borrowed it so frequently, that, in obedience to the promptings of her heart, Octavia freely gave it to her: this being but one of numerous instances of Octavia's generosity, beginning when the girls were yet very young, and hardly out of the nursery.

If Malvinia had not quarreled o'ermuch with Samantha, it was primarily because this child, for many years the youngest of the Zinn girls, struck her as insignificant: so plain, so prim, so pinched of demeanor, with her nose always in a book, or her pencil rapidly scribbling on one of Mr. Zinn's yellow sheets of foolscap!—nay, poor Samantha could not be taken seriously, as a worthy sister, still less as a rival. (So secure was Malvinia in Mr. Zinn's love, that she never troubled to feel jealousy over the fact that Samantha spent so many hours of the day in the workshop above the gorge, playing at being her father's apprentice; for Malvinia had known from the cradle that *she* was Mr. Zinn's favorite, and could not be dislodged from that belief.)

"Am I pretty? Shall I be prettier still?" So Malvinia queried her mirror image, as, with the passage of time, she comprehended that it was *not done,* to speak thusly to others. "Shall I be known as the most beautiful of the Zinn girls?—nay, the most beautiful of all the girls of Bloodsmoor?"

The flawless skin fairly glowed, in assent; the blue eyes shone in certitude; the quick smile was dazzling to see! Yet the impetuous Malvinia could not resist a further question: "Shall I be Father's favorite, throughout his life, and mine?"

It will be no surprise to the reader that the arrival of the orphan-child, Deirdre (then known pityingly as Deirdre Bonner), while distressing in varied ways to the other sisters, was most distressing to Malvinia: not simply because the Zinns were "poor," in comparison to their relatives, and to the important Bloodsmoor families, but because, alas, it did seem, for a time at least, that John Quincy Zinn felt o'ermuch affection (however tempered by his natural absentmindedness of manner) for the orphan, the which inevitably lessened his affection, or, at least, his attention, for Malvinia.

"I cannot think why Father dotes upon her," the affronted Malvinia exclaimed, "nay, I cannot even think why he gazes upon her: for is she not ugly? Is she not sullen? Is she not pitiable? Is she not *common?*"

Little Deirdre Bonner had suffered the untimely deaths of both parents, within a scant fortnight of each other, of the dreaded typhoid: and there had been worry, for a time, that she would succumb as well, less to illness itself as to a most pathetic abandonment of life. She had wept very little, neighbors attested; she was so bereft, even tears failed her—thus believed Mrs. Hewett, the good wife of Reverend Hewett, who had taken for her *particular* charity, amongst the impoverished and unfortunate in the village, this pitiable little orphan. (All the Bloodsmoor ladies, naturally including the Kiddemasters, and Mrs. Zinn, ventured forth as many times as thrice weekly, by carriage, to the homes of the poor, bringing to them such necessities of life as warm clothing, cast-off parasols, and the coarser varieties of food, without which these unhappy wretches would doubtless have expired, over the cruel winter in particular. Of the Zinn girls, only Octavia took heartfelt pleasure in these visits: the others, to their shame, sulked and fretted, and oft refused to smile, shown into an airless and dim-lit cottage of modest proportions, or forced to observe, at rather too close a range, a sickly mewling babe at his mother's breast. "That the poor are so dull, and so tiresome, and, I am sorry to say, so boring, is surely not their fault," Malvinia once declared, her blue eyes flashing, "yet, as it is not *ours,* why must we suffer for it?")

The woeful little orphan Deirdre was not, however, of an impoverished family: for Mr. Bonner had been employed as a manager at a textiles factory some miles downriver (a factory owned by Mr. Clement Whitton, an uncle of Godfrey Kiddemaster's, in truth), and Mrs. Bonner had, within the limits necessitated by her modest social station, participated in church activities, at Trinity Episcopal Church, in which, at infrequent times, she might have been in the company of Mrs. John Quincy Zinn, tho' Mrs. Zinn had no clear recollection of the unhappy woman, and was certain that they had never exchanged a word. Twice-yearly, at Christmas, and in midsummer, great Kiddemaster Hall was thrown open to local residents above a social rank, and it is to be supposed that the

Bonners were included in this general invitation: but, again, no one had any recollection of them, and certain of the Kiddemasters—Edwina in particular—shunned these gatherings, for the very *jolliness* of such persons, wandering agape about the Hall, and eating and drinking all they could, was most distressing, and raised unfortunate thoughts about the wisdom of Mr. Jefferson, and the nature of the American Democracy generally.

Thus, no one claimed to know the Bonners; nor did it help that Mr. and Mrs. Zinn so abruptly made their decision to adopt the orphan, and to bring her home to the Octagonal House, that she would, of a sudden, have not merely a *family,* but *four sisters!* Nor did it help that the child herself, far from exhibiting gratitude, and smiling in response to the Zinns' overtures, sullenly thrust her fingers into her mouth, and shrank from all caresses like a frightened animal, and appeared to have gone mute, out of stubbornness as well as natural grief.

"Why, this Deirdre is naught but a half-drowned river rat!" Malvinia exclaimed, to her sisters, out of earshot of Mr. and Mrs. Zinn. "And we are to be expected to take her to our bosoms, to love her, as if she were one of us?"

"It is a rather grim prospect," Constance Philippa said, drawing herself stiffly up, to her full height, "yet, I suppose, we can rise to the challenge: for it would hardly do, you know, to oppose Father and Mother."

Samantha, then but eleven years of age, thought it most unfair that she should be forced to share a bedchamber with Deirdre: for Deirdre looked, Samantha said, like a wild creature that might *bite;* Octavia, ever the sensible one, bade them all hush, for it would not be their fancy, as to whether Deirdre was welcome or not, in the household: "She is our sister now, and will henceforth be known as one of our family," declared Octavia, in a forthright tone, "and that, I am bound to say, is that."

It may have done some good, that Mr. Zinn spoke quietly to the sisters, each in turn, to assure them that they would not be a whit less loved, as a consequence of having a new sister: but, in truth, the more loved, as Deirdre grew adjusted to her surroundings, and able to return their affections. "And you must speak of her as your *sister,*" Mr. Zinn cautioned, "and never by any other rude term, as *adopted sister:* for I am your father, and would have it so, and it would be very, very wicked of you, to disobey."

Thus, for a spell of some four or five months, even the reluctant Malvinia came round, and determined that she would acquit herself blamelessly, and lavish upon the dumb creature so generous a store of affection, she would be incapable of resisting!—volunteering to teach Deirdre those difficult skills of embroidery, and needlepoint, and cross-stitching, which she had either not been taught by Mrs. Bonner, or had forgotten, as a consequence of her great loss; and to instruct her, in somewhat awkward fashion, in china-painting, and the construction of wax flowers, "phantom" leaves, Valentines, and feather fans. Malvinia's voice being so melodious, and her manner so compellingly dramatic, when she chose to make it so, it was natural that she, and not the other sisters, should read aloud to poor Deirdre, from out that wonderful assortment of children's books in the Zinns' parlor: *Aunt Patty's Scrapbag,* and *Polly Peablossom's Wedding,* and *Blanche of the Brandywine,* and *Knickerbocker's History of New York* (in particular, the part in which St. Nicholas travels through the sky in a wagon), and *Pickwick Papers,* and *A Treasury of Riddles,* and *The Song of Hiawatha,* and many a volume of poesy, by Mrs. Craik, Mrs. Polefax, Mrs. Darley, and divers others.

Alas, very little seemed to move Deirdre, or to rouse her from her melancholy quietude, no matter how thrillingly Malvinia read, and recited, and emoted, with as much spirit, as if she were addressing a worthy audience!

Yet Malvinia prevailed, as much out of willfulness, perhaps, as out of genuine affection, and made an effort to teach her new sister those parlor games she herself excelled in: Pam-Loo, and Boston, and Puss-in-the-Corner, and Snip, Snap, Snore 'Em, and cribbage, and checkers, and Old Maid, and Goff, and Stir-the-Mush: all this, with very little visible success, for tho' Deirdre oft surprised the girls by winning at these trifling entertainments, she gave no evidence of enjoying them, or, indeed, even of exerting herself o'ermuch, as if her melancholy was far too sacred, to be so lightly dispelled.

And the girls sang together, accompanied by Mrs. Zinn at the old spinet piano, that they might entertain Mr. Zinn, or aid him in relaxing by the parlor fire, after his long day's labor. Malvinia's strong soprano led all the rest in such beloved tunes as "Is There a Heart That Never Lov'd," "When the Swallows Homeward Fly," and "What Is Home Without a Mother?" Upon occasion they sang Civil War songs, of the nature of "Stonewall Jackson's Way," and "All Quiet Along the Potomac Tonight," and "The Bonnie Blue Flag," and "The Battle Cry of Freedom," which never failed to bring glistening tears to Mr. Zinn's ruddy cheeks. In frolicksome spirits they sang "Baa-Baa, Black Sheep," and "Tramp! Tramp! Tramp!" (with appropriate stomping, in which gay Constance Philippa was the most demonstrative), and the lugubrious "Come Home, Father," the sheet music of which Great-Aunt Edwina had given them, that good lady being a founding member of the Philadelphia branch of the Temperance Union, and most intolerant of alcoholic indulgence. (It was part of the lightsome comedy of the situation, that John Quincy Zinn was a resolute teetotaler, and oft declared that he would as soon drain a glass of kerosene, as of alcohol!)

Thus, many a chill, windy, rain-lash'd evening was spent, in the snug parlor of the Octagonal House, with all the Zinns gathered together, in boisterous merriment—save for Deirdre, who held herself a little apart, and but rarely smiled, and begged to be excused from the singing: for her voice was hoarse, or her throat sore, or her head ached, or she "had not the inclination to sing."

"Nay, but singing is a pleasure, Deirdre!" Thus Octavia warmly expostulated. "It is not an obligation, or a chore: but a *delight.*"

Whereupon Deirdre stared at her with those o'erlarge silver-gray eyes, all unblinking, and murmured, in a near-inaudible voice, that, to her, singing was *not* a delight: and she would be very grateful indeed, if she might be excused.

"Ah, you are hopeless!—you will *never* be a Zinn!" Thus the exasperated Malvinia declared one evening, when no one else could hear: thereby wounding the unhappy child the more.

That the accomplish'd Malvinia Zinn was secretly jealous of her youngest sister, and in some confused manner envied her, should strike us as highly implausible, if we were not conversant with the mysterious ways of the human heart, and the wanton caprices of girlhood. In truth, Malvinia understood that Deirdre was a most wretched child, and that, in any case, her protracted melancholy was not Deirdre's fault; Malvinia had but to gaze at her own radiant reflection in a mirror, and then at Deirdre, to register the grave distance betwixt them, and all the advantages that were hers.

As the years passed, Deirdre grew taller, and acquired a very little of the soft roundedness of the female form; and some small—indeed, begrudging—measure of social tact and poise, the which she could scarcely have failed to absorb, dwelling amidst the Zinns and the Kiddemasters. Yet her manner remained feral; her cheeks were excessively pale; her thin lips rarely smiled; and her eyes queerly glared, as if with an unnatural light. And the irregular tuft of hair at her forehead!—it suggested a widow's peak, though altogether lacking in the subtlety and delicacy of Malvinia's own.

"How unjust it is, that, to the casual eye, we might appear to be *sisters!*—I mean sisters related by blood, and not by the whim of law!" Malvinia shuddered, making her complaint to Octavia, in the privacy of their bedchamber.

"I fear, Malvinia, that it is you who are unjust," Octavia said with a wan smile: yet such was the tone of her voice, that her words fell upon the air unconvincingly.

Thus Malvinia waged her secret war, and turned upon herself, in dismay and disgust: for *why* should she harbor such feeling, for a sickly creature like Deirdre, who could do her no harm?—and *how* could she be so cruel, as to wish misfortune upon her? (Deirdre was, it seemed, afflicted with a weak chest, and oft succumbed to respiratory ailments, in the winter months in particular. At the age of eleven she was felled by bronchitis, despite Mr. Zinn's "fresh air regimen," which necessitated open windows in bedrooms, in all weathers, to prevent the accumulation of stagnant air, and the breeding of lassitude, lethargy, indolence, short-ness of breath, anemia, chronic fatigue, melancholia, and even consumption: afflictions, Mr. Zinn believed, particularly dangerous to young ladies. At the age of fourteen Deirdre spent upward of a month in bed, in midwinter, so hoarsely breathing, she could not lie on her back, but was forced to sleep in a sitting position: this malady being diagnosed by the Zinns' physician, Dr. Moffet, as a very eccentric species of pneumonia, resistant to all normal medical treatment.)

"Nay, it is very wrong of me, and very foolish," Malvinia reasoned, "to be jealous of so pitiable a creature! And yet—" so the young lady calmly declared, contemplating her image in a tulipwood mirror—"and yet, what a boon to us all, my dear misguided parents as well as my sisters, if, by altogether natural and blameless means, and quite by happenstance, poor little Deirdre should die!"

Yet it would be erroneous for the reader to conclude, from these airy, and, I think, not truly heartfelt words, that Malvinia's dislike of Deirdre was in any way constant: or that, over a passage of time, it did not intermittently alter, to something approaching exasperated affection, or, at the very least, tolerance. For the five Zinn girls lived together, after all, in a household remarkable for its hospitality, warmth, and Christian benevolence; and the frequency of their visits to their grandparents' great house, known throughout Bloodsmoor for its magnanimity, and the espe-cial graciousness of Grandmother Sarah, when she enjoyed good health, could not have failed to have an ameliorating effect upon them. And, as it is surely true, as the poet says, that "Good Fortune breeds Charity," it oft happened that Malvinia's success at a ball, and the appearance of yet another gentleman admirer on the scene, had the agreeable effect of making her more happily disposed toward all her sisters, not excluding Deirdre.

Nay, I think it probable that Malvinia's heart *was* kindly, the while her whimsical thoughts played at cruelty: and we would do best to judge this mercurial young lady by her wisest actions, rather than her careless words!—as, I believe, we should all be wished to be judged, on earth, and by Our Heavenly Father.

Thus, on the very day of Miss Deirdre Zinn's forcible abduction, from Kiddemaster Hall, it happened that Malvinia, acting all spontane-ously, made a gesture of considerable charity, in which *sisterly concern* toward Deirdre was not lacking: with such very mixed results, none of which might have been foretold, that one is forced to marvel at the ironical circumstances, and to puzzle over the nature of *cosmic irony,* and *tragedy,* so rigorously explored by the ancients, of Attic renown, though wisely banish'd in more enlightened centuries, with the coming of Our Redeemer.

For was it not ironical, and was it not pitiable, that Malvinia, moving perhaps *against the grain* of her own sentiment, should, all unwittingly, have caused the darksome rift betwixt herself and Deirdre to widen all the more? With the unpleasant effect we have already seen, exhibited in the gazebo, and quite shocking to all witnesses: I mean the articulated cruelty of Malvinia, in speaking so explicitly of *dowries,* and of *four* Zinn girls, and then *five.*

Inexcusable behavior, on the part of a Miss Zinn, yet explicable, I think, on these grounds: for, not an hour before the handsome Kiddemaster brougham was due to arrive, at the Octagonal House, to take the Zinns to the Hall, Malvinia's eye fell upon Deirdre; and she could not prevent herself from exclaiming aloud, in exasperation, and amus'd pity, that the lady's maid, Chantal, had taken so little pains with Deirdre, the while she, and the other female servants, had fussed over Constance Philippa, and Octavia, and Samantha, and of course Malvinia! that they might strike all eyes as splendid young ladies.

It was with some genuine anger, then, that Malvinia pronounced Deirdre's hair style *impossible:* what could the lazy Chantal have been thinking of, and why had not Octavia taken note, or Mrs. Zinn?—for it was unfortunate enough that Deirdre's hair, being so remarkably dark, should lack lustre; why then fashion it into ungainly *rouleaux* over the top of her head, so that the sixteen-year-old girl actually resembled elderly Great-Aunt Narcissa Gilpin! "Nay, this will not do," Malvinia said briskly. "You will march back upstairs with me, Deirdre, and *I* shall dress your hair, and make amends for this shocking negligence."

The shy, abash'd girl naturally expressed surprise, and alarm, and reluctance, scarce daring to meet Malvinia's scornful eye, as she protested that Chantal's handiwork was adequate enough, for *her:* for she could not imagine (this but rapidly murmured) that anyone should wish to gaze upon her, in any case, throughout the afternoon.

"A nonsensical thought," Malvinia curtly said, "for, tho' your *début* lies in the future, it would be a most naïve intelligence, indeed, that fails to see you as *marriageable,* in truth, as any of us. And you must learn to take pity," Malvinia now gaily spoke, forcibly leading the recalcitrant miss back upstairs, "upon those of us, of either sex, who will happen to gaze upon you, during the course of the afternoon."

Thus Deirdre's feeble protestations were warmly overruled, and, with somewhat pained demeanor, she submitted to her sister's ministrations; and seemed also to concur in Malvinia's pronouncement that she must lay aside her cotton gloves, and wear instead a very pretty pair, made of fine Flemish lace, that Malvinia had tired of; and try on a white satin hat, with enormous green cockades, that Malvinia had worn once or twice, and deemed too distracting, for her own complexion, yet which might suit Deirdre very well.

All the while, Malvinia was working with remarkable skill, employing her own ivory-backed hairbrush, and a crimping iron, and Mrs. Penwick's Oil of Cathay Pomade, and several false braids, and a great quantity of hairpins, of divers sizes: the scene being the small but cozy dressing room, shared by Malvinia and Octavia.

"You are, in truth, a pretty girl," Malvinia spiritedly declared, "and it is yet to be discovered, how *very* pretty you might be: if only you do not foolishly resist."

Malvinia quite enjoyed herself, brushing her sister's long dark tresses, which frizzed and crackled with static electricity, and gave off flashes of extraordinary hues—now a very deep black, now an iridescent brown, now auburn; and weighed agreeably heavy in the hand, being of a considerable length, falling well to the girl's slim hips. From time to time Deirdre winced, as the brush encountered surprising snarls, but Malvinia did not pause in her exertions, for the carriage would soon arrive, and they must be off. "Waves—curls—indeed, a row of curls—and feathery bangs—and ringlets—and once or two of these braids—and mother-of-pearl combs—and cloth rosebuds: and the very prettiest hat we can find, discreetly fitted on top, not large, yet not foolishly small either," Malvinia murmured. "Ah, I shall make you presentable yet!—so do hold still, and hush."

Malvinia's industry, now witnessed by Octavia, and one of the servant girls, was all the more remarkable, and generous, in that this splendid young lady had been fitted earlier into her new white *mousseline-de-laine* dress, finished but a scant twelve hours earlier, by Madame Blanchet of Philadelphia: and how lovely, and how patrician, she looked! Her exquisite gown had been patterned in accord with the latest dictates of fashion, possessing a high-necked bodice, which fitted the wearer tight as a glove; and innumerable layers of wondrously light, near-transparent fabric; and yard upon yard of ruched and pleated flounces; and ruffles of silky *blonde* lace; and pink velvet ribbons. Despite her stiff corset, which made the normal intake of breath somewhat difficult, Malvinia succeeded in carrying herself with the grace of a summer's wisp of cloud; nor did her weight of apparel—some twenty-odd pounds, of skirts, crinolines, and train—have any more effect upon her, than an intermittent shortness of breath, and a numbed sensation in certain areas of her body, the which are too negligible to mention. (Indeed, it may be recorded here that lissome Malvinia was the envy of her elder sisters, and many of her female cousins, in that, despite the weight and burdensome warmth of her attire, she but very rarely betrayed any sign of that unfortunate symptom of corporeal heat called *perspiration;* and if, at times, strength so rapidly left her, that she sank into a swoon, it was never with less than lithesome grace, that she fell, into a chair, or into a gentleman's arms.)

The minutes passed, and Malvinia's fingers lightly worked, fashioning now curls, and now ringlets: ringlets being precisely what Deirdre's rather narrow face required: and how felicitous an opportunity, to disguise, by means of feathery puffs of bangs, that unsightly widow's peak! For this feature, whilst contributing to Malvinia's beauty, did not add greatly to Deirdre's, but rather enhanced her discomfiting air of the feral, and the nocturnal, and the *unnatural.*

Deirdre shyly protested that, in truth, she did not like ringlets: they tickled her, and made her want to sneeze.

Malvinia bade her hush, and assured her that ringlets would quite transform her appearance.

Nor did she like such a quantity of bangs, across her brow.

Nay, Malvinia laughingly insisted, but she *must* hush; for it was painfully clear, that she knew very little about such things. "Am I not correct?" Malvinia inquired of the small gathering behind her, consisting now of Constance Philippa, as well as Octavia and the servant girl. "Does she not look far better, already?"

Some twenty or more minutes of brisk hairdressing activity having ensued, involving brushing, and combing, and crimping, and braiding, and twisting, and curling, and puffing, and oiling, and employing a goodly number of hairpins, Malvinia then stepped back, panting slightly, in triumph, and eyed her creation, and met, in the mirroring glass, Deirdre's gaze, for an instant penetrating her own. "Ah!—now look!" Malvinia murmured. "Only *look:* are you not presentable, indeed?"

She pressed upon Deirdre a hand mirror, and, with a show of reluctance, Deirdre took it, and examined her hair from both sides, and from the back, her eyes widening at first with some surprise: for Malvinia had affixed a remarkable profusion of cloth rosebuds, and very pretty they were, to the back of her head; and the ringlets *were* somewhat excessive, though altogether charming, and skillfully executed.

"Well, Deirdre," Malvinia said, with but a hint of impatience, "we are all awaiting your judgment: tell us what you see."

Deirdre slowly moved the hand mirror from side to side; and raised it above her head, so that she might see, from yet another angle, the effect of Malvinia's extraordinary handiwork. She then peered into the larger mirror, her pallid cheeks now coloring, as a consequence, no doubt, of the unusual amount of attention lavished upon her. Yet her silence grew more prolonged; her forehead lightly furrowed; her lips pursed themselves in an expression very close to disdain.

"*Do* tell us what you see, if you will be so kind," Malvinia said, still somewhat scant of breath, and her own cheeks prettily flushed.

At last Deirdre moved herself to speak, in a voice so low and murmurous one might have concluded it was meant to insult, in that the speaker could not trouble herself to raise her voice, in courtesy; and these were the words that, all astonishingly, fell upon the ears of the listeners: "What do I see? I see a clown; a fool; a bewigged doll; a poppet; a marionette; a manikin; a most garishly prepared *young lady,* not at all different from the rest. I see, in short, no one I recognize, or care to know."

7

Fate would have it that Samantha, and not Deirdre, would be the first to sight the outlaw balloon, as it soared across the river, fairly low, and close to skimming the tops of those hoary old oaks, which majestically lined the shore opposite the Kiddemaster estate—Deirdre being so sunk in an inscrutable, nay, morbid, reverie, that, standing on the bank of the river, her head bowed, her figure motionless, she failed not only to see the horrific vision, as it emerged from out the elysian autumnal sky, but also to hear its extraordinary sound: an uncanny, harsh, diabolical *hissing*.

In truth, I believe it the case that Samantha's remarkably keen eyes had, all unknowing, taken note of something peculiar in the eastern sky, a rain cloud, perhaps—or was it an oddly shaped column of smoke or a funnel of dust-laden air?—the which pricked her curiosity only idly, for she was fatigued by the afternoon's social demands, and by the most unfortunate strain that had arisen amongst her sisters and herself, for which she blamed Malvinia. (Though she could not think very well of Constance Philippa; or even of Octavia and herself, since they had failed to rectify the situation, and had made no move to hurry after the haughty Deirdre. Ah, that exasperating child!)

Thus it was, that Samantha, already agitated and impatient, as a consequence of the words exchanged, and the sweltering weight of her clothing, saw the black silken balloon appear, of a sudden, and heard its eerie intake of breath, and saw, or, at any rate, felt a peculiar conviction *that the monstrous apparition had come for her sister:* and was for some moments so stricken with astonishment, and so doubting of the evidence of her own eyes, that, unhappily, she froze in her place—and could cry out no warning.

Alas, how very different a chronicle this might be, and how spared of sorrow and ignoble shame, the elder Zinns, if Samantha had had her wits about her at this crucial time!—for it was, in fact, not altogether characteristic of her, to register stunn'd incredulity, as to the certainty of her own keen senses; and to sit, meek, with the helpless passivity, of a *lady*.

Of course the astounded girl did finally rouse herself, and wake from her entrancement, to cry, "Deirdre—! Oh, Deirdre, take care!"— but, by the time these words were uttered, the hellish thing was so close upon Deirdre, no human agent could have saved her from her fate.

The while the balloon had been steadily approaching its destination, above picturesque hills of both farmland and woodland, and crickets had begun their merry nocturnal music, in anticipation of dusk, Samantha sat o'erwarm and fretting, a sandalwood fan in her hand, which she opened and closed restively, half hoping she might break, for it would have given her a childish pleasure to discard the thing, in a temper: the fan, for all its charm, being a hand-me-down, in any case, from one of the elder female Kiddemasters.

Unhappy Samantha! Impatient Samantha! She was quite vexed, by the weight of her comely hat, which was made of green satin, and had an elaborate tulle bow, that tied somewhat scratchily beneath her chin; vexed, too, by the damp warmth of her skirts, and petticoats, and crinolines, and cotton stockings; and the ungiving solidity of her corset. Most of all, perhaps, she was vexed with herself, for whilst she stared after Deirdre's retreating figure, and felt some considerable measure of guilt, and regret, for all that had transpired, nevertheless she had made no effort to follow after Deirdre; and had not even troubled to call after her, some words of comfort or sympathy.

"What a wretch it is, despite her Sunday clothes!" Malvinia murmured, vigorously fanning herself, "so exaggerated in her motions, and so *common:* behaving thusly, I do believe, in order to humiliate her family, in the eyes of the Kiddemaster servants!"

"Malvinia, you are extreme," Samantha feebly protested. "You are mistaken; and very cruel."

"And *you* are a silly little chit," Malvinia said.

Whereupon Constance Philippa, as the eldest, irritably interposed: and bade them both be still, for her head ached most violently, and she feared she might run mad, for all this *female chatter* and *female quarreling* and *female nonsense.*

So the four sisters sat in the gazebo, fanning themselves, their veiled faces o'erheated, and their hearts sullenly beating, with emotions not entirely sisterly, at this time.

Samantha silently concurred with Constance Philippa, for such scenes, occurring from time to time amongst the Zinn girls (particularly when no elders were near), struck her as both ignoble and unnecessary; and distracting from serious thought. Gossip, and idle words, and contentious exchanges, and tears, and injur'd feelings, and cruel laughter, and jeering smiles; and forgiving, and embracing, and more copious weeping; and so the days, and the years, passed.

Samantha's pale green gaze followed after Deirdre, and unbeknownst to herself she loudly sighed, and snapped her fan shut, the while thinking, I wish—ah, how I wish!—I know not *what*.

From the point in time, in which this history of the Zinns is transcribed, it is difficult for me to say, with certainty, which of the young ladies, after Deirdre, presented Mrs. Zinn with the most worrisome thoughts: yet I believe it to have been Samantha, who, tho' small-boned, and delicate of features, and, with her luxuriant red hair, fairylike to the eye, nonetheless experienced grave difficulties, in comporting herself with grace, in social situations.

Malvinia said of her, to the others: "How is it that Samantha's skin is so milky-pale, and smooth, I much prefer it to my own; and her upturned nose, so delightful; and her eyes that cold piercing green; and her hair, ah!—that ravishing hair!—which, indeed, I *much* prefer to my own: and yet, withal, the child is sadly plain as a tin spoon; and cannot hope to attract any gentleman who is not, himself, decidedly homely."

Cruel words, yet not greatly mistaken: for it was the case, as all attested, that Miss Samantha Zinn's features, whilst attractive individually, yet did not resolve themselves into that enigma, *Beauty*.

Nor did it help that she had freckles, on her forehead in particular; and that, all unconsciously, she oft gnawed at her lower lip, as if tumultuous thoughts, not unlike those of her father's, ceaselessly tormented her brain, and urged her to take pen to paper. ("Samantha would be quite attractive," Octavia said, in exasperation, "if only she was not always *thinking!*") Allowed to work alongside Mr. Zinn, in the laboratory, Samantha was evidently quite at ease, and perfectly absorbed in her labor: at other times, and especially at social functions, she was visibly unnerved, and distracted, and very far from being agreeable company. Mrs. Craik's gentle observation, in one of her pieces in *The Ladies' Wreath*, that gentlemen are naturally discomfited by an *excess of ratiocination*, in the weaker sex, might have benefited this awkward young miss, had she troubled to seek it. But of course she failed to do so: the books she studied, all out of Mr. Zinn's own library, were very different indeed.

Constance Philippa observed of her, grimly, that she would, one day, *grow up*, and become a *lady*: for had she any choice?

It is hardly surprising, given these impediments, that Miss Samantha Zinn succeeded in intimidating those few suitors who cared to approach her: attracted initially by her petite figure, and the vivacity of which, at times, she showed herself capable, these gentlemen were soon discountenanced by her awkwardness at drawing-room repartee, and the unseemly enthusiasm with which she blundered into discussing *scientific subjects,* and other matters, of a masculine type, beyond her comprehension.

For there were times—indeed, on the night of her own debutante ball!—when, all unprovok'd, Samantha might begin to chatter excitedly about her father's great work, her eyes shining, and her tongue tripping over itself, with a childlike boastfulness: in which, unfortunately, there was not a whit of Mr. Zinn's intrinsic modesty, or sense of proportion. She was quite proud, for instance, that her father had assigned to her, for improvement, his ingenious *spring-stirrup:* this being a special device with which Mr. Zinn had tinkered thanklessly during the War years, for the employment of the United States Cavalry. (The stirrup was equipped with a clever spring mechanism, of Mr. Zinn's invention, which would automatically release the foot of a rider, if he was thrown or shot from his horse; for the greatest danger in such situations was that one might be dragged to his death, by a maddened steed. Many a time John Quincy Zinn, then a lowly private in the 103rd Pennsylvania Volunteers, had sought to demonstrate the efficacy of this shrewd invention, for his commanding officer, and, upon a singular occasion, for General McClellan himself: these efforts being, alas, greeted with no success, and resulting in several injuries to John Quincy, including lacerations of the face and head, and a fractured collarbone.)

On the very night of Samantha's debutante ball, held in the elegant cream-and-gold Federal room of Kiddemaster Hall, with its eight lithesome Doric columns, and its splendid coffered ceiling, Samantha all unwittingly offended one gentleman after another, with her excitable chatter on these unseemly subjects. She did present a charming sight, with her tiny waist, delicate frame, and resplendent costume (a particularly full dress of pale lilac satin and brocade, adorned with innumerable flounces, ribbons, flowers, and Spanish lace, and looped up most becomingly with red and white camellias, this being shrewdly made over from a Worth design of Cousin Felicity Broome's, worn to her own debutante ball some seasons previous): yet, alas, what did it matter, if she chose to speak of inappropriate things?

She rattled on about Mr. Zinn's drawings for a *noiseless electric trolley,* to replace the cumbersome steam engine; and his drawings for an *auto-locomotive,* or *auto-mobile,* possibly to be run by electricity as well, the which wondrous device would replace forever horse-drawn carriages, with their steel-tire clatter, and crashing hooves, and unspeakable horse pollution: an invention to "change forever the face of the earth," as Samantha declared, "and improve it immeasurably." She spoke with immoderate pride of his *burglarproof lock,* which would eradicate theft, and many another form of wrongdoing, from the earth, once a manufacturing concern might be persuaded to produce it; and of his *perpetual-motion machine,* which was nearing its completion; and of a *Utopian paradise,* to be constructed early in the next century, by means of divers inventions, Mr. Zinn's necessarily at the vanguard. Ah, how the child's green eyes shone, as she spoke of cities to be "whitely iridescent, growing vertically into the sky, and beneath the surface of the earth as well!" One day, machines would service machines; great conveyor belts would move unceasingly, bringing forth goods of every imaginable type; there would be no want; no poverty; no yearning; and hence no *crime.* The theory of *interchangeable parts,* initially developed by Eli Whitney, and other American inventors, would be advanced a thousandfold, if Mr. Zinn could but interest an experimental and ambitious manufacturer, for it was his belief—nay, his absolute certitude—that, the secret of the universe being both *interchangeable units,* and *ceaseless motion,* humankind cannot do better than to emulate this law; and to establish, *in material terms,* that harmony of the Invisible Spheres, of which Mr. Ralph Waldo Emerson and others had spoken with such winning eloquence, earlier in the century. "For, as Father believes, if the human margin for error is but eliminated, and only accuracy-tested machines are entrusted with the maintenance of machines, and the conveyors, and the production, are never allowed to wastefully halt, why then how should we fail, to emerge ahead of the other nations, in the great adventure all before us?" Thus the heedless young lady rattled on, speaking with such ill-mannered enthusiasm, and feverish incoherence, as to irrevocably offend the very gentlemen who had been encouraged to dance with her, and, alas! to quite undo the effect of the beautiful lilac gown, and the lilac-dyed ostrich feathers which fell so charmingly backward, from her high mound of hair.

Unworldly, foolish child! She had not discerned the pitying, contemptuous, and amused looks, exchanged by her listeners; she had even been so deluded as to believe (until Malvinia cruelly told her otherwise), that the smile of one gentleman in particular, far from being a consequence of his delight in her words, was but a sign of derision, and thus interpreted by all. "It is your brain that is at fault, and must be brought under rigorous control," Malvinia told Samantha, so vexed that she had to restrain herself from tapping the young woman's shoulder with her fan, "for, in its present condition, it is a *perpetual-motion machine* in itself; and most repugnant."

Samantha alone of the Zinn daughters exhibited no outward jealousy of little Deirdre, being of the practical belief that Mrs. Zinn loved them all as a mother must naturally love her children, in accordance with custom, and duty; and believing, in her innermost heart, that Mr. Zinn secretly loved *her* above any other member of his household, no matter that the vivacious Malvinia had seemed, from the cradle upward, her father's favorite. (For was not Samantha allowed to assist her father, in his work-shop?—ofttimes for as long as eight, or ten, or even twelve, *uninterrupted hours.* And had not Mr. Zinn long since abandoned all efforts to speak of his sacred work, with anyone save Samantha?)

Indeed, Samantha felt some intrinsic sympathy for her adopted sister, both girls being yet childlike in their corporeal development, and so lacking in feminine graces, and beauty, as to have banished from the parlor, forever, any reading of Hans Christian Andersen's "The Ugly Duckling," tho' others of Mr. Andersen's much-loved fairy tales were oft read aloud, with great delight. Both Samantha and the beetle-brow'd Deirdre were ill at ease, in even the most congenial female society: tea-table conversation baffled them, and their dresses were never quite right, and they were given to long maddening silences, as if their minds had, in defiance of all rules of social decorum, drifted elsewhere. From time to time, in such painful situations, they might even have exchanged a swift, covert glance—so fleet, however, as to be undiscerned by their elders, and scarcely remarked even by themselves.

Yet, how ironical it was! Despite Samantha's equanimity of man-ner, and her generosity in regard to certain whims of Deirdre's, it was evidently not the case that Deirdre felt more affection for Samantha than for the others; it was hardly the case that she felt any perceptible affection for her at all.

"Cold of heart!—and secretive!—and stubborn!—and perverse!" Samantha bethought herself, eying Deirdre's rigid back, as the girl sat at her hickory writing table, puzzling over a mathematical assignment from Mr. Zinn, or perusing, in secret, a volume of verse, or a romance of the darksome and gothic type, generally forbidden in the Octagonal House. "And yet, would I wish her otherwise? For I have all that I require—indeed, *more* than I require—of sisters: and find the expenditure of emo-tion very nearly more than I can grant."

From time to time, in great alarm, Samantha might be wakened from her slumber to hear Deirdre's sobs, all but muffled in the bed-clothes: and she would lie transfixed, wondering if she should move to comfort the unhappy child; or if she should allow her some measure of privacy, and secrecy?—seeing that she herself, to Mrs. Zinn's disapproval, prized both. However, if she did ask Deirdre what was wrong, the sobbing oft ceased at once; and the girl lay very still, and very rigid, in a stubborn pretense of sleep. Or, it might be, this instance of whispered solicitude, being unexpected, had the result of causing the stricken child to sob all the more violently—with such despair, and such shameless abandon, verging near upon hysteria, as to make Samantha herself frightened.

(Yet, alas, rarely enlightened, for upon these occasions too Deir-dre would resolutely turn away, hunched up on the far side of the bed, her face pressed into the pillow. Only in the early years had she allowed Samantha to embrace her, all wordlessly, and would even cry herself to sleep, secure in Samantha's arms, the while whimpering most piteously certain incoherent phrases as "No, no . . . no . . . you cannot make me . . . I will not . . . no . . ." and appeals to "Mother" and "Father," which Samantha, even as a young girl, comprehended did not pertain to Mr. and Mrs. Zinn, but to the deceas'd Bonners.)

Samantha also suffered some inordinate distractions, over a period of two or more years, when, shortly after Deirdre's twelfth birthday, their bedchamber began to be disturbed by curious raps, and knocks, and creaks, and near-inaudible "voices," in the walls. This was the onset of the ne'er-explained *ghost phenomena* that were to cause some mischief in the Octagonal House, and elsewhere, and not a little embarrassment; for whilst it could not be proved that any one of the Zinns was responsible for these disruptions, it was always the case that the phenomena did not occur, apart from them: and apart from poor Deirdre, in particular.

Beginning, in a sense, modestly, the disagreeable occurrences increased, both in frequency, and in seriousness: soon moving out from the walls of the bedchamber, to infect the entire house, and, upon occasion the Hall, and several social events, which were then grievously ruined. (Thus Constance Philippa's eighteenth birthday celebration was disrupted, when an invisible force o'erturned the dining room table, and sent all the chinaware, crystal, and silver, and divers victuals, crashing to the floor; and a gay skating party on the river, organized by Malvinia, Miss Delphine Martineau, and several male cousins, in celebration of New Year's Day, was thrown into consternation, when, beneath the skaters' feet, the hard-frozen ice somehow creaked, and muttered, and heaved, and threatened to give way, to cause the young people to plummet into the icy waves—when, at the very same time, the ice was altogether solid! Most distressing of all, the *phenomena* followed the Zinns to old Whitton Hall, on the Delaware, where, one Michaelmas Eve, those elderly relatives of the Zinns and Kiddemasters had given a luxuriant reception, in honor of both the retired Chief Justice Godfrey Kiddemaster, and the visiting Chief Justice of the Supreme Court Morrison Remick Waite, acquaintances of old: the creaks, raps, muffled shouts, heaving of furniture, blasts of icy air, and other familiar manifestations, taking place the while Deirdre herself was all innocently employed elsewhere, in a far wing of the house, doing her schoolwork!)

Deirdre was evidently the victim, as well, of unusual nightmares, and distressing *floating dreams,* which had the effect of quite terrorizing her, for she was certain that ghosts were responsible; and their malevolence was all the more wicked, in that they could not be precisely seen, but only sensed. Mr. Zinn was loath to allow such observations to be voiced, for, as a man of science and rationality, he deplored superstition, and found it very hard to accept that the *supernatural*, in any guise, had to do with these curious events. "The Spirit presiding over the universe, and immanent in every breath we draw, is not, by any wildness of the imagination, a deceitful force," Mr. Zinn said, "nor must it—or *He*, as popular sentiment would say—be interpreted, as springing out of the *supernatural*, and not the *natural*. All that we do not yet comprehend, by means of science and rationality, we are lazily accustomed to call *supernatural*; all that we know, *natural*. Thus," he explained to his alarmed family, and to the trembling Deirdre in particular, "it is erroneous to speak of *ghost phenomena*, and you will displease me greatly, if you persist in so doing."

All his family were in haste to apologize, and promised that, from that moment onward, they should not refer to the strange events as *supernatural*; but only as *natural*.

Yet the curious manifestations not only continued, but increased in frequency, the while poor Deirdre lowly protested that she was not to blame; and quite shrank from the censorious glances of the others. "Perhaps if we administered to Deirdre a strong dose of Great-Aunt Edwina's laudanum," Malvinia speculated, "*she* might sleep for a full night; and *we* might sleep."

Queer wailing winds arose, in the several chimneys of the Octagonal House; and sourceless drafts of air snaked about, ofttimes following certain members of the household, and the little pet monkey, Pip—who was so affrighted, he clamored to be locked safely away in Mr. Zinn's workshop for the night. One morning, it was discovered that Great-Aunt Edwina's dressmaker's dummy had positioned itself some feet *outside* the closed door of the sewing room at Kiddemaster Hall!—and one of the seamstresses confessed that, for some weeks, she had been quite frightened of it, for it gave some small simulation of life; albeit that, when actually examined, it was of course naught but paper, tape, and varnish, and thoroughly lifeless. (More generally, this sewing room at the Hall, crowded as it was with the dummies of ladies no longer living, was a cause of both uneasiness and alarm to the Zinn girls, from childhood onward. Alas, what a lesson here, for even the most brash of young women! So many female figures whose *real* selves no longer inhabited the world; such evidence of Time, and Mortality, and the fickleness of Fashion! Upon one occasion, some years earlier, Malvinia had examined the small, squat, and, indeed, stunted-appearing, dummy once belonging to her great-great-grandmother Lydia Burr Kiddemaster, and expressed some derisory doubt, as to whether it was a *human dummy*, or not. Whereupon Octavia said, disapproving: "Should you like one of our descendants someday to mock your figure, in such wise?" And Malvinia pertly replied: "*My* figure, dear Octavia, is as close to perfection, as nature, art, and craft, might devise: and I find it very difficult to think, that it shall ever be *unfashionable.*")

Pursuant to this bewildering incident involving Great-Aunt Edwina's dummy, a flurry of similar manifestations occurred at the Hall, to the great vexation of the elderly inhabitants, who complained that the house was, by degrees, becoming haunted: no matter that John Quincy Zinn insisted otherwise. Indeed, Great-Aunt Edwina, pressing a beringed hand to her heaving bosom, bluntly contradicted Mr. Zinn to his face, claiming that his *adopted child* was certainly responsible for the mischief: being not only *haunted,* perhaps, but *damn'd!*

(I am sorry to be forced to employ that particular word, in this, or any other, context. for it strikes the ear most harshly, and cannot fail to give offense, to younger readers especially, and to members of the female sex. I believe it to be a measure of Miss Edwina Kiddemaster's sovereignty, at home and abroad, that she, alone of all ladies, might utter this startling word, in all confidence of escaping censure: nay, with every assurance of transcending it!—her gaze stern as a sphinx's, her lips resolutely pursed, her figure stolid as that of an alabaster angel of wrath.)

Mr. Zinn was taken aback, by both this sobering word, with its grave theological weight, and Miss Kiddemaster's vehemence in uttering it; but he managed to reply, forthrightly, yet courteously, that it was quite unjust to speak in this wise of his daughter, who was altogether innocent, and, in any case, a *great-niece* of Miss Kiddemaster's—and therefore to be treated with some consideration.

"Indeed, Mr. Zinn," the marble-brow'd lady replied, "the girl may be a daughter of yours; but she is not, by any liberality of law or custom, a great-niece of mine."

I am compelled to pause very briefly, to explain to the reader that Miss Edwina Kiddemaster was a most formidable presence, in Kiddemaster Hall, and in Bloodsmoor in general. At the time of our narrative's commencement, she was in her late fifties, as to age, and rumored to be exceptionally wealthy, possessing a fortune, as a consequence of her literary activities, well beyond that which was hers by birth, as a Kiddemaster. Her first book, *The Young Lady's Friend: A Compendium of Correct Forms,* had been rapidly penned in the authoress's twenty-first year (although not published for many years), in angry response to what she saw to be a decided loosening of morals, *even amongst her cousins,* during the administration of Martin Van Buren: the most valuable chapter in the manual having to do with proper behavior at balls. (Many a young lady, and her anxious mother, consulted this popular book, to learn that whilst there was nothing inherently indecent about the waltz, it was a matter of great importance that a gentleman never encircle the lady's waist *until the dance begins,* and drop his arms at once when the dance ends.)

Following close upon this auspicious *début* was a related study, *A Guide to Proper Christian Behavior Amongst Young Persons,* which was even more successful, by subscription publication; and so, with the passage of years, book followed upon book, and Miss Kiddemaster undertook a column in *The Ladies' Home Journal,* under the pen-name "Miss K." which, modestly titled "On Etiquette," came to have enormous influence on the genteel classes, involving not only ladies, but gentlemen as well. Thus, it is not erroneous to state that the girls' great-aunt was renowned, in her own right, quite apart from her Kiddemaster heritage; and that her word fell with the weight of law, in all domestic matters.

Certain detractors of the authoress, including, upon occasion, her own brother Godfrey, observed that Miss Edwina Kiddemaster, while being a stern authority on etiquette for others, frequently rose above it herself: having been known to slip quietly from a gathering, before leave-taking was proper; and to introduce certain subjects—party politics, and the tariff, and the scandal of the unions—generally forbidden in mixed company, in the cultivated classes. Godfrey Kiddemaster also speculated, somewhat too freely, as to whether his sister was mad, or merely ambitious, in that she worked so assiduously at her writing desk, whilst the other ladies of her circle occupied themselves with visits, and teas, and charity work, and religion, and fancywork of divers kinds: for he believed it to be quite baffling, that any Kiddemaster should feel the impulse to work, still less to earn money; and fame, of course, was naught but vulgar.

Thus, when Great-Aunt Edwina declared that Deirdre was haunted, or damn'd, the statement was taken up with some alarm, on the part of the Zinns: for Mrs. Zinn knew herself to be a favored inheritrix of her aunt's fortune, and did not wish to offend her. (Unfortunately, over the years, Great-Aunt Edwina had oft expressed forthright disapproval of the Zinn daughters, who seemed unable to please her, no matter how hard they were encouraged to try. Constance Philippa was "uncouth and mannish, as to her carriage"; Octavia, whilst sweet, and agreeably docile, somewhat alarmed the eye, as a consequence of her "corporeal precocity"; Malvinia was "spoiled, headstrong, and vain," despite her beauty; and Samantha, with her stubborn "o'erexertion of the brain," could not fail to displease.)

In time, the disconcerting and unexplain'd phenomena abated; and finally came to an end, not long after Deirdre's fifteenth birthday. Yet it was upward of a half-year before Great-Aunt Edwina condescended to allow Deirdre in the same room with her: and her manner, it hardly needs to be said, remained distinctly formal.

The while the invisible manifestations gradually disappeared, poor Deirdre continued to suffer, on the average of thrice a month, nightmares of a singularly vivid type: oft waking Samantha from a deep slumber, with her childlike whimpering, and squirming, and pleas. "No no no no I will not oh please no I cannot," the stricken girl cried, thrashing about in her sleep, "no no no I cannot come with you I do not belong to you oh please you must leave me alone," as the frightened Samantha made every effort to wake her, sometimes rewarded, for her pains, by a blow to the face or chest.

Nonetheless, Samantha persisted, knowing it her sisterly, and her Christian, duty, and did as well as she might to comfort the wretched child, who oft hid her warm face in her hands, and wept, all uncontrollably, for long minutes at a time. By judicious inquiry Samantha was able to piece together the substance of the dream: a stranger accosted Deirdre, calling her his daughter, and cursing, and shouting, and insisting that she accompany him, on the back of his horse, to HELL ITSELF.

Most puzzling, this strange gentleman—bearded, and wearing a soiled and torn uniform, of an officer in the Cavalry—was *not* Mr. Bonner! Nor could Deirdre explain who he might be, and why he was so angry, and why he had fastened upon *her,* as his daughter, who would accompany him to that unspeakable region, abandoned by God.

On the very eve of that calamitous day, in the autumn of 1879, poor Deirdre was subjected to this remarkable nightmare again: and allowed herself to be comforted by Samantha, who insisted that the "Raging Captain" (for thus he had come to be called) was but a *dream-figment,* and not to be feared. So distraught was Deirdre she seemed not to hear, however, and continued her weeping, and protesting, in such wise: "He has no right to call me his daughter, and to curse, and to swear, and to make such wicked threats!—for he is no one I know, or have ever chanc'd to gaze upon, in this lifetime. But how piteous, for I saw, for the first time, how badly he was wounded!—tho' he would hide it from me —the black blood springing forth, from a wound in his chest—and yet he is no one I know—surely he is nothing human, but a very devil out of Hell! Nay," the near-hysterical girl murmured, her face streaming tears, "I *will not* go to him: I *will not* succumb."

"Of course you will not," Samantha sensibly concurred, "for, as I have said, he is but a dream; and, in any case, you have Father to protect you."

"Father?" Deirdre whispered, lifting her head.

Samantha spoke in a consoling voice to her, explaining that she had suffered naught but a mental illusion of some kind; a phantasmagoria, lacking material substance; a mere wisp of thought. "For you know, Deirdre," Samantha said, "that ghosts do not exist, and that there is nothing to be accurately termed the *supernatural,* as Father has explained. A dream is but a mental fancy, dimly comprehended by our science: it has the power to frighten, with its *seeming* authenticity, and yet, as you must understand, it has far less reality than the furnishings in this room; or your own nightcap, which has, I fear, been knocked awry on your head —do allow me to adjust it."

"You are correct," Deirdre murmured, shivering in Samantha's arms, "you are very wise, and very kind, like all of your family: yet, tho' I understand fully all you have said, and acquiesce to its plausibility, why am I so chill?—so numb?—so apprehensive?—so aware, of *his* loathsome presence, in this very room?"

"It is but a phantasmagoria," Samantha said, chiding, "and you are a very silly young lady, to persist in fearing it."

It was this ominous exchange, with its o'erwrought and unwholesome emotions, which Samantha was forced to recall, not eighteen hours afterward: whilst seated thunderstruck in the gazebo, beside her sisters, as the outlaw balloon approached the wayward Deirdre!

Alas, that she could not draw sufficient breath, to cry out a warning: until it was too late, and the crude mechanism had alighted, and the balloonist's greedy arms had seized hold of Deirdre, to pull her struggling into the basket; and away—to what region of *Earth,* or *Hell,* I know not.

8

Thus it was, that the unnamed and unidentified abductor, clad all in black, and manning a tall black silken balloon, of sinister elegance, came for Miss Deirdre Zinn at approximately the hour of seven o'clock in the evening, on the 23 September 1879: and so swift was his assault upon her, as she stood all unwitting on the riverbank, and so unerring his maneuvers, that he was able to pull her helpless into the balloon's basket, and escape within scant seconds!—whilst her astounded sisters did naught but stare, and no one in the great Hall chanced to observe.

(Tho' it was to be the case that many in the vicinity, including the elder Kiddemasters, and Mr. Zinn in his workshop, would report having heard something most uncanny: this being the throaty, low, chilling hiss of the balloon's flame, which was quite unlike anything experienced in Bloodsmoor, before or since. "The intake of breath, of a monstrous giant!"—thus Malvinia described it, in a quavering voice, afterward.)

But why had they not called to Deirdre, to warn her of the great danger? Thus the sisters were asked, by numerous interrogators.

Yet it was altogether natural, that the four young ladies were so surprised by the unlikely apparition, that they could not utter a word: and even Constance Philippa, the most ordinarily level-headed, was so shocked, in her own words, "my throat closed at once—and not a cry could escape."

Octavia, still very pale, and in danger of fainting yet again, murmured that the black balloon was so very *hideous,* and yet so very *graceful,* she could do no more than stare at it: all the while doubting, in her innermost heart, that it was *real.*

And Malvinia testified that the horror was so enormous, she fainted almost immediately: her affrighted senses took their leave, and left her quite helpless.

And Samantha, with benumbed lips, spoke thusly: "I saw—yet did not see; I cried out to Deirdre—yet sat transfixed, and mute. And then, within a minute, the act was completed, and the balloon was lifting—and it was too late."

"Too late, too late." Thus the sisters murmured, dabbing at their eyes, in which copious tears brimm'd. "May God have mercy upon us!— *too late.*"

9

As the reader may sympathize, it was to be several days before the sisters recovered sufficiently from the shock to their delicate nerves to provide information concerning the heinous abduction, Samantha being the first to summon forth the necessary strength to attempt an account of the kidnapping, and even to attempt, with some small success, a pencil sketch of the balloon.

Though the balloon appeared enormous, as a consequence of the surprise and terror it engendered, Samantha supposed it to be fairly modest in scale, not a dirigible or passenger ship, of the kind she had seen in certain journals owned by Mr. Zinn: not above seventy feet in height, and considerably less than that in diameter. The wicker basket appeared small, by contrast, below six feet in diameter; and of course the balloon displayed no American flag, or any identifying feature.

Ah, the horror of the apparition! The spectral calm, with which it drifted across the river, to the unheeding girl at the shore! Its sleek plump panels might have been made of varnished cotton, or silk: by no means rubber, Samantha declared, since she had seen rubber balloons, filled with illuminating gas, at the Exposition in Philadelphia, several years back: and this balloon was—she felt herself forced to testify—far more beautiful.

Nay, Samantha said, with some reluctance, the balloon was *very beautiful indeed:* and doubtless made of silk, with a sort of French look about it, she could not explain why, save perhaps that she had in mind certain handsome, but wantonly frivolous dirigibles, created by the French, in the early years of the century.

(Her sisters joined her in this judgment, albeit with a similar show of reluctance. Malvinia allowed that the thing was *beauteous* indeed, to the layman's eye, but might, for all she knew, be deemed *ugly* as well; Constance Philippa murmured, with amaz'd awe, that she had never seen anything so *brutal,* and so *comely;* Octavia faintingly said that the vision it had seared into her very soul could not bear close examination—for how could silken beauty be so wed with unspeakable malevolence?)

At the very first, Samantha said, this extraordinary apparition had appeared to be uniformly black, as to the coloring of its panels; but her eye succeeded in absorbing the curious fact that each of the panels differed from the others, in texture, and in shade, and depth, of that hue. One was iridescent, giving off the hard, brilliant, silky sheen of a raven's wing; one somewhat lacy in texture; another composed of imbricated scales, like a pinecone; yet another, a dull, dead, lifeless black, that absorbed the sun's waning rays, and did not reflect them. The effect, Samantha all haltingly said, was necessarily *mesmerizing* for, as the balloon so swiftly skimmed the tops of the trees at the water's edge, and made its silent descent, the panels caught, and refracted, and mirrored, the sunshine, in a most compelling way.

As to the pilot himself, Samantha was less certain, tho' adamant in her belief that there was but one: unless an assistant crouched hidden in the basket. She had a confus'd impression—in which her sisters later concurred—that the balloonist, clad in black, exhibited an agreeable *formality,* as to the style and cut of his costume; and that he wore a hat, of an unobtrusive size, with a narrow brim. His age could not be estimated, and might have been anything, from that of a mere boy, to that of a very mature man: but he did possess a noticeable *agility,* in the swiftness and certainty of his movements; and some evident *strength,* in the feat of pulling the struggling Deirdre into the basket, with no great expenditure of effort. (Tho' Malvinia was of the opinion, but softly voiced, that Deirdre had sunk into a swoon, and, being limp and helpless, had not been capable of putting up a struggle—or so it appeared, to her affrighted eye.)

Sketching being one of Samantha's especial skills, for which, in the workshop, she received much praise from Mr. Zinn, she busied herself with a pencil drawing of the malefic vessel, to aid in the police investigation; and the conical-shaped balloon that emerged, with its compact basket, and numerous ropes (Samantha was assiduous in indicating some *thirty-five* of these), possessed so lifelike a quality, that her sisters visibly shuddered in gazing upon it, and Octavia went deathly pale, and came very close to fainting once again. "Nay, I cannot bear it," the distraught young lady murmured; "the devil's very own device! And our poor lost sister, borne away in it, into the sky—"

"She will be recovered, and returned to us unharmed," Mr. Zinn emphatically declared, his own face warmly flushed, so that the birthmark on his temple acquired prominence; and a fine film of perspiration glowed on his manly forehead. "And yet, Samantha, if only you had seen the villain's face clearly!—if only you might offer us a representation of *that.*"

"Indeed, Father," Samantha stammered, her eyes brimming with tears of shame, "I too wish that were the case: but, alas, it is *not:* for I was at too great a distance, and, like my sisters, too agitated and confused to absorb such details."

"The balloon, after all, might easily be abandoned," Mr. Zinn murmured aloud, plucking distractedly at his beard, "and how should we then know to whom it had belonged, and where he might have fled? And no ransom demand yet made! Ah, it is very, very strange; very strange. You have no recollection, Samantha," the unhappy man again inquired, "of the pilot's features? No grasp of his coloring, or height, or approximate age, or ancestry?"

"None, Father," Samantha humbly replied. "I am greatly aggrieved to say—none."

"I cannot think it an *accident,*" Mr. Zinn ravingly murmured, the while staring at the pencil sketch, with a piercing gaze in which consternation, loss, befuddlement, and virile anger, were irregularly mix'd, "for, in the universe as we comprehend it, there are no accidents: and yet, I am bound to say, I cannot think it a *deliberate act,* for why should my little Deirdre be thus outraged? The aerial balloonist did, as you have said, make his way unfalteringly to the child, that he might abduct her—but how can we rest assured, in assuming that he came for Deirdre herself; for he might very well have kidnapped any one of my daughters who was in a position of vulnerability."

At this remark, the four sisters glanced up at one another, and exchanged solemn, tear-bright looks, not amenable to interpretation, not, in any case, by this chronicler.

"Ah, it is most tragic, it is most outrageous," Mr. Zinn continued, scarce knowing what he said, or how his distraught manner upset his daughters, who were not accustomed to seeing him thus, or to witnessing such extremes of emotion, in their elders, "it is gravely insulting, and *not to be borne.* A rivalrous inventor, it may be, one whose intention is to so disrupt the harmony of my life, that I will not be able to proceed. One who is, perhaps, consumed with jealousy, of my progress—nay, I know not: I know not, why this horror has transpired; or what may come of it."

At this juncture Mrs. Zinn, with ruddy countenance, and red-rimmed eyes, in whose depths some measure of choler, as well as maternal grief, shone, ventured to say: "Mr. Zinn, we none of us know what will come of this horror, nor how, precisely, it came about; but, I believe, we do know *why* it occurred, as it did." She then paused, being stout, and easily made scant of breath, before continuing, in the selfsame adamant voice: "I mean only that the tragedy might have been prevented—nay, *would* have been prevented—had you, Mr. Zinn, chosen to remain in the midst of your family, in order to protect us, *in conformity with your duty.*"

How the anguish'd John Quincy Zinn replied to this grave accusation, and with what divers shocks his daughters o'erheard it, I cannot bring myself to say; for the subject is a painful one, and not even the passage of time can altogether alleviate it. Unhappy mortals! Unhappy Deirdre! It is a sign of that *cosmic irony,* of which, in another context, I earlier spoke, that the innocent girl was borne away in the silken balloon, by the phantom pilot, into an autumnal sky as serene, as elysian, and as soberly a slate-blue, as those graceful Limoges teacups, belonging to Kiddemaster Hall, that Grandmother Sarah had, with such fastidious art, painted, in her girlhood, long past.

II

The Passionate Courtship

10

None of the Zinn daughters was to know—tho' shrewd Constance Philippa did suspect—that their parents, known to them as Mr. and Mrs. Zinn
merely, had once been *young lovers,* indeed: and that Prudence Zinn, née
Prudence Kiddemaster, had succumbed to the ravages of guilty ecstasy
in her youth from which, to her shame and confusion, she was never to
be entirely free.

No poet, this forthright and outspoken Miss Kiddemaster, assistant headmistress of the Cobbett School for Girls by the age of twenty-
nine, no tinkerer with words and loose sentiments, and yet, under the
influence of her tempestuous passion for John Quincy Zinn, she did
recite, under her breath, certain lines from Margaret Fuller's lush "Dryad
Song" as if they were a secret prayer, a dozen times daily:

> I am immortal! I know it! I feel it!
>   Hope floods my heart with delight!
> Running on air, mad with life, dizzy, reeling,
> Upward I mount—faith is sight, life is feeling,
>   Hope is the day-star of night!
>
> Come, let us mount on the wings of the morning,
>   Flying for joy of the flight,
> Wild with all longing, now soaring, now staying,
> Mingling like day and dawn, swinging and swaying,
>   Hung like a cloud in the light:
> I am immortal! I feel it! I feel it!
>   Love bears me up, love is might!

—but only if she was safely alone, out of earshot of her young charges or her parents.

Can it truly be, Prudence Kiddemaster queried herself in her diary, writing by candlelight, secretly, feverishly, in the drear hours of the night when all the house slumbered, *can it truly be that I, who have sworn myself a daughter of Athene, who have spurned so many hopeful suitors—I, Prudence Kiddemaster, a daughter too of Artemis, in whom a love of Independence is as pridefully bred, as in any Man—I, for some 30 years as Maiden in Spirit, as in the Flesh, have succumbed to that giddiness so abhorred in the young females of my acquaintance!—which is to say, have I fallen in love?*

All breathless, she paused; and felt her heart beat solidly in her heated breast; and, as a strand of hair slipped free of its confinement, in her white lawn nightcap, she wrote still further: *And have I fallen in love against all hope?*

Some tumultuous minutes passed, and, it may have been, the distraught young lady bethought herself, whether she should at once destroy the guilty page before her, or allow it to stand, and continue with her astonishing outcry. How Prudence's sternly maiden heart was torn, you may well imagine: for this daughter of the great house of Kiddemaster prided herself on being very different from her numerous female cousins, who thought of little else save balls, and fashions, and engagements, and weddings. Indeed, Prudence scarcely thought of herself as a *female,* so caught up was she in divers activities of an intellectual nature: she was an honors graduate of the excellent Cobbett School, and the Philadelphia Academy for Girls; and, at the time of her fortuitous meeting with the young Mr. Zinn, on October 20, 1853, she was one of the most successful of the women teachers, in the Philadelphia of her day.

John Quincy Zinn, her trembling hand wrote. And, further, to her own mortification, and, I am bound to say, *my* considerable surprise: *John Quincy Zinn: I WILL HAVE HIS SONS, OR THOSE OF NO MAN.*

Reader, imagine that Time has backward fled, some quarter-century before the unhappy September day, on which our narrative has begun: the hapless Deirdre not yet kidnapped, the Zinn sisters not yet born, and, indeed, their parents not yet acquainted.

Then it was that, amidst all the truly advanced Philadelphians of the day, constituting a circle, of a kind, of educators, thinkers, poets, the younger and more rebellious members of the clergy, and certain independent women, no one was more avidly discussed, and quarreled over, than a twenty-six-year-old prodigy named John Quincy Zinn. (Indeed, more than one meeting of the famed Arcadia Club, to which Prudence belonged, had been devoted to a consideration of Mr. Zinn's educational ideas: and many were the passions arous'd!) This young schoolteacher and philosopher, who had come from a rural community known as

Mouth-of-Lebanon, above the Brandywine River, was commonly called *a barbarian prince, a native American genius, a revolutionary of the Spirit,* and *Our Rousseau,* amongst other flattering epithets. And, ah! was he not handsome!

His triumph had come about in this wise: as master of a rural common school, he had been obliged to submit a formal report, to the Supervisor of Public Education for the Commonwealth of Pennsylvania: this estimable personage being, at the time, no one other than the Reverend Horace Potter Bayard, Prudence's godfather, a forthright opponent of all that was old, and crabbed, and conservative, in educational theory. (That Mr. Bayard's position with the Pennsylvania Association for the Reform of Public Schools had led to considerable controversy, and much ignorant insult in the press, I hardly need to state, for these years of valiant struggle are a matter of historical record.) Imagine Mr. Bayard's incredulous joy, in being greeted with a most astounding manuscript, from an unknown source: a report entitled *Out of the Mouths of Babes: A Teacher's Day-Book,* more than fifty pages long, and penned by a remarkable intelligence. "Here is the person we have long awaited," Mr. Bayard tremblingly announced, "and I cannot think it accidental, that he comes not from the Academy, and not from New England, but out of the bucolic rolling hills of our own state!—destined, I hope, to be a prophet in his own country."

Thus it transpired, with near-miraculous swiftness, that the much-loved schoolmaster of a mere common school was invited—nay, summoned—to Philadelphia, to accept a position with the Reform Association (whereby John Quincy Zinn became its youngest member), and an instructorship at one of the better private schools, and to give a series of subscription lectures at the Cobbett Square Church, on "any subject whatsoever, pertaining to *Progress.* " (These six evenings were completely subscribed, and attended by everyone of importance in the city. Mrs. Retta Bayard, Prudence's godmother, one of the most munificent dowager ladies of her day, allowed that young Mr. Zinn might be Philadelphia's match for Mr. Ralph Waldo Emerson: "A scant hour in the presence of that intellect greatly compels me to—ah, I know not!—*to rush out and alter the world.* ")

Naturally, there were those individuals who came to Mr. Zinn's lectures with the studied intention of criticizing, and even ridiculing: rivalrous educators, and opponents of Mr. Bayard's Reform Association, and the more conservative clergy, and journalists of doubtful integrity, amongst divers others. But in many cases, even these persons went away impressed by John Quincy Zinn; and some who came to mock, lingered to praise. For it was a brave, tumultuous decade, in our history: and even those of but limited imagination could grasp the fact, that *change,* of every kind, was swift impending!

The Philadelphia *Inquirer* devoted some four columns to the prodigy, who was hailed as a "native Pennsylvania genius," and "the walking Spirit of Transcendentalism." His espousal of the newest radical causes—not only education reform, but Abolitionism (of the pacifist variety), universal suffrage, Oriental wisdom, German idealism, vegetarianism, temperance, and the New Science—was graced, the *Inquirer* said, with a manly fortitude, and a conspicuous courage, not always to be found in lecturers of his kind; and rarely, in philosophers. The Headmaster of the Brownrrigg Academy (now Free Thinking, but formerly an Episcopal school) spoke of John Quincy Zinn as more provocative, and, it may be, even more valuable, for American educators, than Pestalozzi and Rousseau (whose ideas of education reform were much in the air, in intellectual circles, at this time). So impressed was Dr. Brownrrigg with the twenty-six-year-old schoolmaster, he very publicly offered him a position with the prestigious Academy, at a respectable salary (estimated to be thrice what the young man had been paid, in Mouth-of-Lebanon), and assigned to him an experimental class of exceptionally gifted boys and girls—the sons and daughters, in nearly every instance, of distinguished Philadelphians, in whom wealth had been enlightened by imagination.

It was buzz'd about town that the Arcadia Club, which enjoyed a reputation for being very selective, could induce young Mr. Zinn to join only if dues were suspended: a startling privilege granted him by a unanimous vote of the membership. (Tho' Prudence herself abstained, wishing not, as she thought it, to join in the common stampede.) The president of the Club, Dr. William Everett Tremblay, educator, editor, and philanthropist, boldly declared Mr. Zinn's articulated mission ("a militancy, both *inspired* and *practical,* to transform American civilization") to be as revolutionary, in its way, as the glorious uprising against tyranny of the 1770's.

"I hesitate to make claims, and, by temperament, I shrink from the o'ersimplicities of our journalist brethren," Dr. Tremblay said, "and yet, it does not seem an exaggeration to me, to declare that John Quincy Zinn may be as important for the movement, as General George Washington was to the Revolution."

And, as I have hinted, how wondrously *appealing* the young man was, of countenance, and manly physique both!—a factor that may or may not have been discerned by the gentlemen, but certainly was so, by the ladies.

It was a crisp autumn afternoon in 1853, when Miss Prudence Kiddemaster, who enjoyed, I should say, something of a formidable reputation, even amongst the Arcadians, was introduced to John Quincy Zinn: and suffered such a blow to the heart, her life was *forever alter'd.*

Alas, how to illumine the contours of Romance!—the secret recesses, the labyrinthine ways, so scorned by the uncomprehending, and yet so priz'd, by the initiate! Were she some mere poppet, a creature of frivolous and lightsome sentiment, or yet a schoolgirl, or a member of the coarser classes, one might feel rather more pity, than sympathy, for Prudence's succumbing: but this was Miss Prudence Kiddemaster, a schoolmistress of some reputation and a very outspoken young lady, who, in her secret journal, scribbled thusly, in what shame and anguish, we can scarcely guess: *I am struck to the heart. I am transform'd—I know not how, or why, or whither. Prudence, is it?—or is Prudence no more? Alas, I cannot even resent the Secret Object of my emotion: I plumb my rack'd heart but find no bitterness, no chagrin, no obstinacy, only Awe—and Awe—and yet again AWE.*

Prudence Kiddemaster had several times heard Mr. Emerson lecture, at the Cobbett Square Church; she had dined in his presence, and had, doubtless, surprised that worthy gentleman with the wide scope of her reading, and the passion of her enthusiasm. (For she was acquainted with the theories of Rousseau, Godwin, Owen, Fourier, and many another, and did not scruple to argue with the renowned Transcendentalist, who struck her, as she had occasion to say, as *earnest* enough, and *articulate*, but perhaps somewhat too *abstract*, for her womanly intuition.) There was nothing of maidenly coyness in Prudence, as she matched wits, at the dining room table, or in the drawing room, with certain learned gentlemen; nor was her head turned by compliments or gallantry, or even the whisper'd rumor that Emerson had expressed admiration for her. Thus it did not intimidate her in the slightest, that she should be meeting Mr. John Quincy Zinn, who was, moreover, several years her junior.

Yet, the unanticipated impact of that meeting!—the violence done to our young woman's pride, and stability of being!

For they were introduced, and shook hands, and, *within an instant,* poor Prudence succumbed to—she knew not what, it came so suddenly! —and so without precedence, in her virginal life. "I am pleased to make your acquaintance, Miss Kiddemaster," the young man said, in a murmur almost abash'd; and Prudence had all she could do, to master the flurry of her foolish blood, and speak in her normal firm voice, in saying: "I am pleased to make *your* acquaintance, Mr. Zinn."

This historic meeting transpired in Mr. Bayard's sombre, dignified, book-lined study, with the glazed mahogany bookcases that reached so grandly to the ceiling, and a round-arched fireplace, in which a servant was stirring a fine birch fire, against the encroaching chill of dusk. Miss Kiddemaster in a handsome wool-and-flannel cape, a large, and very striking, feathered hat upon her noble head, firm of voice, and smiling, and resolutely composed, as, alas, she met the young gentleman who would be her fate; and was stricken at once with maidenly anxiety, that he should guess the violence of her feelings, and suppose her a fatuous "society girl" like so many others.

So she addressed some *hard questions* to him, pertaining to his Utopian leanings, and a certain Emersonian inclination in him, which struck her as vulnerable: and took pleasure in seeing the young man blush, and stammer, and fail to acquit himself very firmly in his reply!

(Prudence had also discountenanced John Quincy Zinn by shaking hands with him, for, at that time, the sexes did not needlessly touch: when introduced, a gentleman merely bowed low, with deep respect, to a lady; and a lady kept her gloved hands clasped together, or purposefully occupied with a fan. A custom I think we have been unwise to abandon.)

Seeing the abash'd response of Mr. Zinn, one of the members of the Arcadian circle said chidingly to Prudence, that she had been somewhat inhospitable to the young man, who was, after all, a new arrival in Philadelphia: whereupon Prudence gaily replied, that "the Transcendentalists teach that we are all *new arrivals* on this earth, and must each fend for himself."

"You are right, Miss Kiddemaster," John Quincy murmured, blushing the more fiercely, so that a birthmark at his left temple became prominent, "and a very necessary corrective to the frivolous *sociability*, with which I have been greeted of late."

11

That autumn and winter, the prodigious John Quincy Zinn was a frequent guest in the homes of the Arcadians, and was in some danger (so Prudence feared) of having his head turned, by numerous invitations to the houses of persons less concerned with wisdom than with social fashion. And, alas! it soon became evident, to Prudence's sharp eye at least, that the unsuspecting young genius was being stalked, by many a society matron with a marriageable daughter.

Prudence trusted no living person, but confided nightly in her journal, where her turbulent heart gave itself some small relief, against the anguish of her untoward passion. *Mr. Zinn is like no other man,* she wrote, *erect as a tall candle—burning—brandishing itself—humble yet proud, forthright yet retiring: shy that so much attention is granted him, yet not o'ercome by a disagreeable false modesty. And, ah! he has taken note of me: he has been unable to disguise his forcible admiration, of my courage in questioning him!*

It quite piqued this distraught young woman, that John Quincy Zinn should appear to take as seriously as he took *her,* the eldest (and unmarried) daughter of Dr. Brownrrigg, one Parthenope: proclaimed in literary circles as the *Margaret Fuller of Philadelphia*—an appellation Prudence thought grotesquely unearned, and out of proportion to Miss Brownrrigg's poetical abilities. (And how it vexed her, that, in her very presence, the simpering Parthenope should press upon poor Mr. Zinn a copy of her vellum-bound book of verse, *Hypatia's Summons,* a very sickly sort of poetry, in Prudence's judgment.) That Prudence and Parthenope had been schoolgirls together, some years ago, and had never *quite* warmed to each other, made the situation, for Prudence, all the more disagreeable.

And the dowager widow Mrs. Ferris, as well—was she not advancing her Evangeline, a somewhat more alarming rival than Parthenope, in that she was younger, and considerably prettier?

Yet Prudence knew herself stymied, and frustrated, in that she must hold her tongue: for to speak of such matters to Mr. Zinn, to attempt a warning, would be, alas, to reveal the direction of her own heart.

John Quincy Zinn, she inwardly murmured, scarce caring how she o'erstepped the bounds of native modesty, *I will have his sons; or those of no man.*

Tho' Philadelphia threw its doors open to John Quincy Zinn, and both the Bayards and the Kiddemasters offered him the use of private suites in their respective houses, the independent-minded young man would not comply; but insisted upon maintaining a spartan room in a boarding-house in the city, frequented by workingmen, students, retired gentlemen, and persons of indeterminate background. He was stubborn in his claim that he did not mind—nay, he very much enjoyed—his daily walk of some fifteen miles, to and from the Brownrrigg Academy, through neighborhoods of a decided roughness, and in all weathers.

Fifteen miles—twenty miles—twenty-five miles: such distances were nothing to the robust-bodied young man, who gaily declared that he loved nothing better than a fast-paced *walking meditation,* in lieu of church services on Sunday; and in anticipation of a fulsome ceremonial repast, at one or another Philadelphia home, at midday. (It will come as no surprise to learn that Mr. Zinn was so eagerly sought after, by society, that he was oft forced to decline invitations, pleading the need to work, and "an exhaustion of nerves"—for, after all, his simple rural background had given him very little practice, in social intercourse. Indeed, the poor man laughingly voiced the fear that his *spirit* would be drained from him, by the Philadelphians' exuberant charity!)

"Surely there is no one like you, elsewhere in the world," John Quincy Zinn averred blushingly, to Prudence. "I mean you, and your family, and the esteemed circle, of which you are a part. Such generosity, such support, such boundless hospitality! I see now that the first two decades, and more, of my life, were spent in a sort of exile, in the remote hills above the Brandywine. But you must have pity on me, Miss Kiddemaster, for I am very slow to conform, to this newer-paced life."

How arresting his presence! Thus Prudence confided to her diary, in the nocturnal secrecy of her bedchamber: —*his high proud head bespeaking a native aristocracy, born of Nature, and not Custom; his hair so fair, and so thick, and so wavy; his beard blond, and rich. (And do not a very few silver hairs therein glint? With a most patrician aspect!) His teeth perhaps lack perfect whiteness, yet they appear large, and strong, and engaging in their irregularity, proclaiming, as it were, a sort of rude animal health. His speaking voice is most unusual, and has been remarked upon, by admirers and detractors alike, as partaking of the grave ceremoniousness of a man of the cloth, of the preaching variety: yet herein, I believe, lies his power: and it is not to be scorned. The trifling birthmark at his temple, shaped like a very small dagger (if one gives way to fancy!—for of course the blemish is naught but an inch in length, or less, and does not truly represent any object)—this intensification, as it were, of the natural ruddiness of his skin, whilst it struck my eye at first as disfiguring, now "strikes" it not at all—or with an agreeable cast.* She paused, to allow her tumultuous heart to calm itself, and dipped her quill in ink, wondering if she should register some complaint, to her diary, of Mr. Zinn's sartorial inclinations, for his dark-hued frock coat, of indeterminate age and fashion, and his peculiar headgear (possessing the shape, somewhat dashed, of a bell), and his clean, but crudely ironed linen, and his rundown "farmer's" boots—and, most offensive of all, his black sateen cravat, so ludicrously "formal," and so dismayingly greasy!—did somewhat detract from the charm of the young man's healthful countenance, and his tall muscular frame. She paused, and breathed heavily, and wrote: *That John Quincy Zinn pridefully scorns the exigencies of fashion, I believe to be entirely to his credit.*

But when would he propose?

When would he (with what blushing diffidence, Prudence could well envision) make his stammered request, for a private audience with Judge Kiddemaster? For the months passed; and the seasons; and tho' Miss Prudence Kiddemaster and Mr. John Quincy Zinn were very frequently in each other's company; and in many eyes it was assumed that a courtship of some kind was indeed in progress; and sentiment daily increased on both sides, having passed well beyond mutual regard, and moving toward outright passion—yet *Mr. Zinn did not speak.*

Unhappy Prudence slept but fitfully, and suffered a diminution of appetite so visible, all the family took note: and Aunt Edwina, in particular, made comment. *If I doubt John Quincy,* Prudence bethought herself, *I must doubt myself: nay, the very integrity of the reveal'd Universe!*

They were together upward of a half dozen times a week, by Prudence's estimation. Ofttimes they strolled together, with no chaperon, on Burlingame Street, and Frothingham Square, and even in Cobbett Park; and attended the theater, and even the opera, upon several occasions. (These events being altogether new to Mr. Zinn—and quite dazzling, indeed, to his rustic eye; tho' he could not help, as he said, estimating the cost of such luxuriant entertainment, and the needless expenditure of time, on the part of the audiences.) At the Arcadia Club evenings, they warmly debated, and laughed companionably, and it was surely noted by the others, how handsome a couple they were, both of an uncommon height for their respective sexes, and large-framed, and possessed of commandeering gestures; and, of course, of exceptional intelligence. *Yet he does not speak,* Prudence unhappily wrote, *tho' it is clear that he esteems me highly, and perhaps loves me. He says a great deal (so very eloquently!) and yet—he does not speak.*

Ah, those days! Those turbulent days! Abolitionists of every hue—some genteel, and civil, and of good family; some near-rabid, in their murderous rages, against the slaveholding South. Reformers of society; and woman Suffragettes (possessed of so unnatural a vehemence, and so little modesty, they did their cause scant good, and surely deserved the jeers and abuse visited upon them); and orators of the "Go Ahead" persuasion, who preached that the nation should not give a whit about slavery, "whether it is voted up, or voted down," but continue to expand throughout the Western Hemisphere. The cause of Popular Sovereignty, and the cause of Militant Temperance, and charismatic John Quincy Zinn lecturing at the lyceum, or at Cobbett Square Church (his initial series being so successful, he was recalled for a second season), on the need for radical reform in *Spirit,* in America—this reform, or revolution, then giving way to innumerable small transformations, which would raise our civilization to the height, for which it was destined.

"What we perceive as *Evil* is naught but *Disorder,*" John Quincy Zinn instructed his attentive audiences, "and what our eyes perceive as *Disorder,* is naught but *Order,* unclearly apprehended." The lyceum audiences, being well educated, and of a literary and philosophical turn of mind, were greatly moved by the young schoolmaster's assertion that their children, possessing pristine souls, already knew all fundamental truths—so that their teachers, in all humility, and employing the new *Socratic method,* were but skilled instruments in drawing them out. He oft reiterated his bold declaration, from *Out of the Mouths of Babes,* to the effect that, *The child knows, what the Teacher must recover.* For the old way of rote-teaching must be banish'd; and all old textbooks, crammed with dead, spiritless facts; and, as well, all teachers who clung to the old ways and did not truly love both their charges, and Wisdom itself.

John Quincy Zinn's experimental class at the Brownrrigg Academy did not sit inertly in their seats, but moved freely about, and were encouraged by their teacher to participate in divers conversations, and to ask a good deal of questions. They studied poesy not by committing verse to memory, but by *writing it;* they became disciplined in the exacting art of perception, by *drawing* (with many comical, but surely instructive, results); they were encouraged to invent new words, and new ways of spelling old words—for our great English tongue, as John Quincy taught, is itself a massive machine, an invention of sorts, in which all must participate. They learned geography by applying themselves to actual mapmaking, and anatomy, by studying the skeletons of real animals. Mr. Zinn being a firm believer in manual labor and dexterity, it was necessary that his young charges—girls no less than boys—acquire the use of hammers, saws, files, and planes, and other homely instruments, scorned by the genteel classes. Singly, or in small teams, these amazing children worked on their own machines, and experimented with weights and measurements, and pulleys, and wheels, and water, and fire, and rapid changes of temperature, and direct and indirect sunlight, and the relative buoyancy of feathers, pebbles, blocks of wood, grass, snow, and nails. They designed dirigibles, and submarines, and ideal dwelling places, and model cities. For *Invention*, Mr. Zinn taught, is at the very heart of the Universe, and the especial secret of our great Nation, yet but dimly understood by the rest of the world.

It was Mr. Zinn's fervent belief that all Americans should wish to participate, to the degree of their capability, in the invention of the most remarkable civilization ever to appear on earth: nay, are we not the very civilization, *for which the earth was created?* "Our United States has naught to do with the Old, but only with the New," John Quincy passionately averred, "for, as Mr. Thoreau has said, 'Eternity culminates in the present moment.' We are a New World, of questions and questers; visions, improvisations, and bold experiments; in short, a living *invention.* If I declare myself an American citizen, am I not also an inventor?—for it is our collective destiny, and must be God's will."

Thus the flavor, and the general content, of the young man's public addresses, the which continued to be greeted with exuberant applause, and respectful notices in most of the papers, and an enthusiasm of such wide-ranging aspect, that it was not surprising that the children of such illustrious Americans as Commodore Matthew Perry and Mr. Horace Greeley, and Edwin Booth, were enrolled at the Brownrrigg Academy, to be the pupils, for a time, of the radical young schoolmaster.

Yet why does he not speak? the wretched young woman queried her heart. *Alas, will he not speak?*

12

How astonished the young Zinn sisters would be, to learn that their beloved mother—now so stout, and so matronly, and so grimly practical in her expert housewifery—had once been a fainting, weeping, obsessed young woman!—and the stern-visagèd Mrs. Zinn (who commanded much respect, and not a little trepidation, in the Octagonal House), but a tremulous Miss Kiddemaster, to her shame o'erwhelmed by bitter thoughts directed against her rivals.

For there was not only *Miss Parthenope Violette Brownrrigg,* and *Miss Evangeline Ferris,* but also Vice-Admiral Triem's pretty daughter *Rachel,* and *Miss Honora LeBeau,* and one or two others commonly mentioned, as prospects for John Quincy Zinn. *Shall I live?* Prudence queried, of her puffy and humiliated mirror image. *Nay, can I live? For, if he chooses another, the shame of it shall o'ercome me.*

Rumors flew throughout the city, blown gustily by the winter wind, and piled deep with the fresh-fallen snow; and even if the sadly distraught Miss Kiddemaster betook herself, of a weekend, to her family's country estate in Bloodsmoor, she could not escape certain cruel whisperings: some of which, I am sorry to say, were reported to her by her own cousins, with the pretense of charity. The Brownrriggs' strategic play for the young bachelor involved a formal dinner at which an English baronet was a guest, with some intelligent interest in "American science"; the Mignon Barfields (being the parents of Evangeline Ferris's widowed mother) threw open their fabled dining room, in austere Barfield Hall, that they might honor John Quincy Zinn, who could not know, Prudence thought, with some spiteful gratification, how rare were the Barfields' dinners, and how all of social Philadelphia would have prized an invitation! The Triems boldly made their play at a larger, and less formal dinner, at which (so it was reported to Prudence) John Quincy had quite shocked the company, by speaking of the significant differences in his employ at the Brownrrigg Academy, and his employ in Mouth-of-Lebanon: for, as the young man laughingly recounted, he had not only been obliged to chop firewood, and feed the stove, in his rural common school, but had acted as a carpenter, and a handyman, and a custodian of the outhouses—the which, as he explained, demanded a great deal of ingenuity, to be kept from stinking.

Poor Prudence was an unwilling spectator of Miss Honora Le-Beau's play for Mr. Zinn's interest, and the degree of success of that play: for the LeBeaus had evidently thought so little of her, as a rival, that they invited her and her family to the lavish reception that yearly marked the spring exhibit, at the Academy for the Fine Arts—Miss LeBeau's father being director of the Academy, and an esteemed portrait painter, in his own right. Ah, how it wounded Prudence to espy her beloved in conversational intercourse with the slender, ivory-skinned Honora!—that beauteous young woman being attired, for the occasion, in a new dress by Worth, many-tiered, and amazingly small at the waist (no more than eighteen inches, the unhappy Prudence reasoned: and *her* waist, these past several weeks, was ever growing thicker, and less amenable to her corset); a cambric ruff about her throat, and Mrs. LeBeau's famous emeralds in full display, all over her person, and a smile of such dazzling composure, and charm, that Prudence could not wonder at John Quincy's absorbed interest.

(Alas, so reckless had Prudence become, she ignored her mother's blandishments, and, alone, approached the smiling couple, that she might o'erhear their conversation. And how absurd that conversation was—and how transparent, and how shameful! For, it seemed, Honora had succeeded in engaging Mr. Zinn in a discussion of *balloon ascensions*, in France, particularly that of the aerostatic locomotive designed by Monsieur Petin, which had excited some attention in the press: and in which *Miss LeBeau had herself been a most amaz'd passenger.* It fairly sickened Prudence to observe how John Quincy, failing to discern the base motive behind the young lady's conversation, listened with rapt and very flattering attention, and expressed a great deal of boyish interest in Monsieur Petin's remarkable design, consisting of three balloons of "goldbeater's skin" (made from the intestine of an ox!), of generous proportions, with propellers driven by steam, and wheels with articulated blades: none of which meant a great deal to Prudence, but seemed to, to John Quincy Zinn. For that young man summoned forth enough daring to say, that he would consider it a journey well spent, to travel to France for such an experience, tho', for the most part, he had no interest whatsoever in foreign climes, and could not imagine himself ever leaving his native shores. Whereupon coquettish Honora observed, with a skilled fluttering of her fan, that, her father being an "intimate acquaintance" of Monsieur Petin, it would be no trouble at all, for a lively ride in the air-locomotive to be arranged for Mr. Zinn. And all this transpired with no ironical sense, on John Quincy's part, that he was being boldly *manipulated!* Nay, the flush-faced Prudence thought, and to her shame I must record it, *seduced.* O Reader, you may well imagine, and pity, the ensuing sleepless night, endured by poor Prudence, after this most ignominious of occasions!)

It had been in a chill and drear autumn, some five years previous, that the dissolute man-of-letters, Edgar Allan Poe, was found unconscious on a Baltimore street; and died at the age of forty. Thus, against the vociferous protestations of several older members of the Arcadia Club, a belated tribute to his poetic "genius" was planned, in which John Quincy Zinn volunteered to take part.

"It is a pity, and a scandal," Miss Parthenope Brownrrigg vehemently exclaimed, with an unseemly forcefulness to her voice, "that so rare, so strange, and so unique a poetic talent, has not been properly valued in Philadelphia."

Tho' Poe had dwelt in the city for some years, and had edited *Graham's Magazine,* it seemed that no one amongst the Arcadians had known him; for he had not moved in the best society. There was the unpleasantness of the feud with Longfellow, and a battery of disquieting rumors: the man was ungentlemanly, and morbid, and alcoholic, and his linen was oft unclean, and his hair inadequately groomed.

Yet, the younger Arcadians argued, was he not a native genius? Ah, and consider his wretched death!—brought about, it may have been, by the harshly materialistic and unfeeling world, which despised poetry.

Even Dr. Tremblay, whilst disapproving of the man himself, and doubtful of the value, to posterity, of his *oeuvre,* conceded the brilliance of "Ulalume," "To Helen," "The Raven," and one or two other poems. John Quincy Zinn was, it was revealed, the only person at the meeting to have read both *The Narrative of A. Gordon Pym,* and the remarkable *Eureka,* in their entirety; and he surprised the membership by stating that, in his opinion, certain of Poe's scientific theories would one day be prov'd sound, by future scientists. With a very charming blush Mr. Zinn allowed that, had *he* sufficient freedom, which might only be acquired by financial independence, he might seek to verify Poe's theories himself.

Each law of Nature depends at all points, on all other laws. This theorem of Poe's struck Mr. Zinn as self-evident, and an expression of genius.

The meeting then proceeded, with several recitations of the tragic poet's work, by his especial admirers. (How apt, that the evening was bleak, and drear, and darksome, and the leaded windows of the drawing room beset upon, by unfriendly winds!—so that Prudence, of late fatigued by sleepless nights, and a severe diminishment of her natural robust appetite, felt the chill pierce to the very marrow of her bones, and half-wondered, tho' knowing full better, if the spectre of that wretched man did not stalk the earth, and seek a sort of underbred revenge, by peeking in at his betters, upon such ill-guided occasions.) It was toward the end of the o'erlong evening, during John Quincy Zinn's mesmerizing recitation of "Dream-Land," that something very untoward happened to Prudence: she grew lightheaded, and seemed to see "sparks" in the air, and would have sunk swooning to the carpet had she not been firmly ensconced, in an overstuffed Turkish chair, with substantial arms.

How her senses reeled!—the while her belovèd recited the poem, his eyes benignly shut, and his frame swaying just perceptibly from side to side, in obedience to the uncanny rhythm of the verse:

> By a route obscure and lonely,
> Haunted by ill angels only,
> Where an Eidolon, named NIGHT,
> On a black throne reigns upright,
> I have reached these lands but newly
> From an ultimate dim Thule—
> From a wild weird clime that lieth, sublime,
> Out of SPACE—out of TIME.

At this, poor Prudence's maiden heart beat the more rapidly, and her breath grew so wildly shallow, she was in terror of fainting: for the air seemed of a sudden stagnant, and her corset cruelly tight, and the hypnotic words of her *husband-to-be* so powerful:

> By the gray woods,—by the swamp
> Where the toad and newt encamp,—
> By the dismal tarns and pools
>   Where dwell the Ghouls,—
> By each spot the most unholy—
> In each nook most melancholy,—
> There the traveller meets, aghast,
> Sheeted Memories of the Past—

Whereupon Prudence seemed to lose consciousness, with a scarce-audible sigh (which, fortunately, no one heard, being so rapt with attention, at John Quincy Zinn's performance). She sank into a light swoon, and could not rouse herself for some minutes, until, with the completion of her belovèd's recitation, the company generally bestirred itself: and her strength, and her consciousness, flowed back to her.

Ah, unhappy maiden! She was so ashamed of this curious manifestation of her *weakness,* that she did not care to tell her mother about it: for she believed (how mistakenly, we shall see), that it would never again happen to her: and there would be no public revelation, of her illicit love, for the handsome young bachelor Mr. Zinn!

13

It was the case that the Kiddemasters were well aware of their daughter's *fixation* upon Mr. John Quincy Zinn, and her e'er-increasing turbulence, of mood and temper; but, for numerous reasons, they were somewhat hesitant to speak frankly to her. (Even Judge Kiddemaster, whose reputation on the bench had grown formidable, in recent years, confessed that he "did not like to stir a hornets' nest—*the female soul.*") That their only daughter should, after so many years of stubborn resistance, now *fall in love,* struck them as remarkable; for had they not, with some display of grim stoicism, resigned themselves to their daughter's *spinsterhood?* (I am bound to record here, that it was not altogether true, that Miss Prudence Kiddemaster had spurned numerous suitors: but it was certainly the case that, had the young lady been more congenial, some would surely have stepped forward—the Kiddemaster fortune by no means being a modest one.)

Remarkable, Prudence's impassion'd feeling: and ironical, perhaps: and, should her high regard for Mr. Zinn not be returned, very possibly tragical. Thus the tongues wagged, and no one knew quite what to think. For, on the one hand, Mr. Zinn was quite clearly an estimable young man; then again, on the other— If he *did* sue for Prudence's hand, *was such a match tolerable, in Philadelphia?*

On this issue, as the reader might well imagine, there was much controversy amongst the family: the women being generally of one opinion (tho' arrived at only after much rumination), the men, somewhat stoutly, of another. For, consider: the Kiddemasters and the Whittons (Mrs. Sarah Kiddemaster being a Whitton, of Baltimore) were descended from old English country families, related by ties of marriage to the

Lamberts of Sussex, the Ashbery-Foxes of Warwickshire, the Chuzzlewits of Manchester, the Gilpins of Rowbothan, the Bayards of Norwich, and the Duke of St. Giddings. A Kiddemaster officer had distinguished himself in Cromwell's Army; another had fought bravely at Waterloo; still others had attained eminence, on this side of the Atlantic, as a consequence of their uncommon courage, and manly diligence in the field. The renowned Erasmus Kiddemaster, for instance, had led the noble expeditionary forces of the 1660's, against the Dutch enemy, along the Bloodsmoor River: this fierce gentleman being feared, by his men as well as his foes, for the stern and unbending nature of his *justice*.

Nineteen-year-old Randolph Kiddemaster, a lieutenant in the Continental Army, was credited with saving General George Washington's life, in one of the first skirmishes, in our glorious Revolution; and John Branch Kiddemaster, a controversial figure to this day, had so ensconced himself as Chief Justice of the United States Supreme Court, that, for some three decades after the election of Jefferson, it scarcely mattered who was President, so resolute were this gentleman's Federalist sympathies, and so ingenious his cunning.

In more recent decades, the Kiddemasters had acquired considerable wealth, by way of their iron mining property in the Chadds Ford region, and their several paper mills (the Kiddemasters having intermarried with the Gilpins, as early as 1790), and their import businesses (this being, I believe, primarily a China trade), and scattered investments, too complex and varied to be here enumerated. It is to be kept in mind, however, that this great family's sense of decorum, and abhorrence of all fulsome display of material wealth, dictated their behavior in society; and would never have countenanced the erecting of any house, of a vulgarian sort of splendor, soon to become commonplace in the Union, as our troubled century unfolds.

Godfrey Kiddemaster, though disdaining politics outright, like all cultured gentlemen of his time, knew it his solemn duty to serve his country in some wise, and consequently entered the law: there, by merit alone, and the affectionate support of certain of his relatives, rising with enviable rapidity, having been, for some years, Chief Justice of the Supreme Court of the Commonwealth of Pennsylvania, when young Mr. Zinn was to make his acquaintance. Nor was it entirely out of the question, that Judge Kiddemaster might be called soon to Washington—if only the Whigs were not so bankrupt, and the Free Soilers so churlish a lot, and the future of the Presidency so uncertain.

In this wise various observations were daily made to Prudence, with a semblance of the "accidental," that she might absorb the moral that the Kiddemasters were, by no means, *common:* a fact the proud young lady well knew, but did not care to contemplate o'ermuch at this time—

the spectre of John Quincy Zinn always hovering near, in her inflamed imagination.

I quite realize that I am a Kiddemaster, Prudence bethought herself, biting her lip, but must I remain thus, forever?

To her shame, she began to succumb to those very "spells"—lightheadedness, temper, weeping, melancholy, "fagged nerves"—she so deplored in the females of her acquaintance; nor did she resist her Aunt Edwina's ministrations, as to dosages of Dr. Fayer's Dyspepsia Pills, Essence of Tyre, Woodbridge's Natura, and Miss Emmeline's Remedy—this last medicine being most agreeable to the taste, syrupy, very sweet, with a pronounced orange base, and almost miraculously *calming,* to the distress'd heart.

For some time, God took mercy on the fretting young woman: and the very worst of the rumors subsided.

Alas, then sprang to life again!

Yet, again, ebbed: and Prudence again enjoyed John Quincy's company and, summoning forth all her Kiddemaster pride, gave every indication of *not knowing* how idle tongues wagged.

"I shall not concern myself with anything save the present moment," Prudence wisely counseled her heart, "nor shall I give way to vexations arising out of mere emotion, and particularities. For, as Mr. Emerson teaches, 'I live now: I am a transparent eyeball opened to nature.'"

So John Quincy was invited to tea, and to dinner, at the Kiddemasters' Cobbett Square home; and they went together to one or more of the milder Abolitionist speakers; and to Thursday afternoons at the Arcadia Club; and to the Philadelphia Academy of Art, there to gaze with especial delight upon a watercolor exhibit, of "Autumnal Blossoms." They attended the opening night of that production of *Macbeth,* at the new Varieties Theatre, in which Miss Charlotte Cushman gave an historic performance (for thus the reviewers claimed, in their rhapsodies of praise): tho' Prudence believed that the actress's Lady Macbeth was somewhat too impassioned, and John Quincy expressed some philosophical doubt, less pertaining to the performances themselves, than to the general *violence,* and *gloom,* and *deficiency of beauty,* of the great tragedy itself.

"It may be," the handsome young man allowed, "that, in less enlightened times than ours, and in climes differing substantially from ours, such a spectacle of human nature did not arouse skepticism, amongst persons of intelligence: but we here in America, in our more advanced civilization, have come to believe otherwise, concerning human nature."

Prudence's heart so swelled, as, by John Quincy's side, she heard these forthright words, that she could not speak, save to assent. How judicious his insights, how measured his words!—and how she adored him!

At this strategic time, Miss Rachel Triem was said to be visiting relatives in Richmond, there to remain for some six or more weeks; the ivory-complected beauty, Miss Honora LeBeau, was being assiduously courted by René Du Pont de Nemours (the uncle of Cheyney, at this time but an infant of some six months of age); Miss Evangeline Ferris, accompanied by her mother, had sailed off to London on a line-of-packet ship; and poor Parthenope Brownrrigg, tho' absurdly enamored of John Quincy Zinn, sought to disguise her futile passion by absenting herself from meetings of the Arcadia Club.

Mr. Zinn had of late declared himself somewhat o'ertaxed, as a consequence of his numerous social obligations, and new-arisen difficulties at the Brownrrigg Academy. (For, it seemed, certain dissatisfied parents had complained to Mr. Brownrrigg, that the Socratic method, whilst pristine in itself, seemed to be leading their children into remarkable areas of knowledge, not excluding the *agnostical,* and the *biological.* And there was some small flurry of concern, that the anatomical lessons, whilst conducted with but dry skeletons—of squirrels, weasels, cats, and similar small creatures—nonetheless could not fail to suggest, in the impressionable mind, the grosser private organs, of the human body.)

"I do not care in the least, Mr. Zinn, what rumors are whisper'd about you," Prudence forthrightly declared, "for I know, from having closely perused your manuscript, and from our numerous intimate discussions, the degree of your seriousness as an educator; and I cannot be dissuaded—nay, not even by the priggish Miss Brownrrigg—of your high moral worth."

"You are very kind, Miss Kiddemaster," the young man said, with a somewhat distracted air; and smiled a smile that quite bewitched Prudence's heart, it spoke so much of affection, and weariness.

He loves me, Prudence inwardly exclaimed, *and yet, will he not speak?*

To her sorrow, and protracted mortification, the pricks of jealousy did not abate, tho' certain of her rivals had withdrawn from the field; for there were other regions of John Quincy Zinn's life—obscure and murky indeed—which Prudence but dimly understood, and could not altogether countenance.

For, in the humble boardinghouse, in which he continued to reside (stubbornly resisting his friends' offers of more luxurious housing), John Quincy had evidently made the acquaintance of a number of personages: these being distinctive "characters," it seemed, for whom he felt some puzzling fondness. There was a retired physician, and self-styled phrenologist, by the name of Butler (who, having examined John Quincy's leonine head, fingering the bumps, declivities, and ridges, with a practic'd hand, came to the shocking conclusion that "a God and a Demon warred for his soul"); an unemployed railroad man, of Irish, Scotch, German, and Mohawk blood, who diverted his fellow boarders, at the dining room table, with fantastical tales of gross outrages and crimes to come, with the "triumph of the railroad barons, o'er the hapless maiden, the United States"; and a very young man, by the name of Charles Guiteau, who called himself an artist, but had also worked as a pamphleteer, a printer's assistant, and a dockhand—this person being, according to Mr. Zinn's testimony, an appealing young man, and ofttimes amusing, tho' prone to excitability.

"It is quite touching, how lonely Charles is," Mr. Zinn said, "for simple comradeship, I believe; and for wisdom."

Prudence held her tongue, and said not a word; but she could not keep from wondering, whether, on those frequent nights John Quincy absented himself from the drawing rooms of the Philadelphians, he was consorting with such low creatures. *I despise myself for my jealousy,* Prudence took note, *yet find it near impossible to o'ercome this dread emotion.* And her feeling grew the more problematic, as, laughingly, John Quincy came to speak of young Guiteau as his "hopeful disciple."

So it happened that, against her better judgment, Prudence invited John Quincy *and* his friend Charles to tea; and arranged for them to attend the theater together; and to go for some pleasant Sunday excursions, in one of the Kiddemaster carriages; and for some picturesque strolls, along the Delaware. The three of them attended a lyceum talk by the controversial "Sacred Socialist" Cyrus Feucht, and a most disreputable public debate, betwixt an Anti-Nebraskan, a Pro-Slaver, and a Popular Sovereignty man, that ended with so lurid a free-for-all, that the police swarmed into the building, and made arrests!

Young Charles Guiteau was a good twelve inches shorter than John Quincy, and made a most comical, tho' touching figure, with his pretense of a military bearing, and his high-held head. Prudence could not guess his age, which might have been anywhere betwixt eighteen and thirty: his frame was undersized, his head o'erlarge, and his eyes somewhat beady, and too moist. His dark, thinning hair reeked of brilliantine, and was fashioned into a curious style, with hooklike curls on either temple, and an unwavering center part. He looked ahead, he said, to the day when he would own his own printing press, and might enter politics; then again, perhaps it was his destiny, to leave the city and settle in far-off California, there to organize a Utopian community, which might implement John Quincy Zinn's ideas *in the flesh.* "Ah, how he makes everything clear, that has long been obscured in vile murk! Do you not agree, Miss Kiddemaster?"—thus the strange creature addressed her, with no perspicacity, as to how the sound of Prudence's name, in his squeaking voice, gave offense.

An eccentric trio, I am bound to say: Miss Prudence Kiddemaster in a long, full, black sealskin cloak, that may have emphasized, rather than disguised, the Amazonian stolidity of her figure; Mr. John Quincy Zinn in his ill-fitting preacher's coat, and his bell-shaped hat, the which gave to his healthsome appearance a certain bucolic air; and the diminutive Mr. Guiteau, hurrying alongside them, fairly hopping, that he might keep pace with this handsome couple, whom he plainly admired, and did not scruple to pester with his attentions. (Poor Mr. Guiteau! Prudence thought his overcoat, which fell unevenly to his ankles, was a most piteous sight; and his greasy bowler hat, now much the worse for wear, was somewhat comical; and his high ungainly boots, which flopped, and sighed, and squished, as he hurried along! It was difficult to believe, as Charles Guiteau oft asserted, that his father was a banker, and his mother "of good stock"; tho' Prudence thought it quite likely, that, as Charles said, he and his father had "grievously quarreled," and he had been "expelled" from the home of his childhood, preferring to wander about America, dwelling now in one city, and now in another, in order that he might become acquainted with "all that was most wondrous.")

"Many a young American wanders, that he might seek his *material fortune,*" John Quincy averred, "but my friend Charles wanders in search of his *spiritual fortune.*"

When the two young men had first become acquainted, Guiteau was a staunch believer in militant Abolitionism, and red meat, and Christian determinism: the damn'd were damn'd, the saved saved, and naught further might be said. After a scant three or four months, however, as Guiteau joyously reiterated, to Prudence, he deemed himself a *total convert* to John Quincy Zinn's wisdom—and wished only to have the opportunity, to put Mr. Zinn's ideas into practice.

All eagerly the young man had seized upon John Quincy's theory of the "sacred employment of machinery," in the enhancement of human life; he was wonderfully enthusiastic about the perpetual-motion machine, though, as he laughingly said, he "could not claim to understand a whit about it, or about anything, pertaining to Science." Since Mr. Zinn shared in certain Abolitionist beliefs, that the Negro slaves should be freed, and property belonging to the great plantations redistributed, and that *pacifism, vegetarianism,* and *Spirit* would one day harmonize, to bring this about, this was young Charles Guiteau's fervent belief as well: tho' he did not entirely see (thus he confessed, with an abash'd smile) how such things would happen, the slaveowners being wicked men, and little given to quiet argument. "It would seem to me," Guiteau murmured, with knitted brow, and a childish blush, in cognizance of his daring to speak in such wise, "that the great cause of *pacifism* itself, for instance, might be better advanced, if one were armed."

An eccentric trio, indeed: *yet I have no choice,* Prudence lamented in her secret diary, *no choice & no shame.*

It was sometimes not unpleasant to share Mr. Zinn's company with his impetuous young friend: for Mr. Zinn seemed to enjoy speaking—nay, lecturing—to Mr. Guiteau, whose boyish countenance so readily revealed his thoughts. Prudence did not shrink from stating her opinions. Was it not contemptible, was it not shameful, that President Pierce now wanted to annex Cuba?—*as a new slave state!* All politicians, whether Democrats, or Whigs, or a half-dozen others, were motivated by self-interest, and not by morality: was it not unspeakable, to be in *their* hands?

Led by John Quincy, they discussed, for long impassioned hours, the *profanity* of public life, and the *sanctity* of private life; the *evil* of material interests, and the *blessing* of Spirit. Prudence visibly shuddered, at the recollected thought of certain personages, in her own family, who so craved money, by way of inheritances, that they fawned over their presumed benefactors, and could think of little else. "I had rather be a pauper, and a pauper's wife," Prudence brashly declared, "than so eaten up with covetousness, as I have seen many an inheritrix, of Philadelphia and Bloodsmoor both."

The three young persons talked of the necessity for a *dramatic confrontation,* with the slaveholding South; yet they talked also, with especial warmth, of the impending *World Synthesis,* and the ubiquitous *Love Spirit* (this being the discovery of the Englishman James Pierrepont Greaves, not many years previous), and the problem of whether Humankind's birth in time was intrinsically *evil* (because Spirit had thus laps'd from Eternity), or, in itself, *neutral* (because part of the evolutionary process of Unifying Spirit).

A vexing problem, indeed! (Which, I am somewhat ashamed to confess, I have never been able to grasp in its particulars, still less in its conclusion.)

"And yet," John Quincy Zinn spoke suddenly, with an expansiveness to his voice, "*I see no problem before us: for only look.*"

Whereupon, in one of those impulsive gestures, which Prudence had come to admire, and perhaps even to adore, the forthright young gentleman grasped both his companions by the arms, and sternly bade them gaze out upon the splendid scene before them: for they had been tramping about the birch woods, above the Bloodsmoor River, on a chill and gusty Sunday afternoon in early spring—Mr. Zinn and Mr. Guiteau being, for that weekend, guests of the country estate, Kiddemaster Hall.

(For some decades the family divided their time, with a fair degree of constancy, betwixt the city, and the country; gradually retiring, as it were, to the country, with the advent of Judge Kiddemaster's decline as a jurist, and his increased loathing of his fellows.)

"Nay, my dear friends, *I* see no problem," John Quincy said, in a bold and tremulous voice, "in this heavenly landscape, this living Utopia, in which, all undeserving, we find ourselves placed."

Ah, and it was true! It was true!

Prudence gaped, and stared, and saw that it was true!

That this world, this earth, *was* Heaven: and that they were placed upon it, all undeserving: and that, and that— (But she was in danger, of a sudden, of bursting into tears, of raw exultation: and dared do no more than murmur an assent.)

Little Charles Guiteau, however, suffered no such restraint, but, with an outcry of sheer childish delight, broke away from his companions, and, not unlike a prankish monkey, given to the immediate expression of high spirits, actually dared to run, and hop, and *perform a cartwheel on the grass!*—a cartwheel, in his o'ersized coat, and silly bowler hat, and flopping boots.

How very *curious* he was, this Charles Guiteau!—of whom more will be said, at a later date.

Yet I cannot resist o'erleaping my narrative, to a chill spring day in 1865, after poor Mr. Zinn had at last returned home, from the dread conflict (being wounded in the Battle of Richmond, and made gravely ill, by divers circumstances of spoiled meat, infectious diseases, and unspeakable sanitary conditions): a quite unremarkable morning, in itself, when little Octavia asked, of a sudden, her brown eyes brightly aglow, *Where had Pip come from?*

The seven-year-old child, a plump, sweet, and rarely fretful little miss, was busying herself, at the moment, in sewing yet another charming outfit, for Mr. Zinn's prized pet: this being a miniature vest carefully made over from the green sateen material of an old dressing gown, of Grandmother Sarah's, to which would be added scarlet embroidered flowers, and black velvet trim, and tiny brass buttons. For all the girls loved Pip, and Octavia most of all. (Throughout the war years this spider monkey, gifted with a most remarkable intuition, and some rudimentary intelligence, had *pined away for his endangered master,* as if he knew very well— indeed, better—than Mr. Zinn's daughters, how grave the situation was. Naturally, he did not shrink from playing his usual tricks, and was shrill, and jabbering, and naughty, at times, as if wishing punishment from Mrs. Zinn, or one of the servants; but you could tell, everyone said, that he had lost his spirit—his joy in life. As if, it may have been, the creature's soul were elsewhere! "A most pragmatical time, I am given to say, to rid ourselves of the nuisance," Grandfather Kiddemaster observed, but was o'erruled, fortunately, by the others.)

Dear little Octavia had begun sewing on the very day she learned to thread a needle, in but her third year; and, with wondrous precocity, she busied herself with numerous little tasks, that ranged from the simple darning of stockings and towels and handkerchiefs, to the creation of smocks for her sisters, and some three or four charming costumes for Pip.

With the return of Mr. Zinn from Richmond, and his honorable discharge from the Union Army, little Pip brightened: and spent many an hour stretched out beside his ailing master, who, convalescent, was forced to lie abed, or in a reclining chair (of his own invention), in the healthsome sunshine. Ah, it was a near-miracle to see how the melancholy monkey regained his spirit, and his energy, and was transformed, it would seem, into a very young monkey again!—all sweet, and frolicksome, yet docile, and, for long periods of time, quite tractable. And wasn't Mrs. Zinn embarrassed when pert little Malvinia loudly observed: "How very fortunate, Momma, that Grandfather did not get rid of Pip!—for he is quite settled down now, and *quite* tolerable."

And one day Octavia paused in her sewing, and inquired, *Where did Pip come from?*—and the other little girls looked up laughing, with incredulous countenances, for naturally it had never occurred to them beforehand that Pip, dear Pip, had *come from* anywhere at all!—just as they themselves had not *come from* anywhere, but had dwelt here, in the Octagonal House, from all time.

Whereupon Mrs. Zinn turned a somewhat reproving face upon Octavia, for it was hardly a delicate question, and might lead to yet more unseemly questions, pertaining to the origins of the girls themselves; yet bethought herself, with some hesitation. For it had always been a tacit understanding, within the family, that the spider monkey had been a prankish wedding present, to both the bride and the groom, from one of the several young Philadelphia ladies who had been gravely wounded by John Quincy Zinn's engagement to Prudence Kiddemaster—whether Miss Evangeline Ferris, or Miss Rachel Triem, or Miss Honora LeBeau, or (and this seemed most likely, to Prudence's way of thinking) poor Miss Parthenope Brownrrigg, who was fated never to marry. What a commotion Pip had caused, delivered to Kiddemaster Hall on the very morning of the wedding, a spider monkey outfitted in a miniature bridegroom's frock coat, with a spray of orange blossom in his lapel! The gift was accompanied by a card that read *From an Anonymous Well-Wisher;* and so merry were the spirits, of both bride and groom alike, that they had chosen not to take offense at the prank, and not to interpret it, as some did, as a *malicious trick,* but as a *felicitous omen*—little Pip being at that time hardly more than a baby, and very appealing indeed.

Thus, Prudence had secretly believed that the creature was a gift from Miss Brownrrigg, tho' never acknowledged. But now, confronted with her child's innocent question, and having in mind (she knew not why!) some vague dim memory, o'ertinged with melancholy, and some guilt, of the eccentric Mr. Guiteau, Prudence found herself thinking hard, her brow furrowed, and her breath somewhat short. *Where did little Pip come from? And what did the gift of him mean?*

It occurred to Prudence, with a flash of certitude that rocked her being, and left her quite faint, that the prankster had certainly not been one of the young Philadelphia ladies: it had been no one other than *Charles J. Guiteau.*

Ah, yes! The absurd little man! The monkeyish little man!—who had known beforehand, or sensed, that John Quincy Zinn, once wed to Prudence Kiddemaster, would disappear into pastoral Bloodsmoor, and into domesticity, and sacred fatherhood, and his *destiny:* never again to have time to spare for his disciple of carefree bachelor days.

Of course, Prudence thought, a blush o'ertaking her face, the gift was Guiteau's: and it was meant to insult.

"And yet," she murmured aloud, a knotted handkerchief pressed to her heaving bosom, "and yet, as God knows, *the triumph was mine.*"

14

All doubt in love is swallowed, and lovelier now is she
Than a picture deftly painted by the craftsmen o'er the sea;
And her face is a rose of the morning by the night-tide framed about,
And the long-stored love of her bosom from her eyes is leaping out.
                                                    —WILLIAM MORRIS

Know, O Reader, that, after upward of twelve months' agitation, during which time poor Prudence oft questioned herself, as to whether, in the fever of her own heart's adulation, she might not be *imagining all,* the dread impasse betwixt the young lovers was resolved!—resolved, I am happy to say, most agreeably for all, and, as Chance would merrily have it, in the very house in which Prudence had initially met her "fate."

And, that night, Prudence knelt by her bed, in sobbing disarray, so eager to give thanks to Our Maker, for His sudden mercy, that she could barely speak: nay, it was all the weeping maiden could do, to whisper these words: "O Lord! To think that I had oft doubted You, or doubted Your love for me!—as, alas, I had, so ignorantly, doubted *his!* But will You not forgive this sinner, and bless our impending union?"

The which heartfelt plea, I cannot think but that Our Maker heard, with a most kindly ear!

Deeply saddened in her heart, as a consequence of John Quincy Zinn's most exasperating *silence,* on any matter pertaining to affection betwixt them, Prudence Kiddemaster made the decision (not, I am certain, out of childish spite, or a longing for martyrdom) to betake herself to the country, that she might force her reluctant suitor to feel the pain of her absence. This action came, too, following some weeks of irascibility, lethargy, and distraction, in her classroom, and a growing repugnance for her position, as an instructrix of some repute: for, of a sudden, Miss Kiddemaster bethought herself, that she did not greatly *care* whether her girl pupils learnt their Latin, and did their sums, and memorized the English kings and queens, and perfected their handwriting: nor was it any longer self-evident, that *Independence* was more valued than *Romance.*

Thus, the proud young woman fled Philadelphia, for a certain space of time, accompanied by Mrs. Kiddemaster (who, feeling somewhat enfeebled, as a consequence of the brusque changes in temperature, in the autumn, considered that a retirement to the country might be salubrious); and there Prudence spent some hours daily in prayer, and meditation, and the perusal of philosophical literature: such sombre volumes as Dr. Philipps's *Sacred Annotations of the Seasons,* and Mrs. Wyatt's *Dashes at Life with a Free Pencil,* and the handsome kidskin-bound *Poetical Remains of the Late Lucretia Maria Davidson,* running to some five hundred close-printed pages. It was her intention to purge herself of her morbid *love-thoughts* for John Quincy Zinn, but, alas! his presence there haunted her, as she strolled in solitary repose along the picturesque Bloodsmoor River, or encircled the gazebo, or, with an involuntary sigh, leaned far over the granite rim of the wishing well, to stare into the sepulchral depths below.

(*There* in particular she saw him, as she gazed, and blinked, and wiped a surreptitious tear from her eye: his handsome strong-boned face; his thick blond hair, and full blond beard; his declamatory voice; his impassion'd gestures. Behind the pulpit of the Cobbett Square Unitarian Church—in the company of little Guiteau—in one or another of the Philadelphia drawing rooms, in which he was so welcome—and, alas! in the company of Miss Honora LeBeau, who lifted her flowerlike face to his, in a pretense of intelligent concentration. Poor Prudence tried to summon forth an image of herself, beside his manly frame: but she could not. She tried—and could not. John Quincy Zinn loomed large, in the lightless depths of the old wishing well: but no one stood beside him.)

I shall never forgive you, John Quincy! the hapless young lady wept.

It was reported to Prudence that Mr. Zinn came to call, in the city, and expressed some surprise that Miss Kiddemaster was not in. He inquired after her health; he inquired into the probable length of her stay, in Bloodsmoor; and, upon one occasion, left a missive for her, of substantial length—some seven handwritten pages, on inexpensive but tasteful stationery. (This document was, of course, hastily brought to Prudence, by a servant on horseback: and, Reader, you can imagine the young woman's disappointment, when, in perusing it, she discovered no words of *love, affection, esteem,* or *marital union!* but only a sort of complaint, about the Brownrriggs' treatment of him, and his pupils' lustreless imaginations, and his conviction that a true destiny might be his, if only he were free to pursue it. *Tho' God culminates in the present moment,* Mr. Zinn wrote, with, doubtless, a droll twist of his handsome lips, *it is not always evident, within the high brick walls of the Brownrrigg Academy!*)

Prudence read and reread this letter, and clutched it to her bosom, and halfway wondered—did it not contain, in its very circumspection of language, a declaration of sorts?—a confession, a plea, a proposal?—of sorts?

She then made her decision, to return to the city, unannounced, and to attend a Saturday reception at the Bayards'. *If Fate decrees that we must meet again,* Prudence wrote in her diary, *I cannot resist. I am but a plaything in the hands of God.*

Upward of two hours went into the preparation of Prudence's hair, which was somewhat coarse, and lacking in natural curl or wave, but, with the adroit aid of switches, braids, combs, and velvet ribbons, it was beautifully fashioned into a new Parisian style, which very much flattered her wide forehead. A considerable space of time was required, too, for the ordeal of dressing: for Prudence's striped satin gown, of the previous season, which all the family agreed was *most* flattering, had now become somewhat tight about the midriff and bosom; and had to be let out, by one of the servants.

Yet the toilette was completed, with gratifying success; and, wearing a new satin-and-wool hat, with a comely arcing egret feather, and a long ermine scarf pressed upon her by Aunt Edwina (who knew well, I have reason to believe, the agitated heart hidden in her niece's bosom), and carrying an exquisite Japanese fan, of rainbow hues, and an ivory-handled pink silk sunshade: fortified by nothing more substantial than several cups of black China tea, and a small portion of Miss Emmeline's Remedy, and a negligible breakfast, and lunch, Miss Prudence Kiddemaster stepped forth, to be taken by one of her cousins, to the Bayards' home —and thrust into her fate.

Prudence was ushered into the Bayards' crowded drawing room, there to espy, with frightening alacrity, the object of her passion: John Quincy Zinn himself, so tall, and broad-shouldered, and husky of frame, and, it may have been, so abash'd, by society, that he stood out with prominence —nay, it seemed to Prudence, whose breath was very short, and whose heart fairly tripped, that the young gentleman stood somewhat apart from the other guests: *as if in anticipation of a new arrival.*

And, unless her moisture-brimm'd eyes greatly deceived her, Mr.

Zinn had bought a new frock coat for the occasion!—in itself most remarkable, being of a very dark blue, and skillfully tailored, unlike the
near-shapeless preacher's coat he commonly wore. And, too, he had
exchanged his greasy cravat for a new tie; and wore a pale gray waistcoat;
and—

Of a sudden, the gentleman's head turned, and his eyes fell upon
Prudence, with so swift and, as it were, unlook'd-to, a potency, that the
breathless young woman could not help but step backward, and clutch at
her strained bosom. Across the agreeably murmurous room, the lovers
exchanged a look of such intricacy, in Prudence's assessment, that, in her
very dawning triumph, she felt a kind of despair, that she might never
comprehend him, nor the untrammeled mystery of Romance!

Prudence saw how *alarm,* and *guilt,* and *apprehension,* and *love,*
flowed most rapidly across John Quincy's reddening face; she saw how
his eyes shone; and his movement to step forward, that he might approach her, tho' so many ladies and gentlemen separated them. She was
too astonished, being greeted by that expression of naked *love,* to turn
aside, in confus'd modesty; and is to be excused, I hope, if she remained
stock-still, staring at her belovèd.

And then, a most inexplicable event occurred: Prudence gasped,
and lost consciousness, and, before any startled gentleman could impede
her fall, she sank swooning to the carpet.

So it happened that Mr. Zinn, in great haste, made his way to her,
calling her name, and fairly tearing at his hair, in his consternation. With
no mind for how all gaped at him, he knelt boldly above her; and lifted
her somewhat, so that her helpless back rested against his knee; and ah!
how his manly voice rang, with alarm, and startl'd love, for all to hear:
"My dear Prudence! My love! Oh, do awaken, Prudence! O my belovèd!"

I understand not the paradox of the stricken young woman's mental state: that she was *unconscious,* and yet, to some degree, *conscious.* All
unresisting, with no more muscular volition than a dressmaker's dummy
—and yet, at the same time, was she not capable of *seeing,* through her
shut, flushed eyelids, and *hearing,* with more than ordinary acuity?

John Quincy Zinn continued, the while, to address her, in a veritable paroxysm of tenderness, tears now starting out of his eyes, and his
broad-boned face ashen-white. "My dear, my love, oh, my bride! Do
awaken, dear Prudence! You shall not come to harm!" Thus the stricken
gentleman spoke, as Prudence's pretty feathered hat unpinned itself, and
fell slowly, and with an exquisite grace, from her head, and to the carpet
below. All this while, Prudence was awake, yet in a swoon; she saw and
heard everything, yet could not respond, not even to assure her lover that
she was out of danger, tho' it racked her heart, to see his agitation.

(I hope I will not prejudice the reader, against Prudence, by stating
that it was well for all concerned, not excluding future generations, of

Kiddemasters, that the o'erwrought young woman *did not* enjoy the free use of her arms, at this crucial moment: for I do not consider it an exaggeration, to say that she would have, in full view of the astonish'd assemblage, *entwined her arms about Mr. Zinn's neck; and united herself to him, in a willful ecstasy of love, quite uninform'd by maidenly hesitation, or moral rectitude.*)

Fortunately, Prudence could move neither her arms, nor her nether limbs, so the grave danger passed. It seemed, the while her lover leaned over her, that the scene was ablaze with light, and a thousand angels' voices melodically sounded, in an orison of triumph: and, with that preternatural sharpness of vision, upon which I have commented, she was able to see, past John Quincy Zinn's head, the exquisite stenciled ceiling of the drawing room, at which she had never gazed with especial interest, in the past; and to rejoice in the aesthetic harmony, of the cloud, vine, and pomegranate designs which, skillfully coupled with the rich turquoise of the background, summoned forth the remarkable effect of the out-of-doors, and of the sky, as if the lovers were alone together, in some wild, natural place, in Tuscany, perhaps, or in some unnamed glen, or glade, or declivity, in the ruder region of Bloodsmoor itself!

Yet she sank still deeper, in her helpless soon, whilst her lover cried to her, now from a great distance: "O my dear—my belovèd—my bride—ah, do awaken!—my love, my *bride*—"

15

The anxious reader will be, I know, gratified to learn, that a *formal engagement* betwixt Prudence and Mr. Zinn duly followed, upon the heels of this too-tempestuous scene; and that, after the space of a twelve-month, during which time the love of both parties naturally deepened, and acquired a somewhat more sombre tone, and the Kiddemasters to some degree relented, in their prejudice against Mr. Zinn (of which I will speak more, at a later date)—the handsome young couple was married in a most beauteous and solemn ceremony, at our old historic church in Bloodsmoor, the Reverend Hewett presiding: on the morn of 18 November 1855.

How it would ravish your eye, to see the stone church all sumptuously bedecked, with floral glories, of divers varieties!—and to observe how the quaint old church was happily filled—*every pew, every seat*—with Kiddemasters and their relations, from several states. (Tho' of the bridegroom's family there was, I am sorry to say, no one at all.)

III

The Unloos'd Demon

16

Though Mr. Zinn had instructed his womenfolk to expunge from their minds all fanciful thought of the occult, wisely teaching that what we know as the Supernatural is but the Natural, imperfectly grasped, it did come to seem as if, on that golden autumnal day when Deirdre was carried off, a demon of some sort—bodiless, but ah, how powerful!—was loos'd, upon Bloodsmoor; it truly seemed as if the sacred mechanism of the universe had been grievously upset, and the highest of civilized values —not only gentility, and Christian morality, but Maidenhood itself—were cast down into the mud.

With what catastrophic results, we shall see: for I scarce exaggerate when I say that, from that day onward, *the fortunes of the Zinn family were tragically alter'd.*

The pity of it! Tiny pink velvet rosebuds (with the most beauteous silky-pink interiors) strewn on the trampled grass, of the riverbank.

The pale yellow satin-and-poplin bonnet, its veil hideously torn.

Broken rushes, and sere grass, and a lone branch snapped off a willow tree, from the violent passage of the balloon, in its hasty ascent.

Ah, and the spectacle of the balloon rising, its insensible prey aboard!—a black silken balloon drifting across the wide river—over the line of sentinel oaks—rising, and drifting, and growing ever-smaller—and smaller—the helpless girl aboard, hidden from view—captive, and lost—as her stricken sisters at last begin to scream for help—as the balloon drifts away—now a black sun, against the darkening sky—now a moon, all tremulous and indistinct—and now gone: vanish'd into air!

And, in the confus'd days to come, the onslaught of the dread tribe of *journalists,* amongst them keen-eyed reporters from the Philadelphia *Inquirer,* and the Wilmington *Globe* (the publishers of which dared profess themselves friends of Godfrey Kiddemaster, of old); and the insult of the dignified Kiddemaster name not only printed widely in the common press, but accompanied by illicit daguerreotypes of the great Hall!—and, from time to time, accompanied by crude pencil sketches of the abducted "Miss Zinn" as well, these being entirely fictitious and fradulent drawings, of a young girl not resembling Deirdre in the least.

But tho' the invidious creatures poked and pried as best they could, not scrupling, even, to make their queries in the poorer regions of Bloodsmoor, they remained as ignorant as the authorities, who confessed themselves quite baffled: *how* the resisting young lady was abducted from the riverbank; *why* no one, not even a servant, was near; *where* the balloon sailed, and eventually landed; *who* the abductor was (for surely he must have been a skilled balloonist); and *why,* after the spectacular kidnapping, he chose to make no attempt to contact the grieving family, or the authorities?

"It is an act of singular audacity," Great-Aunt Edwina said, "an assault of the criminal classes against their betters: for I cannot think that, in any wise, the unhappy girl brought this misfortune upon herself."

"It is an insult to the Kiddemaster name," Judge Kiddemaster said, his white-maned, leonine head still held high, tho' greatly saddened by grief, "but one which shall not go unpunished, while I have strength, and breath, and resources at hand."

"I fear," Grandmother Kiddemaster murmured, but very gently wishing to qualify the statements of the others, "alas, I fear that we shall not see poor Deirdre again: for the balloon, as the girls have described it, is surely a balloon out of the darkest regions of the earth; and its pilot, not one to be summarily dealt with."

Whereupon Great-Aunt Edwina, and Judge Kiddemaster, and Mrs. Zinn, and divers others, primarily of the elder generation, soundly took her to task; with every consideration, of course, of her invalid state, and the weaknesses of her mind. Even Mr. Zinn, by nature soft-spoken and courteous, could not restrain himself from observing, to his mother-in-law, that the balloon and its pilot were naught but *natural* phenomena, soon to be discovered by the police—there being a goodly number of policemen employed in this case, owing to the Kiddemasters' importance, and the especial luridness of the event. Indeed, Mr. Zinn near-surrendered himself to some vehemence, in asserting: "Not only is the abduction an altogether *natural* occurrence—by which I mean, it is not *supernatural*—but, it is my prediction that, within a very few days, we shall have our belovèd daughter back, uninjur'd, and untouch'd, and *quite as she was before.*"

Oft the four sisters gathered, in the bedchamber shared by Malvinia and Octavia, or, if no adult or servant was near, in the cozy parlor downstairs, and spoke with tireless melancholy, and not a little continued amazement, of the brute loss of their sister. Ah, and how very strange it was, that the days passed, and the weeks, and no ransom demand was voiced!

"I remember her hair coming loose, that I had labored o'er with such love," Malvinia said, visibly shivering, "and tumbling in a promiscuous tangle, down her back!—a most repulsive sight."

"I remember her bonnet falling, and her skirts billowing about her," Octavia said, dabbing at her reddened eyes, "but most of all I remember her piteous cries for help."

"Her cries for help?" Constance Philippa inquired, with some honest bafflement, nervously turning her engagement ring about her thin finger, for, alas, the eldest Miss Zinn had lost some weight in recent weeks; and her nobly-sculpted countenance displayed a measure of strain. "But I remember no cries at all, Octavia: no cries, save, after some minutes, our own."

Whereupon petite Samantha bestirred herself, and knitted her smooth freckled brow, and came so very close to *grimacing,* that Malvinia felt obliged to pinch her, in chastisement; and said, in a halting voice unlike her own: "I remember poor Deirdre calling to us—I remember the force of certain words—*Oh, help! Help me! Father! Mother! My sisters! Please! Oh, do not let them take me!* And yet," the somewhat breathless girl continued, staring with affrighted green eyes at the others, "and yet, at the same time, I am quite certain that Deirdre uttered no words at all: and that the abduction transpired in absolute, hideous silence."

"That is true," Constance Philippa allowed, with some hesitation. "And, I think, very well put: *absolute, hideous silence.*"

Octavia drew in her breath so sharply, her stays gave her some pain; and protested that she was certain she *had* heard Deirdre crying for help. She then paused, and a very perplex'd expression o'ercame her pretty countenance. "Unless I *am* mistaken, and these piteous cries were somehow rendered *in silence:* or, it may be, in a dream of that night."

"I remember no cries for help," Malvinia said curtly, "neither in *reality,* dear Octavia; nor by *magic.* Constance Philippa does not remember; and I am very certain that, if she examines her memory closely, Samantha does not remember either. You are o'erwrought: you are most unpleasantly *panting,* at this very moment. What *I* recall most vividly is the shameful spectacle of our sister's bonnet knocked awry, and her hair coming loose, in an untidy sort of darksome splendor, of a type not to be glimpsed outside the dressing room." These words spoken with such especial crispness, and such haughty authority, no one wished to contest them; and the matter was closed.

17

That this particularly unhappy period in the history of the Zinn and Kiddemaster families—rivaling the Civil War years, in fact, when Mr. Zinn was away for so long, and numerous young male relatives were wounded or killed outright—is to culminate in the loss of yet two more Zinn daughters, strikes me, upon retrospective study, as less astonishing than it had seemed originally: for there were signs all along, not only that two of the young ladies were infected with the *restiveness* of the era, and wildly susceptible to all that was corrupting in the guise of being "glamorous," but that idyllic Bloodsmoor itself had been tainted, by the shadow of the balloon as it passed so swiftly o'er.

For instance, almost immediately after the alarm went out, and news of the kidnapping was bruited about the countryside, eyewitnesses stepped forward to report to the authorities (and in several impertinent instances to poor distraught John Quincy Zinn himself), a veritable gallimaufry of balloons!—not only U.S. weather balloons and Army dirigibles, which were altogether natural, but an ornate red-and-green balloon said to be of a "chintz" design; and a large "shimmering" golden balloon of the type designed, it was said, by the Frenchman Charles Guillé, but never constructed in the New World; and an egg-shaped green-and-yellow-striped rubber balloon rather like that built by George Hambleton Fussell, the celebrated Boston aeronaut, in the early Sixties—which balloon had suffered a tragic air accident, some years previous, when struck by lightning over the Charles River, killing both Fussell and his young assistant! There was also sighted something resembling the five-balloon aerostat flotilla employed to advertise the famous 1,227-Mile Walking Race of 1868; and a "coppery red sphere"—unless, perhaps, it was a dense cloud of smoke from one of the Whitton factories along the river; and a small, gravely silent balloon of an ivory hue, with an unusually large rectangular wicker basket—this last apparition claimed by Constance Philippa's fiancé, the Baron Adolf von Mainz, by no means an excitable or unreliable temperament, who saw it drifting serenely over a meadow bordering the Philadelphia Pike at a time when, of course, *he could have had no knowledge of the disaster unfolding back at Kiddemaster Hall.* Various witnesses believed they had seen "dark-hued" balloons, up and down the Atlantic seaboard, but no descriptions answered *precisely* to the balloon in which, to the best of the sisters' knowledge (and following closely Samantha's meticulous sketch) young Deirdre had been spirited off.

Mr. Zinn, sometimes accompanied by his father-in-law, sometimes by one or another of Mrs. Zinn's cousins, and sometimes alone, traveled hundreds of miles in the latter part of September, and through October, to investigate these eccentric claims. He tirelessly interviewed persons whose propensity toward hysteria, and whose visible want of intelligence and judgment, would have immediately discouraged a less determined man. For he continued to believe, even in the face of repeated failure, that the balloon phenomenon *could be explained;* and that perseverance could lead him to the explanation. At a time when other members of the family —most conspicuously, Mrs. Zinn—signaled by a depression of spirits that they had given up all hope, and when uncertain health of his own (a resurgence of insomnia, headaches, sharp pains in his old war wounds) plagued him, John Quincy Zinn exhausted himself by his insistence that each eyewitness, no matter how questionable, be examined thoroughly. ("For could not a black *silk* balloon, which Samantha has described as iridescent, somehow acquire another shade, or shades, as a consequence of reflections from the ground? or optical illusions similar to rainbows?" Mr. Zinn asked plaintively. "And could not even its *shape* appear to be distended by the vicissitudes of air currents, and the vagaries of individual witnesses?")

Godfrey Kiddemaster, however, compulsively designating himself, both in private and in public, in muttered exclamations, as the "grandfather of the violated child," believed that far more direct action was required to bring the scoundrel to justice. In short, and bluntly, the former Chief Justice of the Supreme Court of the Commonwealth of Pennsylvania demanded that State and Federal law enforcement officers, working with the United States Army, arrest all known balloonists in the eastern part of the country, and interrogate them ruthlessly, until they confessed all knowledge of the outlaw balloon: for surely the balloonists constituted a compact little world, and knew one another intimately. The authorities should, Judge Kiddemaster insisted, feel empowered to use any method of interrogation that *worked,* including certain techniques of torture acquired from the Iroquois Indians. "We must fight evil, I fear, with its own cruel weapons," the Judge solemnly averred.

As the weeks fruitlessly passed, and other domestic vexations declared themselves, exacerbating the good Judge's mood (among them the news—minor but upsetting—that John Quincy Zinn had, after all, been passed over for election to the American Philosophical Society), the elderly gentleman became increasingly irrational. His high noble forehead, his thick white hair, the penetrating gaze of his stern gray eyes, the vigor of his step and the watchfulness of his posture, as well as the low, husky, but beautifully modulated timbre of his voice, which had handed down so many judgments, and sentences, and pithy observations, in his decades on the bench—all belied the tenebrous state of his soul, and his passion for revenge. "You are pusillanimous, sir," Judge Kiddemaster accused the State Attorney General, a man twenty years his junior. "If I had my full strength—if this outrage had not debilitated me—if I were not, God have mercy! *an old man*—I would bring the scoundrel to justice with these very hands!"

Miss Edwina Kiddemaster, too, behaved in a somewhat extravagant manner, as a consequence of the abduction of the youngest Miss Zinn, toward whom she had behaved, over the passage of years, with distinct coolness, tho' never with less than gracious civility. (Great-Aunt Edwina had, I believe, given Deirdre numerous small gifts, of a kind appropriate to their relationship, the most charming being an ermine muff, and an exquisite French music box with the *jardinière* motif on its cover, in mother-of-pearl —much to the envy, in fact, of Malvinia.)

After the catastrophe of late September, this sensitive lady, and esteemed authoress, retired to her spacious bedchamber: as much desiring a convalescence from the inordinate shock, suffered by her fragile nerves, as desiring some protection, from the e'er-present threat of journalists, busybodies, and gossipmongers, that so plagued our Bloodsmoor during this unhappy time.

There, the invalid found herself in so weakened a state, she could keep very little in her stomach, save her numerous elixirs (including a highly promising new laudanum, brewed, in part, at the Delaware Water Gap, and purified by *mineral application,* and tasting most agreeably of licorice, peppermint, and spirits), and a divers assortment of sweets—the faithful cook being concerned now to outdo herself, in the preparation of cakes, pies, trifles, fudges, and various meringues, that might tempt the enfeebled invalid. For some crucial days, amounting very nearly to a fortnight, Great-Aunt Edwina feared her weakened state would prevent her from completing, to her own satisfaction, a new book: *100 Hints for the Christian Young.*

She feared, too, that she would prove unable to continue in the chaperonage of the young affianced couple, Constance Philippa and the Baron: and what a tragedy, if the responsibility should fall to someone less qualified! Poor Sarah was, of course, bedridden too, with complaints of an arguably more serious nature, than Edwina's. (Dr. Moffet diagnosed Mrs. Kiddemaster's ailments as hypertension, polyarthritis, discopathia, myositis, and neuotis, as well as the more common defatigation, hysteriopathia, and frayed nerves. These grievous maladies, oft visited by other complaints, had plagued the sensitive lady for some years now, since the storm-toss'd winter of 1824, following closely upon the birth of Prudence —an arduous labor that had lasted upward of twenty-four hours. Dr. Moffet, who had overseen the Kiddemasters' vicissitudes of health for many decades, declared, in solemn tones, that one could not expect Sarah Kiddemaster's condition to "improve overnight," but he allowed that there was "some hope" that the invalid might venture downstairs "by next spring.") And Edwina's niece Prudence was, she believed, not altogether trustworthy, in the role of chaperon: for had not that young lady behaved with shocking wantonness, whilst John Quincy Zinn was courting *her*?

Nonetheless, Great-Aunt Edwina thought it advisable to take to her bed. When feeling strong enough she wrote letters, or worked on her manuscript (the which her publishers eagerly awaited), propped up comfortably against a half-dozen pillows, and employing a very clever portable writing desk, of Mr. Zinn's invention and execution. Her lady's maid was never farther off than the next room, for Edwina had many requests, and was always sending out missives, or summoning her brother (for, she believed, this "impressionable" gentleman had been far more greatly upset by the abduction of his granddaughter, than anyone realized), that she might inquire firsthand about the state of the police investigation; or whether or not the distressed John Quincy had yet come upon any genuine eyewitnesses.

For a while, during the first onset of winter, she became greatly agitated, and quarreled with kindly Dr. Moffet when he hesitated to prescribe for her an additional quantity of Professor Forrest's Spring Tonic (the laudanum that appeared to be doing both Edwina and Sarah some minimal good); she quarreled with her brother who, perhaps wearied by the continual sense of disorder and shame, rejected, in unforgivably rude terms, Edwina's suggestion that he hire a small private army— surely no more than thirty men, or forty?—and Steven Bayard, the grandson of Horace and Retta, newly graduated from West Point, could lead them. "It is quite out of the question, Edwina," Godfrey said, standing in the doorway of her chamber (for she refused to allow him entrance). "Private armies are not allowed under our law."

"Then what good, pray tell, you silly old judge," Edwina cried, "is our precious law? Are we *American citizens,* or *Polynesian Islanders?*"

It became an obsession with her, though all the household assured her to the contrary, that her other great-nieces were in danger; or had been, unbeknownst to her, already snatched away and carried into oblivion. She grimly fantasized careers on the New York stage; a succumbing to the blandishments of scheming men, which would lead directly, and fairly quickly, to wretched marriages, slum households, or white slavery in such fetid ports of the world as London, Marseilles, and Calcutta. (Vaughan Kiddemaster had told her about Calcutta, and she had finally pressed her hands over her ears. Even the "Hooghly River"—its uncouth heathen sound!—gravely offended her.)

So the sisters were sent up to their great-aunt's bedchamber one by one, at the most inopportune and whimsical hours (for Great-Aunt Edwina prided herself on waking early: oft as early as five o'clock in the morning), and all save the compliant Octavia greatly resented the ritual; for it necessitated, as one might imagine, not only their very best manners, but their cleanest and most scrupulously ironed dresses, and morning caps that betrayed not the slightest hair-oil stain. "Ah, I see that you are still with us," Great-Aunt Edwina said, not without a tinge of irony, when Constance Philippa presented herself at her aunt's bedside, with a prim little curtsy. "I see that you and your fiancé have not yet *broken away* —have not *eloped.*" Constance Philippa, instructed by her mother to hold her tongue, and under no circumstances to be led into "talking back" to Edwina, stood in sullen silence, her face burning with a pale sickish heat. She would have liked to reply that *elopement* was hardly on her mind, let alone on the Baron's mind: since Deirdre's abduction there had been a decided *diminution* of that gentleman's interest in her; even his gallantry with Malvinia was less pronounced.

Dear Octavia entered the room shyly, and had to be urged forward by her aunt, who, after an initial five or ten minutes of criticism (for the older woman, though complaining of watery eyes and fatiguing headaches, possessed remarkably acute vision, and was rarely satisfied with Octavia's dress, posture, or hair style), suddenly and warmly relented, and, if it were morning, offered her some hot chocolate and oranges, and insisted that she draw a chair up to the bedside and read to Edwina from the Bible (for Edwina, like most of the Kiddemaster women, always began the day with an hour's perusal of the Bible, no matter that the authoress secretly considered herself something of a rebel); if it were afternoon, tea was offered, nay, insisted upon, and Edwina laughingly tho' weakly insisted that her niece join her in a small repast (her first of the day, in fact), a small sampling of *petits fours,* it may have been, or gooseberry jam on crumpets, or thickly buttered cucumber sandwiches. If Edwina was feeling particularly strong, aunt and niece might play a few hands of whist together, and sample a half-dozen bonbons from Vantane's of Germantown, brought out to the invalid by a recent visitor; they might occupy themselves with their sewing—each was, of course, working on something for Constance Philippa's trousseau, since an adequate trousseau consisted of twelve dozen of everything—indeed, *everything*—and the Kiddemasters could hardly trust Prudence to make certain that all was provided for. Linens, teatowels, napkins, doilies . . .

Tho' Octavia professed, to her sisters, to be as wearied of Great-Aunt Edwina as they were, she did indeed enjoy these visits, and hardly minded being summoned from the Octagonal House by one of the Kiddemaster servants, particularly if the servant bearing the message was the son of Patrick McInnes, who sometimes acted as a driver in his father's place, and who would then drive Octavia through the woods to Kiddemaster Hall, and return her home afterward. (The young man's name was Sean, and he had evidently inherited his father's tall physique, and his Irish good looks, but very little of his melancholy: for tho' it sadly compromises our high estimation of Octavia, perhaps it is necessary to remark at this point that Octavia had been well aware of the coachman's son for many, many years—and that she had rarely seen him in a mood other than resolutely cheerful. She was not altogether certain that she quite approved of the brawny robustness of Sean's manner, or his rather too springy red hair, or his habit of whistling as he drove the landau through the woods—a vulgarism the young man would not have dared, she knew, in the presence of one or another of the adults—but she did approve of his smiling high spirits, and his deference to her; and she warmly anticipated the day when he would inherit his father's position full-time, and be responsible for driving the Zinns and the Kiddemasters everywhere.)

Nor did Octavia mind her great-aunt's childish desire for a companion in whist, or Chinese checkers, or Pam-Loo, tho' she always agreed with her sisters, particularly with the rather too brainy Samantha, that such expenditures of mental energy were an intolerable waste of time; and she could not help but concur with Malvinia's judgment—that such games were marvelous if one could impulsively sweep all the cards or pieces onto the floor (as that spoiled young lady did when she played with her sisters), if things were going badly, or if, in an entirely different context, young men were present, and the atmosphere was lively and festive, and one needn't try to win at all. "But with Aunt Edwina," Malvinia said cruelly, "one is not only in danger of falling asleep from very boredom, but in danger of being cheated: for she *does,* you know, perform some quite remarkable sleight of hand, if she fancies she can get away with it." Naturally Octavia protested: she had never in her life, she claimed, heard so outlandish a statement, and it made her almost ill—and, indeed, tears sprang instantly into her eyes—to hear their devoted aunt slandered in such a manner. "Malvinia, you forget yourself!" Octavia cried. ("Indeed, I forget myself only too frequently," Malvinia murmured under her breath, her lower lip swollen with pouting, "and re-member others instead!—a tedious state of affairs.")

In all, Octavia enjoyed these lazy, cozy, fire-warmed visits in her great-aunt's bedchamber, and, despite the innocence of her nature, and her devotion to her parents, she could not prevent her eye from traveling admiringly about, taking note of the crimson damask draperies that hung from gilt cornices, and the Belgian linen wallpaper with its swirling fleshy-pink floral design, and the laminated carved rosewood table by the bed-side, upon which Great-Aunt Edwina's herbal medicines and elixirs were set, and a stack of magazines and novels from the Cobbett Square Lend-ing Library (for it was necessary, Great-Aunt Edwina believed, that she read her rivals—the energetic authoresses of such best-selling works as *Clemence, the School-Mistress of Waveland,* and *Margaret's Plighted Troth,* and *Jessamyn's Wedding Day*).

Lulled by the comfort of these visits, which oft stretched into several hours, Octavia came precariously close to confiding in her great-aunt—as she could not, of course, with her mother. Indeed, Great-Aunt Edwina, frequently in a drowsy, or melancholy, or garrulous condition, as a consequence of her elixirs, was sometimes so lax, as to confide in *her:* alluding to an "unfortunate" affair of the heart, many years previous; and some "grievous happenstance"; and, most enigmatically, a "biologic inheritance" carried secret amongst the Kiddemasters, which emerged in the family rarely, but, when it did, "proved fatal to all—guilty and inno-cent alike." (Octavia wished strongly to inquire of her aunt, as to the details of this *inheritance:* might it be the case that her own blood was tainted, and that her offspring, one day, might carry a sort of curse? But she was too shy to venture the question.)

For her part, Octavia confessed that she had been "gravely wounded," by Mr. Rumford's public display of negligence in his court-ship of her, since Deirdre's abduction; and the more agitated, in that Mrs. Zinn was upset as well. She was too wise, however, to confess to her aunt certain of her feelings, of a decidedly romantic—nay, giddy—nature, pertaining to the coachman's redheaded son: Sean McInnes, whose wide-spaced eyes were so *brightly blue,* and whose hair was so *curly,* and so wondrously *thick,* it quite left her breathless! And he had a habit of humming merrily to himself, and whistling, a gay insouciant sound with the power to pierce her breast like a knife blade!

Octavia confessed to no unseemly sentiment, regarding the coach-man's son; but she did allow, in a small, halting voice, that she was oft "o'erwhelmed" by thoughts of guilt, for the crime she and her sisters had committed, against Deirdre.

"Crime?" inquired the puzzled matron, fixing a stern gaze upon her niece. "I fail to understand you, Octavia. In what way are you and your sisters guilty of a *crime,* against that unfortunate girl?"

Octavia sat for some moments, in distressed silence, biting her lip, and kneading her damp handkerchief in her hand. Finally she spoke, softly, hesitant as an abash'd child: "Dear Aunt, *I cannot say; I do not know.* Perhaps it was my failure to call her back, as she ran weeping from us, to the rough river's bank; perhaps it was my failure to curtail Malvinia's acerbic tongue; or perhaps—ah, I know not!—it was my failure to *love* her, as my parents, and Our Lord Jesus Christ, bade me to do."

Whereupon the elder woman stared at her for some time, in a very peculiar silence, during which one could hear the sombre ticking of the French ormolu clock on the mantel, and see the chaste winter sunshine winking on a little brass statue of the but partly clad Orpheus, on a nearby table. Then, finally, she spoke, in a voice nearly as hushed as Octavia's: "My dear, that we are all sinful creatures, and sow as much misery as a consequence of *omission*, as of *action*, cannot be a surprise to us, at this date. But, do you not believe that Our Lord *does* forgive us such things? —if, indeed, failings they truly be?"

But Octavia had no reply, save a sudden outburst of tears—the which came upon her with such unexpected fury, she hid her o'erheated face in her hands, and wept all uncontrollably, as if her heart would break! —a spectacle the more compounded, and given greater poignancy, by the fact that the esteemed authoress could not withstand such a torrent, *but joined her in these heartfelt tears, for upward of a half-hour.*

Malvinia too was summoned to Kiddemaster Hall, she too was driven through the woods by a whistling, o'ercheerful young Irish driver, she too ascended the broad oval staircase, preceded by a silent female servant. But where Octavia hurried, blushing and out of breath, and grateful to be summoned, the spoiled Malvinia kept to her own indolent pace, yawning, sullen, even defiant: and not at all intimidated by Edwina Kiddemaster.

She curtsied gracefully, her eyes lowered, presenting herself to the older woman as a composed, demure, and even prim young lady, modestly attired in a blue Swiss voile dress with a molded bodice, and a white cashmere shawl begged from Octavia, and an afternoon cap with no more than a half-dozen flounces and ribbons and strips of lace. "And how do you find yourself, Malvinia?" Great-Aunt Edwina inquired, peering suspiciously at her, but discovering no flaw. "Are you well? Are your nights peaceful? Is your digestion satisfactory?" Malvinia answered her great-aunt in a low, respectful voice, her hands clasped together just beneath her bosom. Whether she was well or ill; whether her nights were peaceful, or disturbed by inchoate visions of her lost sister; whether her digestion was satisfactory or not—she surely would not confide in her aunt. So courteous but restrained answers tripped off her tongue, and Great-Aunt Edwina, tho' continuing to stare with a rude suspicion, *seemed* to believe.

"I summon you here," Edwina said, fussing with the sash of her ivory brocade bedjacket, "not because I care to make inquiries about the evidently futile investigation—I am quite resigned to failure along those lines, and to a permanent desuetude of such laws of nature as *honor, chastity, courage,* and *obedience*—for it is, after all, the year 1880—and I fear that some of us, harking back to a simpler, more gracious era, have outlived our time. (Ah!—please do not look so stricken, Malvinia—I assure you that I am in tolerably good health this afternoon, following a slight fever of some days and nights; but Dr. Moffet was kind enough to attend to me, and prescribed bleeding for both your grandmother and me, and I believe we are each the better for it tho' I've felt too weak to venture down the hall to her chamber; and of course the poor thing hasn't been able to see me for months. But do not express such alarm, my dear child, for I halfway suspect we old biddies will outlive younger and healthier persons!) No, my child, I have not summoned you here, and, no doubt, torn you away from far more fascinating company, in order to make inquiries about the police investigation, or to make inquiries about matters at the Octagonal House, how your dear, brave mother is managing her loss, and holding up under the chronic pressure of financial worries; whether your father has abandoned hope in retrieving his wayward daughter, and has returned to his workshop with 'renewed zeal'— that piteous expression not, I assure you, being mine, but that of your slipshod grandfather the former Chief Justice of the Supreme Court of the Commonwealth of Pennsylvania, as we are repeatedly given to know —which exalted position, guaranteeing a certain immunity from criticism, seems to have guaranteed, as well, a corruption of both language and judgment. No, my child," the elderly matron said, now smiling placidly, and looking, of a sudden, somewhat girlish, and even conspiratorial, "I have summoned you to my invalid's retreat on this snow-dimmed day, because your presence is wondrously cheering, to one of my condition; and because I am always anxious to know that my niece's daughters are in tolerable health; and because I am so oft plagued with worry, and must be consoled, by knowing, my dear, that you are still with us: and not quite vanish'd into thin air."

Malvinia stared, and had no need to simulate a pretty startled *moue,* at these puzzling words. Her manner was rather less polished than usual, and her lovely voice somewhat marred, by stammering: "That I—I—*I* am still with you? That *I* am not *vanish'd into thin air?*" She paused, and pressed a handkerchief to her bosom, and, regaining some of her composure, continued thusly: "You must remember, Aunt Edwina, that I am not so quick-witted as Constance Philippa, nor so clever as Samantha; and I lack Octavia's natural instinct, to comprehend the logic of her elders, with no ratiocinative effort. In what way, Aunt, might I *not* be still with you?"

It was oft to be recalled by Malvinia, in years to come, and, I believe, even recounted, with a certain fond nostalgia, in one or two conversations, with that kindly gentleman who would—ah, after what trials!—become her *husband,* how, at this curious moment, Miss Edwina Kiddemaster chose to speak in a casual, and even a perfunctory, manner: the while lounging most comfortably in her bed (uncorseted, it should be noted: but her charming brocade jacket, and her silk embroidered quilt, a China import, tastefully covered the corporeal expanse of the invalid, and truly did not offend the eye), amidst the luxuriant and familiar odors of an invalid's room—that blend of warm flesh; tangy, sweet, and acrid medicines; balm; hyssop; rose leaves; pastries; and black walnut tea cake! Thus the esteemed woman of letters spoke: "Why—I know not—perhaps in the way that headstrong young ladies *do* sometimes disappear—headstrong, and heartless, and doomed—and *very* wicked: in a carriage—by train—by horseback, for all I know—alas, by *balloon!*—or by sailing ship, or— But, truly, my dear, your elderly aunt cannot know such things, save to shrink in revulsion from even their contemplation. The large capitals of our nation are, I would imagine, fairly thronged with your *fallen* and *despicable* creatures, of our frail sex: yet, again, I cannot know, and must insist that we change the subject. You are looking, my dear child, somewhat peakèd?" So, tho' enfeebled by the frequent bloodletting, Edwina made an effort to heave herself forward in her bed, that she might grasp the handle of the Tiffany teapot, and proffer, to her surprised niece, a piece of tea cake: an exertion far in excess of her strength, and greeted with an exclamation of concern, and some gentle remonstrance, by Malvinia, who rose at once to assist.

The subject thus was forcibly changed, and never taken up again, to my knowledge.

It had always been Malvinia's secret conviction, in which, I believe, she was not greatly mistaken, that *she* was Edwina Kiddemaster's favorite niece, favored not only above her own sisters, but above the numerous young female relatives in Edwina's family. Many were the times, when the proud old lady scolded her, with a sort of fussy intimacy; and then pressed upon her some dainty prepared by the cook, for Edwina alone—a coconut trifle, or a sugared pecan date bar, or, upon occasion, a chocolate meringue topped with brandied cherries; and bade her—nay, commanded her—to recline close to her invalid's bed, and read aloud from one of the season's new novels, for she greatly enjoyed Malvinia's mellifluous voice, and needed, she said, to "keep abreast with her rivals, in the field of letters." Upon other, more disturbing occasions, she bade Malvinia to *speak her mind, as frankly as possible*—the which injunction somewhat baffled Malvinia, who was not altogether certain, that she knew *how:* or that, in any case, she dared succumb to her great-aunt's blandishments. (For there were, I hardly need record, divers disagreements and long-lingering vexations, and questions old and new, betwixt the two houses: many predating the Zinn girls' births, and having to do, the sisters surmised, with the choice of Mr. Zinn as a husband for their mother—"Tho' one would surely think," Malvinia protested, "that, after more than a quarter-century, and Father's exemplary work, the high-and-mighty Kiddemasters would have come round!")

There were times, however, when the guarded Malvinia came near to confessing that, alas! she did think o'ermuch about young Cheyney, or not quite so feelingly as she should about Deirdre (in truth, I am bound to say, heartless Malvinia did not care a whit whether her sister ever returned to the Octagonal House). But she held her tongue, and diverted her aunt's interest to other, more lightsome subjects tho', in truth, the elderly woman seemed grateful, and even, at times, greedy, to hear any *gossip* at all: what amusing "outrage" the pretty Delphine Martineau had enacted, at a recent ball; what was whispered about poor Honora LeBeau Kale's health—that unhappily plump lady, now weighing upward of two hundred and fifty pounds, being wheeled, in ermine and diamonds, to the opera, in a *bath chair;* with whom had Malvinia danced, at a recent ball; and whom had she refused in the past fortnight or so, thereby breaking his heart.

"You are not overly cruel to your numerous young admirers, I hope? Nor too capricious, as it is given out?" Thus Great-Aunt Edwina inquired, in a honeyed, and all but coquettish tone.

Whereupon Malvinia lowered her eyes, and adjusted a flounce on her skirt which had become lightly creased. *Too cruel to my young men!* she thought. *How might I be "too cruel"?* Random, unbidden thoughts assailed her: the memory of a long-forgotten gentleman whom, she supposed, she had hurt, many years ago: dear lank-limbed Mr. Malcolm Kennicott, an assistant of Reverend Hewett's: and an acquaintance of her father's. She *had* hurt him, she acknowledged, with both guilt and gratification, but of course she had been too young to grasp the significance of her action— only a child, in fact. The blame, like the emotion, had been his; it had not been hers.

After a courteous moment she said: "Dear Aunt, I should not know —unless by an instinct of my fallen nature, rather than that of my spiritual inheritance—how to be *cruel;* as for vulgar *caprice,* I deem it a feature of the comic operetta, and the 'Haverly Mastoden Minstrels.' "

This remark adroitly, and purposefully, led Edwina to an inquiry into the cultural life of Philadelphia, which, bedridden as she was, she missed with infinite regret. Just the other day Miss Narcissa Gilpin had written an enthusiastic letter about the remarkable lecture, "Walking & Temperance," delivered by Mr. Edward Payson Weston, the Walking Champion of the United States, at the Cobbett Square Church; and the renowned poetess Parthenope Brownrrigg had issued invitations to a small, exclusive group of persons, to attend a recitation of her long dramatic poem *Ivory-Black: or, a Romance of the Shadow World*—a work so moving, Miss Gilpin reported, that several ladies began to weep, and she herself, who had lost so many belovèd members of her family to death in the past several years, quite apart from the loss of a favorite grand-nephew at Shiloh, and four—or might it have been five?—infants at birth, was quite o'ercome.

And of course there were concerts, and pantomimes, and operet-tas, and grand opera (the magnificent soprano Clara Louise Kellogg had recently played Marguerite in *Faust,* which was Edwina Kiddemaster's favorite opera—alas, to have missed that performance!); there were Shake-spearean tragedies, native melodramas, Spanish dancing troupes, light-hearted burlesques. It was a pity, Edwina said, that she would be forced to miss the great Tommaso Salvini in *Othello,* for she had read ecstatic reviews of his New York performance; and the controversial but greatly gifted Orlando Vandenhoffen would arrive soon, at the Varieties, in Daly's *Under the Gaslight*—still on tour after many years. "And, alas, I must miss them all," she said with a half-bitter smile, "confined as I am by my remorseless sensitivity, which seems to intensify with the years, while others of ruder, more robust health disport themselves freely in the world, and take their pleasures where they will."

Malvinia murmured that it was indeed a pity; and, obeying a near-imperceptible gesture of her aunt's that she slice them each another piece of the excellent walnut tea cake, leaned gracefully forward, while Great-Aunt Edwina continued to speak in a mournful voice. She must content herself, she supposed, with a vicarious satisfaction, through the letters of her numerous friends and relatives in the city, who each wrote her, at the very least, thrice weekly (for all the Kiddemaster women enjoyed a lively cor-respondence); and through the firsthand reports of her dear nieces who were young enough, and strong enough, to confront the manifold trea-sures of the *cultural world,* without tiring, or becoming inordinately dazzl'd.

"Indeed, dear Aunt," Malvinia said with the utmost civility, "I pray you are not proved greatly mistaken."

"I shall not, Father," Samantha cried. "Not again! Not so soon! *I cannot.*"

"My dear child," Mr. Zinn said, peering at her over his wire-rimmed eyeglasses, and smiling his gentlest, most delicately ironic smile, "none of us *can;* but most of us *shall.*"

And so she acquiesced.

(In any case, as Octavia kindly pointed out, not sensing the barb her innocent words contained, it was hardly as if Great-Aunt Edwina troubled her very often—many days might pass before a message came for *Samantha;* whereas *Octavia* and *Malvinia* were expected to visit at least twice weekly.)

"Father, I am in the midst of—" Samantha began in a whining voice.

"Daughter, we are always, I hope, *in the midst of—!*" Mr. Zinn said in a tone both gruff and jocular, turning back to the raised pine board upon which he was working.

Samantha's small plain prim face hardened, but already, swiftly, she had snatched off her filthy apron, and was tidying up her end of the long workbench, putting her diagrams and papers and pencils and calibrating instruments and logarithmical tables safely in her drawer. The Zinn workshop, like the workshop of any industrious inventor, was hardly a model of neatness: but Samantha knew from past experience that mischievous Pip, rousing himself from his nap by the stove, might scurry over to see what his youngest mistress had been doing all morning, and, Mr. Zinn's presence notwithstanding, manage to do some playful bit of damage to her drawings. (The remarkable—and, indeed, ingenious—little spider monkey had years ago acquired the habit of tinkering with Samantha's work, sometimes altering it so subtly that hours might pass before the bewildered girl discovered his trick! He possessed by instinct an uncanny ability to mimic those mysterious squiggles and shapes human beings employ as mathematical calculations; but he could, of course, do no more than mimic, and he never dared interfere with his master's cluttered workbench, to anyone's knowledge.)

Samantha alone of the sisters dared to appear in Great-Aunt Edwina's bedchamber in an everyday walking dress, of plain cotton, without a train, trimmed only by horizontal bands of pleating and ruching, and a few limp ribbons of an indefinable hue. Sometimes she even kept on her workshop costume, a loose-fitting flannel dress, long in the sleeves, that had once belonged to Malvinia and had, through repeated launderings with soapwort, borax, and even tincture of benzoin, become quite threadbare. Summoned to her great-aunt, she impatiently tied on her plain woollen bonnet, rarely troubled to bring along her pretty little purse of rabbit fur and beads, though it had been a gift from Edwina Kiddemaster herself, did not scruple to change her shoes; and kept on her everyday plush mittens until she was about to alight from the carriage, when, frantically, she forced her good white gloves on her hands (which, alas, tho' scrubbed with Castile soap, were rarely free of stains), grumbling and complaining to herself in a voice mercifully too low to be heard by the young Irish driver. (Tho' impetuous little Samantha would have preferred to walk through the woods to her grandparents' house, on sunny, mild winter days, Mrs. Zinn necessarily forbade such folly, and their disagreements frequently provoked both to angry tears. "You are hardly a boy," Mrs. Zinn charged her, "and you must not behave as if you were one.")

She sighed loudly, and gnawed at her lower lip, and cast her eyes about blindly as if seeking an improbable escape, led upstairs by the mute servant girl past oval blackwood-and-gilt-framed portraits of her Kiddemaster ancestors—a solemn portly gouty lot, she judged them, who had, despite the acuity with which they stared at her, very little to do with *her*. (And what of her Zinn ancestors, who were represented by no portraits, not even daguerreotypes? What sort of men and women had *they* been? Alas, Samantha knew nothing about them save for the meager fact that a young man named Rudolph Zinn, Austrian-born, a soldier under General Benjamin Lincoln, had been badly injured in a skirmish on the Bloodsmoor River, left behind by the retreating Continental Army, and gradually nursed back to health by a Quaker farm family—Quakers in the region being neutral so far as the Revolution went, and generally unmolested by both the rebels and the British. This solitary Zinn found himself in the Bloodsmoor Valley in approximately the year 1777; he might have been as young as twenty years of age; and beyond that Zinn history was tantalizingly blank since John Quincy Zinn, faithful to his Transcendental beliefs, considered the history of his family, as well as his own history, simply too "personal" to be of significance. . . . And yet Samantha fancied herself a Zinn rather than a Kiddemaster, and liked to think that, generations back, there was a young woman not unlike herself, impatient with housekeeping and women's work, and eager to fuss with numbers and gadgets and schemes to change the world. Deluded child! Had she paid a more scrupulous attention to the examples of her elders, and not allowed her frivolous mind to wander hither and yon, like clouds blown by a capricious breeze, her own history would have been less unruly; and she would not have broken her parents' hearts.)

Tho' she had been urgently summoned to her great-aunt's chamber, she was nevertheless made to wait in an anteroom, and again she sighed loudly, and retied the bow of her bonnet, and calculated how long she would have to remain in Edwina's presence, before she might make a discreet escape. Upon one occasion, back in January, Edwina had been too nerve-sick and fatigued to really converse with her, and had sent her away within a merciful half-hour; upon another occasion, Grandmother Kiddemaster had been visiting, reclining on a block-footed Empire chaise longue beneath a quilted satin robe, too weak to do much more than murmur a gentle greeting to the startled Samantha—for both women had been bled that afternoon by Dr. Moffet, and gave off an air, as they fussed with their crocheting, of virtuous anemia.

When, upon this occasion, Samantha was ushered inside, she was relieved to see that Great-Aunt Edwina was out of bed, seated in a chair, with a brocaded Japanese shawl about her plump shoulders, and a gold cashmere blanket tucked in about her legs. A single lamp burned on the rosewood table for, tho' it was early afternoon, the midwinter day was already dark; the Tiffany shade glowed a rich warm cornucopia of greens, blues, and oranges. Agreeable as the scene was, however, Samantha smiled but thinly, and gave her aunt a stiff, perfunctory curtsy. She was immediately asked to pour two cups of tea and to cut two pieces of fruitcake and butter them as lavishly as possible—for it was necessary, Great-Aunt Edwina said, for one to keep one's strength up, through this everlasting winter.

As Samantha nervously poured the tea, and sliced the cake, her aunt continued in a tone of characteristic irony: "I have dragged you away from your father's side, my dear girl, only because I suspect it would never occur to you to visit me, otherwise; and an old invalid like myself can become very, very lonely for her flesh-and-blood nieces."

Samantha stammered a reply, handing Edwina her cup of tea, and her thickly buttered slice of fruitcake; and in the silence she heard a clock calmly tick. She said, stupidly: *"Flesh-and-blood* nieces?"

Great-Aunt Edwina gestured for her to sit. "As one ages," the old woman said, smiling coldly, "one feels a certain passionate tenderness for one's younger relatives—children in whom, so to speak, one's youthful blood flows. But I hardly expect *you* to understand, my dear; there is no need to look so anxious."

Samantha stared at the carpet, and could not think of a coherent reply. Alas, the clever old lady might well have been speaking in code, and Samantha lacked the wit, at this precise moment, to interpret it. "I am sorry, dear Aunt," she murmured, "if I impress you as looking anxious."

"Anxiety, restiveness, and, indeed, any form of undue mental exertion, are very disfiguring, in our sex; and have been, as Dr. Moffet has said, sadly deleterious to the health—my own, I mean," Edwina said, with a placid frown that yielded to a melancholy smile, "—pertaining to my work: which does, as you may well imagine (tho' I rarely speak of it), demand a considerable expenditure of spirit." Pausing, she then proceeded to make her usual formal inquiries about Samantha's health, and sleep, and digestive faculties; and the states of health, so far as Samantha might know, of the other inhabitants of the Octagonal House. With infinite tact and courtesy Samantha made her replies, and, I hope I will not prejudice the reader against this young lady, if I confide that her mind, *the while she spoke,* fled back to the gorge, and the snug little workshop, and the vision of her belovèd father, who, at the moment, might have paused in his work, to stare out the window at the snowy ravine, of picturesque rocks, and stunted trees, and the fleet darting of birds—all unseen by him: for, tho' John Quincy Zinn oft *stared* out the window, his extraordinary mind was such, that he *saw* not a thing. But ah! how Samantha loved the workshop! How she yearned to be freed from her great-aunt's presence, and back at her father's side, where dear little Pip might even now be perched upon Mr. Zinn's shoulder, gnawing on a sugar cube, unbeknownst to Mr. Zinn himself.

Samantha was roused from her pleasant daydream, by an inquiry of Edwina's, as to the progress of Mr. Zinn's present invention; and so she replied, as best she could, knowing how her mother's family, in secret, valued her father's great effort—how they lightly jested, and laughed, and shook their heads, behind his back! Thus, did Edwina truly wish to know; and how should Samantha most diplomatically reply?

The other day, an inventor named Hannibal Goodwin had come to call, unexpectedly; he and Mr. Zinn had talked together for some time, with animation; Mr. Zinn had spoken quite freely of his work-in-progress ("Alas, *work-in-stasis* might be a more accurate term!" the modest man exclaimed), and he had shown Mr. Goodwin other, interrupted projects, some of them mere sketches, some fairly complete drawings, one or two scale models. . . . Mr. Goodwin, whose own obsession, as he expressed it, had to do with photography—photographic film—and motion—the motion of the eye, and the motion that exceeds that of the eye—was particularly interested in an old toy Mr. Zinn had been working on, for the entertainment of his daughters primarily, in his convalescent years in the mid-Sixties. The toy would have been called the "Zinnoscope," had it been completed, patented, manufactured, and sold. ("An unlikely sequence," Mr. Zinn observed.) Samantha had drawn a half-dozen sketches of Pip in pastel chalk, on the inside of a cylinder of some two and a half feet in length, and Mr. Zinn had set a polygon of small mirrors within the cylinder, to be illuminated by a light from above. As each mirror came before the observer's eye, it reflected the drawing opposite it, and as the cylinder and the polygon turned, more and more rapidly, the successive images of Pip gradually and miraculously merged into one another—so that, blinking and staring, the observer might very easily imagine that he was peeking through a hole of some kind at a *living and motile reality!* Mr. Zinn had also experimented with the notion of projecting these mirror images somehow, perhaps with a magic lantern, tho' he would probably have required more than one, but nothing had come of it: as usual, he had abruptly lost interest in the project since an astounding idea for a new project had suggested itself to him, in a moment of reverie, and he had thought it best not to resist. "And then, of course, as you can see, Mr. Goodwin," Mr. Zinn said apologetically, stooping to blow dust off the model (for the girls had naturally lost interest in it after a few excited evenings, and even Pip, initially fascinated by his own image in motion, was soon bored by its simplicity and repetitiveness), "as you can see, the thing is only a *toy;* and a man cannot content himself with *toys* while the great mass of our fellow Americans pass their days in useful labor."

Great-Aunt Edwina professed very little interest in the forgotten Zinnoscope, other than to observe that it might be a marvelous pastime indeed—for a monkey; she was more concerned with the experimentation Mr. Zinn had been doing with the icebox in the basement, since that large, squat, odoriferous, and dismayingly ineffectual thing caused the household much grief, particularly in the summer months. (A veritable crescendo of odors flew forth as humid August advanced!—and upon more than one ghastly occasion the smells of what might be called "sewer gas" had somehow backed up the drainpipe and into the icebox, *permeating the food.*) But, unfortunately, after a few weeks' puttering and tinkering, Mr. Zinn had come up with the absurd notion that the entire concept of the "icebox" would have to be revised, and that, rather than rely upon the icehouse ice stored in the bottom of the compartment, which inevitably melted and drained away into a pan, in a most inefficient manner, one should work out some sort of method by which the cold of the icebox *creates* the ice!—which would utterly reverse the present procedure, and constitute, in Mr. Zinn's words, another "transmogrification" of reality. When the household greeted this fanciful notion blankly, and even Samantha stared in embarrassed bewilderment, Mr. Zinn quickly lost interest in the project.

Samantha spoke haltingly, fearing that she was betraying her dear father, for the condescending smile with which Great-Aunt Edwina greeted her report of his "progress" only very thinly disguised a more characteristic irony; and she was loath to touch upon the guilt she naturally felt, regarding her unfortunate youngest sister.

Great-Aunt Edwina clasped her shawl more tightly about her shoulders, as if she were suddenly cold, and indicated, with a graceful gesture of her hand, that Samantha should pour them each another cup of tea. And cut another slice of fruitcake, if she would be so kind.

"Thank you, Aunt Edwina," Samantha said, performing the little ritual with a mechanical ease, "but I think I will decline your offer of another slice of cake, myself. The tea, however, is delicious."

"You must eat, you must fill out," Great-Aunt Edwina said, almost peevishly. "You are far too thin, Samantha; and it is not appealing. That you are naturally petite is, of course, admirable—your waist is no more than seventeen inches, I daresay?—which is very, very good, of course—and yet—as you know—a certain generosity of—of—*bodily presence*—a certain attractive *distribution* of mammalian flesh—is thought to be socially desirable; otherwise we shall have to see about padding for you, and I halfway wonder at your mother's judgment, that this problem was not approached before now."

"Yes, Aunt," Samantha said, blushing, so that the scattering of freckles on her face darkened at once, "I mean—I am dreadfully sorry."

"One of your maids would be capable of making something up, I should think," Great-Aunt Edwina said, sipping at her tea, "and, if not, my girl could do it. A small amount to begin with, at the bosom and hips; nothing pronounced; so that your gentleman friends would not take notice. But gradually, gradually . . . You have not buttered this fruitcake, Samantha."

Samantha rose from her chair, apologized, was waved back in place, and blushed more deeply than ever.

"You are not a jack-in-the-box, my dear young lady," Great-Aunt Edwina said. "Nor are you a common servant girl—to blush so ferociously. Can you not control yourself?"

"I am sorry, Aunt Edwina," Samantha said miserably. "I—I—I scarcely know what overcomes me at such moments."

"Thinness is not what we wish," the old woman said slowly, "for we should not, after all, like to see you so skeletal and unappealing as—as your former sister. I mean— your *lost* sister."

Samantha blinked solemnly at these words.

"Yes," she stammered, "I mean—no. Thank you, Aunt Edwina, for—for your kind advice."

"You are blushing more deeply," Edwina said, not without a smile. "As I recall—for he honors me with a visit so infrequently—such blushes are also a characteristic of your father, I believe?"

Samantha murmured a vague assent.

"And Mr. Zinn has a birthmark as well, which asserts itself from time to time," Great-Aunt Edwina said slowly, now chewing her cake, and brushing daintily at her lips with a lace handkerchief, "tho' it is not unattractive, in its place. The success with which he eradicated a similar disfigurement from your left temple, in infancy, is all to his credit: a courageous gesture, and I think a necessary one."

Samantha stared at the carpet.

"You *do* recall the birthmark, perhaps? Or the procedure which eradicated it?" Great-Aunt Edwina inquired.

"I—I am afraid not, Aunt," Samantha said.

"But you know, of course, that you did have a birthmark?—and that your father removed it, with some sort of chemical abrasion, I believe."

"I did not know," Samantha said.

"Your sister Malvinia, for all her pride in her beauty, has a sort of birthmark—a Kiddemaster mark—of her own," Great-Aunt Edwina said, smiling oddly, stirring another cube of sugar in her tea.

"Yes, Aunt," Samantha said, staring. "I mean—I did not know."

"A far less visible defect, and perhaps, to the charitable eye, no defect at all," Great-Aunt Edwina said. "I refer of course to her widow's peak, sometimes considered, I think wrongly, a sign of especial beauty."

Samantha murmured another vague assent. She had grown quite nervous, and was in terror of spilling tea down the front of her dress.

"By one of those peculiar and sometimes disagreeable coincidences, your adoptive sister, Deirdre, was afflicted with a similar mark: tho' hers, I am sorry to say, was far more pronounced, and hardly contributed to her beauty," the old woman said in a slow, queer, flat voice. "I have often asked myself—to what end such grotesque coincidences? —to what purpose, such ironies of fate?"

"I—I do not know, Aunt Edwina," Samantha said.

"Can they be, do you suspect, directed toward our *humbling?*—or our *humiliation?*"

Samantha bestirred herself to speak, miserably. "I do not know that either, dear Aunt," she said in a faint voice.

The old woman, absently stirring her tea with a tiny spoon, stared at Samantha as if looking through her. The fussy prettiness of her afternoon cap and the rich fabric of the Japanese shawl contrasted rather grimly with her face, or with its expression, which was uncharacteristically melancholy; and her soft, fairly unlined skin, usually so high-colored, had a drained, leaden look. "To be *humbled;* to be *humiliated,*" she said slowly, "in God's great scheme. Can we, do you think, altogether trust *Him* to make an intelligent distinction between the two?"

Samantha shivered, perhaps as a consequence of a draft of wintry air from the window; perhaps as a consequence of her great-aunt's blasphemous remark. She could no longer trust her voice, but shook her head, in a negative gesture, like a small unmannerly child, to indicate that she did not know.

"Ah," said Great-Aunt Edwina, suddenly setting down her teacup, so abruptly that tea spilled onto the cashmere blanket, and now bringing her small plump beringed hands to her face, to rub the eyes fiercely, "ah, I will get my revenge!—on *Him!* If I live long enough—if my wit does not soon fail me—you will see!"

These words so astonished our young lady that, for a very long moment, she simply sat, staring; she had not the presence of mind to rouse herself and take her leave, tho' it had become quite obvious that Great-Aunt Edwina, whether through an excess of sudden and unaccustomed emotion, or as a consequence of elixirs quaffed before Samantha's arrival, had lost all awareness of her—and was, in effect, alone: unmistakably alone.

"If I live long enough—if my wit and my courage and my rage do not slacken—yes—you will see—yes indeed—fools and idiots—knaves— men—*Him*—and my belovèd swept from me—my motherhood bereft. You will see, you will see," the stricken woman cried, still rubbing her eyes with an alarming energy, and beginning now to shake, not with sobs but with silent laughter!—which so terrified little Samantha that, unthinking, unmindful of decorum, she rose at once from her seat, and set her teacup down on a table (the cup rattling so against its saucer from her trembling, she feared it might crack), and, backing away from the distraught woman, took her leave with nothing more than a frightened whisper.

But Great-Aunt Edwina did not hear; nor did she, mercifully, notice Samantha's departure.

I shall tell everyone this revelation, Samantha thought, as the horses pulled the Kiddemaster carriage back home, and her heart pumped with a gleeful intoxication, and the very tip of her nose went waxen-cold with excitement; and then, when the Octagonal House came into view, and a certain wintry desolation struck her soul—despite the attractiveness of Mr. Zinn's house, and the dear familiarity of each window, each cornice, each lightning rod—she thought *I shall tell no one this revelation.*

And, to Samantha's credit, this is exactly what she did.

18

Once there were five Zinn daughters dwelling harmoniously with their loving parents, in the Octagonal House on the river: a scant twelve-month later, there were but two daughters remaining.

The grief of losing *one* was soon deepened by the all but incomprehensible grief of losing *three!*

For, as if following their stepsister's infelicitous example, Constance Philippa and Malvinia soon fled decent society—by what flagitious routes, for what unspeakable purposes, I can scarcely bring myself to say.

But did the Baron reject his fiancée, the reader must naturally inquire, fearing the worst; and did the reckless Malvinia elope with her most attractive suitor, Cheyney Du Pont de Nemours? We have reason to believe that the Baron Adolf von Mainz, though devoted to Constance Philippa and her family, and particularly indebted to Mr. Vaughan Kiddemaster for certain financial *coups* of no explicit interest to our history, did suffer the agonies of a reconsideration (however unarticulated) of his decision to align his illustrious family with that of his fiancée's—for one must assume that the Baron, despite a certain insouciant gallantry of manner, was a highly sensitive gentleman; and it must have offended his aesthetic sense, as well as his sense of decorum, to see the names *Zinn* and *Kiddemaster* hawked in the two-penny press, and gossiped over in even the best society. (How pertinacious gossip is in our time! One can hardly credit its longevity, in a dazed age in which fame and notoriety soon blur, and achievement and sin are oft confused.) More than once that worthy gentleman sent a message to Miss Zinn, explaining that he was indisposed, or suddenly called away on business, and consequently unable to accompany her on one of their obligatory visits to the homes of relatives, for, escorted by Prudence Zinn, the proud mother of the bride-to-be, and, less frequently, by John Quincy Zinn, the engaged couple was expected to visit virtually every related family in the southeastern corner of the state, and in Wilmington, Delaware: Whittons, Kales, Bayards, Gilpins, Woodruffs, Millers. "The trapped man naturally resents being dragged about as a sort of trophy," Constance Philippa said with a grim smile, holding one of his messages of deep florid regret out to her mother. "One would hardly be surprised—one would *almost* be sympathetic—if he chose to flee to his homeland." Mrs. Zinn was not amused by her eldest daughter's jest, nor diverted by her challenge. "I forbid you to utter such sentiments," she said, taking the stiff sheet of paper from Constance Philippa, and noting with an irritated satisfaction the propriety of the von Mainz coat-of-arms, in modest gilt, and the graceful contours of the Baron's hand, "even under your breath."

And it was the case as well that Mr. de Nemours, perhaps under the instruction of his wealthy father Irénée (of the firm of Du Pont de Nemours, Père, Fils & Cie, of New York City), stayed away from Bloodsmoor for an awkward period of time, despite his obvious infatuation for the beautiful Malvinia. His *silence* as well as his *absence* struck Malvinia to the core, in her pride rather than her heart; and, as her pride was far more vulnerable than her heart, because more greatly indulged, one can gauge the degree of her consternation. ("I am weary of this constant round of parties, teas, dinners, and balls," Malvinia cried to Octavia, throwing herself down on their canopied bed, and letting her lovely hair tumble in a most unladylike spill across the pillows. "This very afternoon I prowled about Grandfather Kiddemaster's library—as, I begin to recall, I did in late childhood—and quite astonished myself by the joy with which I snatched certain volumes off the shelves—a joy and a hunger combined —for the *mind* seeks nourishing food, as well as the *stomach;* and what is more nourishing than an hour spent in the company, not of the vapid Mr. de Nemours, but of the great William Shakespeare, or Plato, or Oliver Goldsmith?" And Octavia, though undeceived as to the cause of her sister's passionate outburst, did but assent in kindly silence.)

Yet the irony was to be, that the Baron did *not* extricate himself from his obligations to the Kiddemasters, and was the more aggrieved— the more wounded. It is a measure of the perversity of Constance Philippa's behavior that she was not, indeed, rejected by her fiancé: he did in fact fulfill his side of the wedding contract, and take Constance Philippa Zinn as his lawfully wedded wife, at the flower-bedecked altar of our picturesque old Trinity Church, in the autumn of 1880, *as if nothing untoward had ever happened in her family*—as if no invisible prowling demon had been loos'd. For it was not to be Miss Zinn who disappeared from all that was familiar and known, but the Baroness von Mainz . . . !

By a similar irony, within that very week, the impulsive Malvinia cast her lot with a gentleman whose name, though known to society, was hardly known in any intimate sense to her family: in short, not the handsome young heir to the de Nemours fortune, but a stranger to all of Bloodsmoor—a stranger, save for his somewhat meretricious fame, to the drawing rooms of Philadelphia.

(One can imagine the impact of this double—nay, triple—destruction upon a single Christian family: the bewildered heartbreak of the parents, the shame and sorrow of the remaining sisters. Indeed, the deaths of Constance Philippa and Malvinia would have been more welcome, and far more merciful, than the fates that overtook them; and the *humiliation* (for *humbling* is, perhaps, too mild a term) that deepened the maledict cloud already obscuring the heavens above Kiddemaster Hall.)

In the long busy months of her engagement Constance Philippa had ample opportunity to acquaint herself, through her reading, with the sacred duties of Wifehood soon to be hers; she was often to be found hidden away in a corner, alone or with sweet-faced Pip sprawled asleep on her lap, studying one or another of the books Mrs. Zinn, Great-Aunt Edwina, and other female members of her family had pressed upon her. How diligently she read them!—how her forehead creased as she turned back a page, and reread, her lips sometimes shaping the words aloud! The treacherous winds of January and February subsided to the merely cold winds of March; and then, with a wondrous abruptness characteristic of our part of the world, it was early spring—and then spring; and then summer. If the Baron had demonstrated, by an unfailingly subtle restraint in his passion, that he had had *thoughts* about the situation, about marrying the elder sister of a young lady whose fate was so sensational as Deirdre's, he naturally did not speak of these thoughts to his fiancée, or to anyone in the family; and, to the quiet joy of the Zinns and the Kiddemasters, it soon became apparent, as the months passed, as winter shaded into spring and all the numbed, sleeping world awoke, that the Baron's high regard for Constance Philippa and for her family had triumphed over all indecision. Not only would the young couple marry according to plan, but the Baron was reported to have expressed, with his usual cosmopolitan gallantry, and yet not without a trace of sincere emotion withal, the wish that the wedding be held even sooner. (It was Malvinia to whom he addressed this surprising observation, at an evening reception in the palatial Main Line home of Mr. and Mrs. Hambleton Kale. To Constance Philippa's annoyance, and yet to her relief as well, the Baron spoke with far less restraint to Malvinia, and was actually observed smiling and laughing in her presence, while he was quite stiff in the presence of his fiancée, as, indeed, she was in his. Perhaps it had to do with the disparity in their heights, for Constance Philippa "towered" over him, as she expressed it, by at least three inches; perhaps it had to do with the formality of his regard for her—for she *was,* after all, singled out from all of womankind as his fiancée, and therefore a sacred being. Nonetheless Baron von Mainz evidently told Malvinia that "your American engagements are extraordinarily long," and the implied meaning of his statement was unmistakable: the young man was so in love with Constance Philippa he wanted to marry her at once! Or so Malvinia hastened to report to her sister, who blushed ferociously when she heard, and had no reply at all. Mrs. Zinn, to whom all this was dutifully repeated, made only the observation that it was hardly proper for Malvinia to behave as a sort of *confidante* to her sister's fiancé: such intimate exchanges must cease at once. "I thought you might be pleased," Malvinia exclaimed, "by the Baron's very impatience, for surely it argues sincerity? —and affection?" "It argues," Mrs. Zinn countered evenly, "a certain want of delicacy, and a blindness to our Philadelphia customs I should not like generally known, as the Baron's prospective mother-in-law." It was Constance Philippa who observed in her dry droll manner, uncaring of the effect upon Mrs. Zinn: "Ah!—the poor man simply wants to get the ceremony over with, as quickly as possible, before he truly *does* change his mind.")

Yet Baron von Mainz had not changed his mind, and preparations for the wedding continued, gaining momentum as the season warmed. Constance Philippa now spent all her time being driven about in the Kiddemasters' handsome brougham, sipping tea at one or another relative's home, attending dinners, luncheons, and balls (at which she and her fiancé danced with a most agreeable marionette grace); or, at home, being fitted for her wedding dress, or perusing, with an increasing fanaticism, the dozen or more books—including Dr. Napheys's *The Physical Life of Women*—pressed upon her. She oscillated between frenetic activity, and bone-weary indolence; between a lighthearted, rather shrill merriment and saturnine despondency. She read aloud, in private, these powerful words of the poet Shelley—

> Rough wind, that moanest loud
> Grief too sad for song;
> Wild wind, when sullen cloud
> Knells all the night long;
> Sad storm, whose tears are vain,
> Bare woods, whose branches strain,
> Deep caves and dreary main,—
> Wail, for the world's wrong!

—Eliza Leslie North's *Maiden, Wife, and Mother;* Mary Manderly Ogden's *The Christian Mother;* Dr. Elias Riddle's *Counsels on the Nature and Hygiene of Womanhood;* Alice C. Dodds's *A Letter of Advice to a Young Bride;* and, of course, Great-Aunt Edwina's volumes, which the heedless Constance Philippa had neglected to study in the past—*The Young Lady's Friend: A Compendium of Correct Forms,* and *A Guide to Proper Christian Behavior Amongst Young Persons,* and, most valuable of all, as she approached the threshold of matrimony, and prepared to exchange Maidenhood for Wifehood, the best-selling *The Christian House & Home,* which elucidated, in a tone much like that of Edwina Kiddemaster's speaking voice, such priceless advice—

> The young bride crosses the threshold, not into a mere *house,* but into a *home,* which it is her obligation to make blossom as if 'twere a *garden.* How sacred the mission, to be the warmth about which hearts gather; to strengthen, brighten, and beautify existence; to be the light of others' souls, and the good angel of others' paths! And, a mission even more holy, to be a Mother: to give birth to infant immortals!

She read; she gorged herself; and yet was left famished, and susceptible to childish bad moods, that quite astonished the household. Her high-handedness with Octavia became inexcusable; her sarcasm with Samantha shocking; the *pettiness* and transparent *jealousy* of her relations with Malvinia infuriating—though oft amusing, as Malvinia mockingly observed. ("She fears her dwarf-bridegroom will look upon his sister-in-law with more affection than he looks upon his bride," Malvinia told the scandalized Octavia, "and, if she transforms herself into a veritable dragonness, who, pray, would blame him? The Baron *is* human—or, at any rate, one is encouraged to believe so.")

One afternoon, while being fitted for her wedding dress, Constance Philippa read aloud from Dr. Riddle's volume, and quite distressed Madame Blanchet and her young assistant, who scarcely knew how to respond. In a dry, droll, sardonic tone unbecoming in one of her station, and certainly in one being fitted in a lovely China silk dress, with fagoting, handmade lace, latticework, and lace epaulettes, Constance Philippa read: " 'In our most unitary of acts, which is the epitome and pleroma of life, we have the most intense of all affirmations of God's love for us as creatures, and His will that husband and wife participate in a true pangenesis. The supreme holiness of the wedding bond, symbolized in the solemn exchange of rings, is a measure of the holiness of God's bond with His creation. . . .' "

At this very moment Mrs. Zinn happened to enter the room and, blushing an angry beet-red, snatched the volume out of her daughter's hand. But, surprisingly, she said very little about the incident (tho' her grown daughter fairly cowered in fear—Constance Philippa was *most* frightened of her mother's wrath), other than to observe that it was unfortunate, knowing the propensity of Madame Blanchet to carry tales from one house to another, that Constance Philippa had behaved as she had. "I am very sorry, Mother," Constance Philippa said, biting her lips. "I am *very* sorry for everything."

A true pangenesis . . . the epitome and pleroma of life . . . the supreme holiness of the wedding bond: *what,* Constance Philippa tortured herself, did it mean? What did the words mean? She was canny enough at the age of twenty-three to have determined, on her own, that the wedding bond led in most instances to babies; and that the babies (as dimly she recalled from Mrs. Zinn's numerous confinements, for of course Mrs. Zinn had had several stillborn infants, in addition to having given birth successfully to her four daughters) evidently had something to do with the mother's body; and that this phenomenon was a *mystery,* a *blessing,* a *sacred duty,* and at the same time a *cross* all women must bear, as part of God's commandment. What the masculine sex had to do with all this Constance Philippa had yet to determine, but she supposed, vaguely and optimistically, as she supposed she would come to love the Baron after they were married, that she would learn: perhaps he would tell her.

Perhaps, she thought with a wild spurt of hope, Dr. Riddle's promise of *pangenesis* is nothing more and nothing less than the revelation of this profound secret, to be entrusted to the female sex only *after* the wedding vows have been taken?

In addition to the marriage and etiquette manuals, Constance Philippa had also been given, by Narcissa Gilpin, a pretty little volume by Mrs. Katharine Lee Bates called *The Wedding-Day Book; or, The Congratulations of the Poets,* in which she read after her other, more serious reading fatigued her, or after she returned from an afternoon of fifteen or twenty teas, her head ringing with exhaustion, and that sly old tune *A fox went out* tripping and lilting through her very being. *The Wedding-Day Book* was a sort of day-book with a poem for each and every day of the year, all the poems having reference to love, weddings, and marital bliss. *This* volume, attractively covered in crimson papier-mâché sprinkled with tiny gold roses, Mrs. Zinn did not at all mind being read aloud: in fact, on many an evening in those months before the Zinn family was to be irrevocably shattered, and never, indeed, altogether a "family" again, all the Zinns gathered in the cozy firelit parlor after supper, to read aloud from *The Wedding-Day Book:* even Mr. Zinn himself, who had always an especial love of reading and reciting poetry, and who knew well that the domestic hour, close by the hearth, was one of the blessèd features of our American life, rivaling for him the attractions of the workshop and its lonely, exhilarating toil.

Mrs. Bates's *The Wedding-Day Book!* I remember that compact little volume well, its square-cut pages, its gilt edges, its floral endpapers and smart crimson cover! A gift for many a young engaged lady of our time, and one which, it must be imagined, is prized throughout the years as both a keepsake, and a continuing memorial to the power of love—hardly spurned and cast aside as it was in the case of Constance Philippa. (The volume was to be found in the trash by one of the Zinn servants, who promptly rescued it, and, being of so sentimental and loving a nature herself, and so attached to the Zinn family, the distraught girl attempted to clean the stained cover with petroleum naphtha—a grease solvent employed by the servants in laundering Mr. Zinn's workclothes—and badly damaged it. But *The Wedding-Day Book* did survive; it survives still.)

The Zinns passed the book from one to the other, and read aloud, sometimes with pride, oft with a brimming eye, for the impending wedding was a great event in their lives, in which regret, and relief, and joy, and melancholy warred. Mrs. Zinn opened the volume to a favorite poem, and read these moving lines from Langhorne—

> Should erring nature casual faults disclose,
> Wound not the breast that harbors your repose;
> For every grief that breast from you shall prove,
> Is one link broken in the chain of love.

Octavia, her plump cheeks flushed with pleasure, her voice trembling with the *privilege* of good poetry, found it difficult to make a selection, and often paged through the book for many minutes, while her mother and sisters chided her lovingly, even as they continued with their sewing; and Mr. Zinn, stroking Pip, who climbed lazily about his knees, or perched atop his shoulder, said in his kindly voice: "I am sure, dear Octavia, that any selection of yours and Mrs. Bates will prove edifying to us."

Octavia then chose a poem by Mrs. Craik, or Phoebe Cary, or the great Longfellow—

> Sail forth into the sea of life,
> O gentle, loving, trusting wife.
> And safe from all adversity
> Upon the bosom of that sea
> Thy comings and thy goings be!

this recited, with a shy, moist-eyed glance at Constance Philippa.

Malvinia usually made her selections beforehand, choosing two or three poems in place of one, for that young lady read splendidly, and had even, at about this time, begun elocution and acting lessons in the city; so that all the Zinns—even Constance Philippa—found her performances wonderfully gratifying, and excused her rudeness in fidgeting through Octavia's. She always sought out the fragments from Shakespeare which Mrs. Bates had wisely included in her anthology, glowing gems of sagacity of a quality not generally associated with the great Bard (a genius, as all attest, but of an erratic and even slovenly temperament, and betraying at times a disposition quite irreligious—nay, atheistic); she read these lines in as passionate and ringing a voice as if she were on the stage of the Varieties Theatre, portraying the doomed Ophelia, or the still more grievously doomed Desdemona—

> Let me not to the marriage of true minds
>   Admit impediments: love is not love
> Which alters when it alternation finds,
>   Or bends with the remover to remove.
> O no! it is an ever-fixèd mark,
>   That looks on tempests and is never shaken.

And again, upon another occasion, with a frank fond declamatory voice, and a sisterly smile beamed in Constance Philippa's direction—

> I am ashamed that women are so simple
> To seek for rule, supremacy, and sway,
> When they are bound to love, serve, and obey.

Many an evening the engaged girl, out of shyness, sullenness, or exhaustion, simply refused to read; and so Malvinia read the more, and spurred her listeners to outright applause. (All took note of the magical way in which Malvinia came to life at such times: as if drawing a powerful energy from the *attentiveness* of her listeners, who were as absorbed by her beauty and her manner, as by the words she uttered.)

Samantha read with some enthusiasm, yet withal an air of vague bewilderment, as if, despite her effort to please her family, she could not seem to comprehend the subtleties of poesy. Her voice was clear enough, yet hurried and flat—

> My heart is like a singing bird
>   Whose nest is in a watered shoot,
> My heart is like an apple-tree
>   Whose boughs are bent with thickset fruit;
> My heart is like a rainbow shell,
>   That paddles in the halcyon sea;
> My heart is gladder than all these,
>   Because my love has come to me.

—as if Mrs. Rossetti's immortal words possessed no meaning to her at all!

As one might expect, Mr. Zinn read beautifully; to be precise, he did not read but *recited,* needing nothing more than to glance through the poem on the page before him, in order to commit it to memory! (A feat that quite beggars my understanding; and yet Mr. Zinn accomplished it time and again, without effort.) His voice was subtly modulated, almost too rich for the confined quarters of the parlor, and, as in the old days of his lyceum career, mesmerizing. He recited Browning, he recited Tennyson, he recited his belovèd Emerson, and, upon one curious occasion, these lush lines of Margaret Fuller's—

> I am immortal! I know it! I feel it!
> 　　Hope floods my heart with delight!
> Running on air, mad with life, dizzy, reeling,
> Upward I mount—faith is sight, life is feeling,
> 　　Hope is the day-star of night!
>
> Come, let us mount on the wings of the morning

—when, for no visible reason, Mrs. Zinn suddenly rose from her comfortable seat, her sewing forgotten (she was working a complex cross-stitch on a white linen tablecloth for Constance Philippa), her manner distracted and confused and, for some moments, quite alarming to her family—for the poor woman *did* look apoplectic, emotion seized her so suddenly. She stared at Mr. Zinn as if he were a stranger; she steadied herself by grasping hold of the proffered arm of Octavia, who had reacted instinctively to aid her mother; she seemed, as the seconds passed with great pain, unaware of all save Mr. Zinn, whose recitation had naturally trailed off into silence—not even Pip, scuttling in terror behind the ottoman on which Mr. Zinn sat, drew her attention.

Then, at last, as if rousing herself with great difficulty from a kind of dream or trance, she repeated, softly and searchingly: " '*I am immortal —I know it—I feel it—I am immortal—*' "

The moment passed, mercifully; and Mrs. Zinn recovered herself; and resumed her seat by the fire. Mr. Zinn asked if she might like a little lavender and ammonia, mixed with water, to stimulate her spirits, but she assured him no, not at all: she was altogether well, and eager to hear the poem.

And so Mr. Zinn began again his recitation of that excellent work, in as hearty a voice as if no interruption had occurred.

"Sometimes, when I hear poetry read, and particularly when I read it myself," Malvinia said, "I have such a sensation of—of—I know not what! —a sensation of *knowing,* for a brief instant, not simply that I may inhabit other lives, and realize things quite foreign to Bloodsmoor, but that I have already done so, *am* doing so, in another world altogether! I hope," the boldly deferential young lady said, fixing a wide stare upon the countenance of her elder sister, "I do not present myself in too wild a light."

Constance Philippa did not immediately reply. She continued with her crocheting, which, in recent months, occupied her more and more, in those nervous blank periods when she was neither reading nor visiting, and in which her clumsy fingers had grown surprisingly skillful.

"It is a rare concern of yours, dear sister," she said dryly, "to *hope* for anything so modest."

Rebuffed, Malvinia touched a pretty white hand to her slender bosom, and said, in a somewhat aggrieved voice: "I had meant to speak seriously for once, dear Constance Philippa. Particularly since you will be leaving us before long—and when we visit, I shall be addressing a *Baroness.*"

"Shall you?" Constance Philippa inquired, in so bemused a tone, one might have thought her offering a problematical statement rather than a question.

Malvinia gamely returned to her subject, and spoke for some minutes in the same defiantly serious manner, which was, of course, not characteristic of her, even in the days of her innocent girlhood. (It was hardly a household secret at this time—in the late spring and early summer of 1880—that Constance Philippa and her beautiful sister Malvinia frequently had disagreements; and that the elder sister, once so impervious to domestic squabbles, was as prone to bursting into tears as Malvinia, or even Octavia. But not even the least sympathetic servants in either of the houses liked to whisper that the elder, albeit safely engaged, was jealous of the younger or, rather, of her fiancé's attentiveness, as it was diverted from herself and onto the younger: for of all failings, surely jealousy is the most ignoble; and Bloodsmoor confidently expected better of its most prominent inhabitants.)

"So very often," Malvinia continued, undiscouraged by her sister's silence, "when I am reading a book—or when I am watching a play—Shakespeare above all else, of course—and there is Orlando Vandenhoffen in *Under the Gaslight*—and, well—I speak too incoherently, I fear—but my wonder is this: Do others share this sensation of yearning, and yet of *doubleness?*—this sensation of being both *spectator* and *participant?* Do others share this—this—" She paused, but Constance Philippa, frowning at the work in her lap, did not glance up to encourage her. "Ah! —it is impossible to say what I mean. Sometimes I halfway think that the only person who might have understood me was Deirdre; and she is vanished forever."

Still without glancing up, her eyes somewhat hooded, Constance Philippa murmured lowly: "Yes, I have often thought that too—I mean of Deirdre; and of myself."

"Indeed!" Malvinia exclaimed.

For some time, then, the sisters worked, in uneasy and strained silence. Malvinia then roused herself, and, brightly nervous, sought to distract them both, by idle chatter on divers subjects: the resumed courtship of Octavia, by Mr. Lucius Rumford, whilst—as if all of Bloodsmoor did not know—poor Octavia pined away for the coachman's strapping son Sean (who had, it seemed, startl'd everyone by so forthrightly leaving Bloodsmoor, "to strike out on his own" elsewhere); and the lavish wedding of Delphine Martineau to one of the Ormond heirs, scheduled for Saturday next—a social event from which Constance Philippa planned to absent herself with the excuse of a prior commitment; and the Baron, the formidable Baron!—about whom so many rumors circulated, it must be the case, that very few could be true. ("It is most interesting," Malvinia proffered, "to hear that Great-Uncle Vaughan so warmly welcomes him, at Highlands Manor; and allows him to board his stallion there, and his falcon. I have heard, too, that the old Dutch farmhouse—you know, that charming stone cottage—is given over to the Baron's use, when he wishes it. Will it not make a charming honeymoon retreat, Constance Philippa? Ah, I envy you! Your bridegroom will take you hunting on the back of his prancing steed; and, alone of the Zinn girls, you will have the pleasure of a falcon's weight, on your arm. It is all so very romantic!")

Constance Philippa stiffened at these lightsome words, in which a subtle trace of mockery sounded; yet she restrained herself from answering sharply, and chose instead to pursue the earlier subject of their conversation. In a brooding voice she said: "That doubleness of which you speak, Malvinia—that *yearning,* and that *doubleness*—I do believe it is familiar, tho' I scarcely know how to articulate my meaning. There have been certain books, over the years, perus'd in secret, one of them being that wondrously strange, drunken, elated poem, *Leaves of Grass,* by a poet of whom no one has heard—nay, do not frown, Malvinia: I shall not press it upon you! And many another, that seem less to *inspire* wayward dreams, than to *awaken* them. Whilst daydreaming over them, I feel so strong a conviction of another world, and of another Constance Philippa, that I scarce know where I am, or who I am! It is very, very strange. I feel, Malvinia, that there is a hint here, a wisp, a vapor, of a hint, of *the personage God meant me to be.*"

Malvinia was staring at her, uncomprehending. *"The personage God meant you to be!"* she echoed lowly. "Why, Constance Philippa, I cannot understand *that:* put in such terms, it sounds very much like blasphemy."

"Do not be absurd, pray," Constance Philippa said curtly. "Blasphemy, indeed!"

"It is a most eccentric expression," Malvinia said. *"Most* unseemly."

"I should, I suppose, confide in the Baron, on such matters," Constance Philippa said slowly, "but I know that I never shall."

"Nay, you must never," Malvinia said, with some reproach. "He would find it distressing—he would find it a trifle vulgar." She stared, and half smiled, and stroked her handsome plaited hair, and said again: "It *is* a most eccentric expression: *The personage God meant you to be.*"

"We will change the subject, dear Malvinia," Constance Philippa said dryly, "since I see it offends you. Since any subject not your own offends you."

"*My* sense is one of almost painful yearning, and a curious sort of doubleness," Malvinia mused, "as if I were both myself and another person—in a novel, on the stage—Juliet, for instance—ah, Juliet!—I should *be* her so completely!—and then Cleopatra—and Ophelia—and, do you know, I believe I shall begin voice lessons—Cousin Basil has been kind enough to introduce me to some very interesting people in the city —Mr. Danby, who owns the Varieties, for one—and Carla Rowbotham the soprano—and—and others—of whom, perhaps, Mother might not approve; or the great Kiddemaster clan; but they are marvelous people nonetheless. And when this everlasting wedding is over, then I shall, perhaps, move into the city to live, if satisfactory arrangements can be made."

Constance Philippa stared coldly at her. " 'When this everlasting wedding is over'? You are alluding, my dear Malvinia, to my life."

Malvinia continued sewing for some seconds, unmoved. Then her smile deepened; her blue eyes shone bluely; she said, with an intonation quite brazen, as if she were already on the stage: "My dear Constance Philippa, I am alluding to my own."

"*The personage God meant her to be!*" Octavia echoed, when she heard. "But —how is that possible, Malvinia? What could she have meant? The person one *is,* is necessarily the person God *intended;* for how, pray, could it be otherwise? My head spins at the thought. . . . We are meant to be as we are; if we were not, why—God would direct us elsewhere. His plan surely includes us all, for how could it *not?* Constance Philippa knows very well that we are meant to marry, and—" (and here the flustered young lady hesitated) "—and provide grandchildren for our parents—and, if it is at all possible, live close by in Bloodsmoor; she *knows* these things as well as any of us."

With a gay little laugh Malvinia leaned forward to kiss her sister on the cheek. "Of course! How self-evident! She knows these things *quite* as well as any of us!"

The dressmaker's dummy that was *her* began to exert a curious fascination upon Constance Philippa.

When Madame Blanchet and the young French seamstress who was her assistant were not at the Octagonal House, Constance Philippa frequently entered the sewing room, a book in hand, eager to find solitude. The household supposed that she was admiring her wedding dress, and the beautiful green velvet jacket with the puffed sleeves and linen cuffs that would be part of her new suit, and a walking dress in dove-gray muslin decorated with *blonde* lace; the household supposed that, like any young engaged lady, she was thinking of—nay, dreaming of, and who would rebuke her?—her bridegroom-to-be. Alas, it was not so. Constance Philippa sometimes thought of the Baron as she lay in bed, unable to sleep; or, very early in the morning, when she woke prematurely, from troubled dreams; but at such times her thinking had rather more to do with fragments of vision and peculiar recollections of a perverse nature: the almost imperceptible stain at the corner of the Baron's mouth, which she had happened to notice quite by accident while dancing with him at the Woodruffs' midsummer ball; the way in which he slapped down cards, at whist, the whites of his eyes sometimes showing above the iris; the coldness of his touch (which was communicated even through the fabric of his white gloves), the warm meatiness of his breath (which wafted to her at odd times, even while they strolled out-of-doors), the Teutonic harshness of his words, even his softer words—"My dear Constance Philippa," "My esteemed Constance Philippa," "My bride-to-be, Miss Constance Philippa Zinn" (tho' she did not at all mind his accent; she had always admired his accent, when he was barking commands to his handsome stallion Lucifer or his falcon Adonis or the cringing young Negro who was his stable boy).

And yet Constance Philippa did not *think* of her fiancé with any continuity, nor did she *dream* of him, as giddy young girls are wont to daydream of their loves. Instead, her brain was diverted by all sorts of bizarre and half-formed notions, a cacophony of phrases taken from the writings of Eliza Leslie North, Mary Manderly Ogden, Dr. Elias Riddle, Alice C. Dodds, Dr. Napheys, and her own great-aunt Edwina Kiddemaster; and she spent an inordinate amount of time in the sewing room, where it was not the exquisite China silk wedding dress with its many layered skirts that drew her attention, nor even the handsome green suit, but the dressmaker's dummy itself: headless, armless, ending abruptly at the hips: the dummy that was *her*.

While the spacious sewing room in Kiddemaster Hall contained numerous dummies, many belonging, so to speak, to ladies no longer living, the sewing room in the Octagonal House contained only six, and was of far more modest and attractive proportions, being furnished by "cottage" tables and chairs made by Mr. Zinn himself, and painted the cheerful hues of lilac, yellow, and pale orange. The dummy of the most generous proportions belonged, of course, to Mrs. Zinn, tho' its waist was still fairly narrow; next in size was Octavia's; and then Constance Philippa's (this figure being very nearly repellent, to the discerning eye, for its unnatural *breadth* of shoulder, and the *elongation* of the torso); and then Malvinia's, with her lissome waist; and then the very petite figures of Samantha, and Deirdre, who were nearly of a size, tho' Deirdre was perhaps two or three inches taller than Samantha. (I hold it to be a measure of the Zinns' stalwart optimism, as well as their forgiving nature, that Deirdre's dressmaker's dummy had not been removed from the sewing room—as if, one day, it might again be employed.)

Constance Philippa gave herself up to a most unwholesome brooding, biting at her fingernail, and observing her dummy from all sides. She even removed the comely green jacket as if, with no impulse of modesty, she meant to examine the torso *naked!*

This manikin was hers, and, in a sense, was *her:* for its proportions were considered to be her own, when firmly corseted. And yet, with its agreeably slender waist (some twenty inches, when most recently calculated), and its ample bosom (this being a consequence of strategic padding, in compliance with Mrs. Zinn's instructions), it struck the o'erly censorious young lady as not her at all, but a *lie.*

"I *am,*" Constance Philippa softly whispered, touching the dummy's brittle shoulder, "and *am not.*"

Thus she spent upward of twenty minutes, staring, and contemplating she knew not what, and surrendering herself—ah, how unwisely! —to enfeebling thoughts. "I am here represented, as, it seems, my outward form arrests the eye of the beholder," she murmured, with idle industry scratching at a strip of the varnished paper, that had come slightly loose, on the shoulder, "yet *I,* who stand *here,* have naught to do with *this!*—and find it a most maddening puzzle."

At this period in her troubled life, Constance Philippa was not yet so lost to every semblance of decency, as to consult her mirror, *unclothed;* nor did she give herself license to glance down upon her corporeal being, any more than was necessary, while being dressed by the servant girl. (I hardly need state that, like all her sisters, and, indeed, like all ladies of wholesome upbringing, Constance Philippa was never in that unfortunate state termed *nudity:* she was always partly clad while doing her toilette, and bathed whilst attired in a muslin gown, that she might be spared the exigencies of her own flesh, the which would certainly have surprised and disgusted her.) Even as a very small child, at an age when such anomalies have been known to occur, she had never sought to touch herself, and had, indeed, evinced very little curiosity, as to the morbid nether regions of her body: to her credit be it said!

Yet, with a perverse instinct, she seemed to comprehend quite clearly, that her dressed self, which was Miss Constance Philippa Zinn, was not her; the figure molded by her corsets was not her own; and, might it not be the case (for thus her febrile brain ran on and on, in the folly of protracted solitude), that, if this was so, *Miss Constance Philippa Zinn,* as an entity, was not, despite all the laws of logic and custom, *herself?*

"I am, yet am not," the ponderous young lady murmured, the while picking at the glued paper, until, all unwittingly, she had so loosed the strip, that the dummy's smooth surface was seriously marred. "And yet, where *am* I to be located, in this puzzle? Nay, it is most worrisome

—it has made my head spin—I am dizzied by the very deviousness of my own thoughts!''

By late May, both households were greatly pleased that, by Dr. Moffet's prescription, and her own tentative wish, Great-Aunt Edwina had sufficiently recovered from her illness, to come downstairs from her invalid's chamber, upon occasion; and, if the weather did not disturb, by sudden vagaries of temperature, or wind, even to venture outdoors—for this excellent lady dearly loved Nature, and ofttimes went too boldly forth, to partake of it, forgetting the delicacy of her constitution.

She declared herself resolutely cheered, and enlivened, by a renewed *gaiety* about Kiddemaster Hall, difficult to explain. (Even poor Sarah Kiddemaster, despite her enfeeblement, was brought downstairs on her most healthsome days.) For one thing, it now seemed that the scandalous abduction might be interpreted as a *willful absence,* since no ransom had ever been demanded; and it might even be hypothesized (tho' not before the elder Zinns, of course) that a collusion betwixt abductor and victim was likely—to which the name *elopement* might even, at some discreetly later date, be given. So, it would seem, protracted grief was somewhat misplaced, in such inappropriate circumstances.

(Thus did Edwina's circle of lady friends comfort her, reporting to her, with diligence, all that was whisper'd, in Philadelphia: the very *criminality* of the situation, and its *shameless aspect,* granting a sort of respite, from mourning.)

It was the happy case, too, that Edwina was encouraged to leave her invalid's bed, by the resounding success of her new book: the which had attracted a gratifying amount of attention in the papers, and had received a respectful notice in the *Atlantic Monthly,* a gentleman's journal that did not, by custom, usually condescend to take note of female literary endeavors. Thus, tho' she scorned material wealth, and cared not a whit for fame, or posterity, Miss Edwina Kiddemaster did admit to being pleased, for, like any author, of either sex, she hoped to reach the multitudes, that they might be instructed, and elevated, in accordance with their capacities. (At this time, too, she did not shrink from the numerous responsibilities, of a cultural nature, which her social station, and her celebrity, pressed upon her: but, despite her sensitive nerves, acted as a dominant presence in the Philadelphia chapter of the *Women's Christian Temperance Union,* and of the *Philadelphia Grand Opera Association,* and the *Ladies' Society of Trinity Episcopal Church;* and, as the history books have noted, the fledgling *Daughters of the American Revolution* might have foundered at its start, and sunk into a tragically premature oblivion, had it not been for Edwina Kiddemaster's tireless devotion.)

Yet, her attention to her familial duties was such that the primary cause of Edwina's convalescence, and to a certain grim gaiety in her manner, was her recognition of her responsibility, pertaining to Constance Philippa: for chaperonage, tho' crudely despised in later decades, was an art like any other: and Edwina was most anxious that *nothing go amiss,* in the crucial months leading to the autumnal wedding.

"For what if," Edwina said, in a voice whose sternness was somewhat tempered by a quavering apprehension, "what if, through an unlook'd-to accident, or her own headstrong behavior, or, God spare us, a renewed assault by the villainous abductor, *the eldest Miss Zinn fails to become the Baroness von Mainz?"*

And so, sometimes by herself, and sometimes in the pleasant company of Miss Narcissa Gilpin, or one or another of her lady friends, Great-Aunt Edwina industriously oversaw those hours when Miss Zinn and the Baron were in each other's presence, whether strolling at a leisurely pace along the river's path, or through the luxuriant Kiddemaster gardens, meadows, and woods; or sitting quietly in the pretty white gazebo, out of the sun's direct rays, in order to observe the pacific flow of the river, and the picturesque changes wrought in the sky by the action of wind upon clouds of varying shapes, textures, and hues. At such times Miss Zinn wore one of her Sunday dresses, with an attractive train, and carried her prettiest silk parasol, and took pains that her near-opaque veil, liberally festooned about the rim of her hat, and draped across her face, should not be disturbed by the breeze; and her fiancé, attired in fashions rather more American now, and less flamboyantly "foreign," was usually observed to be wearing a dark gray frock coat with a boiled shirt, a handsome hat whose pronounced height added agreeably to his own, and pearl-gray trousers with impeccably ironed creases. A *most* attractive affianced couple, in short—and possessed of perfect manners.

Yet chaperonage was desirable—nay, necessary—as Great-Aunt Edwina well knew, scrupling to keep her gaze always alert, and her attention, though frequently directed toward her companion, or toward the intricate demands of her sewing, never lapsing into indolence or indifference. It was not the case, I must hasten to explain, that Great-Aunt Edwina and the other chaperons distrusted Constance Philippa's modesty, or the depth of her discretion; they knew, and were profoundly grateful for the fact, that they had no such headstrong *flirt* to oversee, as Miss Malvinia Zinn!—and they respected as well Baron von Mainz's maturity. (For he was not precisely a *young* man, and he had been married before—one must assume that the smoldering passions of late adolescence were well behind him.) Yet the elder ladies were obliged to respect the gentleman's expectation of being observed, and, as it were, restrained, by their quiet vigilance and indefatigable concern. More than one Philadelphia engagement had been terminated, within Edwina Kiddemaster's memory, by a profoundly disillusioned man, when, given license by his fiancée's innocence or indelicacy, or by the laxity of her chaperons, he was free to seize his young lady's hand, or, more distasteful yet, to slip his arm about her waist, or brush his lips against her cheek. . . . No matter what turbulence might follow such a breach of custom, no matter the tears, hysteria, and repentance, the injury to the young lady's reputation was such that only the most liberal (or infatuated) of gentlemen could see their way clear to *forgive;* only the most Olympian of temperaments would care to continue with the engagement, as if nothing had happened. So the chaperons comprehended well the gravity of their function, and never strolled farther than some twenty-five or thirty yards behind their young charges, or sat more than fifteen yards away, at an angle almost but not precisely perpendicular to the affianced couple. The elder ladies watched over Constance Philippa and the Baron without seeming to "see" them, and Constance Philippa and the Baron, tho' aware of their chaperons' presence, rarely gave evidence of "seeing" them in turn. In this way many an idyllic afternoon was passed in Bloodsmoor, before the pleasant interruption of tea, when one of the Kiddemaster servants approached Great-Aunt Edwina with deferential grace, to announce the imminent commencement of that event.

On those golden afternoons Edwina Kiddemaster and her companion were kept busy with their sewing, for this was the season of the much-publicized return of the Reverend Hopkins K. Bice from the South Seas, with his tales of heathen infamy, expurgated for ladies' ears, but disconcerting nonetheless, and the Philadelphia circle was much absorbed in its challenging activity, to provide for Reverend Bice, before his return to that part of the world, in mid-September, enough shirts, trousers, vests, and Mother Hubbards, as might clothe the natives under his jurisdiction—for it was a great scandal, and, more than that, in the empathetic words of Edwina Kiddemaster herself, a *pity,* that the South Sea Islands, in addition to being a region of shameless *heathenism,* was a region of rampant *nudity* as well.

The ladies' lace-gloved fingers moved rapidly, then, with the industry of their virtuous needlework, and they conversed together in decorous tones, rarely disturbing the peace of the afternoon—and their young charges' near-unbroken silence—with any sound so jarring as laughter. They talked of the family; of old friends and acquaintances; of Philadelphia society (which was becoming looser with every season—as a consequence, it hardly needs to be said, of the great wealth being accumulated by persons without breeding or education, in some cases of doubtful *ancestry* and still more doubtful *religion*); of weddings and funerals and births (necessarily lowering their voices on this particular topic); of European tours, and illnesses; of Dr. Pennington's Osteopathic Method (for the cure of numerous ailments including nervous dyspepsia, locomotor ataxia, ovarian neuralgia, and general neurasthenia—each of which plagued the ladies from time to time); and Professor Lupa's School of Cognition; and rumors of a new trance medium said to have made a brilliant *début* in Boston, known only as "Deirdre of the Shadows." (The reader will be alerted by the name *Deirdre*, and should be informed at once that a group of Boston relatives attended a séance given by this young lady, soon after her *début;* and Mrs. Zinn herself, accompanied by Octavia, journeyed to Boston to attend a séance—with what disappointing results, the reader shall learn below.) They talked of the stolid granite-and-limestone town house on Rittenhouse Square which Judge Kiddemaster was quietly planning to give to Baron von Mainz and his bride, well within walking distance of Cobbett Square: for the old man, as Edwina Kiddemaster frequently said, with a dry, fond twist of her lips, *could* be generous when the spirit moved him. And, perhaps most enthusiastically of all, they talked of the bridal gown of exquisite China silk, and the green velvet suit, and the dresses and hats and shoes and other necessities of the trousseau, granting, of course, that Constance Philippa Zinn was a Zinn, and not an heiress like most of her cousins, and her honeymoon wardrobe could not be expected to be *brilliant.*

"Your niece has done passingly well, under the circumstances," Great-Aunt Edwina was told, by one or another of her companions; and, not at all taking offense (for these elder ladies *did* speak one another's language flawlessly), Edwina merely nodded, and pursed her lips, and said: "We shall see, my dear—the wedding is, unfortunately, still distant."

By contrast, the affianced couple spent most of their romantic moments in silence, tho' they were intensely aware of each other. From time to time, shyly peering through her thick gauze veil, Constance Philippa was startl'd to see the Baron watching her in an extraordinarily keen manner: which was disturbing, and yet gratifying as well, for Constance Philippa knew that gentlemen should stare at ladies in this way, with that mysterious dark urgency, tho' she could not really comprehend why; nor did she feel the slightest inclination to reciprocate. To a limited extent, she could understand Malvinia's mercurial interest in *her* suitors, who were usually handsome young men, if rather vapid; she supposed she might be capable of feeling an "attraction" for Mr. de Nemours, for instance, if the situation arose, for his conventional good looks, his loud boyish laughter, and his sandy mustache argued forcibly. And there was Sean McInnes, the Irish boy whom poor Octavia was said to be secretly sweet on. (Everyone spoke of Sean as Irish tho' he had been born in Bloodsmoor, and was consequently as American as any of the Kiddemasters; and they commonly referred to him as a boy, despite the fact that he was now well into his twenties, and had made a possibly imprudent bid for independence, by leaving Judge Kiddemaster's employ.) He was tall, broad-shouldered, robust of spirit, with striking red hair and blue eyes that shone with unfailing good humor. Constance Philippa supposed she might feel a girlish enthusiasm for this young man if he had been born to her own social rank; but, as he had not, the situation was hopeless, and she rather supposed silly Octavia deluded herself, in fancying an interest where, in fact, there was none. And yet, if one set Sean McInnes beside old dry-as-dust Lucius Rumford—!

Among her cousins, Basil Miller was surely worthy of a young lady's fluttery interest, and Lieutenant Steven Bayard, particularly when he stood at attention in his dress greens, but they were merely *cousins* . . . and Constance Philippa could feel nothing for them save a somewhat frayed affection.

In truth, strange as I find it, the only person Constance Philippa had felt much emotion for, during her turbulent adolescence, was Miss Delphine Martineau, Malvinia's friend—and as bubble-headed, fickle, and vain as Malvinia herself! Miss Martineau was Malvinia's age exactly, and consequently two years younger than Constance Philippa. A terror at such silly games as Puss-in-the-Corner, very pretty, spoiled, giggly . . . without an ounce of intelligence, Constance Philippa thought contemptuously; and yet everyone adored her, especially the young men, and she very nearly vied with Malvinia as the belle of the Bloodsmoor Valley. Brown hair that appeared burnished, set in curls, braids, and ringlets; lovely cheeks upon which the faintest blush could be discerned; mischievous winking dark brown eyes . . . Alas, the girl had been married only a few weeks ago: and Constance Philippa, whom the very thought of weddings troubled, had absented herself from the ceremony and the surrounding festivities, giving so perfunctory an excuse that both Mr. and Mrs. Zinn commented on it. She did not mean, surely, to be rude to the Martineaus, or to slight a childhood friend on the day of her greatest happiness?

"She was not my friend but Malvinia's," Constance Philippa said coldly.

Long ago the girls had played together, making little dresses for their dolls, long ago the Valley girls had been such good friends, in and out of one another's houses, and Mr. Zinn had made a jack-in-the-box and chickens-pecking (on a paddle) with his fretsaw, and Constance Philippa and Malvinia had painted them, and at casino Delphine had slapped down her cards, one! two! three! and the Zinn girls had exclaimed, laughing. Oh, long ago: and Christmas greetings elaborately scissored out of stiff colored paper and sprinkled with gold dust: and then there were Valentines on rose-scented paper, sometimes stiff with ornamentation—sequins, gilt, lace, strips of braid. Constance Philippa had scorned most of the girls' activities but she had made a Valentine, yes, she had made a Valentine, and a lovely big Valentine it was, eighteen inches high, painted with infinite care in reds and pinks, and the verse had been her own—or nearly:

Four hearts in one I do behold
They in each other do infold,
I cut them out on such a night
And send them to my heart's delight.
I choose you, D., for my Valentine,
I choose you out from all the rest,
The reason is, I LIKE YOU BEST.

But even at the age of fourteen Miss Delphine Martineau had received so many Valentines, from "young gentlemen" as well as from her girl friends, she took no special note of Constance Philippa's card: and so, as Constance Philippa told herself, the *ridiculous* and *degrading* episode passed.

Now she was to be married shortly; and, indeed, Miss Delphine Martineau was already married. And so, and so. She adjusted her veil, as it had grown damp where it touched her mouth, and peered out cautiously at the sun—what o'clock was it? When would they be summoned back to the Hall for tea? Baron von Mainz had been talking quietly of the picturesque vista spread out before them—and the chance configuration of clouds, which struck a particularly aesthetic note—and the fragrance of certain blossoms carried on the breeze. And then he spoke, still in a casual voice, of his tragic history, his personal history and that of the von Mainz family, which involved knighthood, and the Crusades, and the Archbishop Wilhelm IV, and the One Hundred Years' War, and the cathedral town of Mainz, and the great port of Hamburg, and fortunes in wheat won and lost, and the assassination in 1794 of the Baron Friedrich Ferdinand, his great-grandfather, by rebellious peasants—tho' this was perhaps not the time, the Baron allowed, to speak of such uncouth matters. (For Constance Philippa, roused from her daydream, had been staring at him quite openly.)

Strolling back to Kiddemaster Hall, now preceded by their two amiable chaperons, the young affianced couple found themselves more than customarily silent; and at length the Baron said, in a voice perhaps edged with irony: "The Wheel of Fortune, which has dictated the lives of the von Mainz family, and the lives of most of the European nobility of our acquaintance, is perhaps not a familiar concept in your young country?—but it will be, my dear Constance Philippa; it will be."

Very little was known of the Baron's personal history, apart from a brief summary of his business activities, which had been extensive, both before and after 1861, for Great-Uncle Vaughan Kiddemaster had cautioned the Zinns—Mrs. Zinn in particular, whose tongue was unpredictable—against making "indiscreet" inquiries. "It will be enough for you to know," the elderly gentleman said kindly, "that I have satisfied myself as to the young man's *worth*, in every sense of the word; and that I feel no hesitation whatsoever, at the prospect of bringing a foreigner into our family. And since it cannot be said," Great-Uncle Vaughan continued, after a decorous pause, "that suitors are storming the Octagonal House —at least in pursuit of your Constance Philippa—I think we must rest with the sentiment that a *foreigner* might prove, under the circumstances, the very best investment of all."

Enough to know, perhaps, and to rejoice in, that his was a nine-hundred-year-old name, honored and, for a time, feared, throughout Northern Europe. And that *Miss Constance Philippa Zinn* would become, by marriage, as if by magic, the *Baroness von Mainz*.

Gradually Constance Philippa came to learn, however, that her fiancé had studied with Jesuits in Rouen, and had even contemplated for a time entering that prestigious order. (Fortunately for the Zinns, and for Constance Philippa's unborn babies, the Baron had drifted away from his early allegiance to Popery, and was perfectly content to be married in the Episcopal Church—wise, prudent man!) She learned that his father and brothers had been associated with the great English warehousing firm of Anthony Chuzzlewit & Sons, and that they had done a brisk trade in both England and the United States; and that the Baron himself, while still a young man, had acquired a part-interest in the American freighter *Jezebel*, which customarily docked in New Orleans, until its destruction by Union soldiers. (Not only was the Baron forced to suffer this loss—for insurance was inadequate, or the insurers unable to pay—but the vigorous trade with the Ivory Coast of Africa came to an abrupt halt: and the Baron's American partners, it was said, badly defrauded him of his investment.) It was true that "tragedy" had pursued him—and Constance Philippa was both disturbed and fascinated to learn that he had married a fifteen-year-old convent girl, an Italian princess, rumored to be of an angelic beauty and possessing a childlike innocence; that the young lady had died in the seventh month of pregnancy, which had been the seventh month of marriage as well (an abnormally enlarged fetus had "turned to stone" in her womb, whilst the rest of her, poor doomed child, had withered, a sickly yellow). After a twelve-month of mourning, the bereft young husband married again, a fabled English beauty whose slender, sylphlike figure was renowned in London society, and whose father had entered into a business partnership with him; but this marriage, too, ended in tragedy—the young English lady also died within the first year, of mysterious causes, a posthumous examination revealing a most curious distention and atrophying of the internal organs, particularly those of the lower belly, and, in the womb, a very small fetus, hardly frog-sized, which had also *turned to stone*. (This young lady, in submission to the demands of fashion, had had, some years before, an operation to remove her lower ribs, in order to guarantee a satisfactorily slender waist, which operation,

I am somewhat disappointed to report, our own Octavia begged for; but Mr. Zinn, in his wisdom, forbade. The operation, however, being of a simple and mechanical nature, and pronounced altogether harmless by the surgeon who performed it, was deemed to have nothing at all to do with the cause of the young Baroness's death, which cause remained undetermined.)

And perhaps, well, *perhaps* (Constance Philippa held herself aloof from making direct inquiries, and was consequently dependent upon shards and wisps of gossip reported to her by Malvinia, who acquired them by way of their Philadelphia cousins, the *lively* cousins, that is) there may have been yet another marriage, and yet another tragic and premature death: and then the Baron was in New York, dining with the Millers, and then he had entered into some sort of business partnership with the Millers and the Bayards: and then he was in Philadelphia, allied with Great-Uncle Vaughan Kiddemaster, the wealthiest and most powerful Kiddemaster of all, and at a ball at Highlands he had been introduced to Miss Constance Philippa Zinn, and had quite delighted all the family by exclaiming, in his rich Teutonic accent: "Ah!—the daughter, then, of the celebrated inventor John Quincy Zinn?" (For tho' Mr. Zinn was dilatory in seeking patents for his numerous discoveries, and had, by the time of this fateful Christmas ball, only two fully acquired, and a third pending, his reputation was growing at all times; and more and more inventors— Hannibal Goodwin, as we have seen, but also George Washington Gale Ferris, and the bright and rapacious young Thomas Alva Edison—were journeying to the modest cabin in the woods, to make his acquaintance and ask his advice on certain problems of their own and, it may be, simply to shake his hand.)

Constance Philippa struck Baron von Mainz, we may assume, as an eminently respectable young Philadelphia lady, soft-spoken, indeed reticent, possessed of a satisfactorily graceful carriage, handsome rather than pretty (for it was Malvinia, the younger sister, who was truly pretty— enchantingly pretty); no longer, at the age of twenty-one, precisely *young,* as these matters go. But she wore, that evening, a most attractive white- and-lilac organdy dress, and the intricate arrangement of her ringlets, and the peacock feathers in her hair, softened her stern and somewhat bony brow; and she did not offend the gentleman's ear by rattling and chattering nervously like certain of her elders. True, her height exceeded his, tho' he wore inch-high heels; but when they were seated, the disparity was not at all evident.

Constance Philippa, for her part, saw a gentleman of an indeterminate age—younger than her father, surely; far older than Cousin Basil, who had just celebrated his thirty-fourth birthday—attired in garments that bespoke, in cut as well as color, an Old World sensibility: less sombre and restrained than the American, and far more welcome to her eye. In truth, balls stimulated the eldest Zinn daughter to sarcasm, for she did not do well at them, and her sarcasm burnt on her tongue as the evening gaily progressed, and she soon lapsed into a sullen hurt quiet, in which, secretly, she derided her rivals' dresses, and the tiresome blacks and grays of their dancing partners; and so the Baron von Mainz in his fairly bold costume—a blue velvet waistcoat and cream-colored coat lined with velvet of the same hue, a blue satin cravat, white French gloves, two golden breast pins attached by a golden chain, and patent leather shoes that gleamed and winked—*quite* struck her fancy. He was clearly well-bred, showed little emotion save that of a genteel courtesy, did not ask her tiresome questions; and reminded her—tho' not altogether consciously, I suppose—of prankish sweet-faced Pip, with his bright dark ageless eyes and button nose, and the question-mark of a tail, which rose so charmingly above his hunched back.

Constance Philippa grimly judged the meeting "successful," since it happened, as if by accident, that she met the Baron again within that very week, at her Great-Uncle Horace Bayard's home on Frothingham Square, where he was exceedingly gracious, bowing to her, and clicking his heels smartly together. He inquired after her health, and after the health of her family. And she met him a scant fortnight later at a formal dinner at the Rittenhouse Square home of the Hambleton Woodruffs, again as if by accident—she could not prevent a fierce blush from o'ertaking her, as their eyes again met.

That evening, at the long dinner table, the Baron showed himself to advantage amongst his American hosts, partaking of their conversation in a liberal tone, and exhibiting the proper degree of curiosity and appreciation. Topics discussed were agreeably cultured, to Constance Philippa's relief: ranging from the merits of Johann Strauss's *Indigo;* to the most recent lyceum lecture, "Walking, Temperance & Longevity," by the famous athlete-clergyman Dr. Manning Cuthbert of Cincinnati; to the surprising phenomenon of new patriotic societies, virtually springing up overnight: the American Protective Association, formed to "reduce Catholic influence in politics and education"; and the Society of Colonial Wars, to which one or two Kiddemasters already belonged; and the Order of Founders and Patriots, which Baron von Mainz himself thought a necessary bulwark against the influx of Irish, Jews, Negroes, and Orientals of all varieties, which was threatening the complexion of America. In all, these organizations were deemed necessary, though perhaps rather *excitably* publicized; it was the opinion of old Mr. Woodruff, half dozing in his chair, that the country had gone to hell in a handcart since the Federalist bankruptcy—not the murder of Hamilton (for certainly, at that point in his career, Hamilton had deserved death, or worse) but the blunders of Hamilton, leading to the Republican takeover, and, in not many years, the mob triumph of *Andrew Jackson* . . . whose name could scarce be uttered, in the presence of ladies.

There was talk of the Missionaries Alliance; and Mark Twain; and the *All-Blackface Jim Crow Revue* then playing at the Varieties Theatre, direct from the Bowery in New York, with Septimis George in the lead —an absolutely hilarious entertainment. Perhaps it was not exactly genteel; perhaps it was rather rowdy and boisterous; but, as Baron von Mainz insisted, it was surely the most lively, the most ingenious, one might say the most *American* of entertainments, and hence of especial interest to a foreign visitor.

It was then that Mr. Hambleton Woodruff surprised his guests, and his niece Constance Philippa in particular, by doing a spirited imitation of the celebrated Septimis George as *he* imitated Jim Crow. Remaining in his place at the far end of the table, Mr. Woodruff clapped his hands lightly (for it would not do, of course, to summon the servants), and rolled his eyes and made his mouth go slack, and grinned, and grimaced, and wriggled his fat shoulders, and sang in a "negro" falsetto—

> Come listen all you gals and boys,
> I'm just from Tuckyhoe;
> I'm going to sing a leetle song,
> My name's JIM—CROW.
>
> Weel about and turn about
> And do jis so;
> Eb'ry time I weel about,
> I jump JIM—CROW.
>
> I'm a rorer on de fiddle,
> An down in ole Virginny;
> Dey say I play de skientific,
> Like massa Pagganninny.
>
> De way dey bake de hoe cake,
> Virginny nebber tire;
> Dey put de doe upon de foot,
> An stick im in de fire.

—which quite astonished everyone at the table, and moved even the reticent Constance Philippa to laughing appreciation. One might have worried that Baron von Mainz would think Mr. Woodruff's performance vulgar (for it was so often the case, to our bewilderment, that foreign visitors who had enjoyed themselves heartily here, returned home and published vicious satires of American life); but, on the contrary, the vastly amused little German led the applause at the conclusion of Mr. Woodruff's song, and repeated his praise of the blackface music as lively and ingenious and, indeed, marvelously *American*.

It was soon the case that Baron von Mainz had settled, at least temporarily, in a luxurious suite at the Hotel de la Paix (so that he might, he said, repay his American hosts with dinners of his own), and that he had had shipped his stallion, his falcon, and other possessions, to the great country estate of Vaughan Kiddemaster, in Bucks County, where he had been invited to spend weekends riding and hunting: all of which, Constance Philippa was told, might be seen to be "immensely promising." Indeed, within a fortnight she and all of the Zinns were invited to dine with the Baron in his suite and to visit him at Highlands, where, on his proud steed Lucifer, with his hooded falcon Adonis on his upraised arm, he was so arresting a sight—and so *unusual* a sight—that Constance Philippa drew in her breath sharply, and was visited with the thought: *O enviable man!*

Her sisters shrank away from the spectacle of Adonis hunting his small prey (sparrows, mourning doves, and mocking birds primarily), and the elder women of the party, Mrs. Zinn, Grandmother Kiddemaster, and Great-Aunt Edwina, declined even to watch from the terrace of the great house, hundreds of feet away; but Constance Philippa did find the sport fascinating. She was sorry of course that the small birds were snatched out of the air by Adonis's cruel hooked beak, but, after all, they were killed at once (so the Baron assured her), and it was "only Nature"—"only Nature fulfilling herself, as she must." Judge Kiddemaster's grumbling distrust of "foreigners" and "disenfranchised noblemen" was somewhat assuaged, and John Quincy Zinn, tho' disturbed by the bloodiness of the sport, did express some admiration for Baron von Mainz's mastery of his creatures, and was even stimulated to sketch an idea or two afterward—might there be a *machine* bird of prey, a mechanical *golem* of some kind?—attracted to its moving target by magnetism?—a variation upon the military rockets developed by Sir William Congreve at the turn of the century, and fancifully envisioned by Jules Verne?

Constance Philippa stood erect beneath her sunshade as the Baron rode up, and dismounted, keeping his wrist high and steady so that the falcon (now hooded) should not be unbalanced; she gazed shyly at him through her tulle veil, and murmured, as if involuntarily: "How remarkable!—your Adonis!—your Lucifer!" The Baron bowed, yet even then did not disturb his fierce bird of prey, whose burnished feathers rippled in the breeze, and whose blood-stained beak opened and closed spasmodically. Constance Philippa drew a quick wild breath, feeling suddenly faint, and she saw, or seemed to see, an almost imperceptible sensual quiver of the little man's mustache. "My dear Miss Zinn," the Baron murmured, in a near-inaudible voice, wiping his mouth with his gloved hand, and bowing again, as smartly as before, "I am at your service."

And not long afterward he made his appeal to Judge Kiddemaster;

and then to Mr. and Mrs. Zinn; and at last to Constance Philippa herself, who, stony-cold with fear, unable to quite grasp what was happening, accepted his proposal of marriage with numbed lips, and had to restrain herself from drawing away when the overjoyed suitor, still on his knees, sought her hand to kiss it. She could not help glancing over his head, to the doorway of the parlor: for surely her sisters were hiding there, and would burst into laughter in another moment? And wasn't naughty little Pip crouched behind the settee?

Since their dowager chaperons were always nearby, and conscientiously attentive, the affianced couple conversed of little save very general subjects, and, indeed, oft strolled or sat in total silence, absorbed (so I assume) by each other's presence, and basking in the anticipation of wedded harmony to come. Upon one unusual occasion, hardly a fortnight before the wedding, Miss Zinn and Baron von Mainz were strolling along the path above the river, accompanied at a discreet distance by Great-Aunt Edwina and Miss Narcissa Gilpin, when, of a sudden, the Baron evidently took a misstep, and brushed against Constance Philippa, so startling her that she released her silky white sunshade, which was carried off by the breeze, unfortunately in the direction of the river. It was lifted, and fell, not in the river itself but on a rock some yards below, an awkward climb to be sure, and perhaps even dangerous for any but a servant. Constance Philippa's cheeks blushed with chagrin, for she *did* hate any sort of fuss, and the frail white sunshade with its lilac ribbons looked so very silly, caught on the rocks. To her relief, tho' to her surprise as well, Baron von Mainz, in whom gallantry had evidently not o'erwhelmed common sense, did not offer to retrieve it, as an eager American youth might have done. Instead he told her, in his dry dignified voice: "We will acquire another pretty little parasol for you, Miss Kiddemaster—there is a plethora of such female appurtenances in your country, I daresay."

It was shortly before this that Mrs. Zinn and Octavia, accompanied by a trusted manservant (Mr. Zinn having declined vociferously to come along), made their futile journey to Boston to attend a séance given by the new trance medium, "Deirdre of the Shadows."

Alas—"Deirdre of the Shadows" was surely not *their* Deirdre, as they clearly grasped in the first minutes of her introduction: yet they hid their disappointment, and remained for the séance, heavy of heart, and only superficially engaged in the peculiar phenomena that followed.

The séance was dismayingly large, attended by some forty people, as a consequence of the new fame of "Deirdre of the Shadows" in the Boston area. Arrangements had been made beforehand for Mrs. Zinn and her daughter by Aunt Geraldine Miller, who, since the death of a favorite niece two years previously, had made an informal (some would say desperate) exploration of Spiritualist activities in the East, bravely defying family scorn and censure. (The men in particular were doubtful of this new "religion," and had naught but contempt for such sensationalists and charlatans as the infamous Fox sisters of upstate New York, and Colonel McKenzie—many times exposed in the public press, yet continuing to draw zealots withal, and to accumulate sizable fortunes.) That Mrs. Zinn made the long journey not to participate in Spiritualist phenomena, but to seek out her lost daughter, perhaps added to the poignancy of the situation; but it must be admitted that Mrs. Zinn, being of a somewhat stoic nature, and inclined even to cynicism of a kind, had not truly expected to find her own Deirdre. "*Is* it—?" Octavia whispered, clearly frightened, and gripping her mother's arm as if she were a little girl, at the first appearance of "Deirdre of the Shadows," when a tall, slender, alarmingly pale girl with heavy-lidded eyes was led out, in a black silk cloak with ivory lining—but Mrs. Zinn, seeing at once the unhappy truth, said simply: "No. It is not."

Guests that evening consisted of two sorts, those who were seated around a large oak dining table, and others who were of the class of observers, seated in straight-backed chairs lined against the walls. Mrs. Zinn and her daughter, heavily veiled, and rather embarrassed to find themselves in this company, were of the latter class, for Mrs. Zinn had emphatically declined Aunt Geraldine's offer to assure them—through payment so high as to constitute a bribe, made to the gentleman manager of "Deirdre of the Shadows"—a place at the table, and a place, consequently, in the evening's occult proceedings. "My interest in this very odd young woman has nothing to do with her alleged Spiritualist abilities," Mrs. Zinn said, with dignity, "but only with her identity—that, and nothing more. If she is Deirdre I shall bring her back home to Bloodsmoor with me. If she is not—I shall go away again, as I have come."

Since Deirdre's disappearance, now nearly a twelve-month past, Mrs. Zinn had lapsed gradually into a state of mind that might be best described as "inexpressive"—even the Zinns' financial worries (Mr. Zinn was now in debt $25,000 to his father-in-law), even the excitement of Constance Philippa's imminent betrothal could not seem to rouse her to the natural and spontaneous expression of genuine feeling. Her frequent explosions of anger came and went so abruptly as to suggest a curious superficiality, as if the troubled lady lost interest at once in the very spasm of temper that o'ertook her. Whether she exhibited a laudable *stoicism* of a Christian sort, or whether it was a chilling *apathy*, I cannot judge, save to say that Prudence Zinn, after the birth of her third daughter Malvinia, in 1859, involving as it did a forty-two-hour labor of excruciating difficulty, attended by such a loss of blood as to raise the spectre, in her frightened husband's heart, of her death, had never been quite the same Prudence Zinn again—not the forthright, outspoken, boldly assertive young woman, who had been raised to the rank of assistant headmistress of the Cobbett School for Girls by the age of twenty-nine, and who quite held her own, as we have seen, in the drawing rooms of intellectual Philadelphia of the Fifties. It might be said that her spirit was broken: less by the agony of the long labor, perhaps, for that ordeal did result in blessèd life (and from the first Malvinia was a beautiful baby, admired by all), than by the repetition of pregnancies, miscarriages, labors, births, and occasional deaths (for not all of Mrs. Zinn's pregnancies resulted in life, but it would be morbid of me, and distracting from the main narrative, to enumerate these failures). Her love for Mr. Zinn, I hasten to say, remained steadfast, as did his love for her; the *unitary nature* of their wedded bliss could not be shaken, as indeed it cannot be shaken, once God has administered His blessing. And yet—Mrs. Zinn of 1859, still less Mrs. Zinn of 1880, was very distant from Miss Kiddemaster of 1853, and bore her, alas, only a vague family resemblance!

"Who is that, Mamma?" Samantha once asked, pointing at a tinted daguerreotype of Mrs. Zinn in her bridal gown, in the family scrapbook, and Mrs. Zinn, brushing the little girl's hand aside in order to close the book, said: "A creature of vanity."

Yet she loved her daughters, hardly a whit less than she loved her husband; and tho' her love for Deirdre was perhaps not *quite* so fervent as her love for the other girls (such is my assumption: I cannot after all pierce the inviolable mystery of the human heart), she did cherish the unhappy child, and suffered intermittent grief on her account, and dreamt frequently of her—troubled, chaotic dreams in which Deirdre, again a ten-year-old, held her thin arms out to Mrs. Zinn in vain. "Momma! Momma!" the child cried, as she had so rarely cried in real life: but Mrs. Zinn, paralyzed, could not move to her; and woke much disturbed, hardly knowing where she was, except that, with Mr. Zinn slumbering and snoring peacefully beside her, she was much alone.

"Deirdre, my lost Deirdre," she murmured, "how we have wronged you! Yet how can we make amends?"

In addition to Aunt Geraldine Miller, now a somewhat giddy widow in her late sixties, there were a number of female relatives who dabbled, it might be said, in Spiritualism; and even in her girlhood Prudence Zinn and several female companions had experimented with a Ouija board (which they claimed to find intensely boring, far less interesting than a book, say, by Mr. Emerson); but that very new and very American branch of science or religion was vehemently rejected by most of the family, who were after all nominally Episcopalian, or comfortably agnostic, and scornful of religious enthusiasm of a primitive kind. The usually tolerant John Quincy Zinn himself considered Spiritualism "a shameful deception of the credulous, and a still more shameful expenditure of *Time.*"

After the tragic death of nineteen-year-old Annie Miller in Rome, as a consequence of malaria (or so it was given out: the family whispered that Annie might have been murdered by Italians, perhaps poisoned; others whispered cruelly that she might have died as a result of "illicit" behavior with Italians, of an indeterminate nature), Aunt Geraldine and Annie's mother and one or two other ladies sought to make contact with her, by way of mediums in New York City, Schenectady, and Boston; but to little avail. A fair amount of money was spent, and rumor had it that Aunt Geraldine had pressed upon the *chela*-companion of the celebrated Madame Blavatsky, the young Indian Hassan Agha, a costly pearl-and-sapphire brooch that had come down through the family from the reign of William and Mary, yet to no avail: the brooch being accepted as an honorable contribution to the cause of Theosophy, and the erection, in particular, of a new Lamasery in Adyar, Madras; but no contact with the dead girl was promised, or, indeed, was forthcoming. Rather more hurt than discouraged, the grieving Mrs. Miller next applied to the popular trance medium Johnette Whittaker, a former innkeeper's wife of Pike's Falls, New York; and then to the ubiquitous Mrs. Theodora Guilford, whose séances were always characterized by what some observers called an excess of Christian piety (the anxious Mrs. Guilford fearing, not altogether unreasonably, that she might be damned as a witch in some quarters—in Roman Catholic Boston, for instance), alas, to no avail: the deceased Annie, or Daisy, as she was ofttimes called, being as queerly reticent in death, as she was loquacious in life.

It was a measure of Mrs. Miller's desperation that she sent letters and telegrams to the great trance medium Daniel Dunglas Home, now in sumptuous retirement on the Riviera: Home being incontestably the very greatest of mediums in recorded history: Highlander-born (of a long line of "seers") but American-reared, and hence, poor Mrs. Miller wished to believe, disposed to aid her in her search. To these heartfelt applications the redoubtable Home answered only with silence—ungracious man!

Nevertheless, tho' Aunt Geraldine and her companions did not make contact with the dead Annie, they did, in the course of a dozen séances, experience phenomena of a kind to defy all logic, as well as common sense—and became, to the disgust of the men of the family, fervent Spiritualists, contributing much to the cause, by way of both gifts and hard cash.

Deirdre of the Shadows began to hold sessions in the Boston-Quincy-Providence area, in the late spring of 1880; and made a New York *début* not many months afterward, in the lower Fifth Avenue home of a highly respectable widow named Strong, under the auspices of the Theosophical Society, tho' her relationship to the Theosophists, and to Madame Blavatsky, was unclear. As a consequence of her well-born and monied clientele, this young woman soon enjoyed a blossoming reputation, and was duly written up in the papers, and even investigated by the "scourge of the occultists," Colonel Lynes, writing for the *New York Daily Graphic,* who allowed that the young medium *might* possess powers: he had, in any case, witnessed a great deal that could not be explained, either by common sense, or by a suspicion of fraud.

Immediately upon her arrival at the séance, Mrs. Zinn saw, to her relif, that Deirdre of the Shadows was not her daughter; and gave inward thanks (for how very, very bizarre all this Spiritualist claptrap was!—how indelicate, how morbid, how common), tho' she was, of course, disappointed at the same time, to know that she would return to Bloodsmoor without Deirdre. "My poor lost child," she murmured to herself, "lost in the cruel spaciousness of our century . . . !"

Tho' Deirdre of the Shadows was not Deirdre Louisa Zinn, Mrs. Zinn did admit afterward to having been impressed, as much by the young medium's air of innocence and detachment, as by her alleged skills. (These included voices called out of the air; raps and knocks and chimes, and ectoplasmic faces—which did astound the credulous Octavia; a heaving table of solid mahogany; the rattling of dice, or bones; an eerie hunter's horn; an eerie harp; "contact spirits" who babbled in foreign languages, and could not be hushed; and sudden revelations that meant a great deal to the participants at the table, coming, as they evidently did, from "Spirit World," but which sounded like sad, simple nonsense to the uninvolved observers.)

As the young medium seated herself at the head of the table, her cape rustling about her, Mrs. Zinn lifted her dark veil, in order to see as clearly as possible. The medium appeared to be already in a partial trance —or drugged. She had a small, narrow, exceedingly pale face; a perceptible widow's peak; jet-black hair in a shockingly loose style; a small, thin, and somewhat pouting mouth. To be sure, this young woman *resembled* the lost Deirdre (as the impressionable Octavia whispered in her mother's ear), but, in fact, unhappily, and irrevocably, she was *not* Deirdre, but a stranger.

Mrs. Zinn stared openly, paying little attention to the medium's queer halting words, or to the air of nervous expectation in the room. *She* was not, after all, a client; she had not come to communicate with her dead, or with any dead at all; she prided herself on being a steadfast Episcopalian, in manner if not fully in doctrine (for there were elements of the Trinity, and of Mary's role, she found most difficult to accept). Spiritualism might be taken up by the *nouveau riche* of the city, and even by European and English nobility, but it struck a Kiddemaster as being distinctly lowlife, and she had no use for it. And so she watched, she stared, she assessed, quite coolly, and queried herself whether the young woman was truly in a trance, or pretending—or might she be hypnotized?—or under the influence of a powerful narcotic? Ah, there was tragedy here, if one had time to investigate, and the necessary sympathy!

An ironic coincidence, Mrs. Zinn thought, lowering her veil, that this young woman should have taken for herself the appellation "Deirdre of the Shadows." There was, surely, nothing about her sombre face that suggested childhood: and Mrs. Zinn could not help but recall her youngest daughter's small pretty features, and the roses that oft bloomed faintly in her cheeks; and the sparkle of her gray eyes. Lost, lost! And never to be regained!

Octavia again leaned close, to whisper in her mother's ear, and again Mrs. Zinn pushed her gently away. Deirdre of the Shadows was surely a stranger to all sense of decorum and decency, to appear before a paying public as she did, in that theatrically flamboyant cape, and a black silk dress that suggested a nightgown rather than a proper dress, since it was not drawn in tightly at the waist, but fell in loose graceful folds like a pagan tunic; nor was her hair normally fashioned, but tumbled to her shoulders in an unspeakably vulgar style, *Latin* perhaps, or even *gypsy*, Mrs. Zinn knew not. . . . "Deirdre of the Shadows," indeed! And the people who attended her, how very odd they were, a lady's maid with staring agate eyes and a skirt so short her ankles nearly showed, and a young dark-skinned male, slender as an eel, East Indian by the look of him, and decidedly sinister, in a black turban with a scarab brooch, and a black raw silk tunic that fitted his body far too snugly. Behind the scenes, too, offstage as it were, a grossly fat woman swathed in shawls, with a frizzed mop of hair and *no head covering,* bustled about, doing the Lord knew what, and hissing instructions to the maid and the turbaned youth. How shameful, how despicable, it all was . . . !

Mrs. Zinn wiped tears from her eyes, which had begun to soak her veil. She felt a sudden physical loathing not only for the medium and her grotesque comrades, but for the clients as well. Fools! Gulls! So credulous were they, so childlike in their naïveté, they were leaning forward eagerly to take in the medium's every movement, however jerky and spasmodic, and her every half-audible word and moan—as if the entire performance were not fraudulent!

"Mother," Octavia whispered, "are you feeling faint? Shall we step outside for some air?"

"I am *quite* well," Mrs. Zinn said curtly, pushing her daughter's hand away. "Only rather warm. It is unpleasantly close in here."

"I have brought along smelling salts in case—"

"I assure you, I am *quite well.*"

"It isn't Deirdre after all—is it?" Octavia whispered, squinting through her veil.

"Certainly not."

"She is much older—much older than my little sister," Octavia said. "So strange and pale and steeped in sorrow—no longer a child—not, I am sure, our Deirdre?"

"Not our Deirdre," Mrs. Zinn said quietly.

On their return journey to Philadelphia, in the privacy of their plush-lined compartment, Mrs. Zinn and Octavia spoke little of the abortive Boston adventure, and occupied themselves industriously with their sewing. (Each was working on a teatowel for Constance Philippa's household.) From time to time Octavia sighed heavily, but Mrs. Zinn, in her stoic detachment, did not scruple to discipline her.

Before retiring for the night Octavia murmured sleepily: "How *very* strange, that unhappy young lady!—and she appeared to take no notice of *us.*"

The remark was so incidentally made, and Mrs. Zinn so half consciously heard it, no reply was necessary; and neither was to remember it on the following morn, when the coach pulled with a triumphant clatter into sunny Philadelphia.

19

Miss Constance Philippa Zinn and the Baron Adolf von Mainz were joined in holy matrimony on November 15, 1880, at Trinity Chruch of Bloodsmoor, the Reverend Silas Hewett presiding. The bride wore a gown of surpassing beauty, of the finest China silk, with a many-layered skirt and train, and a long veil of Brussels lace; and the groom was impeccably attired in a morning coat and tails, with a sprig of orange blossom in his lapel. There was only a moment's awkwardness, when, it appeared, the wedding band was too small for the bride's finger, and the groom, perhaps embarrassed by his role, seemed to grow impatient, and jammed it on: but an instant later all was well, and, tho' slightly red-faced, the bridal couple continued with the ceremony, and Reverend Hewett pronounced them man and wife; and the organ sounded.

Wedding guests were driven to Kiddemaster Hall in special carriages, and received in the reception room at the east end of the house, which was sumptuously decorated with floral displays of all kinds, and had never looked more elegant. On a raised platform was a six-piece chamber orchestra, which played throughout the evening; in one corner, a display of wedding gifts (a great number of the most beautiful specimens of cut glass, china, silverware, side pieces, watercolors and oil paintings, linens, etc.), which all the guests inspected with delight, and congratulations to the bride and groom.

The wedding repast was served in the larger of the two dining rooms, which room had been given a marvelous *pink* cast, by the judicious selection and arrangement of roses, candles, napkins, and glassware of that hue, to the exclaimed admiration of the guests. The bride's table was circular in form, with a generous mound of tulle upon which were strewn a countless number of pink tea roses interspersed with little bows of pink-and-white-striped ribbon, the appearance of all being most beautiful. Before the bride was placed the bride's loaf, magnificently frosted, and at each of the twelve places about this table, occupied by the bridal party, were bouquets of pink and cream roses, large ones for the ladies, and smaller ones for the gentlemen. (Vivacious Malvinia created something of a scene, by presenting to her elder sister Constance Philippa a prankish little mock-bouquet of tea roses some hours past their prime, interspersed with weed flowers of a common ghastly whitish hue: turkey beard, fly poison, miterwort, and death camas!—a bouquet the bride accepted without comment, and laid beside her plate at the table.)

The long dining table was adorned with pink and cream roses as well, and drew forth unstinting exclamations of delight, as did the delicious ten-course meal, which, as was the tradition at Kiddemaster Hall, disappointed neither in quality nor quantity. Guests were overheard commenting to one another upon the festivities, in tones of fulsome praise: "The most brilliant social event of the Bloodsmoor season," was the general verdict; and I cannot but concur in their judgment.

A fair amount of champagne was consumed, inspiring Cousin Basil Miller to an impudent but high-spirited toast, delivered in rollicking song:

> It's we two, it's we two for aye,
> All the world and we two, and Heaven be our stay!
> Like a laverock in the lift, sing O bonny bride!
> All the world was Adam once, with Eve by his side!
>
> *All the world was Adam once—with Eve by his side!*

The honeymoon journey was to be an ambitious one, involving visits to Washington, D.C., Richmond, Atlanta, and New Orleans; and possibly the West Indies as well—where the Baron's sugar-cane plantation was said to be threatened of late by labor difficulties. So the couple betook themselves to their carriage, and departed for Philadelphia, where they were scheduled to spend the night in the Baron's handsome suite in the Hotel de la Paix, overlooking Logan Square.

They were, it hardly needs to be said, a *subdued* couple, for Constance Philippa in particular was extremely shy, and not even the champagne poured for them by the Baron's silent manservant could loosen her tongue, tho' she drank, it may be unthinkingly, several glasses in rapid succession. From time to time both the bride and the groom glanced around, as if expecting to see, in the room's distant corners, an unheralded visitor or witness. But of course they were alone—quite alone.

"Are you warm enough, my dear?" the Baron asked solicitously, having noticed his bride shivering; and before she had even time to reply, he had arisen, and fetched a lovely white cashmere shawl, and draped it about her shoulders. "Perhaps, my dear Constance Philippa," he murmured, "we can aspire to warmth together."

Constance Philippa murmured an inaudible reply, no doubt an assent.

He regained his seat, and in silence they finished their light repast of ham, scallops, and caviar toast, and drank the rest of the champagne, the Baron now eying his bride steadily, with a look of grimness leavened by some humor (for one must remember that, despite the romance of their courtship, the young man had been married before), and, from time to time, a slight quiver of his mustache; and the bride's cheeks appeared to have acquired a permanent blush, which gave to her ordinarily undistinguished complexion a look, almost, of maidenly delicacy. That the bride was nervous was evident in the trembling of her hand, as she lifted the glass to her mouth, and in a certain quickening of her breath; that the groom was similarly affected was evident in the quickening of *his* breath, which soon became audible. "My dear," the Baron said, in a dry, gentle voice, "perhaps it is time to retire for the night?"

At once the bride rose from her chair, so quickly her husband had not time to help her, and in a soft rushed tone she excused herself, and went into the bedchamber with no evident air of hesitation, and closed the door quietly behind her. The Baron, being a considerate, and, as it were, a practiced husband, lingered behind, idly eating what remained of the ham, and, after some minutes, pouring an inch or two of brandy in a glass, the fumes of which he inhaled with evident pleasure. Time passed: he checked his pocket watch and decided to give the new Baroness another minute or two, to prepare herself. She had brought along for the honeymoon trip such a quantity of suitcases, trunks, and boxes, it would not have surprised him had she searched in vain for her nighttime apparel; and he smiled tightly to think of her growing desperation, should she *not* find it.

After a discreet space of time, the Baron went to the door, rapped lightly upon it, and, turning the knob (which he halfway feared might be locked against him—for that had happened once before), called out to his bride in as controlled a voice as he could manage: "You have no objection, my dear Constance Philippa, if I now join you?"—and, receiving no reply, he added in jest: "Maidenly delicacy, even yours, my dear wife, exerts but a limited charm—and the hour is late."

He believed he heard her voice, and as it did not seem she was asking him to wait, he slipped quietly into the candlelit room, closing the door behind him, and locking it; now beginning to tremble with a necessary and altogether natural masculine desire, lustful only if one subscribes to the scruples of our Puritan ancestors, but entirely normal if one recalls the admonition that Male and Female reproduce their kind, and populate the Earth, under God's command. That the desire to reproduce the human species is native to the masculine sex, and by no means an aberrant tendency, still less an inclination of disgusting perversity, must be kept in mind by the reader, else the behavior of our Constance Philippa will not seem so blasphemous as in truth it was.

The bride had already retired, and lay motionless in the recesses of the handsome canopied bed, near-lost in shadow, and in the flickering phantasmagoric light cast by the candelabrum, upon which twelve candles burnt to great effect. The Baron loosened his cravat, and, taking care to walk lightly around the various items of luggage, so as not to disturb his bride, locked both remaining doors of the bridal chamber—for, upon the occasion of his first marriage, now many years back, an unfortunate incident had transpired, owing to the infelicity of an unlocked door. He then retired to his dressing room where, quickly stripping himself of his numerous garments, he felt his manly lust grow, and could not resist glancing at himself in a mirror, which, tho' dim, presented a countenance of small but regular features, and a mustache of striking fullness, wonderfully black.

Past experience had taught him that it was far more pragmatic to act boldly, than to continue with a pretense of drawing-room manners, and so the Baron strode to the bed, and threw off the heavier of the covers, and, now nearly overcome by his natural masculine inclination, and by the labored dryness of his breath, he slid as adroitly as possible beneath the sheet, embraced his unresisting bride, mounted her, and, in a single gesture of great force and authority, made her his wife in the *Flesh,* as the Reverend Hewett had made her his wife, in *Spirit.*

Grunting, he then flung himself from her, and lay, panting, on the pillow beside hers, one forearm across his face, his eyes half shut, in an effort to recover himself; and, it may have been, the Baron murmured words of comfort or even of love to his spouse, in the throbbing tumult of those minutes; but none has been recorded. After a brief space of time the gentleman's breathing grew more regular, and he bethought himself to glance at his bride, who had, all this while, continued to lie motionless, with infinite tact, not disturbing the sanctity of the rite by moaning or sobbing, as others had done in the past—and I am scarcely able to force myself, to reveal what the Baron Adolf von Mainz saw: not the face of his belovèd bride, and not even her head: *but only the naked pillow.*

With a muttered exclamation he pulled the sheet away, and discovered, to his utter astonishment—alas, was ever a Christian husband so ill-treated?—that no woman lay beside him, no trembling Constance Philippa, nay, not even a human being, but a *dressmaker's dummy:* headless, armless, and possessing no nether limbs!

20

Not two mornings after the furious Baron von Mainz sent word by special messenger to Mr. and Mrs. Zinn, that his bride had disappeared from the Hotel de la Paix, on the very night of the wedding, and that he intended not only to demand an *annulment* of the marriage, but to seek such *financial restitution* as his legal advisors thought just, the following missive arrived at the Octagonal House, addressed likewise to Mr. and Mrs. Zinn, and hastily dashed off in Malvinia's graceless hand:

Dearest Mother & Father,
Forgive me, by the time you read this I will have left Philadelphia —it may be forever!—I had not wanted to disturb plans for the Wedding, & am now satisfied that my action cannot involve any save myself—but I have fallen in Love with the most talented & prodigious Man of our time—who has persuaded me, both to leave Philadelphia under his protection, & to embark upon a career on the stage, for which I have yearned throughout my life tho' hesitant to express my secret wishes, since I know of dear Father's displeasure in Entertainment & the family's disapproval of all Actors & Actresses. I scarcely know how to continue, dear Mother & Father, except to say that I am in love & very, very happy—for the first time in my somewhat troubled life—& a stage career now beckons, to pursue as I wish—for it is none other than the great ORLANDO VANDENHOFFEN under whose protection I am traveling at this very moment (for we wish to make our alliance a fact known to all the world, & not a contemptible Secret). I know you cannot so soon rejoice in my happiness, dear

Parents, but I ask you to think no ill of me, nor of Mr. Vanden-hoffen, & I beg you not to attempt to dissuade me from my Destiny, which lies, tho' it grieves me to be so blunt, not in Bloodsmoor, but in the great great World beyond!

Yr loving Daughter,
Malvinia

A less sensitive chronicler might attempt to convey to the reader, some measure of the heartbreak and anguish experienced by the parents of these two vicious creatures: but I confess myself incapable of such. *Constance Philippa* and *Malvinia!*—scarce am I able to utter their names!—but must content myself with a meditation upon the nature of God's paradoxical plan, and the transience of all things under the Sun, and the wisdom of this poem by the great Mr. Emerson, which Mr. Zinn, on the occasion of his and his family's double affliction, recited in a voice of bell-like clarity for his weeping family to ponder—

> Illusion works impenetrable,
> Weaving webs innumerable,
> Her gay pictures never fail,
> Crowds each on other, veil on veil,
> Charmer who will be believed
> By man who thirsts—to be *DECEIV'D.*

IV

The Yankee Pedlar's Son

21

Exemplary as John Quincy Zinn himself was, and as upstanding a citizen of our nation as might be found anywhere, it must be stated that his background was somewhat inglorious: and that, as a young man new to Philadelphia in the 1850's, his head slightly turned from all the excited attention he received, he had, perhaps instinctively, shrunk from revealing the *entire* truth about his family—and about himself.

Summoned to the city by Mr. Bayard, the State Supervisor of Public Education; taken up by the Arcadia Club; written about in the papers; a frequent guest of the Bayards, the Brownrriggs, the Kiddemasters—the twenty-six-year-old John Quincy Zinn had naturally avoided personal revelations, with the modesty of the born Transcendentalist: for one should after all dwell upon the *Universal,* and not upon the *Particular.* "Zinn, like any of us, might have been born the day before yesterday," he said with his boyish, disarming smile, "in the very Garden of Eden itself, which surrounds us, and is never new."

Even the outspoken Miss Prudence Kiddemaster failed to draw out of him anything like a complete history, which frequently exasperated her, and qualified the wild tone of her praise for him: and then again, as her fancy roamed, argued for his inviolable mystery—and his integrity. "You cannot anticipate marriage with a man about whom so little is known," her father said, badly shaken by Prudence's conversation with him, after the dramatic occasion of her fainting fit at the Bayards', "even if—as you say—he has stepped forward in public to 'claim you.' We are not, I hope, barbarians here in Philadelphia!"

"And yet, dear Father," Prudence said, "I *do* anticipate—a great deal. But we shall see."

The Zinn family was scattered, John Quincy explained, with an air of uncharacteristic sadness: perhaps it had even died out, and he was the last of his line. Certainly both his parents were dead—and his only brother, a sailor on one of Commodore Perry's great men-of-war, had died of a mysterious fever off Smyrna, and was buried at sea.

The farm above Christiana?—ah, long ago sold for taxes! It had never been very productive in any case, and young John Quincy had not greatly desired to take it over.

The first Zinn in the region, John Quincy's grandfather, was one Rudolph Zinn, an Austrian immigrant, who had, as a consequence of a severe wound suffered during an attack led by General Benjamin Lincoln against the British, remained in the Valley, evidently nursed back to health by a Quaker farm family. The young soldier had then married into the family, and taken up farming. A romantic outcome, Miss Kiddemaster judged, to a possibly tragic tale.

"I think not *romantic*, Miss Kiddemaster," John Quincy Zinn said slowly, stroking his beard, "but, rather, *necessary*. For all events occur as they must, in a universe of fluidly interlocking parts."

"I see," said Prudence, staring and blushing; tho' in fact she did not.

Alas, John Quincy Zinn's vague history of his background was *untrue!*—and one can only gauge the depth of his feeling for Prudence Kiddemaster, and his anxiety lest he disappoint his Philadelphia patrons, by our knowledge of how he abominated falsehood. And it may be, too, that the young man's immersion in books, and his frequently obsessive speculation upon the "nature of the Universe," had blurred his memory of particulars, especially as they touched upon *Evil*. (For, as we have seen, Mr. Zinn was passionately resistant to the very concept of *Evil*, judging that it could have no place in God's benign machinery.)

There had been, indeed, a Rudolph Zinn, a private in General Lincoln's infantry, and he was John Quincy Zinn's grandfather; but the "Zinn" connection was less legal than one might like—meaning by this that *illegitimacy* figured in John Quincy's background. *Zinn* was the young soldier's name, but *Zinn*, alas, never became the official name of the seventeen-year-old girl who bore his child, and fled away with it, upon the occasion of Zinn's execution in the spring of 1786. (For Zinn was executed, along with eleven other mutineers, on a parade ground in Morristown, New Jersey—an ignominious death, and yet one befitting a rebel, especially during such perilous times.)

It is not known, and surely the loss is not a significant one, what the surname was of the young woman who was John Quincy Zinn's paternal grandmother: enough for us to record that *Zinn* was the name she appropriated, as she appropriated from somewhere a plain, very thin gold wedding band, thereby deeming herself "wed," and the equal of any married woman she passed on the street! Her lover having been shot by a firing squad, she took her abrupt leave of Morristown and went to live with relatives in the village of Shaheen Falls, New York, where her illegitimate son, though unbaptized in any church, was known by the proud name of *John Jay Zinn*—this name being an indication more of the young mother's impetuous optimism, or of her simple ignorance, than her patriotic regard for the illustrious John Jay: for Mr. Jay, like George Washington, Alexander Hamilton, Henry Knox, and, indeed, General Benjamin Lincoln himself (who had, after all, ordered the mutineer Zinn's summary execution), and many another gentleman of the great Federalist party, was surely no friend of such desperadoes, vagabonds, and shiftless laborers from foreign shores, as she and her family no doubt were; and would have had little patience with her complaints, or with the ceaseless mob demands of her ilk. (And to think that the traitorous Daniel Shays and his rebels were yet to come, in the following year! Indeed, it is a wonder that the young nation did not expire in those early years, as George Washington so feared, beset on every side by rabble-rousers and self-styled "Republicans.")

Rudolph Zinn and his fellow mutineers were partly justified in their discontent, certainly, for they were in the unfortunate position, as soldiers in the Continental Army, of receiving their 22¢ daily salary in Continental currency, first issued in 1775, but, as the war continued, depreciating in its value some forty times—well-nigh worthless, in fact, by 1786, when various isolated mutinies flared up, and soldiers refused to accept payment in such currency, and in some cases (in Zinn's case, it may be inferred) incited others against accepting it. Discontent of this sort, coupled with the hardships of long winters and insufficient supplies, and rumors of Federalist money-making speculations, are perhaps comprehensible; but surely cannot excuse traitorous uprisings within the Continental Army, at a time when unity was so very necessary. So young Zinn was shot down, with eleven comrades, and buried in a pauper's grave, no doubt a mass grave, somewhere in Morristown, New Jersey: and one can hardly fault John Quincy, for choosing not to dwell upon his grandfather's fate. How much kinder, how much more idealistic, to imagine him as a soldier wounded in the service of his young country, and nursed back to health by a Quaker family in southeastern Pennsylvania!

Thus the grandfather, dead at the age of twenty-nine; and the father, tho' living to his fifties, doomed to suffer a particularly horrific death, an execution, too, of sorts—*tarred* and *feathered* and *hanged,* and *set ablaze,* by a drunken lynch mob, in the foothills of the Blue Mountains, in southern Pennsylvania.

For the father, John Jay Zinn, was not, as John Quincy suggested, a farmer; but instead a pedlar—one of that problematic itinerant tribe commonly known as *Yankee pedlars,* about whom so many tales have circulated, by no means of a generally flavorsome nature.

John Jay Zinn, the infamous pedlar: whose trade took him as far north as Bangor, Maine, and as far south as Raleigh, North Carolina. But it was only villages he dared visit—only isolated country settlements, or farms, or shanties up in the hills, stuck on the edge of nowhere.

On foot, or riding a swaybacked mare acquired in trade, or leading a donkey laden with goods. Alone, or with his son. Or with his mulatto mistress from Carolina; or was it Baltimore; or had she been found on a New York street . . . ? Carrying his heavy leather backpack, in the cold slanting rain, in the spring mud, through Maine and New Hampshire and Massachusetts, carrying a staff, limping badly, through Connecticut, his whiskers sprouting gunmetal-gray, *That damned Yankee crook,* through Rhode Island leading a sickly mule, head bowed against the sun, eyes narrowed in a permanent crafty squint, New York and Pennsylvania and New Jersey and Maryland, so many wives for so ugly a man, tall, gangling, sallow-faced, his expression carved out of hickory, his black eyes so sharp they could pick up the gleam of a coin at one hundred yards—in the dark; Shaheen behind him, and the Catskills, and the wintry Poconos, and the Delaware village where a man stabbed him high in the chest for cheating at cards, and no one intervened, *You won't dare show your ugly face here again,* bawling his trade, through marshlands where mosquitoes wouldn't touch him because his blood tasted of brass, along logging roads where screech owls hid from him, else he'd cheat them of their cash, Virginia and Carolina, Cape Hatteras where he had a woman, the outskirts of Lynchburg where he sold his services as a water diviner and walked off with $200 cash in his deep secret pockets, *Look at that blood!—is that real blood of his?—* but the well dried up the next morning, being only a witch-well, and nothing real.

John Jay Zinn, the pedlar. Tho' he went by other names. Alone, or with a fat wall-eyed slackly grinning girl staggering beneath a backpack filled with kitchen utensils and home remedies and outlaw (untaxed) rum, or with the little boy who must have been his son: blond and sunburnt and husky for his age, but crafty-silent. Marshlands, farmland, lanes oozing in black mud, where vultures rose slowly from the carcasses of horses fallen by the roadside, Prince George County, Blackstone, Hungry Mother Mountain, East Stone Gap, Manassas, a black preacher's coat flapping about his knees, loose in the sleeves so that his bony wrists showed, *He won't dare come back here again, he knows what will happen to him,* hawking false teeth for both male & female, young & old, wax-cleaners for ears, his trousers baggy in the seat and knees as if belonging to

another, larger man, solitary, singing and laughing to himself, counting
his money in the dark, long-fingered, selling Bibles and wire-framed
eyeglasses, the rattlers wouldn't come near for fear he'd cheat them of
their rattles, the blue racer snakes flew away in the trees, a tall white
bell-shaped hat stuck on his head, dented in the crown, heavy with gold
coins sewn up inside, the dripping pine forests of Carolina, the red-clay
foothills of Virginia, no flicker of expression in his nut-brown face, no
alarm, no apprehension, no fear, no terror, never a smile except that wide
lipless crafty grin, Ma'am, may I show you, Mister, may I demonstrate to
you, the wooden face, the glass eyes, *What was his name, Zinn?—or was that
the other one?* Alone and on foot and pretending to be penniless. A hacking
cough. Phlegm laced with blood in the palm of his hand, leaking through
the fingers. Alone or with an Indian woman. Or with his son. *The damned
Yankee crook—how did he get away so fast?*—disappearing around the bend
in the road, evaporating like mist, half the village's gold coins in his
pockets and the other half in the crown of his hat. *Yankee!*

John Jay Zinn, the pedlar from Maine. Or was it New York. Zinn
who spread typhoid one wet spring, along the shore of Delaware Bay.
Zinn who had left a wife behind in Shaheen Falls. And another wife in
Front Royal, in the Blue Ridge Mountains. He was six feet ten inches tall
—a loose-limbed gangling giant. Walked hunched forward, using his staff
as if he hated the ground and wanted to cause it pain. One winter, dressed
in beaver skins, short and plumped-out, ruddy cheeks, spectacles with
plain glass in them, to hide his squinting winking mocking eyes; the next
winter, skinny again, in knee-high leather boots stiff with mud, the old
broadcloth preacher's coat that wouldn't have been warm enough for a
normal man, the old soiled white hat dented in the crown: *Is that Zinn
again?—or that other Yankee crook?* Alone and coughing into his hand. Alone
and bawling songs, drunk, at the tavern on the creek in Fayette. He was
a spy for Jackson in the Carolinas, a spy for Calhoun in New England, he
had the power to arrest anyone fool enough to buy his untaxed rum, he
sold Dr. Bolton's Purgative Pills in the little green box with the legend
on the side *Caution: Not To Be Used By Females in the Pregnant State As
Miscarriage Might Occur,* the villagers flocked to him, attracted by a magnet
in the crown of his hat which drew their gold and silver coins and even
the fillings in their teeth. Quadrants for sale, seashells from the depths
of the ocean that foretold the future if you pressed your ear up close
enough, wigs for all sizes of heads made from human hair stiff as
horsehair, Professor Dobson's Portuguese Laudanum, a secret oily po-
tion "for men only," firecrackers and sparklers and gunpowder, even the
laziest woodchucks and possums could not resist, the white-tailed buck
traded his antlers, the squirrel traded his bushy plume of a tail, *Is that boy
of his touched in the head?—what a pity,* the Maryland flatlands, the New

Jersey pine barrens, December days when the sun never rose and the sky was a black lurid soup. *Damn Yankee spy.*

Bawling his wares. Alone or with one of his wives or with his little boy John Quincy. Like father, like son. Five years old, he was. A dwarf, twenty years old. Obedient, quick to duck from his father's fist, staggering beneath the weight of the backpack like a sickly little mule. Leather belts, earrings, wedding rings, "French perfume." Wax candles, candlestick holders, darning eggs, sleigh bells, tin crickets, magnifying glasses, pocket knives and paring knives and quill pens and India ink. Jacob's Antikink Medicine, Curtis's Manhood. Gold fillings *did* work their way out of your teeth, soon as you heard John Jay's bawling out in the road. He fed a sweet orange-tasting medicine to the blacksmith's thirteen-year-old daughter, out behind the cemetery, and walked away scot-free, disappeared around the bend in the road. He read aloud, laughing and wheezing, from *The Rip Snorter,* for customers who couldn't read. A face carved out of hickory, a breath dank and musty as a cellar, unblinking squinting eyes, grizzled eyebrows, *the damned cheating lying Yankee,* spreading influenza from Quakertown to Penns Grove on the Delaware to Cape May on the Atlantic. White hairs stiff as wires sprouting in his ears. Playing the mouth organ. The backpack swung to the ground with a groan, the black preacher's coat pale with dust, *God damn if it isn't him again! Lock your doors and bolt your shutters and plug up the chimney!* The foothills of the Blue Mountains, the steep red-clay roads of the Catskills, twilight in the Poconos, the smell of snow, the smell of winter, a blood blister on the child's left heel, John Jay Zinn treating all the men at the gunpowder mill, John Jay Zinn dragging the child (asleep on his feet) into a corner of the tavern, John Jay Zinn slapping the hysterical woman across each cheek, matching blow for blow as she slapped *him: You got to admire Zinn, playing the game like he was in it to save his life.*

Fancy pocket knives with five blades, bolts of calico, ladies' hats pretty as the ones worn in Boston, pots and pans guaranteed never to tarnish, Dr. Elton's Never-Fail Kidney Pills, paper collars, leather shoes, hairbrushes, tortoise-shell combs. Aquashicola on the Appalachian Trail, Geneva on Seneca Lake, Chazy Landing on Lake Champlain, that cold crafty unmistakable smile, tobacco-stained and gat-toothed, his own false teeth, dentures made of wood. Sometimes with the unprotesting child whose mouth was slack with fatigue, sometimes alone, in his thigh-high fisherman's boots, striding over the hill whistling a tuneless song, or sleeping in a ditch motionless as a dead man. (Nearby were three buzzards on a fence—not *watching* Zinn but *watching over* him.) *But is he dead? Is that real blood?—the damned Yankee.*

Spring mist, a pitiless August sun, cracks in the red soil, *The Old Farmer's* for sale cheap, Rhode Island and Connecticut, pewter mugs with grinning teeth and ears for handles, the five-year-old boy, six years old, husky in the shoulders, shy, a curious birthmark on his temple, the sign of the Devil, New Hampshire and sleet and dogs tearing at their legs, Maine and fever, gloves missing fingers, shoes with paper-thin soles, razors that cut your face so you find yourself bleeding from a dozen little wounds—*John Jay Zinn the pedlar, the Yankee crook.* Cheating at cards but no one saw how. Walking away with so many gold and silver coins, his heels dragged. And around the bend—nothing! Disappeared into the air. Into a raven squawking and jeering overhead. And the little boy—turned into a starling. Flying away, flying overhead, jeering and squawking. Buckshot can't touch them.

A bigamist many times over. Wives in Portland and Concord and Hartford and Shaheen and Wilmington and New Hope and Shenandoah, Dr. Petersham's Home Remedy for Ailments of the Digestive System, Heart Pains, Shredded Nerves, Female Complaints, a sure-fire cure for carbuncles warts inflamed moles cancers of the skin. A spy of King Andrew's. Chest hollow as a drum, nothing behind the eyeglasses, ears baked and cracked like crockery, spreading syphilis, spreading consumption, toes amputated for frostbite, cuckoo clocks that fall apart in a week, razors that cut your fingers as soon as you pick them up, cotton nightcaps stained with blood, the wide slow mocking grin, the tobacco-stained teeth, Yes, ma'am, no, ma'am, I have here, ma'am, let me show you, ma'am, bolts of raw silk from China direct off the ship, buttons of all sizes and kinds—mother-of-pearl and bone and tortoise-shell and jade—he peddled false teeth to the fools in Christiana that never needed them, he peddled tin crosses to the fools in Portsmouth to cure them of influenza, he betook himself ten miles up the road to sell henna rinse to three old baldheaded spinsters, he got married to the old drag-on-widow who ran the Three Bells, and she up and died and he inherited, the same thing happened at West Almond Creek, and in Laurel, Delaware, but her sons got wind of it and chased him hell to leather, would have rode him on a pike if they'd caught him, that was only last year. Forty years old, forty-seven years old, fifty, bastards up and down the coast, nigger brats, the rich Carolina valleys, rain in the Adirondacks, outlaw rum, tobacco chews, spools of thread, beads and sequins and pearls and rhinestones for the ladies, Dr. Roley's Brazilian Hair Curling Liquid, bawling at the top of his lungs, coughing, wheezing, spitting bloody phlegm onto the sawdust floor, Guerlain's Lustral Water, Rowland's Essence of Tyre, Jones's Oil of Coral Circassia, Balm of Columbia, Cream of Lilies, Dr. Kiely's Pomatum, Ring's Verbena, Henry's Chinese Cream, Brown's Windsor Soap, Esprit de Cédrat for the Complexion, Sirop de Boubie, Blanc de Neige, Micheaux's Freckle Wash. Measuring spoons that wouldn't measure, matches that wouldn't

light, doorknobs that wouldn't turn, needles that wouldn't pierce the
flimsiest cloth, bedbug poison the bedbugs lapped up like gruel. He
never blinked when a steel fishing knife slammed into the wall beside
his head, he never did more than cough and sputter when his nose was
broke, and gushed blood, he eased himself up all six feet ten inches
weighing maybe one hundred twenty pounds and walked to the door
and stepped outside into the moonlight and disappeared: just disappeared into the air: and only the blood-splashes left behind.

Taking orders for portable prebuilt houses (Louisiana French
style), $10 deposit, reading from *Mrs. Unger's Manual of Social and Busi-
ness Forms* for the ladies who couldn't read, playing the harmonica, playing the fiddle, tapping his foot, the dancers whipping past him, his eyeglasses winking. Arrested for selling untaxed rum and beaten to death
on the road and left in the ditch and the next year there he was again!
—big as life striding over the hill, raising dust, leaning on his staff, *Lock
your doors and bolt your windows, it's the Yankee pedlar again,* hat racks for
sale, satin cravats only a little soiled, floral-printed oilcloth, last year's
calendar, *The Frugal Housewife's Almanack,* slop jars, children's boots,
glass bells, tincture of benzoin, ginger cough lozenges, heavy carbonate
magnesia, oil of aniseed, Cascara Sagrada Pills, Paregoric Elixir, am-
moniated quinine, oxalic acid powder, essence of pennyroyal, essence
of cloves, eucalyptus oil, belladonna, sugar of lead, liquorice, Buck-
thorn's Syrup, flower of sulphur. Bedwarmers, wool-flock, ambergris
for fertility, Florentine orris-root for toothache, gentlemen's embroidered waistcoats, aigrettes for the ladies, of tinted feathers, shawls of
Spanish rabbit skin, black plush purses, lace collars and cuffs, Yes,
ma'am, no, ma'am, I have here, ma'am, let me shut the door, ma'am, no
pupils in his eyes, no heartbeat in his chest, the boy isn't his son, they
don't look alike, he must be kidnapped, taken somewhere along the
road, buckshot can't touch them.

In Shinnecock, Virginia, the sheriff arrested him and locked him
in jail and by morning the pedlar had beat him at cards so bad, the
inside of the jail was stripped, even the corn-shuck mattress, even the
sheriff's glass eye, and in Oriskany on the Hudson they thought to play
a practical joke on him, put a noose around his neck and dragged him
out of the tavern, and halfway to where they were going he talked them
out of all the coins in their pockets *and* the noose, and ain't been back
since.

The boy was crying and the tears looked real but the birthmark on
the side of his face gave the game away. The Devil's own. A flintlock fired
in the face, his head ducked in the cattle dung pond, *Is that real blood?—
that ain't never real blood,* and next April turning the bend in the road, dry
September hawking Bibles and glass paperweights and water-diviners
along the Trenton Pike, through the Delaware Valley leading a sickly

mule, in Virginia marshlands where the mosquitoes that bit him dropped dead at his feet, in Allegheny County, in Stowe Creek Landing, along the Schuylkill, the boy helping him walk, the boy carrying the heavier of the backpacks, cheeks glistening with tears, like father like son, they ain't never father and son, *You can't hurt them you can't touch them Yankees how did they escape so fast where did they go . . . ?*

22

In the tumultuous weeks and months before their engagement was officially announced, before, indeed, John Quincy Zinn had so publicly claimed her for his own, Miss Prudence Kiddemaster was disturbed by rumors involving not only her suitor's interest in other young heiresses, but his background itself: detractors whispered that the famous experimental school in the hills was less of a success than radical educators knew, and that the Zinns were shrouded in ignominy, as it were, a male Zinn having been executed as a common felon, and John Quincy Zinn, motherless and fatherless, shipped away to an orphanage . . . a Catholic orphanage, in Baltimore, perhaps; or in Wilmington; or New York.

Pride contended with curiosity, in our restless young lady, who refused for a considerable space of time to honor such vaporous rumors by so much as recording them in her diary. *I know not what to think*, Prudence Kiddemaster wrote, *but I know—ah, surely!—what to feel*. She might have followed the example of the self-assured Horace Bayard who, in his role as public educator, invested with a good deal of authority, had for decades airily dismissed all doubts, and many facts, that ran counter to his own interpretation of the world; she might have sought out the source of the rumors—to discover, no doubt, that they were concocted by men jealous of young Zinn's rapid rise to prominence as a popular lecturer, much admired by the ladies, and a member of Dr. Bayard's Association for the Reform of Common Schools, and a man-about-town of sorts, lionized in the very smartest circles. That her reputation—indeed, her very life—would someday be linked to his, the impetuous young woman fantasized almost hourly; and her heart was storm-toss'd with doubt. For tho' she loved him, and thrilled to his words, she was not always certain that she comprehended those words—or could safely believe them.

So discreetly, however, did she broach the subject of *Catholicism* to John Quincy (by way of a warm inquiry into the background of his boardinghouse acquaintance Mr. Guiteau, an admitted Catholic, but one no longer practicing his gothic rite), and learn to her satisfaction that he knew very little about it, and *very* little he found encouraging, that her sensitive suitor never guessed she was interrogating him; discreetly, too, she inquired after his parents, only to learn that his dear mother had been carried áway by tuberculosis, shortly after John Quincy's birth, and that his father had died a martyr's death at an Abolitionists' rally, upon the occasion of the passage of that unspeakable act of 1850, but that, for many reasons, he did *not* wish to publicize the fact.

"I see!—ah yes, I see!" Prudence exclaimed, quite stricken. "You would not—you *must* not—wish to capitalize, or to seem to capitalize, upon such tragedy."

"Miss Kiddemaster," John Quincy said, flushing, and lowering his eyes, "you understand me thoroughly."

If, as the faithful chronicler of the Zinns' destinies, I frequently draw back in trepidation at the task before me, and torture myself with the question —as, indeed, glorious Milton must oft have tortured himself, and the great Bard, and our courageous Harriet Beecher Stowe, to name one close to home, and of my own humble sex—the question of whether *Evil* may be liquefied in *Moral Art;* if, as one laboring to suggest the fructuousness of even the most dismaying and self-serving acts amongst these persons, I am subject to moments, nay, hours and days, of *doubt,* I hope the reader will grant me patience, and some sympathy. For if the *Evil* I must in all sincerity transcribe (being not entirely of Mr. Zinn's admirable Transcendentalist belief that *Evil* by its very nature cannot share the universe with *God*) is to be truly comprehended, and thereby, as it were, liquefied, in the service of a *Moral Art,* how may the chronicler proceed except by way of a fastidious recounting of all that transpires . . . no matter how hideous? For I cannot believe that Evil for all its power is finally inexpungible, in art as in life.

But here is the great Cowper, to express this sentiment in verse—

> But though life's valley be a vale of tears,
> A brighter scene beyond that vale appears,
> Whose glory, with a light that never fades,
> Shoots between scatter'd rocks and opening shades.

It was on a chill October night, by the austere irradiation of the harvest moon, on the outskirts of a nameless little hamlet in the Blue Mountains of Pennsylvania, that the pedlar John Jay Zinn met his sad fate, and the eight-year-old John Quincy became, indeed, an orphan—tho' the reader will be relieved to know that he was certainly not shipped to a Catholic orphanage, in Baltimore or anywhere else, but was brought up in a Christian home, amidst good country people who had taken pity on him, and did not tar him—as it were—with his father's sins.

It may indeed have been as a consequence of Abolitionist quarreling, or a false, febrific rumor, to the effect that the Yankee pedlar was in fact a Masonic spy (for these were the curious years of the Anti-Masons, led by the fiery Thaddeus Stevens of Gettysburg); tho' it is more reasonable to suspect that the murderers of John Jay Zinn simply wished to punish him, because he had cheated them a twelve-month before—he or another Yankee pedlar who closely resembled him, attired similarly in a black broadcloth coat, and a misshapen hat (now white, now gray, now black, now decorated with a pheasant feather in the band, now plain as that of a Baptist preacher's), and accompanied by a child so abash'dly silent, he was believed to be mute. It is reasonable too to suspect that, given the degree of drunkenness of the murderers, and the unspeakably cruel torture to which they subjected their victim, before merciful death at last blotted out his suffering, that *alcohol* itself may stand indicted; and that the pleas of the Temperance Movement, tho' oft derided in the popular press, and even by gentlemen of culture and social standing, must heretofore be granted a greater authority.

Indeed, John Jay Zinn's unfortunate demise may be directly traced to *his having entered a lowlife establishment that served alcoholic beverages,* including cheap gin, beer, and ale; and to his having unwisely joined with a group of revelers, who noisily welcomed him to their party. (This party must not have seemed at first to be hostile, let alone dangerous, if we are to credit the pedlar with the shrewdness for which he was so widely known.) Soon falling in with their camaraderie, tho', at the age of about fifty, he was some twenty years older than the eldest, he treated them to a round of drinks, as is the custom, I believe, in such establishments; and to another; and yet another—as a stratagem to win their good will, perhaps, or out of simple vainglory. (For John Jay Zinn thought well of himself and could not resist, at such times, *throwing his money around,* as the colorful expression goes: and how imprudently, at this particular time!)

And all the while, in an unheated haybarn a quarter-mile distant, little John Quincy slumbered, protected by the deep, dreamless sleep of the child who is both pure of heart and drained of strength by recent physical exertion, for his father had forced him to walk a great many miles that day, burdened by a backpack inordinately heavy with iron kitchen utensils. So exhausted was the child he had fallen asleep midway through his simple repast of stewed mutton and potatoes, and had been slapped awake by his father, never one to cosset the weak, and anxious as ever to reward himself for a day's labor by partaking of alcoholic beverages. (Sleep away, poor child—for you are shortly to be awakened by bestial shouts and screams, which will pursue you for much of your life!)

That John Jay Zinn would willingly step foot inside a crude country tavern, let alone join with a group of drunken ruffians of the tribe who swept Andrew Jackson into office, and rejoiced at the destruction of Mr. Biddle's bank, testifies to something very much amiss in his nature; that he would drink for five or six hours, forgetting his son, and neglecting his own need for sleep, testifies to a want of sense we must judge *ominous*. Unsurprising it is, that the mood of the party gradually altered as the participants grew ever more intoxicated and began to bait the pedlar with various accusations and charges—some of them too shameful to be recorded; nor is it surprising that the foolish man, so overcome with drink that he staggered and all but toppled to the filthy sawdust floor, should have attempted to defend himself, by shouting and waving his fists and attempting to outshine his opponents with sheer vituperative wit. They jeered, and mocked, and grew more restive, and were joined by other louts, and at the closing of the tavern still others came by, there being now a general outcry of sorts, that the criminal *Yankee pedlar* had been caught, who had, some time previously, perpetrated a fraud upon certain members of the settlement by "divining" spring water for a considerable payment (tho' the sum greatly varied, growing as voice was added to voice in the excitement of the moment). He had promised them a well—a well of the sweetest and purest spring water—he had strode about with his divining rod held high, and a crafty-dreamy expression on his face, and after some hours, having traversed the village, and making a great show of the procedure, he had *found* it: allowing them to see how the divining rod fairly leapt in his hands, its fork jerking downward. And they had dug at that spot for water, and found it; and had, in all gratitude, paid the pedlar generously for his service.

But the well had dried up in a few days! Its sweet pure water had turned sandy, and then muddy; and then it had dried up. Some said it was a *witch-well*, and had never had any water at all—only the illusion of water. But by then, naturally, the dishonest Yankee had made his escape, and no one could guess where he might be found.

A wiser man than John Jay Zinn might have allowed that the incident had indeed transpired, perpetrated by another pedlar; but that he, out of a sense of obligation, or sympathy for the villagers, would make proper restitution. A wiser man, surely, would have refrained from shouting back at his drunken tormentors, and suggesting that they were naught but fools and knaves in any case. But John Jay Zinn was *not* a wise man, nor, I fear, a man in whose heart a lucid moral sense had been cultivated; and so he argued with the ruffians, and scuffled with them, and soon all the rabble had gathered, and a small tub of tar was being heated in the blacksmith's shop nearby, and there were war whoops and Indian yells, and no lawman within earshot who gave a fig for the pedlar's fate, and so—and so it happened that John Jay Zinn suffered that excruciating torture of being "tarred and feathered," an American folk-custom still thought, by those unaware of its brutality, to be faintly risible. The tar was brushed and poured on him in great steaming gobs, and soon the moonlit autumnal calm was shattered by his screams of agony, and the poor child in the haybarn awakened in terror, and the bestial prank, once begun, could not be stopped. For one thing, the villagers expressed surprise and delight that the pedlar could be made to feel *pain* at all: they had imagined him a being unlike themselves, whom no one could seriously injure!

(Ignorant, subhuman creatures, the reader may safely conclude: a people so accursèd with bestiality as to give credence to the utterances of such Americans as John Randolph and Alexander Hamilton, who doubted from the first the value, let alone the possibility, of *Democracy*. As for their hapless victim, John Jay Zinn—it is very difficult for me to speak. I see him, I believe, as clearly as I have ever seen any living person, tho' in fact I have never literally set eyes upon him, but have been empowered, so to speak, to *imagine* him, through the recollections of his son; I am capable of "hearing" his voice too, hawking his wares, in one little settlement after another, along the endless ribbon of road that is our nation, lonely to the core, and eluding God's own blessing. His preacher's coat, his eccentric hat, his wooden face and unblinking eyes, the way he leaned upon his staff when no one but John Quincy was a witness, sighing with arthritic pain . . . His solitude, his chilling and relentless industry, so without ambition, and without evidence of a *soul* . . . I see, I hear, I tremble with apprehension for his fate, and share with his wretched son the terror of that night; and yet I cannot *know* him.

Nor do I wish to know him, despite my natural Christian pity for the suffering he endured, a "martyr's" death of a sort, it may be; and the probability of a harsh divine retribution to follow.

That he was the father of our hero is certainly a puzzle, and yet it cannot be an edifying one, and I will not dwell upon it. Pity for the repulsiveness of his death soon crumbles in the face of a profound instinctual displeasure in his being, and a reluctant but incontestable rejection of the immoral life he led. Poor man! poor sinner! That you existed at all, let alone as the father of John Quincy Zinn, argues for the inscrutability of God's ways!—and, it may be, for His vast all-inclusive Love.)

The eight-year-old boy, precociously wise, seemed to know upon the instant of his startl'd awakening not only *what* was happening in the village, but *to whom* it was happening; and tho' he fully grasped the nature of the danger to himself (both as the pedlar's son, and as a witness from the outside world to the crime), and was shivering and whimpering with sheer animal fright, he nonetheless ran after the boisterous mob, calling over and over *Father! Father!*— a more piteous and heartrending spectacle, one cannot wish to imagine.

Alas, the child did witness his father's ignominious death—the aftermath of the tarring and feathering, which involved a clumsy attempt at hanging, and the setting aflame of the limp (and perhaps, by then, lifeless) body, to the noisy satisfaction of the crowd. He heard, he saw, he cried out "Father—!" but there was no help for the doomed man, and no help for the child, who very narrowly escaped with his own life when certain members of the crowd turned their attentions upon him, and quickly calculated, despite their drunkenness, the threat he represented.

There is a tale of my illustrious compatriot Hawthorne's, set in remote Colonial times, in which a youth seeks a wealthy kinsman only to discover that the elderly Major has been tarred and feathered, in protest of British authority, and dragged along in an uncovered cart by a torchlit procession; the persecuted old man is described by Mr. Hawthorne as possessing, even in his humiliation, a "tar-and-feathery dignity." And so absurd is the spectacle, so infectiously merry, that the ingenuous young kinsman joins in the crowd's laughter! One cannot fault Mr. Hawthorne for the precision of his prose style, here as elsewhere, or for the stern wisdom of his vision, but one must question whether "dignity" of any sort is available when one is in excruciating agony from burns to the flesh; or whether laughter, however infectiously communal, is an appropriate human response, to so lurid a sight.

Surely few amidst even that crowd of wretches laughed with true merriment at the death throes of their victim, a bizarre sight in the flames —so erratically covered with white goose feathers, his face seemed hardly human. And the victim's young kinsman, stricken with terror, had no thought now but to escape with his life, his father's life being lost.

And so, pursued by several burly louts, including a beardless drunken youth not many years older than himself, John Quincy ran into the woods—he ran, and ran, and ran—deep into the woods—deep into the chill eerie gloom, where the moonlight could not penetrate, while behind him shouts and whoops rang out, as if it were all a game. He ran until his breath came in shreds, and his small heart beat madly in his chest; and at last, after a very confused space of time, the shouts behind him grew fainter, and dissolved into the night; and a forlorn *whooooing* that must have been the call of an owl, was all that sounded.

In a virtual convulsion of shivering, of both cold and terror, the pathetic child crawled into a thicket to hide; and, when he believed he had brought his trembling under control, he scrambled out, and climbed a tree—a many-branchèd oak—clumsily and yet with great industry he climbed, and climbed—until his hands, though callused, began to bleed

—and still he climbed the great oak—the vision of his defiled father behind him—and the start of the licking flames—and the shouts and whoops of his tormentors—and still he climbed, panting, near-sobbing, until, like a fairy child in one of the old legends, he emerged at last from the gloom of the forest, and entered into the moonlight's realm once more, dazed and exhausted, yet withal not without a sense of animal relief, judging himself (however prematurely) safe from his father's murderers.

So John Quincy Zinn climbed the great oak, his nails torn and his fingers bleeding, and did manage to save himself, the spark of life being so courageous within him. At the top of the tree he secured himself into a kind of cradle, and, clinging to the rough-bark'd trunk, he drifted off into a light, chaotic sleep, waking some time later—how long, he could not hope to judge—to a renewed commotion of voices and footsteps, and an occasional crashing in the underbrush. A lone high-pitched voice arose, a stranger's voice: "Little John Quincy," the voice called, "your father is asking for you, your father wants you by his side, where are you hiding," the voice approached, and then faded, "are you in the bushes here, are you up a tree, come down, little John Quincy," the voice drew nearer suddenly, "come down, I say, come out of hiding, don't you know your father wants you, your father is very angry, he wants you by his side, come down, boy, come *here*—"

But the prescient child, clinging to the great trunk, stayed exactly where he was.

23

Thus, the unspeakable evils of drink and dissipation; and an indelicacy of comportment so extreme as to render all moral judgment superfluous. It is no wonder that the young John Quincy Zinn became an avowed abstainer from drink, and an enthusiastic supporter of the Temperance Movement; and that, many years later—ah, it is a mercy to count how many!—he frequently joined his womenfolk in the parlor, around the piano (which Mrs. Zinn, Malvinia, and Octavia played in turn, being more gifted than Samantha and Constance Philippa), and sang with them, in a voice that never faltered, one or another of the great old Temperance songs. Tho' many were published in sheet music form, and even the least inspired offered wisdom, it is Henry Clay Work's superb "Come Home, Father," that best expressed the spirit of the movement, and the pathos of the child victimized by parental neglect. This melancholy but beautifully melodic tale of a young girl sent to fetch her father from the tavern, that he might kiss his dying son goodnight, must have awakened unfortunate memories in Mr. Zinn's heart; yet of course he gave no indication, and the tear or two he might have surreptitiously wiped from his eyes, as the plaintive chorus echoes, again and again—

> Hear the sweet voice of the child,
>   Which the nightwinds repeat as they roam!
> Oh, who could resist this most pleading of prayers?
>   "Please, father, dear father, come home!"

—this tear, I venture, seemed no more than an o'erspilling of the sentiment of the moment, and could have awakened no undue curiosity in

Mrs. Zinn or the sisters. For even the approximate nature of Mr. Zinn's childhood was unknown to them; and prudently so.

Nineteen years after the events of that horrific night, when pressed to deliver himself of the *particulars* of his background by the Honorable Godfrey F. Kiddemaster, who had summoned him out to Kiddemaster Hall in Bloodsmoor, for a private meeting, John Quincy Zinn looked his prospective father-in-law frankly in the eye, and spoke of domestic tragedy ensuing in part from family illnesses, and in part from impoverishment; he spoke briefly of having spent an intermittent period of time, as a boy, in the hire of farmers in the Blue Mountain region—German, Dutch, Quaker. They were good people, he averred, and treated him well: tho' naturally he was expected to work hard.

He had always been mechanical-minded, and gifted with his hands; but it was in '45 or '46, he told Judge Kiddemaster, a faint blush stealing over his cheeks, at the confusion and, as it were, displeasure of speaking so lengthily about himself, that he deemed himself *born:* born into a sense not only of the miraculous interweaving of spirit that constitutes the Visible Universe, but to a sense of his own place within it, and, it may be said, his own Destiny.

This felicitous awakening was occasioned by his having come upon, in a bookseller's stall in Allentown, the writings of Ralph Waldo Emerson, a name altogether new to him (for he was only seventeen or eighteen at the time, and, tho' decidedly bookish for a rural youth, and set apart from his contemporaries by a unique liveliness of intelligence, he *was* a farmboy without doubt); a name, and a voice, and a commandeering vision hardly to be resisted. He quickly scanned the great essay "Nature," whilst standing at the bookstall, his trembling hands shaking the page, and thrilled to the wisdom therein, that the Supreme Being does not create nature about us, but puts it forth *through* us; that we are immortal, for we learn that *time* and *space* are relations of matter, and that, with a perception of truth or a virtuous will, *they have no affinity.*

A man, John Quincy Zinn dared to lecture Judge Kiddemaster (whom he suspected of wishing to interrupt—for Prudence's father had drawn breath, and was staring most intently at John Quincy), a man is after all fashioned by Nature, and indebted to the culture of the past only as its *Master;* and he must express himself in action in order to influence society, not hide away in his study, or in the woods, or in one or another comfortable retreat from responsibility. It was of course John Quincy Zinn's ambition—to which he hesitated to give the grand name *Destiny*— to influence his nation by the labor of his brain and hands, joining with that *American Destiny* as one individual among many, grateful for the opportunity even, if need be, to sacrifice himself.

The older man regarded him with pale, somewhat frosty eyes, and for a long imperious moment did not choose to reply. Behind and above him, to the left, were six handsome silver tankards (by Paul Revere, in fact —tho' young John Quincy did not know this at the time); to the right, in stately calf bindings, with gilt-stamped titles, the collected works of Hobbes, Machiavelli, and Lord Macaulay. No smile softened the Judge's stern expression (tho' his young opportuner had been smiling a great deal, and freely perspiring); it may even have been the case that his proud posture grew stiffer. And yet his words were gentle—and gently offered. He said, as John Quincy Zinn leaned eagerly forward, as if to hear a verdict handed down, alas, from the bench! "My dear boy, you are young: but you will not always be so."

It may be that the reader, despite repugnance for such details as I have felt constrained to record, in connection with the problematic matter of John Quincy Zinn's orphaning, harbors some small curiosity as to the aftermath of the child's escape, for I have left him, I recall of a sudden, at the very top of a many-branchèd oak; and no succor in view.

Strange it was, this aftermath; tho' no stranger, I must conclude, than much that has transpired, and will transpire, in my chronicle. For in the chill light of dawn young John Quincy awakened to the sound of a woman's voice far below, and tho' he gripped the tree trunk with an instinctive cunning, and did not for some time allow himself even to glance downward (as if fearing so subtle a movement might attract attention), he seemed to understand at once, that the full-throated warmth of this voice, however unfamiliar to him, promised a genuine aid. "Good morn, little boy, do you hear me, are you up there?—little boy?—yes?— will you come down?—and quickly, quickly!—for there is no time to spare."—So the strange voice wafted up to him, and after no more than a minute's hesitation, during which time his red-rimmed eyes worked furiously in his head, the child's heart relaxed: and he made the decision, which quite altered the course of his remarkable life, *to trust the voice, and to climb down.*

And so, indeed, he did. With that cautious and somewhat awkward precision of a cat, lowering itself from a height it has scaled with great alacrity.

In silence John Quincy Zinn returned to the ground, where stood a woman he had never before set eyes upon, yet seemed in a way to know: of no more than modest height, yet sturdy and full-bodied, with a strong jaw, and ruddy cheeks, and glistening eyes that belied the severe furrowing of her brow. She urged him to hurry; clucked at him impatiently; would have caught him in her strong arms and pulled him down, from a height of perhaps five feet, had he not jumped to the ground. She wore a plum-colored cape of coarse wool, with a hood that nearly covered her braided hair, and might have been in her mid-thirties, or younger; she was carrying a woollen blanket, which she immediately draped about John Quincy's shoulders.

"Now come with me, do not tarry: for we have a journey before us," she said, taking him immediately by the hand, and pulling him along. He did not resist: had no thought of resisting: but obeyed her without a scruple. Indeed, it was a measure of the eight-year-old orphan's trust in this woman, as well as the desperation of his plight, that he had no thought to draw away from her, but had in fact to resist a sudden need to burrow into her embrace, and burst into wanton tears. "Come, come," she murmured, taking no time to glance at him, but rubbing his raw, chafèd, cold-stiffened fingers with hers, "it is already dawn, and more than dawn; and we must set you on your way. God has His plans for you, my son—but we must make haste."

She strode resolutely forward, and he followed, his panting breath turned to vapor. Haste!—they must make haste! After some strenuous minutes his knees buckled and he would have collapsed, had his able benefactress not caught him in her arms, and borne him aloft. She carried him out of the depths of the forest into an open place, a hilly meadow —and then down a steep incline—and finally to a lane, where a horse-drawn wagon awaited; and the driver, with a muttered exclamation, leapt down to offer aid. John Quincy was now but partly conscious: he had a confused impression of a rough-hewn but kindly face, and a pair of small, keen, dark eyes, as stronger arms bundled him up into the wagon, and hid him beneath the blanket and a layer of damp hay.

And then off—off they galloped, into the fresh chill mists of an autumn dawn in the mountains. The Devil himself might have been in pursuit, the driver so urged his horse forward, and the old wagon groaned and creaked.

So the pedlar's son was rescued, and carried some thirty-five miles away, to a farming region north of Germantown, on the Granitehill River: which distance might have been a thousand miles from the village in which his father was tarred and feathered, for in those days the valleys had little to do with one another, and village looked with uninquisitive suspicion upon village. News spread slowly, if at all; the fact that a parentless young boy was taken in by a Dutch farm family near Germantown, was a fact of virtually no interest to anyone.

How John Quincy came to be brought to the Van Dusens, and *why* the woman in the plum-colored cape rescued him, were not questions the boy asked himself at the time; nor did he exhibit much curiosity about the past, as the years unfolded. He quite readily adapted to his new family, discovering himself the youngest of five children, and as zealous as the oldest boy (some nine years his senior) when it came to work in the fields, and in and around the barns. He was so profoundly grateful for his having been rescued, and years on the road as a pedlar's son had so accustomed him to fortuities of all kinds, he demonstrated little surprise at his fate; and perhaps even his nights were dreamless—for he worked very hard, and took an evident satisfaction in his labor.

He never did inquire about the circumstances of his rescue. But over the years he pieced together the fairly simple explanation: the woman in the plum-colored cape and her husband had learned of the atrocity committed against his father, and against him; they had pitied him, and sought him out, and carried him off to the Van Dusens of Germantown—the woman being a cousin of Mrs. Van Dusen, and confident as to the family's Christian benevolence.

John Quincy did not torture himself with the questions—did his Van Dusen brothers and sisters know of his father's fate?—did they look upon him with pity?—for he pondered little upon the past, and resolutely turned his thoughts elsewhere. He was soon praised for his quick wits, the dexterity of his hands, and his sunny disposition. He loved books, and so was fondly teased for being a "scholar"; he loved to work with tools, repairing and improving upon farm implements, and so was teased for being a "tinkerer." If his foster family seemed to him at times a dream-concoction, a bubble which malevolent daylight might pierce, it might have been the case that John Jay Zinn himself had been, to his son, something of a dream: and one was as readily accommodated as the other, in a child so young. If the boy suffered visions of a twisted, writhing body—if he saw again the hideous contorted face, blackened with tar, fluttering-white with feathers, splashed with bright red blood across the eyes—he gave no indication; his was a stalwart and forthrightly *physical* temperament, very much at home amongst the Van Dusens.

Thus, the dramatic rescue of little John Quincy; and the radical alteration of his life.

As for the murdered John Jay—no doubt his body was simply dragged away and buried in an unmarked grave, and quickly forgotten. Not a word about him, not a whisper!—and surely no one in the village dared report the crime. Many convinced themselves, no doubt, that the Yankee pedlar, being what he was, deserved any fate that came his way; few indeed were those who believed he had not, however crudely, met with justice. Lest the reader think such persons barbarians, and not citizens of our rural America in those years, he is advised to look into the chronicles of local history if he will—and if he dare.

24

An ineluctable course, or one guided wantonly by Chance? So the school-master John Quincy Zinn must oft have pondered upon the mystery of his life, as he gazed over the bent heads of his twenty students; so he must have brooded, while vigorously sweeping the schoolhouse floor, and sawing and chopping firewood for the old Franklin stove, and making an heroic effort, every few days, to maintain the doubtful cleanliness of the outhouses, some distance behind the schoolhouse, on the bank of a narrow meandering stream.

That his Destiny was enigmatic, he could not doubt. That it *existed* —and lay shimmering before him—he dared not doubt. For was he not, by a fortuitous stroke, suddenly made schoolmaster of the Mouth-of-Lebanon common school?—the former schoolmaster, a young man not many years John Quincy's senior, having made an abrupt departure. (John Quincy had been hired for this position upon the enthusiastic recommendation of the Van Dusen family, and other families in the area, who knew and admired him as a "scholar," yet did not doubt his capacity —evidenced by his husky shoulders and arms, and a certain quiet reso-luteness in his face—to keep the larger and less disciplined boys in line.)

And so, from the age of eighteen to the age of twenty-five, John Quincy Zinn taught eight grades at the Mouth-of-Lebanon school, some twelve miles south of Germantown; and tho', in later years, he frequently alluded to his "schoolmaster days" with an air of fond regret, and won-dered aloud whether Education, after all, should not have drawn the brunt of his considerable energy, it cannot be said—as the reader shall shortly learn—that John Quincy departed Mouth-of-Lebanon with much more reluctance, perhaps, than we might attribute to his predecessor, about whom so little was said save that he "failed to adjust himself" to the rigors of common school teaching in general, and Mouth-of-Lebanon in particular.

His greatest trial came, as one might expect, almost immediately upon his arrival at Mouth-of-Lebanon, for it was then that the older boys tested him, slyly gauging how far they might go in slouching in their desks at the rear of the room, crossing their long legs in the aisles, drawling or muttering answers when called upon, and neglecting to say "Sir"; and in bullying the younger children, some of whom were their own brothers and sisters. Buck, Homer, Carleton—these were the "big" boys, in fact quite tall, tho' only fourteen and fifteen years old: not truly rebellious, in John Quincy's opinion, and surely not bad, but naturally restive in their seats, and angered by the ease with which some lessons were learned by younger pupils. John Quincy saw, and pitied, the half-shamed bewilderment in Homer's face, when one of his younger sisters herself applied the answer for which he had been groping; and the class, tho' cautioned by their schoolmaster against such displays, burst into laughter. It was John Quincy's intention, from the very first, to spare the children the humiliation of *competition,* tho' naturally he had not worked out his thoughts, let alone any theory of education approaching the depth of the long report he would eventually compose, and mail off to the Supervisor of Public Education for the Commonwealth of Pennsylvania, so many miles away in the great city of Philadelphia. He knew only, and at once, with an emotion that caused tears to spring to his eyes, that *educating* might fairly be equated with *loving:* and that one could not succeed in educating, where one had failed to love.

(Granted, John Quincy Zinn's physical stature, his sunny and reasonable manner, and a certain stolid implacability in his face, testified to authority. Perhaps it scarcely mattered, to most of his pupils, what words he uttered and wrote upon the blackboard in his large, careful hand: for they respected him, and feared him, and would not have dreamt of disobeying him; and, it may be, they "loved" him as well—for were not fear and love reversible, in Mr. Zinn's classroom? Granted all this, yet one must conclude, upon the evidence of those unfaulted successes John Quincy did enjoy, that he was as original and brilliant a pedagogue as Dr. Bayard later claimed. And that his precipitous flight from Mouth-of-Lebanon, in the seventh year of his employ, should not cast too shameful a shadow back upon those earlier and happier years.)

John Quincy Zinn's fastidious report, *Out of the Mouths of Babes: A Teacher's Day-Book,* which created such a stir in educational circles in Philadelphia, was surely authentic as to its details, but could not of course convey the e'er-shifting and e'er-changing complexity of the classroom —particularly not a classroom presided over by Mr. Zinn. For teaching of such quality was both a science and an art, and very much depended upon spontaneity. It hardly obliges me to point out how greatly the young schoolmaster's methods differed from those of the majority of his colleagues in the States, in those unenlightened years!—when pedagogical method involved recitation, rote memory, an unquestioning acceptance of all facts, and stupefying boredom; as well as an astonishing degree of corporeal punishment.

Miss Prudence Kiddemaster, having acquired the document from her godfather Mr. Bayard, studied it with extreme interest, for she was, after all, a devoted teacher herself, and one who fully intended to make teaching her life's work, and never to marry. She read, then, young Mr. Zinn's report with more than routine concentration, rejoicing in his extraordinary attentiveness to his pupils—as if they were more than pupils, but fully formed *human beings.*

Out of the mouths and hearts of mere babes, John Quincy Zinn wrote, *a veritable fountain of wisdom!*

The *Day-Book* conveyed a sense of the excitement of John Quincy's revolutionary teaching, but did not, Prudence felt, convey an adequate sense of *him.* (At this time they were not yet well acquainted, having conversed upon less than a half-dozen occasions.) And so, while reading and rereading the document, Prudence frequently closed her eyes in order to summon John Quincy to her: the ruddy, animated face with its scattering of freckles, and its curious birthmark; the staring, demanding, penetrating gaze; the deep resonant commanding voice. She wondered if it was Mr. Zinn's custom to stand, or to sit at his desk; she wondered if, restless as a caged lion, he paced about at the front of the classroom. And what sort of costume did he wear? Not the black preacher's coat, surely? And did he smile? And did he scold? And did he use the hickory cane *very* hard? (For John Quincy, despite his mild manner, did firmly believe that punishment of a sort was a natural accompaniment of affection, and an intrinsic part of education.)

In truth, John Quincy had rarely sat at his desk: he strolled about, up and down the aisles, hands in his pockets, elbows cheerfully akimbo —the most astonishing behavior, for a schoolmaster—and he ofttimes noted, *I should have loved to dance among them—nay, to dance with them.* Since all natural primary truths resided in the child's soul, John Quincy Zinn had only to draw them out, one by one, by judicious questioning. *What was God? Where was God? How did God love? How did God wish them to behave? When were they "good"? When were they "bad"? How could they best please God? Would God make the earth flat—or round? Would God make numbers come to an end—or go on forever?* The first-graders, who could barely hold a pen properly, and whose parents were largely illiterate, were encouraged to "write"—to make lines and squiggles and mock letters, exactly as if they were real; and, far from chiding them, or correcting them, John Quincy praised their messiest efforts, insisting that they must make a beginning, and any beginning at all was excellent. They must only plunge forward —they must not hesitate, or exhibit fear. *All effort in a child is creative,* he wrote; *and all creativity is good.*

John Quincy's vanquished predecessor had insisted upon memorization and drill—drill after drill after drill, up and down the rows— against which the pupils had eventually rebelled; and so it quite amazed them, and delighted them, that the new schoolmaster *forbade* memorization, and would poke them lightly on the head, or squeeze their shoulders, if he suspected them to be quoting from memory and not thinking for themselves. Arithmetic became a lively game, with small prizes—pens, erasers, books—awarded to the best students, and to those who had shown the greatest improvement; spelling bees were so fraught with excitement, the younger children could barely contain themselves. Mr. Zinn recited poetry to them, and read from *The Pilgrim's Progress,* and one or two stories by Edgar Allan Poe which they liked immensely, without completely understanding. The children acted out scenes from *Macbeth* and *Julius Caesar,* the desks pulled about in a large circle. So engrossing were these "lessons" that, at recess and lunch hour, many of the pupils insisted upon continuing them, and even the older boys lingered at the back of the schoolroom as if not wanting to miss a thing.

How is the new schoolmaster working out? people were asked.

The children adore him, and they seem to be learning a great deal; so went the usual reply.

Had John Quincy continued, over the years, with these experimental, and yet not radical, pedagogical methods, he would perhaps have had a less turbulent career: it is quite likely that he would have settled down forever in Mouth-of-Lebanon, and married, and had his family, without even seeking promotion to a better school, in a wealthier district. But so restive was his mind, so insatiable his curiosity, he continued to experiment with his pupils, one season stressing manual skills and gymnastics (never before taught in any school, not even in the most radical Boston schools), the next season stressing natural history and drawing from nature. Geography involved mapmaking, of the very terrain over which the children customarily traveled; poetry involved the writing of poems, and their recitation before the class. Butterflies, frogs, and small creatures like mice and shrews were closely examined, without being killed. One spring, Mr. Zinn having fallen under the spell of Sylvester Graham's teachings, a good deal of time was spent on *human nourishment*—with the conclusion that vegetarianism and temperance were extolled, and "gross" pleasures of the palate condemned. So enamored were the pupils, boys and girls alike, of their handsome young schoolmaster, it was not uncommon for many of them to linger after school, or to return on Saturday, in order to help him with the schoolhouse chores, which, too, became lively games: sweeping and dusting and polishing, chopping and sawing wood, washing windows, mopping up the floor after a rainstorm (for naturally the roof leaked—the shingles were all rotted), tending the old stove and carrying out the ashes, even maintaining the outhouses. Girls sewed colorful curtains for the windows, boys helped paint the walls —bright, bold, sunny shades of gold and green. One of the older boys redesigned the hand-pump at the sink, for greater efficiency, under Mr. Zinn's coaching; and an ingenious revolving coatrack was built, and small hinged blackboards affixed to the individual desks, and a "mechanical hand" at the end of a long pole, for reaching up to the highest shelves. *How is the new schoolmaster working out?* went the query (for John Quincy Zinn was to be called "new" throughout his seven years in Mouth-of-Lebanon), but now the reply might be, *Well—the children like him. And they seem to be learning.*

Complaints arose primarily from parents who felt that their children enjoyed themselves too much, and were too infrequently caned, to argue for the schoolmaster's credentials. Teachers from neighboring districts came to visit, having heard of a "radical" school in this most unlikely of regions, and were surprisingly severe in their judgments. Reverend Tidewell of the Methodist Church in the village expressed worry and doubt and some mild anger as to the "Christian" nature of certain remarks that had snaked their way back to him. What did John Quincy Zinn mean by catechizing his students, and asking them such questions as, *Is God One—or Many?*

Naturally there were complaints: but then there were always complaints: and this enterprising young man was so very *willing* to work for a pittance, without offering any complaints of his own. And, indeed, a virtual blizzard of accusations had swirled about the head of his predecessor (who had spent much of his teaching time simply staring out the window—staring and staring, expressionless, his face doughy-pale and his eyes glassy), and about the head of *his* predecessor (rumored to have been a defrocked Unitarian minister, who had retreated to Mouth-of-Lebanon to lick his wounds, and, as it turned out, drink himself into the grave). Mr. Zinn's methods, tolerated at first, began to be generally disliked, for did not his fellow teachers themselves say they were "too radical"?—and there was considerable, if inchoate, feeling about his "preaching" (on such timely and controversial matters as slavery, and the South, and the Free Soil Republicans, and Abolitionist agitation, and *Uncle Tom's Cabin; or, Life Among the Lowly*—passages of which he read to his thunderstruck charges); but his sunny, uncomplicated personality was so winning, his smile so quick and frank, how could he be faulted? He loved nothing more than to talk with the parents of his pupils, and gave them, during these conversations, an uncanny sense of privilege; he was tireless in the tutoring duties he took on, for no fee, after school and on Saturdays; and, as his employers noted again and again, he was willing to work for a pittance . . . as no one of his manliness might be expected to do. And certainly his students were learning a great deal. Children written off as "slow" were making progress, and even the rebellious older boys rarely caused trouble. How very odd, everyone said, that Homer Feucht should emerge as an outstanding student, Homer Feucht of all people! *Zinn works some kind of spell over them,* it was said, neutrally at first, *He gets them to do anything he wants them to do—so they learn fast.*

John Quincy Zinn's tenure at the Mouth-of-Lebanon school gave little explicit warning of coming to an abrupt end, but John Quincy surely anticipated something of the kind: for the young man was not, despite the smiling equanimity with which he faced the world, insensitive to hostility, however guarded. He knew about the Methodist minister's vociferated doubts—for he had his spies, his adoring spies, among the students. He knew that the parents of one of his female students objected to her peculiarities of diet, which were very much bound up with idealism about Nature and Spirit and the need to free all slaves in the Union. He knew that the Griswolds were jealous of the Feuchts, and the Hyneses angry that their twelve-year-old son lingered after school, to do chores for the schoolmaster, instead of the considerable farm chores that awaited him at home. And there was Eliza, who left little presents for him on his desk —a bunch of bluebells, a poem lettered in a half-dozen pastel colors— and Clara, who was jealous of Eliza; and thirteen-year-old Hannelore, as plumply endowed as any young woman, and disturbingly pretty, who insisted that in dreams Mr. Zinn and Jesus Christ addressed her "in the same voice." And the older boys, as always over the years, proved as difficult *won,* as they had been while being *courted:* for they, too, could be absurdly jealous of their schoolmaster's attention, and as childish as the very youngest students.

And gradually the question *How is the new schoolmaster working out?* ceased to be asked.

It is ironic, and yet significant, that John Quincy's increasing fascination with invention should have brought his sojourn at Mouth-of-Lebanon to an end, for his difficulties as a young man of twenty-five merely prefigured the difficulties he would face in later life—the philistine world's distrust of *genius* being everywhere the same, whether expressed in blunt aggressive terms, or in insidiously subtle ones.

He spoke with great excitement to his pupils, of the inventions that had been discovered, and the still more remarkable inventions that lay in the future. *America,* he stated, and *Invention* are near-synonymous! Hardly a decade earlier Samuel Finley Morse, with the aid of the brilliant Joseph

Henry, had assembled a practical telegraph line, and had sent the prophetic message from Washington to Baltimore: *What hath God wrought?* Peter Cooper had built his famous Tom Thumb—a wonderful contraption with a steam engine at the center—not very many miles from Mouth-of-Lebanon; and everywhere textile mills were improving their spinning frames, to capture the greatest efficiency. There were steamboats, steamships, powerful locomotives, Eli Whitney's "American System" of interchangeable parts, a new repeating pistol, a reaper perfected by Cyrus McCormick that would, in John Quincy's passionate words, "change the face of the North American continent forever." One day soon there would be submarines, that would explore the most forbidding depths of all the oceans; and horseless carriages fueled by electricity or steam. And surely the manned balloons of the previous century would be vastly improved upon, steered by some sort of propeller, and lifted into the air by gases that would not explode. "And this is the world, boys and girls," John Quincy proudly announced, "into which *you* have been born—a new Garden of Eden."

He turned his long rectangular room at the rear of the schoolhouse into a tinkerer's paradise, filled with queer contraptions made of wire, glass, magnets, strips of copper, and wood. His students became his assistants—not only boys, but girls as well. They experimented with electricity by rubbing glass rods with fur, to produce a charge of static electricity. They experimented with radiant heat by carefully placing, on a snowbank, squares of cloth of different colors—thereby proving, to their own satisfaction, that darker colors absorb the sun's heat more readily than light colors. They tinkered with the school stove, they constructed their own lightning rod, they dismantled clocks and built an elaborate orrery, which was at once a mechanical model of the universe and a calendar indicating the hour, the day, and the month. So intense was Mr. Zinn's interest in his contraptions, and so powerfully did it communicate itself to his most sensitive pupils, they were distracted and nervous when away from the schoolhouse; and were oft awakened at night by tumultuous dreams, crying out that their schoolmaster was in danger—the building had caught fire, or had been struck by lightning! Their heads were filled with the motion of pulleys, wheels, cogs, and pistons. They spoke of telescopes, rockets, "auto-wagens" that would someday fly to the moon, machines that would propel themselves, tunnels beneath the rivers and lakes, buildings that rose miles into the sky, underground cities impervious to all weather, the colonization of distant stars, machines that dissolved time, machines that could run forever. A slender, small-boned eleven-year-old named Nahum, the youngest of six children, became particularly obsessed with two of his schoolmaster's notions: the *time-machine,* and the *perpetual-motion machine.*

He dreamt about them, he told John Quincy, every night.

Lessons of a more conventional nature—in reading, writing, and simple mathematics—were neglected, as Mr. Zinn, pacing excitedly about the classroom, speaking in a monologue and taking little note, as to whether the youngest of his charges could follow him at all, speculated aloud on the nature of *Invention,* and the nature of *Evolution,* and the destiny of the United States of America. Now and then a boy might grin slyly behind his fingers, or a girl, suddenly embarrassed by Mr. Zinn's dramatic self-queries—"But how shall I, John Quincy Zinn, figure in this great destiny? How shall Mouth-of-Lebanon declare itself to the world, and to posterity?"—might blush a deep red, and turn away, to doodle nervously in her notebook. But the majority of the students, of all ages and abilities, watched their teacher with rapt fascination, whether or no they comprehended his every word.

It may be said that John Quincy, being still very young, and, as it were, somewhat brash in his expectations, o'erestimated his students' intelligence, as well as the willingness, on the part of their parents, to be tolerant of somewhat eccentric methodology, over a protracted period of time. His sojourn at the Brownrrigg Academy, tho' by no means without attendant difficulties, was to be marked by a comparative *conservatism,* and this in a much more liberal social context, as we have seen. But in Mouth-of-Lebanon, alas, he seemed at times to be totally unaware of the presence of others, and of his responsibility to them. Enough for him, he fervently believed, that he *loved* his small charges: and consequently knew best how to educate them.

The objections of Reverend Tidewell continued, and had their sway in the community, for did not the "mechanical universe" (which very few adults had seen) speak of a godless, lawless, atheistical creation? Did not the schoolmaster Mr. Zinn preach a heresy, in the very bosom of a Christian land? Summoned to a meeting of the district board of education, John Quincy was called upon to defend himself—to answer to certain charges—but he professed only mild alarm that such questions should be asked at all; and declined to answer them, since no one unfamiliar with the *livingness* of his classroom could presume to judge him.

"Gentlemen," he said, his voice quivering, "it is out of the mouths of babes my wisdom springs: I but pluck and gather it, and reap my humble harvest."

So he returned to his small kingdom in the schoolhouse, and continued with his lessons as before, firmly resolved that his way was correct, and that his students, whom he customarily thought of as "his," profited greatly from the very boldness of his enterprise. He believed himself immune to all outside attack, once he was safely home; he knew himself wonderfully privileged; at the same time, a part of his imagination disengaged itself, and considered coolly whether his life might be in danger!—and so he set about systematically preparing a document that would explain, in tireless detail, his educational theories; and he prepared a day-book out of the notes he had been scribbling informally for years, to exhibit to the world the absolute *rightness* of his method, as it blossomed forth in sessions with pupils given names and voices—itself a revolutionary approach. "Thus I consummate the work of seven years," he declared, on the last page of the document.

And he mailed it off to the State Supervisor of Public Education.

The child Nahum, tho' but a sixth-grader, had become so adept at mathematics that John Quincy, ostentatiously seating himself in one of the larger desks, at the rear of the room, empowered him to "deliver a lesson —any lesson" on the blackboard, using colored chalks. These sessions were spirited, but Nahum's shyness erupted into a queer rushed vocableness, which the other children, being unable to follow, began to find distinctly amusing. And so Mr. Zinn felt compelled to "discipline" them, by way of a curious stratagem: he commanded the noisiest offenders to cane *him*.

Which of course they could not do—they simply could not do. The oldest boy in the school, a fifteen-year-old who had grown to a height of six feet, and a probable weight of one hundred eighty pounds, could manage no more than to raise the hickory cane over his schoolmaster's poised hands: and then, flushing red, and coming very close to bursting into tears, the naughty child dropped the cane to the floor; and ran out of the room.

So John Quincy had triumphed—and had, he believed, broken the spirit of all opposition.

As the weeks passed, and no challenge issued from the outside world—"the world of slumbering adults," as he phrased it, tho' not with scorn—John Quincy plunged all the more boldly, one might say brashly, into his teaching of Science. He read aloud from Newton, and Galileo; and William Blake; and Ralph Waldo Emerson; and Edgar Allan Poe, whose fantastical *Eureka* had recently appeared. He had gone on foot to Baltimore, where he examined the newest of steam locomotives of the Baltimore & Ohio, which he diagrammed on the blackboard, in cross-section, for his students to admire. Fire—steam—expanding gas—a closed cylinder—pistons—energy—glorious *Motion!* "And in such ways, boys and girls," John Quincy said passionately, "is the great North American continent made humanly navigable."

Crude "provisional" models of the perpetual-motion and time-machines, each some three feet in height, were set up on the schoolmaster's desk, along with the controversial orrery—which continued, faithfully and precisely, to record the passage of hours, days, and months, as the tiny copper planets revolved around their copper sun. There was, of course, an initial interest in the models; but then they were *not,* after all, the actual machines. "They don't work," many a student murmured in dismay or chagrin. "They never will work"—so a daring student might reply.

Mr. Zinn lectured on the machines, and on invention in general. "What is called, boys and girls, an *invention,* is but the dramatic climax of a vast accretion of details, insinuated, as it were, into Time, by the grace of Eternity. An invention is an *Evolution,* very closely resembling a biologic and a geologic process, as well as the process of human mentality. Do you see?"

He erased the blackboard, and attempted diagrams of the time- and perpetual-motion machine, far more detailed than the models on the desk, and in some cases radically differing from them. Little Nahum at such times was greatly absorbed with his teacher's monologue: he squirmed and writhed in his desk, he waved his hand frantically in the air, and, if not called upon (for Mr. Zinn was much absorbed in his own theorizing), dared to interrupt, and to speak out with a suggestion of his own; which Mr. Zinn, testifying to the charity of his nature, and his innate modesty, accepted with all respect, as if it had issued from an equal. The diagrams grew in complexity, and were abruptly erased with swipes of Mr. Zinn's large hand. And then they blossomed forth again, perhaps with an assistance from Nahum, to last a day or two: and then they were erased again, as being "unworkable."

At such times, John Quincy gave no evidence of minding that certain of his students were yawning rudely, or passing forbidden notes, or jabbing one another with their pens; that a plump German girl, whose seat was near the stove, had fallen asleep and was snoring faintly, to the vast amusement of her classmates; or that one of Nahum's older brothers was lazily digging mud off his boots with a penknife.

(A pity it was, that during these last weeks John Quincy neglected to return to his earlier lessons, in order to reestablish patterns of learning in his pupils: for children forget rapidly acquired skills rapidly, and, undisciplined, tend to revert to their animal ways—charming enough, it may be, under certain restraints, but unruly indeed. So it was that his replacement in the school, a husky, strong-willed, and not overly sensitive widow of Dutch and English ancestry, who had been a Sunday school teacher for many years, found to her bewilderment and gradual anger that Mr. Zinn's alleged star pupils knew but a farrago of unconnected facts and wispy theories; and that the rest of the class—of all ages, sizes, temperaments, and abilities—were "ignorant as savages, and as badly behaved.")

John Quincy Zinn may have sensed that he was losing ground with the majority of his students, even as he gained ground with the precocious little Nahum, whom, indeed, he treated rather like a younger brother, sometimes rubbing his head in play, or stroking his slender shoulder; he may have convinced himself that the passionate pursuit, day by day and week by week, of the elusive machines, would in the end brilliantly justify itself, and silence local opposition—the members of the board of education, and the troublesome Reverend Tidewell above all. He may have told himself, too, that the *imprinting* of certain truths upon impressionable minds was perhaps the most he could hope for, in this backwoods community, where, after all, farming skills were the highest value, and book learning of any sort was looked upon with suspicion. So he strode about the classroom, a tall and somewhat disheveled figure, stroking his beard, clapping his hands softly together, interrupting his own monologue on the history of science and invention from Galileo onward (observations which, not a year later, would strike intellectual Philadelphia as simply brilliant—worthy of a lecture series in themselves), interrupting his own monologue to cast out small glittering gems, to be gathered up by those alert to their value: "The perfecting of a type of object *mechanically,* we must remember, is evidenced by its attainment of *Beauty,*" and "The mass of the Universe is living matter which constantly grows from within, its spiritual gravity necessarily increasing, until such time as it must implode, having no other recourse—and revert to the original fireball of Life, the *Spirit that pervades all things.*"

In the late afternoon, the rest of the students having departed, John Quincy and Nahum labored on the time-machine, in silence for the most part, rarely needing to consult with each other. The machine had now grown to a size of approximately five feet by three, and was set on the floorboards, boxlike in design, and deceptively simple when viewed from the outside. Inside, however, it was a veritable nest of wires, coils, magnets, cogs and wheels and small hammers, and cylindrical mirrors. The principle of *time* being fluid, as John Quincy believed, and having much to do with invisible radiant energies in the atmosphere, contained within the earth's motion as it turned ceaselessly on its axis, the principle of *time-travel* would then involve a resistance to this motion, or an acceleration of it, within, of course, well-defined limits. (For John Quincy and Nahum could not reason how any object could be sent to travel a great distance in time, at least with their present model; nor did they anticipate that any living thing might be sent upon a time-journey, let alone a human being.)

So they labored, and corrected their original diagram, and added to the model, and hours might pass before a rock was thrown up on the roof, to roll noisily down the shingles: a sign, primitive enough, that one of Nahum's brothers had been sent to fetch him, and that he must leave at once. His narrow face at such moments registered a truly adult regret:

and he often backed away from their work, most reluctantly, whilst John Quincy bade him an absentminded but affectionate goodnight.

It was at the very onset of mud-time, the least amenable of seasons, that the *accident,* with its unfortunate results, took place. I hold it bitterly ironic that John Quincy had begun to awaken, many a night, his slumber pierced by uncharacteristic doubt . . . and yet he could never have foreseen what would happen. His thoughts as always tended toward the abstract, for he worried that, in constructing a time-machine, with whatever modest expectations, he was tampering with an absolute Law of Nature; and thereby violating his own principles. Now and then his anxiety touched upon his relations with his pupils, and the community; and in his mind's eye the pale, intense face of little Nahum loomed large; but he made every effort to suppress his doubts, for, as we know, negative mental activities lead to nothing productive, and are fatally exhausting. Mr. Zinn's faith in the Supreme Being was such that he believed his intuition would be guided without ambiguity, should he be inadvertently violating an actual Law of Nature—in which case he would unhesitatingly smash his precious machine, and destroy all the diagrams. Nahum's heart would be broken, but that, alas, would be unavoidable.

It is ironic, too, that the crisis should have been precipitated by the child's reckless behavior, in the face of John Quincy's repeated warnings, and the exemplary model of his own caution. For as work on the time-machine progressed, and excitement naturally grew, the precocious child—who had in fact just celebrated his twelfth birthday—began to speak queerly of "fame" and "riches" and "changing the world forever": and in a breathless, jocular voice that had not the tone of a normal child's voice. John Quincy either paid no heed to such remarks, or countered them with a more practical wisdom of his own: for the pragmatic results of any invention, however ingenious, could not really be foreseen; and the history of invention was strewn with brilliant but finally unworkable and unmarketable ideas. One must after all interest a wealthy patron, or the Congress of the United States, in order to be financed in the systematic *manufacture* of a new invention. Nahum would be wise, too, to recall the discouragement endured by such heroic visionaries as Robert Fulton and Charles Goodyear, whose genius oft invited ridicule and scorn, with rarely a warm wish; and whose lives were surely hastened to their ends by the cruel indifference of the public. The wisest strategy, John Quincy averred, was the hoary old counsel—*Make haste slowly!*

Yet even as John Quincy was speaking, bent over the diagram with a quill pen in his hand, the precocious Nahum chose to follow his own whim—and, having set the gauge on the outside of the machine, to a date in the near future, proceeded to *crawl inside.*

John Quincy worked for some minutes in silence, making emendations in the now alarmingly complex diagram; and it was only a subtle alteration in the atmosphere—a sense of sudden chill, and aloneness—that alerted him to glance around, startl'd, to see that Nahum was no longer present. Whereupon the astonished John Quincy Zinn stood with his quill pen in hand, simply staring. At last he feebly murmured: "Nahum? *Nahum?*"

Whilst the surface of his mind continued with the pretext that the child was still in the schoolroom, but unaccountably hiding from him, the deeper core of his intelligence knew full well, and immediately, that Nahum had plunged ahead with the experiment, with that perverse recklessness of which only the gifted are capable: he had crawled inside the time-machine, into a space that looked as if it would accommodate only a much younger child, and he had, somehow, one surely could not know *how,* caused himself to vanish. That he had penetrated the curtain of time, and traveled, as it were, into the future, John Quincy felt with a sickening certitude must be true—and yet the plausibility of so extreme an action struck the older man as unthinkable.

With what anxiety the next hour was endured, the sensitive reader may well imagine. The unhappy schoolmaster feared for his charge's well-being; indeed, he feared for his very life. Not a thought crossed his mind of the inevitable danger to himself, should Nahum not reappear, for our hero was made of noble substance, and yet he may well have considered his own situation—a schoolmaster who had lost one of his pupils, inside the very schoolroom! But he paid no heed to his own prospects, and paced about the machine, crying the child's name, and tearing at his hair, now and then stooping to peer inside the box at the small galaxy of wires and cylindrical mirrors, all of which (I am surprised to report) struck him as suddenly unreadable, as if constructed by another person altogether. Unreadable, alas, and quite mad!

Then he woke, and roused himself, as it were, and set to fiddling with the gauge, which operated along the general lines of an alarm clock, tho' of necessity it was far more complicated. By now it was late afternoon and the schoolroom had grown dark; it was only with a great effort that he forced himself to pause, to light a lamp, and set it on the table beside him. Again he stooped to peer into the machine, and again he saw that it was empty. Again the fanciful thought crossed his mind that Nahum was playing a trick on him—perhaps in concert with one or two others—and would reappear in another minute, jeering and grinning, from behind the stove, or beneath a desk, or out of a shadowy corner. Ah, how he would have rejoiced! The bitterness he might reasonably be expected to feel, that his most intimate pupil had turned against him, he would gladly have suffered in the interest of knowing that the child was well—and fully present in March of 1853.

Perhaps in response to his desperate adjustments, perhaps quite by chance, the machine whirred into spasmodic life: and the incredulous John Quincy saw that a form—a human figure of some sort—appeared to be taking shape in the machine's dim interior. Seconds passed slowly, as if the figure were reluctant to assume substance, or as if something were very much amiss. "Nahum?" John Quincy murmured. But even before the figure solidified and became, not the twelve-year-old boy who had disappeared, but a much smaller being, John Quincy seemed to realize the nature of the problem, and the certitude that he *had* violated a Law of Nature—however unwittingly—flashed through him like an electrical charge. For the essence of such a violation, the prescient young man knew, was that *it could never be amended.*

And yet of course he must try. He must try to "save" Nahum—now fully materialized, but squirming and kicking and beginning to wail, with all the fleshy vigor of *a six-month-old infant.*

And at this very moment, a rock struck the peak of the schoolhouse roof, and began its noisy tumble downward!

(That John Quincy Zinn should remain detached enough from his own jagged emotions, to reason quickly through the probabilities leading up to the extraordinary materialization of an *infant,* where a *twelve-year-old boy* had been expected, is a testament to his genius—indeed, one wonders how a lesser man, in so horrific a situation, might have conducted himself. The natural husbandly agitation Mr. Zinn would one day experience whilst his wife lay screaming in labor, in another part of the house, was mercifully joined with this selfsame mental detachment: unique, it may be, to his gender; and perhaps allowing for the general superiority of the masculine sex, where emotion and rationality contend. Yet tho' his physical being exhibited many of the symptoms of extreme panic, such as palpitations of the heart, sweating, and flashes of severe cold, combined with a terrifying looseness of the bowels, and the paternal or brotherly instinct in him was to seize the baby in his arms, as if to rescue it (for flesh, God save us, cries out to flesh!), at the same time his mental processes, acting with an almost preternatural accuracy, dictated to him the firm imperative: *Do not touch.* For he grasped the substance of the predicament, tho' the systematical reasoning behind it was not yet available—that is, the fatal error of the time-machine was not only its present primitive form (tho' it is a measure of John Quincy Zinn's skill, that he should have constructed an actual working time-machine, in 1853, out of such homely materials), but a miscalculation as to the nature, indeed the very possibility, of time-travel. For he had not entirely reasoned through the contingencies under which a time-traveler might labor, assuming that no living creature, let alone Nahum himself, would be plunged into the abyss of Time for many years: he had vaguely planned to send inanimate objects into

the future or the past, simply to test whether they could be safely recalled, or no. Laboring with a crude model, tirelessly experimenting
with the *physical,* he had set aside for the time being certain *metaphysical*
problems . . . such as, the question of whether anything, animate or
inanimate, would age if sent into the future, or whether it would maintain its integrity, so to speak, whilst suns and moons whirled o'erhead;
and the question of how the object, once hurtled into Time, might be
retrieved.

(This knotty issue was to be taken up again in John Quincy's
career, but only after a considerable span of years—near the end of his
life, in fact, when he felt called upon to correct certain contemporary
aspirations concerning "time-travel"; and then, only in theory. For after
the *débâcle* of March 1853 he was to destroy his machine, and all his
diagrams, and reject the very notion of time-travel, as a scientific folly,
if not a diabolical temptation. Indeed, it was the American publication of
H. G. Wells's *The Time Machine,* and its popular reception, in 1895, that
roused sixty-eight-year-old J.Q.Z. to a forthright denunciation of Wells's
basic premise, which he held to be a dangerous one, in that it might tempt
inventors and tinkerers to experiment with time-travel *as if it were play.* His
essay was entitled "On the Probability of Time-Travel," modest in ambition, and understated in tone, and consequently doomed to a very limited
readership; unlike the Wells novella, with its romantic appeal to the
adolescent temperament above all. For the esteemed J.Q.Z., despite his
amnesia concerning the specific factors of his own failure, understood
very well both the physical and the metaphysical impossibilities of time-
travel, as the English man of letters and half-baked ideas surely did not.
But enough—I am guilty of an inexcusable digression, and into the future
at that!)

The gist of John Quincy's predicament, as the reader has by now
inferred, had to do with both the susceptibility to time of the wretched
Nahum, and the crude nature of the time-machine's gauge. In plunging
into the future by some years, the child must have rapidly—nay, instan-
taneously—aged; the dial had been set for ten years, but it is impossible
to say whether ten years were in fact bridged, or more, or less. In revers-
ing the machine's motion, John Quincy had naturally set it for ten years
again, but with the astounding results we have seen: the machine o'ershot
itself, in a manner of speaking, and poor Nahum was delivered as an
infant of a half-year, and not in his "true" form. The terrifying sound of
the rock on the schoolhouse roof signaled to the schoolmaster an ignoble
end to his career, for, Nahum's brother having so inopportunately appeared, John Quincy should in another minute have no recourse other
than to confess to him what had happened: and to take full responsibility
for the grotesque accident. No twelve-year-old Nahum, but a kicking,
squirming, wailing infant—the selfsame infant that had emerged into

Time some twelve years previously, now so astonishingly returned! It would beggar all belief, John Quincy thought. Indeed, he himself could not grasp it.

The rock rolled down the shingled roof, and fell to the ground, and, if this afternoon proved no exception, Nahum's brother would probably give him a few minutes' grace, before tossing another rock, or shouting his name. (The rudeness of the procedure, and the insult to *him*, John Quincy had not entirely grasped until this moment. But surely such casual manners in the presence of a schoolmaster, argued for a singular lack of respect.) Seizing upon this temporary respite, John Quincy decided to make another attempt to rescue the twelve-year-old Nahum, and resolutely turned the dial again, with the unanticipated result that the wailing baby, in all its warm flesh, began at once to deliquesce, and melted away before John Quincy's eyes into—into a *vapor,* and then a *shadow,* and then *nothing.* And the wail's echo, poised for an instant in the lamplight, amidst the silent rows of desks and the high windows in which ghost-reflections of the schoolmaster himself danced, gradually faded: and then there was no sound at all.

And, of a sudden, John Quincy found himself staring into his empty mechanism, with no idea at all of what he was doing; or why his heart pounded so queerly, and his body was bathed in chill perspiration.

He remembered the time-machine clearly enough, for he had been working on it all afternoon, alone. But he could not understand why he felt so agitated. Or why, stooped over, he was staring into its shadowy empty space.

"Am I turning somewhat eccentric in my solitude?" John Quincy was to ask himself that night. "Is it perhaps time for me to venture out of these hills, and seek the company of my equals; time, perhaps, to take a wife? And to set aside, for the health of my soul, these damnable vexing problems!"

Another rock tumbled down the roof, and John Quincy, wiping his oc'r-heated forehead with a handkerchief, went to the door, to inquire what on earth was wrong: why such a commotion: who was being murdered? A boy approached him out of the late-winter dusk, one of the Hindley boys, a former student, in fact, who now peered at him with an expression that reflected both arrogance and embarrassment. After a long strained moment it became clear that the boy had no idea what he wanted: some notion had driven him here to the schoolhouse, but now it had fled, and he simply could not remember.

John Quincy, plucking nervously at his beard, inquired again what on earth the boy wanted—and how dared he make such a clatter, rolling rocks down the roof!

The boy came no nearer. He paused, staring; and could think of no word to utter; no word at all. Whatever had drawn him to the school-house on this late afternoon in mud-time, had now precipitantly vanished . . . and the poor blushing creature could not even stammer an apology, before he turned and fled.

25

The singular irony was that John Quincy, in his desperation, must have turned the faulty dial farther to the left, that is, into the *past,* rather than to the right, in order to bring Nahum forward to a more advanced age. Whereupon the unfortunate creature vanished forever!—into that bottomless abyss of Time that preceded his birth, dragging all that pertained to him along with it, into oblivion. Quite as if he had never been born; for, indeed, under these circumstances, he never *had* been born.

An even greater irony, perhaps, lay in the fact that John Quincy Zinn's expulsion from Mouth-of-Lebanon had little to do with the embarrassment of the time-machine and the disappearance of Nahum (whom, of course, no one remembered), and a great deal to do with the mechanical universe: which contraption (in the Reverend Tidewell's contemptuous words) argued for atheism, immorality, and blasphemy, and could not be countenanced in a Christian community.

So objections to the schoolmaster were raised, until a veritable blizzard swirled about his head. He had not the heart to defend himself: of late he had felt unaccountably weary, in advance of his twenty-five years, and even his machines could no longer fascinate him. Folly, he declared them; vanity; and unworkable besides! So he dismantled them, and ripped up the diagrams, and burnt them in the stove.

I must seek the company of my equals, John Quincy told himself.

One moonstruck April evening it happened, quite by accident, that John Quincy, staring out his window, sighted a small group of men in the muddy road, approaching the schoolhouse on foot. Surely, at this hour, they did not intend a social call. Surely, moving with such grim deliberation, they did not intend to give pleasure.

So he betook himself into his narrow room at the rear of the school, and made haste to pack the few things he could readily lay hands upon. A few precious books; his journal; the marvelous letter from Dr. Horace P. Bayard of Philadelphia, which had arrived only a few days before. . . . He gave no thought for his defense, knowing that mere words would not protect him, and that, in any case, it was too late: Mouth-of-Lebanon had expelled him, and he must be gone.

Even as the men approached the schoolhouse from the road, John Quincy slipped quietly out a rear window, and was gone. For he was, after all, despite the passage of so many fruitful years, the Yankee pedlar's son.

26

When, on that blustery sunny morning in November, John Quincy Zinn received a message from the Honorable Godfrey Kiddemaster, in his own hand, all but summoning him out to Kiddemaster Hall at his convenience, he exclaimed aloud at the evident *synchronicity* in operation: for he had been mining his courage, over the days and weeks, to write to Mr. Kiddemaster himself, requesting an audience on a matter of some delicacy . . . !

"Is there a law of coincidences?" he asked of himself, holding his pen aloft, scarce trusting his trembling hand; "an invisible logic to which we must yield, in gladsome surrender?"

The Kiddemaster carriage came to pick him up, at his humble boardinghouse near the warehouse district, and many an admiring (and envious) eye accompanied his departure, for was this not proof positive, at last, that John Quincy, so popular amongst his fellow boarders, and quite the favorite of his landlady, was a prince of sorts in disguise, now being raised to his rightful eminence? Some little envy, of course; but much admiration; and rejoicing for him, on the part of his friend Charles most of all, who may have thought innocently that, were John Quincy Zinn raised to another social station by marriage, let us say, *he*, Charles Guiteau, might one day follow. At the very least, the boyish Guiteau envisioned himself someday riding with his friend John Quincy in that very same carriage—a brougham that would easily seat eight persons, of a gleaming copper with regal ebony trim, drawn by four matched high-stepping bays with long braided tails, and starkly black hooves. And how glorious a sight, the proud Kiddemaster coat-of-arms emblazoned on the side: a fierce-visagèd lion, rampant, grasping in his paws an olive branch!

The crimson silk lining of the carriage's interior, as well as the induced solitude of the long journey, soon made John Quincy restive: and so he rapped for the driver to stop, and quite astonished the man by insisting upon riding *up front* with him—so that they might chat.

Indeed, once the young driver recovered from his natural astonishment, and some suspicion as to the sincerity of the proposal, the journey out to Bloodsmoor was a highly pleasurable one, John Quincy allowing that he learned a great deal from the driver, Mr. Patrick McInnes, late of Cork, Ireland (whose lamentation for his motherland, still suffering from the great famine of 1845, was somewhat leavened by his delight in singing ballads for John Quincy's delectation: one of the ballads, by a preternatural coincidence, being "Deidru the Raging One"); and Mr. McInnes allowing that he had never met so friendly and bright and talkative a gentleman, who clearly wished to make no distinction between an Irish coachman and his betters, or was not aware of a significant distinction, in his passionate talk of his own future plans (John Quincy being much absorbed, at this time, with the proposal he wished to make to the wealthy Mr. Kiddemaster, for the financing of certain experimentations of an eminently practical nature).

At Kiddemaster Hall, as the liveried footman approached to open the carriage door, he was amazed to see Mr. Zinn shake hands with Patrick McInnes, and leap down to the ground. It could not have failed to amaze him still further, and perhaps to offend him as well, that the men not only parted on the most convivial of terms, but the one freely addressed the other as *Patrick,* and was called in turn *John Quincy;* and that some hope was expressed that the return journey should prove as pleasant, and that they should continue their lively conversation.

(Thus John Quincy Zinn's arrival at Kiddemaster Hall; *but,* I am grateful to be able to note, no Kiddemaster was a witness to this curious behavior.)

John Quincy had little time to be intimidated by the Greek Revival façade of the great house, with its high white columns, and its elegant portico; nor could his awed eye do more than scan the gilded interior of the foyer, and rise to the coffered ceiling some thirty feet above. He was immediately ushered into Judge Kiddemaster's private library, empty for the moment, and given a chair; and, seated, fortunately alone, he was able to recover himself, and to rehearse once again the exact words he might use, as his gaze moved slowly about the handsome room, resting here and there on something of especial beauty or charm: the cherry paneling, the tall windows with their panes of stained glass that took the sunshine so boldly, the matching silver tankards on a bow-fronted sideboard, the calfskin-bound classics of English, French, and American literature (which John Quincy's eye lingered upon hungrily: how very much he would have cherished such a library, and how frequently he would have consulted it!). A bewigged gentleman of Colonial times, in a gold velvet jacket, with a generous gathering of lace at his throat, and a black, hatchet-faced look, glowered down at John Quincy from an oil painting above the mantel, as if suspecting him of common—nay, outlaw—blood; ostentatiously laid upon the mantel itself was a long dress sword in a golden hilt, its grip decorated with American stars and the Goddess Athena, also in gold.

The carved oak doors were quietly opened by a servant, and Judge Kiddemaster strode into the room, a figure rather more frail than John Quincy had recalled, and somewhat more grizzled at the eyebrows, but imperious withal, and signaling by a brusque gesture of his hand that the younger man should remain seated. Greetings were exchanged, of a formal nature; the manservant was given muttered instructions regarding tea, and a light repast; and the estimable Godfrey Kiddemaster sank into a rosewood rocker with black haircloth cushions, and fixed his stern, skeptical gaze upon John Quincy Zinn.

After a dramatic pause, during which the younger man felt his face grow mercilessly warm, Judge Kiddemaster observed with cool, dry, aristocratic hauteur, yet not without graciousness: "And so, my dear young Mr. Zinn, I believe you have urgent business to discuss with me . . . ?"

John Quincy blinked at the Judge's prescience, and for a confused half-moment bethought himself that he *had* written the letter he had planned, and mailed it bravely off to Kiddemaster Hall. (This much-debated missive, which he had hoped to discuss beforehand with Miss Kiddemaster, in order to seek her shrewd counsel, was to set forth in fastidious detail John Quincy's ideas for a practical drilling operation in western Pennsylvania, near Titusville, where crude "rock oil" was to be found in abundance. This "rock oil"—one day to be called "petroleum" —was secured at the present time by laborious digging of holes and ditches, and by a still more laborious method of scooping up oil as it floated on creeks; and it had come to John Quincy in a flash, as he read about the properties of rock oil in a Philadelphia newspaper, that one might sink a *well* to *draw the oil up*, precisely in the way that water was drawn to the surface of the earth!—for surely the physical principles were the same. John Quincy's obvious disadvantages were his lack of firsthand knowledge of the Titusville area in particular, and of the actual qualities of rock oil in general: but a natural optimism had fired him, and he had hurriedly sketched a number of diagrams, for the Judge's leisurely perusal, pertaining to the mechanics of the drilling operation.) So startl'd, he could do no more than murmur an expeditious assent, and was at once distracted by the silent manservant, who had reentered the library, now bearing a heavily laden silver tray.

"I—I scarcely know how to begin, Your Honor, my humble plea,"
he said, as the blush rose more savagely up his face, "it—my mission—
the very audacity of my hope—"

Tea was ceremoniously poured, and tiny crustless sandwiches offered, and, as John Quincy spoke—how much less forcefully, than he had
wished!—the elder gentleman furrowed his high, noble forehead, the
which was rendered all the more distinctive, by his prominent widow's
peak; and knit his generously endowed white eyebrows; and nodded, and
murmured "Yes, yes," as he fussed with his teacup, and a sandwich of
thin-shaved beef; and when John Quincy took courage, to inquire nervously whether His Honor might now like to examine the diagrams—for
he had brought them along, carefully folded, in his coat pocket—the
elder man appeared not to hear, but, gazing sternly at the part-devoured
sandwich in his hand, murmured once again an impatient, "Yes."

Which naturally bewildered John Quincy, but did not discourage
him, as he ranged more freely about, talking of past inventions, American
and otherwise, that had been created out of "obvious" principles—the
chronometer, the rotorship, the reaper, the gas-filled balloon, the nefarious rocket weapons the British put to such degrading use, at Bladens-
burg, in 1814. He thought it odd, and verging on rudeness, that in the
very midst of his speech Mr. Kiddemaster should draw out his pocket
watch, and stare into it; but then, he reasoned, the elder man's time *was*
inestimably valuable, and one of his own humble station should be grateful for whatever attention he might be granted. "I hope, sir, that my
boldness does not offend you," he said, tho' with much more diffidence
than his words suggest. "I should perhaps have discussed the proposal
in outline, if not in specifics, with Miss Kiddemaster, who might have—
with her instinctive womanly wisdom!—guided me; or dissuaded me outright. But I have not been so fortunate as to talk with Prudence for some
time now, owing to—well, I scarcely know *what;* and in any case—"

So the poor young man talked nervously, and without direction,
and it soon became evident that Mr. Kiddemaster, for all his air of authority, and the regal nature of his bearing, was somewhat deaf in his left ear;
or, very possibly, in both ears; and that the brusque little nodding of his
distinguished head, and his murmured *yesses,* failed to inspire true confidence. He interrupted John Quincy's remarks on the likelihood of so
developing rockets and torpedoes (along the lines Robert Fulton had
envisioned), that, such terrible weapons being available, war should
abruptly cease to be waged, by snorting in amusement: "Yes—*yes*—such
overtures are always difficult—for *Poppa* and prospective *Husband* alike!"

At this juncture both men fell silent for several minutes, Mr. Kiddemaster impatiently stirring sugar in his tea, John Quincy chewing without appetite a damp sandwich. That there was, in the imposing cherry-
wood-paneled sanctity of Mr. Kiddemaster's retreat, a profound

misunderstanding of some sort, whose consequences would be far-ranging indeed, seemed likely: and yet John Quincy Zinn, in his boyish innocence, could not quite grasp what it might be. *Poppa, husband . . . ?* Were these arcane terms, professional jargon, pertaining to rock oil, or to the financing of fairly radical experiments, by wealthy patrons like Mr. Kiddemaster . . . ? John Quincy reasoned that he could not ask; and, in any case, his host being afflicted with partial deafness, he could not hope of a reply.

(How much shrewder it would have been, he saw now, to have discussed the delicate matter with Prudence! For she oft joked about her father's willfulness; yet hinted that she knew well "how to get round" him, and from which side "he might best be saddled." But he had not seen Prudence for many days. He *had not*—I am most pained to say—seen her at the Bayards' home, on the fateful day of her fainting fit; the simple reason being he had not been invited, and knew nothing of the party. That the febricity of Miss Kiddemaster's passion for him had induced both the *fainting fit*, and the *vision* of John Quincy Zinn that attended it, I cannot help but surmise; that John Quincy Zinn knew anything about it, or, indeed, anything about his friend Prudence's amorous attachment to him, I cannot but deny. In any case, he had not set eyes upon her for some time, and had begun to feel her absence, but casually.)

Some remarks of John Quincy's as to the activities of Know Nothings in Philadelphia, and a diffident query concerning Mr. Kiddemaster's opinion of them, were interrupted by the elder man's irritable ringing for his manservant, and an order given for two glasses of sherry—notwithstanding John Quincy's demurral; and a question voiced, in much the same tone, as to the *particulars* of John Quincy's background. "It being time, after all, for us to speak of such things," Mr. Kiddemaster said frankly.

So John Quincy looked him full in the eye, and did not flinch before a certain half-contemptuous condescension he saw there, and spoke of "domestic tragedy" in his childhood: consumption, influenza, the thin, rocky soil of his grandfather's and father's farm, a series of crop failures. He hesitated, then plunged forward into admitting—stating— that he had spent some years "hired out" to families in the Germantown area, on the Granitehill River; and that he was accustomed to being worked hard, and to thriving on it. And one day, browsing at a bookseller's stall in Allentown, where he had come with his farm family for the day, he had happened upon a slender book by a man unknown to him until that very moment—the great Ralph Waldo Emerson. And the book —he assured Mr. Kiddemaster he did *not* exaggerate—changed his life.

"Indeed!" Mr. Kiddemaster observed, sniffing his sherry. "Emerson, you say?"

The conversation continued, consisting for the most part of the self-conscious young man's presentation of himself, interrupted by *hem's* and *ha's* by Mr. Kiddemaster, and brought to a full halt by the bemused observation: "My dear boy, you are young: but you will not always be so."

There was a pause; John Quincy wondered if he should respond, or sit in blushing silence; and then Mr. Kiddemaster, again drawing out his handsome gold watch, opening it, and staring half angrily into it, said in an orotund voice that might have done honor to the bewigged ancestor above the mantel: "Deambulations, my dear boy, may very well draw us to the point, had we an unlimited fount of time; but such, alas, is not the case, no more for my belovèd daughter, if I may be so bold, as for Mrs. Kiddemaster and myself. And so—to be blunt: I believe that we understand each other, Mr. Zinn, no matter that we seem hardly to speak the same language. My belovèd Prudence has confessed all to me; and, after my initial alarm, I came round to grasping the essence of her case, and to seeing some merit, however eccentric, in it. That my daughter, at her age, should have attracted the affection of a gentleman so forthright, and, if I may say so, so rough-hewn in his manliness, as you, cannot fail but strike a doting father's heart as felicitous—for we Kiddemasters are, after all, altogether *human;* if pricked, we sometimes deign to bleed. That my daughter, at her somewhat advanced and, it may be, level-headed age, with the assurance of both a professional career before her, and a substantial income from numerous investments held in trust expressly for her, should be attracted, in her turn, to any gentleman at all—to *any* gentleman at all—cannot fail to strike a doting father's heart as altogether welcome: for I wish grandchildren as much as any man, and I cannot think (no matter how I humor little Prudence, and my dear sister Edwina) that a woman's place can be anywhere outside the household, if she is to be, in the fullest sense of the word, *womanly.* The weaker sex necessarily being weaker, less by divine ordinance than by simple biological accident, it inevitably follows that the stronger sex *must* provide—if not, in every case, financial support, then surely strength; and guidance; and protection. I had no objections, sir, to my daughter's studying all the books she could lay her hands on, or to her ordering away for e'en more radical reading material, or hobnobbing with every Transcendentalist, Abolitionist, and Free Thinking boobie in the Union; but I did object, sir, and my wife was sorely distressed, that she should profess not only indifference but outright *scorn"*—and here the old gentleman's voice gave way, and began to tremble—"for the sacred obligations of motherhood: yes, sir, I did indeed object!—yes!—I did *indeed;* and you may quote me. For just as one is compelled to look with contempt upon the traitorous soldier who flees his position on the battlefield, so one is compelled to look with e'en greater contempt upon the woman who, refusing to marry, refuses to have children, and to continue her line. Yes, my dear sir: I assure you this is my position, and I shall not budge from it: and you may quote me for the record, and publish it in the damn'd penny papers if you like!"

At this point he paused, breathing rather laboriously, and rang for another glass of sherry. His frost-glazed eyes fixed themselves upon the altogether astonished John Quincy Zinn, and, tho' for a long moment no word passed between them, it did seem to the younger man that *something* quite substantial passed between them: and that he had no alternative, but to tactfully acquiesce.

A profound misunderstanding, John Quincy thought. Ah, indeed! —the aspiration to provide ingenious mechanical means to draw up rock oil to the surface of the earth, supplanted by—can it be?—the prospect of marriage, with the daughter of Chief Justice Godfrey Kiddemaster of Kiddemaster Hall. Somehow, he could not dream of guessing *how,* the one bold aspiration had been jettisoned, to be replaced by the other: so the machinery of the Universe, benign, in perpetual motion, its infinite wheels and springs and cogs and pistons in perfect (if inscrutable) harmony, had brought him, in mute astonishment, to *this.*

And, it may be, the blushing young man saw again that tarred and blazing figure, hauled aloft by a jeering crowd; and saw the mockery of its white fluttering feathers; and smelt the enormity of burning tar, burning hair, burning flesh. The Yankee pedlar that is no more, the rich man's son that *is;* and shall bring forth, for his wife's family, and for himself, and for all the world, the most glorious *issue.*

John Quincy Zinn had given little thought to marriage, and still less to love: his innocence was such, he had but casually meditated upon any course of future action other than his *work*—the work that was his Destiny, and bound up with the Destiny of his great nation. Miss Prudence Kiddemaster with her broad, bold, forthright countenance, and her stolid figure, was his dear *friend;* a kind of sister; and a conscience as well. Of the other young Philadelphia heiresses who had seemed particularly attentive to him, Miss Parthenope Brownrrigg with her ethereal verse had made a great impression upon him, for he thought her worthy —if he might judge such matters—of residing in Concord itself, with her special poetic gifts. And there was Miss Rachel Triem, rather more John Quincy's age, perhaps, at twenty-three, than either Miss Kiddemaster or Miss Brownrrigg, however formidable their qualities; and the slender Miss Honora LeBeau with her astonishing pale skin and crimped hair and billowing skirts—ah, Miss LeBeau struck him, of a sudden, as *quite* an attractive woman!—but perhaps it was too late?

Mr. Kiddemaster, swallowing his sherry, had plunged forward to speak companionably of a dowry; and of a "sizable parcel" of land, on the Bloodsmoor grounds, with an excellent view of the river, and the scenic gorge, for the house John Quincy and Prudence would one day wish to build. He spoke of other matters—he touched lightly upon the "financial"—while his prospective son-in-law, head ringing with blood, stared and blinked and made every effort to follow. So shaken was the young man, he caught himself reaching for his glass of sherry; but drew back his hand in time, as if he had been about to touch a snake.

The Yankee pedlar that is no more, the rich man's son that *is*.

Grandchildren, Mr. Kiddemaster was murmuring fondly. Sons.

"It is less that my daughter becomes a *Zinn*," Mr. Kiddemaster said, his noble lips pursed just perceptibly upon the pronunciation of that name, "than that you, my dear John Quincy, become a Kiddemaster. We shall put it in those terms; we shall think of it that way. *And you may quote me.*"

V

The Wide World

27

So wicked were the Eighties, and so lost to common Christian decency and justice, it is hardly a surprise to learn that the fallen Malvinia Zinn —by brash magic rebaptized "Malvinia Morloch"—was not despised on all sides, but rather elevated—to become one of the theatrical celebrities of New York City within a few years of her *début* (in itself absurdly premature) at the glittering new Fanshawe Theatre at Union Square, as celebrated in the press as the infamous Lola Montez of another era, and the far more gifted Ada Rehan of her own!

It was claimed for "Malvinia Morloch" that, in performance, she was both *audacious* and *tender; angelic,* and yet *provocative; coquettish; noble; enchanting; piquant; subtle; irresistible;* and *unforgettable.* She was a *truly inspired* Rosaline in *As You Like It,* and a *sly, spoiled, outrageous, and absolutely charming* Countess in *Countess Fifine.* She moved audiences to tears with her *spirited yet profoundly tragic* portrayal of Juliet (in a production in which her protector Orlando Vandenhoffen, tho' rather seasoned for the role, evoked an impassioned and convincing Romeo); she commanded peals of laughter as Phronie in *Dollars and Sense,* and awed admiration for her energy, as well as her beauty, in that curious and coarse *Ah Sin: A Play of the Western Life,* concocted for the stage by Bret Harte and Mark Twain. ("Lovely Malvinia is quite the best thing in the play," Mark Twain himself allowed in his amusing opening-night speech, "but I will not ask for a show of hands—whether the poor girl redeems it, or goes down with the rest of us.") The usually judicious William Winter behaved as if he had fallen in love with her, writing in the *Tribune,* on the occasion of her *début* in the silly melodrama *A Flash of Lightning:* "The stage presence of young Malvinia Morloch is nothing less than stupendous. Her feminine charms are

231

electrifying, her beauty mesmerizing, the pathos of her suffering brilliant, her flashes of scorn, courage, defiance, and female sacrifice heartrending. Ladies and gentlemen, we will hear a great deal of Malvinia Morloch in the years to come!"—all this in praise of a performance the unskilled actress merely learned by rote, with her wonderful capacity for imitation and mimicry.

Yet such was the anarchy of the decade, who cared to know? Who cared to judge true merit, amidst the swill of meretriciousness?

("I fear I am really not so good as they claim," Malvinia said to Orlando Vandenhoffen, skimming her notices for the fourth or fifth time, and laughing in perplexity, yet withal defiant as well; for the vain young woman did not truly doubt that she had it in her, to deserve such acclaim, or even to surpass it. Vandenhoffen did no more than laugh heartily, and kiss her lips, and, sweeping the newspaper clippings to the floor, said: "It is your *fear*, then, dear one, we must overcome.")

John Singer Sargent was to paint her portrait—in an immodest low-cut crimson gown that showed her pale shoulders and much of her milk-white bosom to alarming advantage. Mark Twain, acting the fool, would offer her gifts—tho' never marriage; the shameless epicurean Diamond Jim Brady would do likewise, in defiance of Vandenhoffen's prior claim; the railroad magnate Nicholas Drew applied to be her "guardian," and begged her to accept from him not only a parlor car rivaling in vulgar splendor that of the soprano Adelina Patti's (for where Miss Patti's bed-chamber walls were paneled in satin-wood inlaid with ebony, gold, and amaranth, Miss Morloch's were to be in embossed leather and gold, with leopard fur, in a design promised to be "memorable" to the aesthetic eye), but a marble mausoleum as well, of Moorish design, with a jade and alabaster interior: which mausoleum, a twin to his own in Annandale-on-Hudson, New York, was deemed a "fitting future shrine" for the beauteous young actress. Many, and varied, and glittering were the questionable honors heaped upon her—champagne dinners at Delmonico's, a dinner dance at the Plaza, the attention, for a while, of gentlemen so disparate as Jay Gould and Grover Cleveland (that prodigy of immoralism, and sheer animal gluttony), and Mark Twain himself. A reign of some years, with hardened and fickle New York City at her slipper'd feet, all the dazzling spoils of the material world; and her simple girlhood in Bloods-moor, in the Octagonal House, left far behind. And yet one is inclined —nay, compelled—to inquire: Had *Malvinia Morloch* a day's happiness comparable to that once so freely and innocently enjoyed by *Malvinia Zinn . . . ?*

So strangely disheveled, too, were the Eighties, one scarcely knew whether the sun would properly set in the western sky, let alone rise; one scarcely knew whether to be scandalized, or amused, by the prominence of such blasphemous personages as Madame Blavatsky, and the revelations, near-weekly, of the antics of such swindlers as the infamous Ferdinand Ward, whose brokerage firm failed for $16 million, and besmirched the already contaminated name of Ulysses S. Grant. Darwinism and Evolution were making their godless inroads upon American culture, divorce was becoming a commonplace, eight brave policemen were murdered by anarchist dynamite at Haymarket Square, pagan Utopias were discussed by the young with all of the fervor, and none of the restraining moralism, of the old Arcadia Club of a bygone time. Social barriers were so threatened in all but the most distinguished households, one could scarcely be confident, upon entering a drawing room, that a wealthy "prince" of the mercantile-retail trade (in short, a common shopkeeper) might not be present, or even be the guest of honor. There were women so distracted by modern notions of equality, they made fools of themselves by running for public office, when they could not even vote; there were distinguished men of letters who took seriously, and even promoted, the garrulous hedonistic ramblings of Walt Whitman, offered as poesy! That the unseemly decade began with the assassination of President Garfield by none other than Charles Guiteau—alas, a greatly altered Guiteau, and one bearing little resemblance to John Quincy Zinn's old acquaintance—and that outlaws, desperadoes, and common murderers of the ilk of Jesse James were publicized in the papers, suggests but cannot truly describe the feculent airs that assailed the innocent, and that would soon lead, in the prophetic words of the Reverend Tobias Strong, to a "crisis of spiritual Anglo-Saxondom" in this nation—a crisis that continues to be felt in our time.

And surely it is no mystery that, in so disorderly an atmosphere, Constance Philippa simply vanished: or so it was assumed by her grieving family. Whether she met with some species of evil likely to visit itself upon an unprotected woman, or whether she did in fact find protection: no one could know. The deeply insulted Baron von Mainz exposed the deficiencies in his European upbringing, by suing publicly for an annulment to his marriage, on grounds of both *desertion* and *fraud;* and by retaining title to the Rittenhouse Square townhouse, the magnanimous wedding gift of the Kiddemasters to the young couple. (The family was angered to learn that, not one month after the annulment, the wily Baron sold this desirable piece of Philadelphia property for a handsome price!)

Nor is it a mystery that a society so eager for novelty should divert itself with the excesses of Spiritualism, as with the excesses of tobacco and alcohol—evidenced by the financial successes of such mediums as the van Hoestenberghe twins, the "Mahatma" Lotos Bey, Mrs. Daisy Olcott, and Deirdre of the Shadows herself; and by the controversial renown of Madame Helen Petrovna Blavatsky, founder of the Theosophical Society. The penny papers thrived on scandal and sensationalism, and hawked interviews with such creatures as the infamous wife-murderer Brockden Smith, who had advanced as his defense, at his trial in Ipswich: "When they are dead, they are done with"—a pronouncement immediately taken up by the multitudes, as if murder were a cause for hilarity, and the deaths of five Christian women of no great significance.

A wide, wide world indeed! One altogether foreign to the tranquillity of Bloodsmoor; and the simplicity, innocence, and natural goodness enjoyed by the five Zinn daughters, in their girlhoods.

"It is as well, perhaps, that she knows so little"—many a grieving family member said, of the declining Mrs. Kiddemaster, who had taken to her bed after Deirdre's abduction, and never regained her health thereafter. "As well, perhaps, that she may pass from this vale of tears in such serenity"—so the elderly Mr. Kiddemaster himself observed, at his wife's bedside, when, some five months after the week in November in which Constance Philippa fled her bridegroom, and Malvinia ran off under the protection of Orlando Vandenhoffen, the saintly lady breathed her last.

Bloodsmoor observed, with some surprise, and not a little murmuring, that Miss Edwina Kiddemaster, after an initial collapse in November, managed not only to rally her spirits, but to so gird her loins that, upon the publication of her new best seller, *100 Hints for the Christian Young: A Primer of Modern Etiquette,* she was able to address a number of religious and civic organizations in the Philadelphia area; and to accept an award, as Authoress of the Year, given by the Christian Protective Association in Baltimore. It was remarked upon by Dr. Moffet, who was fully acquainted with the history of her illnesses, and the capricious nature of her hypersensitivity, that the gallant lady seemed almost to *rally* in response to certain challenges; unlike poor Sarah Kiddemaster, who had not only turned her face to the wall, in a manner of speaking, after her granddaughters' outrageous behavior, but who had, alas, turned from medicine itself—falling under the influence (or into the clutches, in Dr. Moffet's heated words) of the several Bloodsmoor practitioners of the new and controversial doctrine of Christian Science, a religion not yet a decade old (for Mrs. Eddy's *Science and Health with Key to the Scriptures* had first appeared in 1875).

Great-Aunt Edwina might almost have been gratified, that the *very worst* that might befall the young Zinn ladies had occurred, and she might be absolved of grieving over them, and loving them: for she was curiously distant with both Octavia and Samantha, and quite frugal in her condolences to Prudence; and, immediately upon her recovery, she summoned to Kiddemaster Hall her private attorney, evidently to restyle her will, as well as to direct a number of new investments, kept secret from her brother Godfrey, in speculations as disparate as the Little Rock and Fort

Smith Railroad, John Rockefeller's Standard Oil of Ohio, and Wana-maker's. "I will not be crushed beneath the wheels of adversity," Great-Aunt Edwina stated, in a tone of chill composure, "simply because of the bad judgment of others." She wept, of course, at the death of her sister-in-law, for they had been invalid-companions for many years, and had shared many medicines; but she could not bring herself to feel, as others did, that Sarah Whitton Kiddemaster died a saint and a martyr. That Mrs. Kiddemaster had fallen under the spell of Mary Baker Eddy offended Edwina: for Mrs. Eddy's prose style, set beside her own, was deficient in both *sense* and *aesthetic power*.

Apart from Edwina, however, all of Bloodsmoor mourned the ethereal old lady, who was so very clearly a victim of the young genera-tion's want of delicacy, and something coarse and frightening in the very air—which, tho' Mrs. Kiddemaster read no newspapers or books, her extreme sensitivity allowed her to gauge. A courageous invalid since the 1820's, when illness first forced her to her bed, she had managed, over the years, to triumph intermittently over a host of maladies that would have, in Dr. Moffet's words, "felled any gentleman"—polyarthritis, dis-copathia, myositis, among others, and, since the winter of 1879–80, a new and hitherto unexplored disease, just beginning to be prevalent in the mid-Atlantic region, known as "ovarian neuralgia," in which Dr. Moffet had become something of an expert, before the Christian Science practi-tioners supplanted him in the old lady's affections.

It would have been very difficult for Octavia and Samanatha to believe, had they not the testimony of their elders, and that of an oil portrait painted at the time of their grandmother's wedding—so very long ago, Monroe had been President, and Daniel Webster a handsome young man, and the women's fashions quaint indeed!—that Sarah Kid-demaster had been, in her youth, one of the loveliest girls in the region; and that she had "had her pick," as the saying went, of all the eligible young men. Over the years her more spiritual qualities had strengthened, as her physical qualities waned, and, even as a woman of middle age, she had been admired for the extraordinary slenderness of her waist (a mere seventeen inches, rivaling any girl's), and for the delicate pallor of her complexion, which unseemly blushes never despoiled. Perhaps as a con-sequence of religious devotion, or a natural constitutional inclination, this good lady had gradually conquered *appetite* in all its insidious forms. She allowed no more than two meals to be set before her, of a day; and each was a repast of agreeable lightness, fish and fowl rather than red meat, with no rich French sauces, or unnecessary spices, to stimulate the blood to needless agitation. It hardly needs to be said that Sarah Kid-demaster was a resolute teetotaler, as impatient as Edwina herself with those who regularly succumbed to the weakness of *imbibing*. (Alas, this included her husband, Godfrey, and many a time did he slam out of the room, when they dined alone together, before Sarah's invalidism confined her to her quarters! The family thought it quite a pity, too, that Great-Uncle Vaughan, who had been so attached to Sarah in their youth, was one of that number of menfolk in the family whom the good lady had banned from her bedchamber, in her last illness, for, as she claimed with incontestable accuracy, the men fairly *reeked* of alcohol without being conscious of it, for the poisonous substance had gradually permeated their bloodstreams; and a teetotaler of Sarah's sensitivity could not bear it.)

That Sarah Kiddemaster was a saint, no one in the household could doubt; not even the servants, who oft felt the power of her diminutive will, and responded with alacrity to her frequent calls. Before illness overtook her she was active in numerous church functions, both in Philadelphia and Bloodsmoor; and, in Bloodsmoor, as "first lady," so to speak, she had assumed her social obligations with a resigned grace, and condescended to visit the five or six homes in the village which tradition had deemed worthy of Kiddemaster attention. "Utterly good"—"utterly selfless"—"angelic"—"the epitome of Christian womanhood"—"unperturbed by inordinate thought"; so whispered praise for Mrs. Kiddemaster sounded, well before her death at the age of seventy-nine. Her activities were a thrice-daily reading of the Bible, kept at all times on her bedside table; and her crocheting, to which she applied her flagging energies, with piteous industry, on the very eve of her passing; and near-constant prayer, in which Miss Narcissa Gilpin, as a new convert to Christian Science, guided her. Wickedness, sin, and ill-health *do not exist:* and the soul beset by demonic confusions of "ill-health" has only to pray with doubled intensity, to regain God's blessing of perfect health. (For some excited days it was thought that Mrs. Eddy herself might journey to Bloodsmoor, to more expertly guide the sickroom prayers; but the distance between Lynn, Massachusetts, and Bloodsmoor, being discouraging, and Mrs. Eddy's own health uncertain, nothing came of these plans. Alas, how overjoyed poor Sarah would have been, to see the great Mary Baker Eddy in the flesh!—perchance to shake her hand, and to witness her apply herself to prayer, that wickedness, sin, and ill-health might be banished as the delusions they are!)

For many years Mrs. Kiddemaster had devoted herself to the female arts, with agreeable results: china-painting, egg-decorating, the construction of beautiful papier-mâché flowers, and music of all kinds. In her confinement she restricted herself to needlepoint, knitting, embroidering, and crocheting, sometimes for the poor of the village—who badly needed, as one might imagine, warm clothing for our severe winter months—and sometimes for the trousseaus of her young nieces and granddaughters. Quilts, afghans, coverlets, towels, napkins, handkerchiefs, doilies, antimacassars. . . . Even on her deathbed she was hurrying to complete an antimacassar begun many months previously, for Octavia's trousseau, insisting in her gentle voice that she must make haste, she had not long on this earth, and this pretty little trifle was for her sweetest granddaughter Octavia; the granddaughter she loved above all the rest. No one had told her, of course, of Malvinia's and Constance Philippa's defections; yet that astute lady had seemed to know, and to have resigned herself. She spoke ill of no one on earth, but, it was noted by all, she *did* reiterate her grandmotherly love for Octavia, as the sweetest, most docile, and most worthy of the girls; it may have been that, in the drowsiness of her gradual decline, she forgot about poor Samantha entirely—a possibility that disturbed the child more than I might have anticipated. In any case Grandmother Kiddemaster was crocheting for Octavia's trousseau on her deathbed, no matter that the blushing young lady felt obliged to tell her that, at the present time, she was *not* engaged, and had very few prospects. "Nonsense," Grandmother Kiddemaster said softly, her ivory-pale, curiously unlined, and ethereally lovely face turned for a moment to her granddaughter, "we all marry; you will see."

Death so gently stole into the bedchamber, and gathered her in his merciful embrace, that even Narcissa Gilpin, rapt in prayer not three feet from the expiring lady, took no note of the actual moment of her surcease. That her death was beautiful, befitting her life, none could contest: not even the surly Dr. Moffet, lingering for weeks downstairs, who had insisted to all who would listen that, had he permission to bleed Mrs. Kiddemaster, and to give her medicines for the ovarian neuralgia above all else, he "would have her on her feet in no time."

The elderly judge wept passionately for her, hiding his face in his hands. For a spell the family thought him inconsolable: again and again he moaned, "My belovèd, my angel, my dear girl," and not even his daughter Prudence could calm him. "My Sarah, my perfect one, we will never see your likes again in Bloodsmoor—" until the poor old gentleman collapsed himself, and had to be carried to his own bedchamber, to be tended by Dr. Moffet.

After a brief consultation it was decided that an autopsy might be beneficial, in the interests of medical science, for Mrs. Kiddemaster had died, after all, of no discernible disease—her numerous ailments being of a minor nature, vexing and debilitating, but not fatal. And so the dread but necessary operation was performed, with what astonishing results I can scarcely bring myself to record: it was discovered that Mrs. Kiddemaster had possessed *very few inner organs, and those of a miniature, or atrophied, nature.* The torso, stomach, abdominal, and genital regions were largely hollow; and in these cavities, amidst the pools of pale pink watery blood, were some four or five organs of a size and quality that even the mortician, with his expert eye, experienced some difficulty in identifying. A tiny heart; a tiny liver, of a perplexing grayish-white hue; pebble-sized kidneys; a stomach sac of perhaps three inches in diameter; no bowels at all; a papery-thin conglobate envelope that might have been the uterus, or a genito-urinary canal of some sort, its function too coarse to explore. Having been the enviable possessor, throughout her life, of a skeleton of the most refined delicacy, Mrs. Kiddemaster was found to weigh after her death only *forty-three pounds:* which figure, the mortician thought most extraordinary, a tribute as much to the lady's ascetic Christian practices of diet, as to her God-given anatomy.

Upon being given Grandmother Kiddemaster's crocheted antimacassar, poor Octavia succumbed to fresh fits of sobbing; for she had loved her grandmother dearly, and had never felt worthy of the lady's especial affection. "Samantha, what shall I do; how shall I deal with such grief?" Octavia cried. "Perhaps I am guilty of having allowed Grandmother to deceive herself, as to the nature of my marital prospects!" Samantha comforted her, as best she could, and together both girls examined the crocheting: a wonderfully delicate work, giving no evidence of the lady's ebbing powers, save in its exceptional length. For, Mr. Zinn having measured it with his tape, the antimacassar was somewhat above the conventional in length, being 1,358 yards, or some three-quarters of a mile, and would present problems of practicability.

"I fear that I am not worthy of Grandmother's love, or of her final blessing," Octavia said, dashing fresh tears from her eyes.

Pert little Samantha, staring at the crocheting, and fingering its delicate texture, sighed, and said: "You are worthier than I."

28

The meteoric rise to fame of "Malvinia Morloch" on the New York City stage, as one of the chief attractions of the popular Fanshawe Theatre troupe, was never commented on by her Bloodsmoor kin—for Mrs. Zinn wisely banned all mention of the renegade daughter's name in the Octagonal House, since the mere uttering of "Malvinia" would disturb Mr. Zinn, and seriously interfere with his work; and elderly Judge Kiddemaster, embittered and weary, and given to sardonicism, deemed it a more useful occupation of his twilight years, to keep a close eye on the follies of his time—the Republican "Stalwarts" who wanted Grant back in the Presidency, the Democratic machinery with its boastful crooks, the idiocies of barbarians like William Henry Vanderbilt, "the richest man in the world"—and dictate his memoirs to an amanuensis, and concentrate his grandfatherly love (the meager quantity that remained) on Octavia and Samantha, the virtuous sisters. With a measured smile, and in a voice lightly tinged with gentlemanly irony, he allowed that he "anticipated with subdued hope" the next generation: and that he was prepared to enjoy his great-grandchildren, when they appeared.

Photographs of both Malvinia and Constance Philippa were carefully packed away in silver tissue, along with most of their clothes and personal possessions, for it was better so, that their betrayals be felt as *deaths;* and an appropriate period of mourning undertaken, and completed. (Mrs. Zinn, leading the servants in a flurry of housecleaning one fine day, disposed of the dressmaker's dummies that had once belonged to Malvinia and Deirdre—the one having belonged to Constance Philippa being already disposed of. Certain items of clothing that had belonged to Malvinia—handkerchiefs, sashes, veils, gloves, lace collars were given to Octavia, provided they did not upset Mr. Zinn when he happened to glance at them; Samantha having rejected them, with a contemptuous twist of her lip. And a fan or two, and a lacy morning cap, and a crimson silk sunshade, and a Turkey Morocco case with the golden clasps which —alas, so long ago!—the handsome Cheyney Du Pont de Nemours had surreptitiously given Malvinia: these pretty items Octavia kept, less for their value in themselves than as mementos of the heartless Malvinia. She tied the morning cap's strings beneath her chin, and studied herself in her mirror, and wondered: Would Malvinia laugh cruelly, to see her thus?

At the very rear of one of Malvinia's wardrobe drawers, hidden beneath a sheet of silver paper, was a small yellowed Valentine—pinks and crimsons and creamy-white adorned with strips of lace (badly yellowed as well)—not a homemade card, but charming nonetheless: the signature M.K. in tall playful letters, and quite a puzzle to Octavia: M.K.? But who was M.K.? A young man, a girl?—an older relative? The Valentine, Octavia judged, was *very* old; Malvinia must have received it many years ago; and either treasured it greatly, or had simply forgotten about it.

This too Octavia kept, in secret, hiding it beneath the tissue in one of *her* wardrobe drawers.

At times, alone in the parlor, when she was confident that no one could hear, she clumsily picked out the tunes Malvinia had played with such dash on the piano, and sang under her breath Malvinia's favorite songs—"When the Swallows Homeward Fly," "Is There a Heart That Never Lov'd," "Sunbeam of Summer," "It Is Better to Laugh Than Be Sighing," from the much-admired production of *Lucrezia Borgia* which Malvinia and several of her Philadelphia cousins had attended, at the Stadt Opera House; and her tears often fell afresh down her cheeks. The old Mother Goose book, its pages much-tattered, she again perused, tho' knowing her action futile, and in danger of arousing Mrs. Zinn's ire should she enter the parlor without warning. "It is sinful to confess, as if in defiance of Mother's wishes," Octavia confided in Samantha, "but I miss Malvinia very, very much . . . and believe that, were she to appear in the doorway this very instant, I would forgive her everything, and hug and kiss her till she was breathless!"

Samantha, never a garrulous young lady, had become even more reticent of late, and often did not reply to Octavia's nervous chatter as if, perhaps, she was not seriously attending to it. Her thoughts she kept to herself, guarded; even her small freckled face, so apparently open, and guileless, rarely registered any emotion save that of an innocent and friendly attentiveness. That she was not altogether the childlike sister she appeared, to Octavia's eye, was evidenced by the resistance, and finally the vehemence, she put forth, when urged by both Octavia and Mrs. Zinn to move into Octavia's bedchamber—for Octavia was extremely lonely, and found it difficult to sleep at night, with no companion. But she held her ground: she resisted; she refused. In the end Mrs. Zinn acquiesced, albeit angrily, for Samantha insisted that she had need of quiet in the evenings, in order to work at the mathematical problems Mr. Zinn had assigned her. And Octavia, tho' wounded, allowed that she understood —for she *was* an inveterate chatterer.

"Is it wrong of me to miss Malvinia so very much, seeing that she has abandoned us?" Octavia asked Samantha in a whisper.

Hardly troubling to glance up from a sheet of paper on which she had scribbled the most perplexing figures and shapes, Samantha replied absently: "Not *wrong* so much as *futile.*"

That "Malvinia Morloch" became so successful a stage actress in New York, within months of her theatrical *début,* and that her bright mercurial talents continued to win praise from the most jaded of reviewers and critics, did not truly surprise Octavia, who remembered fondly her sister's childish love of singing, dancing, "dressing up," playacting, and mimicry. At times there had been a certain frenzy to the girl's wish to perform, to however tiny an audience (often only Octavia and Pip—Pip had adored Malvinia), and her troubling wish to *draw praise and applause;* but most of the time Malvinia had been wonderfully charming, and imaginative, and amusing; and had earned the attention lavished upon her. It was impossible to be jealous of her, Octavia felt, for she was so *very* pretty, and so tirelessly spirited . . . ! Octavia had only to glance covertly at Mr. Zinn's countenance, during one of Malvinia's parlor performances, to see how paternal pride manifested itself, and to see that such pride would never be inspired by *her:* yet, such was the girl's sweetness and generosity, she felt only the tiniest pinch of envy, which was then forgotten in a burst of wild applause, as she clapped for Malvinia with the rest. (It is true that she might have liked Malvinia's numerous suitors for herself; and Mr. Du Pont de Nemours above all; but only since Malvinia had said carelessly, upon so many occasions, that she cared for none of them, and surely did not "love" a one!—whatever that vexing word "love" might mean. And even then Octavia was not *jealous.*)

In the old days, when poor Mr. Zinn had been away at the War, and his family had missed him terribly, the little girls and their mother had oft entertained themselves in the parlor, singing, and playing games, and doing pantomimes; and even at that very young age (she could not have been more than four) Malvinia had displayed considerable talent— and considerable energy. She was brash, she was bold, she was silly and funny and reckless: and her sparkling eyes and pretty flushed face and raven-dark flyaway hair (with the exquisite little widow's peak) had usually been sufficient, to deflect Mrs. Zinn's exasperation. But what inventiveness!—what hijinks! Upon one memorable occasion the saucy miss ran into the parlor with Mrs. Zinn's best Sunday hat on her head, all feathers and tulle, and a long lace doily wrapped about her tiny shoulders like a shawl, and, in a high shrill fevered voice she sang her favorite Mother Goose song, "Girls & Boys Come Out to Play," so insistently that the laughing Mrs. Zinn finally relented, and accompanied her on the piano—

> Girls & boys come out to play,
>   The moon doth shine as bright as day;
> Leave your supper, & leave your sleep,
>   & come to your play-fellows in the street!
>
> Come with a whoop,
>   & come with a call,
> Come with a good will—or not at all!

Upon another occasion Malvinia worked up a sort of pantomime with Pip (who was costumed in the darling little sailor suit Octavia had sewed for him), that was such a success it had to be performed at her grandparents' house, for an admiring group of relatives; and how proud Mrs. Zinn had been, tho' she had tried not to show it! Upon another occasion, of a more infamous nature, two or three years later (for Mr. Zinn was now returned from the War, and gradually "becoming himself" again), impudent little Malvinia had stolen out of a closet in Kiddemaster Hall an old corset from the 1780's, which had evidently belonged to Judge Kiddemaster's mother, and she had frolicked about *inside it,* as if wearing it, rolling her eyes and poking out her pink little tongue and acting, in short, supremely silly—until her mother put an abrupt end to the performance, and ushered the child off to bed. (The old buckram corset, tho' much derided in modern times, surely had its advantageous qualities; and was, in my opinion, stouter, more reliable, and generally more effective, than the "streamlined" corsets worn by the ladies of the 1870's and 1880's. Its construction was simple and forthright: betwixt an external covering of firm worsted cloth, and a lining of strong white linen, bound together on the edges with white kid, were ranged a number of stiff whalebones—I once counted one hundred, before giving up—placed close beside each other, with rows of white stitching set between. Seven segments, or gores, divided the stays from top to bottom, and gave them their unique shape, for which they were prized by our ancestors. Stiff and thick and agreeably substantial, tho' a trifle weighty, the buckram corset was laced behind with a leather string, tied to the eyelet-holes, while a broad wooden busk kept the long front as straight and imposing as possible. One has only to consult Copley's paintings, to note the striking effect, in the bodice particularly; and the few remaining works of our "American Hogarth," the brilliant John Lewis Krimmel.) Leaping about inside this stiff garment, the audacious little Malvinia had tried to sing "O What Have You Got for Dinner, Mrs. Bond," but managed only one chorus—

> Mrs. Bond went to the duck pond in a rage,
>   With plenty of onions, and plenty of sage;
> She cried, "Come you little wretches, come, and be killed!
>   —For you shall be stuffed, and my customers filled!"

—before her angry mother hauled her away.

"Was there *ever* such a naughty miss!" Mrs. Zinn muttered. "One might almost think you weren't of our own blood, but were a *changeling!*"

How delightful they were, and haunting too, the old nursery songs!—whose rollicking melodies and simple rhymes dispelled the gloomy thoughts of many an evening, in those days long past! If I listen closely enough I can hear them again; if I close my eyes I can see the girls again, in the old parlor, grouped about the piano as Mrs. Zinn played. Constance Philippa as a young girl, and Malvinia, and Octavia, and little Samantha—and, shortly, Deirdre herself, who, for all her sorrow, *was* capable of a sunny startl'd smile now and then, and a burst of melody that caused her slender frame to tremble with joy.

Octavia's favorite song was "Mulberry Bush," for she loved the bouncy rhythm, and the way all kept going round and round and round: so safe and tidy and delightful! She fancied too, in secret, that she might one day resemble the demure miss illustrated at the top of the page, who stood with her hands clasped at her waist and her eyes lowered, as two husky boys danced about her.

Samantha's favorite song had not a whit of sentiment about it, but went so swiftly it was all over (she had counted) in but three breaths: "Tom, Tom the Piper's Son." Compact as a tiny, perfectly functioning machine, with nothing fussy to impede it; yet what a very *odd* world it must have been, in which a pig—living?—or dead and roasted?—but in the illustration it looked as if it *were* living—was stolen in the street, and eaten at once, as if little Tom were extremely hungry. Samantha did not ponder o'erlong upon the song's mystery, however, but sat on the piano stool, her short legs dangling, and hammered away at the tune, which she had learned by rote, and could play with faultless mechanical skill.

Malvinia loved "Sweet Lavender," for the innocent promise of its words ("Some to make hay, diddle-diddle! Some to cut corn; Whilst you and I, diddle-diddle! Keep ourselves warm"), and for its pleasant illustration, in which a handsome youth, cap in hand, bows before a pretty young miss. And "Little Bo-Peep," despite its insipid lyrics, had a most compelling illustration, which made Malvinia's mouth dry as she studied it in secret: a gorgeous Bo-Peep with long curly tumbling red hair, and an aggrieved expression, and a graceful white gown of a Grecian style, all folds and ripples, which showed her lovely figure to great advantage, as if she were naked beneath it—as one could never be, Malvinia knew, in real life.

Constance Philippa admired the crow in that rollicking song, particularly as he was illustrated at the bottom of the page, in high boots and a pirate's jaunty hat, a mean-looking sabre tucked beneath his wing. Better yet was "The Fairy Ship," which Constance Philippa fancied she would one day sail (no matter that the sailors were mice, and the captain a duck); best of all was "A Fox Went Out," which Constance Philippa found deliciously naughty, tho' her sisters heartily disliked it. "At last he got home to his snug den, To his seven little foxes, eight, nine, ten; Says he, 'Just see, what I've brought with me, With its legs all dangling down O!'" Malvinia clapped her hands over her ears, and cried: "It isn't nice —it's bad to hear—*you're* bad to always want to sing it!" and Constance Philippa said: "It's in the book with the other songs, and I'll sing it all I want!"—her lower lip swollen in an unattractive pout.

The Zinns were poor, but their well-to-do relatives were always taking pity on them, and since the sisters were so winning, and so grateful, they were given a great many presents over the years. By the time Deirdre came to live with them they had acquired the makings of a little orchestra—tiny fiddles, a tiny accordion, a mouth organ, drums and cymbals and even a flute (of a very simple design); and of course they had the spinet piano, which was part of Mrs. Zinn's dowry, and a very fine piano it was, with ivory keys and massive tapering octagon legs, of solid mahogany. Samantha had devised an ingenious method by which a single person could play a half-dozen instruments simultaneously, with the employment of strings, sticks, and wires, attached firmly to the feet. "Isn't she clever!" the family exclaimed, even as they winced at the dreadful noise that ensued. "She takes after her father, doesn't she? What a clever little monkey!"

When Deirdre was adopted by Mr. and Mrs. Zinn she was nearly ten years of age; and the year was 1873. Mr. Zinn having been persuaded by his wife to submit to the nuisance of *applying for a patent*, to secure the rights to certain waterproofing discoveries he had made (which, tho' crude by our contemporary standards, and soon overtaken by others' improvements, were nonetheless valuable), and having been persuaded as well by his vigorous Kiddemaster relatives, to allow them to "talk up" his invention to those manufacturers of boots and raincoats among their acquaintance, the Zinns basked in the delightful if temporary warmth of affluence—and the child might have seemed a sign of that affluence, or one of its literal manifestations. If she aroused their pitying affection with her downcast mourner's gaze, and the tears that seemed forever brimming in her eyes, she nevertheless surprised them with her spontaneous talent for the piano: which was to alter the nature of the music-making evenings entirely, and to embarrass the other girls, Malvinia in particular, who had fancied herself musical.

It came about quite by accident one evening, five or six months after Deirdre's arrival, when all were gathered in the parlor, including Mr. Zinn, who had had an agitated day in the workshop—revising diagrams for his "sun-furnace," which would, he felt confident, entirely revolution- ize the heating of America, if only he could get it right; and little Pip, sleepy after his supper, who lay in his master's lap. Mrs. Zinn went to the spinet and played a few songs at the girls' requests—"Woodman! Spare That Tree!" was a favorite, and "Jeannie with the Light Brown Hair," which Malvinia sang in a breathy dreamy voice; and then Malvinia played, for perhaps a half-hour; and then Octavia, settling herself in her billowing skirts on the stool, with many apologies; and then Samantha hammered fiercely through one or two familiar pieces. Little Deirdre was then en- couraged to come forward, and to sit with Mrs. Zinn at the piano, simply for the pleasure of it, to explore the sounds, and to feel the exquisite smoothness of the ivory keys. Which the child did, reluctantly: for she was naturally shy, and at the same time failed to grasp the sincerity of her new family's affection for her.

"This is the way the hand is stretched," Mrs. Zinn instructed, taking Deirdre's small chill hand in her own, and encouraging her to depress the keys; which she did, tho' very faintly. Malvinia, crowding near, could not resist a demonstration: galloping up and down the treble keys in dissonant chords.

Mrs. Zinn shooed her away, and continued to give Deirdre instruc- tions, of the elementary sort one might give to a very young child, and gradually Deirdre took heart, and depressed the keys more firmly, pro- ducing a sound of crystalline clarity, and startling beauty—as if a peculiar strength were surging through her fingers, to her own amazement. She played with her right hand; then with her left; then both hands together, feebly, hesitantly, then with sudden strength, which immediately ebbed; and returned again, to the astonishment of everyone in the parlor, includ- ing little Pip.

"Why, she knows how to play!—she knew all along!" Malvinia cried, with an air of reproach.

"She does *not* know how to play," Mrs. Zinn said sternly, "it is— it is simply *coming* to her."

And so indeed it seemed: for the frail little girl, her dark gray eyes huge in her face, formed chords and did abrupt sparkling runs, and "played" melodies for a minute or two at a time, before losing the thread, and stopping. Samantha recognized an echo—a queer echo—of "Jeannie with the Light Brown Hair," and Octavia believed she could hear, inside the cascade of unfamiliar notes, the simple tune of "Hey Diddle Diddle."

Mr. Zinn claimed, with some excitement, that *he* could hear musical sense in all the pieces, albeit he was very much an amateur, and was certain he had a tin ear; and Constance Philippa voiced an emphatic agreement, adding, however, that she could not believe Deirdre had never had lessons, or had not been instructed, however informally, by the Bonners. Which statement, tactlessly put, caused the little girl to cease playing at once, and to sit with her hands frozen on the keys, staring ahead, as if seeing nothing.

Whether it was the vociferated doubt of her musical innocence, or the mere mention of the name *Bonner*, the girls' new sister went mute; and would not reply to anyone; and after some distressed moments, Mrs. Zinn noting the degree of her agitation, she was carried off to the nursery, to bed, and settled in with many hugs and kisses, and the promise that she should have piano lessons if she wished.

The child clung to Mrs. Zinn's neck, and whispered into her ear, in a plaintive voice, that she had *not* had lessons before: she was *not* a liar. And Mrs. Zinn comforted her, and stayed with her until she drifted off to sleep. Poor strange disturbing little girl!—the very vision, one is forced to observe, of the orphaned child.

Deirdre stayed away from the spinet for some days, and then returned, and much the same sounds ensued, tho' a pleasant rendition of "Ah! May the Red Rose Live Alway" was interrupted by a sudden crashing of chords, and a run up and down the keyboard, with both hands, that struck all ears as diabolical; and that quite frightened the girl herself. It was a measure of the sisters' sensitivity, to Deirdre's feelings, that they suppressed the remarks they would naturally have made, and the snorts of derision, had one of *them* been responsible for such a noise: tho' Malvinia could not resist a sly chuckle, and the murmured inquiry, as to whether "Father should discern musical sense in *that.*"

Sometimes she played feebly, like any ten-year-old, stumbling through simple Mother Goose tunes; at other times, with a most disconcerting brilliance—snatches and fragments of pieces that, to Mrs. Zinn's moderately sophisticated ear, belonged to the classical repertoire, and might indeed have been written by Mozart or Bach! At such times the child's pale skin appeared to glower, and her eyes grew even darker, and more intense; and Octavia, sitting with her on the piano stool, claimed that she grew *cold*—an emanation issued from her, subtle as a breath, but decidedly cold; and her body temperature dropped so alarmingly, her little fingernails showed bluish-purple. She might play these bits of "serious" music for a minute or two, but then another music would interfere, usually a simple, stumbling, American sort of tune (there was a period of some weeks when "I Wish I Was in Dixie's Land" emerged rather too often, given Mr. Zinn's sentiments about the War; and "Tramp! Tramp! Tramp! or, The Prisoner's Hope," which stirred, with its pounding chords, memories Mr. Zinn had hoped to bury); but sometimes the mad half-angry runs and trills and crashing chords would diabolically assert themselves, to the distress of all the household, including the servants, and the poor child was unable to stop the agitated motion of her hands, until such time as one of her sisters stilled them. She protested that it was not her fault: the keys simply banged down, and her fingers had to follow.

"That's never a little girl playing up there," the maid Vanda once remarked in the kitchen, in Octavia's presence, "that's a grown-up *man:* a *spirit.*"

Indeed, it often seemed that Deirdre did not *possess* the gift, in herself, but that it *possessed her;* streaming through her arms and fingers at the most unpredictable times. It exhausted her, alarmed her, and, less frequently, made her laugh sharply aloud, but it was not *hers,* and was not under her *control.* Tho' Mr. Zinn forbade all manner of superstitious talk, as ill-befitting a household of the mid-nineteenth century, in which rational and scientific evolutionary principles were honored, the sisters whispered amongst themselves that Deirdre's piano playing very likely did issue from another world. ("But where is this *other world* located," Samantha asked skeptically, "and why cannot Deirdre speak of it? She has no more sense of herself, at such times, than Pip!")

That such eerie spells of "music" were deleterious to the child's equilibrium, and to the natural harmony of the Octagonal House, was soon evident, and she was discouraged from exhausting herself at the piano, or to approach it only with Mrs. Zinn nearby; but the natural curiosity of the phenomenon was such, and the intermittent passages of real music so genuinely enchanting, that the child was frequently urged by one or another of her sisters to play—"just for a minute, while Mother is out!" And, sensing that this was a way of pleasing them, Deirdre rarely refused.

(She did, it seems, wish to be liked—perhaps even loved—by her sisters, tho' their affectionate advances to her were frequently rebuffed, out of ignorance, or embarrassment, or an unreasonable terror that they *would* like her, and she should be compelled to like them in return. Unhappy child! One day warm and the next day cold; one day hanging about Malvinia like a puppy, the next day resolutely looking aside when Malvinia addressed her; one day weeping and cuddling in Octavia's arms, because "something bad" had tried to get her in the night, "a great big black bird" like the bird in one of the Mother Goose songs, and her arms and legs were stuck, in something like mud, and tho' she screamed and screamed, no one came to help—another day, wrenching free when poor Octavia sought to comfort her, after a wicked bee had stung her arm. Of course she was younger than her sisters, at an age when every year is crucial: ten years old, to Constance Philippa's *sixteen,* and Octavia's *fifteen,* and Malvinia's *fourteen,* and Samantha's *eleven.* Tho' she shared Samantha's bedchamber, and tho' Samantha made every effort, or nearly, to befriend her, it was still the case that her heaviness of heart, her great, dark, tear-bright eyes, and her habit of going mute for hours at a time, hardly endeared her to the sister closest in age to her; and the sister she most admired—pretty flighty Malvinia—would have none of *her*.)

Deirdre's uncanny ability at the piano might very well have waned of its own, like the disturbing poltergeist phenomena of a year or two later, had not Great-Aunt Edwina summoned the Zinns to Kiddemaster Hall, in order that she might hear her niece play, for tales of Deirdre's remarkable playing had wafted across the park, to the great Hall, despite the elder Zinns' feeling that such reports should be suppressed. (For, wisely, Mr. and Mrs. Zinn understood that anything that served to *distinguish* little Deirdre, in the eyes of her new relatives, would also prevent her from a natural assimilation into the family.) But Great-Aunt Edwina, who had evinced remarkably little interest in the child beforehand, and who had in fact struck both the elder Zinns, and Judge and Mrs. Kiddemaster, as more than ordinarily unaccommodating, in the matter of the adoption, *would* have her way of a sudden. And so Deirdre and the Zinns were brought across the park to the Hall, and Deirdre bade to play "anything she wished" at a piano in the first-floor music room, while, for some eccentric reason of her own, Great-Aunt Edwina insisted upon listening from an adjacent room, through a partly opened door. She wanted, she said, not to disturb the child with her presence; and she also wanted to be alone.

Under such circumstances Deirdre was naturally uneasy, and added to her discomfiture was the foreignness of the Kiddemaster piano, which was made of a bright gleaming satinwood, and trimmed with much ornamentation; and its keys, she murmured to Mrs. Zinn, were "sharp" against her fingers. Nevertheless, the plucky child seated herself on the stool, and played a few faint chords, and began "Looby-Loo," one of the sillier of the nursery songs, experiencing no significant difficulty, yet playing quite without distinction—less skillfully, in fact, than any of her sisters. This continued for some minutes, and rather long minutes they were. The Zinns kept glancing toward the doorway, expecting Edwina to appear, if only to release Deirdre from her obligation: but that lady's stately figure did not materialize, nor did her haughty voice ring out.

The insipid notes of "Looby-Loo" gave way to an uninspired rendition of "I Wish I Was in Dixie's Land," and that to a near-inaudible attempt at "Tom, Tom the Piper's Son," played with very little of Samantha's gusto, and none of her rapid-fire technical skill. Just when, however, the family anticipated an end to the embarrassing little recital, Deirdre sat up very straight at the keyboard, and began pounding maniacally away —her tiny hands flying up and down the keys, up and down, performing arabesques of notes, sly and tinkling as mountain streams, or shattered cascades of ice; guttural and heavy; and mocking; and then again sprightly, and even rather beautiful. Mrs. Zinn rose to her feet, intending to seize hold of Deirdre's hands, and bring the noise to an end, but for some reason she found it extremely difficult to move: crossing an expanse of carpet that measured no more than ten yards took her (according to Samantha's count) some forty-five seconds—and she felt, as she explained afterward, as if she were walking through a cold, dense, sucking element, not unlike mud. By the time she reached Deirdre the music had altered greatly, and was now real music, in fact an extraordinarily lovely air later identified as Schubert's "Adieu! 'Tis Love's Last Greeting," which she hardly wished to interrupt; and so she heard it through to the end, her own bosom heaving with the exquisite sentiment of the piece, and her eyes filling with tears.

After the last notes trailed away Deirdre remained seated at the keyboard, her hands frozen, her dreamy gaze affixed to a point on the wall —as if she were in a trance, but an altogether agreeable one. The Zinns burst into applause, for the music *had* been wonderful, and even Malvinia was quick to praise; but Great-Aunt Edwina not only failed to appear in the doorway, as everyone naturally expected, but the door—incredibly, and so very rudely!—*was pushed shut from the other direction.*

Fortunately, Deirdre was in too somnambulist a state to notice, and, the Zinns, taking care not to call her attention to her great-aunt's rudeness, it was likely she never knew.

Many years later, after Deirdre had been spirited away in the outlaw balloon, her sisters claimed to hear, very distantly, the delicate notes of that Schubert piece: particularly when they crossed a certain stretch of floor, in the small foyer of the Octagonal House, on their way to the stairs. Mr. Zinn allowed that there was *some* sound at that point, but he greatly doubted that it might be characterized as music: still less, that it might be identified precisely as "Adieu! 'Tis Love's Last Greeting." (It was one of the failings of his experimental house—as Mr. Zinn admitted—that queer whining sourceless winds glided through the downstairs rooms, whether windows were open, or no; and that chilly emanations manifested themselves, on even the warmest days. Murmurs, and high hollow dronings, and faint wailing sounds, and ghostly piano music—all scientifically explicable, of course, had one the necessary information.)

Not many weeks after Deirdre's departure, the sisters were about to enter the dining room, when the piano sounded—at a very great distance.

"It is that infernal Schubert composition," Constance Philippa cried, as the blood drained out of her lips. "Shall we never be free of it?"

"She mocks us, she *haunts* us," Malvinia murmured.

"It is not Deirdre," Samantha said, shocked. "It is—only the wind. It is *only* the wind."

The sisters stood for some time, motionless. Octavia's head was bowed, and her eyes closed; and, as the piano faded, and the ordinary noises of the household returned—the loud ticking of a grandfather clock, the sound of servants chattering amongst themselves—she betook herself to say, in a voice of half-amused regret: "But how nice to think —to imagine!—that our sister *considers* us; that she feels sufficient emotion for us, to play again that pretty tune, and rouse our memories."

"It is no tune," Samantha said emphatically. "It is not a piano, it is not Deirdre. *It is only the wind*—as Father has said."

29

With some hesitation, and not a little repugnance, I must now describe how Miss Malvinia Zinn fell in love—violently, and blindly—within the first ten minutes of the tumultuous *Under the Gaslight:* when the virile figure of Orlando Vandenhoffen strode onto the stage, and his fierce dark eyes swept the audience, and his voice rang out with passion of a sort she had never before experienced—save in her most secret and most shameful imaginings.

Ah! so that is the great Vandenhoffen! I must have him, the reckless young lady vowed. *I must—I will!—else life holds no further pleasures for me, and the graveyard warmly beckons—*

So the besotted Malvinia inwardly declared, all the while staring at Vandenhoffen's craggily handsome face, in which a portentous calm now contested the ferocity of the previous moment, and a lofty, tortured dignity sought to display itself: so staring at Vandenhoffen, and following him as he moved swiftly about the stage, that she was oblivious to the other actors, and failed to appreciate the set (a remarkably realistic depiction of the interior of a genteel home); and even to grasp the substance of Vandenhoffen's speech.

She was seated beside her cousin Basil Miller, in the Millers' comfortable box, and tho' it was her custom, with Basil, to whisper and giggle at most theatrical productions, and even during the opera, she was mysteriously silent throughout the first act of the Daly play, sitting quite erect, her gloved hands gripping her fan, her beautiful head held high— as if, perchance, she fancied that Orlando Vandenhoffen might glance up at her.

An extraordinary man—an actor of arguable genius—bold and

251

dashing and impetuous—capable of a virile pathos rarely seen on the American stage, and a profound, raging passion—an aristocrat in every inch of his tall masculine frame—the possessor of a stern, noble, pale brow, and a lofty profile, and those remarkable, fierce eyes which had won so many female hearts: thus the famous Orlando Vandenhoffen, in the second year of his American tour, fresh from a popular success in *Under the Gaslight* at the Fanshawe in New York, and now taking Philadelphia audiences quite by storm. *Was there ever such a man!* poor Malvinia wondered, staring so intensely at him that her eyes began to ache, as if she had stared too long at a flame. *His every gesture—the flamboyance of his walk—the ringing power of his voice—the dark curls at his temples, and his thick mustache, and the perfection of his jawline—the hypnotic spell of his very presence . . .*

Her heart beat tempestuously, but steadily, beneath the molded bodice of her ivory brocade gown, and the cherubic ringlets on her forehead and cheeks grew somewhat damp from a fine film of perspiration that arose, as a consequence both of the o'erwarm theater, and the near-unbearable tension of the play. So infatuated was Malvinia with the leading man, and so convinced that at any moment he might glance up into the Millers' handsome box, that she paid little heed to the other actors, as the play unfolded, and even felt some jealousy of the leading lady (whose conventionally attractive face, and nondescript figure, she deemed unworthy of Vandenhoffen's admiration); yet the general sense of the plot communicated itself to her, and she thrilled with the other members of the audience, female and male alike, who leaned forward in their seats, and held their breaths like children, as, in the final act, Vandenhoffen's villainous enemy bound his insensible form to a length of railroad track (which struck Malvinia's feverish eye as *very* realistic) while, in the distance (again, most realistically depicted), a locomotive bore down upon him! Tho' Malvinia, as an experienced theatergoer, certainly knew that the situation was naught but illusion—melodramatic, and forced, and supremely unlikely—and tho' she knew that, as a spectator, she was being crudely manipulated to feel such tension, nevertheless she could not steel herself against the exigencies of the moment: she uttered a series of breathless little screams, and peeked through her gloved fingers, exactly like the most credulous members of the audience. The hero was so handsome—so noble—so good! What if, by some hideous reversal of fate, he should *not* be untied in time, by his beleaguered leading lady? What if the playwright, like a malevolent jesting God, had conspired to terrorize his audience, by sending Vandenhoffen to his death?

I cannot bear it, the distracted Malvinia thought, leaning so far forward that her whalebone stays cut deep into her flesh, *if he should die! Dear God, I swear to You I cannot bear it—*

(Most of which she would confess to Vandenhoffen, upon the occasion of their first intimacy—giggling wildly, and blushing, and squirming about like an eel, under the mischievous influence of champagne—at a time when a woman of more normal moral fibre would have been crushed with shame.)

But the heroine ran screaming to his rescue, and tho' the massive locomotive bore down noisily upon them, and not a few ladies in the audience swooned in terror, Vandenhoffen was untied, and rescued in time—and the villain foiled. And Malvinia, poor quivering Malvinia, could not stop herself from shedding childish tears of gratitude, tho' she knew that it was only a play, and an ingenious stage setting, and that Vandenhoffen was an actor: that is, one who cannot be killed.

After the cast had taken five curtain calls, and the heavy velvet curtains had swept triumphantly together for the final time, Cousin Basil turned casually to Malvinia and asked, with a slight smile: "Would it amuse you, dear Malvinia, to drop by Mrs. Broome's tonight?—for I have, you know, a standing invitation."

Malvinia was still dabbing at her eyes, and found it difficult to attend her cousin, let alone respond to him with courtesy. But she managed to say, in a faint voice: "Mrs. Broome's? Mrs. *Horatio* Broome? Why, whyever do you ask?—when you know I am not allowed, and I halfway think I should not *wish* to be allowed . . ."

Mr. Miller allowed Malvinia's words to trail off into silence, and the silence to expand dramatically, before he said, his smile now deepening (for the mischievous young man had not been insensitive to Malvinia's agitation throughout the play, and he believed he knew well its cause): "Why, I bring the subject up only because some members of the cast—tonight's cast—have been invited over: you know of Mrs. Broome's *salon,* surely, and how far the poor delightful creature will fling her net!—and I thought, perhaps naïvely, that you might wish to be introduced to Mr. Vandenhoffen, should *he* deign to appear."

Malvinia, still trembling from the evening's emotional strain, the translucence of her lovely cheeks now lightly touched with pink, as if with a virginal blush, and her tear-bright eyes glittering, felt compelled in her surprise to ask Cousin Basil to repeat himself: tho' she had heard him perfectly, the name *Vandenhoffen* having pierced her bosom like a white-hot blade.

(Unbeknownst to her family, Malvinia had behaved very precipitately, in rejecting young Cheyney's hand. She irresponsibly scorned him, it seems, as retaining too much of *Bloodsmoor* to please her! Indeed, the fickle young lady so gave herself airs, on the matter of Cheyney, that, after one of the frequent explosions at the gunpowder mill, which unfortunate accident involved, it was said, upward of a dozen French-speaking workers, of those regularly brought to the States, to work for the Du Pont de Nemours concern—after thoughtless rumors spread across the Valley, from house to house, regarding the fact that sinewy fragments of human flesh, and shattered bone, adorned the barren-limbèd trees, in the vicinity of the mill—why, our haughty Miss Zinn confronted the hapless Cheyney himself, with some histrionic declaration, to the effect that *she* could never countenance such an exploitation of men, whether they be ignorant French peasants, or no: for she deemed it all very *unchristian,* and very *uncouth.* And, this being reported back to her sophisticated city cousins, they roundly applauded her, and showed not a whit of concern, for the nonpluss'd Cheyney!)

Fortunate it was, indeed, that Mrs. Zinn knew naught of this development, but continued in her fond delusion that Malvinia favored Cheyney; and would, one day soon, consent to be his bride.

Over the years, Malvinia had acquired some notoriety, within her family, for always demanding special favors: pouting, and weeping, and cajoling, and begging, and simpering, and persisting, till she had her way. Consequently, her parents were pressed into granting her divers concessions: further lessons on the piano (for it greatly vexed her, that Deirdre could play with such versatility); acting and elocution lessons, at the Philadelphia Girls' Academy (for such lessons, she claimed, would aid her immeasurably at balls, and at other difficult social occasions); French lessons (for someday, surely, she would visit France—and how awkward, to be unable to converse with the natives!); singing lessons (for, after having been enraptured by the magnificent Adelina Patti, in Bellini's *La Sonnambula,* she was convinced that she had a trainable soprano voice). Certain of these requests her parents granted, for Malvinia was so persistent in her demands, it was generally easier to give in than to resist: but a plea for special acting lessons, under Professor So-and-so, made in the autumn of 1880, they had refused for financial reasons, thus incurring their daughter's anger. (Indeed, Malvinia had all but quarreled with her belovèd father, on the matter of these troublesome lessons, her mother having refused them outright, as a needless expenditure. "But I assure you, Father, I *must* apply for these lessons," Malvinia cried, her lovely cheeks blanching, "for all my friends—nearly all my friends—will be taking them: and I shall feel such a countrified little fool!" Mr. Zinn swallowed his amusement, or it may have been his irritation, and said, gently enough: "And *I* shall feel such a countrified fool, my dear child, if you do take them.")

Not many weeks later, the reckless child eloped; and boasted to all the world that she was in love with her seducer. And Mr. Zinn, in great shock, inquired of his wife how it had happened that his innocent daughter had made the acquaintance of an actor!—and how it was, that no one in the family had known of the dangerous circles in which she had been moving. "She is wicked," Mrs. Zinn shouted, covering her ears, "she is marked with wickedness!—it is inevitable, and the blame cannot be laid on us."

Her answer was so unanticipated, and so wildly eccentric, Mr. Zinn scarcely knew how to reply. *"Marked* with wickedness?" he asked.

His wife turned stubbornly away. And would not face him. And said, in a low gratified murmur: "And the blame *cannot* be laid on us."

30

In the months that followed the funeral of Sarah Kiddemaster—an event attended by so many weeping mourners, the old village church was well-nigh filled—a subtle change crept upon Bloodsmoor: and drear, and dismal, and darksome the days proceeded, one upon another. Rare were substantial moments of sunshine, but greatly valued; and the family counted itself blessèd, if something felicitous occurred: the triumph of Great-Aunt Edwina's several Philadelphia lectures, the successful application for a patent out of the Zinn laboratory (for a minor improvement, developed in fact by Samantha, in the printing key frame for the blind, an English invention of the early 1850's: this being a fascinating contraption that had caught the eye of father and daughter alike, who had read of it, and studied its blueprints, in an American inventors' journals).

Alas, reports snaked their way to Bloodsmoor of the increasing fame of Malvinia Morloch, who had played Rosalind in *As You Like It* in New York, with Orlando Vandenhoffen as her leading man; and of the fame—or notoriety—of the controversial trance medium Deirdre of the Shadows, now said to be associated, in ways not clear, with the redoubtable Russian "Countess," Madame Helena Petrovna de Blavatsky. But no news came of Constance Philippa, save cruelly confusing reports: a lone woman answering to her general description (of unusual height, and breadth of shoulders) had been sighted, heavily veiled, in a second-class coach bound for St. Louis, Missouri; a lone woman of similar attributes had been sighted exchanging sharp words with the *maître d'* of the dining room at the exclusive St. Nicklaus Hotel on Park Avenue, New York City —for single women were not allowed into such establishments past six in the evening, and were not generally encouraged to dine therein, at any hour of the day.

"How absurd," Octavia said to Samantha, incensed, "such gossip! Constance Philippa has no reason to journey to St. Louis: no one does. And why would she, of all people, make an attempt to dine at the St. Nicklaus, when it is exactly the sort of place she abhorred, as formality and elegance so badly discomfited her?"

Samantha said softly: "I cannot speculate as to Constance Philippa's motives, any more than I can speculate as to her whereabouts. Whilst she lived in this house, as my sister, I must confess—I scarcely knew her."

Octavia drew herself up to her full height, which was some two or three inches greater than Samantha's; and pressed a hand against her plump bodice. "An extraordinary thing to say, Samantha!—but of course you are only jesting."

It may have been as a direct consequence of Sarah Kiddemaster's funeral (for it was there they met again, however briefly), or it may have been a groundless accident, but Mr. Lucius Rumford suddenly resumed his visits to the Octagonal House, with the obvious intention of pursuing his courtship of Octavia, whose surprise was outweighed only by her delight, as one might well imagine. For Mr. Rumford of Rumford Hall was one of the most distinguished gentlemen in all of Bloodsmoor, albeit a widower of indeterminate age, and a retired Lutheran minister, with a long narrow ponderous horse's face, and a perpetual dry cough.

Dare I hope? the trembling Octavia scribbled in her diary. *Dare I—after so long, and such sorrow?*

She studied herself for long intense minutes in the mirror, in the secrecy of her bedchamber, and felt alternately despair, and encouragement, and despair again: for her face was lacking in beauty of any dramatic sort, yet again her brown eyes were warm, and appealing; but then her complexion—had it not grown sallow in recent months, and lost its maidenly bloom? *I fear I am unworthy of any gentleman's admiration,* she wrote, in a timid pinched hand, *and yet—I must have hope.*

It is true that Octavia had once loved the coachman's red-haired son Sean (now off to make his fortune—who knew where); and true, too, she had once loved Malvinia's handsome suitor Cheyney Du Pont de Nemours (according to rumor, newly engaged to a Charlottesville, Virginia, heiress); but now her thoughts steadfastly attached themselves to Mr. Rumford, who had, she imagined, cared for her all along . . . but had been prevented from continuing his courtship for reasons not in his control. (Rumford Hall had been in financial straits for some time, it was said. There was a mortgage on the buildings, and some of the land had been sold; and the ne'er-do-well elder son—a young man Octavia's age, or older—had accumulated a considerable gambling debt, before abandoning all, and running away to sea.) The vague tale had come to Octavia's burning ears by way of Mrs. Zinn, who had heard it from Great-Aunt Edwina, who had heard it from one of the Philadelphia Butterfields, that Lucius Rumford had "tried his hand" with the young widow Backus, a Butterfield heiress, but had been "sent packing"—for what reason, Octavia had not learned. "Such rumors are the concoctions of idle minds," Mrs. Zinn said stoutly, "and you are *not* to take them seriously. For all we know there is another Lucius Rumford—not of Bloodsmoor —a total stranger—and it is quite futile to become upset. In my youth," Mrs. Zinn added, strangely, her voice for a moment faltering, "in my youth, dear Octavia, I very nearly succumbed to despair, overhearing rumors about your father which I knew, in my heart, were untrue: and how unfortunate for us all, had I not come to my senses!" Mother and daughter were so suddenly moved, they embraced each other, and Octavia, pure of heart as any child, wept upon her mother's broad shoulder. "There, there," Mrs. Zinn said, comforting her. "Mr. Rumford is an honorable man: you can see it in his eyes. And Grandfather Kiddemaster has, I believe, already spoken with him."

And so indeed it was. But the precise terms of Grandfather Kiddemaster's arrangement, and whether he, or Mr. Rumford, had struck the shrewdest bargain, Octavia was never to know.

The austerity & dignity of his face, Octavia carefully noted, writing in her secret diary when all of the house slumbered, *the patience in his smile—that air of God-fearing sobriety—mature virility—a strength forged by suffering—the sagacity of his eyes, which are gray—or a very pale blue—* It alarmed her, and caused her poor silly heart to hammer, that this honorable gentleman loved her: that he had spoken for her; and wished her to be his bride!

How shall I make myself worthy? she wondered. *Only through the counsel of the Lord Jesus Christ. And Great-Aunt Edwina has given me some of her books —a priceless resource.*

Conversation with Mr. Rumford was ordinarily rather strained, for not only were topics scarce, and Octavia's venturings uncertain, but the gentleman was troubled with a dry rasping cough, and the need to blow his nose frequently in his handkerchief. He inquired after her health, and the health of her parents; he inquired as to her particular opinion of the weather—had it struck her as too hot, or too cold; too gusty; too humid; intemperate to any significant degree? He spoke very briefly of his own health, and the weather some four miles away, at Rumford Hall. He did not, of course, ever allude to his first wife (deceased now for some years), nor did he speak except vaguely of his children; and his only outburst, having to do with his misfortune in pipeline investment, as a consequence of "criminal" monopolizing on the part of John D. Rockefeller, terminated in a ferocious spasm of coughing, and was not resumed.

It was a solemn and dignified occasion, upon which Mr. Rumford presented his fiancée with a small but very comely agate ring, set in antique silver; and the young lady's excited shyness was such, she could barely bring herself to speak, and cast numerous wild glances toward the doorway—as if, for some fanciful reason, she imagined figures hiding just outside it, around the corner, eavesdropping, pressing their knuckles to their mouths, to keep from laughter!—only one of several eccentric but harmless excogitations of those last days of maidenhood.

She fancied she rose from her bed to light a lamp, and saw that the agate ring was inscribed in initials other than her own: for of course it was an antique ring, it *had* been used practicably before, she could not demand to be the first woman to wear it!—so she counseled her tripping heart.

But the quivering lamplight revealed nothing: no initials at all. She studied the ring's narrow band, and ran her finger lightly across it, and was quite certain she *did* feel an inscription: but, try as she could, she could see nothing. *A queer phantasmagoria has gripped my heart,* she wrote in her diary, *perchance it is jealousy?—a signal of my budding love for my husband-to-be.*

Nor could she see anything by daylight either. Tho' by daylight, it seemed that she could *feel* the inscription all the more clearly, with her fingertip.

"Mother," Octavia said, some days later, when Mrs. Zinn and Octavia sat companionably in the parlor, doing needlepoint, and a drear but romantic wind howled about the gabled roof of the Octagonal House, "Mother, shall I learn a great deal about the previous Mrs. Rumford; or do you suggest that I make no inquiries, so as not to disturb Mr. Rumford?"

Mrs. Zinn did not reply for so many minutes, it seemed to her daughter that perhaps she had not heard. Her strong fingers continued with their brisk mechanical work; her needle flashed; her gaze was hooded and inscrutable. Octavia looked upon her with both love and trepidation, as the guardian of certain grave secrets: a stout woman of advanced middle age, her pursed lips firmly bracketed in flesh, her color rather ruddy, her gaze either blunt and challenging and intimidating, or oddly evasive. On these informal at-home evenings Mrs. Zinn wore a fairly plain poplin-and-woollen dress, of a neutral shade approaching dark gray, with a tidy white muslin apron, and a lace-trimmed bodice; and her brown hair, now liberally shot with silver, was all but covered by her flounced cotton cap. She had been Octavia's dear *Mother* for a benign eternity, it seemed, and Octavia felt sometimes choked with panic, that she must one day soon leave this warm sewing corner, and her mother, and take up residence—who knew where!

Mrs. Zinn replied at last, with some reluctance: "Such a question indicates, to my mind, an unwholesome sort of introspection—nay, an actual brooding—upon what is *to come,* rather than an active engagement upon what *is.* In the matter of marital relations, my dear daughter," Mrs. Zinn said, frowning at her rapidly moving fingers, as the needle flashed and winked, "it is always best to think *not at all:* in the present, to think not of the future, nor of the past; and not even, if the trick be mastered, of the present itself. For, as the wisdom of the Old Testament instructs us, 'This too shall pass.' "

At this point Mrs. Zinn did glance up at Octavia, who was staring at her, rather too hopefully. But her gaze did not hold: it was only a sort of punctuation. " 'This too shall pass,' " Octavia murmured. "Ah yes: I will remember. Thank you, dear Mother."

Cousin Rowena Kale and her two youngest children came to Kiddemaster Hall for a fortnight's visit, and so Octavia enjoyed the company of a sisterly young woman not so many years her senior: the evident fact that Cousin Rowena was soon expecting another child, and the apparent fact that there was some difficulty with her husband, not being touched upon, as matters too sensitive to be broached, Octavia and Rowena chatted for the most part about details of the forthcoming marriage, and necessities of Octavia's trousseau. Grandmother Kiddemaster's enormous rosewood wardrobe was to be Octavia's—an inheritance of great value, both senti-mental and practical—and so the young women set busily to work inscrib-ing the many drawers, and taking out the year-old silver paper, in order to replace it with fresh, and preparing "sweet-bags" of powdered mace, dried leaves of southernwood and dragonwort, extract of ambergris, sweet marjoram, hyssop, roses, Tonquin beans, Florentine orrisroot, musk, and civet: for the magnificent wardrobe *was* quite old, and badly required perfuming.

When, as happened from time to time, the two young women found themselves safely alone, with not even a servant near, it was oft the case that, in an undertone, topics of a somewhat coarse nature were discussed: whether, "in her present condition," Rowena sometimes craved strange and exotic foods, of a kind not available in Bloodsmoor (for, shyly, Octavia had heard of such cravings, and wondered if she might soon experience them herself); whether details were forthcoming, of the alleged villainy of Delphine Martineau's husband, Mr. Ormond (who was rumored—alas!—to be a secret gambler, and an imbiber of alcoholic spirits); whether Bloodsmoor knew of the "solitary, veiled, broad-shoul-dered" female who had attended each session of the trial of that infamous assassin Charles Guiteau, and had laughed with raucous enthusiasm at the defendant's frequent outbursts of "wit"; whether—and here Cousin Rowena's voice did appreciably drop—the Zinns ever spoke of "Malvinia Morloch."

For the most part, however, the young women in their morning dresses and caps busied themselves with the rosewood wardrobe, taking especial care with the inscriptions for the pretty little drawers, for it would not do, as Rowena stressed, for Octavia, as a young bride, to demonstrate to her husband, in however innocent and inconsequential a way, a natural inclination toward *slovenliness.* Stiff sheets of white linen stationery, each measuring two inches by four, were inserted with care beneath the bone and ivory drawer knobs, on them being written in a perfect hand—

Stockings (Silk)
Stockings (Cotton)
Stockings (Lisle)
Stockings (Wool)
Slippers (Satin)
Slippers (Silk & Cotton)
Caps (Morning)
Caps (Afternoon)
Caps (Evening)
Caps (Night)
Veils (Lace)
Veils (Tulle)
Bands (Velvet & Sateen)
Bands (Cotton & Poplin)
Flowers (Sunday)
Flowers (Everyday)
Shoes (Sunday)
Shoes (Everyday)
Feathers
Embroidery (Sunday)
Embroidery (Everyday)

Lace (White)
Lace (Gold)
Head Dress
Habit Skirt
Collars (Cotton)
Collars (Silk)
Petticoats (Linen)
Petticoats (Cotton)
Handkerchiefs (Cotton)
Handkerchiefs (Linen)
Neckerchiefs (Silk)
Neckerchiefs (Cotton)
Ribbons
Fringing
Muffs (Fur)
Muffs (Wool)
Chemises (Cotton)
Chemises (Calico)
Ruching
Bows
Tinsel, Sequins & Beads

—and, as there were many more of the little drawers, and Octavia and Rowena enjoyed the leisure necessary to accomplish their task, they worked on industriously and companionably for many a happy hour. From time to time Octavia heard her mother's calming words, *This too shall pass;* but she could not stop herself from exclaiming inwardly, rather like a spoiled child, "Ah!—but *must* it!"

31

The Americans are great hero-worshippers, and always take their heroes from the criminal classes, the poetaster and immoralist Oscar Wilde observed, on the occasion of his visit to our too-hospitable shores, in 1882: *Their heroines are more ambitiously chosen: criminals and goddesses combined.*

By an unsettling fortuity, of the kind that affirms superstitious beliefs in the weak-minded, this foppish Irishman so poked about in our native diversions that, along with visits to Niagara Falls, Salt Lake City, Leadville (Colorado), St. Joseph (Missouri), Camden (New Jersey: where he met with a kindred spirit in the reprobate *Walt Whitman*), and elsewhere, he not only managed to see Malvinia Morloch and Orlando Vandenhoffen in *As You Like It* ("a tediously exhilarating transcription of the Bard at his light-hearted worst"), and the Boston medium "Deirdre of the Shadows" ("a *shadowy* venture in truth—amusing and shivery"), but to comment, in passing, with an air of distracted probity, that the "almost too beauteous" stage actress bore a peculiar family resemblance, about the brow in particular, to the medium Deirdre!

But Wilde was far too busy, preening and boasting and gulling his silly American hosts, and offering himself to publicity, as a living exhibition of God knows what (in his tight plum-colored velvet coat, with flowered sleeves and a cambric ruff, and his infamous bottle-green otter fur overcoat), to make any further comment on either of the young American women, save to note, in a letter to a friend back in England, that "the new American religion being Spiritualism, the Americans might do worse than elect to sainthood the clever little charlatan 'Deirdre of the Shadows,'" and to state, upon a number of occasions, until he forgot her name, that "quite the most dazzling thing in the New World, and near to Bernhardt's equal—save in talent—is *Malvinia Morloch.*"

Beyond this, the meretricious young man made no comment upon our great nation or our magnificent geography worth recording; and much that demands censure.

Quite the most dazzling thing in the New World! How Malvinia would have gloated, to learn that so sophisticated, and so captious, an observer as Oscar Wilde had fallen under her spell: for the young woman was of that species of creature, female and male alike, who are capable of measuring their soul's *worth,* only by the ostensible adulation of others.

That Malvinia's history of beguilement was a lengthy one, will come as no surprise to anyone familiar with her character and its defects. As a very small child, in the nursery, she continuously usurped her father-tutor's complete attention, to the dismay of her sisters—Constance Philippa in particular, who, as the eldest, felt that *she* should be the brightest. (A sorry thing it is, the spectre of jealousy haunting a girl of seven or eight years of age!) Mr. Zinn was perhaps partly to blame, for, in his ambitious project to educate his children "in accordance with the sagacity and wisdom of the innate Soul," he was but intermittently enthusiastic, and tho' he could evoke immediate interest in virtually any subject—geometry, poetry, Egyptian history, drawing and painting, elocution—the very immediacy of the appeal, and the necessity for an expeditious response on the part of the pupil, greatly handicapped the slower sisters, and made bright, clever, mercurial little Malvinia the star scholar of the nursery. Mr. Zinn's lengthy Socratic dialogues, seeking Truth through a meticulous examination of the child's mind (or memory), greatly exhausted Constance Philippa, and Octavia, and the very young Samantha (who, even as a child of three or four, took her father's domain of science and wisdom very seriously indeed); yet gave pretty Malvinia an opportunity to perform, as she supplied answers with no evident difficulty at all (as if—as we have speculated earlier—the precocious child were reading her father's mind).

In those early years Mr. Zinn not only divided his time more equitably between his workshop and the Octagonal House, feeling a deep responsibility for his daughters' education, but consented, upon two separate occasions (of seven months and three months each), to accept an untitled position at one of the family-owned factories downriver: for the Zinns were already in debt, producing a worrisome strain in their domestic life. (John Quincy naturally despised the factory, both in itself and for what it represented of the crass materialism of the new post-War era, and his position—one that combined the duties of a manager with the technical skills of an engineer—did not afford him the autonomy he so badly required, in order that his spirit might flourish.) He was, then, necessarily absent from home for long hours, or even for an entire day, which worried his family, little Samantha in particular. (It was amusing, and touching, that both Samantha and Pip languished when Mr. Zinn was away—mooning about his chair in the parlor, glancing through his papers and journals, running every five minutes to the window, to see if he had returned.) These prolonged absences were, however, coupled with exhaustive sessions in the nursery-classroom, for Mr. Zinn felt always that he must compensate for lost time, and he had vague plans, which never altogether materialized, for transcribing his question-and-answer lessons along the lines of *Out of the Mouths of Babes,* which might bring some modest financial reward. It was the case, then, that while his daughters tortured themselves with the silly terror that he should not return home, they also feared that he *would* return, too abruptly, before they had mastered their assignments! Their love for him was so gratifyingly strong, the merest flicker of disappointment in his face greatly upset them. He had no need to punish—ever. He had no need to exclaim: "Your ignorance has wounded me"—for they could read it in his expression: nay, in the calm hurt and bafflement of his eyes.

In this rather feverish atmosphere Malvinia naturally shone, and was her father's darling: and it cannot greatly surprise us that, a scant decade later, upon being presented to the renowned Orlando Vandenhoffen, in the Philadelphia drawing room of a lady of less than admirable reputation (Mrs. Horatio Broome being the handsome widow of a once-upstanding gentleman who, succumbing to madness of some kind, in his late middle years, chose, after his wife's death, not only to marry an artist's model whom he had been supporting in secret, for years, but to live abroad with her, in Paris, Rome, and Venice!), she should skillfully suppress her awe, smile boldly, and reach out to shake his hand: as if she were not a young American lady at all, but a European courtesan. And she gave the air, too, which naturally aroused the actor's curiosity, of being in a way already acquainted with him, and knowing quite instinctively how to best please and flatter and beguile him, and win his heart.

That Malvinia Morloch should possess, and so cruelly exercise, a certain fatal power over the masculine sex in general (tho' not over *every* member of that sex, as we shall see), is perhaps more readily understood if we learn that she was the inheritor of a *disposition toward wickedness,* in her blood; and had half-consciously cultivated such power, from the nursery onward, tho' always in the most innocent manner. She *did not know,* and yet she fully *knew,* what she did; and how her attractions cast their net over others.

For instance, in the case of young Malcolm Kennicott, Reverend Hewett's assistant in the late Sixties, when Malvinia was scarcely eight years old, and, to all eyes, a normal child: albeit uncommonly pretty, and given to spirited tantrums . . .

Mr. Kennicott must have been in his very early twenties, when he came down to Trinity Church, from the Theological Seminary at Princeton. Tho' he declared himself a Christian, and was certainly believed to be such, by the Reverend Hewett, who entrusted him with many churchly responsibilities, the moony, dreamy, lank-limbed youth was rather more of a poet, and spent hours scribbling verses in French, in which religious and romantic sentiments were confusedly rendered. Because he dwelled alone in Bloodsmoor, and was a bachelor of good family, he was naturally taken up by many local families, including the Kiddemasters and the Zinns: and many an hour he spent at the Octagonal House, happily discussing with John Quincy one or another scheme for Utopianism, or his own plans for "America's greatest hymn" (a massive three-part epic poem to deal with the discovery of the New World by Columbus; Pizarro's conquest of Peru; and Cortez's expedition to Mexico), or the very newest and most radical notions of education, social reform, and the dismantling of the "peculiar institution" of the South. He dined frequently with the Zinns, not minding the little girls' presence but rather rejoicing in it: for Constance Philippa, as a grave young lady of ten or eleven, sought to engage in real conversation with him, oft declaring that she wanted him for her older brother, it being so lonely amidst all the girls!—and vivacious little Malvinia won his heart, with her cheerful prattling and teasing.

The lamentable tale of how this congenial if somewhat preoccupied young man seems to have fallen in love, not with a woman of his own age and capabilities, but with the eight-year-old Malvinia, must necessarily be truncated, for it is, at best, an unnatural story, reflecting ill upon both sexes, and calling into question the theological institution that sent Mr. Kennicott out to Bloodsmoor with such excellent recommendations. Suffice it to state that the young man's hazel eyes dwelt too obsessively upon little Malvinia, and his behavior in playing with her and her sisters and Pip, at shuttlecock or croquet, or even at cards, soon attracted attention to itself. "He is a lonely boy, and we must be his second family," Mr. Zinn observed, stroking his beard, to which Mrs. Zinn replied evenly: "He is perhaps *too* lonely—and he is not a boy."

In those days Malcolm Kennicott was clean-shaven, with a somewhat weak chin, and a soft, sweet mouth; and fawn-colored hair that fell in lank waves to his collar. Tho' his clothes were clearly of superior cut, he dressed carelessly, and his rectangular wire-rimmed spectacles gave him an owlish look. Viewed with sympathy, he might have presented an attractive, even a handsome, figure; viewed with detachment, or the oft-cruel caprice of children, he presented an awkward figure—and his pert, prim little glasses afforded some childish jokes at his expense. (On Valentine's Day, for instance, the sisters sent him an enormous homemade

Valentine, constructed of stiff colored paper, dried flowers, and sequins, at the center of which Malvinia had drawn a cartoon face, smiling, and burdened with outsized spectacles: the jollity of which might have blinded him to a certain cruelty in the execution.)

Mr. Kennicott betook himself on long solitary rambles, in the Kiddemaster woods, when in truth he ought to have been working in the rectory, and it was on one of these strolls that he came upon little Malvinia, with Pip, dancing on the stone stage Judge Kiddemaster had had built some years before, in an atmosphere of simulated Grecian ruins. So absorbed was the eight-year-old child in her playful dancing, and so astoundingly beautiful, that Mr. Kennicott sank in a sort of trance upon a stone bench, and gave himself up to simply staring at her—for how long a period of time, I cannot say. Malvinia sang and prattled and frolicked, doing a passable imitation of some of the fairy dances from "The Seven Castles of the Diamond Lake," until even the spirited Pip grew tired. Tho' it was surely the case that Malvinia was well aware of her audience of one —indeed, his presence wonderfully stimulated her—she glanced up with pretended surprise, at his loud, lusty applause, as if she had never seen him before, and was offended at his intrusion. Pip, too, jabbered and squealed and made an absurd show of being frightened. "Malvinia!" Mr. Kennicott cried, rising hastily to his feet; "you know me, surely. It is your friend Malcolm."

But the diabolical child cast a cold eye upon him; a parody, it may have been, of the disapproving glares the elder Kiddemaster females bestowed upon the little Zinn girls, when they were not well-behaved. "Go away," Malvinia sang out, with all the whimsical cruelty of which a child is capable, "go away, you're wicked to be hiding there, we don't *like* you!"

And, after some hesitation, poor trembling Mr. Kennicott did go away—crestfallen, with tears in his eyes.

Not long thereafter he vanished out of Bloodsmoor, and the girls heard nothing of him, save that he had "o'erworked himself" in Mr. Hewett's employ; and that, having become obsessively interested in the Abolitionist cause, he had gone away to join their forces. Then again, it was said that his family had sent him to Europe, for his health: his sensitive nerves being "shredded" by an excess of poetical effort. The Belles Lettres Club of Philadelphia, of which he had been a member, published a slender volume of his verse in French; and Mr. Zinn, reading through the book, declared that, try as he might, he was unable to make sense of the rhyme, let alone the sentiment. "It is all perfumy mists, and fairy dances, and the laughter of invisible children," he said, with a perplexed smile.

Such was the wanton indifference of Malvinia Zinn, however, that she never again gave a thought to her twenty-two-year-old suitor: not until she was of that age herself, and desperately in love. Then, for some reason, stray thoughts of the doomed, lost Mr. Kennicott floated into her imagination, and she felt—however briefly—an uncharacteristic tinge of guilt. "But I was so very young then," she told herself, "I could not *possibly* have known what I did."

32

The great Orlando Vandenhoffen was less imposing of stature in real life, than behind the footlights; but such was the aristocratic authority of his face, and the bemused complacency of his smile (which revealed teeth that seemed almost *too* white), that all who approached him fell under his spell—or were stirred to resist him instinctively.

He was darkish of complexion, with a black mustache wide and full upon his upper lip, and a strong, imperial jawline. The uncanny power of his black eyes was not exaggerated, nor was the potency of his rich, low, elegantly modulated voice. Rumors of his sybaritism, his cavalier treatment of women, the restiveness of his spirit, and the proud melancholia that flashed forth betimes in rage, did not, alas, dissuade admirers of the female sex, of whom Malvinia Zinn was one—ah, how recklessly! Indeed, it is probable that Vandenhoffen's egregious reputation *attracted* willing victims, for each woman alone imagined herself capable of triumph, where others had ignominiously failed.

Upon the occasion of their meeting for the first time, in Mrs. Horatio Broome's drawing room, amidst a great deal of insipid gaiety and chatter, Orlando Vandenhoffen could not have failed to be struck by the beauty of Miss Malvinia Zinn; and by her vivacity; and a certain fey boldness in her manner—for, while acknowledging Vandenhoffen's thespian genius (with some small, half-flattering qualifications pertaining to his interpretation of Ray Trafford in *Under the Gaslight*), the saucy young lady put herself forth as one of the acting tribe too: albeit her status was, at the present time, but that of an *amateur*. Vandenhoffen, amused, could not resist inquiring, which theatrical roles she had performed as an *amateur;* and the blushing Malvinia was forced to admit that her experience had not yet widened to include actual performances, but was in fact confined, at the present time, to *recitations,* of which she knew many by heart. "Ah! I see! A schoolgirl's recitations!" Vandenhoffen laughed, vastly amused. "Well, my dear, you must do one or two for me someday: as a sort of audition."

Another young lady, rebuffed so merrily, might have shrunk away at once; but not Malvinia, who managed, however faintly, to join in the laughter, as her lovely cheeks burned, and her blue eyes, too, appeared to burn, with both girlish embarrassment and defiance. That she was more than ordinarily beauteous that evening, in an ivory brocade gown bedecked with pink velvet ribbon, pink velvet roses, and some seventy yards of lace; and with her gleaming dark hair arranged in angelic ringlets on her forehead and cheeks, and covered in part with lace, velvet tea roses, and ostrich feathers; and her satin-smooth skin glowing with spirit, the self-conscious young lady naturally knew (for she was forever checking her image in mirrors, and had so refined the art, her glance manipulated so adroitly, that few observers knew what she did, or how frequently she did it): that she must—she absolutely *must*—seize the opportunity of the moment, in trepidatious knowledge that it might never again repeat itself, she naturally knew as well. So she did not shrink away from Vandenhoffen's cruel laughter; she did not retreat to Cousin Basil's side, and ask to be driven home; she allowed the hilarity to subside, and said, with admirable coolness: "I shall do so, indeed, Mr. Vandenhoffen, at your convenience: but for the mere sport of it, and for no *audition.*"

The villainous gentleman, taken aback, as it were, by Malvinia's challenge, gave her the honor of a look of evident admiration; and, seizing her hand, placed a kiss upon it, fixing his eyes upon her face all the while with such mock severity, Malvinia felt a decided palpitation of the heart, and bethought herself for a moment—but only, alas! for a moment—that she *had* spoken too recklessly, and she *would* have done best to retreat. But Vandenhoffen was saying, in a mellifluous voice that contrasted vividly with his craggily handsome features, and the slumbering ferocity of his dark eyes: "My dear Miss Zinn—it is *Miss* Zinn, I gravely hope?—there must be, then, at your earliest convenience, a sort of command performance, at which all the splendors of your no doubt vast repertoire will be displayed: nor will I release you from your obligation, since you have prick'd my interest so cruelly."

What manner of man is this, Malvinia inquired of herself, when she was alone, *to arouse such fancies!*

She knew, and refused to know, that she would surrender to him; and surrender, to her shame, with such little resistance, her seducer should be astonished to learn that she was a virgin: nay, a most innocent and sheltered virgin: and a Kiddemaster heiress as well.

Malvinia realized, of course, without needing to inquire of Basil Miller, that Orlando Vandenhoffen had won the hearts of many ladies in America; it is probable, however, that the reckless, inexperienced girl did not know precisely what that expression meant. To "win" a heart; to triumph; to trample underfoot; to despoil, besmirch, shame . . . She did not know, yet knew: and knew she would not resist.

If it were done, when 'tis done, the unhappy Malvinia thought, quite cynically, *then 'twere well it was done quickly!*

Basil Miller, belatedly realizing that he had of course acted rashly, in bringing his impressionable young cousin together with the notorious womanizer Orlando Vandenhoffen, sought a private audience with her, to speak of Vandenhoffen's "hellish charms," and to state, in a voice less airily amused than he would have liked, that *naturally* she would never consent to meet Vandenhoffen unescorted, under any circumstances at all: and was quite dumbfounded by Malvinia's gay response, that *naturally* she should not go unescorted to the Hotel de la Paix (where Vandenhoffen had rented a luxurious suite), nor would she even consent to go unescorted to the theater (for Vandenhoffen had sent her tickets for each of a week's performances, along with a handwritten message to the effect that, no matter which night she came, she was obliged to visit him backstage); she should not go unescorted, indeed, but with Cousin Basil as her escort; for the early part of the evening, that is. "Your services then having been rendered," Malvinia said, showing her small white perfect teeth as she laughed recklessly, "you will then be free to leave us: and to pursue nocturnal adventures of your own."

"I—your escort! In such a scheme—!" Cousin Basil exclaimed.

And before he could continue, Malvinia interjected: *"You,* my escort, in such a scheme: precisely. Else I shall feel obliged to complain to all who will listen—my dear mother and father, and Grandfather Kiddemaster, and *your* mother and father, and anyone who comes to mind, as appropriate in the context—I shall complain of your having brought me to the Broome *salon,* in defiance of all decorum, and your having introduced me to Mr. Orlando Vandenhoffen for, I do believe, *your* sport." She paused, and flashed again her bright insouciant smile, and had an impulse to rumple her cousin's hair, as if he were suddenly a small frightened boy, and she a sophisticated and mature young lady. "That it is no longer *your* sport, dear Basil, but *ours,* is perhaps what disturbs you?"

And so the folly came about, not five evenings after the unfortunate meeting in Mrs. Broome's house, and, at the conclusion of the ten-week run of *Under the Gaslight,* in Philadelphia: the lovers eloped by private carriage to New York City, where Vandenhoffen had rented, in readiness, one of the immense and ornately appointed honeymoon suites at the Plaza Hotel. The heartless cruelty of the letter Malvinia sent to Mr.

and Mrs. Zinn, with its protestations of love, and its boasting of a theatrical career to come, has already been recorded: that the treacherous daughter of such devoted parents should have declared herself not simply "in love," but "very, very happy—for the first time in my somewhat troubled life," will strike the reader to the heart, who has been a parent, or who, perhaps, in a wider sense, has felt the sting of ingratitude of the young, who know not and care not the degree of sacrifices oft made for them, but seize only the hedonistic pleasures of the moment!—much as the rabble swarming forth after the conclusion of the War sought their infamous "eight-hour day," bringing the nation to a standstill with their hellish strikes and labor violence, and demands of a wild anarchic sort, that can never be met. *Folly* of one sort, and *folly* of another: and I am not ashamed to confess myself so agitated at the moment, so sickened with the outrage of impurity of Malvinia Zinn's act, that I can barely force myself to continue. Nay, I shall not continue along these particular lines, save to say that Miss Malvinia Zinn's virginity was as much o'ercome by champagne, verbal flattery, and promises of a sort that any child might have doubted their plausibility, as by the much-vaulted power of Orlando Vandenhoffen's virility; and that the usual exclamations and protestations were made, and continued to be made for some weeks—"I shall love you forever; You have wrenched my heart from out my breast; There has never been anyone so magnificent as you; I adore you; I will do anything for you; My precious one; My adorable one; My infinitely glorious one—"

But this chronicler is sick at heart, and cannot rouse herself even by a brave gesture of amused cynicism. That a lady of good station might stoop to folly is lamentable; that a child like Malvinia Zinn might stoop to folly is unspeakable. "I am very, very happy—for the first time in my life"—thus the deluded girl felt constrained to boast; and surely we are to be excused, if we believe otherwise.

33

I am going to the Lordy, I am so glad,
I am going to the Lordy, I am so glad,
I am going to the Lordy,
Glory hallelujah! Glory hallelujah!
I am going to the Lordy.
I love the Lordy with all my soul,
Glory hallelujah!
And that is the reason I am going to the Lord,
Glory hallelujah! Glory hallelujah!
I am going to the Lord.
I saved my party and my land,
Glory hallelujah!
But they have murdered me for it,
And that is the reason I am going to the Lordy,
Glory hallelujah!
Glory hallelujah!

Thus chanted the assassin of President James Garfield, in a high quivering declamatory voice, on the executioner's scaffold, in Washington, D.C., at midday of June 30, 1882. And the executioner adjusted the black hood over his small, sleek head; and affixed the noose around his neck; and the trap was sprung; and, before a hushed throng of some two hundred fifty spectators (a number of whom had paid $300 for the privilege of witnessing the hanging), Charles Jules Guiteau fell like a shot to within eighteen inches of the ground, whereupon his neck snapped, and he died, after several minutes of strangulated agony, a death befitting the murderer of a President.

His skeleton went to the Army Medical Museum, for display.

The revolver he had used—a .44 caliber British Bulldog with a white bone handle—went to the National Museum, despite the efforts of many collectors to acquire it. (Guiteau had bought an expensive model, he said, because it would look more impressive in a museum display case.)

His autograph, which he had been selling for $1 a card, was scattered far and wide: for such was the avidity of the public in those days, for even the relics of a condemned murderer, and a piteous madman.

John Quincy Zinn, reading of the execution, in the sunlit parlor of the Octagonal House, sighed, and drew his hand roughly through his graying hair, and, laying the newspaper aside, made his way wordlessly to the outdoors: and to the path that led back to his workshop. For June 30, 1882, must be interpreted as a day like any other: a facet of Eternity caught in Time.

J.Q.Z. did not know, for Mrs. Zinn thought it best not to inform him, that, upon several occasions, his former acquaintance and fellow boarding-house resident, the peculiar little Guiteau, had applied to both the Kiddemasters and the Zinns, for "financial restitution"—his argument being that John Quincy Zinn had stolen from him certain ideas of education reform which had been "exploited" in *The Spirit of the Future in America.* In one lengthy letter, written in a wild hand, he had claimed that it was he who had supplied John Quincy Zinn with the "basic fundamentals" of science and invention; in another, he claimed that it was he who had, elaborating upon the Perfectionist doctrine of John H. Noyes, supplied Mr. Zinn with his prevailing philosophy of life, without which he could not have accomplished anything worthwhile. (J.Q.Z., tho' by no means as famous as certain of his fellow inventors—Whitney, Fulton, and Morse, among others—had by this time acquired a modicum of fame: more for his generous contributions to others' theories, than for the completion and marketing of his own.) In the most impudent letter, the ingrate Guiteau laid claim for having "brought together" John Quincy Zinn and Prudence Kiddemaster—the "fortune hunter" and the "fortune," in his crude jesting terms, without which J.Q.Z. "could not have accomplished anything at all."

An unhappy tale it is, and one, alas, from which no moral imperative, indeed, no conclusions whatsoever, can be drawn: the spasmodic stages of Charles J. Guiteau's questionable "maturity," from the feckless and enthusiastic young Philadelphian whom John Quincy, in his generosity, had befriended, to the insane slaughterer of President James Garfield, who had insisted at his trial, amidst much nonsensical giggling and carry-ings-on, that the assassination of Mr. Garfield was a consequence of *Divine Commandment!*

Such was the pattern of delusion into which the unfortunate man gradually fell, that, upon his final expulsion (by servants) from Kiddemas-ter Hall, where he had gone to peddle a staggering quantity of his pamph-let of religious lectures, *The Truth: A Companion to the Bible,* he suddenly reversed his prior claim, and now insisted that John Quincy Zinn had pressed upon *him* the numerous ideas that guided his life, and had flooded his brain for more than twenty years. "You will not be able to silence me!" he shouted from the road, waving his wide-brimmed black hat at the several servants, who had, resorting in desperation to physical coercion, carried him from the front door, and along the lengthy gravel drive, to the gate, and into the public road. "How will you be able to silence me? I know John Quincy of old! We are friends—we are brothers —we are twins of old!"

But he departed that day, and did not return to Bloodsmoor. And Mrs. Zinn, who trembled to hear of his charges, and his very propinquity, made every effort to put him out of her mind. For all of that day, and most of the next, she could barely tolerate poor little Pip in her presence—Pip with his elderly, wise, wizened face, and his sly winking button eyes, and his pink snubbed nose, and his periods of eloquent brooding silence: Pip who, Mrs. Zinn sometimes uneasily felt, might tell them all so much, of his origin and their destiny, if only he could speak.

34

It was on a chill, drear autumn day, when mist rose in narrow curls from
the gorge, and the mood of the little workshop-cabin was somewhat
subdued (for tho' Mr. Zinn had pleased Mrs. Zinn enormously by accepting another assignment from a manufacturer, which was to reward him
with $10,000 in a lump sum, neither he nor Samantha considered the
challenge worthwhile: and perhaps it was rather vulgar)—it was on this
featureless November afternoon, whilst Pip slumbered fretfully by the
stove, and Mr. Zinn, at his workbench, sighed frequently, and Samantha
lost an important diagram amongst her plans, and found it, and then
again lost it, out of sheer carelessness and the effect of strained nerves
(for both Mrs. Zinn and Great-Aunt Edwina were plaguing her of late, as
to her "hopes for the future")—it was at that irresolute—nay, somnolent
—hour of the day, neither daylight, still, nor safely night, that the agitated
Samantha caught sight of something in the gorge, a human figure, perhaps, tho' indistinct, and immediately obscured by twists and curls of fog;
and, standing stock-still for many seconds, her breath withheld, the keen-
sighted young lady waited for it to reappear, and to explain itself, as a
natural phenomenon: no doubt some trickery of the mist, the diminishing
daylight, and her own nervous fatigue.

After a brief while the shape reappeared, some distance away,
defining itself as altogether too bizarre of proportions to be human, or
even animal; and then, before Samantha could call her father's attention
to it, fortunately it disappeared again—fortunately, I say, because Samantha had been quite reluctant to interrupt Mr. Zinn at his work, particularly
on a whim. (As it turned out, the eerie shape in the gorge simply vanished
—had never been, perhaps, more than a momentary delusion.) *My eyes,*

Samantha scolded herself, rubbing them cruelly, *are they playing tricks on me?*

"You seem rather troubled, Samantha," Mr. Zinn observed, from his side of the room. "I hope that nothing is disturbing you?"

"Nothing at all, Father," Samantha answered in haste. "I pray I did not disturb *you.*"

By a coincidence of a purely temporal sort, quite without narrative significance (tho' the propinquity in time must needs be noted, my chronicle of the Zinn family making its claim, however humbly, for historical authenticity), it happened that, not three hours later, near about the time Mr. Zinn and Samantha prepared to close up their laboratory for the evening, to retire to the Octagonal House for the domestic pleasures of dinner and the hearth, there was, at first so softly as to be near-inaudible, a knock on the door: and the skittish Pip awoke from his nap, to leap to Mr. Zinn's shoulder with that exaggerated alarm, which so frequently annoyed his master.

The knock was repeated; and, father and daughter exchanging a quizzical glance (for who could possibly be knocking at the door of their laboratory retreat, away off in the woods, at first dark of a singularly dreary November day?), Mr. Zinn betook himself to answer the door, wiping his stained hands on his workclothes, and cautioning his daughter that the interruption must be merely that of a servant from the Hall, on some errand of harmless principle, which should arouse irritation in neither: for, after all, they were about to lock up for the night, in any case.

And so Mr. Zinn opened the door, expecting to see a familiar face: and there stood a stranger in an oilcloth cape, streaming moisture, and a shabby wide-brimmed rain hat pulled low upon his forehead, and crude farmer's boots that reached to mid-calf, and were badly splattered with mud.

Greetings being exchanged, on both sides uttered with some surprise, and not a little embarrassment (for tho' the young man appeared to know Mr. Zinn, or at least to be familiar with his reputation, Mr. Zinn naturally did not know him), it was explained that the visitor, one Nahum Hareton, was a stranger to Bloodsmoor, and had come on foot, as a pilgrim, simply to shake the hand of John Quincy Zinn: and perhaps to apply (the meanwhile blushing with childlike awe and confusion) for a *position in the workshop.*

Mr. Zinn began to laugh, heartily, and yet kindly, urging the young man to come farther inside, and to take off his wet things. "A position in my workshop! Alas, our financial situation here is such, my daughter and I can scarcely justify our own positions. But let us chat awhile, and become acquainted. I hope you are not too fatigued?"

Now taking in the sight of Samantha (upon whose slender shoulder the affrighted Pip had just leapt), the visitor was even more confused, and began to stammer apologies. He explained that of course he would not expect remuneration of any sort. "I should like only to apprentice myself to you," he said, his pale face mottled with blushes, "for as long, or as brief, a period as you might wish."

"First we shall become acquainted," Mr. Zinn said cheerily, "and then I shall, I hope, dissuade you of your purpose. Samantha, dear, do step forward: perhaps you o'erheard our visitor's name? Nahum Hareton, I believe?" He urged the reticent young lady to come closer, introducing her as his youngest daughter, and the only assistant he had ever had, or would ever require. "Samantha is a scientist of such mental ingenuity, Mr. Hareton, as to one day, surely, eclipse *my* abortive blunderings, and provide the world with remarkable gifts. At the present she is, I fear, somewhat burdened with tasks of every sort of petty nature—but one day her spirit will take flight—and we shall see, we shall see!"

"I am very honored to make your acquaintance," the young man said, bowing awkwardly. His smile was nervous but appealing; his eyes were a pale brown, clear and keen, and quite obviously those of a person of especial intelligence. "I apologize for my intrusion, Miss Zinn, and hope that you will forgive me."

Samantha, curtsying, murmured a vague reply, displaying none of the annoyance and suspicion she naturally felt (for not only did John Quincy Zinn's daughter resent such forthright appeals to her father's good nature, but these were the odious days of Thomas Edison's spies: the much-publicized Wizard of Menlo Park having established his laboratory for the purpose of "inventions by order," not many years before); she made every effort to match her father's congeniality, and bade the self-conscious young man to take a seat by the stove, and to accept a cup of tea, should he allow her five minutes to reheat the water.

Mr. Hareton inclined to her wishes, with many protestations of gratitude, and a reiterated hope that he was not intruding; and, Mr. Zinn drawing a chair forward for him, the two men sat companionably by the fire, and Samantha made tea, scolding in an undertone the trembling little spider monkey, and taking in, covertly, Mr. Nahum Hareton, who might very well be (so the shrewd Samantha reasoned) a spy; or the innocent pilgrim he seemed.

Mr. Hareton was a thin, angular-jawed young man of perhaps twenty-five years of age, clean-shaven, of a stature considerably smaller in height and breadth than Mr. Zinn's own, yet withal possessing a certain quiet confidence. His features were small, and inclined toward a frank, plain, pleasant homeliness; and tho' his manner suggested an origin of some rusticity, and his English was surely not that of an urban dweller, he did demonstrate, to Samantha's critical eye, a pleasing restraint, and a subtlety of personality that argued for a reliable character.

The men, as the saying goes, "got on well" together, and after a while even Pip relaxed, and made overtures to Mr. Hareton, who seemed boyishly pleased to stroke the furry creature's little head, and scratch behind his ears. It rather exasperated Samantha, tho' in truth it hardly surprised her, that Mr. Zinn, within an hour's space, should begin to speak intimately of his projects, and his plans for the future—touching only lightly upon the commissioned assignment (an improvement in the Dumont-Santos pneumatic process for steel conversion, which he and Samantha hoped to discharge within a month and for which, naturally, they would receive no patent royalties); and dwelling at length upon their speculative hopes for the perpetual-motion machine; and an electric-fueled "auto-wagen" to replace the horsedrawn carriage; and "aero-locomotives" of various sizes; and a visual accompaniment to Morse's lightning waves; and a device to record and preserve sound; and "photographic film"; and an electric dirigible, of a size to approach two thousand cubic meters, with an aluminum frame, numerous propellers, and a revolutionary propulsive motor. (This dream-dirigible was but crudely realized in the most recent Parisian experiments, which Mr. Zinn and Samantha had assiduously studied, in the French journal *Patrie*.)

Alas, if he is one of the Wizard's hired spies, Samantha thought, biting her lower lip, and regarding the young man with her level, ponderous, greeny-gray stare, which quite disconcerted the few young society men she met, and very much offended her family. *But there is no subduing Father's generous nature, and not even bitter experience can harden him—dear man!*

Mr. Hareton was too absorbed in Mr. Zinn's warm, rushing words, to stir sugar into his tea; he stared, with burning eyes, at the elder man's handsome countenance, and seemed at moments about to interrupt, out of curiosity and excitement. But he held his tongue, and acquitted himself well, and, despite his fascination with Mr. Zinn's dream-inventions (which Samantha feared might sound rather *too* quixotic, in this cluttered, somewhat shabby little workshop, smelling of tea leaves, wet clothes, and the acrid animal-mustiness of Pip's fur), he did not forget himself so far as to fail to rise, when Samantha joined them, and took her own seat quietly, by the stove.

Samantha, knowing her father so well, comprehended long before he happened upon the idea, that of course they would invite young Nahum Hareton to stay for dinner at the Octagonal House, at the very least; and possibly even to stay the night, in the room that had once belonged to Constance Philippa, and was now designated as the guest room—tho' few guests ever came, the Zinns' domestic budget being a modest one. She knew too, with a flurried heart, and not a few fond misgivings, that Mr. Zinn would most likely agree to allow the avid young man to be his assistant—his apprentice, indeed, for no salary; for of course there could be no salary.

(Afterward, upon being interrogated by his wife, as to the feasibility, let alone the safety, of taking on a stranger, in the intimacy of his workshop, Mr. Zinn would reply with the air of a man to whom certain truths are blatantly self-evident, and accessible to all: "But my dear Prudence, have you not seen young Nahum's *eyes?*—the fervor that burns within them, and the probable genius? And Samantha, too, trusts him: and Pip: and what better recommendations might an apprentice have?")

And so Nahum Hareton came to the Zinn laboratory, as a pilgrim indeed, on foot, precisely as he said, with no genuine expectation that the great inventor would take him in, but much childlike hope, and a spirit of forthright zeal that was delightful to behold. That he would figure so centrally in John Quincy Zinn's life—and even more centrally in Samantha's—could not of course have been anticipated, on that mist-shrouded night so long ago, but three weeks after Samantha's twenty-first birthday.

If I have neglected Samantha of late, in deference to the greater flurry and ado of those sisters who had fled Bloodsmoor, thereby bringing much shame and scorn upon their own heads, and, alas, the heads of their innocent relatives, it is hardly out of a sense of the child's comparative insignificance: for she and Octavia, at this point in our history, are still the most virtuous of young ladies, and models of daughterly deportment. Tho' Samantha's fervent devotion to her father, and her near-obsessive interest in work, did displease the female members of her family—not only Mrs. Zinn and Great-Aunt Edwina, but Octavia, too, and cousins Rowena and Flora and Odille, and every Philadelphia aunt who had an opinion on the subject—her loyalty surely pleased her father; and her assistance in the laboratory, never less than diligent, and frequently inspired, was invaluable to him.

She did his mathematics for him (for he had never quite mastered that discipline); she copied over his inky diagrams and charts, oft expanding them in scale, so as to make their dimensions clearer; she betook herself through the woods, to Judge Kiddemaster's library, to check certain references, unavailable in the scanty encyclopedic volumes kept on hand, in the workshop. In the past several years she had taken from Mr. Zinn the burden of conversing with most visitors, including those manufacturers who journeyed to Bloodsmoor to offer research assignments to him (angered and discouraged, in many cases, by the prohibitive fees and royalty arrangements demanded by the megalomaniac Wizard of Menlo Park—a former associate of the notorious bandits Jay Gould and James Fisk, it is perhaps not generally known: and by temperament very much of their ilk); being a self-possessed young lady, and by no means the simple child her petite figure, plain freckled face, and small features made her out to be, she was able to speak with admirable composure to these gentlemen, and to induce them—in most cases—to raise their offers by at least a few hundred dollars: a feat Mr. Zinn would have been incapable of doing, both out of his innate modesty, and a disproportionate sense of his own market value.

By the age of twenty, this remarkable young lady had acquired her first patent, for a minor improvement upon Foucault's printing key frame (a device by which, it was thought, the blind might learn to write); and, were it not for Mr. Zinn's charity, or carelessness, in discussing this improvement with one Christopher Latham Sholes, of Mooresburg, Pennsylvania, it might have been the case that Samantha would have continued to experiment, until she hit upon the *typewriter* itself—an invention patented, in many stages, by Sholes, and eventually sold for a sadly low figure ($12,000) to Eliphalet Remington & Sons of Ilion, New York, with such extraordinary commercial results, in later years, the reader scarcely needs to be informed. Not long before Mr. Nahum Hareton knocked upon the workshop door, Samantha had been granted her second patent, for a method of waterproofing that was a considerable improvement over Mr. Zinn's earlier method, tho' still far from being ideal (that would come with rubberized fabrics); and from this she earned a small fee—hardly more than a pittance, in fact—every six months. In truth, Samantha thought little of these accomplishments, judging that her real work lay in the future, with the development of such inventions as the aluminum-frame dirigible; but her loving sister Octavia fussed over them, and insisted upon framing the patents in chestnut panels, painted in lavender and gold, to be hung over Samantha's workbench—to Samantha's embarrassment.

At other times, however, Octavia, like their numerous female relatives, professed to be concerned over Samantha's prospects for marriage. Her own engagement to Mr. Rumford having instilled in her a certain measure of confidence and generosity, she was forever nagging at Samantha to fashion her hair more attractively (for, indeed, the lacklustre chignon in which it was, each morning, so hastily fixed, hardly did justice to Samantha's beautiful red hair); and to have the servants unpick one or another of her housedresses, in order to launder it (for Samantha's clothes did have a tendency to lose their freshness, partly as a consequence of the fervor with which she customarily worked, and her negligence in applying deodorizing chloride of lime, or salicylic acid and talc, to her underarms); and to attempt a more consciously *pleasant* manner, befitting a young lady who has, after all, "come out" in society, and is not ignorant of social obligations and responsibilities.

"Do you *want* to be a spinster?" Octavia asked Samantha in exasperation, upon more than one occasion. "Do you *want* to frighten every eligible gentleman away, and have all of Bloodsmoor pity you?"

"A spinister is a lonely old maid who has wished to marry, and been neglected," Samantha said, with an air of pert dignity that quite belied the hotness of heart she felt at her sister's persecution, "and since I have not the slightest wish to marry, and feel no terror of loneliness, I cannot therefore be a *spinster:* and must beg you to leave me in peace."

(Samantha felt a sisterly happiness that Octavia was to be wed within a year; and that, Rumford Hall being not a great distance away, they would see each other frequently. But she could not deceive herself as to the masculine attractions of Lucius Rumford, who put her rather mischievously in mind of Gnasher, one of Grandfather Kiddemaster's retired carriage horses, and she refused to share in the gaiety of spirits, exhibited by her cousins, and by Mrs. Zinn, which she judged somewhat *hysterical*—for did these women have so contemptible an opinion of the single state, and of their own innate worth?—had they feared so *very* much that Octavia might be "left behind"?)

Samantha adjudged Octavia to be superior to her prospective bridegroom in every conceivable way, and took note, to her own satisfaction, that, since the announcement of the wedding banns by the Reverend Hewett, from the pulpit of the village church, Octavia looked prettier than ever before in her twenty-four years. Her warm brown eyes shone with good health, her brow was smooth, and her round cheeks were lightly touched with a pale rosy blush. If Octavia did not possess Malvinia's extravagant loveliness, or Constance Philippa's haughty good looks, or even Deirdre's mysterious, enigmatic beauty, it was nevertheless the case that her warmth, and the excellence of her heart, made her a far more desirable companion for any man—so Samantha thought, in passionate defense of her sister, tho' Octavia *would* nag about Samantha's own prospects.

When next Octavia raised the maddening question, "Do you *want*, Samantha, to be a spinster?" Samantha answered at once: "I had rather be a spinster, and answer only to myself, than be an apprentice to another person—one whom, no doubt, I would hardly know."

Lest the reader suspect that John Quincy Zinn, under the duress, perhaps, of o'erexacting work, was led to *imagine* that Thomas Alva Edison sought to spy on him, in order to steal his secrets, it should be pointed out that certain sketches for an incandescent lamp, first made by J.Q.Z. in the early Seventies, were appropriated by Edison, and released to the world—under Edison's imprint, of course—in 1879. So with numerous minor improvements on Morse's telegraph; and, later in the century, the "discovery" of the wax cylinder phonograph, in which sound was first *recorded* and *preserved* and *replayed,* by the same Edison, the self-proclaimed Wizard of Menlo Park, who gave no more tribute to the honest inventors from whom he thieved, than he gave financial remuneration!

If John Quincy harbored bitter thoughts, and resented the public acclaim so lavishly bestowed upon his rival, he said not a word; no more than he spoke, even to his dear wife, of his disappointment at each spring's failure to find him elected to the American Philosophical Society. (That his father-in-law, Judge Kiddemaster, should feel anger at this slight, and speak of it to all who would listen, is not surprising, given the Judge's rash temper; but the elderly man's rancor caused J.Q.Z. some chagrin.) "I am, it seems, one of those whose duty it is to *stand* and *wait*," John Quincy said, in jest; but Mrs. Zinn was not amused. "This nation shall one day kneel in tribute to you," she said, her stern lower lip quivering, "nay, I would wish the nation might *cower* before you."

"My dear Prudence," John Quincy said, startl'd, "how can you wish the *United States of America* to cower before anyone!"

He threw himself more obsessively than ever into his work, assisted now by both Samantha, and young Nahum Hareton: and his dreams were all of the gigantic dirigible; and the (revised) perpetual-motion machine; and an electric grinding machine to dispose of chicken, turkey, goose, and duck feathers (the marrow of such feathers being treacherously difficult to grind down, as all farmers know); and a thermal suit, for Northern winters, which the wearer would adjust to his comfort; and a new, still vague, sketch for a device called only *The Eye*, to be composed of many electrified mirrors, for instantaneous communication to a central focus or authority, with the hope that crime might one day be eliminated, from the civilized nations.

I very much doubt that so good-tempered, and so industrious, a gentleman, might be subject to fits of jealousy, or bitterness; but, if this was ever the case, Mr. Zinn gave no sign, to the outward world: no more than he gave any sign of the disappointment he so keenly felt, in regard to his three lost daughters. (Whose names, alas, he did not wish to hear uttered, in his household!)

"Do you ever allow yourself, to think of them," Mrs. Zinn sometimes asked, as, yet unsleeping, wife and husband lay abed, "to think, and to envision their probable fates?"

Whereupon Mr. Zinn but heavily sighed, and made no other response, lying stock-still on his side of the expansive bed—feigning sleep, it may be, until, indeed, sleep o'ertook them both.

One day I shall awake, to discover that I have sleepwalked my way through life, Samantha bethought herself, of a sudden, but how is it to be prevented? What, apart from our companionable labor in the workshop, and the delight of Father's presence, and Pip's mischief, is there in this world, to impede my headlong flight?

Thus the small, pale, plain girl with the colorless lashes, and the thin lips, and the quizzical green eyes queried herself, not knowing what her premonition signified; or why peculiar emotions, at unpredictable times of the day, seized hold of her petite frame, and made her tremble with cold. One day I shall awake, she thought, staring at the workbench before her, and at the clutter she so dearly loved, but to *what?*—and *how?*

Nor do I entirely comprehend the motive for such idle thoughts. Yet I would not be altogether honest, if I did not soberly present them in my chronicle, that the reader might judge for himself. For *why* should so cherished and entrusted a daughter, knowing herself infinitely privileged to work in the laboratory of a man of genius, knowing herself, as it were, *set apart from the common run of young women,* think any distracting thoughts at all?

All busily and happily the months passed, and the seasons: and, not long after her twenty-second birthday, Miss Samantha Zinn was granted her third patent, which Octavia, unfortunately, neglected to frame, as a consequence of her own activity, as a new bride, and mistress of austere Rumford Hall. Mr. Zinn, Samantha, and the humble young apprentice Nahum Hareton, working together, yet oft silently, in the rustic cabin above the gorge, passed many a tiring but rewarding day, in their pursuit of divers dreams, primarily that of the aluminum-frame dirigible—the which presented some small, but very nagging, problems, deriving from its extreme weight. For the most part, Samantha acquitted herself admirably, in her father's service; and, living all absorbed in the present challenge, rarely succumbed to the idleness, of which I have just spoken; and rarely to thoughts of remorse, or regret, or wonderment, concerning her renegade sisters.

Indeed, being born in 1862, she felt herself very much a *child of the era,* maturing—nay, being catapulted—into the accelerated times, of the post-War years, in which it was so commonly felt that *one must make haste, else Destiny will be lost;* and greedy rivals triumph. Ah, what a pity it would be, what a tragedy, Samantha oft thought, if other inventors—less scrupulous, more criminal—should rush forward, to discover, and patent, and become millionaires by, the great machines she and John Quincy Zinn had been born to perfect!

35

It was as the slyly manipulative and irresistibly charming Countess in the confection *Countess Fifine,* which ran for more than two hundred performances at the Fanshawe, that Malvinia Morloch achieved her first truly extravagant commercial success, and so succeeded in entering the cultural milieu, by accident rather than merit, that, for a time, she was an object of adoration whose name and picture were likely to be in all the papers, from one week to the next; and whose suitors—among them a number of very wealthy men, both married and unmarried—were so persistent, special doormen had to be hired at the Plaza Hotel, simply to deal with them. Her hair style in *Countess Fifine* inspired a vogue among the most fashionable ladies of New York, and for a while one saw "Countesses" everywhere: none, alas, possessing quite the attractions of the original. (As Countess Fifine, Malvinia wore her magnificent dark hair in a heavy chignon that hung to her shoulders, enclosed in a chenille net snood, with a coronet of purple velvet trimmed in pearls—the effect of which was to emphasize, ironically, the angelic beauty of her features.)

Coquettish . . . enchanting . . . unforgettable . . . simply marvelous: so the critics unanimously responded. Malvinia read every notice of her performances, and saved every scrap of newsprint that mentioned her name, greedy and delighted as a child. If, at times, her connection with Orlando Vandenhoffen gave her cause to brood, and even to weep; if the frequent mention, in the same papers, of "Deirdre of the Shadows" (who was becoming famous as well—for a very different sort of performance), caused her considerable agitation; and if, however rarely, the reckless child cast her mind back upon Bloodsmoor, and the family that had loved her so dearly, she had only to sift through her growing stack of notices,

284

and reread the letters of fulsome praise and adoration she received daily, and tear open the wrappings of yet another luxurious gift, to placate herself, and forget who she was.

I am very very happy, she scribbled idly, on the reverse of a crumpled sheet of gilt wrapping paper, *I have never been so happy in my life. . . . Indeed, I cannot remember my life until now!*

(Yet even then, in what might be called the halcyon, or even the honeymoon, phase of her existence as "Malvinia Morloch," an unmistakable evil was asserting itself in her being: an evil to which I will assign the name *The Mark of the Beast,* since it was in these terms certain members of the Kiddemaster family referred to it . . . the affliction being an hereditary trait, of which I will write in detail at a later time, the prospect is so displeasing, and humanly vile.)

How Malvinia Zinn was transformed so rapidly, and with such immediate reward, into "Malvinia Morloch," had much to do with the arrogance of Orlando Vandenhoffen (who boasted that he could "create" an actress overnight; and who so threatened the manager of the Fanshawe Theatre with a defection to the rival Broadway, the hapless man bitterly surrendered, and cast Malvinia opposite Vandenhoffen in *A Flash of Lightning*), and very little, indeed, to do with Malvinia's natural gifts for the stage. I am not one of that slavish tribe that attributes to the acting profession the accolade *artist* (for such must be reserved for those who have dedicated themselves to a *spiritual* and *moral* idealism), yet I acquiesce in the widespread belief that there may be a certain genius amidst the thespian endeavor, as demonstrated by such stars of the American stage as Charlotte Cushman, Edwin Booth, Charles Coghlan, and Maurice Barrymore. This Malvinia did not possess. She knew no more of genius, than she knew of virtue; tho' a certain low cunning and monkeylike shrewdness were adequate, for a time, to bedazzle her audiences, and even her fellow actors.

That Malvinia could flounce herself about, attired in costly and ostentatious costumes, her face so luridly made up that its charms were broadcast to the cheapest seats in the house; that she could prattle, and lisp, and weep, and laugh, and stamp her foot, and make pretty little *moues,* and pretend to claw at her cheeks with her nails, so that her admiring audiences shuddered; that she could recite to perfection any speech presented to her, with so livid a semblance of sincerity, that even her director and fellow actors might be gulled into thinking she knew what she did—all this she was fully capable of accomplishing; and if this be "talent," then "talent" Malvinia Morloch possessed.

"Isn't it an enchanting little monkey!" Orlando Vandenhoffen exclaimed in an undertone, to his very good friend and confidante Mrs. Agnes Foote, the actress who had retired so notoriously from the stage a decade previously, in order to take up residence, as New York would have it, in the role of "hostess" for the elderly financier Hiram DeHorne. "You see her reciting by rote the speech I instructed her in, only last night: and mark how she animates her face, and uses her beautiful little hands! And this in an actress so *amateur,* any schoolgirl could boast of as much experience."

"She *is* good," Mrs. Foote acknowledged, fanning herself lazily, "and *you* are wonderfully fortunate: for what else, may I inquire, have you taught her to do by rote?"

Orlando Vandenhoffen, smitten with his beauteous young charge, and basking, no doubt, in the dazzling glare of her infatuation for him, would not rest until he had introduced Malvinia to all his friends and associates; and bragged of her even to the press, as "the next Adelaide Neilson"—a remark tactless indeed, for the beautiful Miss Neilson had died so recently as 1880, and was still warmly remembered, and even adored, by not a few among the playgoing public. "Like Miss Neilson," Vandenhoffen said, "Miss Morloch has come from a most alluring romantic background—the details of which I am not privileged to reveal, at the present time."

With a blatant disregard for the mores of society, Vandenhoffen established Malvinia in his suite at the Plaza, and showed her off, as it were, at Sherry's, and Delmonico's, and the Park Lane, and the St. Nicklaus, and the Astor, and the Hotel Marie Antoinette, and the vulgarly sumptuous Fifth Avenue residence of the W. K. Vanderbilts (where, at a fancy-dress ball of 1883, Vandenhoffen and his young mistress came as Romeo and Juliet, in the midst of a crowd of "historical personages," including Biblical figures, Renaissance despots, dethroned and decapitated European nobility, and General Ulysses S. Grant, who appeared, not altogether soberly, as himself); he was proud to have Malvinia on his arm, at the annual game banquet at the Waldorf, in which the main dining room was transformed into a miniature forest replete with stuffed animals and fowl, where freed nightingales sang in groves of rose and hibiscus trees, and artificial arbors were lavishly hung with hothouse grapes, and every manner of meat, fish, and fowl—*every* manner, from walrus steak to hummingbird tongue—was served, on gold plates, to the frenzied delight of the hundreds of guests.

He saw no harm in introducing her to Mr. Jay Gould, and Mr. Russell Sage, and Mr. Edward Daly (who had installed a faucet in his Park Avenue mansion that served champagne), and Mr. James Brady (the infamous Diamond Jim, whose attentions at that time to a "Portuguese" chorus girl were such that his interest in Malvinia was necessarily modest: he sent over to her, at the Plaza, a prankish gift of a gold-plated rocking-horse studded with tiny chip diamonds, sapphires, rubies, and emeralds, and an ermine fur side-saddle for "Countess Fifine to ride upon, bare").

So secure was Vandenhoffen in his vanity, and so convinced of his young mistress's passionate dependence upon him, that he did not even hesitate to introduce Malvinia to the notorious womanizer Nicholas Drew, at that time a frequenter of the theater, and dance halls of a questionable reputation. (Drew, the millionaire railroad man, was soon to be under fire from the Democrats, for having bribed "The Plumed Knight"—that is, the contemptible James G. Blaine—for numerous favors, in excess of $200,000.)

Now and then, of course, particularly as the months passed, Vandenhoffen *did* succumb to attacks of masculine jealousy; tho' he could not seriously believe that Malvinia might have an interest in any other man, however persistent. And it was also the case that a certain piquancy was added to their love relationship, by his own unpredictable flashes of rage, and Malvinia's shocked protestations and tears.

"I cannot believe, Orlando, that you would doubt—that it would cross your mind to doubt—my love for you," the stricken young woman said, in a voice trembling with restraint. "These gifts—these fripperies—these mere tokens of passing interst: you must know how little I value them, and how swiftly I would discard them, if I thought you misunderstood."

"No need, no need," Vandenhoffen said coolly, yet with a certain pragmatic haste, lest his weeping mistress act the fool, and toss an emerald bracelet through the window, as if she were prancing about the stage at the Fanshawe. "You gravely misunderstand me, I fear."

"But do you doubt my love for you?" Malvinia asked, staring. Her blue eyes became enormous, and her lovely skin had gone a deathly ivory-white. "My loyalty to you? My *sacrifice* for you?"

"I doubt everything and nothing," Vandenhoffen responded, tugging impatiently at his mustache, and catching sight of his stolid, virile reflection in a gilt-framed mirror on the wall, "Yet you must recall, my sweet Malvinia, how very readily you fled your native city with me—how abruptly you cast aside your former life. As the canny Brabantio observed to Othello: 'Look to her, Moor, if thou hast eyes to see: She has deceived her father, and may thee.' "

Whereupon the grieving Malvinia lost all restraint, and burst into angry wailing tears, and would have raked her nails across her burning cheeks had not her lover seized her wrists, to subdue her.

"Oh, cruel—cruel—cruel—and heartless!" she wept, with as much passion as if her tears, and her sorrow, were naught but artifice.

So Malvinia Morloch and Orlando Vandenhoffen quarreled, and the hotel room resounded with their high outraged voices, and many an innocent object was thrown to the floor, including vases filled with long-stemmed roses, and crystal decanters filled with wine, and the "fripperies" of Malvinia's numerous admirers. They quarreled; and were reconciled; and quarreled again, more violently; and were again reconciled. There were complaints to the management of the hotel, and lavish tips from Vandenhoffen, by way of apology. There were late-night suppers at Delmonico's, for Malvinia, who was toasted by everyone at the table, and drank rather too much, and would have crawled onto her lover's lap to sleep, like a babe, had he not pushed her, laughing, away. "Ah, but do you love me?" she murmured. "You don't! You don't love me!"—sinking back against the burnt-leather cushions, her half-dozen sapphires licentiously glinting in her hair.

Malvinia was cast as Pauline in *The Lady of Lyons,* but Vandenhoffen insisted that she accompany him to the West Coast, where he was touring in *The Two Orphans* (an unfailing favorite, in which Vandenhoffen played a knife-throwing villain, earnestly hissed by his audiences—the misfortune being that there was no suitable role for Miss Morloch). She acquiesced, but greatly resented her idleness, with the result that the lovers quarreled more frequently than before, and were actually evicted from their lavish quarters in the great Palace Hotel; whereupon they moved, with great pomp and ceremony, to the rival Baldwin—which boasted the longest bar in San Francisco, a billiard room exclusively for women, one hundred twenty-five miles of electric wiring, and interior woodwork of mahogany, East India teak, rosewood, ebony, and primavera from Mexico.

At the close of Vandenhoffen's run they returned to New York City, to a suite at the St. Regis, and rumors circulated that they were soon to be wed: or were wed already. ("But hasn't Orlando a wife and children stuck away somewhere in Europe?" it was asked.) Despite their troublesome reputations, the manager of the Fanshawe troupe was persuaded to cast them together in a revival of *Richard III,* in which Vandenhoffen repeated an old reliable success, as the sinister hunchback king, *loathed* and yet *adored* by his audience; and Malvinia Morloch established a somewhat lesser, but still significant, success as Anne, the widow courted by Richard in the very presence of her husband's corpse!

On many an evening the lovers quarreled backstage, and brought their white-hot nerves behind the footlights with them, so that the theater thrilled with their undisguised passion—whether love, or intense hatred —for each other. Richard was a diabolical villain, Anne a trapped victim, his equal in venom:

> ANNE: Thou wast the cause, and most accurs'd effect.
>
> GLOU: Your beauty was the cause of that effect—
> Your beauty, that did haunt me in my sleep
> To undertake the death of all the world,
> So I might live one hour in your sweet bosom.

ANNE: If I thought that, I tell thee, homicide,
These nails should rent that beauty from my cheeks.

GLOU: These eyes could not endure that beauty's wrack;
You should not blemish it, if I stood by:
As all the world is cheered by the sun,
So I by that; it is my day, my life.

ANNE: Black night o'ershade thy day, and death thy life!

GLOU: Curse not thyself, fair creature—thou art both.

ANNE: I would I were, to be reveng'd on thee.

Upon more than one occasion the saucy Malvinia Morloch, fortified, it may have been, by a half-bottle of French champagne consumed before the performance, so earnestly acquitted herself of the spitting scene that her leading man—muttering a curse beneath his breath, as if he *were* the murderous king, and not his semblance—had to pause in his speechifying, to wipe his face with a handkerchief.

"Would it were mortal poison for thy sake!" Malvinia cried.

"Never came poison from so sweet a place," Vandenhoffen claimed—but not always with the utmost sincerity.

And so they quarreled; and were reconciled; and Malvinia forgave her lover his cruelty, and Vandenhoffen forgave her her ill-temper, and took her in a carriage to the great Thames Department Store on Twenty-eighth Street, where, like a child, she might select as much as she wished, of kidskin gloves, and Japanese fans, and shawls of the finest Highland cashmere, and tortoise-shell combs trimmed in gold, and gold-backed hand mirrors, and French bonbons, and alligator-hide bags. "My favorite place in all the world!" Malvinia said greedily, her blue eyes narrowed and her breath swift and shallow, as, her lover beside her, she rode the palatial elevators, and moved, amidst a throng of shoppers, along the wide aisles of the world's largest store, a very Heaven of costly trinkets. (The Thames was eight floors high, a cast-iron reproduction of a Venetian *palazzo* with narrow columns, spandrels, and small ornate windows, in a design extremely pleasing to the American eye. That P. J. Thames had once been a mere *Yankee pedlar* filled Malvinia with astonishment, for it was quite a miracle, and quite an *American feat*, that the "World's Largest Store" had arisen out of a pedlar's shabby backpack! "Indeed," Malvinia murmured, turning a Japanese sandalwood fan in her fingers, "my favorite place in all the world. Excepting, of course, our private chamber.")

Like all cold-hearted persons, no matter the cherubic nature of their faces, Malvinia Morloch pondered but briefly on the sorrow she had wreaked, in days past: tho' from time to time, when most aggrieved with

Orlando Vandenhoffen, or pettishly incensed by some real or imagined slight to herself at the theater, she recalled with a pang of sentiment the Octagonal House, and the cozy bedchamber she had shared with sweet simple Octavia, and the parlor where, in the evening, the family gathered for music, and games, and reading, and the warm childlike pleasures of the hearth. *Sentiment* was felt; but never *remorse* or *guilt*. She brooded nostalgically upon herself as a child (and so pretty a child! all the relatives exclaimed); and Constance Philippa as a gawky-limbèd young girl, so bony at the pelvis that her corset could be turned freely about; and Octavia who had adored her, and petted her, and fussed over her, warming her chilled feet between her hands, or brushing out her hair, after washing, in a protracted, solemn ritual. And there was Samantha, of course, ugly little Samantha, with that head of beautiful hair which Malvinia had oft coveted; and Mrs. Zinn, who had never forgiven her, perhaps, for the excruciatingly painful hours she had had to endure, at Malvinia's birth. ("Alas, dear Mother!—how was *I* at fault?" Malvinia murmured aloud, in the chilly ostentation of her boudoir at the St. Regis, high above the street in which carriages and horsedrawn cabs clattered. "You might more justly have blamed Providence, after all; or Father himself.")

With many sighs, and a false tear or two in her eye, Malvinia gave herself up to thoughts of Mr. Zinn: not as he was at the present time (for she did not know him, at the present time), but as he had been many years ago, in the nursery, ah, so many, many years ago, when she was his heart's favorite, and performed to his great delight. That Mr. Zinn might have suffered great agony on her account, or might even have wrenched her violently from his affections, the maudlin young woman naturally did not consider: for was she not Father's favorite, the daughter of whom he was most proud?

And then there would sound a timid knock on her door, and it would be her French lady's maid, informing her that a gentleman had come to call; or Mr. Vandenhoffen was awaiting her, in the parlor; or her bath water was drawn, and the warm bubbly suds, liberally spiced with Fleur de lis Oils and Blanc de Neige, in preparation for her: and naturally she would forget all that she had been thinking, for thoughts flew in and out of Malvinia Morloch's head, rarely lingering for long.

"I am so besieged!—so beset-upon!" Malvinia exclaimed to herself, with a gratified little smile.

Significant it is, that Malvinia suffered a kind of amnesia, never recalling the buttonlike eyes of little Pip (save in occasional dreams, in which they were fixed most *sternly,* and most *humanly,* upon her); and never recalling the pallid face of her youngest sister Deirdre.

Indeed, she very nearly called attention to herself, by the way in

which she scoffed at the "Spiritualist nonsense" so many appeared to
believe in: she thought it "ridiculous," and "a consequence of criminal
bribes," that the well-known journalist Colonel Lynes, writing for the
New York *Daily Graphic,* had a moderate word to say for the mediumship
of "Deirdre of the Shadows," after he had exposed so many other popular
mediums, in his inimitable jocular style.

Most of the time, however, she resolutely ignored the newspaper
stories about this mysterious "Deirdre," turning the page impatiently, as
if fearing contamination; and when Vandenhoffen inquired idly, to a
party dining after hours at the Park Lane, "Should we all remove ourselves to a séance downtown, for the sport of it?—since 'Deirdre of the
Shadows' is now operating out of a respectable brownstone on the lower
Fifth Avenue, and it *might* be amusing," Malvinia answered at once, in a
jeering voice, before anyone else could reply: "My dear Orlando, the
Spiritualists are our *competitors* in the theater: they are but actors and
actresses, pretending otherwise."

And the matter was dropped, to Malvinia's great relief.

However—it was on a rain-lashed night in the final week of *Richard III,*
when theatergoers were driven up to the Fanshawe in closed carriages,
and gusts of wind made the gaslight flicker lewdly, that something very
disturbing occurred, to suggest to our haughty lady that the matter could
not be so lightly dropped.

The performance on that evening moved forward as always, perhaps with some diminishment of energy, which is only natural after a
run of many weeks. But tho' Malvinia made every effort to give her Anne
some spirit, it seemed to her—and perhaps to Vandenhoffen as well,
who spoke his lines rather leadenly—that something was amiss in the
theater: some *odd, chill, discomfiting presence* in the audience. Like any
competent actress, Malvinia spurred herself to defeat the mood, pro-
nouncing her lines less mechanically than usual, tho' she was rather disconcerted, feeling a pair of remorseless eyes in the audience, eyes that,
refusing to be taken in by the elaborate illusion on stage, saw her
clearly.

So she recited her lines, she displayed anger, and loathing, and an
almost coquettish resignation, and whilst Vandenhoffen embarked upon
one of his longer speeches, his leading lady took the opportunity, rather
hesitantly, to run her eyes along the rows of spectators, finding nothing,
until she happened to glance up to the box usually reserved for the
wealthy Vander Elst family: whereupon she saw a sight that pierced her
to the roots of her being, and made her doubt for a moment that she
would be able to continue with the farce of Shakespeare, in the light of
genuine malevolence.

For there was no mistaking it: the chill, leaden, paralyzing presence she had sensed, from the very opening of her scene, could be attributed to two personages seated in the front row of the box.

One was a woman of flaccid middle age, who peered at her through a lorgnette, in an attitude of affected refinement, ludicrously at odds with her squat, dumpy figure, and her corpulent face: this woman, attired in a *grande toilette* silk dress with a multitude of ribbons, and an ostrich-plume hat of a jaunty shape and size, with innumerable chains and beads looped about her neck, gazed at Malvinia with more than moderate interest, yet, withal, a not entirely unsympathetic mien.

It was the other person—heavily veiled, small of stature, immobile as a statue—who was staring so intently at Malvinia, and from whom, so the frightened actress imagined, the *odd, chill, remorseless* atmosphere emanated.

Had this evil presence declared itself many months before, at the start of Malvinia Morloch's career; had it—God forbid!—manifested itself on the very night of her *début,* the ascent of Malvinia Morloch to the stellar heights of celebrity would have been hideously crippled: nay, it might have been crushed altogether. But so practical-minded had Malvinia become, as a working actress, and, it may be, so skillful that the ominous presence of the veiled stranger did not incapacitate her, despite her initial trepidation. *I must finish out this scene,* Malvinia thought, in a panic. *I cannot let her o'ercome me.*

And so she continued with Anne's lines, speaking animatedly, so in control of her facial expression, and her rehearsed stage mannerisms, that she was able to disguise the agitation she felt. She experienced a curious numbed detachment, as if she were simultaneously *Lady Anne,* and the actress *Malvinia Morloch,* and *Malvinia* who stood apart from both, no matter that her breath came swift, and her heart hammered, and, involuntarily, her gaze swung up to the veiled lady in the Vander Elst box, with whom she fancied she exchanged a hard, frank stare, despite the stranger's black veil.

And then—God be thanked!—her exchange with Richard was over; and she could escape the stage, all breathless, and close to swooning.

So Deirdre has come to claim me, she thought, in her dressing room, as her hair was being adjusted, and some trifling bouquets of roses were being vased, *but am I hers to "claim"?*

Her premonition was mistaken, in any case. After the first act, the Vander Elst box was empty. And the chill, uncanny presence—the atmosphere of *unearthly menace*—had vanished.

"Hateful creature!—ah, hateful!" Malvinia stormed, in private, striking her fists together. "I do not know her—she is no sister of mine—we have no blood in common—it is intolerable, that she should intrude into my life!"

She told Vandenhoffen nothing of what had transpired, for she dreaded his surprise, and his curiosity, and his inevitable interrogation. And surely he would want to be introduced to Deirdre, surely he would demand that Malvinia arrange for a meeting. . . .

So she did not tell her lover of the agitation that gnawed at her heart, or the image of that slight, veiled, sinister figure, which haunted her for many days and nights. "Hateful—hateful!" she murmured. "Ah, it is intolerable! I will not countenance it!"

Nor did she tell him of an astonishing incident that happened only a few days later, on the very last night of the play: an incident more perplexing, it may be, than the first.

On this final night, the curtain having fallen for the last time, and the cast much relieved, Malvinia made her way to her dressing room, expertly undoing her tresses, when a stranger—a comely young gentleman—all but accosted her, to hand her a bouquet of flowers. "My dear Miss Morloch," he said, in a cool, cultivated voice, eying her with obvious satisfaction, and not a little irony, "you have been a superb Lady Anne: a role lacking in substance, but withal quite poignant. May I congratulate you? And will you accept this small tribute?"

It was rare that any admirer, even so well dressed, and so clearly cultured an admirer, could force his way backstage; unless of course he was known to the manager or the troupe, or had some special function. This handsome young gentleman was a total stranger: Malvinia accepted the bouquet blindly, in some confusion, and was about to inquire of the young man who he was, and how he came to be backstage, when he bowed shortly, and murmured a farewell, and hurried away.

"Wait," Malvinia cried, "sir—please—"

She stared after him. He was a stranger: and yet he had looked familiar. And his voice, tho' a stranger's voice, was familiar too.

An attractive young man, in his mid-twenties, perhaps; no older. With thick wavy dark hair, neatly parted on the left; and thick, severely defined brows; a strong chin; beautifully chiseled, and rather soft lips; a graceful figure; an air of—how to express it?—subtlety, humor, charm, irony—*knowingness*. He was elegantly attired in a tailcoat, trousers, and waistcoat (the waistcoat being of claret velvet, with gold tissue woven into an agreeable, and not overly busy, pattern); he must have been carrying his top hat, and his gloves. So quickly did he thrust the bouquet at Malvinia, so rapidly was the transaction finished, she felt quite dismayed—and rather cheated. Ah, she should have liked to detain the mysterious young man for a few minutes, to question him, and to become acquainted . . . !

Only then did the excited young woman think to examine her

bouquet, and the reader can imagine her astonishment, when she discovered it to be, not the long-stemmed roses to which she was accustomed, but a most curious—a most amazing—bouquet, of a sort she had never received (tho' she remembered clearly having given): an unwieldly assortment of wilted tea roses, and weed flowers distinguished by their ugly pallor: *turkey beard, fly poison, miterwort,* and *death camas!*

"Dear God!" Malvinia shrieked aloud; and, in her alarm, allowed the astonishing bouquet to fall to the floor.

VI

Ivory-Black;
or,
The Spirit World

36

It was not many months after that bodeful visit to the Fanshawe Theatre, by Deirdre of the Shadows and her companion, the redoubtable Countess Helena Petrovna Blavatsky, that the young medium was approached by a representative of the Society for Psychical Research, of Gramercy Park, with the proposal that she apply for membership in the Society, so that she might be registered as a *practicing medium:* which is to say, the Society wanted to investigate her, and publish the results, assuring her of an "objective" and "just" assessment.

Madame Blavatsky naturally warned her young comrade against any such incursion on the privacy of her work, explaining in her hoarse, florid voice, with many an impulsive hug of her little "Lolo"—for such was Madame's sobriquet for Deirdre, for reasons of a particularly maudlin and distasteful sort—that the infamous Society for Psychical Research, the onetime English Phasmatalogical Society, had not Deirdre's welfare in mind, nor even the presumed welfare of her future clients, but wanted merely to persecute; to hound; to pillory; to *crucify.* Skeptics, atheists, boastful agnostics, scientists of a Darwinian stripe, with only a very few fair-minded members, and a *very* few who believed in Spirit World, and its efficacy in this world: they were particularly cruel, Madame warned, to the female sex, for reasons she did not care to explore. "They will write you up in their papers, and cast doubt upon your every achievement, and most of all upon your *motive,*" Madame said. An imposing woman, tho' grossly fat, and costumed in a miscellany of skirts and capes and heavy medallions, giving off an odor, not altogether unpleasant, but uniquely *Madame,* of garlic, warm flaccid mammalian flesh, the strong aridity of Turkish tobacco, and linen that was less than fresh—imposing nonetheless, and not accustomed to being contradicted. "Under the guise of wishing to *help*, Lolo, the Society merely wishes to *expose*, and enjoys in particular the spectacle of a comely young lady tormented in public. I know, my dear; I know only too well. You should have seen how these American gentlemen persecuted me!"

Deirdre did not reply, but continued to frown—in fear, in apprehension, or in simple obstinacy?—at the stiff sheet of stationery in her lap, embossed with the Society's gold letterhead; and Madame, sighing impatiently, rolled a cigarette, her pudgy beringed fingers working expertly and mechanically. "I have only your best interests at heart, child, not only in order to discharge my duties—for the spirits have, after all, entrusted you to me—but because of the bond between us, which is unmistakable. Remember that this is the country, these are the people, who burnt witches not so very long ago, and who harbor a fierce hatred for those of us who would bring them salvation—those of us, I cannot but observe, who are of the female gender. In recent months I have been informed— by my faithful *chelas*, and by disinterested persons who wish only that Theosophy be treated with respect—of the extent and magnitude of the conspiracy against belief in the Mahatmas; and by the passion with which they launch their crucifixion campaign against *me*. Tho' you are not a *chela*, dear Lolo, nor even a member of my society, at the present time, it is impossible that you should have escaped *contamination* from Blavatsky!"—exploding here into hacking laughter, and shaking her massive head so stridently, wisps of her graying crinkled hair sprang loose, and the scarab brooch that fastened her scarlet neckerchief about her neck tore at the thin fabric.

Deirdre raised her large dark limpid eyes to Madame's face. She said softly: "Surely *contamination* is not . . . ?"

"I jest, I merely jest," Madame said, inhaling smoke from her long brown cigarette, and reaching out to squeeze Deirdre's arm with such energy, the many bracelets on her arm rattled. "I am but reading their minds, my dear. For I believe I know precisely how those minds work."

Madame's mirth having now subsided, she settled her bulk more comfortably in her chair, and smoked her cigarette with an angry relish, and spoke again of the evils of "objective" scientific research, and the Darwinian-Luciferian conspiracy to "annihilate" faith in the supernatural, and the insistence on the part of the Mahatmas (in hourly contact with Madame, tho' secreted away in Tibet, in the remotest mountain sanctuaries) that Madame's young charge shun the notorious Society—else she would regret it. Exhaling smoke, coughing, waving her beringed hands, Madame spoke more particularly of the wickedness of one Percy Dodd, the president of the New York chapter of the Society for Psychical Research; and, of course, tho' this had occurred some months before Deirdre's arrival, the scurrility of the infamous Colonel Lynes, writing in the

Graphic (itself a scurrilous gutter paper), who had dared to say in print that Countess Helena Petrovna Blavatsky was an imposter . . . and who had even challenged her aristocratic background. "The gravest, the most unforgivable, of insults," Madame said in a low fierce voice. "Ah, we Russians know what it is, to seek a just revenge upon our enemies!—we have known for many, many centuries! My father, as I have told you, was a captain of horse artillery in the Czar's army, and he did not stint to punish mutineers within his ranks, or any enemy of the Motherland, no matter the sentiments of his own heart. The slightest infraction of the rules might bring a young cadet one thousand blows with a birch rod before the entire assembled Corps—my father being certain that the company doctor stood at attention nearby, to intervene when the boy's heart seemed about to stop. Whippings, floggings, deaths by firing squad. . . . Cruel, you may think, with your New World notions, but necessary nonetheless, as the Czars have always known. Indeed, if a soldier died under punishment, the blows continued until the punishment had been meted out on the dead body. . . . But I digress; I am dreaming," Madame said with a small smile. She fixed her large, pouched, rather reptilian eyes upon the girl's face, and quoted in falsetto, from the slanderous Lynes's piece: " *'We regard this Russian "countess" neither as the mouthpiece of hidden Tibetan seers, as she and her fellow Theosophists claim, nor as a mere vulgar adventuress; we think Blavatsky has achieved a title to permanent remembrance as one of the most accomplished and ingenious impostors in history.'* "

Madame shuddered; with the result that her formidable corset sighed and creaked, and the wattled flesh about her neck trembled. The pouched eyes gave forth a veritable blaze of scorn, yet one might have detected a certain proudful gratification in her manner: for to be heralded, in print, as both *accomplished* and *ingenious,* and *unique in history,* was surely a remarkable feat for a Russian immigrant of impoverished status, who had come to our tolerant shores in steerage, with thousands of other motley European riffraff, as recently as 1873! Indeed, Madame so frequently quoted Colonel Lynes, to all who would listen, one cannot help but conclude that she relished his words, even as they infuriated her.

She exhaled blue smoke in a great cloud, and made a perfunctory gesture to wave it away, for Deirdre's eyes watered, and her throat constricted, in the presence of Madame's strong Turkish cigarettes: yet the child was loath to reveal discomfort. "Yes, yes, to know one's enemies . . . to know, and to take care . . . to contemplate, to plan strategy, and weapons . . . It is a Russian trait, and a noble one; but I fear it is somewhat alien to you, and makes you stiffen with distaste," she said, with an amiable nonchalance, one eyelid winking in Deirdre's direction. "But I am so much older, dear Lolo, than you, on the Earth Plane alone! . . . and so much older, and so much more sadly wiser, in the wisdom of many lives; of which I will not speak at the present time, for it is inappropriate, and would only distress us both. But you must keep in mind, my child, that your career as a medium is still in its early stages, no matter the acclaim you have received among believers, and the interest that widens almost daily, among nonbelievers; no matter, too, the fees and gifts and offers of hospitality that tumble into your dainty little lap, without your appearing (ah, you are so delightful!—may you never change) to condescend to notice. Yet the career is still in its *early stages*, and may well encompass, in its *maturity*, a sphere of influence of an international nature, which cannot fail, I do not hesitate to prognosticate, to bring you a modicum of wealth. Indeed, were I not totally devoted to my own pathway, to the wisdom of my Mahatmas, I would be inclined to take you more securely beneath my wing, and be your earthly mother, nay, mother and father alike—for you *are* so innocent, are you not, dear Deirdre?— and so lonely—"

Another young lady, of a more normal, not to say more delicate, constitution, might have colored becomingly at so florid an outburst; but little Deirdre simply continued to stare at the older woman, her face as inexpressive as a plaster mask, and very nearly as pale. It was true that since the modest start of the mediumship of Deirdre of the Shadows, now some years ago, in Boston, a fair amount of financial rewards had been garnered, including gifts of outright cash (in containers as varied as alligator-hide pouches, and purses of gold thread, and touching little volumes containing the photographs of dead infants in their caskets— infants whose souls, now adequately matured in Spirit World, were able to speak to their bereft parents, through the medium's art); it was true that a great variety of gifts had been received, some far more valuable than others, tho' all honorable; and the offers of hospitality!—at the present time, for instance, Deirdre was living in New York City as the guest of Mrs. Holtman Strong, a widow with more than ordinary interests in the occult, and more than ordinary financial resources (her husband, the late Holtman Strong, had been an early investor in the Little Rock and Fort Smith Railroad, and an associate of the Du Ponts—who, of late, had decided to drop the "de Nemours" from their name): the first floor of the Strongs' sumptuous brownstone, at 2 Fifth Avenue, being given over to Deirdre's use, along with a small retinue of servants, and her own two-seater brougham. (Mrs. Strong was an elderly-appearing woman, in fact not many years older than Madame Blavatsky's robust fifty-three, whose losses to death in recent years—husband, daughter, daughter-in-law, infant grandson—had so greatly distressed her, her psychical as well as her physical health was threatened: one can well imagine the widow's gratitude, that Deirdre of the Shadows had been able to put her in contact with some of her deceased loved ones, and, upon two distinct occasions, to summon forth the ectoplasmic shape of Mr. Strong!) It was true, as Madame Blavatsky observed, that Deirdre's career was but yet in its early stages, and promised a ripe harvest in the years to come: but it was not altogether true that the inscrutable young lady took no notice of these *worldly,* if not to say *materialistic,* facts.

She studied Madame's heavy, ravaged, yet still rather handsome face, with its Calmuck cheekbones, and its almost too ostentatiously "hypnotic" eyes.

A long moment passed: Madame's smile grew somewhat forced, and the creases beside her mouth rather more pronounced.

"That the Society for Psychical Research has been unfriendly to your cause, is certainly regrettable," Deirdre said slowly, in a voice so soft Madame had to strain to hear, "and Colonel Lynes's attack in particular is heinous: but the Society's curiosity about me is something quite different, for, as Mr. Dodd explains in his letter, a judicious investigation would clear the way for my being invited to join the Society, as a practicing medium; and, as it were, licensed. I would—tho' the gentleman doesn't say *this*—become respectable. And as only three percent of the mediums investigated by the Society are judged legitimate, and given the Society's imprimatur, I cannot but think that the opportunity is a felicitous one; and would greatly aid me in what you call, Madame, so very kindly, tho' rather too ambitiously, my *career.* And so—"

"Beware, Lolo, beware!" Madame interrupted, knocking ashes onto her lap, in her agitation, "I catch the drift of your ingenuous thought, and must warn you: the Society is composed for the most part of jealous, grasping individuals, souls very low on the planes of incarnation, and atheistical in the most extreme sense. They are men of science, which they have made their religion—a religion opposed to all we believe in, and dedicated to eradicate your influence. No, no," Madame said, shaking her massive head emphatically, "and again *no:* I cannot allow you to consider such folly. I thought I had explained how such persons are your natural enemies, and how my Russian blood rejoices to do battle with avowed enemies, in the Czar's very spirit: but on our own terms, dear Lolo, not on theirs. To fight in the very sanctuary of the enemy, in the Society's headquarters itself!—folly, pride, Luciferian temerity—"

Deirdre sat without moving, however, staring at the toe of Madame's boot, and a small thin smile played about her lips, evanescent as a firefly. Perhaps because she and Madame were speaking in the parlor of Mrs. Strong's home, and not in Madame's own parlor, at the Lamasery on Forty-seventh Street, she enjoyed a certain calm, and a certain stubborn strength; perhaps because the decision was not in truth her own, but one guided by Spirit World, she could withstand Madame's avalanche of words, and her still more tempestuous outpouring of emotion. Or was it simply a belated manifestation of Deirdre's *perversity*—observed many pages back in this chronicle, on the very occasion, the reader may recall, of her having been spirited away in the outlaw balloon, to a destiny no one could have foretold? Long ago the Zinns and Kiddemasters whispered amongst themselves, "Deirdre goes her own way," and "Deirdre is a troubled young lady," and even—with what unsettling prescience!— "Deirdre is haunted": yet not even the boldest among them (Malvinia, it may have been, or Great-Aunt Edwina) could have prognosticated to what extremes that perversity might bring her, or to what fugitive company.

Madame had been speaking rapidly for some minutes, her pouched eyes glittering with moisture (engendered rather more by anger than by sorrow), the ashes of her Turkish cigarette liberally scattered across her massive bosom; now she paused, breathing hoarsely, and waited for Deirdre to speak, and to give her answer. It would have taken no acute observer to note how the young lady's stare had turned glassy, and her breathing so greatly reduced, she seemed more a waxworks statue than a warm, living, sentient being.

How bitter it is, your heart!—your heart!—so a faint silvery voice sounded, from out of the most shadowed corner of the parlor, where a heavy brocade drape quivered just perceptibly, as if in a summer's breeze: but it was not summer, and the windows were fastened tight.

Madame did not hear; or, being a veteran of such phenomena, chose not to be distracted. She continued to stare at her young charge, awaiting an answer.

And the answer was forthcoming, albeit slow, and halting, and grave, and slyly adamant. "It is the spirits' wish, dear Madame," Deirdre said, her pale lips scarcely moving, and her gaze still glassy and unperturbed, "and not my own. That I submit to Mr. Dodd's proposal—that I go forth, without apprehension, confident of *their* loving protection— and my own honest abilities—that I dedicate myself to bringing the two worlds more closely together: it is not my wish, Madame, but the spirits', and I have no choice, and, indeed, no desire, but to acquiesce."

37

When Deirdre Bonner was but four years of age she contracted an especially virulent strain of measles, and was confined to her sickbed with a temperature of 104 degrees. Her distraught parents kept vigil through the night, day upon day, fearing that their little angel would be carried off, for many a child has died of so minor an illness as measles; and poor Deirdre's skin fairly burned to the touch!

One night, as the twelve strokes of midnight were sounded by the ponderous bells of old Trinity Church, not a half-mile distant, it seemed to both Mr. and Mrs. Bonner that something very peculiar fluttered about their little girl's room. Mrs. Bonner, laying aside the Bible (for she and Mr. Bonner had been reading from it in turns, the Gospels primarily), whispered: "Who—or what—is it? Is something present?" Deirdre slumbered fitfully on her pillow, her dark-lashed eyelids trembling, and her tiny fists clenching and unclenching; her fever gave off a faint radiant heat, it seemed, quivering in the air about the bed. "Who is it?" the frightened woman asked. "What do you want?" Mr. Bonner sought to calm her all the while, by gripping her hand, and then both her hands, firmly in his. There was nothing present, he assured her in a low whisper: nothing: she must be calm, else Deirdre would be disturbed.

No matter Mr. Bonner's brave avowal, it soon became apparent that there *was* something in the room with them: a haze, a glow, a flickering or pulsating presence. The great grave bells of old Trinity tolled, and were silent, save for the faint echo of their sonorousness, which seemed retained in the sickroom, as if time had suddenly stopped.

"Oh, dear God!—what is it, who are you, want do you want?" the terrified Mrs. Bonner queried, looking wildly about, and seeing naught but undulating shadows, that leapt to the very ceiling, and melded dancerlike with one another, cast by the several candles that burned, and the kerosene wick-lamp on the bedside table. "You have not—*have* you?—come for my little girl?"

For long suspended moments the pulsating glow ranged about the room, now hovering in a corner, above an old walnut wardrobe; now snaking indolently across the ceiling; now quivering at the foot of the sick child's bed. Mr. Bonner, as terrified as his wife, continued to clutch her hands in his, but said not a word: afterward, he would claim that he had been *incapable* of speaking had he wished: for his very throat was closed, and his teeth held together with an enormous pressure. (Alas, how might one address a prayer to our Heavenly Father, in such a circumstance!— for, it seems, the approach of spirits, whether blessed by God, or frankly damn'd, so disorients even the good, steadfast Christian, and unlooses all manner of infantile terrors, that one cannot *act;* and only in retrospect might one say, Ah, yes, I should have done thusly, why was I so paralyzed, and so impotent?) Mrs. Bonner's voiced queries faded, too, out of very terror, perhaps, and she froze into silence, afterward concurring in her husband's description of his state of immobility: she seemed to understand, as if instructed by a silent voice that arose, as it were, out of *memory*, that her agitation would communicate itself to little Deirdre, and interfere with the healing process.

And so some minutes passed, between fifteen and twenty, as Mr. Bonner calculated afterward, and the shadowy quivering haze hovered about the bed, and Deirdre's troubled sleep became calmer, and the movement of her eyes behind her feverish eyelids ceased, and her breathing grew soft and rhythmic, and the faint but distinct odor of *fever* and *sickness* lightened; and, Mr. and Mrs. Bonner still fiercely clasping hands, their daughter suddenly opened her eyes wide, and smilingly assured them in a bell-like, limpid voice: "Dear Mother and Father, retire to your bed, and be assured—*I will not die."*

And the child sank back onto her goose-feather pillow, into an altogether peaceful sleep.

("Who was it came to visit you, Deirdre, during the night?" Mrs. Bonner asked, with caution, in the morning, as she sponged the child's face with tepid water. "Do you recall anyone, or anything, visiting you while you were asleep?"

Deirdre blinked, and smiled at her mother, and yawned, with more energy than she had demonstrated in many days; and her cheeks dimpled with something very much—ah, how welcome!—like simple mischief. "You and Father were with me all the night," she said, *"You* would have seen, would you not, if someone else had been here?"

Mrs. Bonner paused, and bethought herself for a moment (for she was, it must be said, not a very complex soul), and could only reiterate her question—whether Deirdre recalled anyone, or anything, visiting her while she slept.

Deirdre giggled, and squirmed beneath the quilt like a silly little eel, and said, with exactly the spirit of naughtiness one expects from, and hopes for, in a healthy four-year-old: "If I was asleep, Momma, how could I *see!* If I had my eyes closed all the while!" And she giggled, and hid beneath the pillow, and was so altogether darling, that Mrs. Bonner's heart swelled to bursting with love of her, and simple gratitude, and she embraced her daughter's warm lively body, and rained kisses upon her still-flushed cheeks; and the matter was closed.)

How the God-fearing Bonners, simple folk as they were, would have been astounded to see into the future, and to learn that their child would mature into one of the most celebrated trance mediums of the Eighties! —compared by Spiritualist aficionados (whether devout believers, or objective observers), to the incontestably greatest medium of all time, Daniel Dunglas Home; and greatly preferred to her rivals Mrs. Whittaker, Mrs. Guilford, and Ambrose Tollers. For tho' little Deirdre did exhibit in childhood a number of queer talents, and appeared to be the center, and perhaps even the occasion, of inexplicable phenomena, she was never so disturbing a presence as the boy Home (who so upset the household in which he resided, he was accused of bringing the Devil into it, and expelled), or the infant Mrs. Guilford (née Parshall, who, in her beribboned cradle, was said to have been sung to sleep by a veritable choir of angel voices, and rocked by invisible hands, and even given suck by invisible means); nor did legends accrue to her, as to the child Helena Petrovna Hahn (who was said to have caused the death of a fourteen-year-old serf when only four years old herself: she called down *russalkas,* or Russian fairy-nymphs, upon him, and he was drowned in a river).

Deirdre was a shy, excitable, sensitive child, of the type called "high-strung"; clearly above average in intelligence; fairylike, wistful, and grave; at times remarkably mature, and at other times babyish and prankish. The schoolmaster of the Bloodsmoor common school praised her as his best scholar, and even worried that she spent so much time buried in books, and compiling long lists of spelling and vocabulary words (for the little girl dearly loved words—their sounds as much as their meanings); but he did report to the Bonners that she could be, upon occasion "devilishly" naughty. She told lies, for instance. She made up elaborate and utterly fraudulent stories. And while she did not steal things, she hid them; and would never admit what she had done.

Mr. and Mrs. Bonner so cherished Deirdre, they were loath to punish her, or even to discipline her harshly. She was susceptible to turbulent dreams and nightmares, and sudden frightening thoughts (or actual visions); and, for a time, the Bonners feared she might be consumptive. (It is interesting to recall that D. D. Home *was* consumptive, stating openly that his spirits came to him most readily, when the physical side of his nature was diminished.) She saw things, she heard things, she even appeared to smell and touch and taste things, not evident to anyone else; and yet it was problematic, whether she understood that these things inhabited only an invisible or internal world—for children are so trusting of experience, they rarely question themselves, as to the *reality* about them. And many are the normal children, after all, who engage in spirited dialogue with invisible playmates, and romp, and disport themselves, in imaginary kingdoms.

Once, at the age of seven, Deirdre ran to Mrs. Bonner and babbled to her, in great excitement, about a "shining" figure in a long white robe, with a "circle of light" about his head, and "wings crookèd like a hawk's": an archangel, by the sound of him, and taller than Mr. Bonner by far. Not long afterward she astounded a Bloodsmoor neighbor by remarking casually that her son was on a "boat all in flames": which, it turned out, referred to the fact that the young man, a sailor in the Navy, en route to Russian America (Alaska), lay abed with a high fever, but subsequently recovered. Upon more than one unsettling occasion the child, always speaking in a spontaneous, lucid voice, said matter-of-factly that someone would be "crossing over" before long: which is to say, dying. (And she was never mistaken—tho' the Bonners deliberately made little of it, not wanting to excite Deirdre, or to call attention to her ostensible powers amongst the villagers, who might misunderstand.)

She could find lost objects around the house; and if an object was brought to her, that had been found (a woman's ring, for instance, discovered in the road), she could describe its owner, and even stammer out a probable name. Once, turning the tattered pages of an old copy of *The Pilgrim's Progress,* which had been in Mr. Bonner's possession for as long as he could remember, she closed her eyes and described, with a cherubic little smile, the white-haired man with the gnarled cane and the strange red speck in his left eye, who had been Mr. Bonner's grandfather—and who had died twenty years before. She astonished her parents by telling them, one winter afternoon, that she had met "the nicest old man" down by the river: proceeding to describe a personage in what must have been a Dutch costume, dating back to no later than the 1660's, when the Kiddemasters had conquered the area, for the British Crown; upon another, more disturbing occasion, she ran to them in tears, and told of a "Raging Captain" whose uniform was soaked in blood, and who shouted at her from atop a hill to come to him at once, else he would punish her and the Bonners. "Little Deirdre," he called her, "little daughter—come to me at once!" Unlike the other presences this "Raging Captain" was horrific, and Deirdre ran in tears from him, tho' she did not seem to recognize that he had no substance: that he was, in short, what is vulgarly called a *ghost*.

"You must not come home from school that way ever again," Mrs. Bonner cautioned, calming her; "you must walk with the others, and not wander off alone."

"Will he get me, then?" the trembling child asked; "if I go off alone?"

"He won't get you," Mrs. Bonner replied, "no one will get you, for your Heavenly Father watches over you; but it is most prudent to stay with the other children, and not to take a shortcut through the fields, or through the cemetery."

"Does he live in the cemetery?" the child asked doubtfully. "I see him atop a hill. His horse is dead beside him."

"He lives in numerous places," Mrs. Bonner said. "But you must obey me, Deirdre: and come home directly from school. Do you hear?"

"Will the Captain get me," Deirdre asked, gazing at her mother with enormous gray imploring eyes, "if I am naughty? If I disobey?"

"I have said the Captain will not 'get' you—or anyone," Mrs. Bonner said, embracing the frightened child, "but you *must* obey, Deirdre, do you understand? Otherwise—otherwise—I cannot promise—I do not know what will happen!"

Alas, as it turned out, both Mr. and Mrs. Bonner were to be carried off, in the typhoid epidemic of 1873, along with some thirty other hapless persons in Bloodsmoor; and the nine-year-old Deirdre was to become, within a fortnight, an orphan—albeit one under the protection of the Reverend Hewett and his wife, who had vowed to the dying Mrs. Bonner (a piteous sight, with her mouth an angry mass of fever blisters, and her eyes deepset in their dark sockets, and her body wasted away to mere skin and bones with the merciless high fever, and the intestinal hemorrhaging) that they would not allow the civil authorities to place Deirdre in an orphanage. "She must be provided for—she is of noble blood—she cannot—cannot—be thrown into the abyss," the delirious woman raved; and it was all the nurses could do, to quiet her, and to restore her soul to some semblance of calm, that she might die in peace.

Poor Deirdre!—poor bereft child!

Yet it had not been many weeks before, after a long Sunday ramble with Mr. and Mrs. Bonner, when the three of them happened upon John Quincy Zinn, that Deirdre had seen, in a waking dream of a particularly vivid sort, the vast Shadow World o'ertaking her belovèd parents, tho' of course the innocent child could not have known the import of the vision, at that time, or the terrible suffering and grief it would entail for all.

Their joyful Sunday ramble had taken them along the river, somewhat farther than their customary walk (for the March air was agreeably temperate, and the sunshine encouraging, and little Deirdre would run ahead, shouting and laughing, and forcing her parents to follow), so that, without knowing it, they found themselves in the area called Kiddemaster Common, not very distant from the Bloodsmoor Gorge: private land, strictly speaking, yet open to the public for such rambles and hikes and Sunday excursions. (Hunting of any kind was naturally forbidden, and the Judge's several gameskeepers were quite justified in expelling from the territory any persons who struck them as undesirable: there having been, during the course of many decades, a number of unfortunate shooting accidents—the Kiddemaster gameskeepers being somewhat o'erzealous in their wish to protect their masters' property, and their masters' game, against incursions from commoners.)

Deirdre ran ahead, an enchanting sight in her pretty yellow coat and lambswool bonnet, and little brown boots, and Mr. and Mrs. Bonner followed, Mrs. Bonner's arm linked firmly through Mr. Bonner's, in the very image of family contentment. Indeed, Herman and Catherine Bonner, of whom so relatively little is known, save their ages (forty and thirty-seven, respectively), and their religious devotion, and love for their daughter, struck those villagers who happened to see them, at such times, besporting themselves in innocent familial bliss, as *upstanding* and *excellent* Christians: not physically handsome, perhaps (for Mr. Bonner was decidedly undersized, with a very narrow, as it were pushed-in countenance; and Mrs. Bonner was hefty and foursquare, with a moon face, and a rather mottled complexion—so very different, one cannot help but observe, from little Deirdre!), nor what might be called, in vulgar parlance, *sharpness* of mind or wit. Nonetheless, they were God-fearing Christians, and faithful members of Trinity Church parish, and Mr. Bonner was said to have acquitted himself fully, and without complaint, of his managerial responsibilities at the Kiddemaster factory—earning an unusual measure of praise from his rather exacting superiors, and, upon the occasion of his untimely death, the expression of deep regret, and the observation that "it would be difficult indeed, to replace so dutiful, and so loyal, an employee."

Bloodsmoor Gorge, as the reader might know, is a region of notoriously craggy terrain, susceptible to sudden fog, chill winds, and inexplicable drops of temperature. There are eerie chasms that appear to open into the very bowels of the earth, and severe cliffs and overhangs, and towerlike abutments of granite and flint, stirring to the eye, but formidable as well, and oft disturbing. It is, in short, as picturesque a place as one, nursed on romantic expectations, might wish: rather too picturesque, in fact, if one's sensibilities naturally curve toward the moderate and the civilized, and flinch from the boldly savage.

The nine-year-old Deirdre ran all unheeding into this place of brute exposed boulders, and her parents, having called after her to no avail, were obliged to follow. Their mood was sunny and good-hearted, for the March day was remarkably warm, and they saw no danger in their impetuous little girl's unleashed energies, for they oft hiked and rambled in fairly rough fields, and, upon more than one occasion, imagined themselves lost—or nearly so—in the oak and beech and ash forests that surrounded Bloodsmoor Village.

So they followed, Mrs. Bonner's arm still linked with Mr. Bonner's, in a gesture of wifely dependency, and harmless public affection, and had no serious thought of Deirdre's becoming lost; until such time as they realized that the cheery yellow coat was not in view, and that, as they called out, "Deirdre! Deirdre!" their voices were drowned out by the low dull thunderous roar of falling water.

Naturally Deirdre's parents became immediately concerned, and Mrs. Bonner, being of a somewhat excitable temperament, inclining, it may be, toward the hysteric, upon the occasion of what she conceived to be a *physical* threat to her child, shouted most vociferously: for what if Deirdre should slip and twist her ankle, or break her fragile leg, on the brute outcropping of rock; what if—God in His mercy forbid!—she should lose her footing, and tumble head-on into one of the cavernous tunnels in which chill foaming water plunged, and quite disappear from view!

The Bonners hurried after their impetuous child, calling her name again and again, oft imagining they had caught sight of her just ahead— her yellow coat, her pretty white bonnet—and then bitterly disappointed, and their strenuous efforts redoubled. "Deirdre! Deirdre! Do you hear? Where are you? Our dear child—*do* you hear? Are you hiding? Deirdre—"

The queerest vegetation grew in the gorge, or along its steep sides —nameless gnarled trees, great spiky bushes and shrubs, and rushes, and sere grasses of all kinds, in appearance as sharp as swords—vegetation that looked, to the botanically untrained eye at least, uncannily o'ersized, as if looming out of a dream landscape. Yet there was beauty withal—I am obliged not to mislead the reader: a lush barbaric beauty of falls, and steep chasms, and shadowed granite cliffs, and enormous beech trees that seemed to possess, in their innumerable branches, and sturdy trunks, the magical authority of mythic creatures of old . . . giants, or gods of a kind, sheerly pagan, and unspeakable to envision. . . .

Just as the Bonners' concern threatened to heighten to panic, they emerged from the boulder-strewn terrain, to a sort of plateau, composed of flat granite outcroppings, and there saw, to their immense relief, the yellow coat of their child!—with what exclamations of joy, we can well imagine, whether parents ourselves or no. And yet, in the very next instant, they were alarmed to see that the child was not alone, but engaged in conversation with a stranger: an extraordinarily tall and sturdily built man, with striking fair hair, and a prominent beard, not immediately recognizable by his attire as a *gentleman*. (For this personage not only wore a somewhat rustic costume, consisting of a leather jacket, and un-tapered trousers, but was *hatless*—indeed, his blond hair shone brilliantly in the sunshine, and seemed, of a sudden, almost preternatural.)

Little Deirdre and the tall stranger spoke together with evident animation, the child chattering happily away, no doubt in her usual airy prattle, and the strange man bent over her, fingers outspread on his thighs, bearded face bobbing in amused agreement. A warm scene; a scene affording vast relief, and not a little joy; and yet, in the next mo-ment, both the Bonners were seized with a sudden terror . . . for this masculine figure had about it a quality *not quite normal*.

It may have been an accident of the vibrant light, or a consequence of the Bonners' frayed nerves, but the stranger looming over their daugh-ter appeared to be unnaturally tall—perhaps ten feet, or more—and his broad smiling countenance was too smiling, having the effect, very nearly, of a beam or beacon. The blond locks, too, as they rippled in an imper-ceptible breeze, did glow with an extraordinary ferocity. Was this crea-ture a wizard of some sort?—a sorcerer—a male witch—the very embodi-ment, it seemed, of the gorge's ominous atmosphere? Yet so sturdy and broad-shouldered was the man, and so generously did his deep laughter sound, that he could not, certainly, have been anything so insubstantial, so pitifully meager, as a *ghost!*

Drawing bravely near, however, the trembling Bonners saw, in the next instant, to what we can only characterize as their enormous relief, that the man was not in truth a stranger: and, indeed, he *was* a gentleman of the first rank: none other than John Quincy Zinn.

A happy conclusion, then, to an episode fraught with more than a little alarm: one's heart swells with joy, to see again Mr. and Mrs. Bonner hurrying to their naughty child's side, and sweeping her up in an em-brace, all the while exclaiming, and admonishing, and fairly gasping with relief, and simple gratitude, and protestations of apology uttered to Mr. Zinn!—for the moment was an emotional one, verging upon the inchoate, and the Bonners are to be forgiven if their hearts pounded most wildly, and tears sprang into their eyes, with an admixture of joy, relief, and parental reprehension.

In an instant, however, all was clear. All was explained, and quite straightforward. Deirdre had wandered onto the plateau of flat rocks, and Mr. Zinn, enraptured by the silence, and completely caught up, as he phrased it, in the "solitude of the Divine Eye," turned to see her—with some surprise at first (for naturally he did not expect to see a child in that wild place, or any human figure at all), and then with delight, and amusement. For what a charming little miss Deirdre was, in her lambswool bonnet, and her smart calfskin boots, new that past Christmas!

The Bonners, conscious of their intrusion into Mr. Zinn's reverie (it being obvious to them that the renowned inventor had been startl'd out of a deep meditation, and no mere idle daydream), and conscious even more painfully of their gravely disparate social status, would have hastened back home immediately, their little girl firmly in tow, had not the handsome Mr. Zinn, with the aristocratic charity of his in-law Kiddemasters, and the yet more impressive spontaneity of friendliness, of his own sunny nature, invited them all to his workshop: there to partake of tea and a light repast, and a few minutes' much-needed rest, before they began their hike home.

The Bonners declined this gracious invitation, with many a blush and genteel protestation; but Mr. Zinn so insisted, and Deirdre grew so lively in her insistence, that, after some minutes, the Bonners acquiesced, and, Mr. Bonner carrying the somwhat o'erwrought child in his arms, they repaired to the cabin, not one hundred yards distant, on a sturdy granite promontory overlooking the gorge's deepest chasm.

The cabin was trim and foursquare, made of plain, stolid, ordinary birch logs, in the weathertight fashion first demonstrated, in the New World of the mid-1600's, by the Swedish and Finnish pioneers, and quite unknown—if legendary history tells truth—to both English and German, and even Dutch, settlers. Mr. and Mrs. Bonner, greatly pleased with Mr. Zinn's hospitality, enjoyed the visit less demonstrably than did little Deirdre: but were pleased nonetheless, to be offered fresh Ceylon tea, and delicious date-nut squares baked (as Mr. Zinn but casually mentioned) by Mrs. Zinn herself—Mrs. Zinn being of course Miss Prudence Kiddemaster, the daughter of the famous Judge, and Mrs. Sarah Whitton Kiddemaster, the wealthy Wilmington heiress.

The Bonners were given chairs by the small but cozy fire, and introduced to Mr. Zinn's pet monkey, Pip, that "naughty little furry-souled devil," as Mr. Zinn fondly called him, and made to feel quite at home, despite their nervousness; and their apprehension, for which they were perhaps justified, that Deirdre would upset something in the crowded workshop, as she prowled and pranced about, Mr. Zinn sunnily ignoring her, or implicitly, as it were, encouraging her. Ah, a lovely teatime visit!—memorable, indeed historic, in the Bonners' lives!—for they would hardly have dared imagine, at the outset of their Sabbath walk, so astounding a conclusion. Yet here was the son-in-law of Judge Kiddemaster speaking warmly to them, as if they were all equals, offering them more tea, and not minding that Deirdre teased and romped with Pip (who had taken to her immediately with all the vivacity of a puppy, and some of the intelligent reserve of a human adult), and even chatting with them about various highly intriguing subjects quite beyond their scope of knowledge: the likelihood of there being, within a generation, an "auto-wagen" to replace the horsedrawn carriage; the possibility of there being, in the next century at least, a revolutionary source of energy, whether solar, lunar, or prised out of the atom by main force; and the pity of it (tho' why it should be a *pity*, the Bonners did not grasp), that oil-drilling in the Titusville mountain range was proceeding with such rapidity, and commercial success, under the guidance of one Edwin L. Drake of the Seneca Oil Company—about whom, Mr. Zinn confessed, he knew very little, save that he felt envy for the man's achievement!

(The Bonners would have exchanged a glance of surprise, that the renowned John Quincy Zinn, who was surely a wealthy gentleman in his own right, should express *envy* of anyone living; but of course they were too courteous to do so, in Mr. Zinn's presence.)

John Quincy Zinn then showed Deirdre a remarkable toy of his own invention—a Zinnoscope, as he playfully called it. It was a cylinder made of some substance akin to papier-mâché, which, when held to the eye, afforded a marvelous fluid kaleidoscopic story: the winsome monkey Pip himself, cavorting and frolicking and leaping about. (The elder Bonners, as well as Deirdre, were fascinated by this creation, and could not guess how it worked. Tiny mirrors that turned and circled; pastel sketches of Pip allegedly executed by one of Mr. Zinn's daughters—and how gloriously talented *she* must be!—it quite beggared the imagination.) Mr. Zinn's generosity was such, that he tried to press this extraordinary toy upon the Bonners, claiming that his own daughters were "fatigued" by it, and no longer had the slightest interest in it; but the Bonners were well-bred enough to decline this offer, with many expressions of gratitude.

"Please *do* take it with you," Mr. Zinn exclaimed. "Deirdre, my dear, will you accept it? As a token of—well, shall we say—an ordinary Sunday?—an ordinary Sunday in March, *wondrously* interrupted by a magical visitation?" But, despite the child's loudly vociferated wishes, the Bonners *did* decline, with finality.

Mr. Zinn begged them, however, to accept from him, as a "mere commonplace of a toy," an ingenious jack-in-the-box he had made, out of hickory wood, with his fretsaw: and this the Bonners were pressed into accepting, for Deirdre, who was naturally o'erjoyed, and expressed her excited gratitude by seizing the gentleman's strong, sturdy fingers, in a somewhat uncharacteristic gesture of childish exuberance, and pumping them up and down as if in an adult handshake.

In all, for Herman and Catherine Bonner, an unforgettable episode in their foreshortened lives—a memorable Sabbath, to be cherished in both this world, and in the next.

It was that very evening, as Deirdre was being tucked into bed, that she murmured, sleepily, with but a modicum of apprehension, that she saw "a big dark cloud, a flaming cloud," approaching the house: but Mrs. Bonner assured her there was nothing amiss, save that the hour was late for little girls to be awake.

Deirdre shifted restlessly beneath her blankets, and groped for her mother's warm hand, and, half asleep, said that "a little girl" would run out the door, and the door would slam behind her, and the "Momma and Poppa" would be caught inside; and the great dark fiery cloud would o'ertake the house, and cause it to explode into flames.

These remarks would have disturbed Mrs. Bonner had they been uttered with more alarm, but Deirdre was so sleepy from her long hike, and so sweetly composed in her bed, with her dark-gleaming hair against the embroidered pillowcase, and her eyelids too heavy to remain open, that only an individual sadly acquainted with occult prophecy, or predisposed to alarm, would have taken note: and Mrs. Bonner, who placed her faith in our Heavenly Father, was neither.

So Deirdre was tucked into bed, and her mother leaned over her, and visited a kiss or two upon her warm cheek, and whispered, in the tremulous voice of loving maternal solicitude: "God bless you and keep you, my child."

The sleep-befuddled child was unable to return her mother's kiss, but managed to caress her cheek, with a vague little hand, and to take hold, for a moment, of the gold locket Mrs. Bonner wore about her neck: a legacy that would one day be hers, and oh! so far sooner than anyone might have known.

38

Tho' the years of Deirdre's sojourn at the Octagonal House, as one of the Zinn sisters—so renowned, and so envied, in the village!—were illuminated by moments, and, indeed, episodes of some duration, of contentment, and even of happiness (deriving most forcefully from Deirdre's adoration of her stepfather), it must be said that her sisters were not unfairly severe, in judging her *heavy of heart,* and *perpetually mourning,* and *scandalously ungrateful*—this last utterance being Malvinia's.

The great dark cloud envisioned by the nine-year-old, in her innocence, ballooned to encompass the entire sky, it seemed: nor did she escape its shadow, tho' her new sisters petted her, and spoiled her, and loved her dearly—for a time. The exiguity of her feeling for them, and, it may be, for life itself, soon discouraged all but Octavia. (For is it not our Christian duty, Octavia inquired, to *love* where no love was *deserved,* or even *desired?*)

For a spell of some months, well into the summer of her first year with the Zinns, Deirdre was mute: not out of any physiological malady Dr. Moffet could determine, but out of sheer grief or, it may be, out of willful stubbornness, tho' the good doctor naturally did not like to make this diagnosis. Shrinking from the Zinns' warmest greetings—holding herself preternaturally still when hugged—composing a face of the gravest sorrow, even when delightful Pip cavorted with a black squirrel, on a fine summer's day, and the Zinns all heartily laughed, and the world was a place of serenity and beauty: so the child resisted *love,* as if the activity of *loving,* of her own, were a treacherous possibility, to be anxiously resisted.

"Momma," she sometimes whispered, "Poppa—are you close by?"

She acquired the extraordinary ability—so her sisters jested, out of the elder Zinns' hearing—to make her cheeks go clammy and cold, when she was being kissed; she had too the ability—hardly an enviable one!—of altering the fragrance of sweet lavender, or powdered roses, or ambergris (sewn up in "sweet bags" for wardrobe drawers), to a dull cold flat must-odor, redolent of the cobwebbed recesses of the cellar, or the grave itself. She was observed as smiling almost with pain, and with a nearly imperceptible brightening of her countenance, when Mr. Zinn addressed her, or squatted before her, to converse; she *might* respond timidly, to Mrs. Zinn's hearty embrace; or to one of plucky Octavia's overtures. Constance Philippa's height, and rather brusque manner, and unconvincing interest in her, were distinctly unsettling as was Malvinia's unpredictable manner—now vivacious and warm and inviting, now petulant and haughty, and cruel. Samantha, nearest her age, a "young-old" child not unlike herself, tried much harder to love her stepsister than the family appreciated, tho' the nervous burden of sharing a bedchamber with a virtual stranger, affected her greatly, and roused her to some resentment, of her parents' fanciful notions of family life, and of Christian charity in general. (Many years later, as an elderly woman, reflecting upon her years as the favorite daughter of John Quincy Zinn—for so, with the passage of decades, *assisting* quite innocently waxed into *favorite*—Samantha was to speak tersely of such domestic trials, observing only that her genius-father did not stint, in introducing the *experimental method,* with its ambiguous consequences, into familial life. But that his intentions were good—surpassingly good, and exemplary—was never in question.)

That Deirdre was a "wizened little cuckoo bird plopped down in our nest," as Malvinia wickedly observed, was surely unfair to Deirdre: for the heart-stricken orphan had hardly wished to be an orphan: and would not have wished Death to o'ertake anyone, let alone her belovèd parents, could she have grasped the nature of it, and the immeasurable losses for the living.

"Momma," she whispered, "Poppa?—are you close by? Do you hear, do you see? Have you abandoned me forever?"

But Spirit World for many years was distant from her, operating by some logic of constraint we know not of: and the Bonners inaccessible: lost in tenebrous confusion, of the kind that attends spirits crossing over in the midst of extreme emotional agitation, or physical distress. And when Spirit World did manifest itself, after Deirdre's twelfth year, it was with such a cacophonous air, and so diffused into raps, knocks, creaks, frissons of every conceivable kind, and frequently vulgar pranks, that the wretched child could hardly have been expected to discern, in such chaos, any personal or human direction; nor did she, being quite untrained at that time, in matters of a psychic nature, seek to exert any control upon this chaos.

Of the numerous chilling manifestations of ghost phenomena the Octagonal House suffered, over a period of many months, and of the household's varying responses to them (ranging from the frightened servants' immediate recognition of *spirits,* to John Quincy Zinn's firm denunciation of all things *supernatural*), I am reluctant to speak in any detail, for fear of drawing upon sensationalist, if not frankly crude, or even obscene, material. The reader will recall Deirdre's capricious musical ability at the piano, which so frequently erupted into sheer ringing noise, said ability at first intriguing, and then evidently disgusting, Great-Aunt Edwina (who closed a door emphatically upon a rendition of Schubert's lovely "Adieu . . ."); but it has not been revealed, that, in Great-Aunt Edwina's presence, the child was invariably o'ercome with an attack of shivering, and a veritable barrage of spirit-voices, including those of her deceased parents, who insisted upon the fact that Edwina Kiddemaster *loathed her,* and *rejected her as a bastard child,* and secreted away in her heart the baffling wish that *she should die!* (Naturally Deirdre could not determine whether these voices were in fact spirit-voices, or whether she simply imagined them; or whether, in some inexplicable way, she was able, at times, to read her great-aunt's thoughts. That she was incapable of determining the actual sense of the whisperings—why, for instance, she should be considered a *bastard,* and why Miss Kiddemaster should wish her *dead*—goes without saying, nor did the o'erwrought child make much effort to interpret such things, abandoning all sense and all logic, and even her peace of mind: wishing merely to be safely out of Edwina's presence, in her bed, perhaps, beneath her warm quilts, where she might sob herself to sleep, or pretend to sleep, in order to elude Samantha's shy ministrations of concern. "Momma," she might whisper to herself, or "Poppa," or even "Heavenly Father," or "Dear Jesus," she might utter beneath her breath, "help me please, oh please, do not let me go mad!")

Her relations with other members of the family, while less dismaying, were equally bewildering, and oft caused the beleaguered girl to question whether what *appeared to be,* in fact *was;* or whether, in all helplessness, she dreamt everything. Perspicacious enough, in the first month of her residence with the Zinns, to recognize that she must express the gratitude she felt, to her new family (for had they not saved her from an orphanage?—from certain misery in some *charitable institution,* in Philadelphia?), Deirdre nonetheless observed that her words, sincerely uttered, were not heard!—as if, by some inexplicable freak, all the Zinns were deaf to her alone.

She quietly thanked Mrs. Zinn for some small, special favor (an extra dollop of cream on her porridge, a cashmere shawl draped about her thin shoulders, an impulsive hug when no one else was near), yet received no response, *as if she had not spoken at all:* and saw only a hurt, perplexed smile on the elder woman's face, and a further crinkling of her brow. She murmured a few words to Mr. Zinn, who occasionally tucked her into bed, along with Samantha, leading the girls in their night prayers, and jesting fondly with them, before he extinguished the lamp: yet *he* seemed not to hear: tho' he heard Samantha perfectly well! "Mr. Zinn," she said (for it was to be many months, before she could call him "Father," and she never called him "Poppa"), "Mr. Zinn, thank you so much you are a good man thank you oh thank you"—but the heartfelt words were not received; and it was quite as if she had never spoken.

"I love you," she tried to say. "I am so grateful. I am so happy here. Please do not send me away, oh please, please!"

But she might as well have remained silent, for all the effect her words had; she might as well have been mute.

As time passed, fortunately, her communications with the Zinns were somewhat more successful: they at least *heard* that she spoke, tho' her meaning was frequently distorted.

One balmy midsummer afternoon Constance Philippa asked her, of a sudden, wouldn't she like to romp down to the river?—toss down her cap, and take off her shoes and stockings, and run barefoot across the grass? (Mrs. Zinn being away on an errand with the maid Vanda, and the younger servants entrusted not to tell tales.) "We could wade in the shallow water—scare up the ducks, and cause them to fly away—what a wonderful squawking and quacking that will be!—and it will be so cool down there—and *no one* need know—" the tomboyish girl said, with an inviting grin, already untying her beribboned muslin cap: but Deirdre must have communicated both surprise and disapproval (which, indeed, she did *not* feel—her heart swelled with gratitude for the suggestion), for Constance Philippa colored at once, as if hurt, and angered: and turned aside with a muttered comment about "fancy little misses with their precious skirts, and patent leather shoes, and delicate ladylike airs!"

And so the opportunity to be friends with Constance Philippa was lost, never to be proffered again.

And there was many an exchange with Octavia, who pressed little treats upon her, in secret—candies, sweet cherries, toast generously spread with marmalade; and who liked nothing better than to give her instructions in sewing, or needlepoint, or crocheting, or cross-stitching; or to fuss with her hair, or her clothing; or to read to her from the Bible, or *The Child's Home Companion,* or *The Child's Jesus:* dear sweet indefatigable Octavia, who also appeared to be hurt by Deirdre's murmured responses, as if mistaking timid gratitude for sullen indifference. Deirdre mumbled "Thank you," her eyes downcast in shyness; and her sister flinched as if she had mumbled, "Leave me be! I hate you."

How *very* strange it was, and exhausting, to be forever misunderstood . . . !

(Octavia, at least, did not turn from her in anger and revulsion: it seemed rather that the good-hearted young lady grimly redoubled her efforts with her new sister, even as she met with evident failure at every turn.)

Since Deirdre was particularly susceptible to uncontrolled outbursts of tears in her bedchamber, when out of the presence of the larger family, Samantha was forever drawing away from her, in helpless perplexity, or in weariness. "Oh dear, *why* are you crying now?" she might ask. "Have I said something bad? Did I upset you? Dear Deirdre, please do leave off crying—you will give yourself a headache—you will give *me* a headache!" But the mood was upon her, the great dark cloud of despair was upon her, and she could almost hear the spirit-voices calling to her at such times—calling, teasing, tormenting, cajoling: *Deirdre, Deirdre, come to us, you are ours.* To her credit, Samantha tried to approach her afresh every morn, as if nothing were gravely amiss, and the agonized tears of the previous night were already forgotten. She did her hair for her, with a touching awkwardness; she helped her dress; helped her with the lacing on her shoes. If Deirdre sniffled, she did not sigh with exasperation (as perhaps she might have liked—she was a very young girl herself at this time), but gamely offered her a handkerchief.

As the days and weeks and months passed, shading into years, Deirdre instructed herself in the wisdom—nay, the pleasure—of befriending Samantha: of becoming a true sister to her as, perhaps, she could not, in regard to Constance Philippa, Octavia, and Malvinia. She recognized the slender child's estimable qualities; rejoiced in her intelligence, and even her precocity; was certainly grateful for her help with schoolwork (Deirdre found mathematics an especial challenge, and even spelling, which she had loved in the old days, was sometimes a problem: for the letters of old, familiar words perversely scrambled themselves in her head); she even believed, contrary to general family opinion, that Samantha's narrow green eyes, and pale freckled skin, and snubbed nose, were attractive features—prophetic, perhaps, of mature beauty.

And yet, despite these admirable convictions, she could not force herself to *like* Samantha.

Your heart, dear Deirdre, a spirit one day whispered in her year, *your heart!—how bitter it is, and how wise!*

A painful episode occurred in her thirteenth year, which she was to remember all her life; and to recall, most poignantly, many years later, whilst watching her elder sister in the role of Lady Anne, in *Richard III*.

For she hated Malvinia—beautiful Malvinia.

She hated Malvinia, and adored her; and oft wished her dead; yet wished—ah, how desperately!—to *be* her. To swallow her up, to sink inside her, to stare at the world through those amused blue eyes!

"Dear Malvinia," she whispered against her pillow, "how can you be so cruel? So lovely, and so cruel!"

At the very start of their acquaintanceship Malvinia had tried to befriend her, less persistently, perhaps, than Octavia; but with far more energy and charm. Hugging her, kissing her, fussing with her hair, pressing little gifts upon her—a sandalwood fan that was *almost* new, a cachet of rosemary she had sewn herself. For it had seemed to Malvinia something of a lark, to have a new sister, so suddenly.

And then, met with Deirdre's silence, and the reproach of her pale clammy skin, and tearful eyes, she had naturally lost interest. "What a drear little wretch it is!" she whispered to the others, scarce caring if Deirdre o'erheard.

So the months passed, and the years, and one afternoon something remarkable happened: the sisters were seated about a round oakwood table in an airy downstairs room of Kiddemaster Hall, receiving instructions from Grandmother Kiddemaster in the painstaking art of china-painting, and Malvinia suddenly wanted one of Deirdre's finest camel's-hair brushes, because her own was ruined—and Deirdre bent more resolutely over the tiny Limoges cup she was decorating, as if not hearing Malvinia, and Malvinia uttered her request again, in a pettish, unreasonable voice, and Deirdre still pretended not to hear, and Grandmother Kiddemaster told Malvinia to hush, and Octavia offered Malvinia *her* brush, but Malvinia knocked it away, and reached across the table for Deirdre's, and, when Deirdre drew back, startl'd, said loudly: "*You!* What do *you* own! It isn't your brush and it isn't your china cup and it isn't your place, here with us!"—and Deirdre rose from the table and hurried away, and ran to hide in the rear of the house, in the servants' quarters, behind a staircase: and Malvinia hurried after her, unerringly seeking her out, with a breathless laugh, and a half-angry sob, and, pulling her roughly around, and embracing her, burrowed her face against Deirdre's neck, and kissed her wildly, and murmured: "Oh, Deirdre, do forgive me! I don't know what devils force their way into me, and gallop along my veins—I don't know *why* I say the things I say—to you and to the others—but particularly to you! Allow me to make amends, oh, do allow me, Deirdre, don't turn away from me—we might share the same bedchamber—Octavia can move out—Octavia can share Samantha's room—we might share the same bedchamber, and become loving sisters—it isn't too late—you are growing up now—and I would try to be good—for I *am* good, truly, in my heart—oh Deirdre, poor wronged sister, *do* forgive me—"

It was the moment long awaited, the moment Deirdre had not dared to dream of: beauteous Malvinia with her burnished dark hair, and her pearline skin, and the fragrance of her slender young body: Malvinia who was everyone's delight, even with the very Devil sparkling in her eyes: now pleading with her despised sister, not only for *forgiveness,* but for *love.* Deirdre feebly returned her caresses, and made an effort to press her cool, moist cheek alongside Malvinia's warm—nay, burning—cheek, and would have blurted out in gasps and sobs her forgiveness, and her love, and, indeed, her worship—had not, at that tremulous instant, a spirit intervened: pinching poor Malvinia sharply on the vulnerable flesh of her upper arm, just beneath her puffed starched sleeve, and crying, in a falsetto voice that was a malicious parody of Deirdre's own: "What! I! Share the same bedchamber with *you!* Never! Not a bit of it! Nay, not a whit of it! *I! You! Never!*"

39

That prankish voice doubtless belonged to *Zachariah,* one of the less civil contact spirits who besieged young Deirdre, when she was in a weakened or fluctuating state of mind: tho' at that time, at the age of thirteen, she did not grasp the astonishing nature of the assailant, let alone his specific identity. She knew—yet could hardly plead!—that the pinch, and the vicious words, were *not her own.*

Zachariah, whom Deirdre came to fear. And *Mrs. Dodd,* whom she most trusted. And *Father Darien,* with his stern yet kindly voice. And little *Bianca,* a child of four, who had died of meningitis in 1867. And, upon occasion, *Mrs. Bonner* herself.

And *Captain Burlingame*—the *Raging Captain,* as poor Deirdre called him—who appeared to her always in nighttime dreams, shouting and admonishing and threatening: with a compelling authenticity the other spirits, oft no more than mere wraiths, could not possess.

Less differentiated, however, and far less human, was a veritable galaxy of noisy spirits, a Babel of protesting, demanding, wheedling, cajoling, furious voices, such as commonly undermine the well-being of the untrained medium, and cast into confusion any household unfortunate enough to contain her. (It was spirits of this ilk, one must assume, that so upset the family of D. D. Home, and played the more diabolical of the tricks ascribed to the Fox sisters; indeed, this species of spirit no doubt interrupted Deirdre's piano playing, jealous of the genuine musical ability of another spirit. Raps and crashes and extinguished lights—all manner of noisome "hauntings"—are characteristic of the lower levels of Spirit World, as I am given to understand.)

Deirdre, however, knew nothing of this—she knew nothing at all.

322 A BLOODSMOOR ROMANCE

So innocent was she that she thought, at first, with a small amazed smile: *Ah! I shall be less lonely.*

Much later she was to think, pressing the palms of her chill hands cruelly hard against her eyes: *Shall I never be free . . . ?*

But such wisdom, alas, lay far in the future: and we have to do, at the present time, albeit in a summary manner, with the Deirdre of fourteen, and fifteen, and sixteen years of age: the embittered and lonely *orphan* who would, out of her heart's pride, and her great yearning anguish, never consent to see herself, in secret, as a *sister*.

Despite her natural fear of such malignant, mischievous spirits as *Zachariah,* and the nameless imps and naughty cherubs who attended him, Deirdre responded with some affection, and not a little gratitude, to the solicitude of *Mrs. Dodd,* a gentlewoman of indeterminate age—now extremely elderly, now of hearty middle age, a contemporary of Washington's, and, indeed, a frequenter of the fashionable *salon* held by Elizabeth Schuyler Hamilton in the days of Hamilton's power and glory; and then again, with what logic Deirdre could not comprehend, and hardly dared to challenge, a contemporary—and a *young* one—of Ulysses S. Grant, the "most unfairly maligned of Presidents," in her opinion.

Mrs. Dodd was in any case a presence admirably maternal, not unlike, in fact, Mrs. Zinn, yet freed of that good woman's ceaseless—and painfully obvious—campaign to love her adopted daughter *as if she were her own.* (A forced issue young Deirdre, with her sometimes cruel perspicacity, comprehended from the very first.) Deirdre did not mind *Mrs. Dodd*'s frequent admonishments, and greatly enjoyed her "o'erruling" of Mrs. Zinn's remarks, tho' she would have preferred her own mother, after all, but *Mrs. Bonner* returned from Spirit World mysteriously altered as to her robustness, and her ability to negotiate consecutive thought; and was rarely accessible to Deirdre when she most wanted her. (How very odd it was, Deirdre tormented herself in thinking, that *Mr. Bonner* did not appear to her, neither as an ectoplasmic shape, nor as a voice. Indeed, this good-hearted man was never to appear throughout the years of Deirdre's active mediumship—having simply been swallowed up, one must sadly conclude, by the farthest reaches of the Void.)

Father Darien was the spirit of a martyred Jesuit, hideously tortured by Iroquois Indians in the Seneca Lake region of upstate New York, a very long time ago, in the 1600's; his nationality being French, he naturally spoke English with a marked accent which Deirdre found, at times, difficult to interpret.

And there was little *Bianca*—headstrong and mischievous at times, yet of a sweet and yielding and, indeed, *sisterly* nature at other times, in response to Deirdre's unarticulated need. She could not delude herself, as other girls did, that hugging a mere *doll,* a silly inert wooden *doll,* was any true comfort when one was in tears, or felt that the world was truly a wretched place: and so little *Bianca,* tho' a ghost child, and the least substantial of all the wraiths, oft wriggled into Deirdre's embrace, and loved nothing better than to burrow there, and cuddle, and fall asleep to a humm'd lullaby of Deirdre's: *Sleep, Baby, sleep . . . thy Father watches the sheep. . . .*

Unfortunately, in Deirdre's own sleep, the strident *Captain Burlingame* sometimes appeared, causing the poor child to awaken in sheer terror, her heart knocking in her breast, and her unseeing eyes opened so wide, Samantha, despite her sound good sense, was led to believe that something *did* crouch in one of the shadowy corners of the bedchamber: and the two girls were almost equally affrighted.

"What does he want of me!" Deirdre wept, striking her small fists against the cotton comforter. "Oh, why does he plague me!"

And the trembling Samantha could only reiterate, in a voice that hardly convinced, for all its equanimity: "There is no *he,* Deirdre, but only a dream-fragment—*only* a vapor of mere thought—mere fancy—in your imagination, don't you see? Come, come now, do stop crying, you know full well that *no one*—and *nothing*—can hurt you, in Father's house."

But there were other dreams. Equally fanciful, perhaps: yet very close to Deirdre's heart. Dreams that were not nighttime vapors, but dominated her thoughts even at midday, when, seated at the dining room table with the Zinns (for, alas, the ungrateful child coldly thought of them thus, chiding herself, over the years, if she lapsed into other, warmer usage), she was obliged to partake of their common, lively conversation; or when, in that cozy hour following the evening meal, and the family gathered in the parlor, she was obliged to take up her sewing in their presence, or sing to Mrs. Zinn's or Malvinia's cheery playing, or, with lamentable clumsiness, participate in a silly parlor game.

At such times Deirdre affixed her eyes to Mr. Zinn's face, as he sat, on most evenings, in repose in his chair, reading, or scribbling notes to himself, or staring into the fire (for Mrs. Zinn so sternly insisted, that he remain with his family in the evening, and *not* repair to his workshop after dinner, as he sorely wished to do, that the good man acquiesced, and came to believe that his "parlor hours" were not only *sacrosanct* in terms of his paternal love, but positively *helpful* in terms of his preparation for the next morning's work). At such times the silent, brooding, pallid Deirdre stared as if mesmerized at her adoptive father's face, and would hardly have noticed, or been alarmed, if the rest of the parlor and its inhabitants had faded into mere vapor, and off the earth entirely. Mrs. Zinn's and Octavia's occasional reading of the Bible—the Psalms, and the stirring Gospels, and the three Epistles of John above all—had the power to engage her interest, but only sporadically; and the rest of the time her mind simply drifted, whilst her gray eyes remained fixed to Mr. Zinn's face, in an attitude of pettish reproach.

O Father I dreamt that my sisters stood over my bed as I slept and tho' I was asleep I saw them clearly and heard their cruel whisperings and gigglings oh and Father Malvinia drew out of her bodice a tiny silver scissors like the scissors in Mother's sewing basket but much, much brighter and sharper—O Father please hear me out oh please do not turn away do not merely smile do not lean to kiss my forehead as you kiss the others—I am not one of them—I am not one of you—O Father please hear me out—please hear how Malvinia your favorite leaned over my bed and snipped at my breast and I cried for her to stop and she paid no heed I was awake yet unable to move even my smallest fingers and toes even my eyelids Father Dearest do not deny me I begged for her to stop but she pierced my flesh she lifted the skin away she touched my heart O O O O Father—

40

On that fateful day in September, of Deirdre's seventeenth year, the sisters betook themselves to the gazebo above the river, in order to await Mrs. Zinn's somewhat delayed departure for home: the numerous guests having at last driven off, with many a vociferous and prolonged farewell, and reiterated expostulations of gratitude, for the extreme hospitality and courtesy of Judge and Mrs. Kiddemaster. The future—ah, how happily!—being *opaque,* to the normal of vision, no one could have foreseen the double—nay, triple—sorrow that would, most ironically, become attached, in the hearts and minds of the Zinns and Kiddemasters, to this particular autumn day. The abduction and disappearance of young Deirdre; the bitter aftermath of Constance Philippa's engagement to the Baron Adolf von Mainz; and, thirdly, a minor issue at best, yet no less abrasive to the honest pride of the Zinns and Kiddemasters, the inexplicable disinclination of the esteemed gentlemen of the American Philosophical Society, to affirm John Quincy Zinn's nomination to membership—and after "the tiresome old fools had ate and guzzled so much!"—in the words of the elderly Judge.

Such disappointments, however, lay in the future: and at the present time, the young ladies, having retired to the charming gazebo, took up with varying industry their sewing, and sighed with an admixture of pleasure, relief, and simple bodily weariness; for the lawn party *had* been a magnificent event, and it *had* been somewhat fatiguing, for young ladies of delicate constitution.

Deirdre, whose head fairly rang with voices, and whose heart was beating most dangerously, found that she had taken up—without knowing it—the crocheting she had elected to do, to replace a scandalously soiled antimacassar on the parlor settee. ("Scandalously soiled," in Malvinia's irrepressible judgment: that sprightly young lady having declared it thus, after a Sabbath in which both Baron von Mainz and Mr. Lucius Rumford had come calling upon their respective sweethearts. Both sisters blushed crimson, upon hearing their suitors mocked by Malvinia, and tho' Mrs. Zinn insisted angrily that Malvinia proffer her apologies, at once, it *did* seem to be the case that the lace antimacassar was irrevocably soiled—with hair pomade of a greasy texture, and a saturnine complexion: and Deirdre, as much to subvert a quarrel, as to be of genuine aid, volunteered to crochet another at once.)

There had been, initially, much resistance in Deirdre's heart—as, it may be, there was in all our female hearts, at one time—to the creation of such commonplace household appurtenances; but as the years solemnly passed, the willful girl had come round to seeing that it might be salubrious indeed, for her to absorb herself in such mechanical manual activity, as a means of guiding, or even suppressing, unfruitful and wayward nervous energies. So too did the other Zinn girls occupy themselves: Constance Philippa laboring over a pink smock for an infant cousin; Octavia working at a patchwork panda; Malvinia addressing herself, tho' without an excessive quantity of concentration, to a needlepoint pillowcase exemplifying the Bloodsmoor River Valley, superimposed upon which was to be, in golden thread, an American bald eagle with spears in his talons; and Samantha decorating a white linen towel with orange cross-stitching, for her sister's wedding.

Deirdre was, as I have said, unusually agitated, as a consequence of the long afternoon (during which she was made to feel, or insisted upon feeling, an ugly duckling in the midst of her relatives' conspicuous splendor; and very much the *adopted orphan,* in the imagin'd thoughts of the guests), and as a consequence of small slights suffered by her, emanating from Malvinia primarily, but also from Samantha (who, since the tumult of the previous night, during which Deirdre had spoken perhaps too despairingly, and too frankly, of her *Raging Captain* nightmare, had shown a distinctly cool demeanor to Deirdre—as if altogether fatigued of her, and contemptuous as well). She had had, moreover, several cups of very black India tea, and no food at all save a single cucumber sandwich, and a mere taste of a quince-custard tart, and hardly more than a thimbleful of scalloped oyster: and was feeling dangerously *not herself.*

(*Dangerously:* for, as I have explained, it was at such times that the very worst of the spirits sought to thrust themselves forward, through the slender fabric that divides their world from ours, and protects us from them.)

Her fingers worked rapidly, albeit mechanically; her thoughts were loath to still themselves; she heard, beyond the complacent prattle of her sisters, the tinkling laughter of a wicked spirit, possibly that of *Zachariah* himself.

Malvinia chattered; and Constance Philippa drawled; and Octavia made her usual sort of observations—pious, cheerful, and uplifting; and Samantha, stirred to a modicum of guilt, interrupted the drift of the conversation to inquire of her bedmate, her opinion on something or other: but Deirdre scarcely deigned to reply.

The spirit-laughter deepened, and a companion-laughter sounded out of the sere grasses that grew so handsomely about the gazebo: a queer trilling noise, which raised the hairs on Deirdre's delicate neck, and made her miss a stitch, out of very horror that her sisters would hear.

Blushing, she stared at the work in her lap; for she knew—ah, how painfully she knew!—that her rude sisters were exchanging a *meaningful* glance amongst themselves.

Thinking themselves protected, the little fools, by the gazebo that was like a small boy's notion of a fortress: complete with lightning rod on the roof!

Thinking themselves immune to the spirits—who threatened to crowd near.

Deirdre's crochet hooks darted and flashed. She knew that something would happen soon, perhaps within the hour; surely before the sun dipped beyond the western hills.

The unnamed spirits giggled, close beside her.

Bianca tugged at the crochet hook in Deirdre's cold fingers.

But Deirdre held fast: for the hook was sharp, and would make a cruel weapon.

The sweet low brow and arched lips of the Grecian profile, the classic timeless beauty: ah, Malvinia! And yet a single thrust of this crochet hook, would destroy the melting limpid blue of that lovely eye forever!

Bianca tugged, Deirdre held fast. *Zachariah* drew near.

Constance Philippa began to chatter nervously about Miss Delphine Martineau, whom the spirits, so a sly voice whispered in Deirdre's ear, had marked for much grief. Delphine was this, Delphine was that, dark and melting brown eyes, hair in irregular ringlets, corkscrew curls, too many Valentines for the boastful young lady to sort, but how passionately Constance Philippa wished to sail away with her!—in an enormous silk balloon, for instance.

You shall all sail away into the sky, Father Darien promised, with an uncharacteristic melancholy, *in time. Ah, my dear children: in time.*

Seize her scissors from out her hand, a voice counseled. Nudging Deirdre to look toward Malvinia. (And, indeed, the very bright silvery scissors flashed. So brightly, it was no wonder Malvinia's veil was drawn past her nose; past her beautiful mouth; discreetly covering her chin.)

No, Deirdre said to herself, *I shall not.*

Mrs. Bonner spoke softly, had perhaps been speaking all along, beneath the other spirits' babble. It was her mission to explain that Deirdre should cease her mourning . . . *for the soul is immortal . . . in God, Who is immortal . . . and thither the soul flies, upon the dissolution of its earthly carapace . . . from eternity to eternity. God is without beginning as He is without end. Grieve no more. Mourn no further. Possess your soul in patience, and in loving kindly deeds. All is finished! All is over. This life is but a dream. There is no death. All that has lived, lives. Do not devour your own bitter heart. The Guardian Spirits hover near at all times. The Angel of Death is not far distant. In a great dark cloud he will come to you, to rescue you, when your earthly suffering becomes too extreme. Trust in me. Trust in God. Do not surrender to the wicked spirits. Love thy enemies, Deirdre, love thy sisters, for they are your trial, as you are theirs. God bless you!*

The sisters, hardly guessing at Deirdre's somnambulistic terror, continued to talk of their insipid cousins and friends: Delphine, Felicity, Odille, Rowena.

If not the crochet hook, then the little scissors, by all means, a spirit-voice murmured shrewdly in Deirdre's ear. So close was he, the fine hairs on her neck quivered with his breath. Malvinia's bright bold gaze, her saucy smile. Finished forever. And no suitor to moon over her beauty: imagine, Miss Malvinia Zinn with a glass eye!

In the shape of an abnormally fat bumblebee the malicious *Zachariah* drifted about them, ready to alight on Constance Philippa's bonnet, to sting her on the scalp; the poison flowing at once to the brain. *She does not want to marry her fiancé, Zachariah* informed Deirdre calmly, *or any man. Shall I put her out of her misery? Extinguish her on the spot?*

Neither the crochet hook, nor the scissors, Mrs. Bonner begged.

Deirdre regarded her sisters through her dense dark lashes. They knew of her rage; yet did not know. Surely they felt the very air tremble with her desire to wound: yet they continued to prattle as if nothing were amiss.

One, two, three swift jabs with the scissors.

And then—flight.

The wishing well, into which one might fall, to sink, to drown, in utter blissful oblivion. *Zachariah*'s arms held wide, *Bianca* whining, whimpering. *I am so lonely, Deirdre, please, Deirdre, please come.*

The bumblebee disappeared. But a spirit hand materialized near the ceiling of the gazebo, a few feet above Samantha's pert little head. And what did the fingers hold? A spike of some kind? A large sturdy nail?

Samantha had tried to calm her, in their bed. "Deirdre please, please Deirdre, 'tis only a dream-vapor, 'tis only a fancy in your head." And then she had shrunk away from Deirdre, repulsed.

The pitiful pitiful orphan.

The wishing well, and a painless death. Or the river. Ah, yes, the river! Swimming out, kicking and thrashing, until your skirts and petticoats pull you down. Sweet dark lightless oblivion. Where even the spirits will allow you to sleep in peace.

And yet: to leave Great-Aunt Edwina Kiddemaster untouch'd!

To leave Kiddemaster Hall unscath'd!

You dwell among murderesses and beasts, sly *Zachariah* said, *how much better for you, to come dwell amongst us! For we cannot sin in the flesh: we are innocent now of flesh.*

The spirit laughter was such—low and throaty and ribald—that all the sisters glanced up uneasily. Malvinia had lain her needlepoint aside.

Samantha wondered aloud: "Where is Mother? Why is she extending her visit so unconscionably?"

Mrs. Bonner's faint voice grew stronger. Deirdre, now very frightened, unsnapped the clasp of her locket: and at once the spirit-voice of her belovèd mother, or the woman who had masqueraded as her mother, counseled her.

Do not listen to the wicked spirits. Do no harm to your sisters, as you would wish no harm done to yourself. Love God, and abide in God. Put down your instrument of temptation. You will not injure Malvinia, whom you adore. You will not drown yourself in the well—nor will you wade and swim out into the river, to a clownish muddy death. Rouse yourself from your dream; get to your feet; clear your head of evil thoughts.

Deirdre stared inside her gold locket at the daguerreotypes of her mother and father. Did she know them? Were they her parents? She was seized with a sudden conviction that they were *not* her parents. After all, they had died. They had been weak, and died. But John Quincy Zinn was strong. Even the *Raging Captain* was strong.

You will not drown, Mrs. Bonner said sternly. *You will not die.*

Suicide is a sin, Father Darien said.

A sin, Mrs. Bonner agreed.

Deirdre continued to stare at the faded old pictures. A woman, a man. What had they to do with her? They had betrayed her by dying. *A great dark cloud. A flaming cloud.* O'ertaking the Bonners' modest house in the village, and causing it to explode into flames.

A sin, a sin, Mrs. Bonner insisted. *Suicide is a sin.*

But murder a delight! prankish *Zachariah* said in a squeaky falsetto voice, as if in mocking imitation of poor *Mrs. Bonner*.

Something shall occur within the hour, Deirdre thought clearly. All her pulses rang: an artery deep in her throat throbbed with passion. To hurt, to wound, to jab, to defile. One, two, three savage thrusts with the little crochet hook.

An axe, Zachariah counseled, now in his own voice. He caressed

Deirdre's shoulders, blew the ribbons trailing from her hat, so that they fluttered gaily as if in an innocent breeze. *An axe.*

I have no axe, Deirdre protested.

An axe. Even a delicate young lady can wield an axe.

But I have none. I know of none.

Behind Kiddemaster Hall, where the land slopes roughly away, hidden by that stand of handsome blue spruce, are outbuildings you have never seen: former slaves' quarters, the washhouse, the bakehouse, the meathouse, the kennels, the henhouses, the stables, the gardeners' several sheds—have you never guessed?—and in those sheds, if you make your way quietly, you will find—

"I cannot," Deirdre whispered inwardly. "I will not."

In the washhouse, for instance, a keen-eyed young miss will find sugar of lead, spirits of salt, ammonia, and ivory-black—all for cleaning, and all poisonous, and so wonderfully close at hand! Zachariah gloated.

"I cannot," Deirdre pleaded.

Many a sister, or a hateful husband, or father, or, for that matter, a hateful mother, has died in agony, as a consequence of my delicious ivory-black! Zachariah insisted.

Impudently, his spirit-hand snapped Deirdre's locket shut.

Deirdre tried to open it, but he held it fast.

Ivory-black, Zachariah whispered. *If the axe is too heavy for a young lady with genteel aspirations. If the crochet hook and the scissors are too fearsome.*

"I cannot," Deirdre said, the pulse deep within her throat throbbing hard, "for—you see—I do not hate them sufficiently—I do not altogether wish them *dead*—"

She looked up, blinking tears from her eyes, and so dazed was she, and so repulsed by the odium of the spirit's counsel, as well as his loathsome masculine propinquity, that for a very long time she could not concentrate upon her sister's words. Did they speak of Mr. Zinn?—one of his new machines?—"Its purpose," Samantha was saying with pert dignity, "is to run forever."

This innocent remark struck Deirdre so powerfully, as if a blade had entered her heart, that, without knowing what she did, very much like a somnambulist, she rose to her feet—rose to her feet, quite shocking her sisters—and let her crocheting fall—and hurried away—out of the gazebo—across the sloping lawn—half running, despite her long skirts and heavy train—stumbling—gasping and panting and sobbing for breath—leaving her sisters speechless behind her.

Yes, said *Mrs. Dodd,* her voice as strong as Deirdre had ever heard it, *yes, come hither, take yourself out of this vale of temptation, come safely to us, come home, sweet Deirdre, do!*

41

Despite how very many millennia spirits have roamed the earth, it is a curious point of information that they began to *communicate,* and to wish most strenuously to do so, only in the middle of our redoubtable nineteenth century: and that their point of entry, as it were, into the Earth Plane, was the aptly named town of Arcadia, New York, the dwelling place of the Fox family, in the year 1848.

Just as the unhappy Zinn family had, for a time, suffered the distractions of inexplicable raps, knocks, creakings, and baffling "presences" in their household, so too did the Fox family report disturbances that gradually grew in intensity, until, one memorable evening (it was in fact March 31, 1848), a gentleman bethought himself to inquire of the "presence" his identity, and what he sought in the Fox home: with the astounding results that, communicating solely by raps, in a laborious session that lasted much of the night, the spirit told a tale of having been a pedlar, murdered for money, and buried in the cellar of that very house!

(The reader will forgive me my small frisson of excitement, when I report that energetic digging in the cellar *did* produce a skeleton, greatly fragmented, but believed to have been human: this no doubt being the remains of the murdered pedlar.)

So Spirit World emerged into the Earthly World, with profound consequences, as we shall see.

Tho' in later years the Fox sisters, by then widely renowned, were to be denounced by a spiteful relative as frauds, and their mediums' powers explained away as simple parlor magic, it was nonetheless the case that, their fame spreading beyond Arcadia, and soon through all of bucolic upstate New York, they were joined, as it were, by other mediums of divers talents and skills. At first but one, in Ebenezer; and then another, in Brockport; and then, lo and behold!—some five or six, in the village of Pendleton alone—and several more, in Ithaca—and, in Syracuse, a most extraordinary Shetland pony, said to be possessed of "second sight"! In Buffalo, the Brothers Davenport soon proved more prodigious in their gifts, and even more adept at the manipulation of gullible journalists, than the Fox sisters. And, in the idyllic rolling hills of Morah, south of the Great Canal, there came to prominence not one, but two, mediumistic canines: the comely tho' shy Lupa, and her more brash, and unfailingly crowd-pleasing son, Remus: these being Labrador retrievers, of some uncertain heritage, who earned for their perspicacious master a gratifying financial reward. (Nor should I neglect to mention, by-the-by, that Joseph Smith, the esteemed founder of the Mormon Church, had dwelt in the sleepy village of Palmyra, also in upstate New York: Mr. Smith's visions and voices being a matter of historical record in some quarters, and surely not to be waved aside, or dismissed, as the babblings of a deranged mind.)

Thus, during the amazing Fifties, the denizens of Spirit World not only greatly increased their numbers, communicating through mediums of all ages, sexes, social distinctions, and species, but increased, as well, their variety of manifestations: for, very soon, mere raps, knocks, and scratchings, were supplanted by faint but unmistakable *voices,* and the vigorous *playing of musical instruments,* and *scribblings* on spirit blackboards; and, upon occasion, in the required twilit conditions—even veiled *ectoplasmic figures!* (Unbeknownst to Deirdre, who knew very little of the larger phenomenon, of which she was so hapless a part, her contact spirit *Zachariah* manifested himself to countless mediums in New York State, and to the formidable Jonathan Koons, in Ohio: this spirit complaining of his ill-treatment, in life, as a consequence of unspeakable sanitary conditions in a field hospital, in northern New Jersey, where he died a prolonged gangrenous death, as a common soldier in General Washington's Army. Whilst this unfortunate fate serves to explain much of *Zachariah's* ill-humor, it cannot hope to explain his intrinsic wickedness—the which, I am sorry to say, he most skillfully hid from most of his mediums.)

Very soon, within a brief span of months, this amazing phenomenon became known as *Spiritualism,* in the public press: and so great was popular interest in it, and so ingenious, as well, the mediums and their consorts, that, by the late Sixties, a considerable amount of money had changed hands; and the gifted Daniel Dunglas Home had swept across the face of skeptical Europe, conquering all, and reaping a most astounding harvest, with his unusual powers—the which involved not only the entire familiar battery of Spiritualist manifestations, but such fanciful variations as the elevating of heavy tables upon which observers and investigators sat. It was a matter of private knowledge to some persons, but by no means a secret, that our great President, Abraham Lincoln himself, received much valuable advice from spirits conjured up by Nellie Colburn, the famous trance medium: Daniel Webster, Cardinal Wolsey, Julius Caesar, and many others routinely gave him counsel, and it was through Miss Colburn's efforts that the Emancipation Proclamation was made in late 1863, and not delayed, as Lincoln's aides strongly advised. (Some say that the War Between the States itself was a consequence of the spirits' fervent wishes, pressed upon an initially resistant Lincoln: but as to the truth of this assertion, it is impossible for me to say.)

By the late Seventies, when Madame Blavatsky emerged to prominence in occult circles, the phenomenon of mediumship, tho' by no means a commonplace, and angrily attacked from the pulpit, had established itself with admirable alacrity as a respectable source of wisdom; its powers to entertain, and to console the bereft, being implicitly understood. The reader will not be surprised, I hope, to learn that many a Rationalist fell under the sway of the Spiritualists, and so eminent a gentleman as Nathaniel Hawthorne, observing the extravagant manifestations of Mr. Home, in Florence, recorded that *the soberly attested incredibilities* were proven, to his skeptical satisfaction, *to be sober facts.* Statesmen and politicians consulted the spirits of Napoleon, Alexander the Great, and Genghis Khan; Conan Doyle became a proselytizer, with embarrassing enthusiasm; Alfred, Lord Tennyson, Poet Laureate of England, was discovered to have been reading Madame Blavatsky's mystical poem, "The Voice of the Silence," on his very deathbed. Such prominent scientists as Alfred Russel Wallace and William Crookes were active believers. The lecturer, pamphleteer, and militant Fabian Socialist Mrs. Annie Besant not only converted to Theosophy, but, with much determination, took over the Holy Cause in Madame Blavatsky's declining years. And Thomas Alva Edison, our American Wizard, was an enthusiastic member of the Theosophical Society . . . to his shame be it known!

In so very peculiar and morbid an atmosphere, then, in which the solemn truths of Protestant Christianity were judged, perhaps, not sufficiently exotic, or not sufficiently entertaining, to hold the concentration of shallow personalities, it is not to be regarded as implausible, that a girl of less than twenty years of age, known to the public only as "Deirdre of the Shadows," should emerge from absolute obscurity, and, within a few fevered years in the early Eighties, win the acclaim of so wide and divers a Spiritualist populace, that she was to be called—for a time, at least—the equal of D. D. Home himself, and a veritable *Princess of the Shadow World.*

("The more fantastical a belief," Madame Blavatsky was to confide in her Lolo, with her hoarse throaty chuckle, and many a squeeze of her nicotine-stained fingers, "the more *they* rush to believe! It is a law of nature, my dear child," Madame averred. "It is not to be *wondered at,* but only *applied.*")

Deirdre's recollection of the immense black silken balloon, and the sombre-garbed personage who manned it, was always to remain clouded, doubtless confused with the floating dreams and visions she so frequently experienced, as a young girl. One shard of memory would have had her believe that she had been borne away by her bridegroom, across the Atlantic Ocean, bade a loving farewell by her bridesmaid sisters, attired in pastel chiffon, and weeping to lose her; another, that the *Raging Captain* himself, his chest wound miraculously healed, and every tear, tatter, and stain in his handsome uniform vanish'd, had not only carried her from that place of temptation, but had spoken kindly to her, and placed a chaste kiss on her burning brow.

Precisely how she was carried, senseless, out of the Bloodsmoor Valley, to awaken upon the morn hundreds of miles away in the scenic wilds of northwestern Massachusetts, unhurt, but gravely fatigued, on a grassy knoll in a park belonging to the estate of the late millionaire F. Holtman Strong; precisely how the alleged *violet-radiance* of her *aura* brought her at once to the excited attention of the Countess Helena Petrovna Blavatsky (then in residence, with her *chela*-companion Hassan Agha, at the Strong manor house); and how, assured on all sides of her mediumistic gifts, and given a carefully orchestrated *début* in Cambridge, Massachusetts, to a small and élite circle of believers, Deirdre gradually grew—nay, blossomed—into so confident a trance medium, as to feel no apprehension of the formidable Society for Psychical Research itself!— how these extraordinary events came to pass, I have some slender knowledge, at secondhand; but fear to burden my chronicle with an excess of historical detail, lest it become o'erlong.

Withal, it happened that Madame Blavatsky's most trusted *chela,* the dusky-skinned young Hassan Agha (of Madras, India—or so it was claimed: detractors within the Society placed his origins firmly, in the West, in Sicily or Athens, or even Liverpool), meditating at dawn, in the park, chanced upon the unconscious young woman; and necessarily sounded the alarm, that help should be summoned; noting, even in the confusion of the moment—as Madame would soon confirm—that the strange black-haired girl, even in her stuporous state, possessed an aura of such magnificent luminosity, violet and iridescent blue, and all the lovelier hues of the rainbow, as to suggest her psychic powers—freely admitted by Madame to be in excess of her own.

So Deirdre was taken into the Strong home, hardly conscious of her surroundings, and put under the care of an eminent Boston physician whose Spiritualist sympathies were not in doubt; and enjoyed a peaceful convalescence of upward of four weeks, attended much of the time by Madame herself, who declared that a miracle "had fallen out of the sky," and that her own "Lolo" had been "restored" to her. And even before rising from her bed, and coming downstairs to meet with company, Deirdre was able, with very little conscious direction of her own, to cause to appear, in her bedchamber, the veiled ectoplasmic form of Mrs. Strong's late husband, and to be the means by which—through her *physical being,* but not by way of her *voice*—this worthy deceased gentlemen spoke to his wife, giving her all manner of advice, both financial and domestic, and consolation as to the reality of Spirit World, and his own continued well-being: with what tearful gratitude on the part of the widow, the reader can well envision. "We have been awaiting this miraculous child," Madame Blavatsky said, "not knowing that she would come to us out of nowhere: materialized like a very spirit!"

At this time, on the two-thousand-acre country estate of the Strongs, in the Landsdowne Valley, there dwelled, not only the charismatic Madame Blavatsky and several *chelas,* but a number of like-minded persons, who shared, not a common belief in Theosophy, or even in the existence of the Tibetan masters, but a general amorphous belief in occult matters, which they took to be the *Religion of the Future*—to fructify most dramatically in the Twentieth Century. (A divers group of individuals, to be sure, yet not deserving, in the aggregate, the condemnation of Mr. Strong's relatives, who spoke of the widow's assemblage as a "swarm" buzzing about a "honey hive"—the honey being, of course, Mr. Strong's considerable fortune.)

Mrs. Strong, having read that great tome *Isis Unveiled,* compiled by Madame Blavatsky in a veritable frenzy of inspiration some years previously, had, after the death of her spouse, sought out the celebrated Russian countess, lavishing many gifts upon her; and would not cease her overtures, that Madame and as many of her *chelas* as she wished, might come to Landsdowne House (for such her enormous manor was called) for a sojourn of as brief, or as extended, time as she might wish. Madame did reluctantly accept this generous invitation, after it was repeated several times, for, tho' she was inordinately busy with the Theosophical chapters in Boston and New York, and absorbed in plans for a long pilgrimage to India, there to commune with the celebrated Swami Dayanand Saraswati, she took pity upon the widow's anguish, which was considerable, and saw no reason not to alleviate her grief, so far as she was capable. It was, however, only with the arrival of Deirdre—soon baptized by Madame *"Deirdre of the Shadows"*—that Mrs. Strong entered into a fully satisfying communication with her deceased husband.

"A miracle," Madame exclaimed, a dozen times daily, "my *Lolo* restored. And in the pretty shape of an *American girl.*"

(It should be noted at this point that *Lolo* was not, in fact, the name of any child of Madame's—but the pet name of Madame herself, given to her as a baby by her mother, long dead!—one eccentricity among many, which constituted the perplexing phenomenon of *Blavatsky.*)

So "Deirdre of the Shadows" was introduced to the Spiritualist community, then very much more populous than now, tho' similarly tight-knit, and possessed of an eagerness to *believe,* which some observers find laudable, as others find contemptible. Financed by the generous Mrs. Strong, and fiercely protected by Madame Blavatsky, Deirdre acquitted herself admirably as a "trance medium"—a *métier* to be explained presently—and, to her grief be it uttered, cast never a backward glance at her Bloodsmoor years, and the charitable Christian family that had given her succor in her time of need. In Cambridge, and in Boston, and in Quincy, Massachusetts; and most conspicuously in New York City; in hotel rooms whose opulence must hardly have compensated strangeness, and abject loneliness; in private homes like that of Mrs. Strong's, "haunted," as it were, by a sickly and morbid obsession with the dead—how her young heart should have grieved for all it had rejected, and oh what lacrimination should have sprung forth, from that tight-skinned carapace of youthful, indeed *witchlike* beauty!—had the heedless child paused to contemplate her situation: both the loving family she had left behind, and the doubtful personages amongst whom she now dwelled.

Despite her arrival as a penniless immigrant in the summer of 1873, Madame Blavatsky had by this time done admirably well for herself: she was known as a Spiritualist who had devoted her life for the past fifteen years to "purifying" the "sacred calling" of mediumship—a calling, I am unhappy to say, rife with fraud, and constantly under attack by both Rationalists and Christians, who lived in terror of its "revolutionary truths." She befriended other mediums, gave séances of her own, cultivated such influential persons as the New York lawyer Thomas Olcott, whose position with the tolerant New York *Tribune* allowed him to write at length, and with unrestrained enthusiasm, for those mediums *innocent of all fraud* whom he encountered; and she had established her secret brotherhood, the Theosophical Society, by which the ancient wisdom of Tibetan Mahatmas was to be communicated to the world, through the person of Madame herself. Recognizing in Deirdre a kindred spirit, and not to be discouraged by a certain withholding of affection, on the part of the young girl, she was most boisterous in her praise of this new medium, and confident that she should "scale the walls" of the "fortress of ignorance and indifference" that characterized America: "A land of great material wealth, in which the most shocking *spiritual impoverishment* is to be found," Madame oft said, "—and in the homes of the wealthy more than elsewhere."

In attendance to Madame at this time were a number of *chelas,* or disciples, her favorite being the tall, cadaverous, dark-skinned Hassan Agha, with his exceedingly narrow, yet attractive face, and his date-soft black eyes, and his Indian costume, which clung tightly to his thin frame: a black silk tunic and pajamalike trousers, and a handsome black turban, in the center of which a large scarab brooch, of Egyptian origin, glittered with uncanny power. (The brooch was a "sacred totem," in Madame's words, a gift not from her but from one of the Masters, who had caused it to materialize in her hand, that she might proffer it to her most faithful *chela*. Madame oft insisted—and begged and cajoled—that Deirdre accept a similar scarab medallion from this Master, to be worn about her neck in place of "that tawdry gold locket," but Deirdre wisely resisted, for tho', in these years, she was to become lost to nearly all sense of decency, and respectable behavior, she did *not*, the reader will be relieved to hear, succumb to Madame's blandishments.)

Even in chilly weather Hassan Agha was barefoot indoors, as befitting an Indian *chela*. He was perhaps twenty-one years of age, and spoke rarely, as if distrusting his ability to employ our tongue. His thralldom to Madame was complete, and thought to be poignant: observers were invariably moved by the way the youth fell prostrate before Madame, upon both the occasion of approaching her, and taking her leave. "An adoring disciple," Madame confided in Deirdre, when Hassan Agha was absent, "and adorable: if one had not become too deathly bored with *boys*."

Madame assured Deirdre, after the early successes in Landsdowne, and Brattle Street, and Beacon Hill, that she would become not only a famous medium, but a great one; and that she would, with her remarkable unforced skills, help countless souls on both sides of the divide—both on the Earth Plane, and in Spirit World. (For many souls, having shaken off this mortal coil in extremities of emotion, scarcely know what has happened to them: hence the prevalence of "hauntings," the preoccupation of a deranged spirit mind.)

"And we are moving, with astonishing swiftness," Madame said, "into the Twentieth Century: which, the Masters grant me, I shall have some small role in guiding. The materialism of our time, given apparent strength by the Darwinians, presents so bleak and unimaginative a spectacle of the Universe, that one hardly knows whether to weep with sorrow, or sheer fatigue!—that Universe being in any case tiresomely *masculine*, in its grim physicality, while our Universe is resplendently *feminine*. Do you follow my sentiments, my dear child? Do you agree?"

Deirdre sipped thinly at her cup of tea, which she drank, as always, unsweetened by either sugar or cream, oft in place of heartier fare, and to the possible detriment of her fragile nerves: she sipped at the tea, without haste, not troubling to avoid Madame's warm and, as it were, fulsome gaze. "I know not, Madame, of the abstractions of which you so casually speak," our young lady said, with a haughtiness of tone, and a frostiness of eye, that might have done credit to Malvinia Morloch herself, "nor shall I belabor myself, as to the forging of an opinion. My life—as you and many others have given me to know—for which I am greatly in your debt—my life *is* my work. I am no *theoretical* Spiritualist, to be found virtually everywhere, but a *practicing* Spiritualist, and must not distract myself with the poetical, but tergiversate, rhetorical displays, which, no doubt, the Masters have inspired in you."

Madame sensed herself rebuffed by this cool speech; yet was not entirely certain of the young lady's meaning. (It is most amusing, as the reader should note, that this noisome Russian immigrant, the self-ordained prophet of a new religion, should pride herself upon her English—yet fail to know the commonest of our words!) To disguise her confusion, and to quell the o'erabundance of energies, which all biographers have remarked as a particular, not to say pathological, characteristic of hers, Madame sought solace in tobacco, taking pinches of ill-smelling Turkish weed out of the bizarre leather pouch she wore about her neck (it was in the shape of an animal's head—yet no animal known to man), and rolling them in a brown cigarette paper, into an irregular cylinder. Her pudgy fingers shook somewhat, as if Deirdre's chill words, and the yet more chill weight of her gaze, quite intimidated her; yet when she spoke she had regained the Blavatsky ebullience, and declared, with a broad smile that came close to cheering the entire chamber in which they sat: "Nonetheless, my Lolo, you shall be *famous,* and you shall be *great;* and you shall—if I have any hand in your destiny—be *rich.* If that prospect displeases you, little one, please allow your most devoted champion to know."

But Deirdre, sipping at her strong dark India tea, said not a word of assent, or protest.

42

The public career of "Deirdre of the Shadows" progressed with a gratifying alacrity in the 1880's, taking the ambitious young woman as far west as Milwaukee, and as far south as Atlanta, and acquiring for her not only a modicum of fame, in Spiritualist circles, but an income deemed more or less satisfactory: tho' Madame Blavatsky, fiercely protective of her young charge, and given to forgivable hyperbole, naturally believed, and did not shrink from telling journalists, that this "miraculous creature" had yet to be honored "according to her deserts"—for which, Madame vaguely threatened, she might have to abandon her native land, and strike out for European, or even Oriental, climes.

Deirdre herself rarely spoke about so external, and so materialistic, an issue as her career, let alone her income, but she might have concurred, silently, with Madame's fervent belief that she was undervalued, despite the attention she continued to receive, and the incontestable mystery of her powers (for, like all genuine mediums, Deirdre had absolutely no comprehension of those powers—and very little control over them); she did not, however, have the slightest desire to abandon her native land—the very thought of sailing for Europe, and leaving her language behind, filled her with secret distress. For not only would she then venture into a world not American, and hence, for her, not imaginable: she would be forced into an even more abject dependency upon Madame Blavatsky, who spoke fluently (or so she boasted) "all the significant European tongues." And this our clever young lady assuredly did not wish to do, for many reasons, primary among them being her e'er-growing desire to free herself of the older woman, whose busyness, commandeering manner, and habits of personal cleanliness, offended her Lolo.

One day, Deirdre murmured to Hassan Agha, Madame being temporarily out of the house on Theosophical business: "How *can* you bear her—is it pretense?—is it Romish *penance?*"—thereby so startling the dusky-skinned youth that he stared bluntly at her, as if he had never seen her before in his life. A look passed between them fluid, and dark, and gravely disapproving on his part, and grayly-chilled on hers: and, with an inordinately clumsy bow, the *chela* took his leave of her in silence, backing out of the room.

In some agitation Deirdre wondered whether he would repeat her words to Madame, whether he would take advantage of her outburst, and betray her. But, in subsequent days, Madame gave no indication that her Lolo had displeased her in any way: so Deirdre felt both relief and some mild disappointment. In Hassan Agha's presence, however, she was resolutely guarded, and could not help but note, to her annoyance, that the *chela* was equally guarded with her, and would not, in fact, deign to look upon her. (Tho' she sometimes amused herself by studying him—taking note of his bony, rather sullen face, and his emaciated frame, and his exotic silken costume, which bespoke, oddly, an arresting sort of masculinity—as did the ingeniously wrapped black turban he wore at all times on his head, completely hiding his hair. She noted his narrow, pale, slender hands—his unusually long fingernails—the black hairs on the knuckles—the large onyx ring Madame had given him, with its indecipherable Sanskrit inscription—the strangely disconcerting grace of his walk, and the absolute silence in which (how very unlike Madame, and most of the Spiritualists!) he was content to dwell, as if brooding upon a deep, rich, unfathomable mystery—a predilection, doubtless, of his ancient Indian soul.) The revulsion Deirdre felt for this most trusted of *chelas* had as much to do, I cannot help speculating, with the fact that, despite his eccentric mode of dress and behavior, he radiated an aura not unattractive to the female sex, as with the covert but unmistakable revulsion he felt for her—manifested, she saw to her angry amusement, by a studious, and at times rather absurd, refusal to meet her gaze, or even to acknowledge her physical presence. "As if I am all spirit!" Deirdre laughed interiorly. "As if I am *only* spirit!"

Tho' the public career of Deirdre of the Shadows had progressed, as I have noted, with a satisfactory speed, and the financial rewards garnered were, for the most part, not disappointing, it was nonetheless the case that no one—not even the timidly bold medium herself—might have predicted the *triumph,* and the *scandal,* that would result from the investigation of the Society for Psychical Research into her mediumship: tho' the calculating young woman was correct in her assumption that, daring to take on the Society's scrutiny, she should have fashioned a break with Blavatsky and the Theosophists, and won for herself that degree of independence so eagerly, and so unwisely, desired by certain American females of the latter half of our century. "If you agree to this examination," Madame said, hoarsely and sadly, her pouched eyes fixed upon Deirdre's with very little of their power of old, "I shall interpret your action as both impetuous and ungrateful—my cruel Lolo!" And Deirdre said with equanimity, shrinking from the harsh odor of Madame's cigarette, and the hardly less harsh fragrance that hovered about her person, redolent of garlic, and Indian incense, and mammalian flesh but sporadically washed: "Madame, you must calculate your interpretations as you see fit—perhaps the Mahatmas can guide you."

Deirdre was dwelling at this time in a handsome apartment in the Fifth Avenue home of the widow Strong, whose altruism had not abated over the years; whilst Madame, with a varying contingent of *chelas* and Theosophists and devotees of the occult, maintained a somewhat shabbier household—the famous Lamasery, in fact, whose exotic furnishings were soon to be sold on the auction block—unfashionably north and west, on Forty-seventh Street and Eighth Avenue. This unpleasant disagreement having arisen between them, as they dined alone together, the older woman had no recourse but to take her leave at once, with a blood-suffused face, and that occasional dignity of which the very corpulent, and the very abash'd, can be capable. "I bid you *adieu,* my vainglorious American miss," Madame said; and Deirdre, her gaze fixed upon the carpet with the selfsame stillness, and the selfsame obstinacy, that had so maddened her sisters years before, murmured only: "And I, Madame, bid you *goodbye.*"

The first sittings offered by Deirdre of the Shadows had been held in private homes, like Landsdowne House, with very little publicity, and all who participated pledged to secrecy: for Madame had a predilection for secrecy, believing it to be the most practical fount of self-promotion. Did not the world's greatest religions spring, at their source, from mystery?—from disciples sworn to silence? "Nor must we offer you too cheaply," Madame advised. "A democratic people value *only* what is o'erpriced."

Deirdre's early clients, assembled by Madame Blavatsky in concert with the widow Strong, were female for the most part, incontestably well-to-do, and genteel even in their bereavement. So desirous were they of communing with their dead, and so desirous were the dead of communing with them, that the young and inexperienced medium would barely be seated at the table, and Hassan Agha and the other attendants

would scarcely have settled the clients—*guests,* as they were called—and
subtly dimmed the lights, when the spirits of the deceased relatives would
rush forward!—oft pushing violently past Deirdre's contact spirits, *Mrs.
Dodd* and *Father Darien,* to cause a considerable upset in the room. Oh!
the confusion!—the thrill of abject terror that communicated itself from
person to person, around the oval table! A clatter as of china and cutlery,
and an occasional smashing of glassware; a maniacal rapping and bang-
ing, as if it were All Hallows' Eve; gay, drunken, importunate voices
interrupting one another, and clamoring to be heard; a flood—a Babel
—a cacophony punctuated by isolated cries of genuine, and heartrending, despair: "Mother!" a voice sounded, and "Daughter!" and "O my
son, my son!"

The young medium, attired in sombre black, with a black lace cap
on her head, and the little gold locket about her neck, sank at once into
trance; and then into a deeper trance; her eyes partly open, the lids
fluttering, and the eyeball itself sometimes rolling upward—a ghastly
sight, which, coupled with the extraordinary pallor of the medium's skin
at this time, and the queer crackling and frizzing of her hair, as if with
static electricity, produced a most disconcerting, yet most satisfying,
effect around the table. As she sank into deeper, and yet deeper, trance,
the mature spirits were able to restore calm, and the alarming pan-
demonium of the opening minutes would subside.

The voice of *Mrs. Dodd*—stern, peremptory, and subtly amused—
would issue from Deirdre's throat, assuring the guests that their loved
ones were present, and would speak with them in turn: there was no
cause for anxiety about time or sequence, or any vestige of *earthly protocol,* for Spirit World was all of a simultaneity. *Those who have loved you
continue to love you, and those whom you have loved continue to require your love,
that they may be less lonely: for even Paradise can be lonely, when families have
been split asunder.*

So the voice of the estimable *Mrs. Dodd* assured the little gathering,
issuing through Deirdre's frail vessel of a body, a voice not her own, as
even the most detached and skeptical observer would note.

(Indeed, at such uncanny times, Deirdre's mind broke into shards,
and she experienced dream-images of such compelling vibrancy and
authenticity, it would have been very difficult for her to realize that they
were *not real,* but only phantasms, visual, and without sound or thought:
once she discovered herself, bodiless, no more than an optic nerve that
quivered with mute astonishment, in the ruins of a great Mayan city, in
the Central American jungle, the tall adobe buildings with their narrow
windows absolutely empty—empty of all human inhabitants—yet with an
unsettling air of being only *recently* emptied; another time, she discovered
herself in her adoptive father's workshop above the Bloodsmoor Gorge,

and there was Mr. Zinn himself, absorbed as always in his work—but ah! how changed!—for he had become wizened and bald, and his skin had turned a queer metallic texture, silvery and metallic, wondrous to behold: and he had no consciousness of Deirdre, or, indeed, of any of his surroundings, being so rabidly hunched over his machine, a machine-man hunched over a machine, scarcely five feet tall. Still another time, during one of her most successful séances, in fact, conducted by *Mrs. Dodd, Father Darien,* and a surprisingly sober *Bianca,* Deirdre discovered herself, again bodiless, in a remote and bitterly cold place where the earth, encased in ice, curved most abnormally away, and no vegetation showed itself, and not even an outcropping of rock, and solitary birds flew close over the ice, their dazzling white feathers perfect as if *they* were ice: ah, and their long crooked necks and cruelly hooked beaks!—and their small gleaming eyes, invulnerable as rock!—and her heart cried out in rapturous yearning, to be one of them, alone, in utter isolation, where no spirits could follow, for no *life* had ever been *lived:* for what need had the polar cap of *life,* encased in such beauty? The solitary white birds, the great dazzling-white birds, their beaks, their long crooked necks, their staring eyes . . .)

There is no death, *Mrs. Dodd* assured the agitated people around the table. *Your loved ones await you—they are always present.*

There is no death, Father Darien said. His voice was firm and manly; the intrusive French accent, scarcely perceptible.

There is no death, the child *Bianca* lisped, with as much heartfelt joy, as if the news were gladsome.

(And how was the trick accomplished?—the innumerable tricks? How did mere girls like Deirdre of the Shadows not only present themselves, in the late 1800's, as intermediaries between the *visible* and *invisible* worlds, boldly making sorties, as it were, into the religious domain, by custom and by natural law the province of masculine authority? How did they not only present themselves as conduits by which the Dead might address the Living, and vice versa, but, through some unspeakable sortilege, manage to convince others, including many objective observers, that theirs was a mission undefiled by fraud, and chicanery, and dementia? How did they, like Deirdre, surrender themselves to contact spirits, who, in turn, brought forth other spirits, warmly desirous of communicating with the living, and entirely convincing in both content and manner of delivery?

My answer is—and I am half-shamed to confess it—*I simply do not know.*)

However she did it, with whatever innocent or less-than-innocent strategies, Deirdre appeared to bring into contact many who had been divided by death: she took her place with very little self-consciousness as a focal point, a juncture, a mere vessel—in short, a *medium*—whereby children spoke with their long-deceased parents, and widows communed with their dead husbands, and secrets were revealed, and tales told, and posthumous explanations for inexplicable behavior given, of a sort that, in nearly every instance, *no one living might have known beforehand.*

The séance attended in secret by Mrs. Zinn and Octavia, at 2 Fifth Avenue, was typical of Deirdre's early successes; tho' initially, as we have seen, the atmosphere was unsettled by the pranks of a malevolent spirit, doubtless *Zachariah* (this spirit being loos'd as a consequence of the emotional tension emanating from Mrs. Zinn and her daughter—however ignorant Deirdre herself was of their presence): hence the rappings, floating lights, music, and other tomfoolery. The wicked spirit being routed, however, by the mature spirits *Mrs. Dodd* and *Father Darien,* a period of relative calm was achieved, and the proceedings were wondrously rewarding, as all testified afterward. Amongst those who enjoyed the privilege of speaking with deceased family members, some of whom death had divided for more than fifty years, was a female descendant of Aaron Burr, who was assured by that gentleman that, while guilty as charged of certain political machinations, he was altogether innocent of the libelous statements published by the New York Federalists, as to his wiles as a *seducer:* indeed, his sojourn in Spirit World had convinced him that celibacy is the highest state known to man or angel! Another distinguished participant was Congressman Wallace G. Tunstall, a pork-bodied gentleman with shiny red cheeks and glaring eyes, who did not scruple to weep unashamedly, when addressed by the spirit of his lost, English-born cousin J. H. Tunstall, murdered in 1878 on his Felix River ranch in notorious Lincoln County, New Mexico—the very Tunstall who was later to be revenged, a hundredfold, by the actions of his loyal young employee William Bonney (which is to say, *Billy the Kid*). J. H. Tunstall communicated to Congressman Tunstall the fact that a considerable fortune in silver and gold was buried at a certain fork in the Felix River, and untouched to that very day: this fortune belonging by moral as well as legal rights to no one more deservedly than him. After giving elaborate instructions as to the location of the treasure, which Congressman Tunstall, for weeping, could barely transcribe, the deceased cousin went on to speak, in his charming British accent, of the New Mexico terrain, with such vehemence, and such great love, that the brilliant sunrises, and chill hovering mists, and the cactus flowers of early April, and the very *air* itself, so clear! so sharp!—were most miraculously, and convincingly, present, in lower Fifth Avenue, of this bustling city.

Nor did the impassioned spirit pause, at this, but continued to speak of his transmogrified state: "You see, my dear Wally, it is nothing more than *crossing over.* I cannot put it more succinctly, or more accurately —*crossing over.* When your time is imminent, Wally, you will have naught to do, but extend your hand: and I shall be there to help: and the mortal scales will fall from your eyes, with great alacrity, I can promise! For only consider: I am here now, tho' perhaps *not visible* to you, as a consequence of intrinsic weakness of vision, amongst mortals: yet I am here, I assure you, and able to communicate with you, with no great difficulty; and you can communicate with me; and there is nothing mysterious, or repugnant, or frightening, about it, for it is but a *crossing over*—" whereupon the voice, which exuded such gratifying confidence, began suddenly to fade, and in a moment was lost, to leave in its wake a shocked hush, and the sound of divers weeping: which did not exclude, so moving had the testimony of the deceased Englishman been, even the much-experienced *chela* Hassan Agha!

Perhaps it was not amazing, to Spiritualist believers and adepts, that the Tunstall treasure was located in *precisely the spot,* that the spirit had promised it: but I am bound to say that it was amazing to others, of a more skeptical nature; and it continues to amaze, and perplex, and, indeed, *disturb,* this faithful chronicler.

For such curious *concidences,* if they may be thusly termed, were by no means remarkable in the course of Deirdre's mediumship, but came to be quite habitual.

"How, may I ask, does your charming friend accomplish it?" Thus the query was put, ofttimes with a rude conspiratorial wink, to Madame Blavatsky, who, it must be said, enjoyed immensely a *man-to-man* rapport with the most worldly, and the most cynical, of gentlemen, not excluding journalists. "You may confide in me, Madame," it was commonly said, "for, I swear under oath, I give you my absolute word, I shall not reveal your *secret.* It is simply that my curiosity is so prick'd, I can scarce sleep at night, for a tumult of thought, and speculation, as to how you and the charming young lady accomplish your *craft:* for thus I call it, and not *trickery,* as others have charged."

Whereupon Madame smiled an enigmatic smile, and said, with dignity of a gentle, rather than a haughty, aspect: "My dear sir, your question as to *how* cannot be answered, by me: for *how,* in this instance, resides with God."

Still they plagued her with their questions, they begged for her confidence, if only she might reveal the secret to *them,* and to *them alone:* for it was a most tortuous puzzle, as to how Deirdre of the Shadows managed all she did—the voices, the ectoplasmic apparitions, the revelations of certain truths, that, given the evidence, simply could not have been known, by her, or by anyone in the room!—for, surely, it was a most ingenious—nay, a most diabolical—trick, which might lend itself to rational explanation?

But Madame Blavatsky did naught but shake her head, so that her jowls quivered, with a most affecting air, of humility, and again spoke: "*How,* my dear sir, must *always and forever* reside with God; and not with man."

43

The famous investigation of Deirdre of the Shadows by the New York chapter of the Society for Psychical Research, with its scandalous—nay, tragic—results, and its sombre implications for all who would examine too closely the machinations of Spirit World, took place on a mild April evening in 1886, at the old S.P.R. headquarters at 11 Gramercy Park, a town house in red brick and brownstone with imperial granite trim, and twin sphinxes, also of granite, who stared over into the park with placid blind eyes. Deirdre was escorted to the examination by two gentlemen, Dr. Percy Dodd and his young assistant Dr. Lionel Stoughton, and a lady, Mrs. Minnie Cunningham, who enjoyed a membership not only in the S.P.R., in which very few places were reserved for members of the female sex, but in the powerful Missionaries' Alliance, which had recently spoken out with great reservation and some animosity against the "pagan-phenomenon of Spiritualism"—Mrs. Cunningham being, as she conde-scended to inform Deirdre, not *altogether* convinced that her sisters' harsh judgment was correct. "I shall maintain an entirely open mind, in viewing tonight's proceedings," Mrs. Cunningham said.

It may have been obligatory for Deirdre to thank Mrs. Cunning-ham at this point, for both gentlemen looked at her, Dr. Dodd most emphatically: but Deirdre, seated in a corner of the plush-lined carriage, and so swathed in black shawls of cashmere, Spanish lace, and brocade subtly trimmed with black swansdown, that one might have fancied the evening chill, and not unseasonably balmy, chose to interpret the good lady's statement as complete within itself, and needing no further com-mentary. So she remained silent, her gaze affixed to a corner of the carriage some inches to the left of Dr. Stoughton's shoulder, and her manner eerily serene, some small apprehension indicated only by her fondling of a gold locket worn on a chain around her neck—an item of adornment of unexceptional quality, as her observers could not fail to note.

(There have recently been, I should hasten to inform the reader, in order to prevent a premature condemnation of Deirdre's judges, vulgar gossip in the *Graphic*, and one or another of the cruder three-penny papers, to the effect that "Deirdre of the Shadows" had been the recipient of a diamond- and ruby-studded serpent bracelet, some twelve inches in length, and fashioned to be worn curved about the forearm, costing upward of $20,000!—a trinket from Mr. Diamond Jim Brady himself, doubtless as a gesture of extreme gratitude for the young medium's services, or of especial interest in her on a more personal plane. That Deirdre, acting upon inscrutable but surely praiseworthy impulses, had sent the meretricious item back to Mr. Brady with but the single word *"No,"* was not of course reported: and what a pity! for the young woman had but little comprehension of how such gutter publicity should rouse *spite* and *envy* against her, and a general wish that she should *fail.*)

"The entire assemblage, Mrs. Cunningham," Dr. Dodd said quietly, "is sworn to the necessity of *open-mindedness:* we would naturally assume you to be no exception."

That the Society's investigation into her mediumship—which is to say, frankly, into the *authenticity,* or the *fraudulence,* of it—might have justified some signal anxiety or, at the very least, concern, on Deirdre's part is but natural: unnatural, perhaps, was her peculiar affectless serenity, shading very nearly into light trance, as the hour approached. She consented without protest to the private examination of her person, which involved *partial disrobing,* by several members of the Ladies' Committee: an accommodation to the Society's scrupulosity that might very well have offended the taste of a delicate young lady (as, indeed, it greatly angered many mediums, who avowed that they could not, and would not, comply); she seemed to view with equanimity, if some slight ironic humor, the close guard put upon her by Mrs. Cunningham and two other ladies, afterward escorting her upstairs into the Society's grand parlor. Nor did she view with alarm the large gathering that awaited her—some seventy-five persons, at the very least—and the rather grave countenances of the eight gentlemen of the examining committee, seated at the front of the room, at a long table draped in deep crimson velvet. *It is but your outward form they perceive,* a wise spirit-voice assured her, *your truest self, residing safely with us, the fools cannot apprehend.*

Yet such was the young lady's maturity, or, at any rate, the condition of her being so greatly practiced in her skill, that she had no true need even of the spirit's consolation: for she doubtless knew the fools would never apprehend her, without being told of the fact. Indeed, her mind was already detaching itself from the high-ceilinged parlor, and the assembled ladies and gentlemen, with their great variety of expressions —some of which, despite Dr. Dodd's assurance, frankly communicated *suspicion* and even *contempt,* and not a little *inquisitional appetite:* her mind, sinking into passivity, withdrew from the jarring diversity of the visible world, and took solace, in a manner of speaking, in the invisible, where she might think and dream and summon forth all manner of memories, while the spirits advanced, to gather themselves close about her. In this state of *light trance,* which the medium would systematically deepen, by some mysterious volitionless volition of her own, she would be free to entertain such thoughts as those stimulated by her visit to the Fanshawe Theatre some time previously, and by the frequent accident of her sharing a page in the *Tribune* or the *Graphic* with the acclaimed stage actress Malvinia Morloch—now enjoying yet another conspicuous success, in a lavishly produced presentation of *She Stoops to Conquer;* she might passionlessly contemplate the angry, tearful farewell between herself and Madame Blavatsky that had occurred not a week before, just prior to Madame's removal of herself and her most cherished *chelas* to Bombay—the anger, and the tears, being exclusively on Madame's side, as well as unseemly accusations of "betrayal," "wanton cruelty," and "Luciferian pride." Indeed, so impenetrable was the trance into which Deirdre of the Shadows sank, while her inquisitors gazed upon her *outward* and *material form,* that she freely visited the parlor of the Octagonal House, where, at that very moment, her adoptive father and mother, her stepsister Samantha, and sleepy-headed Pip, had gathered; Mr. Zinn in his usual chair, Mrs. Zinn in hers, knitting an item of clothing for "Little Godfrey"—but who was "Little Godfrey"?—and chatting companionably about "Nahum" and "Mr. Watkins"—but who were *they?*—in total oblivion of Deirdre's spirit-presence. To her credit, the imperturbable Deirdre gazed almost with longing upon this warm domestic scene, and bethought herself that, had she her physical being, she should want very much to —nay, she *would*—bestow a light kiss not only upon the brow of the handsome Mr. Zinn, but upon the somewhat creased brow of Mrs. Zinn, and the small palely freckled cheek of Samantha! and then depart, in the very next instant.

Such were the perplexing skills of the medium's mind, *during the very time when the examination was beginning,* and when, still in her own voice, she forthrightly if rather mechanically answered questions put to her by the gentlemen of the committee. There she sat, on a slightly raised platform, in a sturdy C-scroll chair with a velvet cushion and velvet arm-rests, at apparent ease, tho' exhibiting satisfactorily good posture; there she sat, unalarmed by the multitude of eyes fixed upon her, a young woman of decidedly exotic countenance—with her prominent widow's peak, and her loos'd black hair that seemed frazzled and stiff with electricity, and the uncanny gray eyes which glinted with an impersonal authority, like mica (how totally altered from that furtive, feral, shrinking child of thirteen years previously, when she was first brought to dwell with the Zinns!); there she sat, I repeat, calmly answering questions asked by Dr. Dodd, and Dr. Stoughton, and Professor Crosby, and Mr. Sinnett, and Dr. Eglinton, and Sir Patrick Koones, and Mr. Oakley-Hume, and Professor Bey—while her mind was fully occupied elsewhere, and the spirits, unbeknownst to the others, silently gathered.

(How Deirdre of the Shadows managed the following harlequinade, I do not know—no more than the mystified Nathaniel Hawthorne could grasp how Daniel Dunglas Home summoned forth *his* spirits, and made lights fly flashing about the room, and immense pieces of furniture dance, all the while being closely observed. Since the official investigation of Deirdre of the Shadows of April 21, 1886, is included in the eleventh volume of the historic fifteen-volume compendium, *The Transactions of the American Society for Psychical Research*, it is a matter of public record, and one dare not doubt its veracity—however unsettling to the Christian mentality, and to common standards of decency and sanity.)

Dr. Dodd, as the President of the Society, began by asking certain formal questions of Deirdre—her full name, her birthplace, background, and so forth—and the young woman, gravely composed, replied succinctly that she was no more than "Deirdre of the Shadows," and could not explain herself further. "The spirits have thus baptized me," she said, "and I cannot contradict their wishes."

    After a startl'd pause, Dr. Dodd proceeded to inquire into her professional background, receiving this response: "My first séance was conducted at Landsdowne House, in the late autumn of 1879, as the Society doubtless knows—if its records are thorough."

    "And this *début,*" Dr. Dodd said, "was it not under the auspices of Mrs. Helena Petrovna Blavatsky, the founder of Theosophy?"

    "It was under no one's auspices," Deirdre said, "save perhaps Mrs. Holtman Strong's—or that of the friendly spirits themselves."

    "But Mrs. Blavatsky *was* present, I believe?" Dr. Dodd asked.

    "She was present," Deirdre said evenly, "along with divers others, whose names I am afraid I have forgotten."

    "And where is Mrs. Blavatsky at the present time?"

    "She has allegedly departed for India," Deirdre said, with a very slight curl of her pert upper lip, "and I doubt—I strongly doubt—that our paths shall cross again, in this life."

    Here was intercalated some questioning by Professor Crosby, and Sir Patrick Koones, who wished to know more about the medium's association with Mrs. Blavatsky, and with the "discredited" Theosophical Society in general; and then Dr. Stoughton (happening to be the youngest gentleman on the committee, with a handsome, forthright countenance, and a strong but courteous voice) observed that "Mrs. Blavatsky is not tonight under investigation, her case having been decided some time past," and that the questioning should continue, "along a more temperate line."

Despite Dr. Stoughton's wise counsel, however, Professor Crosby continued his line of interrogation, asking the medium whether she was familiar with one "Count Youry," a trance medium residing for a time in Boston, and long since exposed as a fraud, and arrested as a common felon, said "Count Youry" having been an early protégé of Mrs. Blavatsky's. Whereupon the medium paused for the briefest of instants, and replied, in a voice of great dignity: "Should you desire to bring to trial the Countess Blavatsky, you must transport her hither by your own efforts: for my spirits have assured me, *they* are not capable of doing so."

This response was so fluidly offered, it was a moment before the audience comprehended its wit: and the gentlemen of the committee, Professor Crosby in particular, glanced out, annoyed, at a small flurry of laughter. Dr. Dodd, too, frowned as if distinctly annoyed, and the laughter at once subsided.

Next, Dr. Eglinton, a blunt-featured gentleman in a gray frock coat that ill fit his massive frame, asked the medium, in an imperial voice, whether she would reconsider, as to informing the Society of her background, for "it could not be a matter of any anxiety, in an *honest* and *law-abiding* career," that such information be made public.

Whereupon the medium said: "I know only that I am baptized 'Deirdre of the Shadows,' and that my life previous to this baptism is of no account. The spirits have selected me, I am given to understand, as *the bearer of good tidings, heralding the New Dispensation.*"

"The 'New Dispensation'?" Dr. Eglinton asked sharply.

"Whereby the Resurrection of the Spirit is properly understood," Deirdre said without hesitation, "and the material world is transform'd."

"But precisely how, my dear child," Mr. Sinnett asked with a fond, if rather peremptory, smile, "is the material world to be transform'd!"

Deirdre paused; and it might have been observed that her large gray eyes had become somewhat glassy. After a placid moment she said: "Mr. Sinnett—for I believe that is your name?—you must not condescend with me, or suggest familiarity: for the spirits will be displeased, and I cannot answer as to the punitive capacities of the least mature among them."

"Ah! The young lady threatens us!" Dr. Eglinton said, with a startl'd laugh.

"It was not a threat—not precisely a threat," Mr. Sinnett said. "I interpret it as a rather charming rebuke, the which I own I probably deserve! My apologies, *Mademoiselle.*"

Dr. Dodd, clearing his throat, returned briefly to the subject of the medium's background, inquiring of her whether, to her knowledge, there was an *hereditary history* of psychic powers in her family—this information always being valuable, for the record: but the medium greeted this question with an imperturbable silence, as if beneath her consideration to answer.

After an uncomfortable moment Sir Patrick Koones said to Dr. Dodd: "Is she already in trance? I say, she is a *most* peculiar lass!"

"Perhaps she means only to indicate that questions concerning personal background will not be answered," Mr. Oakley-Hume said in an uneasy voice.

"And yet," Professor Crosby said, *"why* will they not be answered? It strikes me as distinctly suspicious."

"Professor Crosby," Dr. Dodd said, "you forget yourself. Please, sir."

"Is the medium in trance?" Mr. Sinnett said, leaning far forward. "Are the spirits present?"

"The spirits are always present," Deirdre said in a slow sepulchral voice. "Hence they must not be trifled with."

"Ah, surely no one means to trifle with them!" Professor Bey ejaculated.

"Or to trifle with so haughty a miss!" Dr. Eglinton observed.

"Dr. Eglinton, *you* forget yourself as well," Dr. Dodd said, and there was a stir of approbation from the audience. "I must ask you to keep in order."

The questions then proceeded, pertaining more exlcusively to the medium's comprehension of her exact role, as an intermediary between the "two worlds," and Deirdre's answers were forthcoming, if rather slow and glacial in tone: to the point at which Mr. Sinnett (the "layman" of the committee, and, in fact, a journalist for the Boston *Journal*) could not restrain himself from exclaiming: "Gentlemen, is this young lady in a trance? She looks decidedly unwell—perhaps we should stop. It is all very, very queer—"

Dr. Dodd assured Mr. Sinnett, with barely concealed impatience, that the medium might very well have put herself into a light trance, preparatory to the séance itself; that being her prerogative if she so desired.

Mr. Sinnett replied, embarrassed, that so long as the other gentlemen were not alarmed, and several physicians were present, he supposed that the young lady was not in danger: but she *looked,* he murmured, so deucedly strange! "So deathly-pale a complexion, in a living creature," he said, "I swear I have never seen."

The other gentlemen remonstrated with him, and even young Dr. Stoughton demurred, stating that such *personal observations* were irrelevant to the investigation, and distracting moreover. Whereupon Professor Crosby resolutely said: "It is the *odylic force* that renders her so pale, gentlemen. She summons it forth, out of the female organs—by a process but dimly understood. When it is in full flower, so to speak, she will utilize it—you shall see!—to read our minds."

"Professor Crosby, that is most injudicious," Dr. Stoughton said, blushing. "It is—most unfair."

"Odylic force?" Mr. Sinnett inquired of Professor Crosby, leaning in his direction. "What, sir, might that be? I am quite in the dark!"

Before Dr. Dodd could rule him out of order, Professor Crosby said, as if lecturing to the entire assemblage: "O-d-y-l-i-c. Odylic force. A form of electricity, Mr. Sinnett—magnetism. By which the medium penetrates the minds of others—heaves furniture about—causes a general consternation of the air. First proposed by the Baron Reichenbach, deriving obliquely from Mesmer's animal magnetism, and quite a viable hypothesis—in fact I am publishing a little monograph on the subject in the fall—"

"Professor Crosby, you forget yourself," Dr. Dodd said sharply.

Tho' the gentleman declined to apologize, the examination continued along more conventional lines: questions being put to the medium not only by members of the committee, but by several members of the audience, regarding her understanding of "powers" and of their value to the world. These questions the young woman answered in a slow, halting voice, tho' her words were distinct enough. "The dead are not dead . . . the living are not separate from the dead . . . the worlds are so vastly, vastly populated . . . our dead . . . our belovèd dead . . . close as every breath we inhale."

(At which Professor Crosby could not resist interjecting, to Mr. Oakley-Hume: "Chemical excitations in young females arise from the reproductive organs, to flood the brain. It may be an epileptoid dysfunction as well—I have seen it often in 'psychic' mediums.")

The medium, while evidently in trance, her head held high and her frost-hued eyes fixed upon an indefinite point in space, nevertheless o'erheard this remark, and said in an even, but forceful, voice: "If you continue to mock, sir, the good spirits will be o'ercome by the malicious: and I cannot promise sufficient control over them, to fully protect you."

Sir Patrick Koones murmured to his colleagues that they *must* show respect, whatever disdain they truly felt; and Professor Bey, shifting about restlessly in his chair, observed that he should like very much to examine the medium's skull—he had been promised that he *might* have this privilege—for it was highly likely that Deirdre of the Shadows suffered from the phreno-organization of the classic *psychopathological spondylosoid:* the symptoms being a distinct ridge of bone at the crown of the skull, and numerous small bumps at the base.

Mr. Sinnett interrupted excitedly to say that he had seen something—a spirit, perhaps!—sliding under the door.

Whereupon all the gentlemen turned to look, in the direction he pointed; but professed to see nothing. Dr. Eglinton exhibited some impatient amusement, stating in a low voice that the profession of journalism doubtless accommodated certain excesses of the imagination, not enjoyed by the scientific mentality. Sir Patrick Koones adjusted his *pince-nez*, which were fastened to his waistcoat by a silver chain, and said, after a strained moment, that he fancied he did see something in the room—now in that corner, above the gilt cornice—now entwined about the chandelier overhead. "A manifestation, it may be. Ectoplasm in a very amorphous state."

"Nonsense!" said Professor Crosby. "And yet, it is very peculiar, I am suddenly *chilled.*"

"I too am chilled—my legs in particular," Mr. Oakley-Hume said, with some agitation. "There seems to be a draft in here."

Mr. Sinnett rose to his feet, smiling in great perplexity. "Perhaps Miss Deirdre too is cold? *Is* there a draft? Shall I check the windows, or the door?"

Professor Bey too arose, tho' slowly. He had drawn out of a leather satchel a peculiar instrument, something like a headdress, tho' of metal, with several joined curved bands. "Perhaps it is out of order—perhaps it is premature—but I should like—ah, I should so *very* like—to be assured of—to be allowed—" he said, with a smile no less perplexed than Mr. Sinnett's, but a great deal wider.

Dr. Dodd and the others stared at him in amazement, and urged him to be seated.

"It is that—that *thing* in the chandelier," Sir Patrick Koones whispered. "Cannot someone make it go away?"

"There is *nothing* there," Professor Crosby said irritably. "I see nothing."

"Nor do I. *Where* is it?" Dr. Eglinton asked, amused.

"Now it is expanding, and growing very thin," Sir Patrick Koones said quietly. "It means to envelop, I halfway fear, the entire room."

"It has a slight acrid odor, does it not?" Mr. Oakley-Hume said.

Professor Bey remained on his feet, albeit somewhat shakily, his bony shoulders hunched forward, and his mustache now glistening with saliva. He was a gentleman of some years, yet possessing, withal, a reputation for youthful vigor of purpose: it was to be said of him, after this particular evening, that *whatever got into him* simply could not be dislodged, and *was not him* in any case. For he suddenly dropped his measuring instrument, and began speaking in a voice of great urgency: "I—I—

I must know, and know upon the spot: *Is* my Saviour awaiting me? In that other world? Are His promises legitimate?"

"Why, he is babbling," Dr. Eglinton said.

"Professor Bey, what is wrong?" Dr. Dodd asked, in astonishment.

"I must know this one thing, and then I will be content," Professor Bey said, his voice quavering. "All else—all such tomfoolery—" and here he indicated, with a careless gesture of his hand, the metallic instrument, the leather satchel, and, indeed, his colleagues at the long table! "All such vanity is merely a waste of our time, and *our time,* alas, is fast running out."

"Dear Rodney," Dr. Eglinton said, tugging at his arm, "you must be seated: it is not quite the place for jesting."

"I do not jest, sir! How dare you!"

"He is unwell," Professor Crosby whispered to Dr. Dodd. "Perhaps a mild stroke—an incursion of senile dementia—"

(And all the while Deirdre of the Shadows remained unperturbed —quite oblivious to the drama! Where her unfeeling soul had drifted, I dare not speculate; but those "windows of the soul"—the eyes—now reflected very little that was *warm with life,* let alone *human.*)

Some minutes were taken up by Professor Bey's distress, the members of the committee being unable to agree whether to persuade the unfortunate gentleman to leave, or to allow him to stay, or to adjourn the séance for another time—this last being rather impractical, under the circumstances. He continued to address Deirdre of the Shadows in a high, forlorn voice, quite at odds with his wide smile. *"Is* my Saviour awaiting? *Is* He close by? Of a sudden I am so very, very frightened—I believe we are all frightened—as the dread year 1900 approaches—the dread and *unimaginable* year 1900—and I am visited by a sudden terror—that He has departed—and that we cannot even mock Him any longer! For what shall we mock, my colleagues, if not *Him?"*

"He is not jesting, he has gone quite mad," Dr. Eglinton said. With a large white handkerchief this gentleman wiped at his brow, which was freely perspiring, despite the chill of the room.

"I see naught but a great, great expanse of water—serene and oily —all waves abated, all storms—thousands upon thousands of tons of sheer dead pressure—millions of tons—*billions*—"

Dr. Dodd, Dr. Stoughton, and Mr. Sinnett attempted to calm the o'erwrought man, and to lead him from the room: and were joined in their struggle by a youthful member of the Society, Professor Bey's grandson, himself a physician. Seeing himself trapped, the old gentleman made a rush toward Deirdre, now crying in a loud aggrieved voice: "Why is He so rarely present—even when we abuse Him? You must tell me! You must cease this charade! For *nothing, nothing, nothing* matters save that Jesus Christ is a hoax, or is not a hoax—"

In the embarrassing contretemps a decanter of water was knocked to the floor, and Mr. Oakley-Hume was struck in the face by Professor Bey's flailing arm. At this most inopportune moment the gas jets everywhere in the large room faltered, and grew bright again, and again faltered, as if about to go out: which, I hardly need to note, further alarmed Professor Bey, and disturbed everyone in the room.

During all this time the young medium remained immobile in her chair, her waxen hands clasped tightly in her lap, and her sightless gaze fixed in space. A voice sepulchral as hers, yet not hers (it was that of an elderly, weary man) sounded from the air:

"Jesus is you, and you are Jesus, and He is in you, and everywhere; and nowhere. Prepare for His coming."

These grave words, however, far from calming Professor Bey, so greatly distressed him that it was deemed advisable, by all, that he be led out of the room, and home: and in this he gratefully concurred.

"I shall prepare—I shall prepare—ah, yes!—I shall prepare this very night," he was heard to say, as his grandson escorted him out of the room, and along the corridor.

After this unfortunate interlude there was a brief respite, as the committee members conferred with one another, in low tones. A gathering restiveness in the audience, however, suddenly manifested itself in an unauthorized question, put directly to the medium, by a stout veiled lady at the very rear of the room: "Is there hope? Is there hope? As the old gentleman asked, *Is there hope?*"—but this importunate individual was immediately hushed.

Now a great many voices sounded simultaneously, from out the very air: and were perceived as spirit-voices. And the gas jets flickered once more. The chandelier swayed; or, it might have been (so many attested afterward), *the parlor swayed,* rocking gently from side to side, whilst the chandelier remained fixed! One or two ladies exclaimed aloud, in voices that communicated both fear, and thrilled apprehension, and were answered by a series of raps—loud, sharp raps—which came also from the empty air.

(*Rapping* being a phenomenon commonplace in Spiritualist circles, these unpleasant noises had a salutary effect upon the gathering—imposing quiet, and, as it were, respect, upon the ladies and gentlemen.)

Yet the abrasive Dr. Eglinton could not resist observing, in a voice in which righteous anger and amusement were arrogantly blended: "My dear colleagues, do you see? *This* is standard séance claptrap. This above all. The Fox sisters invented it, to a credulous rural audience; the Davenports deviously patented it; and this industrious young lady merely peddles it—snapping her knee joints in secret—or her toe joints—and *throwing the sound.* So that it appears to the untrained ear to come out of nowhere—out of 'Spirit World'!"

"Her knee joints?" Mr. Sinnett asked, astonished.

"Or her toe joints," Dr. Eglinton said.

"Indeed," Professor Crosby said sharply, "it is standard practice: every medium knows how to do it. And ventriloquism as well. They are all masters—*mistresses!*—of the nefarious skill."

The rapping noises were now coming at the gentlemen from numerous directions, and were mixed with a more uniform drumming or droning sound, which, even to recall in tranquillity, is most chilling to this chronicler: not in its actual sound, so much as in the *persistence* and the *pressure* of it, which seemed to threaten madness. Several of the gentlemen believed that the drumming was in their own heads, and Mr. Oakley-Hume, who suffered a mild condition of the heart, believed that the sound was that of his own heartbeat, grotesquely magnified.

After some minutes this most distressing assault abated, and the gas jets ceased their flickering, and, some twelve or fifteen members of the audience having made their exit (in fact a wise decision, as we shall see), a modicum of order was restored; and Dr. Dodd insisted, in a voice gone shrill, that the investigation *must* proceed along traditional lines—or it would have to be terminated.

A faint titter of impish laughter attended his pronouncement, which he did not deign to hear.

Dr. Stoughton then noted, with some solicitude, that Deirdre of the Shadows was not only excessively pale, but sitting in her chair so rigidly, and in a posture of such extraordinary tension, that her slender body was quivering with strain. "I wonder, Dr. Dodd, whether it might be advisable to rouse her from her trance, before something unfortunate happens. Her eyes, you see, have rolled partway up into her head," the young man observed.

"Not at all, not at all, it is standard practice, it is back-parlor charlatanry," Professor Crosby said. "We *shall* proceed—we *shall* expose her! They can make thousands of dollars at a single sitting, these young ladies! Imposture and fraud! Impertinence!"

Whereupon the spirit *Zachariah*, invisible, caused the table at which the gentlemen were seated to heave itself upward, suddenly, and violently, at one end.

Again calm was restored, and Professor Crosby, unchastened, said: "Telekinesis."

Mr. Sinnett asked in a tremulous voice: "What did you say? Tele—?"

"*Telekinesis,*" Professor Crosby said.

And now the chandelier swayed emphatically, and the air again hummed and droned, and Dr. Eglinton said in a queer changed voice: "I shall examine her—I shall penetrate to the heart of the mystery—an autopsy of her inner organs—the female parts, and the brain: I shall not rest otherwise! The upstart little trollop!"

"Dr. Dodd," Dr. Stoughton repeated, in a voice that too seemed alter'd, "the young woman *is* under a tremendous amount of strain: why, I fear her very backbone might snap! Look how it arches, like a bow—"

"You can feel the vibrations in the air," Mr. Oakley-Hume said, shivering. "That they emanate from the witch I cannot doubt—that they have naught to do with the dead, I firmly believe—and yet, and yet!—I am so very stricken, I fear I must leave— Ah, gentlemen, do you *feel* the intensity of the pressure? Will it not injure us?"

"It is the odylic force," Professor Crosby said. "Telekinesis—mere animal magnetism."

"Yet I fear for my heart," Mr. Oakley-Hume murmured.

"Nonsense, sir! Sheer nonsense," Professor Crosby said.

"I must excuse myself—I believe I am in danger—and yet, and yet—" the stricken man said, "I dare not move for fear of exciting the witch further!"

The voice of a mature man (doubtless *Father Darien*, the martyred Jesuit) sounded from directly overhead, protesting, "Gentlemen! beware!"—but was at once interrupted by a shrill braying, as of an adolescent boy imitating a donkey; this in turn interrupted by the stern admonishings of a woman, whose words, in the din, were unintelligible.

Dr. Dodd rapped for order with his fist, grown greatly impatient, and sought to follow customary séance procedure, by addressing the spirits directly. In a quavering voice he asked them to identify themselves —to explain their presence—to speak one at a time, and as coherently as possible. The spirits quieted at once. Then an outburst of giggling occurred, and the woman's voice arose, seemingly out of the floorboards beneath the carpet. Her tone was fondly scolding: "*Willy!*"

Dr. Dodd staggered to his feet, to stare blinking at the floor. For a long moment he did not speak; then he said in a faint voice: "Momma? Is it—Momma?"

The spirit-voice began to speak, in an admixture of scolding and crooning, no more than babble to other ears; yet producing a remarkable effect upon Dr. Dodd. Professor Crosby tugged at his sleeve, saying quietly, "Ventriloquism, William, sheer parlor ventriloquism," but the agitated Dr. Dodd, a white-haired gentleman well into his seventies, knelt on the floor and pawed frantically at the carpet, saying in a piteous voice: "Momma? Is it you? Momma? Momma! O dear belovèd soul—*Momma*—"

The voice then sounded from out the ceiling, so that the elderly gentleman was obliged to get to his feet, and, turning awkwardly about, staring overhead, continued to address his mother: a most heartrending sight. And tho' Professor Crosby, aided now by Dr. Eglinton, laid restraining hands upon him, and insisted that the "spirit-voice" was merely that of the medium, projected by skillful magic across the room, Dr. Dodd paid them no heed—in fact, he urged them away, and shook himself free.

This pathetic spectacle continued for some minutes, Dr. Dodd turning in wild circles, crying, "Momma! Momma!" while the other gentlemen made every effort to calm him, and to explain the phenomenon by plausible rationalist terms: *telepathy, hypnosis,* and *ventriloquism.* Dr. Eglinton insisted that one could very nearly see the medium's lips moving, if one observed closely; Sir Patrick Koones noted that he had been present at a similar incident, in London, during the investigation of the notorious Florence Cook, a trance medium whose tricks had never been fully exposed.

A vague spectral emanation appeared in a corner of the parlor, near the ceiling, naturally exciting much comment; and this, I am unhappy to say, so excited Dr. Dodd that he staggered and lost consciousness, falling to the floor in a dead faint. His colleagues immediately ministered unto him, but to no avail—the poor man could not be aroused: and so it was thought best to carry him from the room, and to attempt to continue with the séance, as quickly as order was restored.

"A very clever trick, Miss!" Dr. Eglinton said, shaking his fist at the insensible medium (who had not moved for some minutes, and gave no indication even of breathing), so trembling with rage that his jowls and chins quivered, and his eyes fairly started out of his head. "A very clever trick, but one, as you shall see, that can only be played on an old fool who has already lost half his wits!"

(That this peculiar voice, and the ectoplasmic manifestation that appeared to accompany it, belonged to the spirit of Deirdre's *Mrs. Dodd* —and that *Mrs. Dodd* was in actual fact Dr. William Dodd's mother—I simply cannot verify, having no way of knowing. In any case the unfortunate gentleman so fiercely *believed* his mother had appeared to him, that his reason was to be permanently unhinged; and, after a number of embarrassing episodes involving him in his position as President of the Society for Psychical Research, in Spiritualist circles of the lowest and most suspect nature, he was to be not only divested of his office, but, by a judicious action of his sons and heirs, declared *non compos mentis* and hospitalized in a private sanitarium in Newport, where he died not soon after. These sorrowful events lying still in the future, and no one guessing at them on the evening of the investigation, the séance continued, with Dr. Stoughton uneasily assuming command.)

As if even the spirits had grown sober, after the spectacle of so distinguished a gentleman being o'ercome, and carried bodily out of the room, there was an interlude of some time—upward of an hour, by most estimates—when the séance, skillfully and yet courteously guided by the young physician, assumed the contours of a more traditional session, in which the spirits of certain deceased relatives of members of the audience spoke forth, moderated by *Father Darien* (who introduced himself briefly and modestly, choosing not to dwell, as he ofttimes did, upon the grisly nature of the Iroquois's methods of torture). The great-grandfather of Dr. Phineas O'Shea, a Society member of many years' standing, who had always prided himself on his ability to sympathize with both the *Rationalists,* and the *Spiritualists,* among his wide circle of acquaintances, addressed him in a hearty, jubilant voice, alluding to such private information as regards the O'Sheas in general, and Dr. Phineas in particular, as to leave the respected gentleman "in no doubt whatsoever" concerning the authenticity of the spirit, and the miraculous gifts of the medium. The husband of Mrs. Minnie Cunningham addressed her, in a voice in which concern and amused impatience were intermixed, at first greatly startling the lady, and then consoling her, when he spoke to her "pressing concern"—the vexations she was suffering in her home, as a consequence of an old housekeeper who had acquired *loose and clacking dentures,* and who, Mrs. Cunningham thought, could be neither dismissed nor "spoken to," considering the delicacy of the situation. (The deceased Mr. Cunningham promised his wife that, upon the morn, the problem would be resolved: for he would see to it that the offending creature was visited in the night by a spirit, doubtless a relative of hers, who would impart the much-needed information, that the dentures should be attended to at once.) An interlude of some tearful emotion occurred, when the spirit of *Mrs. Jane Clemens* was brought forward, in quivering luminous ectoplasmic form, calling out to her belovèd son Sam: with the result that, the disguised Samuel Clemens (our own "Mark Twain") tore off his false beard of curly black whiskers, and, stammering, announced that he *was* present: and most eager to hear what his mother had to say. The deceased Jane Clemens informed her famous son that she spent nearly all of her time praying for him, and attempting to supervise his life, so far as she could, meeting with "some resistance," of a kind he doubtless comprehended —for, in certain manuscripts of his, there were still egregious cuss words to be found, and unspeakable infelicities of idiom, having to do with clothing of a private nature ("bloomers," "pantalets," "breeches" being among the most offensive): all of which, I am relieved to say, the author promised to excise from his writings in the future. Mrs. Clemens chided him further for the improvidence of his ways—his penchant for the theater, rich food and alcohol, fancy dress, and billiards—and the repentant gentleman, tears streaming down his manly cheeks, hastened to kneel in the aisle to receive his mother's blessing; and promised, from that day forward, to live his life more honorably. (Which, I am unhappy to say, "Mark Twain" failed to do!—for we know how the life of luxury drew him, and the spiritual sloth of sybaritism, and the even greater sloth of rank pessimism. Nor did he acknowledge Deirdre of the Shadows with anything approaching respect: it was, in fact, to Malvinia Morloch herself that the cynical man of letters would dismiss Spiritualism as "mental dyspepsia"—"*spooks* being a higher form of *flatulence.*")

This interim passed, however, with increasing excitement, the proofs of the medium's authenticity being such that, by common consensus among the membership, she would surely have gained a resounding majority vote in her favor: much of the credit to be attributed to the courtesy and efficiency of young Dr. Stoughton, who tempered his questions of the contact spirit *Father Darien* with a constant regard for the physical condition of the medium—who, it must be said, gave so ethereal an appearance, with her staring sightless eyes and waxen skin, as to seem hardly more than a spirit herself. Perhaps because the séance was progressing with so little difficulty, and the audience so clearly disposed in Deirdre's favor, those gentlemen of the committee who harbored a secret loathing for all things supernatural—Dr. Eglinton and Professor Crosby primarily—interrupted, insisting to Dr. Stoughton that control was too slipshod: it was often the case that an investigating committee monitor more closely the medium's physical condition, by checking blood pressure, pulse, temperature, and so forth, and by determining whether the "spirits' voices" were in fact ventriloquist tricks.

"I cannot, for my part, pass any judgment approaching the favorable," Dr. Eglinton said, "if I am forbidden to examine the candidate more closely. This sort of thing, after all—highly entertaining as it is!—has hardly the rigorous control of the scientific laboratory, where truth is investigated without sentiment."

"And I concur," Professor Crosby said at once, half rising in his chair, to stare at the insensible medium. "It is all most unscientific. It is all most slipshod and sentimental."

Dr. Stoughton quietly objected: the hour was late, Deirdre of the Shadows was clearly exhausted, and perhaps in danger of collapse; and even the audience, for all their rapt attention, doubtless suffered fatigue. Tho' the youthful physician spoke with necessary deference to his elders, he did not draw back from suggesting that, a good deal having transpired that evening, which should deserve the contemplation of *all* witnesses, it might be best now to adjourn. "For I hardly believe that Dr. Dodd would countenance much further strain on the young lady's powers," he said.

"Nonsense," Dr. Eglinton said. "The medium is always proud of her 'trances'—she does not want to be awakened, and the carnival stopped."

"I shall examine her," Professor Crosby said, rising from his chair. "I have here—as you see—one or two pertinent instruments."

"*I* shall examine her," Dr. Eglinton said. "Dr. Dodd clearly indicated that *I*, as an internist and gynecologist of some modest reputation, should examine the young woman, under the auspices of the Society."

"And yet," Sir Patrick Koones said, in a low rapid voice, "it can hardly be done in public. We must clear the room of spectators, or adjourn to a more suitable place."

"If Dr. Dodd were present—" Dr. Stoughton began, but was interrupted by Dr. Eglinton's sneering aside: "But the old man is *not* present, is he?—and *we* are now in charge."

Whether the three gentlemen would have succeeded in clearing the hall of the invited guests, or whether the proposed examination would have taken place in another part of the building, one cannot know; it is likely, too, that Dr. Stoughton, and one or two others, feeling keenly the injustice of the procedure, would have insisted upon an adjournment, thereby averting disaster.

However, Dr. Eglinton had no sooner uttered his abominable remark, than the gas jets flickered anew, and Mr. Oakley-Hume shuddered aloud at another severe chill, which appeared to pass up his legs from the floorboards; and Mr. Sinnett snatched at his notebook, which suddenly rose from the table, and spiraled away out of sight. "The deuce!" Mr. Sinnett exclaimed. "What has happened?"

Dr. Stoughton was to state afterward, in making his deposition to the Chief Magistrate of New York County, that he had known immediately that something irremeable had occurred, by a subtle alteration of the temperature, and by his uneasy recollection of the medium's warning words—to the effect that, should wicked spirits be loos'd, she might be incapable of restraining them. ("Indeed," Dr. Stoughton explained to the authorities, and by his testimony quite exonerated the medium herself, of any possibility of wrongdoing, "it should have been a miracle for the poor young lady to have affected the course of the events at all, since her delicate constitution was so taxed by the examination, she was very nearly in a dead faint; and must have been entirely insensible of what happened about her.")

Professor Crosby, clutching several instruments of a gleaming surgical nature, had pushed back his chair, and was about to proceed boldly to the medium, in order, as he put it, "to forcibly examine her, and expose the shameful fraud to the assemblage of gulls and dupes"; but was restrained by Mr. Oakley-Hume, who murmured, with great compassion and distress, that it was a "most ungentlemanly procedure, in which he could have no part." Mr. Sinnett had wandered to one side of the oval parlor, seeking his notebook (which appeared to have vanished, tho' it was to be found, upon the morn, in one of the horse troughs on the north side of Gramercy Park), being aided in his activity by several sympathetic members of the audience. Sir Patrick Koones complained aloud, with some alarm, of the truly severe chill, which not only arose from the carpet, but descended from the ceiling, with a disconcerting effect upon his bald head; and Dr. Eglinton began to wipe and swat the air close about him, as if driving off flies, being afflicted, of a sudden, with something invisible but highly persistent, that both *bit* and *kissed* at his face. "What is it—who is it—how *dare* you!" the astonished gentleman cried.

Attention was now turned to Dr. Eglinton, who stumbled to his feet, continuing to mutter excitedly, and swatting at the air. A child's voice was suddenly heard—singing and crooning—high, shrill, mischievous, yet of an almost distressing *sweetness,* uncanny to hear. Dr. Eglinton did not find the presence sweet, however, but cried angrily: "The Devil! —the very Devil! D——n creature! Away with you! None of that, d'you hear! I am *Dr. Percival Eglinton!*"

Out of the empty air came the melodious voice: "Love love love love *love*"—followed by a tinkling giggle.

"I say, how dare you! I say, none of that!" Dr. Eglinton remonstrated, his face flushing red.

"Love Doctor! Love Doctor! *Kiss kiss kiss kiss!*" the naughty spirit cried. (This was of course the child *Bianca,* and never had she possessed, at any previous séance, so extraordinary a charm! Indeed, I am powerless to evoke, for the skeptical reader, the nearly unbearable beauty of her voice—its winsome sweetness, its pristine innocence, yet, withal, its *teasing girlishness.* But every witness to Dr. Eglinton's collapse was to attest, afterward, that the child's voice—to whomever it belonged—must have had a heavenly origin, being so angelic: and that the physician's furious swatting and pummeling of the air, seemed greatly in excess of the situation.)

"Lips brushing mine—arms about my neck—murderous little teeth—I say, stop! D——n slut! I will have you put in chains! I will have you flogged!—flayed!—dissected!"

And the darling little girl merely crooned and teased, quite invisible to the assemblage, save in her remarkable effect upon Dr. Eglinton.

This contretemps involved perhaps as little as ten minutes, tho', in the judgment of most witnesses, the time appeared to be much protracted for so it is, that eyewitnesses can rarely gauge the duration of time, without falling back upon mechanical means. Very little sympathy was evoked by the spectacle of the dignified gentleman stumbling about, in rage, and then terror, for it was generally believed that the child's teasing was altogether innocent, and the *kissing* merely *kissing.* (Which would have been quite shocking in a mature female spirit, but was, surely, no more than a sign of babyish affection in *Bianca.*) Dr. Eglinton shouted —begged—whined—whimpered: and his fellow committee members made every effort to calm him, tho' risking the danger (which poor Sir Patrick Koones did not entirely escape) of being struck by him in his frantic pummeling. As if to expose Dr. Eglinton to the weakest eye, the gas jets not only regained their full strength, but appeared somewhat brighter than ordinary; and, as I have said, the poor gentleman drew no sympathy from the audience, and even, it is sorrowful to report, some merriment at his expense—for he *did* look a fool, stumbling and crashing about, as if set upon by a hive of hornets, and not merely a child-spirit's kisses!

Dr. Stoughton remonstrated with Dr. Eglinton, not guessing at the seriousness of the situation, and perhaps believing, in his own confusion, that Dr. Eglinton was *imagining* the assault, and that argument could reason him out of it. Professor Crosby stood with his surgical instruments at the ready, a sneer twisting his lips: for his old rival Eglinton was being quite humiliated, and he saw no reason not to enjoy the spectacle. Mr. Oakley-Hume, his hand pressed to his heart, pleaded in a low voice to the frightened Mr. Sinnett to help him from the "accursèd chamber before it was too late, and all were destroyed," which Mr. Sinnett needed no further prompting to do: whereupon both gentlemen left the parlor, under cover of the general confusion. (In writing up his famous account of the evening for the Boston *Journal,* Mr. Sinnett averred that it was only the feebleness of his companion's constitution that saved both their lives —which was, I am convinced, a grave exaggeration. "In any case," Mr. Sinnett declared, for the *Journal*'s thousands of fascinated readers, "there can be no doubt from this day forward: *Spirit World does exist, and is hardly to be trifled with, by even the most distinguished scientists.*")

Now Dr. Eglinton pawed and clutched at his clothing, so writhing about that his gray frock coat tore under one arm: a sight that repulsed the ladies, and many of the gentlemen. Dr. Stoughton and Sir Patrick Koones being temporarily routed, Professor Crosby set his instruments aside, and went to seize his colleague by the shoulders, declaring that "the charade was about over," whereupon, to everyone's astonishment, he too began at once to swat and strike at the air, and rub his bewhiskered face roughly, muttering: "Begone, d'you hear! Begone! What is it! Who—!"

I should have noted, perhaps, that during this time the entranced medium remained seated as before, rigid as a statue, and as sightless, on her raised platform, discreetly apart from the gentlemen's difficulties. Where her etheric body roamed—where her imagination dwelt—I cannot say; nor could Deirdre herself, recall upon wakening. And during this time members of the audience had risen to their feet, in amusement, alarm, or simple keen interest, crowding to the front of the room, tho' not o'erly near—wisely fearing the contagion of the child-spirit's assault. (A number of Society members, primarily ladies, made their exit from the room, feeling great strain and fatigue, and not a little apprehension, that perhaps—tho' they were *not* Popish in their fear of Spiritualism—the Devil might have a hand in it, and not merely disinterested private spirits.)

Now both Dr. Eglinton and Professor Crosby were being attacked by the invisible *Bianca,* perhaps with the aid of other spirits, for so it seemed afterward, judging from the extent of their injuries; and the situation, tho' ludicrous to behold, soon darkened, and revealed its sinister aspect, when Dr. Eglinton crashed heavily to the floor, and rolled and pitched about. Poor Dr. Stoughton clearly had no idea what to do, for relative youth and inexperience, and a certain reserve of character, ill equipped him to handle such emergencies: he clutched and tugged at his hair; ran to Deirdre of the Shadows and begged her to awaken, and put a halt to the spirits' persecution; then ran back to the struggling gentlemen, remonstrating with them, and near-sobbing in his distress: for how unfortunate it was, that his first experience as comptroller of a Spiritualist session, should end in such chaos!

"Gentlemen! Gentlemen! You must come to your senses!" the distracted young man cried. Whereupon a vast assemblage of spirits laughed heartily—and the cruel gas jets glowed stronger than ever.

The investigation of the Society for Psychical Research into the mediumship of Deirdre of the Shadows became a landmark in American Spiritualist research, and acquired notoriety, as I hardly need record, far beyond Spiritualist circles. That two examiners were tormented by spirits *to their deaths,* and a third examiner so deranged that his relatives were soon obliged to hospitalize him, impressed upon the scientific community the gravity of taking too lightly Spiritualist claims; and impressed upon the public in general the formidable powers of Spirit World. It goes without saying that Deirdre of the Shadows became so famous, and so sought after, that she was obliged to go into seclusion for some months—and to afterward accept, as her clients, only a very élite group of ladies and gentlemen, whose fidelity to Spiritualism, and whose fervor in supporting its necessary worldly accoutrements, were exemplary.

"How *very* extraordinary!" Mr. Orlando Vandenhoffen was to observe, the following midday, when, at a late breakfast, he saw the blazing front page of the *Tribune,* with its lurid photographs, its two-inch red headlines, and exclamations. "How very—*very*—extraordinary!"

Malvinia, sensing that the news must concern her despised sister, grew deathly pale, but said not a word: indeed, she turned innocently aside, and occupied herself with rearranging a bunch of white and pink orchids, which had been delivered only minutes before.

"Ah, this medium—this 'Deirdre of the Shadows'—I am grateful to you, dear Malvinia," Vandenhoffen said, "for dissuading us from going to one of her sittings: for, as it turns out, she is not only a *genuine* medium, but a *lethal* one."

Not noticing that his mistress remained silent, her back to him, he continued to read the article, muttering aloud, and sucking and pulling at his mustache, frequently interrupting himself with ejaculations of alarm and horrified amusement. "Egad, *how* is it possible!—and yet, and yet—it seems that it *is* possible—for the *Tribune* would hardly lie," he said.

Malvinia succeeded in remaining silent, tho' her heart fluttered, and a violent pulse raced in her throat; and she very nearly drew blood, by biting so hard upon her lower lip. *I shall not inquire, I shall not know, she is nothing to me, I feel no curiosity, I am untouch'd. . . .*

And finally, after much muttering and *tsking,* Vandenhoffen relieved her suspenseful curiosity, by saying, in an amazed voice: "It seems, my dear, that two gentlemen—a Dr. Eglinton, and a Professor Crosby— of whom, I must say, I have never heard—were tormented to death last night, before some fifty eyewitnesses, here in the city—*by spirits.* It is evidently the first such instance in recorded history, and it took place but a scant mile south, at Gramercy Park! Amazing! Two gentlemen said to be in excellent health, in the prime of life, staunch Rationalists, *tormented to death by spirits*—have you ever heard anything more astonishing? It was discovered that their faces and throats, and much of their bodies, were mutilated by thousands of tiny serrated teethmarks, which had filled in with blood. How *very* extraordinary," Vandenhoffen mused uneasily. "One might suppose that—granting the existence of spirits, to begin with —they might have had the power to frighten the men to death: but to *bite* them to death, with such tiny teeth! Each of the victims, it says, lost less than a pint of blood; the wounds were quite superficial. Don't you think, Malvinia," Vandenhoffen said, turning to her, "it is *all* most extraordinary? And perhaps even 'historical,' in a manner of speaking?"

But Malvinia was staring sightlessly at the gorgeous orchids, which revealed, at their very centers—or did the terrified young woman imagine it?—tiny, almost imperceptible dots of red. For a long moment she was so transfixed, she could not speak; indeed, she could not move.

"I said, Malvinia," Vandenhoffen repeated, his voice edged with a coolness that had become, alas, all too familiar in recent months, "I said, don't you think it is all most extraordinary? This 'Deirdre of the Shadows,' and her carnivorous spirits, and the fact that two men were evidently murdered, not very distant from this room?"

Malvinia summoned the false, bright, brave strength of the stage, in giving an answer; and managed even to turn a pale, but quite composed, countenance to the gentleman who so resolutely addressed her. "Extraordinary? Such monstrousness? I might have said," she murmured, pausing for dramatic effect, "that I expect nothing less, from such low and vulgar quarters."

VII

"Unsung Americans..."

44

Loving, unquestioning obedience! Dependence! Cheerful resignation! What can be sweeter? To submit oneself wholly and contentedly into the hand of another; to surrender all appetite for the grossness of Self; to cease taking thought about oneself at all, and rest in safe harbor, at last, content to know that in great things and small we shall be guided and cherished, guarded and helped—ah, how delicious!—how precious! Even the poet Alexander Pope, who in other instances reveals a low, coarse, jesting soul beneath his smooth-tongu'd verse, spoke with rare wisdom when he penned—

> She who ne'er answers till a husband cools,
> Or, if she rules him, never shows she rules,
> Charms by accepting, by submitting, sways,
> Yet has her humour most, when she obeys.

Our subject of course is *Christian marriage:* that treasure so ignorantly spurned by three of our young Zinn ladies, in their frenzied quest for their own fortunes in the wide world, and, for a long period, held in contempt by a fourth: but never doubted by the fifth, our dear Octavia.

Octavia Theodora Zinn, blessèd in her station as *Mrs. Lucius Rumford,* of historic Rumford Hall. Wife and mother and mistress of a household: and as exemplary in all roles, as she had been while dwelling in the Octagonal House, as the loving daughter of excellent parents!

That a devout and dutiful Christian wife accepted with gratitude the vicissitudes of marital life, seeking rather to fulfill herself as her husband's belovèd helpmeet, than to pursue her own vanities, was never doubted by sweet Octavia; and accounts for much of the *placidity* and *industry* and *prayerful contentment* of her nature, during even the perilous years of this chronicle. By intrinsic temperament docile, trusting, and unquestioning, this well-bred young lady did not pine after an unseemly independence, whether of fortune or spirit; nor did she truly require instruction, by her religious mentor Reverend Hewett, or the elder ladies of the family, or such conscientious handbooks as those authored by Miss Edwina Kiddemaster, to comprehend the fact that the Husband is the natural head of the household, and that Our Heavenly Father is never more pleased than when His authority is honored, albeit on the humble, earthly plane, in the eager submission of Wife to spouse. *To love, honor, and obey*—never were these sacred words more gravely whispered, than by Octavia, as she knelt trembling at the altar of Trinity Church, beside her God-chosen bridegroom Mr. Rumford.

(If I feel compelled, at this point, to introduce the unhappy fact that, within a scant fourteen years of her marriage, the courageous Octavia was to mourn no less than *three deaths,* it is not with the coarse intention of dismaying the reader, but only to assure, in the very next breath, that these several tragedies merely strengthened Octavia's Christian faith, and compelled the innocent young woman to assume a stoic and matronly dignity all observers were to find most exemplary. "Dear child!" Great-Aunt Edwina herself was to exclaim, with tearful visage, upon the occasion of the third of these unlook'd-for deaths, forcibly clasping her niece's chill hands in her own; "how far you have journeyed, in so brief a span of time!—and with what remarkable bravery, equal, indeed, to any exhibited by any Kiddemaster, male or female, throughout our long history!" Whereupon the silently weeping Octavia replied, with dignity, and, it may have been, some slight pity for her agèd relative, who, in these final years, was increasingly susceptible to emotional spasms: "Ah, dear Aunt! It is Our Heavenly Father who guides us, and Jesus Christ who hourly grants me strength! I cannot claim a mortal source for bravery, not even in my precious Kiddemaster blood; nor in that fortitude I have some small hope of having inherited, from my belovèd father as well." The piety of such an answer splendidly revealing, to even the most skeptical of observers, the Christian excellence of which I have been speaking.)

Thus smooth-brow'd Octavia; whilst her wanton sisters plunge ever more distantly outward, in the perilous waters beyond Bloodsmoor.

That Octavia nonetheless harbored a protracted, albeit surreptitious and even outlaw, interest in their fates, and sought news of "Malvinia Morloch" and "Deirdre of the Shadows" whenever she could (usually by laying hands upon Philadelphia papers and magazines thoughtlessly brought to the country, by visiting relatives), and eagerly, tho' futilely, sought news of Constance Philippa, is surely not to be charged against her, but attributed, I insist, to a chronic softness of sentiment in her nature: as well as to her stubborn *sisterliness*, kept wisely hidden from Mr. Rumford (who would have been greatly incensed by it), as it had been hidden, for years, from Mr. and Mrs. Zinn. (Both the elder Zinns continued to forbid all mention of their renegade daughters in the Octagonal House, which sometimes caused confusion in Mr. Zinn's devoted assistant Nahum, who had reason to *guess* that Samantha had other siblings beside Octavia, yet hesitated to inquire, for fear of seeming impertinent, or awakening an old distress. By the time of Octavia's wedding to Mr. Rumford, however, all visible traces of Malvinia, Deirdre, and Constance Philippa had vanished from the household, and even those melodies favored, at the piano, by Malvinia, stood permanently banned. For such was John Quincy Zinn's hurt, and, it may have been, his manly pride as well, that he contented himself with believing his daughters *dead*, as well as *disgraced;* and the obedient Prudence wordlessly concurred in his judgment.)

Nevertheless, the mistress of staid Rumford Hall secretly knew of each of Malvinia Morloch's stage triumphs, and saved such clippings and magazine features as she could, hiding them beneath the silver-tissue in certain of the drawers of Grandmother Kiddemaster's wardrobe. She knew, tho' she dared not speak of it to anyone, of Malvinia's early success as a "saucy and mesmerizing" Rosalind, in *As You Like It;* she knew of Malvinia's Broadway fame as an "inspired comedienne" in *Dollars and Sense;* she knew of the relative failure of *Ah Sin,* and of Mark Twain's generous praise of Malvinia before the opening-night audience—as she was to know, to her incredulous dismay, some years later, of the crude gossip that alleged a *liaison* between her sister and that famous man of letters. She knew of a triumphant tour to the West Coast, with the road company of the popular melodrama *She Lov'd Him Dearly,* from which Orlando Vandenhoffen was to withdraw with such surprising abruptness. It goes without saying that Octavia never spoke of Malvinia to her husband or his numerous relatives, no more than she would have voiced a wish to journey to New York City in order to attend a theatrical entertainment!—such meretricious vanities now being excluded forever from her life.

Octavia followed, too, and likewise followed in earnest secret, the parallel career of her sister Deirdre, in which she was aided by the happenstance that the housekeeper of Rumford Hall, an elderly German widow, received in the mail such Spiritualist periodicals as *The Seer, The Far Shore, The Spiritist,* and *The Theosophist,* which regularly took note of "Deirdre of the Shadows," soon proclaimed as the "unquestioned Seeress of the Age." Octavia read avidly, albeit with a necessary repugnance, for she knew that Spiritualism was fraudulent, and her sister quite lost to all standards of civilization and decency; she knew that Our Saviour redeems us, and assures us of immortality in His bosom, and that Heaven is presided over by Father, Son, and Holy Ghost, and that, according to Episcopal doctrine, mediums could have no role in any of this—the mechanism of the church being one of masculine authority, and beyond all usurpation, as it was beyond all comprehension, by persons of the weaker sex. Nonetheless, Octavia did follow Deirdre's career, and knew of the early accolades bestowed upon her, and of the generally respectable coverage by the Spiritualist "muckraker" Colonel Lynes, for the New York *Daily Graphic;* and, of course, of the infamous investigation by the Society for Psychical Research, which had resulted in the deaths of two —nay, three—gentlemen, from causes never to be satisfactorily explained in the public press. How Octavia would have liked to speak of such things to her housekeeper, how she would have liked to broach the subject of Spirit World in general, and "Deirdre of the Shadows" in particular! But, fortunately, the credulous young mistress of Rumford Hall was saved from such folly, by a sober awareness of the necessary distance between herself and the servant class. "One does not speak *with* servants, but only *to* them"—so Miss Edwina Kiddemaster herself had oft counseled, in such manuals as *The Christian House & Home,* and *The Young Wife's Almanac;* and tho' she sometimes felt o'ercome with loneliness (Mr. Rumford being of a taciturn nature), Octavia successfully resisted speaking to her housekeeper, on any matters save those strictly regarding the house.

And she would have as readily raised the subject of *Spiritualism* to Mr. Rumford, as she would have the subject of *theatrical entertainments!*— knowing with what astonished scorn, and choler, that sombre Christian gentleman would have greeted it. (For, despite his husbandly concern for her physical enfeeblement, upon the occasion of her first miscarriage, Mr. Rumford had been incensed at Octavia's delirious assertion that she had had a *premonition* of the catastrophe—for such bespoke pagan superstition in his eyes, and "the crudest sort of women's prattle.")

So the years passed, and the new mistress of Rumford Hall shared her secrets with no one: having become estranged from Samantha (who, fanatically engrossed in Mr. Zinn's numerous projects, had simply no interest in Octavia's married life, or in her children—and made no pretense of it); and seeing but rarely her younger cousins from Philadelphia, who frequently visited Bloodsmoor, but found Rumford Hall "too distant," and Mr. Rumford possibly too forbidding. Of course Octavia often visited with Mrs. Zinn, and enjoyed visits from her, but naturally she could not speak of Malvinia and Deirdre to her mother—she dared not even allude to them. (Save to say, with a sigh, that she sometimes missed her old bedchamber!—her dear cozy old room, and the cozy double bed! —but knew it was mere foolishness, so childish a sentiment.)

Yet, a most peculiar incident occurred one dark wintry afternoon, when Mrs. Zinn and Octavia were companionably knitting together, in the drafty parlor at Rumford Hall, and Octavia's eye chanced to fall upon a copy of the Philadelphia *Ledger* which she had perused at some length, and which was about to be discarded, and her tongue got the better of her, as it ofttimes did: and she thoughtlessly blurted out, that she should very much like Mrs. Zinn to look at a photograph in the paper, and deliver her opinion.

In silence Mrs. Zinn took the much-folded newspaper from her daughter, and in silence she adjusted her reading glasses, while Octavia bent over her knitting, her face flushed with excitement, and some little apprehension. (The dear child! How impetuous, how ill considered her whims might be! It was a custom in these days for mother and married daughter to knit and sew baby things, month upon month, and, indeed, year upon year, in anticipation of an imminent birth, without once descending to the coarseness of mind that would feel the need to *state their mutual purpose:* such indelicacies as "pregnant," "going to have a baby," and "expecting" being quite out of place in genteel surroundings. Yet such had been Octavia's childish excitement, upon the occasion of her first pregnancy, in the first year of her marriage to Mr. Rumford, that she had, of a sudden, as soon as she and Mrs. Zinn were alone together, blurted out: "Oh, Momma! I think it has happened! I mean—I think it will happen! Mr. Rumford shall have another son!"—these words uttered with such incredulity, Mrs. Zinn had hardly the heart to chastise Octavia, for the unseemliness of her diction and deportment.)

Now Mrs. Zinn frowned at the *Ledger,* and the bracketing creases beside her mouth deepened. What had this photograph of a stranger to do with her? A gentleman not yet thirty, with emphatic dark eyebrows, and calmly gazing eyes in which some measure of irony might be noted: smooth-shaven, angular of face, the lines of the jaw bespeaking stubbornness, the thin-lipped mouth set firm. He was, perhaps, with difficulty, *handsome*—yet a certain arrogance of demeanor quite offended the eye. "Philippe Fox" of the Rock Bluff Mining and Milling Company, of the San Pedro Valley in Arizona, recently appointed Deputy Assistant to the United States Marshal for southeastern Arizona. The singularity of this appointment, the *Ledger* noted, was that the telegram was received not five minutes before Fox was to be hanged, by local authorities, in Tombstone—"a happenstance not greatly irregular in the West," the *Ledger* continued, "though the precision of the timing must surely be noted."

For a very long time Mrs. Zinn contemplated the young gentleman in the photograph, and then, making no haste, with an expulsion of wearied breath that might have been a maternal sigh, she hoisted her considerable bulk forward in her chair, and thrust the offensive newspaper into the fireplace, where it burst into gladsome flames at once, and was extinguished in a moment. Octavia, staring sightless at her knitting, felt her pulses race, and murmured boldly: "That gentleman—whosoever he may be—caught my eye—I know 'twas foolish—the features very distantly resembling those of—of— Ah, I *know* 'twas foolish, and I hope you will not scold, Mother!"

Mrs. Zinn picked up her knitting, and one could not have judged, from the mechanical rapidity with which her well-practiced fingers worked, and her rigorous posture, whether she was displeased with her daughter, or no. After some minutes she said: "It is hardly a time in your life, dear daughter, in which to allow your imagination free rein. If you are troubled by wild, scattered, unproductive thoughts, I shall insist that you spend more time at prayer, both in the morning, and before retiring at night. And I shall leave for you, this very day, a small bottle of Miss Emmeline's—which, as you know, Dr. Moffet most strenuously prescribes for my sensitive nerves, and which, I am pleased to say, does have some minimal effect. At this time in your life, dear Octavia," Mrs. Zinn said, deliberately spacing out her words, so that, with great subtlety, she was able to make explicit what must needs have remained unspoken between them, so causing sweet Octavia to blush with embarrassment and pleasure, "at this sacred time in your life, in which, alas, the blood oft runs riot with fanciful notions delved from God knows where, and one conjures up fatuous ideas, as exotic and unspeakable as a sudden ravening appetite for fruit out of season, it is wise, my dear daughter, to surrender yourself fully to Our Heavenly Father, that nothing go amiss: Our Heavenly Father, and Miss Emmeline's—which, if you do not allow me to forget, I shall leave for you today."

Chastised, yet gratified, Octavia glanced up shyly from her knitting: but Mrs. Zinn did not meet her eye, and was now as placidly knitting, as if no problematic exchange had occurred. The sudden outburst of flames in the fireplace having died back, and the birch logs burning as steadily as before, perhaps nothing *had* occurred.

"Miss Emmeline's Remedy—ah yes!—I am very grateful to you, Mother—very grateful indeed: but I am already under Dr. Moffet's prescription for that very medicine, and do find it salubrious," Octavia murmured.

There being nothing further to say on the subject, mother and daughter continued to knit companionably, until teatime, in agreeable silence.

45

The trials of Octavia Zinn in her alter'd state as Mrs. Lucius Rumford, wife, mother, and mistress of old Rumford Hall, are of so dark-visagèd a character, and so redolent of despair, that, were I, as the narrator, not confident that the young lady's fortitude in meeting them, and her exemplary Christian behavior throughout, would not inspire rather than horrify the reader, I would throw down my pen forthwith: for of what value is a book, or any manifestation of art, or, indeed, any human experience whatsoever, that does not contribute to the moral betterment of mankind, and the strengthening—nay, universalizing—of the Christian religion? That this sacred mission is inexorably bound up with the chronicle of Progress in our great nation, and that *Christian morality, Progress,* and the *American People,* are to be grasped as one resounding anthem, doubtless sounding through Heaven even now, cannot be too stridently claimed, especially in an epoch in which all standards of behavior, and even, alas, all standards of grammatical discourse, have been thrown into tumult; that it is the Author's sacred obligation, no matter his or her subject, to conform to these requirements, and to present withal a smiling countenance, in the face of all adversity, seems to me incontestable. It is not remiss to quote from a sovereign address made to the Senate at about the time of Octavia's second confinement (her first having blessed Mr. Rumford with a hearty little male heir, splendidly formed, and of perfect health: Godfrey II, named for his belovèd great-grandfather, who held with palsied hands, and stared at with urgent, somewhat protruding rheumy eyes, this hallowed infant), the address delivered, in fact, by the very Albert J. Beveridge who would, in later years, become one of John Quincy Zinn's strongest advocates in Congress, and a vociferous supporter of government-financed scientific research. (Alas, I trust the reader will forgive me in leaping ahead of myself for, fired by my duty to transcribe Octavia's tale, and half tremulous at the challenge, I find that my nerves are all shatter'd this morn, and I scarcely know the date on my calendar, let alone the date of my narrative.) In any case, Senator Beveridge's charge to the Senate is very akin in spirit to this author's sense of her own sacrosanct mission, tho' it emanated, surprisingly, from the crude Midwest, and not from the portals of old Philadelphia or Boston:

> Of all our race, God has marked the American people as His chosen nation to finally lead in the regeneration of the world. This is the divine Mission of America, and it holds for us all the profit, all the glory, all the happiness possible to man. We are humble trustees of the world's progress, and guardians of its righteous peace!

Thus the good Senator from Indiana; and so, too, it is to be hoped, this yet more humble trustee, your narrator.

The vicissitudes of fate, heaped upon the pious head of our poor dear Octavia, are such that almost call into question the sovereign justice of the universe: yet, Octavia's final happiness being so profound and lasting, one must concur, as Job did, that the ways of God are not our ways; and to be but dimly understood. That this sweetly docile, resolutely uncomplaining, and perfectly obedient young wife should experience not merely the agonies of several miscarriages (not markedly uncommon in our day), but the death of her beautiful infant daughter Sarah, her second-born, at the age of nine months, as she lay napping in her crib *undisturbed by any prior symptom;* that she should—alas, my eyes well with tears merely with the act of recording such sorrow!—be forced to witness the drowning of her firstborn, Little Godfrey, at the age of seven, on a beauteous and serene summer's day; and that she should suffer the heart-rending loss of her belovèd husband, in *the very unitary act of their connubial bliss,* in what was scarcely the thirteenth year of their wedlock—all this would paint a spectacle so deathly of visage, as to be quite unfit for perusal, save for the fact that our heroine *triumphed over despair* in each event, and emerged, in her forty-first year, as serenely unquestioning of her Maker's judgment, and as smooth-brow'd, as she had been in her childish virgin state! Such was Octavia's piety in her suffering, and her resolute refusal to cry her woes aloud, like other weak-minded creatures of her sex, that even the gentleman who was to become her second husband promised to bethink himself of his "irreligious nature," and "give some possible credence" to the Christian faith, upon which, I am troubled to say, he had, in his youth, turned his back for reasons rather of ignorance than of congenital wickedness. (This second marriage, which I am quite content to see as a *happy event,* despite the bridegroom's free thinking, will take place beyond the temporal confines of this narrative; and the reader is begged to think no more of it.)

It is strongly advis'd that the bride shall not succumb to unseemly or ill-timed emotion, in the bridal bed: neither to an outburst of tears, nor to an abrupt expression of fright. So Octavia read, and was duly perplexed by, in Dr. Mudrick's *The Christian Marriage and Family,* pressed into her hand, with a wordless smile, by Cousin Rowena Kale, some weeks before Octavia's wedding. *Unseemly or ill-timed emotion! Tears, nor—fright!* The impressionable young maiden tormented her curiosity, for many an hour, over the precise meaning of these words: at a time when she might better have occupied herself with more fructifying tasks, such as the completion of her trousseau, and the monogramming of her linen. She could not seek an audience with Mrs. Zinn, who was greatly absorbed at this time, and quite happily so, with a thousand and one details pertaining to the wedding; nor would she have dared approach Mr. Zinn, who, throughout that difficult decade, the Eighties, labored most piteously on his aluminum-sided dirigible, for which he had, alas! such noble hopes—only to see them dashed to the ground, and shattered in a million fragments, when, in 1888, the German aeronaut Wolfert made an ascent in a large dirigible of similar construction, *equipped with a Daimler gasoline engine:* an advance poor John Quincy Zinn was forced to assess as truly revolutionary, tho' it came from abroad, and not out of his native country.

"I know I should not succumb to ignoble self-pity," Octavia murmured to her only remaining sister, "but I should dearly like, Samantha, to speak with someone—someone, I mean, who has trod this particular pathway before me, and might offer some advice. But Mother has no time for me now; nor does Father; and Great-Aunt Edwina merely presses her books upon me, which, I own, I have already read a dozen times, and very nearly memorized."

Samantha stared at her sister with unsmiling eyes, as if vexed that Octavia should detain her thusly, in the corridor outside their bedchambers, when the morn was so fresh and promising, and the workshop above the gorge beckoned. She wore her plainest calico gown, with an apron not inordinately fresh; her fine red hair, hastily arranged in a chignon that owed more to practicability than to feminine grace, was covered by a morning cap barren of all lace, and adorned with but a half-dozen spiritless ribbons. Tho', of late, for some quite unfathomable reason, Samantha appeared to be maturing almost daily, and growing, to Octavia's surprised eye, ever more lithesome and pretty, her manner in regard to Octavia was very frequently impatient, and, at its best, condescending, despite the significant fact that Octavia was several years older than

Samantha, and ought to have commanded both respect and affection.

Now the malapert young miss said, in response to Octavia's heart-felt declaration: "Dear Octavia, Mother has time for no one *but* you. She rushes about the two households, commandeering all the servants, sending away to the city for every sort of fribble and furbelow, and worrying aloud that all her plans will go asunder, if the *weather* does not cooperate on your wedding day, or Mr. Rumford vanishes into thin air—which, considering the dryness and gravity of that excellent gentleman, I think an unlikely possibility. And Father, our dear Father: naturally he has no time for you, who has no time even for himself. Have you marked of late the o'erabundance of his beard, and its asymmetry; the fatigue that underlies his cheeriest smile; the nervousness and distraction of his manner? The John Quincy Zinn who resides with us, Octavia, is but our father by a happenstance of nature, for which we must be grateful, and not greedy: his true allegiance, like his true identity, resides elsewhere, in the pantheon of the ages, where he shall someday assume his rightful place alongside Da Vinci, Michelangelo, Newton, and Franklin. And you wish," Samantha murmured, with a cruel pitying half-smile, "*you* wish to discuss wedding-day flummery with him!"

So abash'd was Octavia by this well-delivered speech, and so intimidated by her sister's cool green gaze, that she fairly shrank away, with many profuse apologies; and allowed her impatient sister to pass.

Poor Octavia! It was a measure of her loneliness, within her own family, and the somewhat disordered state of her sensibilities, that, in those weeks preceding the wedding, she succumbed to many a lachrymal outburst, and would dearly have loved to be but a carefree child again, sharing her bedchamber with pretty little Malvinia. "How you have deserted me, my heartless sister!" Octavia murmured, seeing again the winsome image of her younger sister, and the bright-glittering mischief of her periwinkle eyes. "But I shall have my revenge upon you—I daresay —for *I* shall be a married woman within a fortnight, while you—piteous creature—are but a *fallen* woman, scorned by all decent persons, and bent upon the pathway to perdition!"—this ejaculation so little pleasing the unhappy girl, she surrendered to a fresh spasm of weeping, and hid away in her bedchamber, behind a locked door, to be summoned out only by the repeated demands and protestations of Mrs. Zinn: for Madame Blanchet and her young French seamstress had arrived, and the day's fittings must begin.

Miss Octavia Zinn's emotional vagaries, in those confused days before she became Mrs. Lucius Rumford, will afford perhaps a morbid interest, to those harboring a curiosity concerning such extreme states of mind; but cannot have a general interest, nor, I am confident in asserting, would Octavia herself have granted them any value, after she had become initiated into the honorable obligations of wifehood. That she alternated between ecstatic flights of *fancy,* and moments of unmitigated *dread;* that she hurried about the house humming and singing beneath her breath, like a very young child anticipating Christmas, and then stopped short, and began to tremble, and weep, as if knowing that something hideous lay ahead; that she dwelt o'ermuch upon the grave, communing, in her heart, with her belovèd Grandmother Kiddemaster (whose spirit, the impressionable young lady halfway believed, dwelt in the enormous rosewood wardrobe with its happy abundance of drawers), or that, in impetuous reaction against such thoughts, she betook herself for long unauthorized walks in the wild forest above the gorge (so startling Mr. Zinn, Samantha, and Nahum, upon one embarrassing occasion, that the inventors believed they had seen a veritable ghost in the woods nearby!—a stumbling aimless figure in a light-colored gown, with a white cap upon its head that quite obscured its face); that she was continually dropping stitches in her knitting, or pricking her fingers with her needle, whereupon her fine Irish linen became dotted with blood—all this is hardly to Octavia's credit, yet has some small historical veracity, and suggests a surprising parallel, inaccurate in other respects, with Constance Philippa, in the weeks and days preceding *her* wedding. Indeed, so unbalanced did Octavia's judgment become, and so beclouded by spurious sentiment, that she found herself yearning for the companionship of her lost older sister, whose abstergent wit, and scorn for such frivolities as dress fittings, she believed would be most refreshing. But how dismaying, how unspeakable, Constance Philippa's crime!—to have broken the sacred bonds of matrimony *upon her very wedding night,* and to have brought such disgrace upon her family: for which she might never be forgiven, save perhaps in the other world. (And Octavia even found herself thinking, with a wistful melancholy, that she should not have minded, even, seeking solace from Deirdre: she might have crept into her bed, and the two of them might have shivered and hugged and wept, and Octavia could then speak of her own sudden terror of being *orphaned*—of all the imaginable fates, the most cruel.)

Cousin Rowena might have been expected to be of some aid, but her spirits were somewhat depressed, as a consequence of an apparent recurrence of the pregnant state, following close upon a grievous miscarriage, and several months' difficult convalescence: and so, apart from pressing into Octavia's hand Dr. Mudrick's invaluable book, she behaved rather evasively, and offered advice of an agreeably sunny, but rather general, nature, stating that Octavia, as a young bride, must remember at all times that the marriage bond is sacred, and the issue springing from it blessèd, and that Jesus Christ would never be far from Octavia's side, should she require His guidance. (She went on to say, with a queer gratified vehemence, that Delphine Martineau, who had once held her head so high, had truly backed *herself* into a tight corner, having married a "genuine" brute of a husband, who drank, gambled, and, it was rumored, *consorted with females of a certain classification.*)

On the very eve of her wedding day, Octavia found it difficult to sleep, and quite exhausted herself, with a feverish scribbling in her diary, of a most unnatural—and, indeed, uncharacteristic—nature. *I am visited by such thoughts!* the wayward young lady wrote, *I scarce know how to gauge them: a sudden hideous image of a skinned rabbit on the hearth, the poor thing freckled with blood; Grandmother Kiddemaster in her casket; a confus'd memory of the son of that Irish coachman of Grandfather's—I shall not sully the page with his name—for 'tis of little moment—as a young boy of perhaps twelve or thirteen, in the company of rough boys like himself—workers' sons, it may be—frolicking some distance downriver—bathing and splashing one another—and our little drawing and sketching class, led by the French governess Grandfather had secured for us for a brief spell, taken all unawares—and most affrighted—and—and I forget—* And, indeed, the o'erwrought girl did seem to have forgotten, not only what sight had so astonished her and her sisters, on the riverbank so many years before, but why, in fact, she was attempting to record it.

So she ripped the offending page out of her diary, and, bethinking herself of the entire project, that of recording her intimate thoughts over a period of some years, decided emphatically that the entire diary must be destroyed, before the morn: and spent an hour or more feeding the pages into her fireplace, that no evidence of *Octavia Theodora Zinn* should be preserved, when she took her rightful place as *Mrs. Lucius Rumford.*

46

It will come as no great surprise, to the mature reader, that our distraught heroine's apprehension regarding the wedding ritual, and the matrimonial bed, and Mr. Rumford himself, proved to be totally unfounded.

Indeed, upon the sunlit morn of her first day as Mrs. Rumford, the deeply gratified Octavia spent upward of an hour upon her knees, in the privacy of her dressing room, giving fulsome thanks to Our Heavenly Father, and to His belovèd Son, that she was at last a *wife,* and had been brought forever under the protection of a loving *husband.*

Octavia so lingered in the tearful bliss of prayer, and in fussing over a small wound on her right shoulder, which she had not wished her maid to see (for, negligible tho' the wound was, and emitting hardly a thimbleful of blood, it did present an angry, reddened, alarming appearance), that, upon descending at last to the breakfast room, as the hour chimed seven, she found Mr. Rumford already gone: and had to content herself with eating alone. It may have been the unfamiliarity of the room, with its high ceiling, and featureless walls, and somewhat grimy wainscoting; it may have been the curt manner of the elderly maid, whose oft-reiterated *Missus* had a singularly hissing sound; it may have been that Octavia dearly missed her bridegroom's presence, at so momentous an occasion as her first breakfast in Rumford Hall: in any case she had little appetite, forcing herself to swallow but two or three mouthfuls of coffee, and a mere half-piece of cold buttered toast.

Her heart beat in a flurry, and she closed again her moist eyes: summoning forth Mr. Rumsford's cherished countenance, and the dry, acerb odor of his muttonchop whiskers and hair, and the several words of affection and esteem he had uttered, the previous night, in the midst of his strange, protracted exertions. She hoped she had proven worthy of the *sanctity of the marriage bed,* of which her elders had spoken so emphatically, and yet so evasively; she dared to hope that blessèd issue would one day spring—she knew not altogether how—from that *unitary act,* into which Mr. Rumford had initiated her.

(As a consequence of her assiduous application of the cautionary words of Dr. Mudrick, to her own situation, Octavia had completely triumphed over a gross inclination to "succumb to unseemly or ill-timed emotion," and had, through a generally voluntary stratagem of her own discovery, succeeded in overcoming a childish propensity for both tears and fright. This was accomplished thusly: upon the very onset of Mr. Rumford's most vigorous, and, as it were, *corporeal* attentions to her body, Octavia had stuffed a considerable quantity of her lace-trimmed pillowcase into her mouth, to stifle her surprised screams; and, when that expedient proved but a stopgap, she had turned her head sharply, in order to gnaw at her own tender shoulder—not drawing a sufficient quantity of blood, fortunately, to attract Mr. Rumford's notice, or to deflect from the energetic procreative travail, to which that worthy gentleman had applied himself.)

The bride's most treasured reward being, upon the cessation of Mr. Rumford's prolonged wheezing and plunging and pumping, a scarce-audible, but unmistakable, blessing: *". . . wife."*

Rumford Hall was as distinctively an historical dwelling place as Kiddemaster Hall, tho' lacking grandeur and ostentation; and somewhat overcast, it may be, by an appearance of crabbèd gloom, emanating from the steep turreted roofs upon which mold, or dull-hued moss, grew in some profusion; and the tall narrow windows, many of them shuttered against the chill; and the flinty dark granite of which the building was constructed, which bespoke stolidity rather than grace, and sombre dignity rather than charm. The mansion house was composed of three storeys, with cellar and attic, and enjoyed no extraordinary vista, having been built not atop a hill, like Kiddemaster Hall, but rather in a sort of sunken glade, in which the ground was forever somewhat spongy underfoot, and, in springtime, badly puddled. About the main property a fifteen-foot brick wall had been constructed, with a narrow porter's gate, and a generous quantity of iron bars and spikes—not o'erly sharp, Octavia was quick to note, rusted with the years, and doubtless quite dull.

"Rumford Hall!" the young bride murmured under her breath, when, her bridegroom beside her, she had been driven through the main gate, still in her pretty wedding finery, with her filmy veil upon her head. "And I—*mistress!*"

Mr. Rumford being a gentleman of few words, and those judiciously chosen, with no flair for meretricious display, or drawing-room gallantry, he expended little time in introducing the new Mrs. Rumford to the senior members of the housekeeping staff, all the while stroking and fumbling at his sandy-hued beard (not in nervousness, I should hasten to report: for Mr. Rumford was of a settled, grave disposition), and told her, in a voice she might have wished were lowered, that she would not find her duties o'ertaxing, but they were demanding, and required a very early rising, and constant surveillance, and extreme discipline; for, servants being of a naturally lazy disposition (and a number here *were* Irish), they were most perspicacious in regard to any laxity, let alone slovenliness, either of a corporeal or a spiritual nature, in the mistress of the household. "And yet," Mr. Rumford said, his pale lips shifting in the semblance of a husbandly smile, whilst his pebble-colored gaze retained its necessary dignity, "and yet, my dear Mrs. Rumford, I do not doubt you: I do not doubt that you will fulfill your duties more than satisfactorily."

At which kindly words, the young woman did not trust herself to reply, but, with tear-brimming eyes, modestly bowed her head.

Where, during the romantic days of their courtship, Mr. Lucius Rumford had been to Octavia a scarce-grasped phenomenon, most readily approached in its elements (a top hat of gray silk and cotton correctly laid upon a table, or upon the carpet, with a pair of dark gloves correctly laid across the rim; a calling card of precisely the correct weight and quality of paper, the engraving having been done by Rilker & Sons of Philadelphia, in the typeface employed by all the best families; a pair of muttonchop whiskers in which sand-colored hues, and white, and silver, were unevenly blended, and which gave to his hoary face an almost youthful dash; and a distinctive odor, as of dry leaves, or ash), he was now, as her lawfully wedded husband, and the master of Rumford Hall, an altogether different experience: no less formidable, perhaps, and certainly no less impersonal, but a great deal more immediate, upon the necessity of their retiring to their bedchamber each night.

"My dear Mrs. Rumford," Mr. Rumford said, in a not unkindly voice, rising from his chair beside the fireplace (in which, to save fuel, a modest fire of somewhat damp oak logs burnt), "I believe it is, is it not? —time to retire."

Whereupon Octavia let fall her knitting, as if startl'd, and said, with alacrity: "Yes, Mr. Rumford, I am certain it is."

And the required servants were rung, and the married couple ascended the staircase, to their bedchamber on the second floor of the old house, and each retired to a dressing room, attended by a servant, and performed the necessary ablutions, and was helped to dress for the night: each step of which Octavia followed without question, tho' it did puzzle her, at first, but only at first (Octavia being not of a restive or skeptical mind), that, after she had bathed, she was required to put back on not only her chemise, and her petticoats, but her stiff whalebone corset as well—tho' she was allowed to leave off, for the night, her wide-rimmed crinoline, for which she was meekly grateful; and, of course, her wire-and-horsehair bustle, which was out of the question, under such nocturnal circumstances.

It is a radically different nighttime attire, from what I wore in my childish maidenhood, Octavia bethought herself, dressing in haste, but so, I must remember, is my elevated station in life now radically different, from all that preceded it.

Ofttimes Mr. Rumford allowed Octavia to know, by way of her lady's maid, that the master wished her to wear "her prettiest morning cap" too, or "her prettiest bonnet": which quite ruled out the possibility, for poor Octavia, of undoing her heavy hair, and extracting the "rats" and other false pieces, which so vexed her during the day, and were quite horrific at night. But she could comprehend the gentleman's distaste at being forced to glimpse a *bare head,* and gave some inward thanks, for her own part, that, whenever, in the privacy of their bedchamber, she chanced to catch sight of her husband, his nightcap was firmly ensconced on his narrow head, and not a single offending hair protruded.

Mr. Rumford had evidently a weakness, as well, for every variety of attractive trim—silk ribbons, and bows, and ruching, and fringing, and feathers, and beads, and tinsel, and sequins, and crocheting, and lace, and embroidery, and even gold brocade—some of which, taken from a massive cherrywood wardrobe in one corner of the bedchamber, must have belonged to Mr. Rumford's deceased wife. (Or wives: for Octavia had not been informed, and did not like to inquire, whether Mr. Rumford was a widower twice over, or but once; similarly, she was not altogether certain of the precise number of his children, and of their specific ages.)

"And here, ma'am, from the master's own hand," the maid might whisper, looping about Octavia's neck a feather boa of the softest swans-down, or entwining in her plump bodice a chain of sateen rosebuds: the which our Octavia accepted without question, and even with some nervous relief, for it would greatly embarrass her to feel *exposed,* in her physical self, even in the bridal bed: for the puritanical sternness of Mr. Rumford's Calvinist faith would brook no carelessness in such matters.

Upon many a night, then, and particularly during the first several months of their marriage, before Octavia's initial pregnancy became too evident, the young Mrs. Rumford was led by her lady's maid to the enormous fourposter bed, with the sombre silken canopy, and the high, hard horsehair mattress, to await her bridegroom, attired in a most re-markable, but certainly fetching, costume, of a sort that, in her virginal ignorance, she had not guessed *married women* wore: this costume consist-ing, for the most part (tho' naturally it varied from night to night, according to Mr. Rumford's instruction), of cotton chemise, and calico "cover," and whalebone corset (laced as tightly, alas! as its strings would bear), and yet another lightsome cover, and a half-dozen or more petticoats of silk, or satin, or cotton, or muslin, or poplin, all flounces and frills and puffs and draped folds, over which was arranged, by the harried mistress and her silent maid, as many as fifty or sixty or even seventy yards of trimming: in order to prevent, one must infer, Mr. Rumford's nocturnal gaze from encountering any unnecessary exposure of female flesh, which would surely have been repugnant to him, despite Our Heavenly Father's blessing of the bridal bed, and His emphatic imperative that Adam and Eve, and all their progeny, *increase* and *multiply*, that the earth may be inhabited, and Christianized.

The bride being carefully arranged on her side of the bed, some distance from the tasseled cord by which the servants were summoned, the maid noiselessly extinguished all but a single candle, and left the room; and, within a minute, bearing his own candle aloft, the bridegroom made his entrance from out his dressing room, in what might have been his slippers, or even his stocking feet, judging by the hushed quiet with which he approached the bed. The degree of darkness in the bedchamber varied considerably from night to night, as Octavia gathered, without, it cannot be too firmly stressed, making any deliberate effort to *recall*, or *compare*, or *analyze*, or *assess*, one marital night in terms of another, or any marital night in terms of a virginal night, from days long past: the precise degree of darkness being, in any case, problematic, since Octavia was not invariably in a position to know, Mr. Rumford either pointedly requesting, or wordlessly allowing her to know his request, that she acquiesce to a hood, of some lightsome and altogether agreeable material (muslin, it may have been, or the finest silk: but never wool, linen, or satin, which would have interfered gravely with her breathing, and become uncomfortably warm), the which accoutrement was generally drawn over her head, hair and head covering and all, with no haste, and certainly no roughness or impatience of manner, on the part of the master. Thus blinded, the young woman could not, with confidence, determine whether Mr. Rumford extinguished both candles, or one, or none: or whether, his mood quite naturally varying from night to night, he varied too the degree of illumination, and might even, unbeknownst to Mrs. Rumford, light an additional candle or two, or even the kerosene lamp, for his own purposes. (So scrupulously devoid of all unseemly curiosity was Mr. Rumford's new wife, that, upon the morn, oft finding herself alone in her bedchamber—Mr. Rumford having earlier departed, in order to lead favored menservants in prayer, and the daily Bible reading —she rang at once for her maid, and did not allow her frivolous gaze to wander about, to determine whether any curio of the previous night was in evidence, or even whether the wick in the kerosene lamp was more greatly scorch'd, than she could recall. For the lessons she had eagerly learned from out Miss Edwina Kiddemaster's many handbooks of wisdom, coupled with her dear mother's diplomatic hints along these lines, and, it scarcely needs to be said, her own intrinsic delicacy and feminine reticence of soul, cautioned her against any foolish expenditure of attention, in matters not of her concern, and which might provoke, in her belovèd husband, any acrimonious rejoinder, or—tho' it *rarely* came to this, as I am obliged to record—any exaggeration of manly force, during the *unitary act,* which might result in severe and punitive pain, in the nether regions, or elsewhere, in Mrs. Rumford. But I do make haste to explain, to the fair-minded reader, that the alarm and terror of the bridal night, and, indeed, the excruciating pain our childlike virgin endured, all the while most considerably grinding her teeth against her milk-soft shoulder, was but *rarely* repeated—and then, only, one infers, with the greatest reluctance on Mr. Rumford's part, rather out of a sense of castigatory discipline, than any animal passion, pleasure, or corporeal lust! *It cannot be a human member, not even a masculine, virile object of reproduction,* the affrighted virgin thought wildly, in her agony, upon the occasion of her bridegroom's laborious consummation of their love, that first night: *it must be, ah! I know not, dear God! of wood, or stone, or hardened wax, or some unnameable substance!*—these very words, near-sinful in what they suggest of rebelliousness, and indelicacy of character, being banished forever from the bride's thoughts, upon the dawn, and the resuming of the pure and unpolluted daylight world, in which she was again Mrs. Rumford, the new mistress of Rumford Hall.)

The bride being modestly arranged, as I have said, on her customary side of the bed, it was the usual procedure that her husband join her without any unnecessary word, let alone vulgar amorous prattle, either slipping over her docile head a hood of sufficient thickness, as to discourage her *witnessing* any incident, or the exposure of any bodily part, or expanse of skin, that would naturally offend her decorous eye; or so totally extinguishing the flame, that this precaution was rendered unnecessary. For which, despite her uneasiness, she could not fail to be grateful: tho' she had never doubted the assertions of her elders, that Mr. Lucius Rumford was a gentleman of the highest quality, and an excellent match for any young lady. ("This too is a great departure from all I had known, as an ignorant young girl," Octavia murmured inwardly, regarding the hood Mr. Rumford oft drew over her head, with its drawstring, tied sometimes rather tightly about her throat, and presenting problems of inhalation—about which the young wife did not complain, I should hasten to say.)

The actual methodology of the connubial union, so far as I am able to judge (being of maiden status myself, and altogether innocent of experiential knowledge, or any gross sort of speculation), is allowed to vary from husband to husband, within certain delimitations—procreation being, of course, the primary, indeed, the sole, enterprise. Yet in all instances of Christian wedlock it affirms itself as a sacred communion, but dimly understood even by the blessèd participants, who conform to God's prescription; and it does, surely, declare itself as that *true pangenesis,* in which the *epitome and pleroma of life* are rightly celebrated. All this is a mystery, I know, and its secrets are to be forever hidden from one residing in the celibate state, like myself!—yet I fully comprehend the grave obligation, free of the slightest taint of sin, the Christian Man and Wife perform, in the pangenesis of their sacred union.

In the absolute darkness in which she lay, Octavia would commonly hear divers noises: a prolonged, and sometimes quite noisy, rustling of fabric; an accelerated, laborious respiratory activity; the eruption into moaning, grunting, and exclamatory mutterings, in Mr. Rumford's own voice, surely, yet rarely recognizable as his. It was a measure of that gentleman's intrinsic fastidiousness, that he employed all restraint in addressing his wife directly, doubtless sensing that such blunt intimacy would disconcert her, whether in the privacy of their bedchamber, or in the public rooms of the Hall.

It was a measure as well of Mr. Rumford's high breeding that, for all his fussing and fumbling and pawing amidst her petticoats, and the accelerating frenzy of his passion, with its curious and oft-alarming results, Octavia but rarely noted that her things were seriously ripped, nor was her cap dislodged: tho', it should be confessed, the undergarments usually became badly stained, and required immediate laundering upon the morn; and Octavia's stockings were frequently so damaged, as to render mending impractical.

Blindfolded thus, the young wife could but conjecture, over the months, and, eventually, the years, the methodology of her husband's attentions to her, grasping that, from time to time, new accoutrements were employed: she might, as she lay obediently unmoving, be beaten (but lightly!) with wet gloves, presumably her own, or belonging to a previous Mrs. Rumford; she might be rapped about the bosom and nether regions with a fan, or a silk sunshade, or an unidentified object of a lightsome construction, to the accompaniment of Mr. Rumford's stentorian breath, which sometimes dissolved into short, shrill whistles, before the final cataclysmic explosion. Then again, varying according to no logic that she could determine, Mr. Rumford might choose to employ feathers to tickle her (tho', alas, the docile and rather frightened young woman perhaps did not oblige, as her husband might have wished); or he might smear upon her an odoriferous medicine or liniment, or, then again, sweet jam, honey, or marmalade, the which he then greedily lapped up from her, and licked, and sucked, emitting noises of great variety, ranging from gasps and low whimpers, to gargling outcries, of so powerful a volume as to throw Octavia into terror, in apprehension that the servants would surely hear, and in a natural wifely concern for her husband's health—Mr. Rumford being, alas, no longer precisely young.

All this the new Mrs. Rumford bore with saintly diligence, and sweet acquiescence, and not once, in the many years of their wedlock, did a murmur of complaint escape from her tight-pursed lips: not even in the extremities of fright, or pain, or childish bafflement; or the delirium of illness. She understood that a married woman's duty is solely to her husband, who is her rightful *lord* and *master*, and to have sworn to *love*, *honor*, and *obey* such a chosen person, at God's own altar, is no burden, but a privilege of the highest type. She understood too the fact that, in Mrs. Zinn's frequent words, the married state "is not one to be explained, nor yet doubted": and we must forgive her an occasional expression of pride, in the midst of sisterly affection, in addressing poor unmarried Samantha. (Alas! unmarried at the age of twenty-six, and with no prospects whatsoever, amongst socially acceptable gentlemen—the fault not of her family and relatives, but solely her own.)

That Mr. Rumford's intrepid fulfillment of his connubial obligations was to result in sacred issue—Godfrey II, Sarah, and Lucius Quincy, among those who survived beyond infanthood—is an outward manifestation of Our Heavenly Father's satisfaction in him, and in his belovèd wife; nor had Octavia suffered any doubt in this undertaking, proving as excellent a mother as she had a wife, to the delight of all observers, and to what we must assume to have been Mr. Rumford's gratification and pride. His early and generous prediction of her capabilities as mistress of Rumford Hall, made upon the very day of their wedding ("My dear Mrs. Rumford, I do not doubt you: I do not doubt that you will fulfill your duties more than satisfactorily"), possessed a startling prescience, and quite affirmed, what many had surmised, that Mr. Lucius Rumford was an individual of exceptional, if modestly hidden, resources.

And yet, alas!—the sorrow that lies ahead, for both husband and wife!—a tragedy of so astonishing a scope, that I cannot continue in this vein at the present time, but must withdraw, wishing to leave the reader with these gentle words of our poet Pinkney, who might almost have been penning his thoughts in regard to Mr. Rumford and his loyal Octavia—

> Intent to blend with his her lot,
> Fate formed her all that he was not;
> And as, by mere unlikeness, thought
> Associate we see,
> Their hearts from very difference caught
> A perfect sympathy.

47

One sun-warm'd April morn a near-catastrophic accident involving Mr. Zinn's experimentations with his hydrogen-filled balloon occurred (which accident, occurring above the Bloodsmoor River, resulted in a fiery plummet of young Nahum into the waters—thereby saving his life): in a season in which the respective notorieties of both Malvinia Morloch and Deirdre of the Shadows were waxing to their short-liv'd zeniths, and old Judge Kiddemaster fired off daily—nay, hourly—missives to Washington, couched in the most atrabilious of vocabularies, in protest of the new Interstate Commerce Commission, which, if "given its leash," would "strangulate" free enterprise in the nation forever, thereby decimating the Judge's own railroad investments: at a time, ah! so ironically! when the heroic John Quincy Zinn was beginning at last to doubt, not his own genius, still less his own good spirits, but the hospitality, in a manner of speaking, of the great democracy in which he resided—it was then that the cheerily ebullient Mr. Watkins of the *Atlantic Monthly* appeared, unannounced, at the Octagonal House, with a request for an *interview in depth* with Mr. John Quincy Zinn, the inventor "of probable genius," said to dwell so "reclusively" in Bloodsmoor, a "legend" amongst his more prosperous fellow-inventors, yet "gravely unknown" amongst the masses, who wanted only helpful instruction, in order that they might honor him as a "near-avatar" of the great Benjamin Franklin himself!

Since it was the stern-brow'd mistress of the Octagonal House who greeted Mr. Watkins upon that momentous day, accepting from his hand a gilt-engraved calling card, and listening in silence to the flood of loquacity that issued from his smiling lips, one might have supposed that the journalist's boldness would have been matched by an equivalent

389

boldness, on the part of Mrs. Zinn (who had been surprised, moreover, in the midst of supervising the monthly wash, done by the servants in the cramped, ill-lit, and steamy cellar): one would have supposed that that excellent lady, who did not deign to suffer fools gladly, would have sent him on his way with dispatch, and forgotten him entirely.

Such was not the case at all, however, *but rather the reverse!*

For, tho' Mrs. Zinn remained unsmiling, and offered the brash gentleman no seat, she nevertheless allowed that he might return again, past teatime, perhaps, of the subsequent day, where, by her arrangements, he might speak, tho' briefly, with John Quincy Zinn himself.

Immediately upon Mr. Watkins's departure, she sent one of the servants to fetch her husband; who, arriving in his shirt sleeves, breathless, with wild staring eyes, had to be assured with repeated emphasis that nothing was amiss in his household (for rarely was Mr. Zinn summoned from his workshop, and never for anything less than an emergency); but that, in fact, something wondrous had occurred, with profound significance for the future.

Whereupon she seated her perspiring husband, and forced him to listen, and showed him Mr. Watkins's handsome little card, and, when he tried to interrupt, continued speaking, in so knowing and maternal a tone, that he soon surrendered.

"The tentative title of the piece is, I believe, 'Unsung American Geniuses,' or 'Unsung Americans of Genius,' " Mrs. Zinn said, with satisfaction. "If all goes well—if you cooperate—and if it appears, as the young man has promised, in the *Atlantic Monthly:* why, then, you see, my dear John Quincy, they will no longer be able to deny you your due! They will be forced to kneel at your feet, as they should have done all along."

"They?" Mr. Zinn asked doubtfully.

"Now, at last, after so very, very long," Mrs. Zinn said, more vehemently, her cheeks grown ruddy and her eyes unusually bright, "they shall be forced to grant you justice."

Mr. Zinn stared absently at the calling card, turning it over in his grease-stained fingers. His untidy beard had grown so yellowish, in recent years, and his hair so ferociously stood out in tufts, that we must count it a blessing, that Mr. Watkins had not glimpsed him that day. For a very long time Mr. Zinn said nothing, but only sighed noisily, and blew out his lips, as if he were alone, and unobserved.

"Now we shall reap our reward," Mrs. Zinn said, quite surprising her husband by the *crooning* and *gloating* rhythm of her voice, "oh yes we shall, Mr. Z., oh yes, now we shall reap our mutual reward, oh yes, yes indeed, and fly in the faces of our enemies, and grind them underfoot, and hold our heads as high, oh yes, as high, as any of them, and as any Kiddemasters should, by rights!—*oh yes!*"

To her startl'd husband's protestations that she "surely exaggerated," and that in any case he hadn't time for "rambling conversations with amateurs—no matter their good will," Mrs. Zinn, shaking off the last jot of the cozy lethargy, usually induced in her, in the mornings, by Miss Emmeline's Remedy, simply unpris'd the calling card from Mr. Zinn's vague fingers, and held it triumphantly aloft, for both to see—

Adam P. Watkins, Esq.
Journalist-at-Large
The United States of America

—and murmured once again, with bright-glittering eyes, and a heaving bosom, and a warmth Mr. Zinn had not observed in her, for many decades: *"Oh yes!"*

And was Prudence Zinn correct, in envisioning that their lives would be permanently alter'd, by the industrious Mr. Watkins, and that *justice* would at last be granted, by way of the much-heralded essay that appeared, after some delay, in the *Atlantic Monthly,* in February of 1888? Was that excellent lady correct, in prophesying that "they" (by which she meant, I believe, not only the entire nation, and the prosperous inventors who had thieved from John Quincy Zinn, but her very own relatives, in Philadelphia, Wilmington, Baltimore, New York, and Boston, above all else) should at last be moved—nay, *forced*—to acknowledge the rare worth of her belovèd husband, and her own fortitude, loyalty, and devotion, in standing by him for more than three decades of supreme sacrifice: should be forced to "kneel" at his feet, in a manner of speaking, by the appearance of a single essay, with the grandiloquent title "Unsung Americans of Genius Living Now Unknown"?

I am not so cruel, as to keep the reader in suspense, and am eager to share my delight with all: for the answer to the above questions is a resounding and joyful *Yes*—precisely in Prudence Zinn's gratified tone!

48

In this troubled age to which the censorious (yet richly deserved!) appellation "Gilded" has been given, by Mr. Mark Twain, when our indwelling American optimism has been cut to the quick by such national scandals as the exploits of the Tammany Ring, and Jay Cooke & Company, and the Big Business Republicans, and the "Noble" Order of the Knights of Labor, the heart thrills to learn that there reside, still, in the bosom of our land, those selfless, devoted, and courageous individuals— how few, alas, might they now number?—who embody the great ideals of Jefferson and Franklin: the "Unsung Americans," as I have seen fit to designate them: "Unsung," it may be, O America, but not unheralded!

So began Adam P. Watkins's famous essay for the *Atlantic*, in which unstinting enthusiasm for his subject and patriotism for his country were subtly blended, to produce a highly gratifying paean to the lives and works of four "unknown" Americans, in whom, it would not be remiss to charge, true genius did flower. Our own John Quincy Zinn was, of course, the primary concern of the author, and it was to his life, with its numerous vicissitudes, that Mr. Watkins devoted most of his well-chosen words; but he spoke most generously of three other "unsung" Americans —the poetess Amelia Fairleigh of Elmhurst, Massachusetts, of whose voluminous outpourings since the early Fifties a scant dozen sonnets had seen print, the which situation had not evidently discouraged the spinster toiler, but inspired her all the more; the lawyer-elocutionist Stanley Gummidge of Hawthorne, Illinois, whose "life-project," as he called it, was to see the United States of America annex Canada and Mexico to its "rightful" territory; and the notable physician Dr. Benjamin Rush, who had discovered, by treating a Negro male diagnosed by other doctors as suffering from *leprosy*, the astonishing, and equally loathsome, disease *Negritude!*—which disease is evidently a skin condition whereby great patches of the natural white skin become discolored, and even blackened, resulting eventually in *Negritude*, for which, the good doctor fervently believed, he would one day discover the cure, and thereby restore the suffering "blacks" to their original, and natural, whiteness.

Young Mr. Watkins, wishing not only to formally interview his subject, but to quietly observe him "at his daily labors," so impressed Mrs. Zinn with his earnestness, that she invited him to stay at the Octagonal House, for as long as he might require: this duration of time being, all told, some six days. The journalist's manner was sunny and ebullient, his questions steady and unrelenting, and his "indefatigability as to trivia," as Mr. Zinn amusèdly phrased it, remarkable. The Zinns soon grasped that the journalistic profession was one which saw, and seized, and exclaimed, and expanded upon, with both a childlike wonderment, and a curious cynicism. For tho' Mr. Watkins's praise of Mr. Zinn's endeavors was so fulsome as to frequently embarrass his subject, his vituperative denunciation of other persons was startling: the more so, that by his own admission, he had not a *precise* knowledge of all he denounced, but was "going by what he had gathered," from the newspapers, or "confidential" conversations with knowledgeable individuals. (Mr. Watkins's mocking scorn of the Wizard of Menlo Park, gratifying to the Zinns at first, soon became troubling, when the young man let drop, quite inadvertently, that he had once applied for an audience with Edison, so as to do a "humane study" for one of the New York papers, but had been rudely rebuffed: the inventor being so "swollen with pride" as to suggest that he had not *time* for the project! "As if," Mr. Watkins observed with both anger and merriment, "*I myself* were not daily pressed for time!")

Yet the young man was an agreeable presence in the household, and did not disturb the workshop activities so greatly as one might anticipate. In fact, the questions he addressed to Mr. Zinn himself were fewer in number than those addressed to Mrs. Zinn: for it was from her he sought his "humane interest," greedily accumulating all the "idiosyncratic facts" she could recall, pertaining to Mr. Zinn's earlier life, and their marriage of upward of three decades. He evinced a flattering curiosity about Mrs. Zinn—the Prudence Kiddemaster of old, who had forged a substantial career for herself, as a schoolmistress in an excellent Philadelphia academy; he was naturally interested in the Kiddemasters, whom he did not fail to call "an historic American family"—tho', for the purposes of his article, as he scrupled to explain, he would *minimize,* or *edit out,* most references to John Quincy Zinn's powerful in-laws: this alliance provoking, in the general reader, the wrong sort of inference. ("I cannot allow it to be speculated, that Mr. Zinn's in-laws have financed his projects," Mr. Watkins said vehemently, "for that would quite distort the meaning of all that John Quincy Zinn symbolizes: and, moreover, I am confident that it is not true." To which assertion, Mrs. Zinn, cutting the young man another slice of white fruitcake, did not strenuously object.)

Fortunately for the Zinns, Mr. Watkins had but a glancing interest in the Zinn girls, assuming rightly that Mr. Zinn "must have hoped for a son and heir," yet was not "gravely disappointed" at the female issue he had sired, being, by nature, a "kindly and indulgent father," and "hardly given to the sort of tyrannical outbursts," characteristic of other men of genius—in whom, Mr. Watkins waxed poetically, genius and madness contend, like Indian mongoose and snake. That the Zinns had had four daughters, and adopted a fifth, was a fact to be merely noted in Mr. Watkins's article, tho' he questioned Mr. Zinn with bright, pleased eyes, and an enlivened countenance, on the subject of the *birthmark remover*, with which he had experimented, on both himself and his infant daughter Samantha, who had been afflicted at birth with a fiery, dagger-like blemish on her left temple, a miniature of her father's. (The chemical application Mr. Zinn had devised, while effective—after many experimentations—on his baby girl, was ineffective on him: and, in fact, caused extreme pain: so that he felt obliged to discontinue the applications, and lost interest, almost immediately, in the project.) Mr. Watkins dwelt upon the subject of progeny but briefly, in the written essay, not choosing to mention any of the Zinn daughters by name (tho' he did list "Nahum Hareton" as J.Q.Z.'s "disciple and assistant"), the focus of his remarks being upon the published theories of Ebenezer Gilfillan of the Royal Society, as to the correlation between the number of children of outstanding inventors and their patents. (This correlation, as advanced by Dr. Gilfillan, is necessarily controversial, and, in any case, vexingly difficult to prove. That the size of the *average* inventor's family correlates .878 $\pm$ .014 with the intensity of the patenting rate, is not helpful as regards Mr. Zinn, who made so little effort, after all, to acquire patents for himself.)

Mr. Watkins evinced more curiosity in the "gadgets" Mr. Zinn had made for household use, and the "architectural wonderment" of the Octagonal House itself—which the Zinns, having dwelt therein for so many years, had long ceased to notice (tho' Mrs. Zinn did have her complaints about the drafts and "moaning winds" that ofttimes sprang out of nowhere). He was to underscore in his essay the likelihood of the theory that an *eight-sided* domicile was salubrious as to general health, and highly stimulating as to the "higher mental faculties"—an issue that would be debated, with colorful pros and cons, in the Letters Column of the *Atlantic,* throughout much of 1888.

As it was published, Mr. Watkins's lengthy article gave as much space to the "legendary" and "oft-eccentric" mode of behavior of his subjects, as to their accomplishments. It delighted in little Pip, "his master's constant shadow," and in the "cluttered and cobwebbed *profusion*" of the Zinn workshop; it made much of John Quincy Zinn's "charming idiosyncrasies" of dress and manner, his habit of going about in his shirt sleeves "like any honest workingman," with his silver-hued beard "of noble proportions," and his "dreamy saint's eyes" in which both kindliness and native Yankee shrewdness were to be found. That J.Q.Z. sometimes turned aside from his work "in a frenzy of coughing," that he had acquired, over the years, an "ascetic," and "much-ravaged," and "yet childlike" countenance, and that, above all, he felt "not a *whit*" of bitterness or regret, that other inventors had so freely betaken themselves to "imbibe at his well"—all were offered as proofs of his *genius,* and his *patriotic character.* He was the living spirit of Ralph Waldo Emerson's idealism; the incarnation of Benjamin Franklin's selfless sagacity, the "brother" of Abraham Lincoln in his modest birth and background, and belief in the Democracy of Mankind. "A veritable paragon of American manhood," Mr. Watkins boldly averred, "even *apart from* his astounding intellect."

In Mr. Watkins's discussion of J.Q.Z.'s technical accomplishments, he did not, it seems, distinguish sharply enough between those that had been emphatically Mr. Zinn's own, and patented by him or by Samantha, and those that belonged in part to other men, and those that were, at the present time, still in the planning stage—still, that is, in Mr. Zinn's fertile but not reliably pragmatic imagination. He seemed to find amusing the "quest for the Perpetual Motion mechanism," no less than the sketch for a Thermal Suit (whereby the individual, in all weathers, might regulate his own atmospheric condition), and the machine to grind up barnyard nuisances like feathers and bones, and the various insecticides and "fly-stickers"; he declared as "infinitely significant for the future," Mr. Zinn's present experimentations with a hydrogen-filled dirigible (built, of course, to scale, as a consequence of his workshop's severely limited resources), and his improvements in weaponry, which would one day make war "so horrific a prospect, no sane men would wish to indulge in it." His spring-stirrup for the U.S. cavalry was a "small masterpiece" of "tinkering ingenuity"; his notion of paper (disposable) collars for men, simply brilliant. A road- or auto-locomotive would be a godsend to the American people, as would a flying machine, and a cure for snoring, and a "sun-furnace," and waterproofing methods that were 100 percent reliable: all projects upon which Mr. Zinn had worked, with widely varying results. Mr. Watkins was particularly struck by the visionary notion of a single Great Eye, driven by electricity or some other clean power, that would exert a constant moral surveillance over the nation—"a force for good gravely needed," the journalist intoned, "in these troubled and uncertain times."

The typewriter, the zipper, the incandescent light bulb—and many another "brain-child"—had resided, in their embryonic forms, in Mr. Zinn's "great teeming mind," only to be snatched away by "plunderers," whose names need not be given. Most remarkable of all was Mr. Zinn's *sweetness* and *charity* toward those very personages who had stolen from him, and thereby made their fortunes!—and his continued optimistic faith in the future of his great nation, initially expressed, long ago, in his writings on educational reform (which, Mr. Watkins abash'dly confessed, he had not had time to read, prior to the preparation of his article), and his oft-reiterated hope that, in the forthcoming decades, the United States might "assume its rightful mantle" as a supreme World Power. *"Do you believe in the Utopian Ideal?" I inquired of John Quincy Zinn. His eyes flashed with a courageous, if somewhat wearied, zest of life; and his reply came without hesitation. "Indeed, Mr. Watkins, I do: its time may be the future, but its place is here, in the United States of America!"*

"I do not recall having made such a statement," Mr. Zinn said, in some perplexity, after repeated dazed perusals of Mr. Watkins's article. "Indeed—I do not recall Mr. Watkins asking that particular question."

"No matter," Mrs. Zinn said, her cheeks grown ruddy and warm, with what appeared now to be a permanent blush, as of maidenly shyness, or intense excitement (for the brief paragraph on *Mrs. John Quincy Zinn, née Prudence Kiddemaster of Philadelphia,* with its depiction of Mrs. Zinn as "that paragon of wifehood—an uncomplaining helpmeet to her belovèd spouse," had deeply moved her). "No matter, John Quincy: it is accomplish'd at last: your public vindication! At the end of which," the somewhat flurried woman said, with a trilling laugh, and a flamboyant gesture of her hand, "I should like to pen, in five-inch red letters, AMEN."

"Prudence, surely you exaggerate," Mr. Zinn said, plucking nervously at his beard.

Yet she did not; or, very little; and Mr. Watkins's generous "Unsung Americans of Genius Living Now Unknown" not only stirred much comment amongst readers of the *Atlantic,* and, indeed, caused the issue in which it appeared to be entirely sold out on the stands, but brought the name and plight of John Quincy Zinn to the Congress of the United States, where he was championed in impassioned speeches by such divers legislators as Congressman Arlin C. Cayce of Pennsylvania, and Senator Albert J. Hackett of Indiana. Debate on the floor centered less upon the advisability of easing the financial plight of an "unknown genius," than on the specific terms of the allotment; and on the nature of the invention, or research, to be underwritten.

And so, one sunlit May morn, a servant from Kiddemaster Hall delivered, to Mr. Zinn's trembling hand, a lengthy telegram from Washington, D.C., containing a message of such import that the astonished man could scarce absorb its content, but was forced to require Samantha to peruse it, in his stead. (The telegram was delivered, of course, to the workshop above the gorge, where Mr. Zinn and his two young assistants had been industriously working for some hours, before the momentous interruption.)

"Ah, Father!—what is it!—shall we all journey to Washington?" Samantha gaily cried, holding the telegram aloft. *"Special project—commiserate with the talents of—in dire need by most States—annual honorarium—research pertinent to—* Father, do my eyes decieve me? Can this figure—$15,000— be correct? *An annual honorarium of—"*

But so o'erwrought was the usually self-contained Samantha, that she allowed the wondrous yellow missive to slip from her shaking fingers; and might, indeed, have staggered in a daze, and fainted, had not young Nahum, close at her side, leapt with alacrity to steady her.

Upon the liveried servant's arrival, Pip woke crankily from his midmorning nap, and began to chatter and scold, and creep about the workbenches, his jabber increasing, as always, as his human associates failed to give him significant notice. Now he leapt and danced about in spirited merriment, his long slender tail looping over his tiny head, and there may have been an element of mischievous mockery, as well, in the very *gaiety* of his manner: and the frenzy with which he snatched up the fallen telegram, and pretended to read it, with high-pitched staccato cries. He brought it close to his face, as if he were near-sighted; and crumpled it; and might even have eaten it, had not Nahum taken it forcibly from out his fingers.

"Ah, now let me see!—it is so very unexpected, Mr. Zinn—and so deserved—let me see, the remainder of the message—" Young Nahum fairly stammered, his own face flushed, and his eyes behind his schoolmasterish glasses grown round and moist with wonder. "Ah yes, here: *An annual honorarium of $15,000—research pertinent to—and the construction of a working model—for the adoption of all, or most, States—a more humane and more efficient technique of—of—"* And here the excited young man paused, and blinked, and made an effort to smooth out the crumpled sheet of paper, in order to read more clearly. *"A more humane and more efficient technique of —public execution."*

For an astonished moment there was silence in the little workshop: and even sensitive Pip ceased chattering!

At last Samantha broke the spell, by saying in a voice childlike with surprise and dismay: *"Public execution!* Ah, no!"

And Mr. Zinn left off pulling and plucking at his beard, to extend a dazed hand to Nahum, and, adjusting his half-moon glasses, reread the missive in a halting, stumbling voice, which nonetheless gained strength as it proceeded, and partook of his daughter's righteous dismay: *"A more humane and more efficient technique of public execution.* You are correct, Nahum, you have read correctly."

"Execution!" Samantha exclaimed, now more angrily. "And of course you must refuse!"

"How *dare* they make such a request," Nahum cried, snatching off his glasses and waving them, in a gesture of impotent defiance, "of *you*? Do they not know to whom they have directed their impious declaration?"

Then, of a sudden, Mr. Zinn's furry little companion leapt to his shoulder, and, in a sympathetic gesture in which natural monkey spirits contended with a heartrending sweetness, brought his small wizened face close to Mr. Zinn's—so that, for a startling moment, the young people could see how both monkey and master had aged, in their long years together.

For a brief spell the haggard, yet still distinctive-appearing, John Quincy Zinn was silent, staring at the offensive paper in his hand, which, we may surmise, only a stoic detachment prevented him from crumpling, and tossing it to his feet. When he did deign to speak, there was very little expression to his face, save an uncharacteristic droop of his nether lip; and his voice was slow and grave and sonorous, with a plangent dignity, that quite prick'd the hearts of Samantha and Nahum, and was to be embedded in their memories forever: "Yes. Of course I shall refuse."

49

During these fateful months in the lives of the Zinns something quite miraculous was transpiring, remarked upon only inwardly, and cursorily, by Octavia and Mrs. Zinn, but unbeknownst to John Quincy Zinn: the Zinns' only remaining daughter at home, Samantha, was, at her "advanced" age, growing ever more beauteous by the day!

An improbable development, the skeptical reader may scoff: and yet, I assure you, it was so. *In her late twenties the Zinns' youngest natural daughter, whom Malvinia had once cruelly described as "plain as a spoon," was growing more beauteous daily!*

No single feature appeared to have alter'd and yet, by a bewildering alchemy I cannot hazard to explain, in terms other than the *romantic* and the *sentimental*, the young woman was fast shedding her customary "plainness," and acquiring a most striking "beauty," beneath the noses of those who saw her each day: those who, save one, were blind to her, and rarely, in fact, "saw" her at all.

In addition to a considerable facial beauty, this peculiar girl was also acquiring a somewhat alter'd *character:* for, where she once worked in silence, hour upon hour, and turned but a distracted, and, it may even have been, a crabbèd countenance, upon the world, and indulged herself in no girlish chatter or whims, considering such behavior not only repellent, but, more significantly, *a waste of valuable time,* she now—ah, how delighted I am to note!—found herself singing and humming under her breath, in the very workshop itself, and oft, on the path connecting the workshop and the Octagonal House, skipping along, and smiling for no cause, like a little girl of four or five, instead of a mature woman, of more than two decades older. Nor were grace, lightsome spirits, and frequent laughter unmatched by an assiduous application of Samantha's keen mind in the service of what we might call her "feminine" appearance: for where that young lady once dressed in haste, and allowed the servant girl to fashion her hair in any style, so long as it "went quickly," and cared not a whit whether her lace be graying, or her ribbons lank and dispirited, or the bow of her sash but meagerly tied, she now spent upward of a half-hour upon her morning toilette alone, and, tho' her weekday dress remained a plain calico, and her apron not altogether fresh, she took small pains with the trim on her bodice and skirt, and wore the prettier of her two morning caps, and oft found herself gazing in rapt but near-mindless contemplation, at the fairy-stranger who regarded her from out her mirror: whom (for such was Samantha's modesty!) she did not dare see as *beautiful*, but, she hoped, as *pretty*.

And if I reveal that young Nahum too appeared to be acquiring, as the weeks and months sped, a new attractiveness, and a distinctive maturity of manner, freely mingled, withal, with a boyish exhilaration, and a propensity toward loud and spontaneous laughter—if I reveal that the two young people, far from keeping their jealous distance from each other, as, at the start, they did, were now cooperating on nearly all their labors in John Quincy Zinn's sacred workshop—if I reveal, moreover (and here, doubtless, I expose my hand!), that Samantha Zinn and Nahum Hareton oft found themselves glancing at each other for no purpose, and stammering, and laughing, and blushing, and finding a dozen breathless excuses, daily, to seek each other's counsel, while the oblivious J.Q.Z. continued all absorbed in his work: even the most hardened reader, to whom *romance* be naught but a scarce-recalled, and doubted, relic of youth, will rejoice in the knowledge that love, all unexpected, was blossoming in the famous workshop above the gorge: where, one would have thought, only the most *mechanical* blooms could flourish!

So, indeed, Samantha and Nahum fell in love, over a period of many months, in all innocence, and but slenderly grasping the phenomenon that overcame them: for each, I hardly need aver, was virginal in soul as completely as in body, and had never before given a thought to love, let alone surrendered to its spell. Indeed, I would go so far as to declare that each young person would have vociferously *scorned* the possibility, but a few years before!—that possibility that had, by degrees, become a dizzying reality, bringing a rosy blush to Samantha's pale cheek, upon the meagerest provocation, and a catch in the throat of the manly Nahum, when he chanc'd to spy upon his belovèd, as she tripped her way, just past dawn, along the graveled pathway to the gorge.

A lover's eye, they say, is notorious for what it invents: yet the innocent Nahum, inventor tho' he was, succumbed to very little self-deception, in his remarking upon, and absorption by, Samantha's growing beauty. For, warmed by her deepening affection for him, as the vegetation of April is warmed by the e'er-waxing sun, and grows more lush thereby, Miss Samantha Zinn *was* growing in her beauty, and would surely have caught the eye, and riveted the attention, of many a suitor, had she still acquiesced to her family's wishes, that she mingle in society, and attend balls, with the hope of attracting a suitable husband. Nahum gazed upon her, in reverent silence, and all virtuous were his thoughts, and wholesomely removed from the grosser masculine emotions: he observed his belovèd in the words of the great Tennyson—

> A maid so smooth, so white, so wonderful,
> They said a light came from her when she moved.

—and did not dream of uttering his love aloud. For not only was Samantha petite as a fairy sprite, and wondrous to behold, with her clear eyes and pale freckled skin and gleaming red hair, but she was also Nahum's equal, or even his superior, in intelligence; and she *was* his master's most cherished daughter.

Why, for her part, Samantha should have succumbed to the softer feminine emotions, after so many years of proud—nay, insolent—indifference, I cannot determine: save that Nahum's manner was so shyly winning, and so unstudied, and unsullied by vanity, even a hardened female heart could not fail to be moved. He did not, it is true, possess striking masculine beauty, nor was he so tall, broad of shoulder, and vigourous of expression as Mr. Zinn had been, in his younger manhood: but his oft-smiling countenance radiated calm, and patience, and a capacity for loyalty, that was altogether appealing. Nor did his deference to Mr. Zinn displease Mr. Zinn's daughter.

For the first several months, however, after Nahum's arrival at the workshop, Samantha had, with grim resolution, *not* allowed herself to observe, and certainly not to speak with, her young comrade: for, I am unhappy to say, she suffered some jealousy of him, and some resentment, that he should so readily be welcomed into the workshop, and entrusted, from the very start, with Mr. Zinn's most treasured secrets. "He may be a spy of Edison's," Samantha said, her green eyes narrowing with malice, "or of Westinghouse's: you know well, Father, that plans of yours have mysteriously vanished, from out this very place, only to turn up elsewhere, with much vulgar ballyhoo!—and yet you continue to allow strangers into your workshop." Mr. Zinn, not sensing, perhaps, the true, tremulous motive behind his daughter's petition, replied in a curt voice that both those gentlemen—Edison and Westinghouse—had, not many months previously, approached him through intermediaries, as to the enlistment of his talents on new projects of their own, involving electrical current: and he had of course declined their offers. (Mr. Zinn did not know that Samantha knew of a shameful episode that had transpired, a twelve-month previously, when, being in such financial distress that he could not buy materials for his aluminum-sided dirigible, save by way of a desperate appeal to Judge Kiddemaster, or Great-Aunt Edwina, which Mrs. Zinn angrily opposed, the unhappy John Quincy Zinn had been so "backed into a corner," as he phrased it, that he had sold a rudimentary, but highly promising, notion of his, dreamt up in an impassioned half-hour, to the Edison workshop in Menlo Park: an elaborate amplification of the processes involved in the cylindrical toy in which Pip, in drawings executed by Samantha, "performed" in motion, of the sort that might one day evolve into a *projected* and *moving* view upon a *screen*—the value of which, for society, Mr. Zinn had not had time to speculate upon, being so harassed, and unquiet of mind.)

"It does not do you proud, Samantha," Mr. Zinn said, knitting his brows, and absentmindedly stroking his ragged beard, "and is hardly a beneficent reflection upon your mother and myself, that you should harbor low suspicions of a young man in possession of such sterling qualities, whose loyalty, I, for one, cannot question."

A most uncharacteristic speech for John Quincy Zinn to deliver himself of: and the abash'd Samantha had no recourse, but to blush fiercely, and murmur a daughterly apology, and retreat.

And yet: it may be that Mr. Zinn's warm words, and his depiction of young Nahum as *loyal,* and in the possession of *sterling qualities,* sank deep within the contumacious heart of his daughter: there to stir much mischief, and cause much distress, over a passage of time.

The wonderments of love!—its soft-petal'd and unexpected blooming! Many years were to pass, during which time Samantha came gradually to warm to her father's apprentice, gauging him first as a rival; and then as a working associate; and then as a brotherly presence; and then —ah, her heart scarcely knew, what designation to choose! She found herself one day taking note of each motion made by the lank-limbed young man: each word that dropped all artless from his lips, and each smile that illuminated his angular, boyish face. Why, of a sudden, his unexceptional brown eyes should be *of interest;* why his habit of polishing the lenses of his spectacles, with a chamois cloth stained with grease, should be *appealing,* she could not have explained. With a prick of amusement she watched as, staring off into space, Nahum allowed his tea to go cold, and devilish Pip to gobble down his toast. With a prick of affection she noted his threadbare gloves, his mud-spattered boots, the shabby oilcloth cape he continued to wear in wet weather. One day—in a voice so stern it might have passed for Mrs. Zinn's—she inquired of Nahum (whom at that time she still called "Mr. Hareton," or addressed by no name at all) whether he would give her the pleasure of allowing her to mend his shirt collar, which was so badly frayed, it had actually torn behind: or whether he wished it to remain as it was, out of some "purposive eccentricity" of his own.

The startl'd young man, so accustomed to a frostiness of demeanor on Samantha's part, or, at the very most, a benign indifference, scarcely knew how to reply: and made rather a fool of himself, in his stammering that he had not known—he was grievously sorry, not to have known—that he presented, to others, so ill-kempt a spectacle: and begged his master's daughter to forgive him. So distraught was he, by our lady's inquiry (which was, I do believe, somewhat too arch and "Kiddemaster"-like), that the poor young man went away in shame, and neglected to reply, that of course he should be greatly honored—nay, overcome with delight—were she to condescend to sew anything for him —oh, anything at all!

Given this development, it is most plausibly the case that Samantha's love for Nahum, and his for her, would have as naturally blossomed, as the myriad dogwood trees in the surrounding woods, in the spring: for these were two young persons, after all, of extraordinary caliber, as accustomed to ratiocination as other young persons might be to dinner dances, and balls, and riding to hounds. Then too, the repugnance aroused in other young men, by Miss Samantha Zinn's persistent *intelligence,* which she waved about, as Malvinia once observed, like a fringe of the cheapest velvet, evidently did not occur to Nahum: for he was, tho' I hesitate to say so, for fear of alienating the reader, not of a good family: not, so far as anyone could determine, of *any family at all.* His origins were as shrouded in mist as the Bloodsmoor Gorge, on the very day of his arrival, not, it would seem, out of any willful prevarication, but out of sheer forgetfulness; and it was hardly counted amiss by John Quincy Zinn, with *his* charming absentmindedness, that, from time to time, relaxing at tea, or at dinner in the Octagonal House, the youth should speak vaguely of having been a pupil of Mr. Zinn's, as a child: recalling with sporadic vividness certain classroom events, and diagrams on a blackboard, and models of machines. . . . But beyond that Nahum's memory failed; or, to be more accurate, he simply drifted off the subject, as did his host, for both were wonderfully beset by all sorts of random ideas and notions, of a kind that I, attending so reverently, yet at such a mental distance, cannot hope to characterize. And of the question of *origins*—well, as we have seen, Mr. John Quincy Zinn was somewhat loath to speak, sensing himself, still, after a passage of so many years, but *reluctantly* admitted to the wide circle of his wife's distinguished family!

In any case, remarkable as it may strike the ear, Samantha Zinn's superior intelligence seems not to have repulsed her young man, but to have actually *attracted* him! Which is, I suppose, entirely to Nahum's credit; tho' one should remember that his family background was lamentably obscure, and his breeding, in general, very much in question.

I am confident, however, that the dawning of love between Samantha and Nahum would have grown at a natural pace, and the disaster for the Zinns merely forestalled: but two events served to accelerate the natural progress of the powerful emotion, and to force it into a premature, and, it may have been, a somewhat feverish, eruption. The first was the regrettable accident involving Mr. Zinn's heroic dirigible; after so many months of labor, the balloon crashed within ten minutes, when one of the propellers struck a riverbank tree, and cut back into the balloon, not only allowing the hydrogen gas to escape with a furious hiss, but causing at the same time a small explosion, and a terrifying conflagration! —so that poor Samantha was forced to witness her belovèd Nahum, who alone had manned the experimental model, leap all aflame into the Bloodsmoor River. (And, for some wretched minutes, it almost seemed that the youth had disappeared forever . . . sinking beneath the surface of the turbulent waves, and withdrawing from the Zinns' lives, as abruptly as he had entered them. *But it was during those agonizing minutes that Samantha knew her heart.*)

The second event, alas, I am forced to say, was that very article of Adam P. Watkins's, which was greeted with such unstinting enthusiasm, by Samantha's mother, and by all of her mother's relatives. For not every reader of "Unsung Americans . . ." found it completely pleasing, in its details rather more than in its general scope.

Samantha could not have liked it, that her name went unmentioned; as if, being of the female gender, she *had* no name, and was merely her father's daughter—his "daughter-assistant," in Mr. Watkins's perfunctory words. (Her feeling for Nahum, however, was so strongly developed by now, that she experienced not the smallest pang of jealousy, that *his* name should be revealed, to the *Atlantic* readers—on the contrary, she took a happy pride in it, and read that passage aloud many a time, to her blushing companion. "Now, you see, Nahum, you have become famous!" the high-spirited girl teased. "Now you shall desert the Octagonal House, for Menlo Park!") What distressed Samantha in Mr. Watkins's essay, was the account of the *birthmark removal*, which had allegedly transpired during her infancy—and of which she retained but the cloudiest recollection. Or did she not remember, at all; had she been *told*? All dimly, and uneasily, her memory yielded a most puzzling episode in Great-Aunt Edwina's bedchamber, some years previous: the which episode had proved so peculiar, and so obdurate, as to its secret meaning, Samantha had cast it out of her thoughts altogether, and addressed herself to more useful activities.

Now she studied her smooth forehead in a mirror, and satisfied herself, that she could detect not the slightest trace of the old blemish. How difficult it would be, to imagine a birthmark there, on her left temple! A small galaxy of freckles had been sprinkled across her face, and altogether charming they were, tho' I am fully conscious of a fashionable repugnance for freckles, and a predilection for lily-pale skin: but these freckles were, for the most part, quite unobtrusive, and not even the thickest cluster resembled a birthmark, let alone an actual blemish. If the child had been afflicted with a birthmark resembling her father's, she should certainly have wept with gratitude, that he labored to remove it; for no young lady, not even one who had, for so many years, haughtily scorned prettiness and all its trappings, could have failed to regret so disfiguring a mark. Yes, Samantha *should* have felt naught but gratitude, and might even have been expected to grasp her father's hands, and thank him, so many years after the event: and yet, for some reason, she did not.

For some reason—the distraught young lady could scarcely have said *why*, even to herself—she did not. She felt no gratitude for having been relieved, in her infancy, of an ugly blemish; she felt, on the contrary, a most childish resentment.

An odd, a very odd sort of reaction! the reader thinks. As, indeed, the writer thinks as well. For, any normal young woman would have been not simply grateful for her father's concern, that she enter life *unblemish'd;* she would have been profuse with daughterly thanks—and tears, and hugs, and kisses, and declarations of lifelong devotion.

Yet Samantha, that perverse child, was not. No, she simply, and stubbornly, was *not.*

Of course she breathed not a word of her resentment to Mr. Zinn —for they were not in the habit, father and daughter, of discussing personal matters of any kind; and Mrs. Zinn's pride in the article, and her repeated perusals of it, and memorized quotations from it, did not inspire confidence in Samantha, that she would be sympathetic with any criticism. Were Octavia still residing in the Octagonal House, it is possible that Samantha would have unburdened her heart to her: for Octavia had always been the sweetest of all the sisters, and truly attentive to the others' needs. But Octavia now lived some distance away, and was now, most conspicuously, *Mrs. Lucius Rumford;* and cruel Samantha did not stint, in her inward contempt for that worthy gentleman—whom she persisted in seeing as a pompous old dullard, a bewhiskered fool, a dry-as-dust hypocrite, with all the worst trappings of a Calvinist man of the cloth, and none of the virtues: and far less wealthy, moreover, than the Zinns had believed.

So there was no one, at this time, with whom Samantha could speak; no one to whom she could unburden her heart, and release the poison festering the rein.

Unhappy daughter!—and, alas, soon to be *unhappy father!*

50

"Mr. Zinn," Mrs. Zinn addressed her husband, one wintry eve when the two of them sat alone in the parlor, with only the sleeping Pip as a companion (Samantha having early retired to her bedchamber upstairs), "may I disturb you from your book? I have something troublesome to discuss, and have put off broaching the subject to you, not wishing to worry you unnecessarily, or deflect your energies from your new project."

Mr. Zinn glanced up blinking from his book, which was a crudely-illustrated history of the Spanish Empire, sent out to him, at his request, by a Philadelphia bookseller; and, in deference to a certain gravity in his wife's tone, which always presaged issues of no light moment, he even laid aside a little sketch he was doing, in pencil, in his notebook. "Yes, Prudence?" he said, with a tentative smile, beginning already to stroke his beard, and peering, in utmost attentiveness, over the tops of his half-moon glasses. (For John Quincy Zinn had remained, lo, these many years, the most respectful of husbands: even when, it may be, his wondrously fertile mind was attuned to its own interests, and did not altogether concentrate upon those given utterance by his wife.) "I hope it is not something *gravely* troublesome?"

Mrs. Zinn's reply was admirably succinct: "Not *gravely*, at this very moment; but in time—in time."

The which, failing to enlighten Mr. Zinn, gave him cause to knit up his brows: and to widen his already perplex'd uxorious smile. "You intrigue me greatly, Prudence; but I must beg you—for I am feeling less than zestful this evening, having passed a workday of no demonstrable value—I must beg you, not to stir me to anxiety, at this late hour."

Mrs. Zinn did not break the rhythm of her knitting, as she cast upon her husband the briefest, and the most mildly remonstrative, of glances. "Your daughter, sir," she said curtly. "And your assistant."

Mr. Zinn stared, and was so bewildered, that, for a moment, he left off stroking his beard. "My daughter, you say?—and my assistant?"

"Your daughter Samantha," said the grim-visagèd Mrs. Zinn, allowing a forciful caesura to punctuate her words, and even, by way of further punctuation, raising the strip of knitting to eye level, in order to examine it, before returning to her rapid work, "*and* your assistant Nahum."

"I see," Mr. Zinn said, most readily, "and yet," the good gentleman laughed, now drawing a befuddled hand roughly through his hair, "and yet I fail to see."

"That you fail to *see*, Mr. Zinn, more than a twelve-inch past your nose," Mrs. Zinn said, resuming her knitting, which was so mechanically adroit that the needles flashed, and, to Mr. Zinn's vague eye, appeared at times to fairly blur together, into a single glowering image, "is not a characteristic your loved ones have missed in you; but it is one, for all that, not invariably helpful."

Mr. Zinn sat in silence for some moments, gazing now toward the fire, which, no longer giving off annoying sparks and crackles, had subsided into a warm, near-phosphorescent glow. It may be that he was puzzling out his wife's words, or it may have been that, vexed of late by the myriad technical problems his new project was causing him, he had drifted back into a contemplation of *that:* the which Mrs. Zinn seemed to sense, in that she gave her knitting an impatient shake, and caused the needles to click smartly together, and said: "Mr. Zinn, I am referring to the unfortunate, indeed, the outlaw, romance that is breeding in your very workshop, beneath your abstracted gaze: a romance of which I have hesitated to speak these many weeks, not wishing to distress you—for I know full well, my dear husband, how deeply immersed you are in your new project, and how important that project is, not only for the Zinns, but for the welfare of the nation."

"Romance?" Mr. Zinn whispered, slowly taking off his glasses, to stare with myopic alarm at his wife. "Breeding in my workshop?"

"Perhaps, in a mother's fond foolishness," Mrs. Zinn continued, in a nobly controlled voice, "I *had* placed some small hope on Samantha, that she would one day contract a satisfactory marriage, despite her contumacious heart. My father is in the midst of renegotiating his old friendship with René Du Pont, for what reasons I cannot discern, but he has let drop the fact that, some miles west of the village of Hope Ferry, a considerable property of his adjoins a considerable property belonging to the Du Ponts, and, given that *we* have a daughter left over, so to speak, and the elderly Du Pont has a grandson similarly unaccounted for—I refer of course to poor Cheyney, about whom such troubling things have been said—it had crossed Father's mind, and it hardly seems, to *my* mind, an unreasonable proposition, that—"

But Mr. Zinn did not appear to follow. He turned his eyeglasses slowly about in his large, blunt, stained fingers, and continued to stare at Mrs. Zinn's stolid countenance. "A romance? In *my* workshop?" he murmured with numb lips.

"Unless, of course, I am simply imagining it all, in my morbid state of mind," Mrs. Zinn said. Here the good woman sighed heavily, and again lifted her knitting, and quietly contemplated it, with an expression in which habitual resignation, and habitual impatience subtly contended. Mr. Zinn remaining silent, she said: "And yet I believe—I *fear*—that I am imagining nothing at all: that I am (God help me!) altogether too keen-sighted."

John Quincy fumbled for the shabby leatherbound tome he had set aside, and his sketch, and pencil, not in order to resume his speculative work, but, as it were, in a sort of daze, needing to occupy his trembling hands. His *daughter*. And his *assistant*. Nay, the good man, so accustomed to the merciless but fair-minded logic of machines, and mechanical motion, and the all-seeing Benevolence that suffused the universe, found it most difficult to grasp Prudence's words: and shaped them again and again with his numbed lips. His *daughter*. And his *assistant*. An *outlaw romance*. In his very *workshop*.

Mrs. Zinn continued to speak, in a rambling monologue, now peevish, now philosophical and stoic, with an occasional glance at her stricken spouse, who, as the minutes passed, began unseeingly to sketch and doodle, his pencil moving slowly at first, and then with increasing speed: tho' his eyes, I am unhappy to say, acquired none of their customary lustre, but remained grimly narrowed. The passing years had been exceptionally kind to John Quincy Zinn, for, as a gentleman in his sixties, he looked admirably youthful, and were it not for his somewhat disheveled beard, and his thick, stiff, silvery hair, he might have been mistaken for ten or even twenty years younger. Mrs. Zinn, alas, *did* look her age, or more—that age being near to seventy, I believe. Ah, how greatly she had changed, from the vigorous, clear-eyed Prudence Kiddemaster we had first known in Philadelphia, as an independent young woman! How flaccid her skin had become, and how darkly pouched her eyes! Her somewhat square jaw would have been sadly disfigured by some three or four stiff, wirelike hairs that sprouted from it, had she not (upon the emphatic advice of her Aunt Edwina) taken care to pluck them regularly; her bosom and stomach and hips would have strained more liberally against her confining clothes, had she not worn a whalebone girdle of more than ordinary strength. Yet such was John Quincy Zinn's love for Prudence, and his high regard, that he seemed hardly to notice the grievous changes in her: it may have been, in fact, that he did not notice, and had long ceased to recall, even in reverie, the handsome young woman of the Fifties, and the giddy romance of their youth.

Mrs. Zinn addressed her distracted husband for upward of an hour that evening, tho' you should not think she spoke continuously: rather, she touched upon one subject (the unspeakable betrayal of the three daughters), and sighed angrily, and drifted to another subject (the happy match between Mr. Rumford and Octavia) and yet to another (Mr. Watkins's superb article), and to another (the handsome honorarium bestowed upon John Quincy by Congress: which Judge Kiddemaster, by arcane negotiations it were better not to dwell upon, caused to be raised to $20,000 *per annum*), and to another (the extraordinary rise to genuine wealth of the Du Ponts, who had begun, not so many decades ago, with a modest powder mill on the Bloodsmoor, and a substantial loan from the Kiddemasters: their fortune being made, of course, by the happenstance of the war against Mexico, and the *still more* fortunate happenstance of the Civil War). Which subject brought her to the matter of young Cheyney, who had returned from a trip to the Orient, mysteriously broken in constitution, but withal said to be still charming: and desirous of making his permanent abode at the Du Pont country estate, but a scant twenty miles away. "He is said to be under the care of the finest physicians," Mrs. Zinn commented, "several of the very staff who had made so valiant, if doomed, an effort to save poor President Garfield from his fate."

In this wise Mrs. Zinn held forth as she knitted, and Mr. Zinn's lead pencil moved, as of its own volition, creating one rudimentary but inspired sketch after another. By an irony of history it would be, in later years, Samantha herself—who was, alas, to cause her father such grief! —who most clearly characterized John Quincy Zinn's genius: a veritable flood of inspiration, lasting upward of several hours, during which his pen moved, and moved, and moved, and one sketch after another was made, and allowed to drop to the floor at his feet, until, by some process never to be known by the mind of man (for how, pray, can the *mind* know the *mind?*), the *perfect,* or *near-perfect,* sketch was realized: and the fatigued gentleman then sank back in his chair, his face slack, his eyelids drooping, a haze of perspiration on his brow, but, let us hope, a small still smile on his lips.

Thus Mrs. Zinn spoke; and spoke by degrees companionably, and then peremptorily; and, reverting to the original subject of Samantha and "that penniless Nahum," turned suddenly to her dazed husband, and inquired of him, her mouth bracketed by deep ironic creases: "And what, Mr. Zinn, do you propose to *do* as a consequence of our dialogue?"

Mr. Zinn, in his exhaustion, did not precisely hear his wife's words, nor had he, I fear, been attending to their general sense, for some minutes; but this pointed question struck him, with no great difficulty, and, extending his most recent sketch for Mrs. Zinn to see, he seemed to indicate that this surprisingly elaborate, tho' hurried, drawing was a reply of sorts to that question.

"Yes?" said Mrs. Zinn, frowning, and taking it from his fingers. "What am I supposed to make of *this*? After your furious scribbling—after your scant pretense of attention—after your near-unforgivable dereliction of your duty, Mr. Zinn, in overseeing your daughter's behavior: what am I to make of this—this—why, is it a bed? Is this contraption, with all its knobs and wires and nonsensical coils, a mere *bed*?"

Despite his considerable fatigue, and the lateness of the hour, and the sorrow that clouded his heart—and would, I hardly need to aver, continue greatly to cloud that noble heart, for some time—Mr. Zinn made an effort to smile at his wife's fondly chiding words, and, leaning forward in his chair so that, with one forefinger, he might tap forcibly on the sheet of paper, which his wife held in such doubtful fingers, said quietly: "Yes, my dear, a bed: but an *electric bed.*"

51

There came a day, not many weeks after this impassioned conversation between John Quincy Zinn and his wife, when, at a small and elegant reception in Kiddemaster Hall, Samantha was brought near-forcibly into the company of her old acquaintance Mr. Cheyney Du Pont, and, in silent rebellion against the chatter ringing on all sides, consoled her hot beating heart with these secret words: *I love Nahum, and I shall claim him, and run away with him I know not where, whether we be married or no—for, what is marriage after all?—but I shall make my claim nonetheless. And who is to prevent me!*—all the while extending her pretty little hand, and staring coolly at the handsomely attired young gentleman before her, who bowed with some awkwardness, and muttered a few startl'd and embarrassed words in her direction, and stared with perplexity at her, as if the young Mr. Du Pont no more recognized Samantha, than she recognized him.

For Samantha, as I have said, had grown most alarmingly beautiful, over a mere twelve-month, and, with her graceful petite figure, and small porcelain-smooth face, she resembled nothing more than a lovely little china angel, of the kind wrought by the gifted Rogers, for his most privileged subscription customers. Great-Aunt Edwina had insisted that Samantha prepare herself for this social event (such events, alas, having become rare at Kiddemaster Hall in recent years), so the reluctant young miss was attired, not in one of her old best dresses, but in a striking new peach-colored Swiss voile gown, in the fashion of the late Eighties, with an exaggerated long bodice, an angular bustle, and a wide, heavy, layered skirt flounced in Chantilly lace; and she wore, upon her tight-molded red hair, with its fringe of charming ringlets, a tall hat—well over eighteen inches in height—very prettily adorned with peach blossoms, peacock feathers, and white silk ribbons. Indeed, *could* this young beauty be the "brainy, strange, homely one" amongst the Zinn sisters of old?—so every countenance seemed to proclaim; and the elderly René Pierre Éleuthère Du Pont, leaning on his cane, and wiping a negligible clot of saliva from off his trembling chin, said, in a hoarse chuckling undertone to Judge Kiddemaster: "Ah, sirrah, your trump card!—yes indeed!—no more than sixteen or seventeen, I wager!—and most luscious! And if the sickly young pup cannot whelp her, why, sir, I shall volunteer—it shall be my final sacrifice for my family"—thereby provoking himself into a hacking spasm of laughter, which in turn shaded into a spasm of coughing.

That Cheyney Du Pont, blinking with watery red-rimmed eyes at Samantha, failed at first to recognize her, is perhaps to be attributed not simply to Samantha's alter'd appearance, but to certain mysterious changes in the young Du Pont heir himself.

I know not what tragic illness had o'ercome this charming young gentleman, in the years since he so passionately wooed the heartless Malvinia, or even whether it arose as a consequence of his long romantic journey to the East, or had its origins close to home: whether it was an "illness" in fact, or a "condition"; an infection from without, or from within. It is altogether likely that the heartbreak suffered by Cheyney Du Pont, upon Malvinia's elopement with Orlando Vandenhoffen, so precipitated a crisis of some sort that, the sensitive young man's bodily constitution being weakened, any manner of disease might successfully assault it: nor did his style of living, which involved a considerable expenditure of his income, in New York City and elsewhere, contribute to his physical stamina. In any case, tho' Samantha was very wrong to behave coolly to poor Cheyney, in the presence of both their families, her bewilderment at his appearance, and her difficulty in recognizing him, are perhaps comprehensible.

Where the Cheyney Du Pont de Nemours who had so gallantly courted Malvinia, in those halcyon days of old, pleased the eye in every respect, with his tall trim manly bearing, and his strong-boned handsome face, about which, withal, a boyish smile oft played, *this* Cheyney could not hope to please any eye at all, I am afraid, save one dimmed with familial love, or wifely Christian forbearance. No longer precisely tall, and disturbingly soft, in a queer red-flushed voluptuousness, not truly fat, nor yet obese, but rather puffy and bloated—awkward in his motions, as if he had yet to grasp how radically his virile grace had been qualified—his skin, which had once been a fine hearty bronze-tan, now reddened, dry, and flaky on every visible inch, but most grievously between his fingers, and about his lips—the hair, once so thick and wavy, now retreated almost entirely from his forehead and temples, to reveal a patched and flaking scalp—the eyes, once so finely-lashed, and so impudently masculine, now small, squinting, reddened, and virtually lashless—and his once-proud mustache so sadly depleted, it was but a grayish wisp on his tremulous upper lip: that this agèd and broken creature had once been that paragon of young manhood, Cheyney Du Pont de Nemours, over whom even Malvinia had shed a tear or two, and in whose veins flowed the blood of an *historic*—it may even be a *noble*—family: ah! quite beggars the understanding. For he could not have been above thirty-five years of age at this time.

Cheyney Du Pont was, however, attired in the very latest fashion —a dinner jacket of black velvet, startlingly informal in it shortness, yet with an elegant roll collar, and black trousers which, cuffless, fell quite properly to the heel of his shoe; his waistcoat was of white Marseilles quilting, and almost too sumptuous to the eye.

His stammered greeting to Samantha was but the prologue to a somewhat awkward exchange, during which it became gradually evident to Samantha, that Malvinia's former suitor had undergone not simply a physical transformation of the most mysterious sort, but a mental transformation as well. That a young gentleman of our time should converse with a young lady, in a drawing room of faultless propriety, chiefly on matters concerning the weather, did not surprise Samantha (tho' of course it greatly wearied her): that the gentleman in question should proceed so slowly, with such hesitation, drawling and repeating his words, and surreptitiously wiping at his mouth with a stained handerker-chief, did naturally alarm her, and cause a most unbecoming frown to appear between her pretty pale-red brows. *I love Nahum, and am confident in his love for me*, Samantha told herself bravely, *and we shall not be cheated of each other: nay, not even Providence shall part us!*—words of such extraordinary brazenness, I can scarcely bring myself to record them.

And these heretical thoughts were transpiring in one of the most beautiful drawing rooms at Kiddemaster Hall, in the heart of a fairy-sprite young lady, who looked but half her age, and bestowed upon the world an angel radiance!—well-observed, on every side, by her family: Mrs. Zinn and Miss Edwina Kiddemaster in particular, who might *guess*, but could not *know*, of the serpent lurking in Samantha's heart.

Indeed, there was nothing in Samantha's overt behavior to incriminate her. She attended to Mr. Du Pont's lengthy, halting, stammering monologue, which, drifting from the subject of Bloodsmoor weather, reached an early plateau of interest when it touched upon weather in the Orient (monsoons, tempests, heat of 130 degrees Fahrenheit, droughts of such severity "you could see," as Cheyney mumbled, "that God detests the heathen"), but descended swiftly to tedium, when it drifted onto the subjects of the tariff, and the rabble-rousing Democrats, and the "anarchist thugs" who were seducing the American workingman—issues which Samantha had heard many times discussed by her grandfather, and other of her older relatives, in the same terms.

After a strained pause, during which time Cheyney sipped at his glass of sherry, one hand steadying the other as the glass was brought to his lips, and Samantha, standing immobile, allowed her green gaze to dart about the room—retreating, at once, when it met that of Great-Aunt Edwina, who was watching her quite overtly—Mr. Du Pont inquired of Samantha whether she visited New York City at all: and Samantha replied in a courteous and well-bred voice, that, unfortunately, she did *not*.

"Nor shall I," Cheyney said, sighing. Unconsciously he had begun to scratch at the red flaking skin about his mouth; and small scales fell liberally, with a deleterious effect upon his elegant black jacket. "I am, they have probably told you," he drawled, with an almost disrespectful wag of his head, in the direction of his elders, "home in Bloodsmoor for good." His puffy-lidded eyes so contracted, Samantha feared he was about to burst into tears: but, on the contrary, he began to laugh quietly. "*For good,* as they say. Which may be interpreted in one way, or in the other; or in both. 'For good' in the sense of being permanent; 'for *good*' in the self-evident sense. Of course I am altogether happy that Providence has arranged it so," he said, his bloated chin creasing as, in deference to Samantha, or in mockery thereof, he attempted a clumsy bow, all the while laughing and giggling quietly, so that his soft body quivered, "and that I have the honor of meeting you again, Miss Zinn. And this time, I trust it shall turn out properly: you shall not run off: in your balloon or whatever. Or was it—" he said, an infantile bewilderment o'ercoming his countenance—"or was it on horseback, eloping with that blackguard actor—with whom my honor obliged me to duel, but my natural good sense—and my cowardice—instructed me otehwise: nor was the whore worth it. But excuse me, Miss," he said, blinking and staring, "You seem to be return'd to me: and much smaller this time, and, so they have promised, much easier to manage: and this time," he said, with a heaving, spasmodic fit of silent laughter, *"you shall not escape.* And we shall see, Miss Zinn, what prodigious issue shall spring from our—union."

At which point Samantha, tho' having always judged herself a strong-willed individual, given to no foolish female weaknesses, quickly raised her fan to her lips, and, opening it wide, stared with affrighted green eyes at her companion's merry face.

"He is an altogether agreeable young gentleman," Mrs. Zinn said to her youngest daughter, the very next morning, "rather more subdued in spirit than I recall; and quite the better for it, your Aunt Edwina and I think. In the old days, provok'd, no doubt, by your departed sister, Mr. Du Pont disported himself in almost too exuberant a virile manner: and, I am bound to think, pressed upon that hussy illicit notes and gifts, if I dared believe the servants' tongue-wagging. The which, my dear, I hope *you* will resist: for no gentleman can respect you, who sees that you accept favors from him, before the banns are officially announced. Your father and I noted too," Mrs. Zinn said, her voice deepening as if to confront her daughter's protestations, "an altogether pleasant hygienic air about Mr. Du Pont, an uncommon *immaculateness,* both of body and of linen; the consequence, it may be, of his vigorous regimen, and a renewed asceticism. That Mr. Du Pont will not only make an excellent, upstanding, and altogether gentlemanly husband for some very fortunate young lady, but provide also an invaluable opportunity for the generous exercise of *Christian love and charity,* I do not doubt: such love, and such charity, being not inordinately exercised by your generation, in these atheistical times."

Mrs. Zinn having delivered herself of this speech, which, conveyed thusly, in cold print, cannot suggest the maternal warmth which emanated from it, she then drew herself up to her full height, so as to best confront her red-haired daughter's response: and was greatly surprised, and not a little disconcerted, by Samantha's slow, hesitant, benumbed voice, and the just faintly perceptible trembling of her lips.

"I know you are right, Mother," Samantha said, "tho' my heart wishes it were otherwise: for, in truth—in truth—" she murmured, faltering, "I had hoped not to marry at all, but to remain here at home, with you, and dearest Father, and—and—simply to continue as I have been: your daughter Samantha, and Father's most trusted associate. I had hoped," the moist-eyed girl continued, a becoming blush spreading across her cheeks, "I had hoped to remain a maiden, all the days of my life."

Mrs. Zinn was so moved by this speech that, forgetting her usual composure, and the whalebone armor that restrained her bosom, she reached out to embrace her daughter: and folded her in her arms, all the while comforting her, and half weeping, and then, indeed, truly weeping, for Samantha's meek words had quite penetrated her heart, and for a brief poignant moment she realized all that it imported: she should lose forever not only sweet Samantha, but her *last daughter.*

So mother and daughter embraced, and exchanged tearful words of endearment, and Mrs. Zinn surrendered Samantha to Cheyney Du Pont, and to Christian charity; and Samantha, her cheeks streaming with tears, espied little Pip over her mother's shoulder, there in the doorway, in the midst of scrambling nimbly upward against gravity—and spider monkey and young lady exchanged a long, level, unblinking, uncanny stare, the nature of which I am no more able to define, than to countenance.

It may have been that Mrs. Zinn, thinking more calmly, and with more native suspicion, upon Samantha's unlook'd-for acquiescence, believed that another step must be taken; or, it may have been that the good woman, succumbing to a pang of regret, that someone—that is, poor

Nahum Hareton—must be injured, in these new developments, came to
a sudden decision that he should be addressed: in any case, not three days
after this heartrending scene, a manservant brought a letter to Nahum,
as he sat dallying in the sunshine above the gorge, attended by a subdued
Samantha (surprised in the act of pouring tea into his cup, as the servant
approached): and, tearing the envelope open, with shaking fingers, the
youth announced that it was a *summons from Mrs. Zinn.*

The young lovers' eyes snatched guiltily at each other, and for a
long terrible moment neither could speak.

Then Nahum said: "Your mother wishes an audience with me,
Samantha; and I must go."

Samantha pressed a small pale hand against her forehead, half
shutting her eyes, yet did not allow herself to stagger, or to exhibit any
further sign of weakness. In a low calm voice she said: "Yes. You must
go. But do not allow the dragon to devour you alive."

"Samantha!" Nahum exclaimed. "She is your mother, after all—
how can you speak of her thusly?"

"She is not my mother, but a dragon," Samantha said slowly, "tho'
I shall not contest the point, at the present time: indeed, I have no great
interest in debating the issue. You must go, and you shall: and, I implore
you, do not allow her to devour you. And all will be well."

"Alas—*will* it?" Nahum asked. He looked from the face of his
belovèd, which, from having gone deathly pale a scant moment before,
was now regaining its color, to the stiff importunate missive in his fingers;
and back to Samantha's face again, with a most piteous expression upon
his own, the which might well rend my heart, were this guilty couple not
acting both in defiance of the elder Zinns, and of propriety in general.
(Indeed, I am not in full possession of the knowledge—and have no
desire to be so—of when, precisely, and in what outlaw circumstances,
these two *confessed* their feeling for each other: but such is the startling
intimacy of this scene, that I am led to conclude that a confession of sorts
must have occurred, however "innocent," in a carnal sense, the two
remain.) "Samantha, my dear, *will* it?" Nahum whispered.

"We must trust in God," Samantha said, a faint line appearing
betwixt her delicate eyebrows, "and in our own ratiocinative powers,
which are, I do believe, at least the equal of poor Mother's: for she is, you
know, *poor, impoverished,* in both heart and in spirit, and cannot do us a
great deal of harm, once we elude her. The sole danger, dear Nahum,"
the brazen miss said softly, laying her hand upon his, in an extraordinary
gesture of comradeship, and blatant public intimacy, "the sole danger is
that Mother will so mercilessly interrogate you, as to cause you to reveal
our situation—not in actual words, for you are too clever for that, but in
emotion, for you are too honest, and know nothing of prevarication."

"I shall do my best to compose myself," Nahum said, and, with a stealthy glance toward the doorway of the workshop, a distance of some fifteen or twenty yards thither, dared to squeeze Samantha's fingers in his; and then abruptly released them. A dazed frightened smile warmed his sober countenance. "To compose myself, and to reveal nothing: tho', I must confess, your mother does in fact terrify me, as your father could never."

"Nay, you are too generous," Samantha said, with a bitter little laugh, "for surely you have noted the *apparent reluctance,* and the *actual fervor,* with which Father has capitulated to that offer from Congress? *She* is terrifying, yes—but so is *he*—in the alacrity of his surrender—in the very ingenuity with which he has approached the project: considering and discarding, early on, all the 'humane' measures of execution that would involve no mechanism, and hence no genius. Nay, hush," the half-angered girl commanded, "do not defend my father to *me.* I was his first human experiment, and shall not have been his last. An *electric bed,* indeed! And the miserable felon to be strapped to it, in full consciousness, no doubt, and high-voltage A.C. to be directed through his being! And Father murmurs of Justice, and Law, and Sacrifice, and Patriotism, and all that he owes to this great nation, and the remarkable kindness of the Senators—nay, my dear, do *not* interrupt, you are *not* obliged to defend any Zinns or Kiddemasters to me—and it is only his current want of materials, and the delay in the honorarium, that keep us from witnessing God alone knows what 'necessary' experiments, here in this sacred place! No, each is terrifying, Nahum, in his own way: indeed, all of Bloodsmoor terrifies me. So you must approach Mother with caution, my dear, or not at all."

Nahum was staring most intently at his young lady, during this wild, indeed incoherent, speech; but I know not whether her demented words most absorbed him, or the ruddy blush on her cheeks. All transfixed he was, for an uncanny moment, as if—God help us!—he were about to utter the crudest words of outright love, or move to fold the impetuous girl in his arms, and place a searing kiss upon her audacious lips. But at this moment the sunshine was eclipsed, and then quite obscured, by a massive rain cloud; and the lovers stood staring at each other, as if locked invisibly together, with no notion of what had happened, or what was to come.

Silence brimmed between them. Minutes sped past, with the weight of hours, or days. And finally Nahum bestirred himself: "Or not at all?" he echoed.

Samantha, clad in her weekday calico, an old woollen shawl about her shoulders, could not prevent herself from shivering, with anticipation, or with the damp chill that eased upward from the depths of the gorge: and smiled queerly at her lover. "Or not at all," she said. "For, you know, there is no power on earth that forces you to obey her summons—just as there is no power on earth that forces me to remain here, as the last of the Zinn daughters."

"And yet," Nahum said quickly, "you would break their hearts if —if you left with no warning."

"How else is there to leave," Samantha said as quickly, with a brave, nervous little smile, "except with no warning?"

Nahum solemnly folded the missive from the Octagonal House, and would have slipped it into his breast pocket, had not wicked Samantha snatched it out of his fingers, and torn it swiftly in two, and let the pieces flutter over the cliff's edge, and down into the mist-obscured depths of the gorge.

"Samantha!" Nahum exclaimed. He adjusted his wire-framed glasses, as if to peer sternly at her; but his gaze eased away, guiltily, and slyly. No one stood in the doorway of the cabin-workshop, and no one observed from out the window: the lovers were alone. John Quincy Zinn, immersed in his work, was oblivious to them as always; and the aging Pip, coiled asleep near his master, had not the faintest notion of the sin that blossomed in the lovers' hearts.

Fingers of mist rose silently from the ravine, and where innocent sunlight had rayed, but a brief while ago, now the bare flat rocks stretched bleak and expectant.

"It is true, I confess, that your mother intimidates me," Nahum said quietly, "and your father as well. They are giants, Samantha!—giants in a child's dream."

"Yes," Samantha said. "But we must wake from that dream."

"Am I a coward, Samantha, to fear her?" Nahum asked. "And to fear *him*? Tho' I love him as well."

"You are no coward," Samantha said, wrapping her shawl tightly about her shoulders, as if in preparation for a journey. "You are brave, and wise, and gentle."

"Shall we marry, then?" Nahum asked in a quavering voice. "When we are out of here?—when we are free?"

"I know not about *marriage*," Samantha said, her pert upper lip curling, as if the word gave her no pleasure. "I have all I can manage, to contemplate *love*."

And, so exclaiming, the bold young woman seized both her lover's hands, and urged him forward, to stand at the very edge of the ravine, where the damp chill mist grew thicker with every minute. They may have exchanged further words—I do not doubt that they did—but the words were lost to me, and, stricken with revulsion as I am, I cannot wish to retrieve them.

And so, on that day, without warning, Miss Samantha Zinn and Mr. Nahum Hareton disappeared: descended into the mist, as into the bowels of Hell: with every step drawing farther from me, and from Bloodsmoor, until at last the fog closed over their frail figures, and swallowed them up entirely.

Ungrateful children! Shameless sinners! But my words cannot touch them, for they have escaped utterly; and none but the lewdest fiends in Hell might guess where they have gone.

52

It was unjust of Samantha, and certainly intemperate, to accuse her father of having been casual or self-serving, in his consideration of various "humane" measures of execution: for the good man taxed himself greatly over this problem, internally debating the morality of the entire procedure, and many a time ready to give up in dismay, save that, as Mrs. Zinn so wisely said, the project, and the generous honorarium, would then be awarded to another man, possessed of inferior moral fibre.

"You are right, Prudence," Mr. Zinn said, sighing. "And then, too, I am but a tinkerer, and must leave the administration of justice—and, indeed, the entire legal profession—to other men, who have made it their lives' work."

Many a sleepless night John Quincy Zinn spent, perusing dusty old volumes, and causing his eyes to ache, and his stomach betimes to heave, in his diligent search through the centuries, and through many cultures, for a means of capital punishment that would satisfy Congress's demand for both *humanity* and *efficiency!* Not scholarly by nature, and restive away from his belovèd workbench, he nevertheless devoted himself to the preparation of a formal report for Congress, in which numerous traditional methods of execution were considered, and analyzed, and their suitability weighed. Flogging, whipping, knouting, slow strangulation, burning at the stake, starvation in prisons, cages, stocks, etc., mutilation of the body, being torn apart by wild carnivores, and other such heinous means were, in John Quincy's eyes, automatically rejected, as being both inhumane and inefficient, and unworthy of a Christian nation. Nor did death by firing squad, or hanging, altogether strike his fancy, despite their popularity in most of the states. Garroting by way of "slave collars," a favorite device of the old slaveholding South, was also rejected, even for Negroes: tho' Mrs. Zinn cautioned her idealistic husband against speaking too bluntly on this issue, and offending the Southern gentlemen in Congress. ("It is not, after all, as if slaveholding were unknown in the Kiddemaster family," Mrs. Zinn said. "I mean amongst relatives who lived farther South—and with whom, of course, we Philadelphians did not sympathize.")

It was certainly the case that Mr. Zinn, with his Transcendentalist soul, felt grave reservations about this project, at the start; but his native Yankee ingenuity soon came to the rescue, and he was able to apply himself to it as a problem of technique, or technology, thereby releasing his greatest energies. The old Roman method of suicide, by opening a vein, struck him as a distinct possibility: particularly if the condemned man were to be allowed the privilege of *administering the execution himself.* And there was the guillotine, which, his reading on the subject soon convinced him, was a wondrously humane and efficient procedure; tho' he doubted that the American public would take to it, as the French so greedily did, being less eager to see blood spilt, and, in general, less desirous of actually mutilating the human body. The employment of powerful poisons—hemlock, cyanide, arsenic, etc.—struck him as reasonable, tho' no poison that induced agonizing convulsions could be considered. Sleeping draughts in excess would be as merciful a means of death as one might hope for, Mr. Zinn thought, after the sudden death, in her crib, of his nine-month-old granddaughter Sarah Rumford. (How untimely, and how tragic, that infant death! Poor Octavia simply discovered Baby Sarah no longer breathing, one day, in her white wicker crib, as peaceful as if she were merely asleep, with her brother Godfrey close by, quite unaware of the disaster, and innocently asking "if Baby would wake soon, and wish to be pushed in her perambulator"—for little Godfrey, a husky high-spirited lad of three, had enjoyed nothing more than helping Octavia push his baby sister along the estate's tree-lined paths.)

Yes, Mr. Zinn concluded, transcending his private grandfatherly sorrow, and seizing upon the idea of *sleep-death:* for could anything be more humane, more peaceful, more gentle, more—inviting? And if the condemned criminal were allowed to *administer the overdose himself,* within, of course, a delimited period of time, the entire procedure could not fail to be eminently civilized, and exemplarily Christian.

And so he drafted a proposal for Congress, enumerating all of the above, and concluding that the method of *sleep-death* seemed to him most viable: and you may well imagine his consternation, when, after much delay (indeed, weeks and months), he was informed that the proposal had been vigorously rejected, with *not one vote*—Republican or Democrat—in its favor.

"I am quite bewildered by this, Prudence," Mr. Zinn said, plucking nervously at his beard, and examining the official missive yet another time. "I am quite demoralized, and cannot comprehend why they have rejected me so vehemently."

Mrs. Zinn allowed that *she* was not greatly surprised: for, after all, *self-administered death* was tantamount to suicide, and suicide was a sin against God, and the United States government could hardly countenance, let alone provide the means for, such an egregious act.

"But think of how merciful such a procedure would be!" Mr. Zinn protested. "No bloodshed—no agony—no writhing at the end of a rope —no damage to the physical being! My dear Prudence, what could be more Christian—more humane?"

"Humane it may be," Mrs. Zinn said, "but Christian it is *not.*"

Fortunately for Mr. Zinn's prospects, it happened that one of Prudence's cousins was a Congressman, from a Philadelphia district, and when he journeyed out to Bloodsmoor to spend a few days hunting, he sought out the perplex'd J.Q.Z. in order to inform him that his notions of the *humane,* the *peaceful,* and the *gentle,* were all very good, but totally unacceptable. For, it seems, the legislators wanted a means of capital punishment that was uniquely "American"—even, if you will, "showy"—a means that would "do us proud as a billion-dollar country."

"Something new, and flashy, and bright, and inventive," Heywood Kiddemaster said, clapping Mr. Zinn robustly on the back. "Something, you know, *ingenious.* And tho' the 'humane,' business is important, it needn't be the prime consideration: for, tho' my gentleman colleagues did not expressly say so, in their debate, I do believe it would be politic, my friend, to make death hurt a little."

"Ah! I see," Mr. Zinn said slowly, gazing at Heywood Kiddemaster, and blinking, with so vague an expression as to quite belie his words, "I see: death should be *showy,* and *flashy,* and *ingenious,* and—what was the other?—ah yes, *American.*"

"And it should hurt," Heywood said, snapping his fingers for emphasis. "Yes, indeed, if *we* are paying for it: it should hurt at least a little."

"And it should hurt," Mr. Zinn repeated, in a hollow dull voice, *"at least a little."*

53

Amongst Octavia's female relatives there was more than one, I believe, who solemnly wondered at that steadfast young woman's courage, and bethought herself frequently, as to whether *she* possessed the like strength, and the unwavering Christian faith. The tragic untimely loss of the infant Sarah!—so close upon the heels of a miscarriage, and a prolonged convalescence!—and, tho' such matters were necessarily kept from the ears of womenfolk, it was dimly known too that Mr. Rumford had suffered substantial losses in grain speculation, and had had to borrow heavily from the Kiddemasters: which did not, the reader may well imagine, knowing a little of that stern-conscienc'd gentleman's heart, inspire a household cheeriness, or a free commingling betwixt husband and wife.

Yet, all uncomplaining, the grieving young mother took comfort in all that she *had:* a belovèd husband; a precious and angelic son; devoted parents and family; and, above all, the guidance of Heaven, which became ever clearer to her, in her darkest hours of need. *Forgive me a mother's impertinent sorrow,* was Octavia's daily—nay, hourly—prayer, *for if You have called Baby Sarah to Your side, it was out of a desire to have the prettiest angel of all in Heaven with You!*

Thus her innermost heart; as, a never-resting and resolutely genial mistress of Rumford Hall, she busied herself with one hundred and one household tasks daily, and supervised the servants, and discussed all the menus with her housekeeper, and paid her necessary visits to neighbors of a like social station, and to the elderly rector and his wife; and, even more resolutely genial, and certainly uncomplaining, she accommodated Mr. Rumford's conjugal demands, which, with the passage of time, grew gradually more exacting, and more challenging of definition. Yet it was her bliss in her duty, and no mere grim stamina, that gave her the required strength, and sealed her lips, against any outcry of repugnance or simple pain: and more than once, enduring her spouse's protracted labors in the *unitary act,* the amiable wife consoled herself thusly, with an inward recitation of J. Monckton Milnes's powerful verse—

> Thou must endure, yet loving all the while,
>   Above, yet never separate from thy kind;
> Meet every frailty with the gentlest smile,
>   Though to no possible depth of evil blind.
> This is the riddle thou hast life to solve;
>   But in the task thou shalt not work alone,
> For while the worlds about the sun revolve,
>   God's heart and mind are ever with His own.

Even so, I am led to wonder if Octavia's strength, and, above all, the placidity of her heart, might have been sustained throughout her trials, had she not been blessed with her golden-curled cherub, Godfrey II: *Little Godfrey,* as the household warmly called him, with much amazement at the boy's precocity, and the robust high spirits that gave to his every shout or footfall a joyful ring.

Ah, the delightful little gentleman!—his mother's constant worry, for all his tireless mischief; and his mother's constant blessing, upon whom the good woman shamelessly doted, in the warmth of that maternal love which beggars all description, and certainly all analysis!

Master Godfrey was, at the age of three, a large-boned, husky, wondrously energetic little man, with curly locks in which gold and fair brown contended; and pale blue eyes, lit with a gay impudent twinkle, set rather close together, but inordinately beautiful, and thickly lashed; and a squarish, firm face, the cheekbones broad, the chin well-defined, the pretty little ears somewhat elongated, and tapering sharply at the lobes. So well-defined was the child's widow's peak, which grew, it may have been, a full inch down into his smooth broad brow, that it gave an impish, yet utterly captivating, cast to his entire countenance, and might well have been the envy of many a young lady, with pretensions toward beauty. (For tho' the old superstition would have it, that this distinctive mark signified *early widowhood,* or *disaster* of some less defined nature, it was generally considered, by the enlightened, as an unusual sign of beauty: and so indeed, in Malvinia, and even in Deirdre, the widow's peak was striking rather than disfiguring, and surely did not detract from their comeliness.)

Dear Master Godfrey! How dare I attempt to describe that indefatigable imp, who, from the scant age of nine months, was gaily "into everything, high and low," as his mother exclaimed? How dare I attempt to fix, in cold unyielding print, the sprightly glow of his eyes, and the inquisitiveness of his every glance, and query, and poke? The unabash'd animal spirits that enlivened his husky little form, and the shrill sunny chuckle that erupted from him one hundred times a day, were so irresistible as to wring a smile from Mr. Rumford's thin lips, and inspire a moist tinge of paternal pride, in that gentleman's preoccupied gaze: and to cause him, of a sudden, to summon his lawyer to Rumford Hall, that he might significantly alter his will, in order that Little Godfrey be named as his main heir, and his other children—scatter'd, and doubtless grievously disappointing to him—allotted smaller portions. (Octavia, being of the female sex, naturally stood to inherit nothing at all: yet we can imagine her great joy, on being informed, however obliquely, by Mr. Rumford, as to his intentions. "And, named as he is," Mr. Rumford observed, "I cannot doubt but that my son will do handsomely, in your grandfather's will too: for the old fool must leave his fortune to someone.")

True it was, that the elderly Godfrey Kiddemaster—now in his mid-nineties—would become inordinately fond of his great-grandson, despite the boy's mischievous high spirits, and his numerous pranks: but the relationship began rather oddly, quite bewildering poor Octavia, and offending Mr. Rumford. For some reason Judge Kiddemaster insisted upon seeing Little Godfrey immediately following the baby's birth—as soon as common decency, and Dr. Moffet, would allow; not only did he wish to see, and to hold, the newborn infant (all red-faced and squalling, and kicking with a fury wondrous to behold!), but to *examine* it, in full daylight. So he carried it to a window, and, peering close, took note of the tiny widow's peak, and the shapely little ears, and murmured, "Ah! I like not that, nor *that,*" and continued for some minutes to examine the raging infant, despite the protestations of its father and mother, and the kindly Dr. Moffet: until such time as, puzzled, brooding, and, as it were, *undecided,* he handed the infant back to its nursemaid, his palsied hands shaking, and betook himself back to Kiddemaster Hall without another word.

The which, shyly, Octavia described to Mrs. Zinn, when the two women were alone together, save for the exuberantly suckling baby (who tugged and tore at the breast, and flailed his little fists, as greedy a little darling as one could imagine—and a fine ruddy color all over): whereupon Mrs. Zinn spoke for once in some alarm, without composing her thoughts beforehand, and, in fact, fixing her daughter with a gaze of unalloy'd surprise: "Why—Octavia!—it is very strange—it is *very* strange —but so my dear father did with each of *my* babies—with each of *you*— and never once did he explain his mysterious action, and never, of course, did I dare inquire—nor did Mr. Zinn—and—and—why, I can only repeat, tho' I mean no criticism of him—tho' I am *sure* there is a comfortable logic behind it: I can only repeat, *it is very strange.*"

And so indeed it was; but, I am happy to say, the entire incident was soon forgotten, in the general rejoicing amongst the three households, and Judge Kiddemaster's fluctuations of temperament, by no means excessive in a gentleman of his advanced years. (Nor can we doubt that the baptism of the infant, as Godfrey Lucius Rumford, and, informally, as "Godfrey II," did indeed please the kindly old Judge.)

So great-grandfather and great-grandson became friends, and there were innumerable visits back and forth, between Rumford Hall and Kiddemaster Hall, to the delight of all concerned. Octavia made every effort, and was frequently successful, to subdue the healthy animal spirits of her firstborn, who, despite his wide cherubic grin, and his bouncing golden curls, did oft deserve the fond epithet bestowed upon him by the several households—*Little Demon.*

In truth, as soon as he gained the use of his legs, and could walk unassisted, he was indeed "into everything," and ran his laughing mother most ragged: tho', stopping him from one little mischief or another, or soothing an alarmed or weeping housemaid, Octavia never failed to hug her boy close, against her warm palpitating heart, and kiss his o'erheated brow, and declare that "little angels ought not to be so naughty—for fear of being mistaken as *little demons"!*—the which teasing gave pleasure to mother and baby alike. As Godfrey grew able to run, and to escape from his cradle at will, oft very early in the morning, before the sun had risen, it happened that he wore out and discarded "as if they were but cheap cotton gloves" (in Samantha's censorious words), one valiant nursemaid after another. On his most jolly days, when he entered his eighteenth month, he eluded all his pursuers, laughing and shouting and jumping, as if life were naught but *play,* and *sheer delight;* and it must be a hard-hearted person indeed, to scold him, or to register displeasure at his antics.

The little imp danced, and sang, and whirled about, and "sounded the alarm" by running Mr. Rumford's hickory cane up and down the rungs of the staircase banister; he rocked so energetically in a zebrawood rocker, with a rush seat, that the seat broke through, and he would have injured himself, had not his vigilant mother run tearfully to his aid. Many a time was the solemn quiet of the old house punctuated by Little Godfrey's shouted laughter, and Octavia's alarmed cries. "My baby! Godfrey! What on earth *are* you doing? Have you hurt yourself? Oh, my dear, my dear—let Momma look—" Octavia fairly wept, wringing her hands. And, suddenly docile, the high-spirited child would allow himself to be snatched to his mother's heaving bosom, and might even share a tear or two with her, until, smiling with an angelic radiance, he assured his affrighted mother that he was not at all injured: "I am quite all right, Momma—*please* leave off crying, or you will break my heart!"

Most of the time the little darling did no genuine mischief, and certainly no deliberate harm, but, as he grew older, and ever more husky and exuberant, it sometimes happened that, quite accidentally, he broke things; or made poor Pip scream in terror, by hugging him too hard about the middle; or, intrigued by the "pretty tiny sounds" that came out of Great-Aunt Edwina's jeweled French music box, could not rest until he had pried the delicate little mechanism open, and quite destroyed it. Tho' forbidden to do so, he could not resist "playing general" with the beautiful old sword in Judge Kiddemaster's library, and not only nicked and tore the antique furnishings in the room, but managed to stab a hole in the portrait of his bewigged Kiddemaster ancestor!—to the genuine distress of both his great-grandfather, and Great-Aunt Edwina, who declared, taking Octavia aside, that "something *must* be done about him: he will drive us all to our graves otherwise!"

Whereupon Little Godfrey was contrite; and sincere in his contrition. And, with no need to be instructed by Octavia, he knelt before the elder Kiddemasters to tender his apologies, couched in near-formal terms, and lisped in a voice made soft by regret. He acknowledged that "he had been naughty," but he had not meant to be so: and hoped he might be forgiven.

And his shy, hopeful, abash'd smile was such, who among mortals could deny him?

Betimes, it is true, particularly after the birth (so unexpected to him) of his baby sister Sarah, he did fly into a temper, and bang at anything within reach of his hard little fists, and smash his teacup against the wall, and throw himself hard upon the floor, where, flailing his arms wildly, and kicking like a veritable dervish, he pounded with his heels so powerfully against the carpet that, to the consternation of the servants, a fine cloud of pale dust arose! In play become overly rough, the precocious three-year-old came near to injuring the five-year-old son of one of the servants, himself a husky lad with a freckled Irish face. Little Godfrey in all innocence struck the child with a flat rock from out the kitchen garden, having mistaken it, as he tearfully explained, for a cushion. And there were pranks, or mishaps, most of them too inconsequential to record, involving puppies, and cats, and baby chicks, and other small creatures, which, it may be, Little Godfrey *loved* too energetically, or was o'ercurious, as to the workings of their delicate inner mechanisms.

One day, after the servants had accused their little master of torturing, stabbing to death, and partly dissecting, a young mongrel dog belonging to one of the groundsmen, Octavia took her son aside, and bade him be still: for she had something solemn to tell him.

And he gazed at her with his thick-lashed baby-blue eyes, somewhat moistened with tears of contrition and defiance, and whispered: "Yes, Momma?"

Octavia began her lecture sternly, telling her son that it was a sin to hurt the little creatures—*any* creatures, no matter how ugly, or in-consequential—whether belonging to a servant, or otherwise—because these creatures were part of God's creation, just as he was: all had their place in God's love.

"Yes, Momma," Little Godfrey said meekly.

And so it was very wrong of him, and very naughty, to injure that mongrel dog, even in innocent play. Did he understand?

"Yes, Momma," Little Godfrey whispered.

And the cherubic little gentleman did look so contrite, and so chastened, that his mother could not resist kneeling before him, and hugging him; and in this wise continued her solemn little lecture, which had such an immediate effect upon the boy, that he remained altogether still in her embrace, and did not struggle to escape. "You should not have injured that nasty old dog, my dear, or any creature of God's, because they are all God's creation, just as we are; and, by injuring a one of them, you are injuring God as well. And should you, my sweet, wish to injure Our Heavenly Father?"—so the fond mother queried, all the while hold-ing her firstborn close against her beating heart. Little Godfrey fought to hold back his tears, but could not withstand the waves of contrition in his heart, and at last began to sob; and so mother and son were locked in an embrace of such love, and such sombre understanding, that my eyes fill with tears merely to record the scene.

"I am very, very sorry, Momma," the weeping cherub said, "but, you know, Our Heavenly Father was watching, and did not seem to care: and did not, in any case, stop me: and so I was much confus'd."

Little Godfrey adored his baby sister, however, and, in her pres-ence (no matter that she was but an infant, and could hardly know him), oft danced, and sang his little songs, and scampered about the room in imitation of Pip, seeking merely to delight her. He was, it is true, some-what distressed by the baby's evident inability to recognize him, and to respond with appropriate laughter, and admiration; but Octavia ex-plained to him that "Baby Sarah was too little to understand, but would, in time, grow to love him"—and that he must love her, and be patient with her, for he was a strapping big boy, and she but a tiny thing.

All of which Little Godfrey appeared to understand: but he con-tinued his energetic frolics nonetheless, and begged a dozen times a day to be allowed to hold Baby Sarah, or to push her in her perambulator; and was never more lively and mischievous than when "showing off" for her—racing about the lawn, somersaulting, and tumbling, and rolling, with his high-pitched chuckle; and, upon one summery occasion, on the terrace of Kiddemaster Hall, the little imp "played mousie" and crawled across the flagstone to poke his head beneath Great-Aunt Edwina's volu-minous skirts, and to lunge beneath them, and *disappear from view!*

What consternation followed, what amaz'd exclamations—the

reader can imagine, with no assistance from me. And how Great-Aunt Edwina gasped, and shouted, and struck at her frothy skirts with her rolled sunshade: and how Mrs. Zinn, ever-vigilant in the presence of her adored grandson, acted with surprising alacrity, to grasp the young rascal by the ankles, and haul him out. That Master Godfrey was roundly scolded on all sides, and severely disciplined by Mr. Rumford (who grew fearsomely red-faced during the interim), and, at last, was allowed to retreat in tears from the scene, attended by his blushing mother, and the new nursemaid—I scarcely need to remark: for it was indeed a scene that repeated itself, with great variation, of course, as to its particulars, over a period of years . . . until that tragic culmination of his young life, at the scant age of seven, of which, alas, I must one day speak, for not even the truly execrable events of our history will be excluded from this narrative.

"Was I naughty again, Momma?" the little dear would inquire, lifting his angelic, tho' tear-stained, face to Octavia, in order to receive her fond scolding, and her exasperated kiss: and to feel her sometimes tremulous, but at all times reassuring, fingers on his warm forehead, as she brushed away his golden locks. "I do not mean to be naughty, Momma; or to make you cry," the diminutive gentleman said stoutly, "and I *shall* be good from now on: to please you."

"Ah, I know, I know, my dear," Octavia exclaimed, her fond mother's heart near-swollen to bursting, "I *know*, my dear—and in fact you can do only good, and God, Who sees into your heart, can understand, as I do: for the pure of heart are pure in their every action, and cannot sin, but only, it may be, *disturb*, as a consequence of spirits tuned rather too high, for the staid elders of Kiddemaster Hall."

54

The morn of that day of unprognosticated sorrow, when nine-month-old Baby Sarah was discovered no longer breathing, in her pretty white wicker crib, carried with it no omens that might be feared by those in whom Christian piety and intellectual enlightenment have agreeably mated: for, in our advanced epoch, we cannot take serious note of the fact that, throughout the midsummer night, one of those cacophonous members of the owl family, the screech-owl, disturbed the tranquil darkness with his heinous calls; and poor Octavia woke from a distressing dream, most puzzlingly familiar to her, in which her belovèd son Godfrey appeared monstrously transform'd, into I scarcely know what—a creature of some six feet or more in height, with burning lewd eyes; and greatly protruding, and glistening, incisors; and tufts of thick dark hair, or fur, on the backs of his hands; and the inverted V of his widow's peak grown down savagely into his forehead, so that it nearly met his eyebrows, which had, in turn, grown bushy and shaggy. (How the alarmed mother recognized her son, in so grossly alter'd a state, I cannot guess: save that, even in her sleep, Octavia had wit enough to comprehend the Devil's agentry here, in his slanderous masquerade of the innocent child. *Get thee gone!* was the dreaming mother's hissed prayer, even as her bloodstream raced with ice, and each hair on her head rigidly defined itself.)

Immediately upon waking, however, Octavia cast off the insipid distractions of the night, and, retiring to her dressing room, spent upward of an hour upon her knees, giving thanks to God as she customarily did, and begging especial grace for her lost sisters (whom she could not believe beyond the largess of God's forgiveness, tho' she knew she had not the right to forgive them, of her own), and enumerating, as always, those amongst her family, her relatives, and her wide circle of acquaint-ances, whom, she hoped, God would deign to bless. The satanic disturb-ances of the night, those vaporous profane fittings known as *dreams,* Octavia did not honor by considering weightily: for, like all who are of robust, normal spirits, and have naught in their hearts to hide from God, she knew that it is the *daylight* that beckons, with its joyous, simple clarity, and its unwavering designations as to our task here on earth, and not the *night,* that abode of empty chimeras!

There followed, then, no uncommon routine, but, rather, the happy pursuance of Mrs. Lucius Rumford's daily regimen, involving a half-hour's blissful nursing of Baby Sarah (the dimpled dear!—so very gentle in her suckling at the maternal breast, she oft fell asleep in the midst of her nourishment); and an hour busily occupied with ablutions, and dressing, and the tidy and practical arrangement of her hair (these three activities assisted by Octavia's personal maid, a reticent but amply competent Irish woman of indeterminate years); and some forty-five min-utes devoted to the Bible, which Octavia was compelled to read aloud to the female members of the household staff (compelled, that is, by Mr. Rumford, who, in another room, generally read the Scriptures aloud to the male servants); and then breakfast, sometimes in the company of Mr. Rumford, and sometimes alone; and then a gladsome reunion with Little Godfrey, and with Baby Sarah, characterized by many joyful kisses, and exclamations, and those visible displays of mother love, as are too com-monplace to require explanation: and so the day properly began: and one did not greatly differ from the next, in the paradisical confines of old Rumford Hall.

"Are we not the most fortunate creatures on God's earth?" Oc-tavia gleefully whispered, as, hugging her precious baby to her bosom, she plumply stooped, that she might kiss the rosy cheek of Little Godfrey as well, and receive his morning kiss. "Are we not happy? Are we not blessèd? I pray only, my dears, that we deserve this bounty—and that our very felicity will not tempt Satan!"

As I have said, Little Godfrey was devoted to his baby sister, and made constant appeals to Octavia, and to the nursemaid, that he might hold Baby Sarah in his arms (which he was rarely allowed, being somewhat clumsy despite his surprising strength, for a child of three years); or push her in the heavy beribboned perambulator that had once been his own (which he was frequently allowed, tho' his excitement was such that he sometimes pushed the vehicle too fast, and caused Baby to scream); or feed her those favorite foods, that the kitchen staff, in shameless doting upon him, could not resist providing—tarts, trifles, puddings, and such (which of course he was not allowed, these foods being inappropriate for a nine-month-old infant). When Baby Sarah cried, Little Godfrey alternated between an anxiety—most touching to behold!—that she was "un-happy for some reason, I know not," and a stern disapproval, in that she was making Octavia upset: "For it is very, very naughty," the golden-haired child claimed, "for anyone to worry Momma—*I do not like it.*" Whereupon Octavia, even as she soothed the squalling infant, made every effort to comfort her diminutive protector, explaining to him that Baby Sarah did not *mean* to upset with her cries—but was simply behaving as a baby must, and as *he* had done, some years before.

It was sheer delight, to see the precocious lad rear back, as if insulted, and exclaim: "No, my dear Momma, you are mistaken—you are *very* mistaken—Godfrey did not ever carry on thusly, he did not *ever* wail and kick and stir up a fuss, and release a shameful odor—I insist, Momma, that *he did not.*"

"Was there ever such a boy!" Octavia said laughingly, to the at-tendant nursemaid, who, being somewhat new to Rumford Hall, and unaccustomed to Little Godfrey's strong-volumed voice, did not yet feel entirely comfortable in his presence. (The young woman had not, for instance, known how to accept Little Godfrey's immediate gift to her, of a lovely orange-and-black butterfly with slow pulsing wings, pinned to a strip of satin cloth.)

Little Godfrey's love for his sister being great as it was, I can imagine no worse catastrophe, than that, Baby Sarah ceasing to breathe as she did, of a sudden, in her crib, it was Little Godfrey who first gazed upon her—but who, fortunately, being a mere babe himself, had no notion of the horror that had transpired. The sequence of events was confused, and, of necessity, poor Octavia could never piece it together satisfactorily, but it unfolded something like this: Baby Sarah had been placed in the nursery, in her crib, for her midmorning nap; the nursemaid had retired to her own chamber, on a private mission, meaning to be out of the room a scant five minutes; Little Godfrey had entered the room, to see if Baby Sarah was awake yet, and desirous of a stroll in the peram-bulator; Octavia was giving instructions to the housekeeper, at the rear of the house, yet, by way of the backstairs, not so very far distant from the nursery—and, suddenly overcome by a vertiginous sense of horror, as of suffocation, she broke away from her conversation, and hurried upstairs, as quickly as her petticoats and crinoline and affrighted heart would allow—only to rush into the nursery too late, for Baby Sarah had already ceased breathing, and lay in her wicker crib as peaceful, and as angelic, as if she were merely sleeping, her brother Little Godfrey in attendance close by, fixing his mother with wide blue luminous eyes, and querying, in his exuberant voice: "Will Baby awake soon? Will she want to be pushed in her perambulator?—for *I* am ready, Momma, at any time."

Octavia leaned over the crib, and snatched her baby in her arms, but, alas!—it was too late. *The dimpled babe had passed from this earthly realm forever.*

Precisely what transpired next, Octavia retained but scant knowledge: she clutched her warm yet unbreathing infant to her bosom, and would have swooned straightaway, and sunk heavily to the floor, had not Little Godfrey strode manfully forward, crying, "Momma! Dear Momma! What is it, Momma!"—and acted to assist her to a chair. It would wring the most calcified of hearts, to witness this child's grave concern for his mother, so tragically contraposed with his utter ignorance of the catastrophe at hand!

With Baby Sarah's elfin corpse in her arms, poor Octavia did indeed sink into a swoon, for the shock was o'ermuch: and it is God's great mercy to us, in our hour of most unbearable grief, that He grant us a semblance of oblivion, and weigh our eyelids against that very *daylight world,* that, in all well-intentioned innocence, I had praised, but a moment before. In short, the o'erwhelmed mother *fainted:* but not before she heard her little boy ask anxiously, "Is Baby being naughty again, Momma? Is she worrying you? Momma? Momma? *I* am at your service, Momma, you know—pray, do not despair!"

VIII

The Mark of the Beast

55

It is scarcely to be believed, by those of us who know her so intimately, that, as her public career advanced, and her talent matured (for, I suspect, her myriad admirers could not be totally mistaken, as to her possessing a modicum of that vulgar commodity "talent"), the infamous Malvinia Morloch became increasingly doubtful: that, upon a hundred occasions, in the late Eighties, and the early Nineties, when her celebrity was at its meretricious height, the flamboyant actress was oft seized by not only a sense of her having done something wicked, but of her *being* wicked: an accursèd mechanism, devoid of Spirit, and "natural" in naught but the most egregiously bestial of ways!

I shall not succumb, Malvinia Morloch instructed herself, with bitter deliberation, pouring wine, or, it may be, a yet stronger liquid, from a decanter into a glass, gripped in a shaking hand, *I shall not this time succumb,* she vowed, scarce daring to confront the cold-glazed blue eyes in the mirror (whether a mirror in a hotel suite in New York City, or San Francisco, or Chicago, or St. Louis, or New Orleans, or Boston: ah, wherever!), *I shall not succumb, or, I swear, I must do away with myself . . . !*

And she quaffed the powerful beverage, the like of which no lady would desire, let alone deign to imbibe, and, all atremble, waited in vain for a narcotizing effect to transpire: yet, such was her spiritual condition, and so accustomed by this time was her frail physique, to alcohol of any degree of potency, that no glow of confidence ensued, or faint blossoming of strength. And so the wretched woman shivered, and half sobbed, in a realization that her depressed mood was but the more depressed by this shameful indulgence—of which, I hardly need confide, I can bring myself to speak only with great effort.

An accursèd mechanism, she named herself, and knew herself, indeed; and from the inside. Without a soul, whether graced by God, or merely mortal: without the softer, gentler, feminine impulses, by which in all civilized Christian societies decency is judged. By the most ironic of coincidences, the gentleman who was now pressing himself upon her, with little attentions, and gifts, of a cynically costly nature, appeared to be of like mind, tho' Malvinia, in her coquettish despair, had never hinted of her dread self-assessment. This gentleman, whom the reader will know as Mark Twain, was doubtless a perfect mate for Malvinia Morloch, tho' she made her usual show of resistance: for even as he excoriated the money-maddened society of his day, he boasted to all who would hear of his own wealth, and his own schemes for yet more wealth; mouthing a disdain for the public's high regard of his "genius," the captious man of letters nonetheless strutted along Fifth Avenue every Sunday afternoon, or descended the sprawling staircases of the most elegant hotel foyers, proudly attired in full-dress, white tie, white silk waistcoat, and all, that his giddy admirers—most of them, I am sorry to say, of the weaker sex —might flock about him, clucking and lunging like barnyard fowl. *An accursèd mechanism,* Malvinia secretly adjudged herself, the while she made up her face as heavily as she dared, to be viewed in the cruelty of daylight (for our capricious young lady was no longer twenty years of age, but, as this segment of our history begins, a rather more sobering thirty-three), *a machine of beastly inclination,* she inwardly muttered, as, adorning her body with ever more costly and flamboyant articles of clothing, poor Malvinia thrust herself upon the "stage" of her own life, with a play of zestful appetite her fickle attentions belied—and was deeply shaken, despite her show of outward coquetry, by Mr. Mark Twain's proudly voiced negativism, which so queerly and coincidentally matched her own.

"What is Man?" the aging, but still handsome, gentleman rhetorically inquired, sprawled in a booth at Delmonico's, or at his specially reserved table at Sherry's. "What are *we,* my dear Miss Morloch, but machines? No, no, pray do not turn so startl'd and innocent a visage upon me, my dear, but only consider: machines moved, directed, and commanded by *exterior* influences, *solely*—or, if animal-like, exactly along the ignoble lines of the chameleon, who takes his color, in order that he may survive, from his place of resort."

Whereupon the beauteous Miss Morloch, not many minutes from a triumphant, but exhausting, performance at the Broadway, in the leading role of a negligible concoction entitled *The Lost Heiress,* saw fit to respond not with the shocked sympathy she felt, but with an arch, and prettily disapproving, query to Mr. Twain: "But, my dear sir, you must exempt me, for, as you can see," and here she made a childish gesture, and turned upon him a dazzling and inspired smile, "as you can see, I am *hardly* at one with my setting, and would not, in the crude state of affairs of which you so gleefully speak, survive for an hour!"—dressed as she was, the vain creature meant, in an evening gown of indecent décolletage, made of a glimmering, clinging, iridescent Oriental fabric, bright crimson, upon which jewels and pearls weighed heavily; and slender-bodied ermines, three in number, grasped one another's tails firmly in their small clenched teeth, their extraordinary beauty in the rank service of keeping warm her near-naked shoulders. "I should, you know, be picked out at once by any hunter: and must then depend solely upon the mercy of kind-hearted gentlemen like yourself, that you will not pursue me for my hide."

The mustached man of letters could not resist an admiring smile, at his would-be mistress's wit, however artificial it might strike the ear, and however coldly glinting her blue eye might strike another eye; nor could he, in all good sport, refrain from acknowledging a kindred *soul,* or a kindred *soullessness,* as remarkable as his own. And, laying a chunky, beringed hand upon Malvinia's bare forearm, above her silken white glove, he chuckled deep in his throat, and intoned, in a voice just loud enough so that rapt eavesdropping admirers at the next table might hear, and cherish forever in their memories (ah! to have stolen away with a *bon mot* fallen from the sacred lips of Mark Twain!): "My dear Miss Morloch, it quite astonishes me, that a young lady of your wisdom, and your notable experience, should prove so naïve: for yours truly has rarely been mistaken as *kindhearted,* still less as a *gentleman:* and I hope you will soon allow me the privilege, of disabusing you of that notion."

And what had become of Orlando Vandenhoffen? the startl'd reader may well ask; what had become of that great impassioned love, for which, at one time, the distraught Malvinia had threatened to "do away with herself"?

Gone. Lost. And, yes—forgotten.

Whether cast aside by Malvinia, in one of her insane fits of jealousy (which occurred with increasing frequency, in the mid-Eighties); or contemptuously free of her by his own volition, and reconciled with his long-suffering wife and family, in Italy: I am not altogether certain. That Vandenhoffen had disappeared utterly from Malvinia Morloch's life, however, by 1892, I am quite certain; for, in fact, his place in her affections had been filled many times over, by a shameful diversity of gentlemen, of varying degrees of charm, wealth, and social position.

Impossible! you exclaim. Had Malvinia not vowed to love Vandenhoffen forever, and to die at once, if their sentimental union were dissolved? Had she not wept, and thrown herself about, and threatened to rake her beautiful cheeks with her nails, if he but glanced upon another woman, or alluded to another woman in his speech?

Was it not the matinee idol Orlando Vandenhoffen of whom Constance Philippa's most beautiful bridesmaid had sung, in secret, so many years ago, at that fateful wedding celebration in Bloodsmoor?—mouthing the merry words like any other participant, in all ostensible maidenly innocence—

> It's we two, it's we two for aye,
> All the world and we two, and Heaven be our stay!
> Like a laverock in the lift, sing O bonny bride!
> All the world was Adam once, with Eve by his side!
>
> *All the world was Adam once—with Eve by his side!*

whilst, imprinted upon her lustful heart, the image of *Orlando Vandenhoffen* surreptitiously smoldered!

And had the faithless daughter not cruelly bragged, in her hastily scribbled farewell to her loving parents, that she was happy for the first time in her life, under this cad's protection: not minding, for a moment, how the wicked boast should strike their ears? And had she not believed Vandenhoffen to be more than a mere man, but her *Destiny*?

Indeed, yes: you are not mistaken in your memory, dear reader: but much mistaken, I am afraid, in your credulousness. For Malvinia no longer adored Vandenhoffen, nor did he adore—or, it may be, very clearly recall—his bewitching protégée, whose career he had overseen, and, most repulsive of all, a certain unspeakable *inclination* in her carnal being, that, at last, he experienced an altogether masculine repugnance for her; and squeezed out of his heart, forever, any sentimental illusion as regarding *love* for such a creature, let alone lightsome *romance*.

In any case, this much-heralded union of two great "stars" had unloos'd itself, and dissolv'd utterly, to the malicious delight of all observers, some four or five years before the advent of Mr. Mark Twain.

I shall not succumb, Malvinia inwardly vowed, pacing about her hotel room like a caged tigress, as she awaited the ring of the telephone, and the discreet announcement, from the desk clerk, that her importunate suitor was in the lobby, and would shortly ascend, to rap at her door. *I shall not succumb to it again,* the near-frantic woman beseeched herself, *or, I swear, I will do away with myself at last: for what other punishment is equivalent to the crime?*

56

After her premature, and, indeed, unearned, ascent to theatrical fame, in the early Eighties, Malvinia Morloch inevitably found herself on a sort of plateau—high enough in itself, but possessed of very few acclivities; and some surprising declivities. She learned, to her untutor'd astonishment, that the theatergoing public could become ecstatic over a new, and younger, Juliet; that, the very season following the success of "Countess Fifine," one "Baronne Zoë" might appear—a flaxen-haired Nordic beauty whose crown of braids, and whose somewhat affected Scandinavian accent, would inspire hundreds of imitators, amongst the fashionable female set.

Poor Malvinia could not help but feel that the public's clamorous interest in another young actress was a literal rejection of *her*—and one of her stormiest, and prolonged, sessions with Orlando Vandenhoffen, was a consequence of a simple notice in the *Tribune,* to the effect that, upon the removal of Miss Malvinia Morloch to a new play, her understudy Miss Nelly Lockwood had acquitted herself superbly: the suggestion that Malvinia leave the long-running *Bride of Llewellyn* to open in *Fatal Secret* having stemmed from Vandenhoffen, who stood accused, tho' he hotly contested the fact, of being a secret protector of Miss Lockwood! (The critic for the *Tribune* said of Nelly Lockwood: "This lovely young actress possesses in abundance a piquant maidenly charm quite in contrast to Malvinia Morloch's more tempestuous and, as it were, exhilarant, powers; and is altogether her *equal* in mesmerizing an entire theater. Miss Nelly Lockwood, a hearty welcome from one and all!")—an amiable notice which inspired a most unamiable rage in Miss Morloch.

"She is yet another protégée of yours—*do not deny it,*" Malvinia charged, her maddened eyes flashing, and her teeth bared in a malevolent grimace, with unpleasant connotations of the carnivore, quite at odds, I hardly need emphasize, with the young beauty's costly attire, and the heavy strands of pearls looped about her slender white throat. "Pray do not turn that visage of *righteous denial* upon me, Vandenhoffen, who know your stage technique so well: do not insult us both, by attempting a spirited denial, of what, no doubt, all of New York is whispering."

Whether Vandenhoffen was this time altogether innocent of any infidelity, or whether the veteran thespian so controlled the range and timbre of his voice, that the most egregious lie might be uttered with the most compelling sincerity, I hardly know: but in any case that vexed gentleman, making his exit, gloves and top hat in hand, paused only to make a speech of distinctive brevity. "If you forbid me, my dear, to affirm my high regard for you, by a *spirited denial* of the charges brought against me—why, then, I find myself most powerless, and must simply leave!"— the while his nobly craggy brow darkened with the contention of storm and portentous calm, and his profile strongly defined itself, as both cruel and tender, outrageous and just.

"Liar! Adulterer! Murderer!" Malvinia cried; and would have flung a vase of purple orchids at the villain's handsome head, had he not prudently made his exit.

And even in this scene, in which the grossly physical, and the carnal, play no evident role, one can discern—albeit with hesitant, shrinking eyes— *The Mark of the Beast.*

The capricious nature of the theatrical world is such, however, that, by merely taking on new roles—new costumes, new hair fashions, new "characters"—Malvinia could retain a sizable number of admirers, gaining some, losing some, and again gaining some, from season to season. If her passionate emoting as the betrayed wife in *Fatal Secret* met with but restrained enthusiasm, in New York City, it was certain to receive a fonder reception in Buffalo, or in St. Louis; and, in any case, her gifts for "innocent comedic malice," tho' "most remarkable in a woman," would, the next season, regain her applause on Broadway, in a bright confection called *Love's Labors Won,* a spoof from the pen of Mr. Mark Twain—at that time in his career when, tho' immensely famous and wealthy, and scornful of both fame and wealth, that satirical gentleman evidently desired more. "You can't be wealthy enough to satisfy your heirs"—so Mr. Twain has informed us.

And so the years giddily passed. And Malvinia Morloch, tho' taking on, with admirable if misguided ambition, any number of disparate roles, remained essentially the same young woman: a precocious girl, to be more exact: a scheming *ingénue.* She was so incontestably beautiful, as even her enemies were forced to agree, that a great deal was forgiven her; there were even those pitiable gentlemen, some of them in possession of considerable wealth and social rank, who exhibited a contemptible *greed* for ill-treatment—altogether perverse, to any normal way of thinking, in the masculine sex.

Malvinia Morloch prided herself on her exquisite *perfection* as a woman. Tho' hilariously scornful on the subject of Bloodsmoor mores —the examples of Grandmother Sarah Kiddemaster, and Great-Aunt Edwina, in particular—Malvinia did not in fact radically stray from certain prescriptions laid down by those excellent ladies, who knew that the *physical* by its very nature is *gross,* and that the flesh of the female sex, whilst required for habitation on this earth, is yet angelic in aspiration, and partakes not at all of the lusty carnal appetites of the male. All this Malvinia knew, and it is to her credit: she was excessively fastidious in her daily—nay, thrice or four times daily—toilette; she bathed in French oils, and Portuguese minerals, and pink-toned sparkling bubbles that filled the air of the entire hotel suite with the most lovely fragrance; she abhorred plump women, and disapproved prettily of fat men—even Diamond Jim Brady; she recoiled in exaggerated disdain from all unpleasant odors, particularly those originating from the human body. Tho' hardly a maiden at this point in her shameless career, Malvinia Morloch yet played the maiden in her coquetry; she was bright, brittle, arch, chill; virginal in manner; affecting a flirtatious reluctance to be touched—so that a gentleman, kissing her proffered hand, *even if gloved,* was rewarded with an involuntary frisson from her, and, it may be, knew himself all the more fired, with a passion to conquer her nymphal resistance. From the very start in her relations with Orlando Vandenhoffen, when she allowed herself to be seduced, in his lavish hotel suite, in Philadelphia, Malvinia's role was that of the *violated virgin:* shy, coy, blushing, bold, resisting, and then unresisting, but never exactly acquiescent: and, of course, never moved by any ignoble impulses, let alone carnal passions, of her own. In all this, I suppose, the young Zinn girl *did* comport herself well—and was, in a manner of speaking, an incarnation of Grandmother Sarah Kiddemaster, despite the public immorality of her life!

I shall not succumb, the beauteous young girl proudly declared, and, indeed, for some time, her boast was not o'erturned.

The seasons passed, however, and the years: and it was not long before certain inclinations were aroused in the young woman, of a sort that baffled and disgusted her, in secret; and, as they errupted into visibility, must have equally baffled and disgusted her seducer—and frightened him as well, for *the Mark of the Beast*, as it asserted itself, could not fail to intimidate the most manly of individuals.

(*The Mark of the Beast* being that ominous trait for which Judge Kiddemaster had looked, in his great-grandson Godfrey, and, many years previously, in his four granddaughters. The precise details concerning the Kiddemaster taint, which evidently surfaced, in varying degrees of severity, from generation to generation, were never available to me: tho' it may be helpful for the reader to learn that while Judge Kiddemaster and Great-Aunt Edwina knew fully of this genetic curse, Prudence did not: nor, of course, did John Quincy Zinn.)

In any case, as regards the intimate relations between Malvinia Morloch and Orlando Vandenhoffen, it seemed to transpire, as the young *ingénue* strengthened her talent, and achieved a substantial reputation in the theatrical world—soon acquiring not only an ability to endure, but a positive exhilaration in, daylong rehearsals in ill-heated and rat-infested theaters, and performances made under great emotional strain and excitement—and, it may be, as Vandenhoffen impressed her less as a figure of mythical dimensions, and more as a near-equal, the impetuous young woman troubled but infrequently to hold her emotions in check; with unlook'd-for consequences, as if a veritable Devil sprang up in her, in quarrelsome moments, or in moments of carnal intimacy.

Alas!—coarse jests, and ribald remarks, and an extreme physicality, of a type perhaps not known save to pathological medicine; the occasional release of unspeakable odors, emanating from the nether regions; as well as an unnatural lubricity, of the female organs, that could not have failed to arouse grave repugnance in Vandenhoffen—as, indeed, it did in the hapless Malvinia, who was utterly astonished at the demonic caprices of her body, once the lamplight was extinguished. (Malvinia soon discovered that The Beast's most repulsive antics did not emerge, if the room were not bathed in total darkness. But, as no self-respecting female, even of the fallen ilk, would submit to any amorous embrace, save in the pitch-dark, this proved of little practical aid.)

At such times it was not unusual for Malvinia to wrestle with her lover as if she were no frail female creature, but another man: and she might yank at his hair, or kick him, or walk over him with her hot bare feet! Possessed by indefinable urges, she grunted, and cursed, and clawed, and bit, and pummeled with her fists, ofttimes causing genuine pain in Vandenhoffen, and arousing much alarm, chagrin, and fury, in addition to simple disgust. That she begged for forgiveness, afterward; and dissolved in tears of abject humiliation, claiming that she "had no idea what came over her," and that "it would never, *never* happen again," was but scant consolation to the matinee idol, who must have inquired of himself, with increasing frequency, whether he might not be best served by returning to his lawful wedded wife, and to his children, in Europe, being assured by past experience that *that* good woman behaved, at such times, with saintly passivity, and had never given him the least grounds for offense.

Still, Vandenhoffen's young mistress provoked such visible envy in other gentlemen, and had acquired such an agreeable renown of her own, in Café Society, that he was loath to give her up. Her creamy-pale skin and luminous blue eyes and dramatic dark hair, as well as her sloping shoulders, slim waist, graceful carriage, and the impeccable style of her couture, were all to *his* credit, as the most exquisite Arabian steed is to its rider's credit, and a significant aspect of his public self. Vandenhoffen responded with icy anger, when his mistress received gifts, and even marriage proposals, from other gentlemen: but he was secretly delighted, and may have kept closer tabs on her admirers, than she would have thought to do herself. And, it might be noted, the shrewd thespian did not stint from partaking of the bounty that was showered upon Malvinia Morloch, whether in such trifling forms as liqueur-filled bonbons, or fresh-cut roses, or sybaritic repasts at the most exclusive restaurants and clubs in the city; or in such extravagant forms as jewels and furs and other finery, that might, in extremes of financial need, be exchanged for cash. (For Malvinia and Vandenhoffen lived with lavish abandon, as if deriving a frenetic, childlike joy out of spending money, and riveting the public's attention upon them: such behavior, in such circles, being by no means remarkable during these "gilded" years, despite the fact that periodic economic depressions struck the nation, and it was not uncommon for frivolous theatergoers to pass, in the street, the most piteous "gentlemen-beggars," their expressions registering naught but a blank stupor, as a consequence of the disaster that had befallen them.)

And so, Vandenhoffen thought it politic to forgive his mistress her occasional bizarre behavior, in the light of these considerable advantages; and, for her part, Malvinia made every effort to overcome her congenital deficiency—which, of course, she could hardly have known was congenital.

The more The Beast haunted her, the more Malvinia bathed, seeking to purge herself of offensive odors; she applied harsh depilatories, to rid herself of ugly hairs, that sprouted in her armpits, and elsewhere, with brutal persistence. She found that The Beast was somewhat subdued, if she went for most of a day without eating, and drinking naught but water. And, when the *unitary act* was unavoidable, as a consequence of her companion's natural lustful appetite, and his imbibing of copious quantities of alcohol, the cunning young woman acquired the discipline of lying immobile, as if paralyzed, or a veritable corpse, the better to overcome unspeakable inclinations: and so, much of the time, her pride was maintained. (For she could not bear it, that Orlando Vandenhoffen, who had adored her from the first as his "Princess"—his "Angel"—his "Snow White"—should have any true suspicion, of the degree to which The Beast ofttimes permeated her being.)

I shall not succumb, Malvinia grimly instructed herself, but, alas, she had not always the choice.

57

It was many years later, at a private dinner in a most sumptuous dining room, in one of the newer and more palatial Fifth Avenue mansions, that Mark Twain said of Malvinia Morloch that he "would, but for his rheumatism, fall down in worship at her feet: for he greatly admired such vivacious *life*, to the extent that his own heart was *dead*."

This drawling observation was greeted with somewhat confus'd laughter, and, from her position farther down the table, the greatly flattered actress made a show of opening her silk embroidered fan, that she might display her slender fingers, upon which many a jewel licentiously glittered; and, cleverly choosing not to have heard these words with any precision, tilted her head coquettishly, and said, in a charming mock drawl (in a pretty imitation of Mr. Twain's slow, twangy, Western speech): "It would be a regrettable waste, sir, that so distinguished a man of letters, attired, moreover, in so dazzlingly resplendent a white costume, might so misconstrue the natural order of things, as to concern himself with my *feet*." A speech greeted with even more appreciative laughter, from both the ladies and the gentlemen present (for, I hardly need say, the "ladies" in attendance at a banquet of such a kind, were possessed of no more natural feminine reticence than Malvinia herself).

It may have been the case that Malvinia Morloch's cheeks *did* betray a light rosy blush, as if in girlish consternation at such words; but the blush, I assure you, had been *cosmetically* applied, some hours earlier, by the young woman's adroit hand.

Malvinia's slight acquaintanceship with the famed man of letters harked back nearly a decade, when, as I have recorded, she played an agreeably fresh *ingénue* in *Ah Sin*, and caught the erstwhile playwright's eye. She had, however, glimpsed him but rarely in the intervening years, less I might infer, as a consequence of the married gentleman's moral disapproval of her liaison with Vandenhoffen, than of the fact that, business and professional exigencies having arisen, Mark Twain had found it more pragmatic to dwell, for much of the year, in Europe.

The great man's public person was so widely known, and his frequent presence in New York City so noted, that even the self-absorbed Malvinia Morloch could hardly fail to be aware of him, and to admire him, rather more for his enormous success and prosperity, than for his writings. (There is a distinct possibility that, as a girl, she might have glanced through a copy of *Roughing It,* and *The Innocents Abroad*—that lively book being one of Judge Kiddemaster's great favorites, for, as he phrased it, "he had badly needed instructions not to feel *guilt,* that Europe, with its interminable cathedrals, and madonnas, and gibbering jabbering culture, had left him stone cold every time.") And, too, a merry imperative of Twain's—*Earn a character if you can, and if you can't, assume one*—had struck her innocent ears as altogether sensible, rather than cynical: tho', for many years, she had believed it to be yet another of Franklin's waggish epigrams.

Like all observers who gazed upon Mr. Twain, knowing in fact that he *was* Mr. Twain, and not a mere nobody with a sudden surplus of cash, that allowed him to hire a tailor, and give himself a swaggering mock-modest style, Malvinia admired his manly countenance, and thought him, for his age (he was fifty-eight years old, when Malvinia was thirty-three), wondrously appealing: with his thick unruly gray-white hair; and his bushy eyebrows that gave him a look of leonine but playful ferocity; and his slow, guarded, twangy "bumpkin" speech; and his bristling mustache —so large, it covered his entire upper lip, and subtly masked his expression—whether he smiled or grimaced, or merely pursed his lips, in habitual amused censure of the folly glimpsed on all sides. She could not fail, like any young woman of her ilk, to admire his ostentatious clothes, and his evident wealth, which displayed itself in the size and elegance of the carriages he hired, and, tho' I must not give the impression that, over the years, Malvinia Morloch truly took note of the illustrious author, with anything approaching a systematic interest (being frantically absorbed in both her professional career, and her tumultuous private life), she would certainly have concurred with popular sentiment, because it *was* popular, that Mr. Mark Twain ranked with the highest literary geniuses of all time, whether American, or European; or whatever. ("I have read your books, Mr. Twain," Malvinia said, upon the occasion of his taking her to dine at the Park Lane, on canvasback duck, turbot, and roast beef, "tho' perhaps not *all* of them," she allowed, so dipping her melodious voice, that her archness was for once infused with a most pleasant sweetness, "and, I must say, they have made me laugh, and made me think; and I am most grateful to you." Mr. Twain then tugged at his generous, manly mustache, and allowed himself a small gratified smile, and inquired of his pretty companion which book of his she most cherished, *Thrice-Told Tales,* or *The Fall of the House of Usher?* Whereupon the shrewd Malvinia, sensing something amiss, pouted, and murmured that she did not like to be interrogated, let alone trifled with: for it was in her nature to be *artless* and *sincere,* and to speak her heart fully, with no thought of being quizzed or judged.)

The obsessive pursuit of Miss Malvinia Morloch by Mr. Mark Twain was to occupy that bemused gentleman for but eight or nine months, out of a most complex and troubled lifetime; and within, as well, a particularly troubled year, so far as Mr. Twain's chronic business difficulties were concerned (his investment in the doomed Paige typesetting machine taking precedence over other vexations); and his heartrending familial problems, of which he took care never to allude to, in Malvinia's presence (for his faithful wife, Livy, at that time dwelling in Europe, continued to suffer ill-health, as did his epileptic daughter, Jean); and his own deepening perceptions as to the "malign thug" who ruled over the universe. (Such heretical usage giving me pause, as I hardly need inform the reader, in the very act of recording it: for is not one susceptible to wickedness merely by *taking note of it?*—and is the chronicler, however innocent, and proceeding but along the lines laid out by Duty, perhaps guilty of *disseminating* that very wickedness she would *transcend?*)

That the licentious "love affair" came to a most disastrous, and, indeed, humiliating conclusion, for both principals, is a fact that should be softened by our superior knowledge that it figured but slenderly in the lifetime of each; and that, in particular, the episode for Malvinia is most cogently comprehended as a *stopgap,* and a near-desperate means of *distraction,* as the storm clouds that brooded over the unhappy young woman's life began, with grim resoluteness, to close in.

(For, yes! Miss Malvinia Morloch, envied by so many, was a deeply unhappy young woman: no matter that her public gaiety would seem to deny it, and the lavishness of her jewels, and elaborately fashioned hair, and her ermines and minks and other furs; and the stern-willed *defiance* of her beauty.)

The fiery liaison with Vandenhoffen had ended, it is true, some years back: but, lest the romantic-minded reader immediately deduce that it was this loss that had pierced Malvinia's heart, to render her incapable of contentment, let alone those paroxysms of euphoria she almost daily simulated, I must inform you that the loss figured comparatively little in Malvinia's emotional life—to her shame be it said. For the sharp-eyed career woman had cruelly, but accurately, seen that her lover was past his prime, both so far as his thespian activities were concerned, and his youthful energies: she had noted the frequent slurring of his words, on stage, and an increasing slovenliness in his performance, as a consequence of the imbibing of alcohol, and a general indifference. ("Our audiences are but sheep, idiots, and love-starved females," Vandenhoffen had observed. "Why, then, must we memorize each line to perfection, for *them?*") If she suffered some small pang of regret, now and then, it was as much for the fact—which she and her associates at the Fanshawe had done their best to correct—that the public might believe *he* had left *her*, in order to return to his wife: and naturally her vanity was prick'd.

No, the loss of Vandenhoffen did not deeply distress her, nor inspire many genuine tears: rather less, I suppose, than she was accustom'd to shedding in her nightly performances, when she portrayed, with a singular *authenticity*, now an aggrieved widow, now a betrayed wife, now a heartsick daughter, now a fiancée whose lover was in jeopardy.

Vandenhoffen was at once replaced by a new lover, and he in turn by another: a middle-aged manufacturer of ladies' parasols; a gentleman-attorney in the hire of the copper trust; a widower-banker with several anxious sons (and heirs); an associate of Chauncey Depew; an amiable ne'er-do-well, the youngest son of a wealthy family, who spoke often of having "quite pulverized" Theodore Roosevelt, at Harvard, in the semifinals for the lightweight boxing championship. And, one giddy evening, when, it seemed, a political victory of some sort was being celebrated, by gentlemen conspicuously *not* in the company of their wives, but of another sort of woman altogether, Malvinia had even come face-to-face with —of all people—Cheyney Du Pont: so hideously chang'd, as to his physical being, and so pathetically drunk, that she no more recognized him at first than he did her.

"My dear *Mademoiselle*," the bulbous-nosed creature began, attempting a leering smile, and a bow so clumsy he nearly toppled against Malvinia, "unless I am gravely mistaken—and I am ofttimes so mistaken —are we not, to your knowledge, previously acquainted? Or are you but a part of my dream? My dream that goes on—and on—and *on:* and is so hideously compelling, I am tempted to believe it is real!"

It was that night, whilst tossed by chaotic dreams, that Malvinia experienced, *for the first time in more than twenty years,* a sudden and unmistakable flood of grief—and loss—and anguish—and, yes, heartrending *guilt:* not for her cold-blooded treatment of Mr. Du Pont, nor even for her heinous treatment of her belovèd parents: but for her inexplicable disregard for that gentle man of the cloth, the *Reverend Malcolm Kennicott!*

You may well register surprise, as I do; and yet it is so. Some obdurate rock in Malvinia's soul must have been o'erturned, by the ghastly reappearance in her life of the once-dashing Cheyney; and by the frenetic gaiety of the revelers, which had left her more than ordinarily exhausted, and desirous of being alone. Her toilette but half completed, she collapsed upon her bed, and, by way of the great mystery of the night, in which all the laws of nature and logic are suspended, the glamorous *Malvinia Morloch* found herself transform'd into the child *Malvinia Zinn:* but eight years old, and weeping copious tears, as if her heart would break!—for the childish cruelty she had unwittingly perpetrated upon Mr. Malcolm Kennicott, whom she adored above all men, save her father.

Mr. Malcolm Kennicott—whom she adored above all men, save her father!

Hoarse shuddering sobs roused her from her alcoholic slumber, and, for some affrighted moments, Malvinia scarce knew where she was: murmuring in a piteous voice, "Octavia? Octavia? Why have you slipped out of bed, and left me alone? I am so very, very frightened!"

Gradually her senses returned; she knew she lay in a bed not her own, in a hotel, in a great city (for down on the street, even at this godless hour, the clatter of horses' hooves sounded on the cobblestones, and drunken masculine laughter arose), she knew she had traveled a great distance—a tragic distance—from her lost, belovèd Bloodsmoor, and from the innocent little girl she had been, at the age of eight years.

Lost—ah, lost!

And never to be retrieved!

Whether Mr. Malcolm Kennicott was deceased, and now dwelt in Spirit World, from which his phantom might be freed at such exigent moments; or whether it was but hallucination, I cannot say: but Malvinia so clearly beheld his melancholy visage, she would have sworn he had entered her bedchamber. His dreamy, poetical countenance—his shy-smiling eyes—the hair which was fawn-colored, and wavy, and silken-soft —the boyish air, suffused with wounded reproach!

"I am so sorry—I did not know—O dear Mr. Kennicott! I was but a heedless child, *and did not know—*"

Had Malvinia thought to fling aside her luxurious covers, and throw herself to her knees on the floor, appealing to Our Heavenly Father for forgiveness, and for counsel, these dark hours might have been transform'd to joy: but the distraught woman was so unaccustom'd to prayer, and so bewitched by the phantasm, that, to her shame be it said, she gave no thought to God; and abandoned herself to violent spasms of sobbing, which wracked her body with as much barbaric force as The Beast itself might wrack it.

"I am so sorry! O dear Mr. Kennicott, forgive me—forgive a heedless child! *I did not know!*"

58

There followed then a period of some heightened days, when, convinced
that Mr. Kennicott was dead, Malvinia greedily perused all the Spiritualist
publications she could find—*The Theosophist, The Spiritist, The Darkling Tide,
The Psychical Letter,* and others, many of them published on cheap pulp
paper, and all of them given over to numerous columns of classified
advertisements. *Mountain Seeress—Highlander Visionary—Trance Medium of
Lake Champlain—Priestess of Amazing Gifts:* the self-proclamations alternately intrigued Malvinia, and disgusted her. Her dread that she would
suddenly discover herself reading about "Deirdre of the Shadows" came
to naught, for she found not a word in any of these publications, pertaining to her lost sister; and wondered, not without a small thrill of regret,
whether Deirdre had given up her peculiar profession, or had somehow
failed at it. (Malvinia being unfamiliar with Spiritualist protocol, she
could not have known that the most exalted and prestigious mediums
never advertised their services: they would not have condescended to do
so, and, in any case, being so constantly in demand, despite their high
fees, they had no need. And, after the historic investigation at the headquarters of the Society for Psychical Research, Deirdre of the Shadows
had so enviable a reputation, she gave but a few sittings a month, and
these generally in very private circumstances.)

It was Malvinia's intention to arrange for a private séance, that she
might be put in contact with the spirit of the young clergyman whom she
had so wantonly mistreated, for she was quite certain he *must* be dead.
So she scanned the numerous publications, murmuring, "It is my fault
—he did away with himself, for me—because of me—I alone am to
blame": still in a heightened state from that night of tempestuous emo-

tions, and somewhat disoriented, in her ratiocinative powers, as a consequence of the liberal doses of ether and water she daily prescribed for herself. "If we can but greet each other, face-to-face," she whispered, "surely he will forgive me—surely he cannot help but forgive his little Malvinia, once he grasps the burden of sorrow and repentance I bear!"

Yet in the end she wearied of the pamphlets, her inborn drollery aroused by so many insipid advertisements for "visionaries," and "seers," and "miracle-mediums," and "priestesses." She gathered the publications in her arms and threw them away, at the very instant the telephone began to ring in the next room.

In a moment her maid would rap gently at her door, to inform her that a gentleman was on the line: and who, Malvinia wondered with a sudden smile, would it be this time?

And poor Malcolm Kennicott became, at that moment, a *shade* indeed!

59

It was a bitter, yet not an unjust, irony, that The Beast should emerge with especial malevolence, when Malvinia Morloch had at last—after so many months of coquettish retreat!—abandoned herself to the intimate embrace of Mr. Mark Twain; and at a most precarious time in her career, when she was about to tour the Far West in *She Loved Him Dearly*—a trifling romance written for her particular talents.

Having no capability, and, indeed, no desire, so far as graphic descriptions of "love embraces" are concerned, I shall make no attempt to sketch for the repelled reader precisely how The Beast emerged, to make a loathsome mockery of the love declarations, kisses, caresses, and other amorous indulgences, which transpired between Malvinia and Mr. Twain, in Malvinia's sumptuously appointed bedchamber in the Hotel Nicklaus, in the late hours of January 13, 1894; I shall make no attempt to record, even for the interest of those employed in the profession of *morbid psychology*, with what suddenness The Beast blazed forth, in the midst of an embrace of extreme intimacy, announcing itself by a chuckling deep in the damsel's throat, and a brash flurry of activity, involving hands, feet, knees, and mouth, of a sort never experienced in his lifetime, we may infer, by the incredulous man of letters. That an interlude of sybaritic dalliance should erupt so violently, and so lewdly, against all normal expectations, plunging mistress and would-be lover into a struggle of brute physicality, the one cursing and grunting, the other crying aloud in alarm and fear, and begging, finally, for help—that a love scene of illicit (and, some would say, *romantic*) proportions should be o'erturned, with such alacrity, to become a spectacle of buffoonery, may indeed strike the Christian contingent amongst my readers as *fit punish-*

ment for such projected wickedness: and, were I not stirred to a vague pity, for Malvinia's extreme degradation (and its attendant effect upon her career), I would surely concur.

"I know not what has happened, or why—save that it is not my fault —it is not my doing!" the shamed woman cried, her eyes gleaming a lurid black, and her hair disheveled, and the widow's peak prominent above her furrowed brow: *"It is not my doing, and I own it not! I am innocent!"*

Lest you pity the grappling lovers, being moved to sympathy by the embarrassment of the distinguished author (who, having dined royally that evening, on oysters, tripe, roast suckling pig, and crêpes suzette, was perhaps not in prime condition), I should remind you that there could hardly have been any genuine love between the principals, and but a modicum of meretricious sentiment. Doubtless, yes, Miss Malvinia Morloch and Mr. Mark Twain liked each other well enough, or at any rate admired each other, beneath the stylized carapace of their "romance," for over a period of months they did have, it seems, an occasional serious conversation. (You may well imagine with what astonishment Malvinia greeted Mr. Twain's casual remark that *his* father, John Clemens, had spent a great deal of his time laboring on a perpetual-motion machine, back in Hannibal, Missouri!)

But both were celebrities, jaded with the proffered adoration of strangers, which, coming so freely, could not escape being valued as cheap. They were magnificently self-absorbed, and blithe in their common intercourse with others; they made clever speeches, and did not listen; and were always glancing about, in public rooms, to take note of who took note of *them*. No, they could not have felt any tenderness toward each other, and one would be misguided to pity them. Only a queer "mental telegraphy"—a coinage of Mr. Twain's—drew them together; and this tenuous connection was blasted forever by the brute emergence of *The Beast*.

Like any seasoned courtesan, Malvinia professed to admire her admirer. Upon the occasion of their first late-night supper together, after an evening performance of *She Loved Him Dearly*, Malvinia confessed that, a decade previously, she had been "o'erwhelmed, and struck to the heart" by his personage, as he had stood on the stage to make his "wondrously witty" speech, on the opening night of *Ah Sin*. His mastery of the English language—his aristocratic, yet unassuming manner—his generosity toward *her*: all were quite remarkable.

All this Mr. Twain appeared to absorb with a bemused, even skeptical, smile, beneath his prominent mustache: but he did not stint, upon the morn, in the quantity of red roses he caused to be delivered to Miss Malvinia Morloch's suite at the Nicklaus!

How attentively Malvinia appeared to listen, as her white-suited admirer, a carnation in his buttonhole, a whisky-slurred drawl to his words, spoke in lengthy monologues, in which melancholy and drollery contended, of his childhood in Hannibal, Missouri, where he oft saw men shot and stabbed in the streets, and "niggers" sorely abused, and where his father had gone bankrupt, before a premature death; with what amused sympathy she attended to his speechifying on the "good, rough, man's world" of Nevada and California, in the old days; and the "unparalleled ambrosia" of the riverboat world. Florid-faced from a substantial dinner at Sherry's, consisting of claret, champagne, bourbon, brandy, and rum punch, among the liquid refreshments alone, he recounted loving anecdotes of General Grant, "the iron man," and recited, for Malvinia's benefit, and for the benefit of diners at nearby tables, a speech evidently given some years ago, by one Colonel Robert Ingersoll: *"Blood was water, money was leaves, and life was only common air until one flag floated over a Republic without a master and without a slave!"*—the climax to a masterpiece of oratory that brought five hundred Union veterans to their feet in clamorous applause. And Mark Twain had himself given so wickedly amusing a speech, in ostensible honor of General Grant, that he had broken that giant into pieces with laughter: "I did it! I licked him! And I *knew* I could lick him!" Mr. Twain mused, filling his glass again with more claret. "My dear, if only you might have been there!—or, ladies not allowed, if only you might have *eavesdropped!* For once in Grant's life he had been knocked out of his iron serenity, and it was little Sam who did the job—shook him up like dynamite—racked all the bones of his body apart. And the audience *saw* that I had done it: five hundred witnesses. Ah, what a night! The house came crashing down! These Broadway ovations are piddle. Not to insult you, my dear: *everything* else is piddle. Shall I tell you, Miss Morloch," he said, leaning uncomfortably close, as if in confidence, but with his voice still raised, *"everything else is piddle.* But we must keep the lid on our secret, eh?"

Malvinia was pleased to learn that Mr. Twain's "billion-dollar baby," a typesetting machine patented by a genius-inventor named Paige, was being manufactured—or was it *not* being manufactured, owing to difficulties?—in a factory at Eighteenth Street and Broadway. Paige was not simply an inventor of surpassing genius, but a poet—a most great and genuine poet—"the Shakespeare of mechanical invention." There were certain difficulties with the machine, at the present time, Mr. Twain conceded, and there *were* financial snarls; but once the Paige typesetter was manufactured in quantity, and on the competitive market, why, its boon to mankind would translate into hundreds of millions of dollars—solid cash—solid *gold:* and Mr. Mark Twain would be "up there in the Parthenon" with Vanderbilt, Astor, Carnegie, and the rest. "I hope we shall have *sustained,* if not to say *deepened,* our acquaintance by that time,

Miss Morloch," he said. "For it is but a matter of time!—piddling time."

"You are very compassionate, Mr. Twain," Malvinia said. "But tell me, please, about the miracle-machine: for tho' my ear is untutor'd, I have some small interest in the great inventions of our century." A stratagem on the courtesan's part to keep her admirer talking, and talking, and talking, and drinking, so that, for this night at least, his importunate invitations that she join him in his modest suite at the Players' Club, in order that they watch, together, the sun's first slant rays penetrating the lacework of the great elms of Gramercy Park, might be bypassed.

So Mr. Twain talked, his twangy bumpkin's voice oft rearing to an impassioned height, as he spoke in unabash'd adulation of the Inventor, who was but second to God Himself: for was he not, after God, the "creator of the world"? Where the Old World pimped for its tiresome hodgepodge of castles, and cathedrals, and worn-out anemic Czars, and so many madonnas, you could pile them to the moon, the New World had the right idea: Hadn't the Connecticut Yankee opened a patent office right in King Arthur's England, to get things going? Didn't every Yankee with a head on his shoulders do the same kind of thing, in his own life? "Now a writer like myself may be acclaimed, Miss Morloch, as those in your profession are frequently acclaimed, but we are but entertainers for the masses. At best, we can hope to be teachers and moralists, and other such tedious bearers of wisdom. But the inventor, ah, the inventor!—the great American inventor!—he is the poet—the *true* poet—and nothing in any degree less than the poet. If I could trade in my feeble scribbling for a patent on a brilliant mechanism like the cotton gin, let us say, or that new contraption for executing criminals, the 'electric chair,' is it called? —or my own James W. Paige's jewel of a machine, why, *that* would be true redemption, and let the suet-headed missionaries have the other!"

Malvinia listened; and, with many a nod of her lovely head, appeared to concur, whilst her eyes roved the festive interior, seeking to observe who might be observing her, and her illustrious escort. She was not disappointed: for it was a rare diner, in this sybaritic enclave, who did not recognize Miss Malvinia Morloch—and even those wealthy foreign visitors, dining with robust appetites, and queer continental manners, knew at sight the great man of letters Mark Twain.

She listened; she sympathized; she encouraged her suitor to tell her more; and, at the conclusion of a long and particularly impassioned speech on the "exquisite and fastidious and altogether beautiful miracle" of the Paige machine, she roused herself to some thoughtful commentary, to indicate the depth of her attention. Nay, she acquitted herself admirably, fetching out of some dim reservoir of memory—one of her theatrical speeches, perhaps?—these stirring words: "To my amateur's ear, Mr. Twain, it sounds very much as if this machine is indeed extraordinary, and will do you proud. Not merely to supply wealth, which you, as our greatest American author, scorn by instinct; and still less to supply fame, which you already possess in vertiginous abundance: but to hasten the progress of our great century, and promote all that is rare, and good, and wondrous, in Democracy itself! Why, it may be, Mr. Twain, that, owing to your prescience, future generations of mankind will be irreparably *altered—enhanced—revolutionized.* I am but a woman, and consequently hesitate to make such judgments, but it sounds very much to me as if this machine is no tinkerer's dream, but a device that will *revolutionize the continent.* And you are to be applauded, my dear sir, for not only having recognized this fact, but for doing all you can to bring it to fruition." A speech of such boldness, and such contagious enthusiasm, that the aging gentleman's susceptibility to Miss Morloch's female charms can be well understood.

"Your thinking, Miss Morloch," Mr. Twain said, after some seconds of rapt silence, during which time he stared quite fully into his companion's face, "has the timbre and resonance of a man's thinking!—which is quite, quite remarkable. But," he added, his mustache quivering in a smile that was almost boyish, despite his creased face, and the fatigue that registered in his bloodshot eyes, "but, I am happy to observe, you possess nothing else, about your person, that might be mistaken as a *man's.*"

In such wise the "mental telegraphy" between these two celebrities drew them together, and allowed them the admittedly considerable pleasures of self-deception, unavailable to those of us who hoe far humbler rows. From time to time, Malvinia's heart was pierced by sudden recollections of that wronged and lost man of the cloth, Mr. Malcolm Kennicott: yet, being a most wondrously resilient heart, how readily it mended itself! The frequent and animated discussions about the Paige machine, which Mr. Twain conducted generally, in the company of divers others, could not fail to have had the effect of causing Malvinia to recall, and to brood upon, and perhaps even to shed a tear over, her rejected family, and Mr. Zinn most of all: whom, she supposed, she *did* love, and would one day be a more dutiful daughter to, if only Bloodsmoor were not so very distant, and its custodians so tiresome. (In her quieter moments, forced by the exigencies of the body to endure yet more prolonged, and hotter, baths, Malvinia bethought herself sadly that Mr. Zinn as he had been in the nursery, so many years ago, would remain, perhaps, her most priz'd admirer: she had recited for him, and memorized for him, and preened herself for him, and ah!—how he had applauded! Now, her various audiences might very well applaud, with gratifying enthusiasm, but, as Vandenhoffen had sourly observed, they were *perhaps* not altogether meritorious arbiters of taste: and quite, quite impossible to love, as she had loved her father.)

She thought of Mr. Kennicott, and forgot him; she thought of Mr. Zinn, and forgot *him*. At odd times, oft in the midst of a histrionic speech, in the blaze of the footlights, she thought of her sisters: and wondered what the roles were, that they now played; and whether they were quite so cynical about them, as Malvinia was becoming—alas, almost day by day —about hers. (Constance Philippa, Malvinia realized, would now be thirty-seven years old: a sobering age. Had that strong-willed young woman changed greatly? Malvinia wondered; did she repent of her wedding-night escape from the Baron, or had she entered an utterly new life? It was difficult for Malvinia, vain as she was, and obsessed with the inevitable incursions of aging, in her own much-vaunted beauty, even to attempt to imagine her older sister as thirty-seven years old: she preferred to cozen herself with memories of the brash, blunt, handsome Constance Philippa as a young girl of eleven, or fourteen, or seventeen, so very awkward in her Sunday finery, and vexed by the weight of her hair, that Malvinia could not help but burst into a spasm of giggling, and risk incurring her rage. At the very most, Malvinia was willing to summon forth, in her mind's eye, Constance Philippa as a bride: in that beautiful silk gown, the lace cap and veil so beguiling upon her high-held head, her dark eyes glittering with an unarticulated emotion, not unlike that glimpsed in the eyes of certain noble steeds—saddle-broken by a skillful trainer, yet mercurial, and shrewd, and always on the alert, for weakness in any other handler. "Ah, my dear Constance Philippa!—my *courageous*, and altogether *fantastical*, older sister!" Malvinia laughed softly to herself. "That you did right, to escape your gnome of a husband, I cannot doubt: that you have succeeded as well as I, in conquering the world beyond Bloodsmoor, I cannot believe: but I hope that, wherever you are, in whatever unguessed-at circumstances, you are happy—indeed, happier than I." This uttered with a sigh of atypical weariness, in which not a little genuine sentiment for her sister might have been discerned. And, in a mood of reverie, her laudanum-drowsed mind drifting upon the others, Malvinia saw again the warm brown eyes, flushed cheeks, and loving smile of Octavia; and the small, pinched, pale, homely, and rather mysterious countenance of Samantha; and the melancholy, brooding visage of Deirdre—whom, by some happenstance, she unthinkingly recalled as her *sister*, rather than her *adoptive sister*. Had her relations with Mr. Twain touched more sincerely upon personal matters—had, indeed, her relations with *any* gentlemen done so—Malvinia would have dearly liked to speak of Deirdre, and of Samantha, who now struck her, in retrospect, as having been, in potential at least, exceedingly interesting; she would have enjoyed telling a spirited anecdote about Constance Philippa, and the sinister little Baron, and the dressmaker's dummy; and there was Octavia too—so very *dear* a sister, one forgave her her piety, and all the tedium it engendered! But Malvinia Morloch shimmered, like a beautiful mirage, quite alone: it was part of the glamour, impressed upon her by Orlando Vandenhoffen, and by the manager of the Fanshawe troupe, that she stand by herself, of mysterious origin, unique in her beauty, *one of a kind.* "And I very much doubt that they should be interested in my family life," Malvinia said with a bemused sigh, "my zealous gentleman-admirers.")

With her moods swinging violently from the brooding and near-elegiac, when she was alone, to the vivacious and festive, when she was in the company of others, Malvinia had cause to wonder if Mr. Twain's strictures on the shallowness of man, and his mechanistic psychology, might not be woefully precise. When, his tongue loosened by Angostura bitters, and hot toddies to forestall the "January void," Mr. Twain railed on and on about the meanness, the selfishness, and, most damning of all, the pointlessness, of human existence, Malvinia quite spontaneously played the *ingénue* (as she suspected the unhappy gentleman required), and pretended to be scandalized; when he drifted from his adulation of the Machine, to an alarmingly bitter attack upon the Machine, and the entire "universe of Machine-Men," she pretended to disagree, and to wish to point out, prettily, that *he* was surely an exception to his own philosophy. ("Am I?" Mr. Twain asked, staring and blinking, his expression gone quite blank, and, as it were, greatly moving in its childlike appeal, "Am I? Am I? Am I?"—turning the poignant moment into a joke, and really a very witty joke, in its improvised mimicry of a machine: whereupon the others of the company uproariously laughed, and Malvinia herself could not resist.)

"Life has absolutely no dignity or meaning," Mr. Twain catechized, his soft-twanging Southern drawl amusingly at odds with the bleakness of his words. "Absolutely no dignity or meaning, my friends, except that suggested by the agreeable bubblings, seethings, and airy emissions, engendered by an excellent meal. . . . Gentlemen, and ladies, and all the rest of us, I propose a toast to the Father, the Son, and the Holy Typesetter, which is to say, *the mind of man,* of which we try so very hard, to be so very proud. Will you join me?"

Malvinia laughed shrilly, as if in delight, and protested: "My dear Mr. Twain, you do not mean half of what you utter! You wish only to shock."

Whereupon the slow twanging voice rejoined: "My dear Miss Morloch, I do not *utter* half of what I *mean.*"

Yes, she secretly concurred, who had, so many years previous, heard from the lips of the Transcendentalist spirit, John Quincy Zinn himself, words that were so completely the reverse!—words of faith, and hope, and charity toward all mankind—and unswerving, tho' unconventional, belief in the undefinable *Spirit of the Universe.* How far, how tragically far, poor Malvinia has come, you may note, from Bloodsmoor, and its happy vales and hillocks: how far, too, our sovereign nation has come, from the poetical faith, the dream-certain bliss, the *sacred certainty,* of Mr. Emerson, to the blasphemous half-mad rantings, of the "humorist" Mr. Twain! Where the great Emerson declaimed with unswerving faith that God is All, and All is God, the besotted Twain declaimed, like a lowlife preacher stood rudely upon his head, that God is just a machine-notion, a machine-thought, put forth by the "coffee-mill" mind of man! Were it not too demeaning to do so, I would set forth the tenets of the Episcopal faith, as they confront, and, one by one, conquer, the heretical ravings of Mr. Mark Twain; were it not an exercise in superfluity, I would measure the great, the profound, the God-ordained wisdom of the Bible, against the nonsensical mutterings of an adulterous bully and drunkard, who, perhaps, scarce knew what his lips babbled, only that his constant circle of admirers was amused, and the beauteous actress Malvinia Morloch laughed with the others, and *seemed* close to being won. (Unbeknownst to Mr. Twain, Miss Morloch *was* in fact close to being won, in the bitter winter of '93–'94; but only as a consequence of the defection of a wealthier gentleman-suitor, a vociferous supporter of President Cleveland, who had found an Egyptian hootchy-kootchy dancer more to his liking, than the temperamental Miss Morloch, who was, after all, hardly in the first flush of youth any longer. A revelation not known to Mr. Twain, certainly, and known to Malvinia herself but indirectly.)

"Do not look so aggrieved, my dear Miss Morloch," Mr. Twain said, seizing her fair hand, and raising it to his lips, "tho' we *are* but machines, and tho' we *are* guided by naught but coarse self-interest, I hardly deny that there frequently occur *mutual* self-interests, indeed, *mutual* pleasures, of a kind best satisfied in tandem."

The romance came most abruptly, and hideously, to an end, upon the night of January 13: said night having begun when, after a performance of *She Loved Him Dearly,* Mr. Twain arrived at Malvinia's dressing room to escort her to a private party, where much drinking transpired, and a heated discussion, between partisans and antagonists, as to the feasibility of Mr. Carnegie's scheme for absorbing Great Britain, Ireland, and Canada, into an entity to be called the "American Commonwealth." Mr. Twain brayed with laughter at the nonsensical idea; for who would want impoverished Ireland, and moose-ridden Canada, and dumpy Queen Victoria? It was quite loathsome enough, after all, to have won back the Alamo.

A quarrel later arose, I cannot say how, or why, over the comparative merits of Mrs. Eddy's Christian Science mind-cure, and Professor Lupa's School of Cognition and Memory: the latter favored by Mr. Twain, the former by Sir Charles Nook, who was, Malvinia gathered, a $10,000

investor in the Paige typesetter, and a somewhat precarious friend of Mr.
Twain's—tho', to be sure, all of his friends were "precarious," if not fully
in flight.

"Come, Miss Morloch," Mr. Twain commanded, "come away with
me: this is a vulgar lot, and you and I are degraded to remain in their
midst."

So a cab was hailed, and Malvinia and her suitor were taken up-
town to the Nicklaus, and, Mr. Twain gripping her arm with a viselike
attentiveness, and allowing her to know that, should she *not* allow him to
escort her to her suite, and well into the interior of her suite, within the
hour, she should *not* expect to hear from him again, the somewhat o'erwrought Malvinia heard herself acquiesce: for, after all, she thought,
staring mesmerized as the gas lamps along Park Avenue appeared to trot
backward to her, and past her, in a jolting unending stream, after *all,* the
noisy old fool has perhaps paid his dues by now.

Once in the perfum'd privacy of Malvinia's bedchamber, however,
the couple was thrown into a nervous constraint: and Mr. Twain was so
stumblingly inept, in merely disrobing, that Malvinia's heart lifted with
the momentary hope that he might collapse harmlessly upon the bed, and
do no mischief—and, upon the morn, be convinced that he *had.*

But the determined man of letters righted himself, and, after some
difficult moments, during which time his flushed face grew yet more
reddened, he managed to extricate himself from his starched shirt, which
was stiff and unyielding as armor; and from that vulgar species of masculine undergarment popularly known as *long woollens,* Mr. Twain's being
of a coarse gray wool, surprisingly soiled for one of his reputation and
alleged wealth. He then turned to his hoped-for mistress, who stood in
a pose of virginal detachment, prideful, and yet shy as a girl, not unlike
the young Juliet in one of Miss Morloch's first successes on the stage: he
turned to her, with a show of lusty spirits, sighing, and cackling with
nervous laughter, and rubbing his hands together: and seized her by the
shoulders, that he might plant a moist, and strangely boyish, kiss upon
her part-yielding lips. Glancing then uneasily about the luxuriously appointed room, with its several ornamental mirrors, and its numerous
vases of flowers, that, in the shadowy light of so late, and so illicit, an
hour, gave an eerie appearance of being *witnesses* to this degrading spectacle, Mr. Twain ordered that the candles be snuffed out at once, and
"darkness be the order of the day."

In jest he said: "For it is necessary that some rituals be *performed,*
my dear; but not that they be *observed.*"

"Yes, Mr. Twain," Malvinia said in a gay, benumbed voice, as she
hurried unthinkingly to do his bidding, "yes, you are quite correct."

Whereupon the oblivion of pitch-dark night ensued!—with what
tragic consequences, I can scarce bring myself to record.

There followed immediately, upon the opened bed, with its silken canopy and massive fourposters, some minutes of dalliance, clumsy, and hopeful, and wicked, yet, I am led to believe, hardly unnatural, in a couple of adulterous intent—kisses of an adolescent fervor, and dampness; and awkward, tho' forceful, caresses; and an attempt at a manly embrace; and divers amorous whisperings, and murmurings, and cajolings (there being the continued posture, agreeable to both principals, that Malvinia was of a recalcitrant and maidenly disposition); and many declarations, made in a drawl now heightened with urgency, as to the astounding beauty, voluptuousness, and general desirability, of Miss Morloch. (That Mr. Twain had entered into sacred Christian matrimony, many years previous, and that his invalided wife, Livy, wrote to him faithfully from Europe, during his long courtship of Malvinia, was not, of course, a fact the blackguard husband cared to mention; yet it was a fact Malvinia knew well enough, from other sources. So this "love embrace" was to be not simply unblessed by any churchly vows, but in positive defiance of Holy Wedlock! —an action beset with enormous risks, for Our Heavenly Father does not like to be insulted. Shameful, too, was the fact that Malvinia cared not a whit for the existence of a loyal and betrayed wife, whether invalided or no: for who among her numerous "bachelor" suitors was *not* married?)

Some minutes of animalistic loveplay, and the gradual "surrender" of the female, and the gallant attempt upon the part of the male, to initiate the *unitary act:* and then, alas, of a sudden, *The Beast!*

The Beast! Announced by an abrupt chuckle in Malvinia's throat, low and ribald and insinuating: and a sudden tugging of Mr. Twain's wet mustache!

And then, the fit having come upon her, unstoppable, hideous, Malvinia gnashed her teeth, and ground them furiously together; and gave herself up to coarse, guttural, jocose—indeed, *bestial*—imprecations, which issued forth from her lovely lips, which, in the candlelight of scarcely ten minutes ago, had looked so pristinely innocent! These profanities and obscenities and primitive "names" for bodily parts are not only so evil in themselves, as to bear no consideration whatsoever, in this chronicle, but they are, I am proud to say, so foreign to my experience, in even the verbal sense, that I could not begin to guess how they might be *spelled;* and will make no attempt herein.

Mr. Twain's amatory boldness, more the consequence of alcoholic ingestion, than of a natural inclination, was, as you may imagine, quench'd at once by this development: yet Malvinia Morloch took no mercy upon her lover's consternation, and may, in fact, have had no clear awareness of it, so exuberantly did The Beast force himself into her slender, writhing body—fitting her arms, and limbs, and torso, and the nether regions of her being, like a powerful hand thrusting itself into a snug and slightly resistant lady's glove!

The unlucky gentleman cried out, in surprise that halfway wished to be *amused,* as if his mistress's wild paroxysms were but a joke: but no amusement was forthcoming, as slim female fingers grown brazen with the dark groped, and slapped, and twisted, and poked; and a knee wedged itself upward, with painful results; and the burning soles of frantic feet "walked" all over Mr. Twain's body, both front and rear! The obscene chuckling increased in volume, issuing, evidently, from deep within the damsel's throat; unspeakable—nay, ineffable—odors were released, from the primeval orifices of the body; there was a brute wrestling, and scrambling, and grunting, of a kind to summon forth, in the stunned author's imagination, an image he would have supposed long forgotten: he saw again, in his paralysis of terror, the antics of a pet monkey on board the cholera-struck sailing ship *America,* in January of 1867: this comely little creature, cinnamon-brown of hue, and wondrously appealing as to its tiny, wizened, childlike face, had been grotesquely costumed in black velvet trousers and braided jacket, and black string tie; and, to the depraved amusement of the passengers and crew, who sought to distract themselves from the horror of the cholera epidemic, had been fed brandy-soaked bananas, so that the poor crazed creature jabbered, and twirled about, and foamed at the mouth, and rolled about the deck in convulsions. A piteous spectacle, which Mr. Twain had successfully buried, for nearly three decades, but which now sprang forth, unbidden, and in great confusion, as he struggled, as if for his very life, with the beauteous Malvinia Morloch. . . .

(Thus The Beast—the delineation of which, it quite sickens me to write; and would have an equivalent effect, I am certain, upon any normal personage, of either sex. But I am obliged to continue, in accordance with my authorial responsibilities, confident that God will absolve me of any inadvertent sin, in the process of transcription, as He has given me the task to begin with—to justify the eccentric ways of man, in our great century, to God Himself.)

The transformation of a romantic, however adulterous, love episode, into an episode of such baffling quality, would have been disorienting enough, in a man of fewer years; in Mr. Twain, who, you may remember was nearing his sixties, and suffered moreover from rheumatism, and gout, and various dyspeptic ailments, augmented upon this occasion by the heavy dinner of oysters, pork, crêpes suzette, and other delicacies, including many alcoholic spirits, the effect was severe: I am only glad that it was not catastrophic, in bringing about a fatal attack of angina pectoris, in that rank, adulterous bed, for think of the grief, and the horrific humiliation, to poor Livy Clemens, dwelling in all wifely innocence, in the invalided state, in Paris!

But Fortune, tho' grimacing, did smile upon Mr. Twain, who, tho' so frightened that his teeth chattered, and his blood ran cold, and his heart thundered, yet *did not die,* or even faint with terror: a testament, doubtless, to his rough bucolic childhood, and his frontier experience. Malvinia poked, and slapped, and pinched, and jabbed, and tugged at his hair and mustache, and scratched at his face, and, cursing and laughing the while, like a veritable demon, *yanked at his masculine organ of regeneration!* —but the astonished gentleman had now gathered his wits sufficiently, and what remained of his strength, to defend himself, and to finally extricate himself: and, gasping and wheezing and sobbing, he crawled from that bed of bestial extremities, to flee, naked as a newborn babe, out of the bedchamber—and through the candlelit outer room—and into the plush-carpeted corridor, where gas lamps in gilded niches cast their somnolent glow upon his hobbling and piteous figure—

And thus to safety!

And to a generous remainder of years, sixteen in all, doubtless informed, and refined, by this humbling and chastising experience, as to the hazards that await the *faithless husband,* straying from the ordained marital bed.

(Mr. Mark Twain did flee to safety, from the heinous embrace of The Beast: but also, I am afraid, to extreme embarrassment, in regard to those members of the hotel staff who were on duty at that suspect hour, and to the management of the Hotel Nicklaus in general, who, tho' respecting the renowned author's literary works, did not stint in spreading malicious and amusing tales about this peculiar episode. I cannot, however, bring myself to follow his fleeing naked form any farther, down the corridor, but must close a door upon him, so to speak, and remain with the grunting, cursing, pulsing, palpitating Malvinia Morloch, now on hands and knees in the damp tangled bedclothes, dazed and ferocious as a tigress—her prey having escaped.)

Yet even her protesting voice, her wailing lament, partook of The Beast's unmistakable tones, as in baffled outrage she cried: "I know not what has happened, or why—it is not my doing!—not mine! Mr. Twain, I command you, return!—at once, return!—it is not my doing, and I own it not!—I own it not, do you hear!—villains!—blackguards!—I am innocent!—*do you hear!*"

60

It was but a scant fortnight later, at the very end of January, that Miss Malvinia Morloch precipitated much buzzing discussion amongst the theatergoing public, and the Broadway savants, by fleeing from the stage of the Fanshawe, in one of the opening scenes of *She Loved Him Dearly:* her dead-white complexion, and the inelegant haste of her flight, lending credence to the theory that the celebrated actress had been o'ercome by a *morbid seizure* of some kind. It was advanced by some that a "tragic disappointment" in love had cleaved her heart; by others, that her "well-known predilection" for alcoholic spirits was responsible.

Miss Morloch not only ran stricken from the stage, leaving her fellow thespians, and the audience, quite astounded—she ran from the playhouse as well, pushing aside all restraining arms, and, so far as anyone knew, from the very city itself!

Unprecedented behavior, in so exceptionally professional an actress, and quite inexplicable: for no letter of explanation or apology was received by anyone at the Fanshawe, nor did any journalists discover motives, amongst the numerous acquaintances and associates of the popular actress whom they interviewed. A disastrous love affair—an alcoholic crisis of some kind—a neurasthenic collapse—a sudden breakdown of that audacious *confidence* which those in the acting profession require, simply to exhibit themselves before an audience: many were the theories, as tongues freely and maliciously wagged, but no one, not even Miss Morloch's fellow actors, could lay claim to any certainty.

Could they have known that whisperings of "The Beast! The Beast!" drove the wretched young woman from the stage, and had, indeed, pursued her for many hellish nights, since the shameful episode in

466

the Hotel Nicklaus, they would surely have been astonished—yet no more enlightened.

And so it was, that Miss Malvinia Morloch disappeared, leaving no trace behind, that might help to explain her whereabouts, or the uncanny mystery of her behavior. Speculations were rife, and would have the distraught woman drowned in the river, having committed the sacrilege of suicide; or hidden away in a mental asylum, or a Catholic convent; or simply fled, in abject humiliation, into obscurity.

And whence she has fled, it is to be hoped that, sinner tho' she be, that hideous imprecation, "The Beast! The Beast" does not attend her!

61

In the turbulent decade following that historic evening in Gramercy Park, Deirdre of the Shadows acquired an international reputation as a "seeress," and, no doubt, a considerable fortune as well: as a consequence of both her talent and the ruthless determination of her ambition.

The general decline of public interest—indeed, public credulousness—in Spiritualism, noted in the latter half of the Eighties, and unmistakable in the Nineties, might be attributed in part to a reawakened comprehension, in Christian men and women, as to the inviolable truth of that religion; or to the numerous revelations of fraud, amongst the Spiritualist seers and mediums. Yet this decline affected only those with mediocre gifts, or no gifts at all, and such acclaimed practitioners as Deirdre of the Shadows continued to thrive, being sought after by as multitudinous a number of clients, as the great Home himself—perhaps by more, for, where Daniel Dunglas Home assumed that smirking sardonicism toward his talents and his clients, oft noted in the effeminate male, and gravely insulting to those of normal persuasions, Deirdre comported herself impeccably in public, behaving very like as one might expect a young woman to behave, who was under the spell, and, indeed, in the selfless service of, Spirit World. She was meek; docile; possessed of an increasingly ascetic, and beauteous, countenance; her voice a feathery whisper, her lovely dark eyes never bold, her movements sombre and studied and wondrously graceful—so that many amongst her impressionable clients spoke of her as an "angel emissary," ordained by God Himself to help bring about a revolution in human awareness, as to the *fluidity* of the barrier betwixt the two worlds! A blasphemous claim I can scarce record, without trembling to the roots of my being.

To her credit, Deirdre never publicly acknowledged such assertions, and took care, indeed, to behave in a suitably modest manner. *She*
did very little, save to surrender herself as a vessel so that the spirits of
the deceased might approach the living, and speak. "It is not I," she said
quietly, "but the others: our friends in Spirit World who, through their
kindness, and their infinite wisdom, make all things possible."

Yet I do not attribute it solely to sheer spiteful resentment, the
remark made by the unhappy son, of one of Deirdre's clients (who had
gifted her with an invaluable emerald bracelet, in a transport of ecstatic
gratitude), that, tho' the "spirits" were attributed with all the virtue, and
performed so tirelessly, *they* were not being paid: nay, not a pittance of
the medium's exorbitant fee! Tho' the Society's investigation of Deirdre
of the Shadows had tragic consequences for several gentlemen, and
brought untold grief upon their loving families, it served to point up a
moral, hitherto rigorously observed in the better Spiritualist circles, that
one must never tempt the spirits to "prove" themselves. And it brought about the
considerable beneficence, for the young medium, of the Society's invitation to join its august group: an imprimatur withheld from all but two
previously examined American mediums, both of the masculine gender.
"And now, do you see, how very mistaken you were, Madame!"—thus
Deirdre murmured to herself, as she stood, triumphant, and alone, with
the delectably gratifying letter in her hand.

One mellifluous day in late spring, when the greenery of Gramercy Park
fairly pulsed with tender life, and it would have required a considerable
—and a considerably morbid!—imagination, to summon forth the hor-
rors of that memorable evening, Deirdre had a most eccentric interview
with Dr. Stoughton, in the Society's headquarters. That upstanding
young physician had now assumed the mantle of the presidency of the
New York branch of the Society, and, it may have been, the responsibility
of his office, as well as the doubtless pleasurable authority it involved, led
him to invite Deirdre to the handsome brownstone building, where he
spoke with her of the membership's *unanimous* vote that her mediumship
be affirmed; and that she be granted the honor of membership to the
Society.

Whereupon Deirdre naturally thanked him, but continued, with an
air of maidenly puzzlement: "I accept your invitation, with gratitude—
nay, with a sense of profound humility. For, despite the 'talent' of which
you and your associates are so kind as to speak, I know myself but a means
by which the spirits address the living, and do very little of my own
volition, save prepare myself, by *releasing* myself!"

Young Dr. Stoughton, in whom a sensitivity of manner was subtly
tempered with that stolidity of masculine authority, which makes those of
the healing profession so very like ministers of God, paused but a mo-

ment, and said then, these words that Deirdre was not to forget for many years: "Deirdre—for such I am obliged to call you, and I hope you do not mind!—my *dear* Deirdre, it is perhaps a grave infraction of my professional duties at this time, and no doubt offensive to you, but I feel I must speak openly, and frankly, and, indeed, warmly, like a brother, and not like one with the queer power of 'licensing' you: I must open my heart, and tell you that, in my *personal*, as opposed to my *professional*, judgment, you would do well to abandon your career as a medium: for it is not one suited for any young lady, and not one, if I may be so bold as to assert, suited for *you.*"

Deirdre slightly recoiled from these unexpected words, and so great was her astonishment, her customary mask of meek, resigned, and ofttimes *ecstatic* serenity gave way, of a sudden, to an expression of near-indefinable complexity: alarm, and anger, and defiance, and childlike curiosity, tumultuously admixed.

"Dr. Stoughton, your words are most peculiar indeed," she said forthrightly, "and I really must acknowledge that they *do* offend. That the Spiritualist profession is not suited for any young lady, is hardly a premise I grant; yet I find it more presumable, than your impertinent statement that it is not suited for *me.*"

Dr. Stoughton bent his gaze upon her, with a look of profound contemplation and searching inquiry, his manly brown eyes narrowing, but for a half-second, at the petite damsel's response. (For the gentleman was accustom'd, I would imagine, to frightened feminine submission, and acquiescence in all matters, in his professional practice.) He then said, in a seriousness that was informed by some humility, and with a small grave smile of his handsome lips: "My dear Deirdre, I risked offense by speaking so boldly, and yet I cannot regret it: for I was gripped upon awaking this morning—nay, upon the very first sight of you, some weeks ago—with an altogether queer, and yet not unpleasant, sense of my being an instrument, a means, a vessel, a *medium*, if you will!—entrusted with the utterly simple obligation of informing you all that I have said, and more, if you will condescend to hear."

Deirdre made a faint motion, as if to arise; but sank back in her chair, quite pale, save for a feeble rosy glow about her cheeks. "Dr. Stoughton," she said, "you honor me by this interest: yet I cannot agree with your assessment, that it is *not unpleasant.* I find it very odd indeed, stemming from one of your professional caliber, and entrusted, as you are, with the presidency of your Society—the unfortunate Dr. Dodd being, I have gathered, now retired."

"You may indeed find it odd, Deirdre," Dr. Stoughton said, speaking always with a studied and delicate formality, as he pronounced her name (for he could not address her as "Miss Deirdre," nor as "Deirdre of the Shadows"—an abominable appellation, I have always thought), "but no less odd than I find it. Yet I hardly exaggerate my conviction that I alone have been entrusted with this advice: believing, as I have reason to, that those with whom you are associated at present, and those with whom you have been associated, until very recently (I refer of course to the notorious Countess Blavatsky), would not offer it to you, their interest in your career having the weight of a decided *investment.*"

"I scarce comprehend your language, Dr. Stoughton," Deirdre said palely, "but pray continue: I would not interrupt."

"My meaning is, I hope, not obscured by any ambiguity in *my* motives," Dr. Stoughton said, as a singularly painful expression passed over his countenance, "for I, as the new President of the Society, am obliged to welcome you into our midst, and to invite you to any and all occasions—whether of a professional, or a social, nature—the Society has cause to sponsor; and it would be contrary to my own interest, as it is to the Society's, to suggest that you put all this behind you, and retire to another mode of life altogether."

Faint mocking laughter sounded, as indistinct as thunder erupting a great distance away, beneath the earthly horizon: the laughter of *Zachariah,* it may have been: but it shaded at once into Deirdre's own, in which she indulged but for a moment or two, her pale countenance betraying no mirth. "That I have been *chosen* from birth, and consequently *will-less,* is as much an aspect of my being, Dr. Stoughton, as these hands—and this face—and this hair—and this physiognomical curiosity called a widow's peak," she said in a low breathless voice. "So, should it interest a gentleman of the scientific profession, like yourself, the experiment of defining myself against, or in opposition to, my very nature, would not only result in disaster: but would, I believe, be an impossibility. The terms of my contract on the earthly plane are such that, I would not *be* here, in this very chair, had I not this particular *being*—the which, I gather, you find so very disagreeable."

"Not at all, Miss Deirdre—I mean, Deirdre—not at all, not at all," the startl'd gentleman stammered, as, continuing to gaze upon her face, he seemed near-o'ercome with the brave insolence of her eyes, in which myriad fiery rays, of a possibly preternatural origin, converged into a burning focus. "You are hardly disagreeable, in any of your selves; you simply could not be so! I refer, instead, tho' dismayed at the difficulty I am having, in making my meaning clear, only to your professional employment of yourself, in Spiritualist circles, under the moral and worldly guidance of no guardian, whom I am able to discern at the present time —*that* is what my clumsy words sought to express, and that is *all.*"

"Yet it is a great deal, sir," Deirdre said with a semblance of calm.

Rising suddenly from his chair, and beginning to pace about, as if in inordinate anxiety, Dr. Stoughton murmured almost brokenly: "My conviction is, *I alone am obliged to offer you succor.* And yet, if you do not wish it—! And yet, if I am mistaken—! It would be, I fear, an unforgivable transgression on my part, the more intensified, perhaps, by my professional qualifications, and my subsequent *pretensions* to wisdom. For, clearly, you are one of the most gifted 'mediums' of *all* time, as well as being, I hardly need inform you, without parallel in this country, at *this* time; and why should you not employ yourself, as you wish? Why should you not be swept up in the frenzy of others' demands, so long as they constitute a reasonable—I should think it a *most* reasonable—means of livelihood? Ah, I know not! I know not!" the distraught young man said, his face now ashen pale, and his eyes snatching at Deirdre's, as if to measure the degree of her revulsion. "That I imagine myself *entrusted* with any sort of mission, however well intentioned, is perhaps as much a self-delusion as—as—" And here, in grave embarrassment, Dr. Stoughton paused; and swallowed; having made such a blunder (for of course our keen-witted young lady knew precisely what he meant—her sensitivity being natural as well as supranatural), that he scarce could continue, but leaned back against the book-filled shelves of his office, and, for a brief spell, gave himself up to a posture rather more suitable for a common derelict, of the kind, alas! now glimpsed so frequently on the streets of our metropolis, than for a physician and scientist, of the highest reputation. His handsome face colored; and colored more deeply; and he said, now in a more discreetly restrained voice, "The entire phenomenon of self-deception is not one I can bring up, at the present time; for our subject is another, and far more significant. *Deception* is provocative enough a subject, and rarely, I think, truly understood, but *self-deception* —alas! A veritable cornucopia of riddles, each with its own distinctive flavor, or poison," he said, now smiling abash'dly; and making, even, an attempt to laugh, as if to dispel the unmistakably *strange*—indeed, *uncanny* —atmosphere, that had begun to pervade the room, in the past few minutes. (An atmosphere, I hazard to guess, that was hardly alleviated by a near-inaudible continuation of that low mocking laughter, nor by a queer, scarcely perceptible flickering of the gas lights: tho', if Dr. Stoughton looked resolutely about him, and listened with assiduous concentration, he could discover nothing amiss.) "Deception—self-deception—no, I shall not tread upon *that* precarious ground, for I am unduly distressing you, or, it may be, angering you—and unwisely too!—ah yes!—unwisely! —as the wretched Eglinton would now attest and the others—unwisely, unwisely," he nervously said, coloring yet more deeply, and with a shy intensification of that abash'd, and even boyish, smile, which he bent upon the solemn young lady.

"You forget yourself, Dr. Stoughton," Deirdre said evenly. "You are o'erheated: you will, in another moment, cause that pretty Egyptian vase to dislodge itself, from its perch atop the shelf, and fall, to shatter in a dozen pieces, introducing an element of *material* upset into our discussion, which will quite alarm you: your pulses having begun to flutter already, I sadly suspect, with an anticipation of spirit mischief, or vengeance, in response to your treading too close, in your own figure of speech, to that cornucopia of which you spoke. And so, I pray, *do* seat yourself: and disburden yourself, of all you have to say, by way of your *sacred mission."* These last words uttered with a very light, tho' unmistakable, irony, as subtle as the bitterness attendant upon even the finest China tea, that has been allowed to steep past three minutes.

Whereupon Dr. Stoughton cast his eyes downward, as if surprised in the most secret recesses of his being; yet, with an air of some relief, which blended most agreeably with his nervous, boyish manner, he did return to his desk, and to his seat; and managed to sustain his hopeful smile. His voice had near-calmed, and regained something of its authority, as he spake: "I can hardly be surprised, my dear Deirdre, that you have taken this tone—indeed, it is a tone *well* taken—for in my stumbling, blundering, altogether graceless way, I have requested of you something I should be unable to supply, should anyone—however kindly of intent—request it of *me.* I mean by this, as you so finely phrased it, that I have asked you to consider a mode of action so contrary to all you believe of yourself, and of your unique destiny, that it is a virtual impossibility for ratiocinative exploration: as if some doddering old fool of a philosopher should demand of Substance that it define itself, denuded of its qualities; or some crazed scientist should wish to 'cure' a person of that which—whether inclination, or habit, or something so merely superficial as a birthmark—*is* himself! Yes, I see, indeed I see," the young man mused, his strong-boned face still ruddy, as his eyes were still somewhat dilated, "and yet, you will forgive me, I hope: I persist in believing, with an unwavering stolidity, that the *public career* of mediumship is not a destiny forced upon you, by 'spirits' or by your own stubborn decision, but one which is *accidental* to your *essence:* and one which," he said, hesitating but an instant, before plunging with great audacity forward, "—one which you might yet be saved from, by the proper guidance, informed with the proper high regard for your worth."

Again sounded that distant laughter, faint, susurrous, and quite uncanny!

But Deirdre was replying in a calm, albeit melancholy, voice: *"Proper* has much to do with *propriety,* I think; and neither, Dr. Stoughton, has much to do with *me."*

Dr. Stoughton raised an alarmed gaze to her countenance, and for a long trembling moment could not speak. Then he said hurriedly: "Alas, have I offended you irrevocably? And I meant no harm, I assure you— no harm! I meant only," the agitated gentleman said, "to suggest with the warmth of a friend or a brother, that a life as a professional medium need not be your fate: for there are others, I assure you, bringing far more rewards, and far greater contentment."

"And what, may I inquire," Deirdre said, her expression impassive, but her great dark brooding eyes bright with barely withheld flame, "what are these other fates, Dr. Stoughton?"

Again he bent his gaze upon her, and again looked away, as if confus'd, or, it may have been, dimly apprehensive, as the low distant laughter sounded, ominous as thunder, or invisible waves lapping about the very floorboards of the study!—the which this forthright man of science did his best to ignore. "Ah, perhaps it is wrong of me to speak! —to answer to the compulsion of my heart—to offer succor, where none is desired! For what, after all, have I to set against your destiny—your public career—your practice—your life as 'Deirdre of the Shadows'? I— I know not—I know not— Perhaps it is even the case that I am grievously deluded, in imagining that I can offer you aid: perhaps it is *you* who should offer *me* aid! Nevertheless, Deirdre," the blushing gentleman said, with an abjuring gesture, and an uneasy smile playing about his manly lips, "nevertheless I must speak bluntly, tho' I risk your anger, or, excuse me!—the anger of your spirits: I must warn you against sacrificing yourself to a life of Spiritualist 'service'—answering always to the demands of others, whether deceased spirits, or living clients. Ah, to drain away your life's blood, in such employ!—in ghoulish darkened rooms, amidst the perpetually mourning! My dear girl, it is a most *piteous* fate!"

Whereupon Deirdre of a sudden brought both hands to her face, and, in a curious gesture, pressed the gloved fingertips against her closed eyes: at first lightly, and then with more force. It may have been that the agitated young lady was attempting to suppress tears, or a similar untoward response; but when at last she spoke, her voice was not greatly changed, and her manner retained its semblance of glacial calm. "And shall I inquire, Dr. Stoughton, what a fate might be, that, in your professional assessment, is *not* piteous?"

Dr. Stoughton's stolid cheeks burnt yet a richer crimson, as he spake, in a voice somewhat quavering, yet withal assertive: "The joyous fulfillment of your sex: the sacred duties of belovèd wife, and helpmeet, and mother. In opposition to the vulgar and mercantile hurly-burly of the great world, the idyllic pleasures of the domestic hearth—the which, I firmly believe, make of one small room an everywhere, indeed; and provide us with that small measure of bliss, which is, if we are greatly fortunate, and deserving, Our Lord's promise to us, of the Heaven to come."

Hearing these impetuous words, Deirdre cast upon her interlocutor a gaze radiant—nay, fiery—with maidenly disdain. And, rising with great dignity from her chair, she said: "What, *wife*, and *helpmeet*, and *mother!* And did you say *sacred* as well, Dr. Stoughton? Ah, it is too amusing: *sacred!*"

Dr. Stoughton rose with clumsy alacrity from his seat, and would have tendered his apologies, for having spoke, as it were, rather *too* bluntly, but the haughty young lady inquired of him: "And is *your* wife, Dr. Stoughton, so joyously fulfilled as to her sex, and so ecstatically immersed in the sacred duties of her lot, as to speak with equal passion of that fate, as *you* have done? Would that she were here to bear witness!"

"I have no wife," Dr. Stoughton murmured, "I am unmarried."

Again the low laughter sounded, and a sourceless sibilancy issued from out the very air; and the gas jets coquettishly quavered. And Deirdre, in some apprehension that her mischievous spirits would rush forward, to make a shambles of the office, and of Dr. Stoughton's strained composure, betook herself to the door, the dignity of her small erect carriage reflecting none of the emotion she felt—neither the angry amusement, nor the pain. Yet she could not resist a parting remark, uttered in a low and falsely genteel voice, the which I record only with hesitation, for it bespeaks a sensibility formed neither by that devout Christian couple Mr. and Mrs. Bonner, nor by the Zinns, and is, indeed, a libel upon her Bloodsmoor background itself! "I am deeply grateful for your suggestion, Dr. Stoughton, uttered out of that special reservoir of wisdom that is yours, both as a consequence of your profession in life, and your maleness: but you will forgive me, if I demur, in that I much prefer intercourse with the Spirits."

62

Tho' it was not until the autumn of 1895, after the successful, albeit difficult, exorcism of a malicious spirit, from out an old country manor in Fishkill, New York, that Deirdre of the Shadows was forced to retire from her mediumship, I am hardly amiss in stating that the *seeds* of the young woman's destruction were sown many years earlier: I am almost tempted, alas, to say, *upon the very day of her birth!*

(By which I do not mean solely that that birth, in the autumn of 1863, had been perhaps more shrouded in mystery, and shame, than we would care to think: I mean in addition that, God's infinite love and mercy notwithstanding, and the sacrifice of Jesus Christ operative at all times, there do seem to be, in our fallen world, souls distinctly *marked* for sin, and consequently for sorrow, from the first instant of drawing breath. No doubt this is what the Christian religion means by Original Sin: and yet, why are some of us joyously freed from its taint, by God's grace, and Jesus' love, while others remain damn'd? A profound mystery here, the which has been explained patiently to me, many a time, by gracious men of the cloth—yet, the frailty of my sex being as evident in me, as in my untutor'd sisters, I am bound to confess that I have never understood; and, at my hallowed age, it is unlikely that I ever will.)

Yes, O Reader, speculate a moment with me, and consider: had Deirdre any intimate companions who valued her, and respected her; had she, let us say, the sweet solace of a loving and devoted *sister,* or even a *brotherly* guide, it is possible that her pathetic collapse in the wilds of Fishkill might have been averted. ("Pathetic," I say, and not "tragic," for one must consider the circumstances of the breakdown, and the caliber of the young woman's moral character.) And yet—if we recall Deirdre's

476

lifelong perversity of will, and her spiteful insistence upon going her own way, I very much doubt that even a sister with the infinite well of sympathy of Octavia Zinn, or a brotherly guide with the steadfast integrity of handsome young Dr. Stoughton, might have saved the headstrong creature from her fate: a fate easily the equivalent in horror, and in degradation, to the loss of maidenhood itself: by which I mean *the loss of sanity.*

It happened that less than a twelve-month after the exchange with Dr. Stoughton, that gentleman of surpassing integrity, and Christian compassion, Deirdre boldly betook herself in 1891 to the historic Old World of Europe: and there, traveling with a modest entourage of less than ten persons, the American medium enjoyed a continued success, and was fulsomely rewarded, with both praise from her numerous clients, and money and gifts. In Paris, in Munich, in Vienna, in Zurich, in Rome: in the sunny clime of the South of France, in the beauteous chivalric mountains of Old Spain, in the snowy-white Alpine heights of Switzerland, along the magnificent castle-haunted rivers of Germany, in the graceful albeit melancholy city of Prague, and the tragic city of Warsaw: in that city of incomparable gaiety, charm, picturesque palaces and cathedrals, and steep hills, Buda-Pest, risen like a fairy city on the placid Danube: and even in exotic Turkey, abode of mosque and seraglio!—know, O sympathetic reader, the little American medium found herself most welcome, her fame having been hawked before her, by Spiritualist compatriots in these foreign climes.

Deirdre of the Shadows was reported to have been a houseguest for several weeks of Count János Krúdy, in his great castle on the gloomily picturesque Lake Balaton, in Hungary; and of the Duke and Duchess of Bellegarde, at their country estate in Provence; and of the wealthy shipowning family the Björkös, of Old Uppsala, Sweden. Lord and Lady Kellynch, of Kellynch Hall, Sussex, were said to have been enormously gratified, by the aid of Deirdre of the Shadows, in their communications with their son, lost on a voyage to India: as were the Ingolstadts of Gondol, who had lost a belovèd daughter some years previously: and the Szczyrks of Warsaw, whose anguish at the loss of a belovèd wife and mother, quite overcame their Catholic repugnance for "witchery" and "sorcery."

It was noted by all, believers and detractors alike, that Deirdre of the Shadows, with her stark, blackly-burning eyes, and her near-translucent skin, and her hushed voice, appeared rather more a spirit herself, than a young woman of some twenty-odd years of age: and that, whether mesmerist, or ventriloquist, or magician, or genuine psychic, she was so clearly convinced of her occult powers, and so totally absorbed by them, the most contemptuously savage of skeptics could not wish to accuse her of fraud. "How wraithlike!—how pallid! She is an angel-emissary, surely," Lady Kellynch was said to have exclaimed, "and yet, the singular curse of *being* her!"

It was during this ambitious, and greatly exhausting, European tour that Deirdre began to take note of an alteration, at first so subtle as to be near-imperceptible, in the contact spirits' manner: in both the timbre of their voices, and the messages they conveyed. *Mrs. Dodd* had long since vanish'd, it is to be supposed as a consequence of her son's misfortune, and his "crossing over" into Spirit World; yet *Father Darien,* so generally sober, and wise, and, indeed, fatherly, succumbed upon some occasions to an unexpected testiness, and revealed a most surprising bellicose tone. (The saintly Jesuit had become, Deirdre gathered, to her amaz'd puzzlement, somewhat anti-Catholic in tone!—for, it seemed, the "Popish harlequinade," to use *Father Darien*'s own phrase, was a grave disappointment beyond the Earth Plane: there being, evidently, not a whit of truth to its confident assertions, throughout the centuries, regarding the entire pantheon of saints, Popes, and Mary herself.) Puckish *Zachariah* was no less problematic, and quick to take advantage of the other spirits' indecisiveness, or the medium's exhaustion; but, added to this, was an increased malevolent hysteria to his behavior, as if he were no longer capable of controlling his caprices, but quite at the mercy of a demonic pleasure in playing all sorts of tiresome pranks, such as a naughty twelve-year-old boy might conceive of; and in muttering, and cursing, and babbling incoherent threats against his enemies "in both worlds."

There had appeared, it was true, a new, and gentle, spirit identified only as *Sarah,* possessed of so frail and tremulous a voice, and, in general, so undependable as to her aid to the medium, that one might presume her to be extremely elderly: albeit a lady of obvious grace and breeding. And, from time to time, a *Red Indian* emerged from out the cacophonous murmurings, bearing with him, fortunately, no ill-will for the race of white men, and blessed with a surprising command of the English language; and there was a *royal son of Thebes,* and a *lost Czarina,* and, infrequently, the loving *Mrs. Bonner* herself—but so very faint, Deirdre could rarely determine the sound, let alone the sense, of her words. These were, it might be said, "helpful" spirits: but there were others who were less helpful, indeed mercurial and alarming, among them *Bianca* (who had dramatically changed from her impish state, and was now a shrill and even sluttish girl of some fourteen years of age, noisy with apocalyptic mutterings of the "Great Cataclysm" ahead); and one *Margaret Fuller* (so choked with rage, she could scarce express herself: save to warn that *Mankind*—by which she meant the entire masculine gender!—would soon reap the harvest they most deserved, by the terrible year 1900); and the *Raging Captain,* whose bullying manner, and incontinent imprecations, earned him, one storm-toss'd eve in Buda-Pest, a vicious response from his fellow spirits: *Zachariah* in particular, tho' with the aid of a hot-tempered *Father Darien,* and a shrill-laughing *Bianca,* administering to that contumacious shade so severe a beating, as to render him silenced forever!—to the relief of the exhausted young medium, whose head pounded with these invisible battles, and whose sensitive nerves so rang, that, after the most disorderly of sittings, the balm that "knits up the ravell'd sleave of care" would not descend upon her for as long as eighteen, or even twenty-four, desolate hours.

And, on the rain-streaked night of May 8, 1891, a grotesque and altogether unlook'd-for episode occurred: in the midst of a tearful but nobly restrained reunion between the ninety-year-old Baroness Ambaaren of the Norwegian fortress-town of Otterholm, and her deceased spouse, who had died, as a consequence of galloping consumption, at the age of twenty-eight, there suddenly intruded—with what coarse effect, both buffoonish and painful, in the midst of the Baroness's drawing room, the sensitive reader can well imagine!—a familiar female voice of singular stridency: throaty, rudely jocose, slyly insinuating: the very voice, unmistakable, of *Madame Blavatsky!*

Madame's remarks, some of which had to do with "enemies," and "pernicious detractors," and the "Great Conflagration" to be visited upon the globe with the advent of the new century, were not entirely coherent: for the poor creature was at that time suffering from the dislocation of "crossing over" (having died but that afternoon, in her sickbed in a patroness's home in London). She laughed hoarsely; and uttered one or two ribald comments on "rascal celibates"—perhaps in reference to *Father Darien,* who was trying to restrain her; and chided Deirdre for her cruelty, and "maidenly cunning"; and railed at some length against the apostate *chela* Hassan Agha, who had, evidently, defected in Madras, reverting to the "bloodless Low Church Anglicanism" of his mother. This shrewish interruption of a poignant love-exchange betwixt the Baroness and the Baron was, of course, most unfortunate: unfortunate, too, was the fact that Deirdre, sunk deeply in trance, her opened eyes glassy and her pulses but faintly beating, was in the painful position of being aware of *Madame Blavatsky's* mischief, whilst being at the same time totally powerless to curtail it!

After some minutes of great confusion, Madame's spirit was satisfactorily subdued, and vanquish'd by the others; and the séance continued with no further disturbances. But the mischief *had* been done, and it was quite some time—upward of two hours, in fact—before the affrighted spirit of the long-deceased Baron could be coaxed into resuming the dialogue with his widow. (Poor Madame Blavatsky! She had, it seemed, never truly forgiven her Lolo for having rejected her; and had been quick to imagine, or to perceive, a most subtle attraction between Deirdre of the Shadows and the comely young *chela.* Grave financial problems had attended her Indian pilgrimage, and not a few embarrassing episodes, too tedious here to recount; and, returning to Europe, she eventually settled in the Avenue Road house of a London Theosophist, who tended to her, until her death by way of heart trouble, rheumatism, influenza, and Bright's disease, on that May afternoon of 1891. Along with the rather more gracious William James, who died in 1910, "Madame B.," as she came to be called, was the most familiar of all famous spirits who found their way, unbidden, into séances in America. But the uncouth Russian immigrant never sufficiently mastered our great language, as to be capable of communicating, with the forcefulness she desired!)

These numerous startling—indeed, frequently terrifying—séances did not, as the reasonable observer might suspect, bring upon Deirdre of the Shadows anything more than a negligible disapprobation: but did in fact (alas, the folly of the times!) so fan the desire to witness them, on the part of even the most genteel of Spiritualists, that Deirdre and her associates had all they could do to deal with demands for sittings—and to deal with the angry disappointment (oft shading into bizarre expressions of threat) of those whose petitions were denied.

    Nay, the increasingly frequent eruptions, from out of Spirit World, of spirits who were not only unsolicitous, but positively unhelpful, and, in some instances, *unrelated* to the proceedings entirely, had not the anticipated effect of so disgusting Spiritualist believers, that they turned aside from the young American medium (a development that would certainly have "saved" her—at least temporarily): and this was as true in the States, when she returned, near-broken in health, and oft dazed for many hours after a séance, as it was in historic Old Europe, where one might expect *primitive*, and certainly *foreign*, manners.

63

As close to madness as a cobweb has breadth—so Deirdre mused, of herself and her condition, with that curious detachment in all personal matters that came to characterize her, at the peak of her career. *As closely akin to the earth beneath my feet,* she continued, in idle anxiety, *as a cobweb has weight!*

The death of Madame Blavatsky, and the intermittent disturbances that formidable woman caused, might have stimulated Deirdre to truncate her European tour, and to return home without satisfying numerous engagements: that, and the betrayal of an associate (who absconded with a considerable amount of money); and repeated yieldings to extreme fatigue, which had the additional consequence of so affecting Deirdre's sensitive eyes, that she could barely tolerate daylight, and much preferred to remain inside, on the sunniest, most pleasant of days, dwelling in candlelit seclusion.

Do I object? Deirdre queried herself. *Do I raise my voice, in opposition? Not at all, for I have grown enamor'd of the dark.*

It has been observed that monetary gain did not greatly excite this young woman, tho' she took a cold pleasure in the waxing of her fortune, and felt some panicked anger when it ebb'd. Avaricious greed she knew not, no more than she knew sensual indulgence: yet, alone in her chamber, she oft contented herself with a consideration of her accounts, and a perusal of those gifts—most of them ostentatious trinkets, like the emerald bracelet, forced upon her by grateful clients. "Yes; good; this is my desert; it is earned with my blood," Deirdre counseled herself, "—nay, with my soul."

About her slender neck she continued to wear the little golden locket given her by Mrs. Bonner, so very many years ago: perhaps not "golden" entirely, for it had long ago begun to tarnish; and was, in fact, rather shabby and diminished in appearance. In contrast to the costly items Deirdre now received, which she never deigned to wear, the locket was decidedly modest, and "did not do her justice," in Madame Blavatsky's words. Yet she wore it, on its thin chain (which had tarnished so thoroughly, it no longer even resembled gold), inside her dark raiment, hidden from sight: as tho' it were a secret, of which she was ashamed.

The tiny likenesses of Mr. and Mrs. Bonner, Deirdre's true parents, had, alas, so greatly faded with time—it being, now, some thirty years since the daguerreotypes had been taken—that, had Deirdre opened the locket, to contemplate them, she would have been greatly saddened at their loss: for one might scarcely have distinguished Mrs. Bonner from her spouse, and both had faded into sepia-pale wraiths! But Deirdre did not distract herself from her absorption in the present, by so purposeless an activity. If she continued to wear the shabby locket, and even to caress it, at times, half consciously, it was not perhaps for sentimental reasons, but solely, I am saddened to say, out of habit.

Consider, O Reader, how far—how tragically far—this heedless young woman has come, from her innocent origins in Bloodsmoor! At the time of her collapse she dwelt alone, in public accommodations, moving restlessly from one hotel to another, having no companions but only associates, of a managerial nature; and counting amongst her friends only that coterie of Spiritualist enthusiasts, widows and widowers primarily, and those afflicted with severe loss, or with such a terror of personal mortality, an unchristian fanaticism had sprung to life in their souls. It hardly needs to be said that she had no gentlemen suitors, for only a very brave-hearted man—or a very unwise one!—might have wished to approach her, with *romance* in mind: risking thereby not only the jeering interruption of the contact spirits, who were evidently always present, but the unmanning frost of Deirdre's own scorn.

"*Alone* I assuredly am," the vain young woman declared, "but, as assuredly, *lonely* I am not."

Thus Deirdre of the Shadows at the advanced age of thirty-one: "advanced," I mean, for a young lady not married, or with any prospects in sight.

You will be surprised, then, to learn of her emotion, in which astonishment, gratification, and pain were commingled, when the news of Malvinia Morloch's humiliation came to her: for the gutter press so luridly hawked the pathetic incident, as to insist that the distraught actress had fled from the stage as a consequence of a "tragic affair of the heart," and an "overindulgence in alcoholic spirits"! So crude speculation was abbreviated into still cruder fact, and that, into two-inch head-lines; and, in some ghoulish versions of the story, it was proposed as a certainty ("according to authentic police conjecture") that Malvinia Mor-loch had taken her own life—in some wise not yet known.

Indeed, witnesses had already stepped forward, to noisily assert that they had seen the figure of a woman plummeting from one bridge or another, into the river: in some cases they swore they had seen the "beauteous, damn'd" countenance of the celebrated actress. Already a "phantom woman" had been sighted, wandering at midnight along the walkway of the gloomiest of the bridges—to dissipate into mere vapor, and vanish, when approached by a policeman!

Greatly agitated, Deirdre hid herself away, to peruse all the news-papers, and to pace about her bedchamber, murmuring to herself, and laughing softly, and stumbling upon the carpet as if she had no notion where she was. It was nearly as much of a distressing revelation, to read that her sister was now *thirty-three* years old, as to read of her public humiliation, and even the possibility of her suicide: for Malvinia had always been so indefatigably young, so brilliantly vivacious! Ah, the shame of this Malvinia Morloch, driven from the stage, in full view of an audience, vanquished utterly, and for so pathetic a reason: a mere love affair!

"This," Deirdre said aloud, "this scandal is *her* just desert, and I can feel no pity for her."

Yet she found it surpassingly difficult, to set aside her thoughts, and her emotions, with the ease with which, after a few days, she disposed of the newspapers. For she was haunted by Malvinia's image, and could nearly hear that melodious, sly, inimitable voice: not so much as she had heard it, and had thrilled to it, in the Fanshawe Theatre, upon the occa-sion of that performance of *Richard III*, but as she had heard it—ah, so many times!—so many cruel times!—in Bloodsmoor.

"A pathetic half-drowned river rat," Malvinia had once called Deir-dre, in her hearing. "And this sorry specimen is presented to us as a 'sister'!"

Sister. Adoptive sister. Despised.

"I hate you," Malvinia had said, turning the chill contemptuous gaze of her lovely eyes upon Deirdre: "I hate you, and wish you too had died of the typhoid, and I am most vex'd with myself, that I should even trouble to *hate* such a wretch as you!"

But were these cruel words *uttered*, or only *imagined*?

Beautiful Malvinia, Mr. Zinn's favorite! So capricious, so wanton, so utterly charming, who could resist her sporadic outbursts of affection, even while cowering against the lancet of her wit!

Malvinia, who had eaten of Deirdre's heart. Greedily, and yet—who could forgive her!—disdainfully.

"I know that I am not your sister," Deirdre once murmured, in Malvinia's presence, when the two girls had chanced to meet alone, "I know that I am but your stepsister: but, for all that, I refuse to be despised: I *will not* be despised."

Whereupon the slim-bodied maiden, trailing a dozen ribbons, and giving off a fragrance of powdered rose and hyssop, merely bestowed so mock-startl'd a glance upon her, as if a contemptible creature—indeed, a river rat—had reared back upon its hind legs, to speak, that Deirdre felt the full and incontestable weight of *being despised:* and knew that it was her fate.

Never, never will I forgive, Deirdre bethought herself, her eyes spilling salt-stung tears, even had I in me, as these Christians teach, to forgive, why, I should not!—I should not!—ever!

Malvinia the loveliest of the Zinn daughters: the loveliest of all the Kiddemasters: Malvinia whom everyone of her age, and of the female gender, could not help but envy: nor was the cowering river rat any exception, despite the bitterness of her heart.

Malvinia, in the frothy white dress, new for that very occasion— that fateful occasion!—of the Kiddemasters' high tea, in honor of Constance Philippa and the Baron, and those bewhiskered gentlemen from Boston, who had belonged to some sort of august society, in which Mr. Zinn was a candidate for membership. Malvinia, erect in the high-necked bodice that fitted her so smoothly; one could not guess at the apparel beneath, no more than one might have guessed at the flesh, the young woman, beneath. Malvinia, in yards and yards of fragrant floating translucent fabric, adorned with hundreds of flounces and ruffles and pink velvet ribbons: Malvinia, commandeering, imperious, yet altogether magnificent. "I insist that you allow me to refashion you," Malvinia said crisply, "to make of you the striking young lady you assuredly are, somewhere beneath that dowdy hairdo, and that peevish sickly unutterably *stubborn* expression—!"

Deirdre had of course protested, and feebly resisted: but who in all of Bloodsmoor was ever capable of thwarting Malvinia's will?

And so she had submitted, meekly enough, for all her sullen stubborn soul. And Malvinia had refashioned her, in ringlets and plaits and ingenious curls: a very pretty miss, indeed. But Malvinia's handiwork had naught to do (so the embittered Deirdre reasoned) with Deirdre, but only with Malvinia: Malvinia's industry, Malvinia's charity, Malvinia's legerdemain in prettifying the half-drowned river rat.

Why should I thank her for this exhibition of her vanity, Deirdre bethought herself, even as her cheeks flushed with involuntary pleasure, at her sister's warm propinquity, and at the attractive stranger in the glass. Why should I thank her who despises me, and whom I in turn despise!

Thus—alas!—the bitterness of Deirdre's heart!

Thus it was at the tender age of sixteen years; and thus, still, at the sober age of thirty-one. For in some hearts, prematurely shriveled, as it were, or touched from the very moment of conception in the womb, with that *Original Sin* that falls upon our race like a shadow of granite, there is, and can be, no spiritual progress!

I did not thank her that day, and I was right in refusing to do so, Deirdre thought, pacing her bedchamber, which was shielded against the bright blazing sunshine of a clear January morning, by heavy velvet drapes, which Deirdre had bade the servant girl not to pull: for the daylight pained her eyes, and caused vexing tears to stream down her cheeks. She despised me as an *orphan*, and never loved me as a *sister*, Deirdre continued, her small angry fist of a heart knocking against her ribs, no matter the foolish adoration I felt, in my girlhood ignorance, for *her*.

So she counseled herself, locked away in a hotel suite, in a city it is purposeless to name, for it carried not a whit of meaning for Deirdre of the Shadows, but was nothing other than a place, tolerable since temporary, for the brazen enactment of her mediumship.

Nay, this heedless young woman not only refused to pity Malvinia's public shame, or to concern herself with the possibility of Malvinia's death (as if the shadowy realms of Death were *her* province solely): she took pride in thus hardening herself against any natural feeling, and wiped the stinging tears harshly from her eyes.

It was to Mr. Zinn that her mute but impassioned plea was directed, tho' she had resolutely hardened herself against him as well, for all the years she had been away from Bloodsmoor: *O Father please hear how my cruel sisters despise me O Father do not turn away do not deny me O hear how Malvinia drew from out her bodice a tiny silver scissors and with it snipped at my breast and pierced my cringing flesh and lifted the skin away and touched my heart my living heart O Father hear how she broke off a piece of my heart and ate it and* Ah! this is bitter *she spat* how bitter! *she mocked and jeered* How bitter it is, her heart!—her heart!

And so indeed it was; and continued to be; until the very day of her downfall.

64

It is fitting that Deirdre of the Shadows, in seeking to exorcise a spirit, should find herself, in a manner of speaking, *exorcised*—so o'ercome at last by malicious Spirit World contention, and by the prolonged strain to her own nervous system, that she fled on foot into a marshy woods, and had to be forcibly rescued, by those of her assistants who had accompanied her to Fishkill, and by those employees of Fairbanks House who had not been earlier frightened away. "Help me! Save me!"—so the hysterical young woman cried; and yet, such was the extremity of her condition, that she sought to beat her captors away, and seemed not to recognize them. "Do not touch me! Oh, help me! Save me!"—thus she raved.

This pathetic episode occurred in the late summer of 1895, at the Fishkill estate of General Darius Fairbanks, known locally as Fairbanks House, a handsome mansard-roofed stone mansion, set atop a majestic knoll o'erlooking the Hudson River—that grandiose and invincible monarch of rivers—and surrounded by great copper beeches of a Palladian hauteur. The princely country estate had been in the Fairbanks family for many generations, since the first settlement of our country, and not even the vicissitudes of the Revolution had divided its fertile acres, which numbered in the thousands. In recent decades, since the retirement of General Fairbanks, and the onset of a protracted and undiagnosable illness in Mrs. Fairbanks, the elderly couple had chosen to live all the year round in their Manhattan dwelling place, leaving Fairbanks House untenanted: and uninhabited, save for a small staff of servants and grounds-keepers. (The rich farm- and orchardland was rented out to neighboring farmers, and was said to yield a rich return, save in the very driest of summers.) If you know the Fishkill region, scarcely a two-hour carriage ride from the bustling Fifth Avenue of Manhattan, you know its idyllic beauty, and the aristocratic grace with which its grassy hills rise one above the other; you know the grandeur of the old forests, which hark back, it might seem, to the very beginning of time, before our mere *human* history had its origin. And if your eye has chanced to fall upon the imposing Fairbanks House itself (for it is partly visible from the road, tho' the sloping front lawn is richly cultivated, and aged vines grow thickly upon the wrought-iron fence), you have, perhaps, registered naught but pleased surprise, and unstinting admiration, for so splendid an abode. But know, O Reader, that Fairbanks House yielded, for its tenants, very little save vexation, and a good deal of distress—this regal dwelling place, for all its manly stone, and the strength and weight of its four-square structure, being *haunted!*

It was not so much the house itself, but the garden to the rear, that gave evidence of contamination by a malicious spirit, tho' at any time on the estate, and at virtually any spot, according to servants, the spirit might manifest itself—or herself, to be precise, since it was generally believed that the spirit was female. The garden, laid out in a classic Italian style, most pleasing to the eye, consisted of every variety of rosebush, including rose trees, and was dissected by a long rectangular pond, some fifty yards in length, and perhaps two yards in width, but rather deeper, at five or six feet, than the casual observer might believe. Tho' in recent years, as a consequence of the elder Fairbanks' marked lack of interest in their property, the rosebushes had been allowed to grow somewhat shabby, and the pond to become choked with water lilies, the garden was still charming, and exerted an eerie, bittersweet spell, upon all who chanced to enter it. An especial pity, then, that this spot had come to be the favorite habitation of the ill-tempered spirit!

According to those servants who had not been driven away over the years, this preternatural creature was rarely visible to the human eye, save occasionally at dusk, when her form assumed, for a brief period, a phosphorescent glimmer—so tremulous and uncertain, as to be naught but mist. The estate's animals—dogs, cats, and horses in particular— ofttimes demonstrated, by every variety of startl'd response, that *they* had no difficulty in sensing, or actually seeing, the malevolent interloper: and many were the nights (so the elderly housekeeper told Deirdre) that all were kept awake by the furious and terrified baying of the dogs, which might continue for as long as six or eight hours at a time!

The spirit did not generally behave like a *poltergeist*—that species of household nuisance who slams doors and windows, and throws china about, and causes tables to heave into the air—but rather like a melancholy ghost of old, disturbing, and, as it were, contaminating, the happiness of the living, with a spiteful sort of persistence, not unlike that of a cranky and bilious guest who ruins a social occasion by his mere presence yet will not go away. She gave off emanations of flat dead air—indeed, the rank air of the tomb—and made sounds so peculiar, and so indefinable, as to cause a chill in this chronicler, merely as I transcribe them! Moans, and sighs, and stifled outcries of pain, and near-inaudible protestations, and gurgling noises, and chokings, and wild lunatic laughter, and panting, and hysterical weeping: she caused doors to swing slowly, and creak on their hinges; an invisible harp to sound its ethereal notes with a crazed repetition; a slithering and rustling sound, best identified as *snakelike,* to arise, in odd corners of the house, including the mistress's drawing room, and the master bedchamber. And she sang and hummed to herself: the which many witnesses found most repellent of all, her voice being distinctly unmelodious, and the *repetition* of the simple tunes she chose to sing, quite unnerving.

Upon occasion, it is true, this unhappy spirit's venom discharged itself in more dramatic ways: she caused large sparks to leap from the wood-fire stove in the kitchen, onto the floorboards, or onto one of the terrified servants; she worked some unspeakably cruel magic, so that the hounds might suddenly tear at one another, in a frenzy of dog lust, and one of the most majestic of the copper beeches sickened and died within a fortnight, and the quaintly picturesque golden carp in the garden pond turned upon one another, and, in a very short period of time, before any of the groundsmen guessed what was transpiring, gobbled one another up! At the first formal dinner party given by General Fairbanks's grandson and his bride, some eighteen months before Deirdre of the Shadows was summoned to Fishkill, the spirit wantonly disturbed the convivial gathering by stealing the ladies' gloves one by one (these gloves resting, as is customary, upon the ladies' knees, during dinner); and causing the atmosphere to be "perfum'd" by her peculiar odor of rankness, and interrupted by the scarce-audible ghost harp; and, most unforgivably, o'erturning an antique French sideboard in the dining room, so that, to the terror of the diners, hundreds of pieces of china and glassware crashed to the floor, and may very well have injured someone, had not one or two quick-witted gentlemen acted with extreme alacrity, to shield the ladies from flying chips of glass!

That, in general, the spirit did restrain herself, as I have noted, from behaving with the buffoonish caprice of the *poltergeist,* is surely to her credit: but one can sympathize with the Fairbanks family, in having conceived so great a repugnance for their ancestral abode, that they scarce wished to visit it, let alone dwell within it, despite its princely grandeur, and the bucolic splendor of the Fishkill countryside!

So for some twelve or fifteen years the magnificent house remained untenanted, until, given as a wedding present to one of the General's grandsons, it was refurbished, and reopened, in the early spring of 1895. Young Darius Fairbanks III and his pretty bride, of the

Maryland Nashes, were courageous enough, or impetuous enough, to establish their household in the midst of the spirit's domain; or, it may have been, their good-natured "modern" skepticism (shaped in outline, if not in detail, by the corrupting Darwinism of the times) prevented them from grasping the magnitude of the situation. "How quaint!—how wonderfully eccentric!" young Mrs. Fairbanks exclaimed. "To own a *haunted* house! Why, there is nothing like it in Baltimore; and surely not in New York City."

The brave young couple moved into Fairbanks House, bringing with them a number of servants new to Fishkill, and, for some weeks, perhaps because she was disoriented by their presence, and the busyness of the household, the spirit kept her distance: with naught but the ethereal harp sounding, very late at night, and so indistinct that Mr. and Mrs. Fairbanks had to talk themselves laughingly into *hearing* it. "There! There it is, Darrie!" Mrs. Fairbanks cried. "You do hear it now, don't you?" And the fresh-cheeked young man cocked his head, and listened hard, and finally allowed that he did hear something: tho', most likely, it was nothing but the wind in the beech trees. "The wind in the trees!" Mrs. Fairbanks exclaimed laughingly. "Why, it is nothing of the sort: it is your family's renowned *ghost*. And I will not have the poor thing belittled."

After some weeks, however, the "poor thing" grew bolder, and began to make her presence known, both in the house and out; and not in the most palatable of ways. That her dissonant singing and humming might be characterized as "quaint" was arguable; her other pranks— causing doors to creak on their hinges, sparks to fly from fireplaces, china to shatter—were most annoying indeed, when not genuinely frightening. One by one the new servants gave notice; within a month the handsome rose garden was so sinister, no one wished to stroll in it; the carefree marital climate was o'ershadowed, and close to blighted; young Mrs. Fairbanks succumbed to purposeless bouts of weeping, and Mr. Fairbanks found himself hot-tempered, raising his voice upon the slightest provocation. "It is the *spirit*," Mrs. Fairbanks said, tearfully, "your family's *spirit*, that comes between us." Whereupon her young bridegroom retorted: "Never mind such claptrap! There is no *spirit* on the premises; and, if there were, it is assuredly not my family's spirit, but a *stranger* entirely."

And so, indeed, it was proved to be. But only after many mishaps, and one very serious incident—this being the collapse of the antique sideboard in the dining room, which so terrified Mrs. Fairbanks that she sank into a swoon from which she could not be roused for many hours, and, upon the morn, suffered a most piteous miscarriage, which plunged all the household into mourning; and fired her young husband with a desire for vengeance against the malicious ghost.

"I will not rest until the thing is banish'd from my property," Mr. Fairbanks vowed. "And money will be no object."

And so it came about that, in the late, and very dry, summer of 1895, Deirdre of the Shadows was approached by the estate manager of Fairbanks House, with a very simple and challenging proposition: if she should be successful in *exorcising* a spirit, from out of a house belonging to one of the oldest families in the state, and keep the exorcism a secret, she would be most liberally rewarded: indeed, she might set her own price.

In a medieval fortress-castle on the Rhine, and in the alabaster villa of the Marchesa di Tito, in Nice, Deirdre of the Shadows had been successful in driving out unwanted household spirits: less "driving them out" than so reasoning with them, and so cajoling them, that they left voluntarily, and crossed over into Spirit World, as they should have done upon their natural deaths. So worrisome had Deirdre's contact spirits become of late, so unreliable *Father Darien,* and so unpleasant the shrill-voic'd *Bianca,* that Deirdre preferred an *exorcism* to a *séance,* since it would involve no other personages than herself, and the hypothetical spirit.

After some hesitation, and not a little negotiating, Deirdre accepted the challenge; and journeyed out to Fishkill in her private carriage, accompanied by her French maid, and two assistants. It must be said that her health at this time (not many weeks past her thirty-second birthday) was somewhat precarious: the delicate-boned young woman was susceptible to fainting spells, attacks of nerves, hammering headaches, and flashes of near-blindness, during which tears streamed liberally down her cheeks. And there were hours when, unbidden, her contact spirits intruded upon her, with wild garbled messages delivered out of the void, having to do with that subject so strangely familiar to all Spiritualists, in the closing years of the nineteenth century—the *End of the World.* ("I do not care to hear it again," Deirdre cried, "I beg you, not again: *Fire, Flood, Earthquake, Famine, Pestilence!* Take yourselves thither, and leave me be, for I find that I cannot care whether the world endures beyond 1900, or no!" Yet the belligerent spirits—those known to her, and outright strangers—crowded close, and made a din, that great conflagrations should o'erspread the globe, in the year 1899; that fragments of a moon of Jupiter's should smash against the earth, annihilating entire continents; that Jesus Christ should return in glory, athirst for the blood of sinners; that the polar caps should shift, and the temperate zones freeze; that the Black Death should return, spread by rats; and Time itself would come to an end. "O sinful man," *Father Darien* intoned, in a sepulchral Jesuit's voice, "remember: from dust thou hast come, and to dust thou shalt return. Blessèd is the name of—*dust!*" And on and on, sometimes for hours, when Deirdre was at her feeblest, and could not resist.

Until she railed at them with the fury of a fishmonger's wife, and bade them begone, to hell if no other place would have them!—for she was heartily sick of their prattle, and wished only to be left in peace.)

You may be the judge yourself, Reader: as to whether the young medium was wise, her health being so precarious, to undertake so arduous a task as the exorcism of a malevolent spirit.

Once at Fairbanks House, Deirdre questioned the estate manager, and the housekeeper, and one or two of the more articulate servants, that she might form some notion of the history of the phenomenon: whether the identity of the spirit was known to anyone, whether there was a story or romance behind the situation, which might account for it. A spirit trapped on this side of the barrier being, in the medium's words, "one who is trapped in an old legend he or she has spun about himself, whereof he cannot break the bands, to breathe freely again." The estate manager professed to be new to Fishkill, having come into the elder Fairbanks' employ but ten years previous; the housekeeper, tho' filled with the wildest of tales, pertaining to the ghost, could offer very little by way of factual information, save that there had been a story, many years ago, when *she* was but a young woman new in service at the house, to the effect that a crazed girl had scaled the walls of the garden, one moonlit midsummer night, to drown herself in the lily pond!—but this was many years back, and might even have been a century ago, in the days of Federalist rule.

(If Deirdre of the Shadows felt the slight to her esteemed personage, that neither Mr. Fairbanks nor his comely wife condescended to greet her, as if *she* were but a hireling, naturally she gave no indication: her manner being impeccable and assured at all times, so far as observers might note.)

"A drowning," mused Deirdre, "a suicide by drowning: no very pretty death, and one I cannot envy. No wonder she remains bitter." And then, aloud, she queried the housekeeper as to whether there might be, in the records of the local church, any notation concerning this death: but was told that, assuredly, there was *not;* for no gentleman of the cloth would care to register, for posterity's eyes, so unspeakable a sin. The which did not surprise Deirdre, but grimly amused her. "Of course, you are correct," she said, but with a slight ironical twist of her lips, "our deaths must *not* be recorded, else our lives too will demand rumination."

It was on the third day of her domicile in the austere old house, after a particularly troubled night, in which unbidden spirits promiscuously mingled with dream personages, and much incoherent exhortation was voiced, that Deirdre of the Shadows confronted the first manifestations of the Fairbanks House spirit: these being but the mild phenomena I have already noted. That Deirdre evinced little surprise at these uncanny developments, and no alarm, quite impressed the household servants, whose custom it had been to rush shrieking out of the room—a response exactly as extreme, and as demeaning, Deirdre sought to explain, as the unhappy spirit *wished* to provoke. "A spirit trapped on the Earth Plane," Deirdre said, in her low, level, near-inflectionless voice, "is not unlike a spiteful child, who wishes to punish others by punishing himself: one must be on guard against the *spite,* but ever aware that it is a *child* with whom we deal."

Ah, how calmly Deirdre of the Shadows lectured her frightened little audience!—how assuredly, how resolutely, she comported herself, in those final days of her mediumship! If the staff of Fairbanks House thought her extraordinary, and not very unlike the spirits with whom she traded, they could not help but think, too, that, in her black silk-and-muslin dress, with its fashionable long bodice, and loosely draped sash of braided satin, she was incontestably *of good breeding:* for all her independence, and rumored eccentricity, *a lady.*

"No spirit can harm us—" Deirdre spoke with equanimity—"save with our complicity."

So she strolled in the rose garden, which did indeed contain a scent—near-imperceptible, but distressing nonetheless—of corruption, and contamination, and grave *wrong.* So sear was this August, in its days of pitiless heat, and no rain, that when she strayed from the tiled path, the earth crumbled beneath her feet; and the many rosebushes, tho' assiduously watered by the bravest of the gardeners, turned limp-petaled and mournful countenances upon her, and seemed hardly blooms, but papier-mâché, molded by a distracted hand.

The sighing grew louder, and was suddenly very close: but Deirdre wisely did not turn, nor even give much indication of awareness. She opened her fan, which was made of fragrant sandalwood, painted in black arabesques, and adorned with tiny puffs of black swansdown: this elegant accoutrement having been a gift from the late Madame Blavatsky, at the peak of Madame's affection for her wayward Lolo. She opened the fan, and fanned herself languidly; and tho' the smallest hairs on the back of her neck did stir, as if of their own volition, she truly felt no alarm, and surely no sense of danger, at the approach of this creature who was neither *living,* nor peaceably *dead!*—the very thought of which, I am bound to confess, fills me with extreme agitation.

Some minutes passed, with a sullen slowness—as, indeed, the entire exorcism would proceed very slowly, requiring, in all, some twenty-five hours of continuous concentration, on the part of the medium: the which doubtless contributed to her emotional collapse. But we must remember that Time evidently possesses no value, and, indeed, no meaning, in Spirit World, and that five minutes, five hours, or five days might very likely seem, from that vantage point, identical. Deirdre of the Shadows was so accustomed to the vagaries of spirit behavior, so familiar with the curious oscillations between reasonable conduct, and totally bizarre conduct, that, it may be, she had become somewhat complacent, as to her ability to determine the contours of an exchange; nor she did take cognizance of these extreme durations of time, as if, in all unconscious vanity, she fancied herself but an ethereal spirit—requiring no rest, no sleep, and no human nourishment.

"I wish you no harm, and come here as a friend," Deirdre said softly, "for, I have been told, you are greatly unhappy."

Again some minutes passed, it may have been with coy resistance: and then there was a stirring, to Deirdre's left, and an emanation of dank odoriferous air, which gravely offended Deirdre's fastidious nostrils. She made, of course, no sign of displeasure, but, seating herself on a stone bench, close by the lily pond, continued to fan herself with the handsome black fan, in slow precise motions. Scarcely raising her voice, she repeated her words: her sensitive eyes darting about, yet discerning nothing, save the rosebushes in their pleasingly regular pattern, and the pond, and a stone bench that faced her across the pond, some seven or eight feet away; and the vine-bedecked stone wall beyond.

How many times Deirdre repeated these simple words, I cannot say; but surely they induced a hypnotic calm, in both the spirit and herself, which, tho' disrupted from time to time by a shrill fit of giggling, or an explosion of incoherent curses, did serve to reduce the spirit's suspicion of her, and to establish some modicum of rapport.

"I am your friend," Deirdre whispered, "your friend, your friend. And I have been told you are greatly unhappy; and that your heart is very bitter. But I come as no enemy, tho' in *their* arrogant hire: I come as a friend."

Abash'd silence; and ostentatious sighs; and a spell of coughing, which shaded into such a spasm of choking, and gasping, and the unmistakable sounds of suffocation, that Deirdre's impenetrable poise was all but shaken. But then silence returned: and a considerable period of time passed, during which any but so seasoned a medium as Deirdre of the Shadows, would have concluded that the spirit had gone away.

But Deirdre remained where she was, immobile save for the slow, sombre, mesmerizing motion of her fan; and the heat of the afternoon began at last to slacken, in its ferocity; and the first intimations of dusk heralded themselves. "Your friend, your friend," Deirdre intoned, her eyes somewhat glazed with the strain of this long vigil, and her throat hoarse, "your friend who wishes you no harm; but only to alleviate your suffering."

As twilight deepened, Deirdre's vision grew more acute: and, as the minutes passed, she began to see the spirit, or at any rate a brooding, motionless form, on the stone bench which faced her, across the dark pond. This figure had not the irregular density of the ectoplasm that ofttimes materializes itself, at séances, and which has been, in fact, photographed: it was rather to be characterized as a *uniformly dark aura,* transparent, yet unmistakable: and unmistakable, too, as the figure of a young girl.

At this materialization Deirdre noted in herself the *involuntary* physical responses that might have belonged to a less courageous, or a less practic'd individual: the subtle raising of the hairs on the back of her neck, and an acceleration in her pulse. (For so we respond in the presence of the *uncanny*—whether there is actual danger to us, or no.) Yet she indicated no alarm, and sat quietly, her gaze avidly affixed to the vaporous, and darkly pale, countenance of the spirit, which defined itself with exasperating slowness, yet withal a regularity, moment by moment, and minute by minute, until it was as substantial as the laws of nature would allow it to become. "Ah!" Deirdre exclaimed; and, startl'd, she allowed the fan to slip from her loos'd fingers, and to clatter to the stone beneath her feet.

For this girl, or, rather, the materialized spirit of the girl, seated directly across the pond from her, no more than eight feet away, seemed to her distressingly familiar, tho' clearly a stranger: a *stranger,* yet a *sister:* and one whose palely glowering, brooding, petulant countenance could not fail to strike her as sympathetic.

Whereupon an interview ensued, of a strained, awkward nature, during which Deirdre repeated her declaration—that she was a friend, that she meant no harm—innumerable times, as if speaking to a very small child; and in a hoarse reproachful voice the girl replied, enunciating her words with a curious intonation—shy, yet bold, untutor'd, yet genteel and affected.

Deirdre was now hunched forward in her seat, and stared with amazed, and undisguisèd, interest, at this long-dead female adolescent, who told a halting, disjointed, and probably quite false tale, of having been a kitchen maid "cruelly used" by one of the Fairbanks sons, and thereafter shunned by him, until, in desperation, that he might take pity on her, or at least acknowledge her, she scaled the garden wall—and threw herself into the pond—and succeeded in drowning herself, her weakened physical condition, and the great weight of her water-soaked petticoats and skirts, preventing her flailing limbs from saving her.

"A suicide!—ah yes," Deirdre breathed. "It could not be otherwise."

Our repugnance for so extreme a sinner, and for so shameless a liar (it being quite questionable, that a scion of the great Fairbanks family should behave in an ungentlemanly fashion, or even consort with a female of the servant class in this wise), should not prevent any natural upsurge of pity; for, indeed, the drowned creature *was* pitiable, the more so that her face was so pinched, and her pallid complexion so unwholesomely roughened, as if with smallpox scars; and her plaited and banded hair was disheveled, and sluttishly frizzled, giving off an odor, after more than one hundred years, of stagnant damp! Her small, bright, suspicious eyes were set deep in her narrow face, and so shadowed by indentations in the bone, she appeared rather more like a woman of advanced, and ravaged, age, than a mere girl of eighteen or nineteen. Her reedy voice whined and droned, as she recited her tale, to a most unfortunate effect; tho' she held herself stiffly, observing very poor posture, she could not prevent spasms of near-convulsive shivering from passing over her thin frame. The gray cotton dress she wore, and the torn and soiled apron, would have been quite appropriate for one of her station, had the vain creature not sought to prettify it by a most pathetic and sickly assortment of ill-matched ribbons: all of which, I hardly need say, had become markedly shabby, with the passage of years.

Nonetheless, this sorry personage held Deirdre's rapt attention, as she recounted her story, the doubtful tale o'erleaping itself, and twisting back, and offering embellishments, and contradictions; and then it was interrupted by a spasm of angry sobbing; and then by a spasm of laughter that greatly resembled sobbing. All of which Deirdre attended to, scarce allowing herself to breathe.

A tale so jumbled and incoherent, and fraught with libel, does not require summary here, in a chronicle determined from its outset to Truth: yet it may be helpful to note that the suicide (who not once, in the course of more than twenty-four babbling hours, was to show proper remorse for her sin) died, by her own spiteful efforts, on a moonlit night in the summer of 1787, so very long ago, our noble General Washington had not yet been elected to the Presidency, and our proud states not yet united, under the Constitution. Alas, that bitterness, and every kind of ill-feeling, and a mean-hearted *lack of Christian charity,* should pursue so young a woman, into the grave and beyond! And that a shameless disregard for her own failure of chastity should give rise to audacious sentiments, and still more audacious charges, leveled against such illustrious personages as the Fairbanks, those gentlemen who were the trusted associates—nay, the intimate friends—of such Founders of our nation as John Adams, and Alexander Hamilton, and General Schuyler, and Washington himself!

Yet it is foolish indeed, to expect from so gross a sinner, as one who has died by her own hand, in blasphemous defiance of God's will, any modicum of rational behavior, let alone moral scruples: so the drowned girl raved on, with no sense of her violation of propriety, and very little concern that she exposed herself, with every churlish innuendo, and vulgar accusation. Perhaps it is to her credit, that Deirdre of the Shadows, practic'd in her intercourse with Spirit World, did not once seek to interrupt this stream of foul babble, tho' hour upon hour passed, with excruciating slowness, by human measurement: perhaps it is a reflection of her waning judgment, and the accelerated frailty of her nerves, the which she had been straining to the limits of endurance, well before consenting to journey to Fishkill.

"A suicide—by drowning—yes—yes of course—it could not be otherwise." So the fatigued medium murmured, gazing all the while at her scurrilous communicator, whose spectral form, in the ghastly pallor of moonlight, seemed of nearly as much substance as her own: and cast a faint reflection in the turbid pool of water that lay between them.

After a most protracted spell, the drowned girl lapsed into silence, and Deirdre, with the greatest semblance of composure, again repeated her simple words, and went on, to speak of the "Earth Plane" and "Spirit World" and the vastitude of space, in which "deceased souls" were reunited with their loved ones, in a communion too mysterious to elucidate, and too evident to doubt. It was both *mistaken,* and *self-injurious,* to refuse to "pass over" into Spirit World, at death: a volitional act that brings with it unforeseen consequences, quite in excess of all anticipation. For, if the homeless (and bodiless) spirit imagines he will exact revenge upon those who have injured him, it is more often the case that revenge so contaminates the aggressor, he becomes blinded to his circumstances, and fails even to notice the ineluctable passage of *earthly* time—with the remarkable result that his "revenge" falls upon totally innocent persons, as one generation succeeds another. "That there is some small pleasure in the exercise of *revenge,* for *revenge's* pristine sake," Deirdre said uncertainly, her throat grown hoarse, "I cannot doubt, and would not deny: and yet, I am bound to instruct you, your imagin'd transgressor, or transgressors, has long since 'passed over,' and has not dwelt here at Fairbanks House for a very many decades. Indeed, my dear Florette"—for so the affected young baggage had called herself—"indeed, it is the case that those whom you *love,* as well as those whom you *hate,* have all passed over into the other plane—and are waiting with great impatience, and infinite compassion, for you to join them."

This speech, falteringly uttered, yet impeccable in its logic, did not evoke any immediate response in the drowned girl, who, it may be, had for so long been isolated from all human discourse, that she had difficulty in the simple comprehension of commonplace words and diction: but Deirdre tirelessly repeated it, and expanded upon it, pointing out that Christian charity obliges us to forgive our enemies, and to love them, despite the wrongs they have inflicted upon us, and the hardness of their hearts. If one's cheek is harshly slapped, one must, in imitation of Our Saviour, bravely turn the other cheek: for such is the mystery of the Crucifixion, that it brings about the Resurrection, in the flesh as well as the spirit: and this is *a mystery pertaining to all mortals*—to all Christian mortals, that is, who embrace Jesus Christ as their Saviour.

So the skillful medium averred, I know not how sincerely, all the while gazing upon the spectral countenance of the sullen Florette, who held herself rigidly as before, and continued to succumb to convulsive spasms of shivering, the which were soon contagious, as Deirdre herself began to shiver, the hour fast approaching midnight, and the nocturnal air markedly cool. *That is the face of Death,* Deirdre's thoughts ran, disjointed from her articulated argument, *that is the face, the very face, of Self-Death,* she mused. Brooding, and morose, and sickly, and spiteful, and characterized by a perverse admixture of *angry resignation,* and *lethargic righteousness:* the very image of the child who seeks to punish others, by punishing himself, and cannot comprehend why his energies bring him no satisfaction, but the more hot tears.

For a very long time Deirdre spoke, and then too lapsed into silence, and the birds of night sang lewdly to one another, and the glaring lantern of a moon made its journey through the star-twinkling sky, and the mood was reminiscent of nothing so much as this passage of that wicked but ah! so greatly gifted Mr. Poe—

> Said we, then—the two, then: "Ah, can it
> Have been that the woodlandish ghouls—
> The pitiful, the merciful ghouls—
> To bar up our way and to ban it
> From the secret that lies in these wolds—
> From the thing that lies hidden in these wolds—
> Have drawn up the spectre of a planet
> From the limbo of lunary souls—
> This sinfully scintillant planet
> From the Hell of the planetary souls?"

—words of great mystic import, not comprehensible, perhaps, to those of us of unpoetical bent, yet, withal, fraught with wise counsel, in the dim nether regions of the soul.

Thus the agoniz'd night unfolded, and once again the spirit took up her plea, and droned, and whined, and cast a gaze of ember-hot fury at Deirdre; and Deirdre with infinite patience and compassion repeated her expostulation; and again silence ensued; and again the spirit made remonstrance, that the profligate had savagely "misus'd" her, and "cast her into the dirt, when he had had his fill"; and yet again the valiant medium put forth her advocacy, even as (in Mr. Poe's awesome words)

> —the night was senescent
> And star-dials pointed to morn—
> As the star-dials hinted of morn—

and the lusty cock crew, to be answered by another, and yet another: and all the world cast off the sickly eclipse of *Night,* to take up the bright mantle of *Day:* save Deirdre of the Shadows and Florette, who remained locked in their dispute, which exerted the more power over the human participant, in that her energies were fast fading, and her judgment uncertain, and a terror leapt and frolicked along the precarious pathways of her nerves—that, should she suddenly weaken, her contact spirits, and divers others (she scarce knew who, or what, they might be, having felt them gather behind her, so to speak, all the long night), would rush forward shrieking and gibbering, in total control Ah, and then—! And then—!

It is hardly my pleasure, to reveal to the reader, at this point, that Deirdre's premonitions were exactly correct: and that, upon the very moment of what should have been a considerable victory (to be, in fact, considerably rewarded, by young Mr. Fairbanks—the payment made to Deirdre of the Shadows by way of her financial advisor, rather than to the stricken medium directly), these altogether undisciplined—nay, savage—spirits broke loose, of the mysterious bonds which had restrained them for so many years, and so flooded Deirdre's being that she could not for more than a heroic minute or two withstand them: and quite succumb'd, to that dread *loss of sanity,* of which I have previously spoken.

Alas, the pathos of the situation!—the hideous irony!

For, after so very many hours, after so very selfless and courageous an ordeal, Deirdre of the Shadows did indeed convince the kitchen wench to surrender her resistance, and to "pass over" into Spirit World—not, I am sorry to say, as a consequence of her admirable argument for Christian *charity,* and Christian *forgiveness,* but rather as a consequence of her patient explanation that the profligate, and all of his family, now dwelt in Spirit World, and were best apprehended there: a happy, and all but unlook'd for, development indeed! So the spirit acquiesced, and hid her pinched face for a long moment in her hands, and appeared to be weeping, indeed, racked with sobs: and Deirdre, tho' dazed with the long effort, continued to stare with the utmost concentration, and no sign of her internal distress: and, ah! how wondrous! the slatternly Florette enunciated the words, "Yes: I will: I will at last *die,*" and, lowering her wasted hands, cast upon Deirdre a queer ghastly joyous smile, the which struck deep into the medium's heart, and brain.

So saying, Florette rose from her bench of sombre stone, and began to dematerialize, as Deirdre continued to stare, and stare, in hapless fascination; and surely it is to the credit of Deirdre of the Shadows, whose hardness of heart has so oft been remarked upon, in these very pages, that, the penitent spirit making a gesture of spontaneous sisterly affection—extending her arms toward Deirdre, across the pond—Deirdre responded at once, with no prudent hesitation: with the consequence, so very confus'd I cannot satisfactorily explain it, that, *despite the significant distance that divided them,* Florette managed to snatch off Deirdre's little golden locket, and, grasping it triumphantly in her clenched fist, stole it away with her to Spirit World!

Ah, the unhappy, the wretchèd Deirdre! "Deirdre of the Shadows" that was! Where is your composure now, whence has fled your much-priz'd calm, and control, and icy-cold self-determination?

Deirdre's initial outcry was one of simple physical pain, for, in snatching off the locket, Florette broke the chain, tugging it hard against Deirdre's neck. Alas, to be treated thusly, after such patience, and such sacrifice! To lose the belovèd locket that Mrs. Bonner had so long ago given her, as a reminder of the bountifulness of maternal love! It were well that the spirit of Mrs. Bonner had, in recent years, so greatly faded, so that the good-hearted woman might be spared this act of sacrilege: and the witnessing, too, of Deirdre's sudden collapse: which followed the loss of the locket by not more than five minutes.

Spirit vengeance! Spirit madness! The ravening as of ghouls—wild beasts—greedy—clamorous—the once-gentle *Father Darien* transform'd into none other than the *Raging Captain,* hellbent on possession—the once-pretty *Bianca* shrieking in triumph, and raking furiously with her long nails—*Zachariah* a lewd horn'd Cupid—the *Red Indian* screaming out his blood-chilling war whoop, against all the White Race—*Mrs. Dodd,* too, transform'd into a trumpet-voiced termagant, in the company of an elderly woman who very much resembled *Grandmother Sarah Kiddemaster*—now greatly changed, and as crazed as the others, in her blood lust!

Thus the unspeakable horror, which the prescient medium had half anticipated, broke upon her: and no mortal effort would have been adequate to save her, as she fled from the garden, crying most piteously for help, her voice shrill and broken, a voice scarcely hers at all: "Oh, help me! Save me! Oh, do not touch me! Save me!"—so loud that all the household was summoned, and those incredulous assistants who had accompanied her to Fishkill: all, I am aggriev'd to say, *to no avail.*

65

It will be hardly required, I am sure, for this historian of the Zinn family, to speak at any length on the difference between the fates of "Malvinia Morloch" and "Deirdre of the Shadows," and the courageous equanimity with which their sister Octavia endured *her* trials.

On the one hand, reader, we have *selfish, vain,* and *deluded* creatures; on the other, a gentle Christian heart, greatly strained, it is true, by the tragic losses of her loved ones (ah, within so brief a span of time! —not only Baby Sarah, but agèd Grandfather Kiddemaster; and Mr. Rumford; and, most heartrending of all, Little Godfrey himself), greatly strained, and, doubtless, *tempted* to despair: yet unyielding to the Serpent, her trust all in her Saviour, that He would give her strength beyond the frailty of the flesh; and dwell always by her side. And, as mistress of old Rumford Hall, no matter her afflictions, and the heaviness of her heart, Octavia had little choice but to busy herself with one hundred tasks daily, great and small: and this too, I am bound to observe, contributed to her forbearance. For as we read in the sacred Book: *She looketh well to the ways of her household, and eateth not the bread of idleness.*

The sorrows of the Zinns!

The unspeakable losses!

For, not very many weeks after the shocking defection of Samantha (the which betrayal, the elder Zinns shrank from calling an *elopement*), it happened that our grand old gentleman, one of the last of an expiring breed, was found dead of a stroke in his study at Kiddemaster Hall: Former Chief Justice Godfrey Horatio Kiddemaster, discovered by a terrified manservant, on the carpeted floor, his ancestral sword atangle in the skirt of his dressing gown, and his *jubilant voice still sounding*—from out of one of those recording plates or discs, revolving mechanically on an apparatus known as a "phonograph." (This apparatus, popularly credited to Mr. Edison, had been ingeniously if casually improved by J.Q.Z. himself, who, tho' greatly absorbed throughout the Nineties in his research for the United States government, nonetheless found time in his busy day for that "tinkering," which he so dearly priz'd, and would not abandon for all the riches and acclaim in the world.)

Alas, poor Grandfather Kiddemaster! He passed from this vale of tears but a twelve-month after the demise of his elder brother Vaughan; and some sixteen years after that of his belovèd wife, Sarah: the last of a breed, I daresay, of *giants* rather than *mortal men:* the likes of which, this nation shall not again see.

For some weeks prior to his fatal stroke, Grandfather Kiddemaster had been behaving with uncommon secrecy, locking himself away in his study for very many hours at a time, with that contraption his son-in-law had built for him: his evident intention being to record his voice for posterity, his heirs, and as a means of communicating to those "fools" and "knaves" in his own party, who seemed incapable of smashing, for once and forever, the triple perils of *socialism, communism,* and *devilism,* which the Democratic Party freely endorsed, out of blindness as much as wickedness. (Grandfather Kiddemaster had suffered a mild stroke in June of 1894, when the Democrats in Congress had vociferously enacted a 2 percent tax on incomes in excess of $4,000; and the fact that the Supreme Court later declared the tax unconstitutional, scarcely cheered him, in his philosophical gloom and pessimism about the future of our nation. Reader, you may well imagine, and doubtless sympathize with, the patriotic old gentleman's fury at that traitorous upstart William Jennings Bryan, then campaigning for the Presidency, against McKinley! And, yet, his bitter resentment of Mr. Mark Hanna, whose "extortionist" methods within the Republican Party, could not fail to offend the sensibilities of a Kiddemaster.)

I am in possession of very few details, surrounding the tragic death of the old Judge, save that, as a consequence of his repeated experiments with the recording machine, the household staff had grown somewhat benumbed, as to his raised voice, shouts, and wild climbing laughter, whereby he signaled contempt to his enemies; and his sister Edwina, in somewhat depressed spirits herself, as a consequence of age, and of the extraordinary popular success of a rival etiquette expert, so avoided that part of the house in which his voice sounded, that she scarce saw her brother save at formal meals—at that time reduced, by mutual consent, to but one daily repast, at two o'clock in the afternoon. Mrs. Zinn, ever a loyal and dutiful daughter, thought it wisest, to limit her visits to her father, to but once a day, after teatime had commenced: and yet, alas!—

many were the afternoons, when Grandfather Kiddemaster's manservant informed her, that her father was "so absorbed in his patriotic task, he must beg to be excus'd." That J.Q.Z., energetically absorbed in *his* labor, delayed from day to day, and from week to week, his visits to Kiddemaster Hall, must have gone unremarked by Grandfather Kiddemaster, who never spoke of his son-in-law save in the vaguest of terms, and even gave evidence, from time to time, of confusing him with Mr. Lucius Rumford! (Nor did he remember him, I am saddened to say, in his will—but with the casual observation that, his daughter Prudence's household being so lavishly *in debt* to him, a mere erasing of that debt, upon the occasion of Godfrey Kiddemaster's death, should constitute a substantial *inheritance*.)

All of the household being, then, so accustomed to Grandfather Kiddemaster's noises, behind the locked door of his study, it was some hours before the most sharp-eared of the servants took note that the Judge's words, and the exact modulation of his voice, appeared to be *repeating* themselves: whereupon, the door forc'd, it was far too late, the terrified witness being greeted with the sorry sight of which I have spoken, yet much confus'd, to hear that noble voice ringing out nonetheless!

So extreme were Judge Kiddemaster's terms of abuse, in these recorded messages (even, I am sorry to say, in those messages intended for certain of his family members), the milder amongst them being such expletives as "blackguard," and "villain," and "blockhead," and "lack-wit," and "donkey," and "d——'d fool," and "d——'d a——e," and "h——t," and "m——b," I cannot see the exercise as fructifying, to record them here; and would worry that, granted even the genuine admiration and interest of historians of this period, in the great Kiddemaster heritage, some misinterpretation of the Judge's sensibilities, and the wide range of his intellectual capabilities, might result. Indeed, I concur with Great-Aunt Edwina's wisdom, not only in commanding that all of the record discs (estimated at above two hundred) be destroyed immediately, but in personally presiding over that action, and even volunteering some aid, in thrusting the offending "records" into the flames, and dealing with them soundly, with a poker.

"The old ruffian," Edwina declared, red of cheek, and panting, to her astonished niece Prudence, "cannot even be excused on the grounds of drunkenness, or common senility: I smell nothing other than *The Beast*, emerging in *him*, who had imagin'd himself *immune!*"

This dreadful news was borne upon that very day to Rumford Hall, by Mrs. Zinn herself, who, strengthened by ministrations of smelling salts, ether and water, and one or two other remedies, prescribed by Dr. Moffet, knew it her mother's duty, to inform Octavia of her grandfather's sudden death: and of the surprising revelation Great-Aunt Edwina and Prudence had chanc'd upon, in the general confusion of papers on the old man's death, as to the directing of the Kiddemaster fortune, in all but some trifling instances, to a most surprising party: *Miss Edwina Kiddemaster herself!*

"I cannot comprehend the meaning behind this queer—indeed, bizarre—outburst of generosity," the elderly woman averred, in a stately voice, grown tremulous by the several shocks to her delicate constitution, "and would give half my fortune, and half *his,* to learn what caprices had leapt about in his inflam'd brain, in these late weeks. A loving brother's natural concern for his maiden sister's well-being, surely underlies the spirit of the gesture; and yet!—I am hardly *maiden* in years, or in vulnerability; and I daresay my own fortune quite approaches his—my sex notwithstanding, and the lifelong feebleness of my health."

"Dear Aunt," Mrs. Zinn declared, her stolid countenance gone pale, and her daughter's eyes brimming with tears of grief, "dear Aunt, there is no one more deserving than you, who bear the great *Kiddemaster* name, regardless of age, station, personal accomplishment, or personal fortune: and I daresay it is this Father sought to honor, as well as expressing, in the way he knew best, his brotherly affection for you."

Miss Edwina Kiddemaster surely heard these words, as she was but negligibly deaf, for a woman of her advanced years; yet she chose not to respond to them explicitly, but to murmur, with a perplex'd smile: "And it was so freely thought that Little Godfrey would inherit!—that angel-imp having so captivated the old man's heart, it was believed, in recent years!"

Thus it was, Mrs. Zinn ordered her carriage, and was driven to Rumford Hall posthaste, that she might tell Octavia of Grandfather Kiddemaster's death, and prepare her for the news, necessarily tentative (the actual will being locked away), of the curious inheritance, which had so lavishly rewarded that very sister whom the old man had affected to dislike: and which had slighted (ah, so cruelly!) both the Zinn and the Rumford households, where simple gratitude would have much more zestfully blossomed, as finances were needed. (For tho' J.Q.Z. had enjoyed a conspicuous success with the inaguration, in 1893, of his "electric chair" —the *chair,* rather than the *bed,* being Mrs. Zinn's contribution, for she thought it "unsightly, that a felon would die in a posture of *repose*"—and tho' Congress had increased the amount of his annual honorarium, that he might continue his research, it was still the case, I am sorry to say, that that visionary gentleman's material expenses were extraordinarily high: and Mrs. Zinn suffered much silent anxiety, over the maintenance of her household, in an era of inflated prices, and servants' venal requests for higher wages.)

Mrs. Zinn found Mr. Rumford not at home, a fact her grievèd heart must be excus'd, for deeming fortuitous (for, indeed, Mr. Rumford *was* to show considerable perplexity, and displeasure, over the surprise of Judge Kiddemaster's will): and so mournful was her countenance, and so immediate the tragic communication in her eyes, that poor Octavia, but glimpsing her mother at some distance, divined at once the import of her message!—and hurried to her, to be embraced in her strong maternal arms, and to embrace in turn, offering such daughterly comfort, and commiseration, as the elder woman could not fail to find gratifying.

Octavia was, on this mild spring day, seated on the west terrace of Rumford Hall, in the company of the frolicksome Little Godfrey, and a tall, somewhat stout, but altogether pleasant-faced gentleman, possessed of burnished-red hair, and a forthright manner, who was presented to Mrs. Zinn as "Mr. McInnes"—a United States Congressman from the Chadsworth district, and an attorney, and "something of an investor" in mining, railroads, and munitions manufacturing: this gentleman being, I am startl'd, and pleased, to note, none other than Sean McInnes, the late coachman's son!—involved now, in what circumstance I do not know, in Mr. Rumford's financial speculations, or in the interests of one or another of Mr. Rumford's Philadelphia creditors; and much alter'd from that inconsequential Irish youth, of whom I had scant occasion to speak, some time ago. But such was Mrs. Zinn's tearful grief, and so violent Octavia's immediate response, that it is doubtful Mrs. Zinn even heard the name *McInnes* clearly, let alone grasped the quaint connection, between *Sean the coachman's son,* and this fully mature, and clearly affluent, *gentleman* who stood before her. And, Mr. McInnes being sensitive to the extremities of the moment, he at once summoned the servants, that they might be of aid to their mistress; and bowed; and took his leave: correctly divining that mother and daughter should wish to be alone, at this poignant, and heartrending, moment.

"Break, heart!—I pray you, break! break!" Octavia wept, in a convulsion of granddaughterly sobbing, caught fast in Mrs. Zinn's embrace; "for it is too pitiless, it is *too cruel,* to suffer the loss of Grandfather so suddenly!—with no word of farewell, no final kiss!—indeed, no warning at all!"

"Well may you weep, my dear daughter," Mrs. Zinn grimly, yet withal tearfully, declared, "yet, I do not doubt, Our Saviour will guide us, as He has not failed to, in the past: if we but pray with sufficient zeal, and offer the vanities of our hopes, as well as our heartstruck grief, to Him, and do not succumb to the sin of Despair!"

Thus mother and daughter commiserated, and comforted each other; and it would wrench the most callous'd heart, from out its breast, to see how that affrighted cherub Little Godfrey, *tho' but five years of age,* sought to placate this demonstration of grief, by leaping about, and circling the sobbing women, and clutching and pawing at them, that they might acknowledge *him:* and see, in his own words, that *"Little Godfrey* is not injured, but quite well!—indeed, very, very happy—and healthy—and quite hungry for more apricot cake!"—for *why*, then, should they weep?

66

Wise indeed was the hand, that writ *Troubles do not singly come!*—for it was to be on Palm Sunday eve, in April of 1897, not long after the death of Grandfather Kiddemaster, that poor Octavia was plunged yet more deeply into mourning: this unlook'd-to occasion being, I am very griev'd to report, *the loss of her devoted spouse.*

Unhappy Lucius Rumford! Pluck'd before his time! Yet, withal, he left a worthy heir for his lands and fortune, in the child *Little Godfrey*, whom, I am sure, he loved with a deep paternal pride, no matter that, his temperament shrinking from the vanities of display, of outward affection, he exhibited a countenance somewhat stern and forbidding; and chose to leave the rearing of his son to Mrs. Rumford, and a succession of governesses. It is true that Mr. Rumford was considerably displeased with the eccentric formulation of the Judge's will, the which stimulated him to observe, with acrid brevity, to his timorous spouse: "It is hardly the first time, Madame, that your *distinguished family* has prov'd disappointing to the world"—a statement not elaborated upon, and rich in ambiguity. It is true too that this displeasure o'erspilled, in a manner of speaking, onto the cherubic little boy himself, with the saddening consequence that Mr. Rumford's natural fatherly tendencies were suppressed, in Little Godfrey's presence: and that, on the matter of Mrs. Rumford's having again conceived, he had succumbed once or twice to a cold fury, uttering such imprecations as "shameless," and "harlot," and "Whore of Babylon"— the which poor Octavia was able to accept, with Christian humility, and all the more readiness, in that her pure—indeed, *maidenly*—mind scarce grasped the meaning of such words.

Know, O Reader, all these observations are true: yet it would be a most erroneous judgment, to see Mr. Lucius Rumford as anything less than an upstanding Christian husband, possessing qualities of such modesty, sanctity, and truthfulness, as to make him a model for all of the neighborhood, as well as for his wife and heir: and, indeed, so lavishly mourned by his wife, she lay abed senseless for a fortnight, after the unspeakable event, and, one rain-toss'd night, rang feebly for her nurse, that a writing board might be given her, and a sheet of stiff paper, and a quill pen and ink, in order that she might transcribe an elegy in his honor: our dear Octavia, who never before writ a line of verse, nor aspired to such heights!

Yet this remarkable poem flowed, with no discernible hesitation, from the widow's pen, which moved with a wondrous feverish haste, in great contrast to the beatific serenity of her countenance, and the brimming brown warmth of her lovely eyes!—

> When evening dews are falling fast,
>   When stars are shining clear,
> We'll think of hours so sweet tho' past,
>   When thou wert with us here.
> And thou too, wilt thou hover near,
>   If thus to thee 'tis given,
> To meet with those on earth so dear,
>   While thou art blest in Heaven?

—after which, the graceful pen slipp'd from the grieving woman's hand, and ink was blackly splattered across the paper: and never again, in all her lengthy and bountiful life, would Octavia be so stirred by inspiration —or, it may be, by inconsolable *loss*—as to write another poetical line!

The actual circumstances pertaining to Mr. Rumford's demise are somewhat clouded; and even the zealous Dr. Moffet was not able to determine, to his professional satisfaction, the exact cause of death—save the obvious factor of *heart failure,* as a consequence of an o'erexertion of some kind; and *choking,* or *suffocation,* which appeared to accompany the former. (The distraught widow, invalided with shock and grief, was surely not to be interrogated: the more so in that her condition was deemed precarious, and a miscarriage gravely feared: and the sagacious Dr. Moffet had cause to be apprehensive of a recurrence of that *brain fever,* which the unhappy woman had suffered, immediately following the death of Baby Sarah.)

As it was, I hope I am not o'erleaping my story, by confiding in the reader, that Octavia was not allowed to rise from her sickbed, despite her vehement wish that she be allowed to do so, for she greatly worried about Little Godfrey, and the household, it being prescribed by her physician, and vigorously affirmed by Mrs. Zinn, that she remain safely abed until the birth of her baby, some months thither—a most wise, and prudent, decision, in that an infant son of a somewhat undersized development, was born to her in early September, several weeks before he was due. (This child was to be baptized *Lucius Quincy*—and I hope I do not offend, by leaping yet further into my story, to remark that the greatly priz'd angel, tho' sickly in infanthood, would acquire strength, and grow, and thrive, and be a heartfelt blessing to his mother, in her hallowèd twilight years: and, yes, to his stepfather as well! But such a culmination of the present agoniz'd grief, lies so far in the future—indeed, in the next century, into which I shall not venture—that it is to no helpful purpose, to comment upon it here.)

A beneficence we must deem it, that Mr. Rumford should have expir'd, if God had so decreed, that his time had come, in his bed; and in the embrace of blissful wedlock: not upon the drear streets of Philadelphia, where naught but strangers might have hurried to his stricken side; not upon the lonely road, or in foul weather—the wind, and the hail, and the snowstorms of that most bleak of seasons, winter! Nay, but in his faithful wife's arms, where, coupled in that sacred *unitary act*, of which, in ignorance, I am hardly worthy to speak, he might have found some solace, and some measure of boundless love, as to compensate for the sudden termination of his life on earth!

Tho' the circumstances of Mr. Rumford's death are, as I have noted, somewhat obscure, it would seem that, in the several months preceding it, he had seen fit to introduce, in his conjugal relations with his spouse, an element of forcible exertion: the which may have been for purposes of penitence (so that, even as the chaste gentleman succumbed to an involuntary spasmodic bliss, of a brute animal quality, he chastis'd himself, in homage to Our Saviour's sacrifice), or for purposes of discipline (it being, at times, lamentably the case, that the obedient Octavia, for all her intention, could not prevent herself from a display of struggle, and even of muffled protest, particularly if severe discomfort, or outright pain, were endur'd).

In any case, Mr. Rumford's principles being unknown, his practice was such that, in addition to the hood, and the corset, and the petticoats, and the numerous pretty accoutrements I have mentioned, he began to employ a *noose* of some lightsome—indeed, flimsy—fabric: silk, it may have been; or satin; or mere cotton. This device being placed over Octavia's head, *over* the hood, and secured about her neck, it perhaps helped to keep the protective covering in place, during the strenuous *unitary act*, so that the chaste wife's eyes were the more shielded, from any startling or untoward sight, of a kind that must be occasional, I suspect, in the marital bed, no matter the purity of the husband and wife, and the Christian nature of their intentions. That Octavia silently acquiesced to this strategy is to her credit, for she knew herself resented, and even, at times, despised, both for the frequency with which she conceived ("a bitch in heat might display more reluctance," were Mr. Rumford's words), and for her grandfather's insulting negligence.

Thus Mrs. Rumford's abash'd docility, in the light of her husband's natural displeasure; nor did the young woman fail to observe the predicament of the once-headstrong Delphine Martineau, who, having protested her husband's drinking, gambling, and "consorting with low personages," was said now to be confined to a single chamber of her husband's ancestral house, and under a physician's close ministration, that her *hysteria,* and her *imagin'd fancies,* should not have a deleterious effect upon her young children, or besmirch the noble name of Ormond, her husband's family. And there was the example, too, of Cousin Rowena Kale, sent back penniless to her father's house, as a consequence of some disagreement, involving the treatment, or mistreatment, of her children: the unhappy woman, having incurred the displeasure of her lawfully wed husband, hardly failing, now, to incur an equivalent displeasure, on the part of her father, all the more that her dowry was "squander'd," and "thrown down a rat hole," with nothing to show for it. And, I am sorry to say, there were other whisper'd tales, which shall have no place in this narrative, partaking, as all such prattle does, of shallow gossip: and casting an unpleasant shadow upon that holy institution, marriage, in which God binds man and wife as *one* flesh, and *one* spirit.

So it is fully to Octavia's credit, that she submitted to Mr. Rumford's divers requests, and did not demur, even when she suffered some physical discomfort, and attacks of irrational panic, as a consequence of the tightening of the noose about her tender throat: nay, she did not allow her mind to roam that freely, that *complaint* might be an option. Nor did she object, when, after a passage of some weeks, Mr. Rumford of a sudden requested that *she,* whilst still blinded by the comely hood, lower the noose about *his* head, and tighten it about *his* neck.

I cannot say how frequently this divergence from custom occurr'd, through that long drear winter, when the frigid winds from Canada howl'd, and the solar orb shone but faintly, and Little Godfrey made the servants sigh with fond exasperation, wanting now to be dressed for the chill out-of-doors, and now to be undressed, that he might remain indoors: nor can I say, with any degree of certitude, why it was that Mr. Rumford fell into the habit of requesting, from his complaisant mate, a gradual *increase* in the degree of tension, which the noose exerted upon his throat. Yet it was so; and to *his* sorrow, and *her* grief!

"Tighter," Mr. Rumford would ofttimes pant, in the midst of his strenuous labors, "—and yet tighter—and *yet tighter,* Mrs. Rumford—" until his words were garbled, and his breath turned shrill and wheezing, and not even his fond wife might determine what he said, but only divine, by intuition's aid, his desire. If, out of exhaustion, or a fear for Mr.

Rumford's safety, Octavia allowed the noose to slacken, before the crucial moment, she earned a sharp rebuke, and, not infrequently, a chastising pinch or twist of her flesh, which would betray a considerable redness, by the morn's light. "Tighter—tighter—and yet tighter, Mrs. Rumford— else I shall be displeased!"—so Mr. Rumford commanded; and Octavia grew habituated in her obedience, sometimes pulling both ends of the silken cord, in a simple fashion, and sometimes, by Mr. Rumford's express desire, evidently "choking" him by a kind of *twisting*, and *tightening*, procedure, the which, of course, she could not see, her vision being annihilated, by the hood.

And so it came about, upon that Palm Sunday eve, that, Mr. Rumford's exhortations to his wife being to *tighten*, and yet further *tighten*, the noose, she unthinkingly obeyed: her thoughts drifting free, it might have been, to glance in upon the slumbering Little Godfrey, in the nursery; or to shed a quiet tear o'er the elfin grave of Baby Sarah; or to ponder upon those mysteries of Free Will, Determinism, and Grace, as expounded by the Reverend Silas Hewett from out the pulpit of Trinity Church: this gentleman of the Protestant cloth now well into his tenth decade, and sadly deaf, yet, for all that, as vigorous and clear-minded an orator, as might be found anywhere in the land. Or, her fond thoughts might circle about Mr. Zinn, the proud inventor of the "electric chair"; and, more recently, a toothbrush operated by a small crank, for remarkable efficiency, in removing tartar from the teeth. (Mr. Zinn was now deeply immers'd in a project, of a secret nature, in conjunction with a branch of the Du Pont organization, whereby the demands of Captain Alfred Mahan of the United States Navy for more efficient torpedoes might be satisfied —Captain Mahan being that eloquent warrior who, in his numerous books, argued for the forcible extension of the American nation, not only to those small, troubled countries, Cuba and Hawaii, but throughout the hemisphere, and, God willing, throughout the world.) Or, her thoughts might touch upon the pathos of her lost sisters, which a harsher judgment might have called *damn'd:* yet, withal, such was her sweetly affectionate nature, she could not resist suffering a pang of remorse, that Malvinia was not still her bedmate; or that Samantha had so cruelly betrayed the parental hearth, with no word of farewell, and no express'd concern, that she might ever glimpse her belovèd nephew again, in this world. . . .

So, the while her adoring spouse toiled manfully, in the *unitary act,* urging her, by mutterings, grunts, and impatient groans, to tighten the noose, and yet still further tighten it, Octavia's thoughts, in all maiden innocence, drifted hither and yon: and it is perhaps not altogether surpising that, habituated as she was to these marital customs, she should have too vigorously complied with his command—or, it may have been, a simple misinterpretation ensued, as a consequence of which Mr. Rumford of a sudden ceased his *toil:* and, alas!—ceased his *breathing!*

Reader, you may well imagine the affrighted wife's response, when, sensing something amiss, or, in any case, irregular, in the proceedings, she dared—shyly, and hesitantly—to draw off the hood from her head, in order to investigate the situation (Mr. Rumford having not only ceased his exertions, but fallen ominously silent, upon her breast), she saw, with amazed eyes, the countenance of her husband so *empurpled,* and *contorted,* and the eyes so hideously *bulging,* that she gave a shriek of horror, as if not recognizing him!—and, a scant moment later, yet another shriek, in her comprehension of the poor man's expiration!

For, indeed, in this wise Mr. Lucius Rumford came to his end: and I count it a sign of God's especial mercy, toward His most cherished children, that Octavia, in her grief, and the precariousness of her health, sank at once into a swoon—*and was never to clearly recall the precise circumstances of Mr. Rumford's death.*

67

Of the death by hideous drowning, of that golden-tress'd child Little Godfrey, upon a mellifluous midsummer's day, at Kiddemaster Hall, ah! —I have neither the words, nor the corporeal strength, to speak.

Nay—I have not the *heart*.

Know only that the dread event occurred but a scant year after the demise of Mr. Rumford, the grieving widow persisting in her mourning attire, but prepared to bend, I believe, to the admonitions of her mother, and her great-aunt, and divers other ladies of the neighborhood, that she set aside her widow's raiment, and wear again the colorful hues of life, and of joy: bearing in mind (as, doubtless, any young widow must bear in mind, who is also a mother) that it is now her *children* for whom she must live; and not her *spouse*.

Too cruel—too bitter!

The loss of any minikin innocent: but the loss of *this* innocent!

Nay, I cannot speak, for the task is too oppressive, the sorrow too great. In transcribing my *Romance*, I had certainly known that *Pathos* and *Heartbreak* could not be skirted: but, O Reader, I had not known that the chronicle would swerve so pitilessly toward the *Tragic*, and tax my heart so enormously. Tho' we are told by the eminent poetess Miss Jane Woolsey that "*Stars* are the angels' alphabet,/ Who write in light above,/ Full many a pure and gentle thought/ Of holiness and love"—it is far, far different here below, with those of us who aspire to the patient and fearless recording of an *Earthly* truth!—ah, how greatly, how cruelly different!

For, in this instance, I am obliged to speak of an event so charg'd

512

with horror, it can scarce be contemplated by the sane mind, let alone given adequate voice: the loss of a child.

My feeble energies being so drained, and my aging eyes so brimmed with tears, I can scarce see this page, or the slow sad halting motions of my quill pen, I must turn to the enduring wisdom of poesy, in order that the reader might comprehend, even dimly, the *loss* which poor Octavia must endure. In the words of the Reverend Hargreave Tupper, from out of his popular collection, *Proverbial Philosophy*—

A babe in a house is a well-spring of pleasure, a messenger
of peace, and love;
A resting-place for innocence on earth; a link between
angels and men.

And how much truer this declaration must be seen to be, pertaining to the robust, tireless, bright-countenanc'd, and gloriously high-spirited *Little Godfrey!*

Nay, I cannot force myself to speak, save in the most circuitous of ways: the reader being obliged to envision for himself a scene very much similar to that with which this history began, back in September of 1879 (ah, *that* ill-omen'd day!), on the beauteous grassy lawn that sloped so gracefully from the rear terrace of Kiddemaster Hall, to the peaceable river some hundreds of yards below. You will recall the gazebo, in which the sisters sat, in their pretty Sunday dresses: that very gazebo (alter'd not a whit) from which the uncouth Deirdre fled—to her shame, and her destruction! You will recall, so picturesquely in the near-distance, a most elegant rose garden, and a wisteria garden, and fields of natural sere grasses and ornamental rushes: you will recall, perhaps, the old stone wishing well.

Alas, indeed: *the old stone wishing well.*

For it was in these dank, lightless, sepulchral waters, that, trapped in the embrace of the crazed Pip, our dear Little Godfrey met his end.

But how to articulate, how to record, the elements of that flailing, choking, sputtering, *furious* death!

And the incalculable ironies of the death: in that, the worrisome monkey having mistaken Little Godfrey's *playfulness,* for something more *severe,* he reached out with his surprisingly long, and surprisingly muscular, arms, to seize the smiling child, *and pull him into the well with himself.*

All this being, as the reader can grasp, naught but a misunderstanding on Pip's part, if we allow that the furry little creature might have been capable of "understanding," in any case. For such was his nervous temperament, and the superficiality of his animal shrewdness, that he mistook Little Godfrey's prank, in snatching him from the terrace (where, beggar that he was, by preening and cajoling, he had succeeded in win-

ning from Octavia, and Miss Narcissa Gilpin, and one or another of the
ladies, some dainty morsels of Bavarian cream cake), and bearing him to
the wishing well, and gaily tossing him o'er the rough-stoned rim, for an
act of *cruel mischief,* rather than the simple, high-spirited, innocent act of
child's play, that it was.

Alas, I am scarce able to continue!

For, quite apart from the obscene, unspeakable, piteous spectacle,
of *angel-child* and *mere beast,* drowning in an embrace, in those waters of
the Kiddemasters' wishing well which, by tradition, had no practicable
function, other than that of the ornamental, and the diversionary, and
(may God save us!), the *whimsical:* quite apart from the horror in itself,
which was witnessed not only by the ladies at their tea, but by tiny *Lucius
Quincy* as well, on his mother's lap (that dear child being now almost
twelve months of age, and, apart from some small respiratory weakness,
and an exaggerated timidity in the presence of his boisterous, but adoring, elder brother, grown to a reasonable size—the recipient of his
mother's bountiful love, as the puniest weed-flower partakes, with as
much glory as the rose, of the solar beneficence): quite apart from the
deleterious effect the event was to have, upon the already weakening
constitution of Great-Aunt Edwina—we have, alas, the hideous irony, that
Mrs. Rumford was being admonished, *up to the very moment of Little Godfrey's
prank,* by the elder ladies, for her excessive grief, and her prolongation
of mourning, which, they averred, "Mr. Rumford himself must surely
have become uneasy with, in his Heavenly abode"! Gently, with infinite
tact and compassion, and regard for the sanctity of Christian grief, the
young widow was being admonished: but admonished she *was:* and urged
not only to leave off mourning, and to partake more wholesomely in the
pleasures of this earth (amongst which must surely be included, the
delicious Bavarian cream cake, and the walnut tortes, and the Swiss chocolate almond ladyfingers, being served at the tea), but *to rejoice in her two
beautiful babes!*

Nay, the irony is too bitter: I am enfeebl'd, and can continue but
for another scant page.

To say only that, despite the smiling, laughing, and chattering
congeniality of the scene, and the ambrosiacal taste of the cakes, tortes,
and ladyfingers, which, with reluctant appetite, she had acquiesced in
nibbling; despite the idyllic beauty of the midsummer day, and that
dreamlike indescribable serenity, of the Kiddemaster estate—indeed, of
all that great family possessed; despite the gradually increasing strength,
which hours of daily prayer, and immersion in the Holy Book, were
allotting her—despite all this, Reader, Octavia's maternal intuition was
such that, she seemed to know, before the crazed monkey had pulled her
son into the well with him, before, even, Little Godfrey had toss'd the
creature over the side!—whilst, in fact, the exuberant imp was still glad-

dening the afternoon with his shouting laughter, and *not a thing appeared to be amiss,* the monkey's terrified screeches being but a commonplace, when Little Godfrey chose to play with him: yet her mother's quickened instinct was such, she *knew* something terrible was going to happen: and, tho' she willed herself to set the warm weight of little Lucius Quincy on his grandmother's ample lap, that she might, gathering her skirts, run to the well, and divert the catastrophe, *she found that she was paralyzed, and could not move—nay, not a muscle!—not an eyelid!—nor could she call out, that one of the servants might be alerted, and save her son, from his watery fate!*

68

Tho' the career of the genius-inventor John Quincy Zinn had at last begun to flourish, in the closing years of our glorious century, it is no secret to us, his intimates, that, in his injur'd father's heart, he had to contend with the memories of his treacherous daughters, the which haunted him nightly; nor were the cruel wounds soothed, even by Mrs. Zinn's scrupulous action, in casting unopened into the fire, immediately upon receipt, those two or three letters sent by Samantha—from some commonplace address in the "wide world," of little significance here.

Thus, it may have been as a consequence of private brooding, upon these losses, or, the inevitable effects of overwork, which, more frequently than ever in his life, left him unclear in his mind, when engaged in conversational intercourse of a lightsome social nature: or, it may even have been as a confus'd consequence of his grandfatherly grief, for the tragic loss of Little Godfrey: or (for who can plumb the depths of another's heart!) it may have been an expression of simple thoughtless nostalgia, for all the furry little creature had represented, reaching back to that wedding morn of 1855, when every songbird seemed to cry *Romance!* and every flowery countenance seemed to smile *Romance!* and, indeed, all the world thrilled, and wept, and lifted a gladsome choral voice *Romance!*—the wedding morn, that is, of the maiden Prudence Kiddemaster, and the blushing young gentleman John Quincy Zinn. Ah! —we cannot know; we cannot say.

Only that, some five or six days after the funeral of Little Godfrey, J.Q.Z., distracted, and stroking at his long beard, glanced up from his uneaten midday meal, to fix upon Mrs. Zinn a brooding and half-reproachful gaze, and to murmur, all but inaudibly: *"Yet Pip too must be mourned."*

IX

"Adieu! 'T is Love's Last Greeting"

69

And years flew by, and the tale at last
Was told as a joyful one, long past.
—S. L. SEABRIGHT-BOUGH

Through these many difficult months, in transcribing so labyrinthine a chronicle, it has been my task, and my modest hope, to both allow the reader some small sense of its *contours*, clear, forthright, and, it is to be hoped, unconfus'd; and to allow him to savor, out of the generous bounty of the Zinns' and Kiddemasters' family histories, a sense of its profusion of *detail*—the which, numerous as the blooms in flowery Bloodsmoor, have, I confess, quite enthralled me, and have given me many hours of meditative—nay, brooding—puzzlement: as to whether our mortal lives here on earth most candidly reveal themselves *from a distance*, discernible only to the objective, or Godly, eye; or whether they reveal themselves solely *as they are experienced*, which is to say, in finite parcels of time, weeks, days, hours, and minutes!

Oft have I ponder'd: ah, and would I not have greatly rejoiced, if, for a scant hour, I might have sat at the knee of Mr. Zinn, to put these questions to him, who dedicated his life to such philosophical puzzles! Tho', doubtless, my frail female capabilities, in such areas of mental wizardry, might have taxed his patience; and excited some pity; and bafflement. (For, in the final years of this distinguished man's life, waning, as it did, with the century, he was frequently in so remote a world of ratiocination, as to return but reluctantly to *this* world: where even his workshop came to seem to him, as he expressed it, "insubstantial"—and unreal, and lonely as well, the irksome little spider monkey being gone forever, and no assistants being desired, after the treachery of Samantha and Nahum.)

Alas—this is not a privilege allowed me: nor am I entirely able to grasp, after many perusals, J.Q.Z.'s intricately worded response to that curious work by Mr. H. G. Wells, *The Time Machine,* Mr. Zinn's monograph being entitled, "On the Probability (And Impossibility) of Time-Travel," and appearing in a philosophical journal, in March of 1896.

In any case, the authoress's solemn task being, then, to mediate between *contour,* and *detail,* I am bound to confess that, as my Bloodsmoor history draws to its appoint'd close (not many seconds before the initial stroke of midnight, of December 31, 1899), I find myself the more beleaguered, by all that, for purposes of *brevity,* I must omit: by all that enthralling multitudinousness, of weeks, days, hours, and minutes, which the Zinns experienced *as their lives.* Ah, to omit—to be forced to omit!—so very much: to awake in the midst of the night, my poor head ringing, and clattering, and clamoring, with the vociferous demands of a dream-double, of Samantha, or Mrs. Zinn, or Charles Guiteau, or the Baron, or Pip, or "Mark Twain," or Little Godfrey, or "Malvinia Morloch" that was, or "Deirdre of the Shadows" that was!—to the effect that, I have not done the complexities of their souls *justice,* and, in shaping them to the contours suggested, by a labyrinthine profusion of others' lives, I have, in fact, *betrayed them,* who entrusted their beings to me.

That *A Bloodsmoor Romance* presents itself, with humility, and hope, as an allegorical—indeed, exemplary—narrative, I should be very foolish to wish to deny; that its numerous personages are instructively enjoined, as to most clearly lend themselves, to *moral interpretation,* I can but affirm. In so doing, however, I am not conscious of having betrayed the individuals who discover themselves herein—and make my plea to them, that, the capacities of readers, no less than of authors, being resolutely finite, I am obliged to continue with my general favoring of *contour.*

(Which is to say, that tho' not one of the personages described herein, would consent to naming himself, let alone interpreting himself, as an *allegorical figure,* nonetheless it is necessary for me, as the historian of these proceedings, and, it may be, as the judge thereof—to the limited extent to which, of course, a member of my sex may be considered a *judge,* that position being by hallowed tradition a masculine prerogative!—it is necessary, I fully believe, for me to extract what is *exemplary,* rather than what is merely *idiosyncratic,* and *eccentric,* from these individual lives, in order that a wholesome moral lesson may be drawn.)

Thus, I choose in this brief introductory space, to speak of the *contour* of the concluding book, which will take us from January 28, 1899, to the very end of that tumultuous year; and from a place in San Francisco, which no lady might wish to enter, even were she allowed entry, back home to Bloodsmoor—the which, I hardly need stress, I have never truly left, in spirit. The reader shall become reacquainted with those Zinn daughters who, it might have been thought, had so violated the customs of propriety, good sense, and daughterly obligation, as to be lost—indeed, *damn'd*—forever: reacquainted, and, it is hoped, sufficiently stirred, by the compassionate motions of Christian charity, as to rejoice in the numerous *reconciliations* that Fate saw fit to decree, in these final months of our century. That those Zinn sisters who have abandoned their parents, and the domestic hearth, in order to plunge into the wide world, find their divers ways back home, I take to be a triumphant affirmation of God's grace—operative, as it is, in ways so o'ersubtle, as to beggar our human comprehension.

70

I shrink from the scene, which it is my oppressive task, to now convey: and I beg the reader's indulgence, both for my timorousness, and for the unwholesome—indeed, loathsome—nature, of what follows.

For we are to be plung'd into the *vile, unnatural,* and altogether *morbid.* Nor are the details, of a physiological kind, completely clear.

Indeed, upon rising from a night of troubl'd dreams, yesterday morn, I had fully hoped to plunge at once into this chapter, despite my wanness of countenance, and a deep revulsion of the soul. It had been my authorial strategy to thus introduce, as the very first note in this concluding book, both the central issue (the astonishing Last Will and Testament of Miss Edwina Kiddemaster, and the yet more astonishing "Confession of a Penurious Sinner," by the selfsame hand), and the issue of "Mr. Philippe Fox," which has long dismayed me, for reasons soon to be made evident. Yet such was my repugnance for "Mr. Fox," or, "Constance Philippa Zinn" that was, that, not trusting my enfeebl'd powers, I turned my pen to other, more general concerns, the which I hope have proved instructive to the reader, the while they have allowed me some measure of restorative time. But, "Haste, ere the gathered shades/ Fall on thee from the tomb where none may work," as Mrs. Sigourney reminds us!—and I must now confront my long-dreaded task.

Indeed, I am bound to confess here that I have, upon several occasions, shrunk from taking up this strand, in my intricate fancywork, out of that timidity of my sex, that has rendered us so generally unfit for the creation of great works, like those by Mr. Dickens and Mr. Balzac, and, in our own clime, Mr. Melville—a timidity that has its unapologetic basis in natural *ignorance,* and *innocence,* of the cruder aspects of life: and a gracious wish that naught but "rainbows of unearthly joy" (to quote Mrs. Sigourney once more) irradiate our literary attempts, as, it is devoutly hoped, they irradiate our lives.

The scene, which I hope will not offend your sensibilities, to envision, is the dim-lit and murmurous *gentleman's bar*, in the sumptuous Baldwin Hotel of San Francisco: one of those much-priz'd sanctuaries of the confirmed hedonist, to whom it is not uncommon to wish to repair to even by day, in order to partake of those excesses of alcoholic consumption, to which such personages have abandoned themselves. Here, amidst gilded, mirrored, tessellated, polished, and glittering splendor, of the most ostentatious sort, repulsive to the healthful mind, gentlemen of divers backgrounds commingle: imbibing such spirits as bourbon, whisky, gin, vodka, rum, brandy, and liqueurs of every imaginable species, all the while giving license to their gluttonous inclinations, by devouring such delicacies as smoked oysters, and squid, and buttered snails.

As our eyes become accustom'd to the smoke-hued dimness, we observe a lone gentleman standing at the far end of the bar, reading a copy of the San Francisco *Ledger*, which he has just found, discarded, beside him. It is difficult to judge the gentleman's age, whether he be fairly youthful, as his manner suggests; or well into his thirties, as the graying hair at his attractive temples would indicate. He is smooth-chinned, and sports not the smallest hint of a mustache: indeed, there is a pleasing *softness* to his complexion, which not even the sun's insistent rays, and his own frequent scowls, have been able to mitigate. Tho' his clothing is not altogether fresh, and might in fact have been worn for several days, it is of evident quality, and not greatly out of place here at the Baldwin, where men of wealth commonly stay: a white linen shirt with ruffled cuffs; a dress-suit of fine dove-gray broadcloth; a waistcoat patterned in gilt arabesques; a black Western string tie; a pearl lapel-pin. At his elbow lies a pair of well-worn pigskin gloves; and he has brought into the bar with him a broad-brimmed white wool hat, redolent of the Southwest. His cowhide boots are custom-made, sporting remarkable two-inch heels (with the desir'd result, that he is agreeably tall, and possesses, despite his lithe frame, an air of swaggering menace).

A *snakelike* sinuousness informs his being, yet, withal, he is comely enough, and intriguing enough, to both attract and repel the eye of the casual observer. Is he uncommonly handsome, with his marble brow, and his exquisitely sculpted lips, and his sly, deepset, dark-lashed eyes, which move boldly about? Does he give an impression of cunning, rather than of sinewy masculine strength; and of the dandified, rather than the forthright and robust? Is his manner stealthful? Might his fashionable gray coat hide a pistol, carried in secret? Might he be a well-to-do Eastern gentleman, of good breeding; or might he have sprung from the lowest level of society? Is he one of those numerous young men who are "with the government," or "with the railroads," or "with the law"? Is he a wandering journalist, a bigamist in flight, a gambler, a cardshark, a gold prospector, a "law enforcement officer," a bankrupt, an outlaw, a murderer, a "desperado"? When he addresses the bartender he reveals an accent that might well be Eastern, yet o'erlaid with an emphatic Western twang: but whether this be natural, or mere affectation, is not clear.

Despite the gentleman's evident wish for privacy, and even secrecy, there is something resolutely impudent, and even reckless, about his manner: as he lights a small thin Mexican cigar, and continues to peruse the newspaper, impatiently scanning the columns, the while muttering and laughing contemptuously under his breath.

Until, of a sudden, quite by accident, his eye fell upon this item, the which so startl'd him, the cigar nearly slipped from his fingers, and he murmured aloud: *"Her—!"*

ESTEEMED AUTHORESS
MISS EDWINA KIDDEMASTER DIES

UNUSUAL STIPULATIONS SAID
TO COMPLICATE WILL

With great rapidity the slim-bodied gentleman read this news item, which, I am sorry to report, did not receive, from the *Ledger,* the amount of space so solemn an event surely deserved: nor was its placement, on page 17, in the midst of numerous other obituaries, of unknown persons, sufficiently respectful, in terms of our loss to American letters. But, tho' abrupt, and composed in a singularly graceless style, the article contained no distortions; and from it, the increasingly agitated gentleman learned the following facts: that Miss Edwina Kiddemaster had succumbed to a brief illness, and died, at her ancestral home in Bloodsmoor, Pennsylvania, at the age of seventy-eight; that she had authored "upward of seventy works, pertaining to moral, domestic, and religious subjects, the which, sold by subscription, were read and cherished by millions of Americans"; that her "sorrowful passing," in the words of Mrs. S. T. Martyn, the editress of *The Ladies' Wreath,* "is a cause of great mourning, amongst her devoted readership, the more so in that it is unlikely—nay, it is impossible—that our nation will ever see Miss Edwina Kiddemaster's equal again, in the troubl'd years to come." There was some unnecessary comment on the curiosity that Miss Kiddemaster had, in recent years, become litiginous, bringing suit not only against "rival etiquettresses" who, she claimed, had "appropriated" her teachings, and "capitalized shamelessly" on them, but against her publisher as well, who, in her opinion, and in the opinion of her legal advisors, "had failed to advertise her most recent book, *The Hearthside Guide for Young Christian Wives,* and to satisfactorily sell it," with the consequence that, in the first twelve-month period, the volume had sold only eighty-four thousand copies, a grave disappointment to the authoress.

All this might have been adequate to stir the gentleman's compassionate distress; but it was the final, and, alas, all too brief paragraph of the obituary, that truly struck him, so that now his slender cigar *did* slip from his fingers, to roll harmlessly on the bar: this paragraph informing the reader that Miss Edwina Kiddemaster had possessed a "considerable fortune, in properties, businesses, and investments, in the East," augmented in recent years by several inheritances, and by the continued sales of her popular books; and that, by her decree, the breaking of the seal of her Last Will and Testament, was to be postponed, *until such time as her five great-nieces might assemble together, in Bloodsmoor.*

"The deuce!—the *hell*—d——'d Bloodsmoor—never!"—thus spoke—nay, sputtered—the alarmed gentleman, in whom, as we see, all normal sentiments of love, Christian charity, and moral lucidity, were so gravely atrophied, by long residence in the lawless West, and, doubtless, by congenital inclination, as to cause him, at so poignant a moment, to *curse!*

"Bloodsmoor: *never!*" And, so saying, indeed, spitting these words, he folded the paper over, and toss'd it down, and signaled for the bartender, that he wished another whisky-and-soda at once.

71

Yes, it is true: the saddening news, that Great-Aunt Edwina, tho' appearing, in Dr. Moffet's measured opinion, to "having taken a decided turn for the better," after some months of convalescence, died one gloom-ridden January day, very early in the morning: to be vociferously mourned by her family, and the devoted household staff, and her Bloodsmoor neighbors, and her wide circle of friends and acquaintances and literary associates, along the Eastern seaboard.

The brief obituary, doubtless toss'd off by a crude-minded male journalist, whose knowledge of Miss Edwina Kiddemaster's renown, and great worth, was naught but secondhand, was correct in its assertions, in the main: but could not, of course, have hinted that the elderly lady, tho' industrious as ever, in terms of her authorial labor (she had just completed a new volume, *A Compendium of Morals for All*, in spirited answer to the rival authoress Mrs. D. E. E. Brownwell's *101 Most Frequently Ask'd Questions, With Answers: A Handbook for Young Christian Americans*, one of the best-sellers of 1898), nonetheless suffered from a certain *increasing melancholy*, and *heaviness of heart*, the which her niece Prudence had reason to attribute to the numerous tragic losses sustained in recent years. That Great-Aunt Edwina might weep over the untimely death of Little Godfrey was indeed plausible; that she might, upon occasion, weep over the "defection" of Samantha, and the "heartlessness" of Malvinia, and the "stubbornness" of Constance Philippa, and, even, the "ingratitude" of Deirdre, struck the Zinns as remarkable. In Mrs. Zinn's words, gravely uttered to her spouse, who gave every show of listening with concentration, this brooding upon their daughters must have been "as much a symptom of her afflict'd health, as an expression of her familial love—which, until these past few months, had been conspicuously absent."

After a lengthy pause, during which time it was a distinct possibility that J.Q.Z.'s thoughts had flown far from the connubial scene in the bedchamber (husband and wife quietly preparing for bed, as they had done for many a fond decade now), Mrs. Zinn was startl'd by the *warmth*, and *sympathy*, of the reply: "But, my dear, you seem not to comprehend, that your aunt is no longer a young woman, nor even a woman of middle age. She must set her thoughts to Eternity, and doubtless regrets that she has no daughter of her own, to love, and to be lov'd by in turn: and to leave her immense fortune to."

Prudence turned stoutly to look at her husband, who very rarely, in recent years, delivered himself of so forthright, and so pointed, a speech; and almost never, on a subject of domestic interest. Thus, his response took her somewhat aback, and caused an abash'd blush to color her cheeks; and her tone was almost humble, in replying: "You are correct, John Quincy. Would that the wealthy old spinster had one of *ours!*—for those very same purposes, which you have so reasonably cited."

Nor did the obituary speak of the numerous maladies the esteemed authoress had had to endure, in the final years of her life, which added greatly to her ill-temper, and doubtless stimulated her to bring lawsuits against various persons who, whether in her inflamed imagination or no, had "gravely insulted" her. Amongst these were several rival authoresses, including the o'erprolific Mrs. Brownwell; and Aunt Edwina's publisher John Twitchell & Sons, of Philadelphia; and the writer William Dean Howells, who, in Aunt Edwina's opinion, had "savagely lampoon'd and libel'd" her in a "scurrilous" novel of his, titled *Indian Summer*. She had, for a time, even considered bringing suit against her own attorney, who had dealt with her legal affairs for upward of fifty years!—but finally relented, contenting herself with discharging him, and hiring one of her nephews, Mr. Basil Miller, who had acquired, over the years, a respectable Philadelphia reputation, for both his keen mind and his discretion. "My will must be revised, and revised *ab initio*—if you recall your Latin," the stately dowager said. So confidential did she wish the proceedings, she would not hear of conferring with Mr. Miller in even the most private of chambers, in Kiddemaster Hall; but insisted that they repair to the out-of-doors, to the gazebo, where, as they spoke, they might cast their eyes freely about, on all sides, to see that no one crept near: that neither an inquisitive *servant*, nor an inquisitive *relative*, might press his ear against a wall or a locked door!

If this lamentable excess of suspicion troubled Mr. Miller, he gave no outward sign, and may even have concurred with his aunt, that her precautions were all to the good; for this estimable gentleman had considerably matured, and gained in the canny wisdom that all lawyers require, since those youthful days, so many years previous, when he had—ah, so irresponsibly!—escorted Malvinia to the theater.

Whether the increasing obsession with legal matters was a consequence of illness, or aging, I cannot say, but it was certainly the case that poor Aunt Edwina suffered a multitude of complaints, in her twilight years. None was precisely "serious": none should have proved "fatal": yet the accumulation of polyarthritis, and spondylosis, and spondylarthritis ankylopoietica, and neuotis, and catarrhous inflammation of the female organs, and simple discopathia (the which poor Sarah had suffered as well), and undiagnosable complications of the nerves, and chronic defatigation, surely proved too burdensome, for even that brave constitution to endure. The household was saddened, when Edwina angrily discharged the faithful Dr. Moffet, and betook herself off, in a private carriage, to numerous watering places and sanatoria—amongst them Saratoga Springs, and Margitzpara Spa, in Virginia, and the "Miracle Waters" of Lockport, New York: but was relieved when, not many weeks later, the ailing lady returned to Bloodsmoor, and summoned Dr. Moffet back, with the cynical observation that "she might as well die in familiar territory."

Nonetheless, after the zealous physician had given Edwina one or two new medicines, and bled her substantially (for it was his diagnosis that the invalid suffered "an excessive richness of 'plasmon' in the blood"), it seemed clear enough that she was improving: and so regained her old spirit, as to denounce him from her bed, as a "charlatan and sawbones"!

In late December of 1898, however, whether through the therapeutic purification of her blood, or through a gradual instinctive refinement of her being, as her soul drew ever nearer her Maker, the once ruddy-cheek'd dowager grew wondrously pale, until her skin was smooth and waxen, and of a saintly serenity approaching that of Grandmother Sarah Kiddemaster, some years before: until, one sorrowful morning, at the very turn of the year, Dr. Moffet arrived for the seven o'clock bloodletting only to discover—alas!—*his renowned and belovèd patient expir'd in the night.*

And, on the bedside table, was the very same phonographic machine that Judge Kiddemaster had so earnestly employed, in *his* final days: tho' Edwina had not been recording her voice, but only listening to a well-worn disc, of the tenor Guiseppe Luigo singing Schubert's beauteous song, "Adieu! 'Tis Love's Last Greeting." Indeed, the ingenious machine was still working, and the groov'd disc still turning, tho' silently, when the peaceful corpse was discovered—as loftily tranquil in her high canopied bed, as an angel effigy upon a tomb; with the subtlest, and most aristocratic of smiles, shaping her pallid lips.

72

Great-nieces of the late Miss Edwina Kiddemaster, of Bloodsmoor, Pennsylvania, are URGENTLY REQUESTED to make contact
with Mr. Basil Miller, of the law firm of Southerly, Butterfield,
Ruggles & Miller, Philadelphia.

Thus the zealous Mr. Miller placed discreet notices in newspapers, and
in the better journals; and he refused to stint, in employing the generous
resources of the allowance stipulated for him, in traveling about in the
late winter of 1899, oft with a small staff, to make inquiries after the
possible whereabouts of the sisters, in numerous cities along the Eastern
seaboard. "If they live—and I am determined they *do* live, each of them!
—I shall locate them," he averred, "and bring them back to Bloodsmoor."

Yet many days passed; and weeks. And no word was received.

"It is hopeless," Mrs. Zinn declared flatly, "not even the prospect
of money can tempt them: that being, I am afraid, one aspect of the
deformity of their characters, which led them astray in the first place."

"I cannot grant that," Mr. Miller said. "Not money but curiosity:
that shall tempt them."

The reader will be pleased, I hope, to learn that Mr. Miller was to
be prov'd the more nearly correct, in this exchange: and that, after many
weeks, and innumerable false leads and disappointments, he did succeed
in discovering three of the renegade sisters—and his office was contacted,
by telephone, by one "Philippe Fox," who designated himself as an agent
"empowered to represent the legal and financial interests of Miss Constance Philippa Zinn."

And so, whether it was *money,* or *curiosity,* or *repentance;* or an unlook'd-for recrudescence of *familial love and duty,* in bosoms long thought hardened, I cannot say: nor, perhaps, could the principals themselves have lucidly stated their motives. Nonetheless they did agree, in turn, after a great deal of argument on Mr. Miller's side, in which he appealed to them as a *cousin,* and then as an *attorney,* and then, most convincingly, as a *man of the world,* to meet at a strictly appointed time, in the Golden Oak room of Kiddemaster Hall, there to be witnesses to the breaking of the seal of their great-aunt's will, and to the reading of the will, and any other relevant documents on hand. "You will not regret this incursion upon your privacy," Mr. Miller told the sisters, with whom he had personal contact, "not that I promise material reward: for I cannot. But, I think, you will *not* regret returning to Bloodsmoor, for some very interesting revelations our aunt chooses to make, from out the grave."

Malvinia and Samantha concurred; but Deirdre, tho' modest and docile in every other respect, could not resist saying: " 'Our' aunt, Mr. Miller? I think you are confus'd, in the excitement of the moment: and have forgotten that I am not a Zinn by *blood,* but only by *law.* "

Mr. Miller gravely bowed. And added: "I would not, if I were you, Miss Zinn, too earnestly scorn the *law!*"

And so it transpired—and I cannot but choose to think it emblematic—that, on the third day of Easter Week, of 1899 (this being in late April, a most mellifluous season in our fragrant Bloodsmoor), the four "lost" sisters did meet with the fifth, and all five, in the presence of their parents, were witness to the ceremonial breaking of the seal of Miss Edwina Kiddemaster's Last Will and Testament.

An historic meeting, fraught with so many startl'd glances, and sudden tears, and fierce embraces, and surprises of both a small and monumental scope, as to render me near-powerless, in attempting the task of faithfully transcribing it!—yet I must proceed, as fastidiously as possible, with the authorial hope that the larger, and distasteful, revelations to come, will not despoil for the reader, some of the small pleasures the scene affords.

Firstly, the handsome setting: the Golden Oak room of Kiddemaster Hall, the which, I believe, you have not yet seen, for it was employed primarily, in the old days, as a meeting room for gentlemen—politicians, military men, business associates of the Kiddemasters, and others, mainly of the Whig persuasion, tho', I believe, some conservative Democrats did secretly join them from time to time, in the hope of steering our Ship of State through troubl'd waters. This room was paneled in the most exquisite golden oak, with a stenciled ceiling in which motifs from *Paradise Lost* were beauteously delineated, in rainbow hues; and three ponderous chandeliers, in which gold, brass, and crystal formed an agreeable harmony, and tall tapering white candles lent a distinct air of nobility. Ah, and the sun-warm'd spectacle of the stained-glass windows, in which motifs from Shakespeare's great tragedies were depicted!—these windows, from the workshop of Mr. Baines, of Philadelphia, being employed as frames for the windows of clear glass, which looked out upon one of the pastoral slopes, which dipped gently away to the Bloodsmoor River, sparkling and glinting in the sun, like a serpent so imbued with health, all his scales wink!

That the atmosphere might suggest itself as less formal, with the hope that any strain and anxiety the principals, and their parents, might feel, would be ameliorated, the thoughtful young Mr. Miller had commanded the servants to take out certain heavy items of furniture, including a massive table, wrought of solid mahogany, about which as many as fifty gentlemen had comfortably seated themselves: and to bring into the room, and judiciously arrange, a number of cushioned chairs, and small tables, and étagères, and even a few trinket boxes, and other aesthetic objects, so as to induce a feeling of elegance and calm, the which would make, I am bound to say, certain lurid revelations to come, strike an altogether *nightmarish* and *unreal* note.

At the appointed hour, Mr. and Mrs. Zinn, and Octavia, and the gentleman whom Octavia had seen fit to retain as her legal advisor, Mr. Sean McInnes, had already seated themselves, with some uneasiness, to await in silence, and, no doubt, great apprehension, the others: scarce knowing, of course, whether these renegade others would fulfill their promise, and appear. (All the family rejoiced in Octavia's good fortune, in that an attorney of such caliber, and possessing so *gentlemanly*, and *warm*, and *patient* a character, should step forward, and, *for no fee*, agree to defend the widowed and many-times-bereft Mrs. Rumford, from certain libelous charges made against her, by the grown children of her late husband: in that Mr. Rumford's impulsive will, giving over all his property, possessions, and cash investments, to the boy Godfrey, was unjust, and must be broken: with the look'd-for result that, Mrs. Rumford having inherited *from her son*, she would then be penniless!—and cast out from Rumford Hall, with naught but her two-year-old son Lucius Quincy to accompany her. It had been, for many months, the courteous task, on the part of Mr. McInnes, to both *console* the aggrieved widow, and *advise* her, as to the most pragmatic legal maneuvers—all the more so in that, of late, Mr. Rumford's investments in certain agricultural interests had begun to yield a healthful return, with the advent of the new Christianized rule in Hawaii, and the stabilization of the sugar beet crop.)

"I cannot think—I cannot dare *hope!*—that, within the hour, I will embrace my belovèd sisters once again!" So the tremulous Octavia warmly exclaimed, despite the gravity of the setting, and the taciturn countenances of her parents, who were seated beside her.

Mr. and Mrs. Zinn remained silent, each with lowered gaze: whereby, to alleviate the tension, Mr. Basil Miller allowed that the prospect was past mere *hoping,* and was in fact a *certainty;* and Mr. McInnes concurred.

Yet the elder Zinns sat in brooding silence, Mrs. Zinn with drear pouched eyes, and a nervous twitch in her cheek, and a resigned and melancholy smile, of that resolute "social" cast, that had been taught to her—ah, how many decades ago!—by her mother; and Mr. Zinn, tho' attired in his best suit, his long patriarch's beard newly trimm'd, with that brooding, shadow'd, nervous, and, I am saddened to say, unwholesome look, that anticipated the infirmity to come. (Alas, the paradoxes and riddles of our earthly sphere! For tho' J.Q.Z. now enjoyed some measure of success, and was, indeed, seized many times a day by euphoric eruptions of triumph, and glee, and boyish gloating, in that his newest experiments, with "detonation at a distance," and "nightscopes" for rifles, and "robot soldiers," and other ingenious inventions, of which I know too little to speak, were being greeted with cautious enthusiasm by manufacturers, nonetheless he was, for the most part, more distracted, and anxious, and peev'd, than anyone could recall. That this disconsolate air had much to do with his daughters' behavior, I cannot doubt, for, most of all, he bitterly grieved the loss of Samantha, and had some reason to think that, in a supreme act of betrayal, she and the villainous apprentice Nahum had sold certain of his most priz'd secrets to Mr. Edison! Yet the sallow and sickly cast of his complexion also prefigured this great man's final illness, which, even in the resplendent sun-graced warmth of the Golden Oak room, upon this idyllic April morn, had set its teeth cruelly into its victim—and was not to surrender its hold.)

Upon the last stroke of the clock, signaling *eleven,* the old butler entered, in his liveried costume, to announce in solemn tones that "Miss Malvinia Zinn has arrived."

Reader, you may well envision the scene: the shock'd alarm of the elder Zinns, at once suppressed; the gladsome, and irrepressible, joy of Mrs. Rumford—who, behaving in all defiance of the protocol of the scene, and very much against the note set by her heavy-skirted widow's raiment, and the penitential nature of her black satin bonnet, could not prevent herself from leaping to her feet, and hurrying to the door, that she might, in tears and stifl'd exclamations, and great confusion, fold Malvinia into an embrace—the which that criminal sister may have resisted, for some scant seconds, before, dissolv'd in tears herself, she surrendered: and a scene of such sisterly rejoicing, and lavish weeping, and fulsome ejaculations, ensued, as to make it near-impossible for me to continue in this wise, at the present moment—my eyes brimming with salt-tears, and my heart fairly hammering, as Octavia's and Malvinia's hearts hammered, in that heavenly embrace!

Ah, that Malvinia should appear, after so many years, and such mortification!—after her family had oft wished her dead, as, doubtless, the fallen woman must have wished herself dead, and freed of her earthly wretchedness!

That she should have summoned forth the strength, and, I do not hesitate to say, the courage: which all but deserted her, in those first confus'd minutes, when, extricating herself from her sobbing sister's arms, she advanced with dutiful courtesy to her parents, to greet them in subdued tones, and to be similarly greeted by them, wisely offering no hand for either to grasp, and taking no apparent note, it would seem, of Mr. Zinn's rigidity of demeanor, in that he did not rise to his feet.

Thus Malvinia: much alter'd since we have seen her last, her silver-threaded hair now fashioned into a graceful and modest chignon, the sides affixed in sweeping wings, to cover her ears; the old stealth of her eyes now calmed, or, it may be, hidden, by the tulle veil that drooped from the brim of her traveling hat, and by a solemn, and chasten'd, cast to her pale face. Tho' past the rosy flush of youth, Malvinia remained a most attractive woman still, pleasingly soft-spoken, and conservative of attire (in a traveling cloak of gray-lavender, lined with gray raw silk, and a matching dress of wool-and-silk, many-skirted, but without a bustle, and very plainly trimmed); and agreeably *undramatic* in her gestures, and employment of her corporeal being. It is not a cruel observation, to say that one might candidly guess her age to be *thirty-eight:* but one could not guess, I am pleased to say, the Malvinia Morloch of old, with her extravagant beauteousness, and her childish, and captivating, ways!

Whilst Malvinia seats herself, succumbing yet again to another embrace from Octavia, and scarcely repressing (by a visible effort of her will) a fresh fit of tears; whilst she declines, in a somewhat shaken, but resolute, voice, the toneless offer of Mrs. Zinn, that she "accept some refreshment, if only a chilled glass of water, after your long journey," I shall take the opportunity to explain, with necessary brevity, the circumstances of Malvinia's life since that pathetic night, at the Fanshawe Theatre; and the fortuitous steps that led her cousin Basil to her.

Fortuitous, indeed!—for, you will grant, the circumstances that resulted in Basil's discovery of Malvinia, as "Miss Malvinia Quincy," spinster instructress of Elocution, Music & the Thespian Arts, at the St. Veronica Academy for Young Episcopal Ladies, in Lawrenceville, New Jersey, would challenge those invented by such masters of the novelistic craft as Mr. Dickens or Mrs. Southworth—and would be, perhaps, distasteful in a work of fictional fancy, for the strain placed upon normal credulity. Such uncanny circumstances in real life, however, strike us as wondrously pleasing—proof, if proof be required, to fling in the teeth of the Darwinists, that Our Heavenly Father dwells in our midst, as both *progenitor* and *guide,* and that His earthly creation is naught but harmony, if properly observed.

Consider: Was it happenstance, or Fate, that led a travel-weary Basil Miller to the Knickerbocker Club of Manhattan, upon a night of pitiless sleet and wind; was it happenstance, or Fate, that led him to seat himself in one of the massive leather chairs in the smokers' lounge, and, drawing out his pipe, sigh with such amused resignation, that he attracted the sympathetic attention of a gentleman seated nearby?

A casual greeting ensued, an exchange of names, and a handshake, and some ejaculative commentary on the weather, and on the general topics of the city of New York, and the nation itself, both of which seemed, to the friendly stranger, "greatly fallen from past grandeur, and well on the way to Decadence: the new century being no herald, it is feared, of *rebirth.*"

Mr. Miller heartily concurred: for his native city of Philadelphia had fallen even more sharply from what it had been, before the War; and it was unspeakable, how the vulgarians and bullies had seized control of the Republican Party: there being little hope for improvement, with the noisome "Teddy" Roosevelt rough-riding over his betters, and drowning out all opposition with his pip-squeak's voice.

Each being alone for the evening, the gentlemen decided, most reasonably, to dine together: whereupon, during the leisurely course of an excellent meal of salmon, canvasback duck, and roast beef, Basil Miller saw fit to reveal that he was in search—"perhaps futilely"—of four female cousins of his, amongst them the former actress *Malvinia Morloch:* her real name being *Malvinia Zinn.*

Remarkable to see, how his companion reacted!—expressing some shock, and, after a moment's troubled silence, haltingly inquiring of the details of the search, the which Basil offered him, stressing rather the legalistic nature of the problem, than the personal. During these minutes Basil closely observed the gentleman, and bethought himself, did he not find those features somewhat familiar?—round-rimmed glasses giving to the man's eyes a scholarly cast; and the long slender nose, not without a hint of nobility of blood. He was perhaps in his mid-fifties, and of moderate height, rather bald, yet, withal, a fringe of curly graying hair low upon his skull gave him a most appealing, and even boyish, appearance. When Basil finished he spoke quietly, and modestly —but you can imagine Basil's surprise, when he averred that "perhaps he might aid in the search for Miss Malvinia Zinn: having, by a coincidence too wondrous to be explored, a missive on his person, *from that selfsame young lady.*"

And so it was, against what odds, I cannot fathom: for this soft-spoken gentleman was none other than *Malcolm Kennicott!*—whom we had last known as a young, and sadly immature, clergyman, assisting the Reverend Hewett at the Trinity Church in Bloodsmoor. It had been Malvinia's self-absorbed fancy, that young Mr. Kennicott had done away with himself, for *her:* but such was not the case, and I am even uncertain as to whether, in his protracted melancholy (which led him to precipitantly resign from his church, and to remove himself to the Old World, there to study classical languages and literature, and toil at his epic poem), he even made any serious attempt to do so: the sin of suicide being the most grievous of all sins, and the most harshly punished by Our Lord.

In introducing himself to Basil Miller, Mr. Kennicott had but murmured his own name, for, the recent public success of *The Vision of Columbus: An Epical Hymn in Three Parts,* having made the shy gentleman abash'd, he did not wish to call Mr. Miller's attention to himself, and to deflect from the normal course of the conversation. (In any case, it was not altogether certain that Basil would have recalled the name "Kennicott" —for he had heard but snippets of the sorry tale, laughingly recounted by Malvinia, some years after the unfortunate clergyman had banished himself from Bloodsmoor. And how very puzzling a tale it was, that a young gentleman of good family, ordained in the Episcopal Church, should fall in love with an eight-year-old child!) But these were the circumstances: after much delay, and many disappointments, the six-hundred-page epic had at last been published, by the relatively small firm of Rogers & Sons, of New York City, only to be heralded in the press, as a classic, which exposed in "deathless rhymes" the *savage* and *bellicose* nature of the Spanish soul (this being a time in our history, the reader should recall, when the sensationalist newspapers raged and foamed daily against Spain, urging war, that American "honor" and "commercial interests" might be upheld, in the Caribbean and elsewhere). And so it had come about, to no one's astonishment more than Malcolm Kennicott's, that his tripartite poem, long dreamt-of in the claustral sanctuary of his imagination, and grown most intricate, and most difficult, with the passage of years, was not only sprung into the public domain, with considerable notice, but had gone through some fifteen editions in a scant twelve-month!—which popular success, tho' having the agreeable effect of bringing the poet monetary reward, and the offer of a distinguished chair from his own college (for Mr. Kennicott was Professor of Classic Languages and Literature at Columbia), had as well the troubling effect, of making him decidedly self-conscious in society, and embarrassed, before his literary and academic peers, whose praise and congratulations he found most difficult to accept.

All this is of course worthy of notice: but it is more crucial for our narrative, that, with the publication of *The Vision of Columbus*, Mr. Kennicott came into such renown, as to capture the attention of the exil'd "Malvinia Morloch," then in disguise, in a small town in New Jersey, as "Malvinia Quincy," an academic spinster, habituated to solitude, and attired, for the most part, in plain, shapeless, and decidedly unfashionable clothes. How Malvinia had lifted herself from the ignominious depths to which she had fallen—how she had rescued some small particle of self-respect, and of mental sanity, from the chaos of her life (for the last we have glimpsed of her, she was fleeing in graceless terror from the stage of the Fanshawe Theatre!) is an exemplary tale in itself, involving much hardship, and prayer, and Christian humility, over a passage of years: not all of which, I must admit, was to be revealed, upon her reconciliation with her family, and the rekindling of that courtship—so shrouded in the mists of distant romance, in 1867 or '68, it was scarce recalled by the participants!—betwixt herself, and the faithful Malcolm Kennicott.

The reader will forgive me for o'erleaping myself, in my pleasure at this unlook'd-for twist of events, and my rejoicing in the visible harmony of Our Lord's creation.

Let us return to the discreetly appoint'd main dining room of the Knickerbocker Club, upon that fateful night in January of 1899, where Mr. Malcolm Kennicott could not forestall a blush, as, withdrawing a much-folded letter, in blue stationery, from out his breast pocket (where, he confessed, he had been carrying it for nearly a half-year), he informed the incredulous Basil Miller that he had been the grateful recipient of a missive from the "lost" Malvinia Zinn—the which, under these extraordinary, indeed, unprecedented, circumstances, he thought it no violation of gentlemanly discretion, to share.

Mr. Kennicott did not, I hasten to say, hand over the letter to Basil Miller, but simply showed it to him, that he might form a glancing familiarity with the hand (which was indeed Malvinia's, so far as Basil could recall). He then proceeded to summarize and paraphrase its contents, all the while flushing in a most abash'd, and charming, manner: "... *Regret, and affection, and high regard for his poetic genius ... and a plea for forgiveness, for the events of more than a quarter-century ago. ... The wonder, and manly precision, and poetic splendor of rhyme and rhythm, displayed in the epical hymn ... most astoundingly in the book devoted to Cortés. ... He would not recall her, perhaps: a vain, foolish, infantile creature at that time: and she begged him now, to forgive her for the past, and forget her utterly, releasing her to that desir'd Oblivion, which, to her surprise, she found almost comfortable. Tho' by penning this letter, she was risking exposure, she felt necessitated to write, to express her* infinite relief *and* gratitude, *that he lived (for she had feared otherwise) ... and her* joy, *that* The Vision of Columbus *was receiving the critical and popular acclaim, which, her feeble aesthetic judgment told her, was no more than his due."* So greatly moved that, for a long moment, he could not continue, Mr. Kennicott shook out from his pocket a fresh linen handkerchief, with which to wipe at his eyes, beneath his somewhat misted glasses. Even Basil Miller felt constrained to swallow very hard, for he heard—ah, so clearly!—so captivatingly!—his dear lost cousin's voice therein, and summoned back her especial sweetness, and grace, and maidenly charm, which, he could not help but think, he had had a villain's hand in squandering, in bringing her to the *salon* of a "lady" of *déclassé reputation:* and in allowing her to be addressed by the notorious Orlando Vandenhoffen.

Mr. Kennicott took strength, and concluded the summary, in a broken voice, reiterating that the authoress of the letter felt compelled to *insist,* that her secret abode not be revealed; that no attempt be made, on his part, or on the part of any other, to seek her out in her exile: and that—most cruel!—the "impulsive and, it may be, unwelcome" letter *not be answered.*

Greatly excited, Basil Miller asked to examine the envelope: and saw clearly that the postmark was "Lawrenceville, N.J."

"Why, that is very close by!" he exclaimed. "But a morning's drive!"

But Mr. Kennicott took back the envelope, and folded the letter, to slip it inside, the while murmuring sadly that he could not, under any circumstances, disobey Miss Zinn's command: for he respected her too much, and, even after so many tumultuous years, loved her too much, to do so.

Basil Miller then expressed some incredulity—for it had, after all, been *many* years, since his companion had last glimpsed Malvinia.

"Nay, not so," Mr. Kennicott said warmly, "I had quite naturally recognized her as Malvinia Morloch, and must have attended upward of one thousand performances of hers, in this city, and elsewhere: forbidding myself, I hasten to say, from ever imposing upon her, or calling attention to myself in any way, save by sending her, from time to time, trifling gifts of flowers, and trinkets, and whatnot: along with her numerous other admirers!"

You can imagine how deeply moved Basil Miller was, when the soft-voiced poet went on to explain, that he had taken his present position, with Columbia College, in order that he might dwell in Manhattan, close by Malvinia. And he had been, of course, quite devastated, in fact ill with brain fever, for some weeks, after her much-publiciz'd disappearance, and the vicious rumors that she had drowned herself.

"But Lawrenceville, New Jersey, is wonderfully close by," Basil Miller said, with agitation, "not many miles from Princeton, I believe. We shall hire a carriage, Mr. Kennicott, and drive out there, upon the morn!"

Again Mr. Kennicott demurred, nervously stroking his chin, and blinking warm tears from out his eyes. "Indeed, Mr. Miller, I *cannot* do that: I am very sorry, but I *cannot*. You, as her cousin, would doubtless be welcome at her door; but *I—!*"

Basil Miller made a gesture of amused impatience, and pouring more wine into their depleted glasses, said in a forthright voice, of a kind that had agreeably impressed Great-Aunt Edwina, and his elders in the profession of law, in Philadelphia: "Come now, Mr. Kennicott, tho' you are a poet, you are also a man of the world: if you take so curious a stand, I shall think you more conversant with the merely *epical* amongst poetic compositions, and not the *romance*."

And thus it came about, that Basil Miller discovered the first of his four lost cousins: and the reluctant, and greatly distraught, suitor of old, Mr. Kennicott, was reunited with his love! Indeed, it was Mr. Kennicott who had escorted Malvinia to Bloodsmoor, upon the occasion at hand: but, discreetly wishing to remain unobtrusive, he had chosen to take rooms at the Bloodsmoor Inn, there to await his lady-friend, and to learn of what might transpire. (That Malvinia and Mr. Kennicott were not yet joined in holy matrimony, but only engaged, will not, I trust, arouse distaste in the sensitive reader—for Malvinia had quite reformed, and would not now, I am certain, have consented to remain overnight, even in a public inn, beneath the same roof as a gentleman not her spouse. Indeed, so extreme was her revulsion, for the *bestial* side of her own nature, that she had agreed to Malcolm Kennicott's reiterated proposals of marriage, only on the condition that they dwell together as *sister and brother:* to which the adoring suitor gratefully agreed, having been celibate for his entire life, and rather more of the Platonic persuasion, than otherwise.)

The gathering had had scant time to compose themselves, after Malvinia's arrival, before the elderly butler announced "Mr. and Mrs. Nahum Hareton"—and there appeared Samantha!—and the treacherous apprentice Nahum: the criminal couple who had broken Mr. Zinn's heart, and now seemed, by the resolute boldness with which they entered the room, hardly repentant.

But if Malvinia had aroused surprise, at the numerous changes time had wrought, in both her meretricious beauty, and her comportment, it was quite the reverse with Samantha: arousing surprise, perhaps, that, in the years since her departure, she had changed so very little. Now a married woman of mature years, and, in fact, a mother, she nonetheless strode forward with the brazen energy of a young and headstrong girl; and so healthful was the glow of her complexion, and so childishly appealing the freckles scattered across her face, that one might have sworn she was no one other than the Samantha of old!—her father's belovèd disciple, and long the favorite of his heart.

The overjoy'd Octavia, in rushing to embrace this sister, was per-

haps less unrestrained, than she had been with Malvinia: in part, because
not so many years had passed, since the two had last glimps'd each other;
and in part because they had not been exceedingly close. Nonetheless,
Octavia's tears freely sprang, and her words of exclamatory welcome, and
admiration for Samantha's appearance (for her face, now very slightly
fuller than it had been, was lovely still; and her green, silk-lined traveling
cloak was *most* becoming), were delightful to hear, the more so in that the
elder Zinns were greeting this arrival with as much, or even more, restraint, as they had greeted Malvinia's. And there was a forc'd warmth,
as well, in the exchange between Samantha and Malvinia: who, staring
and blinking at each other, and dazedly smiling, might have been strangers, and never sisters at all.

One could clearly see the sharp vertical crease, that, of a sudden,
appeared between Samantha's eyebrows, as she approached her parents,
and made a half-curtsy before them, and bespoke her sober words of
greeting. Indeed, the atmosphere was quite strained, as Mrs. Zinn responded in a voice all but inaudible, and managed but the faintest twist
of her stern lips; and Mr. Zinn, now grown ghastly pale, seemed incapable
of lifting his steely gaze from off the carpet at his feet, to grant this
daughter the courtesy of a glance, or the murmur of a reply.

Nor did the visibly nervous Nahum fare any better: tho' some
minutes were mercifully taken up, by Basil Miller's friendly conversation,
and by Malvinia's show of flushed pleasure, in being introduced to her
younger sister's husband, when, of course, she had not known of any
marriage; and had not dreamt that any suitor would prove so convincing,
as to deflect Samantha's interest from that of *invention.* Samantha, however, remained standing before her seated parents, and, at last, biting her
lower lip, said in an even, tho' rather hoarse, voice: "I am sorry, Mother,
and dear Father, that our lives have so evolved, as to have necessitated
this meeting: and I beg your Christian forgiveness, for having come into
your presence this morning, and so clearly giving you cause for displeasure." A speech that embarrassed all, not simply for the import of its
words, but for the grave silence, and tacit agreement, with which it was
received by the elder Zinns.

So quickly did Deirdre—black-garbed, and discreetly veiled—follow upon the heels of the Haretons, that I have not sufficient space, or
time, to inform the reader of Samantha's life, since her elopement a
decade previously: save to remark that, without J.Q.Z.'s guiding genius,
both Samantha and Nahum had settled in, with surprising equanimity of
temperament, and some occasional laziness, to the life of *an ordinary
married couple,* Samantha helping her husband out, as the spirit moved her,
in his self-styled "inventor's workshop" (which dealt primarily in repairs,
particularly of electrical gadgets, and horseless carriages) in the small
inland town of Guilford, Delaware. Apart from the Haretons' concern

with money—for their finances were always uncertain, and inflation steadily increased—and some occasional concern with their children's health, which might be seen to be only natural, it was quite remarkable, that Samantha and Nahum led so peaceable, and unambitious, a life!— after the consuming passion of the workshop above the gorge, which had, one might have thought, infected Samantha for life. Indeed, had this renegade couple but consented to allow Our Saviour into their lives, and to arrange for the proper baptism of their children in the Episcopal Church, I would be inclined to think them altogether enviable: or, at any rate, so little fired by a desire for worldly advancement, or for the vertiginous pleasures of Fame, as to constitute Christian models, of mutual love and esteem, and connubial bliss.

Yet—here is Deirdre!

The unfeeling *"sister"* Deirdre: the *adopted daughter* Deirdre: *"Deirdre of the Shadows"* that was, and is no more!

So quietly did this lithe young woman enter the room, so stealthy was her motion, it was a very long moment before her staring family quite grasped the fact of her presence—and, it may be, realized in her slender form, and in her pallid countenance, the very origin of their misfortunes.

Not a mere girl of sixteen, but a mature woman of thirty-six: and doubtless aged beyond her years, by her unseemly experiences in the wide world, the nature of which Bloodsmoor might never know, or wish to know!—how very amazing to see her there, in the Golden Oak room of Kiddemaster Hall, an intruder in a world that, in opening its gates to admit her, had been grievously injur'd. And yet—there she stood: a veil of fine black lace discreetly screening her eyes.

How fitting, her breathless exclamation, which began with these words: "I am sorry—"

73

The reader will be surpris'd to learn that Miss Deirdre Zinn was persuaded to respond to the classified notices that appeared with such regularity in the New York papers, and to acquit herself of her responsibilities to that generous family that, in stooping to adopt her, had unleashed such harm, by one of the most estimable personages in this chronicle: *Dr. Lionel Stoughton.*

Indeed—the revelation comes as a considerable surprise!

Yet more surprising still, the unlook'd-for development, which had its clouded origins in the early autumn of 1898, that the spinster Miss Zinn (now supporting herself on the meager salary of an amanuensis, for a retired Islamic scholar) was being courted by not *one*, but *two*, gentlemen, both possessing considerable fortunes!—and that she did not so much hesitate between them, but shrank from both, out of a fastidious dread that she might marry, simply from fear of poverty; and out of the more reasonable dread, that she was *unworthy* of either gentleman, and, indeed, of the sacred matrimonial state itself.

One of the suitors for her hand was Dr. Stoughton; the other, I am most reluctant to report, was the swarthy-skinned Hassan Agha, who, having returned to the States after some years of meditation in India, had made a display of renouncing his Theosophical ties, and, more generally, his interest in "all things Oriental and tiresome," and had most desultorily taken up the Anglican faith of his deceased mother: the which he also rejected, after a shamefully brief period, tho', shrewd as he was, and blessed with that craftiness we oft note in the pagan, he did not reject the handsome fortune that had come to him, by way of his mother.

The blond, upstanding, selfless Christian physician, on the one hand; and the olive-skinned, black-eyed, part-Indian ne'er-do-well, on the other: and yet, such was the unwholesome nature of Deirdre's judgment, she dared hesitate between them, *as if they were equals.*

"I shall not press my suit, Miss Zinn," spoke Dr. Stoughton, the modesty of his bearing scarce concealing a tumultuous heart that beat within, "for, I believe you well know, the *breadth,* and *intensity,* of my high regard for you: and I shrink from bringing more discomfiture to your troubl'd life." Thus the courteous Dr. Stoughton, upon several occasions, and numerous times, employing divers language, in formal epistolary guise.

Now hear by contrast the rude imperatives of Mr. Hassan Agha, whose years of ascetic discipline, as a *chela* of Madame Blavatsky's, and as a novice, more generally, in one of the most austere of the Hindoo sects, had scarce had any discernible effect, upon his latent animal nature: "Miss Zinn, I shall not let you rest, until you have given me an answer: nay, until you have given me the only answer that *your* nature, and *mine,* as well as the curious adventures that bind us, require. I declare myself with pride the son of an Indian prince, and an Englishwoman of excellent breeding, and commendable passion (if little common sense): with no slackening of that pride, I declare myself your slave, one who has known himself under your spell, since that prodigious morn at Landsdowne House, where, upon a beauteous grassy slope, I discovered your reclining, and insensible, form, and succumbed at once to your authority. Yes, even amidst that crowd of fools, quacks, dupes, and charlatans, in which I enacted some dictated role, which only the grotesquerie of *karma*-wisdom might explain, I had manliness enough, to realize my passion for *you.*"

Coarse words!—and accompanied by a hot dark gaze, and an intensity of manner, of such visible animalism, I cannot even attempt to convey, in the verbal art, its effect.

That Deirdre fully felt the barbarism of such utterances, is to be inferred, since, her silken cheeks flaming crimson, she sent Mr. Agha away with dispatch: that she wavered in her judgment, and succumbed to no little anxiety, during her insomniac nights, is clearly evident, in that she failed to *forbid* this importunate creature to indulge his passion for her, in sending voluminous missives to her, the which made disquieting reading, and struck a very exotic, and jarring, note, in the unadorned solitude of the single room which Deirdre now rented, in a modest, but altogether respectable, rooming house for "single ladies." (This stolid brownstone on Stuyvesant Square, very near St. George's Episcopal Church, accommodated some ten or twelve spinster ladies, all of good middle-class families, and most of an age advanced beyond Deirdre's. Without exception, all were employed in those feminine skills—that of teaching the very young, or tutoring the invalided, or acting as librarians, or pastoral assistants, or amanuenses—which, tho' by tradition affording but meager financial reward, are nevertheless gratifying as occupations, and inestimable, in their quiet contribution to our industrious society. And not only was the subdued atmosphere of this excellent rooming house a palliative to Deirdre's uncertain nerves, and vexing memories, but the tranquillity of East Seventeenth Street, and, indeed, the genteel atmosphere of the square itself, mercifully free of that bustling traffic that, elsewhere on the island, so plagued and endangered the lives of the city-dwellers, could not fail to act as a restorative, to her soul.)

"I shall not press my suit," declared the one, in a manly voice made tremulous, by emotion; "I shall not let you rest," declared the other, scarce minding that his animal exigency, and the smold'ring black gaze he bent upon her, were deeply distressing, to one of virginal status.

As if there were any reasonable grounds for the slightest hesitancy, in choosing between them!

Yet hesitate the perverse Deirdre had done; and continued to do; all the while further taxing her fragile nervous constitution, by inquiring as to whether, "fallen" as she was in so many respects (I refer to the egregious worldly *career* she had forg'd for herself, out of vanity and ambition, as well as to the outlaw nature of her flight from Bloodsmoor), she deserved *either* man for a husband; or *any* man at all.

"It is my fate, I am sure," Deirdre languidly mused, many a night, in the frugal solitude of her spinster's abode, "to dwell alone: husbandless, and childless. And, tho' I feel naught but relief, how apt it now seems, that even my 'spirits' have abandoned me!"

(For, indeed, those diabolical creatures *had* abandoned their "medium": and had not even teased her, during the long months of her convalescence, when, one might think, her enfeebl'd state might have tempted them.)

Plagued by sleepless nights, and rarely soothed by the robust tolling of the bells, of old St. George's, Deirdre nonetheless absorbed herself in a subtle species of *pride,* in musing thusly; and in so fastidiously interrogating herself, as to whether, impoverish'd as she was, and granted so very little in the way of security, as to the future of her employment (her elderly master, the retired professor of Islamic studies, being both forgetful, and ill-tempered), she might not, in spinster desperation, marry for *money:* the mere possibility of which repulsed her.

"While it is the case that Dr. Stoughton has, I believe, a more modest yearly income than Mr. Agha, I can hardly make *that* the basis for choosing," Deirdre tormented herself, "and who can say, but that a spirit of malevolence continues to haunt me, and would misdirect me, even when I dared to fancy I was behaving well!"

So troubled was this young lady, she found it increasingly difficult to enjoy the company of others; and, upon one singular occasion, greatly surprised, and offended, her landlady's daughter, when after the evening repast one night, this pleasant-voiced girl sat herself at the piano in the parlor, and sang but a few words of a song, with the consequence that Miss Zinn *fled in tears up to her room.*

A mystery to that startl'd gathering, no doubt; yet hardly a mystery to *us,* for the song was that heartrending melody by the musical genius Paul Dresser, to become so deservedly popular in the late Nineties:

> 'Tis the grave of an outcast who died long ago,
> Who has sinned, and no mercy was shown;
> So one cold winter's day, her soul passed away,
> And they buried her there all alone.

—this classic being, I hardly need inform the reader, "The Outcast Unknown," whose words struck very deep in poor Deirdre's heart.

That it was Dr. Lionel Stoughton who advised Deirdre to contact Mr. Miller in Philadelphia, as the numerous advertisements bade, suggests a certain intimacy between them: which, I must hasten to clarify, was not the case.

On Dr. Stoughton's part, there was the continuance of a *professional* concern with the erstwhile medium, which, whilst not uncontaminated with romantic aspirations, was noble in itself, and disinterested. After her ignominious collapse at the Fairbanks estate, Deirdre was, for some eighteen months, a patient at a private sanatorium in the Adirondack Mountains: this enforc'd convalescence, in salubrious surroundings, being initially paid for out of her own savings, and, as these rapidly dwindled, by funds from an "anonymous well-wisher"—none other than that very same doctor of medicine, and President of the New York branch of the Society for Psychical Research, who had, years previous, warned "Deirdre of the Shadows" against embarking upon her perilous career!

Yet, when at last they did meet, Deirdre's condition having substantially improved, and her melancholy having partly lifted, this considerate gentleman naturally did not press his advantage; nor did he allude to her former life, and her notorious "career," which was still avidly discussed in Spiritualist circles—and may be, for all that I know, still discussed today, if such occult enclaves exist. Dr. Stoughton's conversation had to do with positive matters: primarily with Deirdre's future, whether she would now return to her family, or whether she would seek employment in some wise, appropriate to her talents. "I cannot return to my family," Deirdre said quietly, "for, in truth, I have none: I was but an *adopted* child, and was never allowed to forget it. *Zinn* is my adopted parents' name; *Bonner* my real parents' name; and all, alas! are lost to me now. So I shall seek employment in the city, Dr. Stoughton, and hope to lay by some savings, so that, in time, I may repay you, at least in part, for the kindness you have shown."

"Not at all," Dr. Stoughton said, reddening. (For he had imagined his secret safe—that the object of his Christian beneficence might never guess his identity.) "I cannot—I will not—hear of *that*, Miss Zinn!"

So pitiful were the wages Deirdre received for her labors, as the assistant to the Islamic scholar, that, to her extreme embarrassment, she was able to save but a few pennies a week; nor did the future look brighter. Ah, what a queer dream it had been, the years of her relative wealth! She could scarce believe she had once commanded such exorbitant fees, and had believed them but her due: for now she had naught to show for those years save certain items of clothing, of resolutely sombre hue; and some very upsetting memories.

"Nay, I count myself blessèd," she oft murmured, in solitude, "tho' I be near-penniless, I am my own woman at last: *and I am not mad.*"

Nor did she miss the intoxicating powers, her wicked spirits had once afforded her. Was it a dream? Had she imagined all? *Father Darien,* and *Mrs. Dodd,* and the *Raging Captain,* and *Bianca,* and fork-tongued *Zachariah?* And, beyond them, the black silken balloon that had borne her so silently away, from the peaceful countryside of her birth?

Ofttimes she queried herself: *Had Bloodsmoor itself been naught but a dream?*

It was not many weeks after her discharge from the sanatorium, and the establishment of her residency, in the spartan brownstone at 207½ East Seventeenth Street, that her benefactor, Dr. Stoughton, tendered to her his proposal of marriage: worded, at the first, in such abash'd and recondite language, she scarce grasped its import.

Dr. Stoughton made haste to assure her, that he wanted nothing less, than to bring further upset into her life; and that she should bear in mind that he was, first and foremost, her devoted *friend,* who desired only her *happiness,* and *well-being.* "If you should ever consent to return my love," he murmured, his gaze affixed to the floor, "and to be my wife, why, I would be transform'd into *the happiest man on earth:* but you must feel no obligation, toward that end, nor any pressure whatsoever."

Thus spoke one of the most magnanimous gentlemen, who ever drew breath: his thick blond hair but lightly touched with silver, and his forceful countenance betraying but a very few lines and creases, to indicate the deepening maturity of his years.

Deirdre's reply was faltering, and near-inaudible. "I cannot consent," she murmured.

"You cannot consent," Dr. Stoughton slowly repeated. "And yet —dare I hope?—*you do not absolutely deny me?*"

At this the agitated young woman could not force herself to speak: to indicate *yes,* or *no,* would have cost her weakened constitution far more strain, than it might have endured.

Yet, if she did not accept his plea, she did not reject it: and if she did not banish the hot-blooded Hassan Agha from her life, she did not encourage him either: and seemed, indeed, to her own way of thinking, near-helpless in her fate, as a fly entrapped in a spider's elaborate silver-tinged web.

Dr. Stoughton first called her attention to the classified notices in the *Tribune,* which she read with great alarm: and a rush of emotion, in which regret, and guilt, and fear, and a sense of prickling curiosity, were commingled. Her initial response was violently negative: nay, she *would not* comply. But, as days and weeks passed, and she turned the prospect over in her mind, she bethought herself that the tyrannical old lady, Miss Kiddemaster, had not been *altogether* cruel to her: perhaps—ah, perhaps! —there had even been some affection, but awkwardly expressed, and never reliable.

And one morn she woke to the thought: I *shall* do as Dr. Stoughton counsels, and return to Bloodsmoor; and perhaps, by so doing, I will give the wheel of my own fortune a helpful turn—and be awakened from this paralysis, to know whether I dare marry, or no; and whom it might be.

Thus, her arrival at Kiddemaster Hall, some twenty minutes past the hour: breathless, and stricken to the heart by the assault of so many eyes upon her, and, ah! by the ravages of time, so harshly evident in the faces of the elder Zinns. (For, in truth, poor Deirdre scarce recognized the once-handsome John Quincy Zinn: for a confus'd instant she wondered if that sallow-skinned bearded old gentleman might have been *Grandfather Kiddemaster!*)

Startl'd silence greeting her, she heard her own voice—graceless, and throaty, and rushed—offering a feeble apology. "I am sorry—I am very sorry—it seems that I am late—it is an inexcusable tardiness, which might be accounted for, yet cannot be excused—"

So her words nervously rattled; and Mr. Basil Miller, with his practiced social instinct, advanced upon her, to welcome her with kindly reassurances that she was not seriously late, for they were also awaiting Constance Philippa. And, after a moment's hesitation (doubtless fearing a rebuff), Octavia, too, advanced upon her, and folded her in a solemn embrace, the while murmuring: "Ah, my poor Deirdre! My little sister! It has been incalculably long! It has been piteously long! We are sisters, yet we are strangers—*yet we are sisters, still!*"

Dear effusive Octavia! Deirdre weakly offered to embrace her in turn, yet felt o'ercome by the sentiment of the moment. She would not have recognized this full-bodied matronly woman with her handsome, high-colored countenance, so liberally glistening with tears: nor would she, in other circumstances, have recognized Malvinia—was it truly Malvinia?—suddenly before her, who offered a gloved hand, and a droll searching smile. Malvinia, so changed! A mature woman! Striking, still, but ah!—no longer young!

And there arose Samantha—might this woman be Samantha?—her bedmate of childhood, *Samantha?*—with her cool green eyes and quizzical expression, yet wondrously alter'd, and now radiantly lovely: the once-plain and graceless girl who had offered, against the grain of her own heart, some small measure of patience, and affection, and sisterly concern, to the ungrateful Deirdre. Now they grasped hands, and managed a ceremonial embrace, not affectionate, and surely not sisterly, but adequate to the flurried circumstances.

Dazed, wiping a stray tear from her eye, Deirdre next found herself meekly standing before Mr. and Mrs. Zinn. Ah, how she had dreaded this moment! How she had deluded herself, in never seeking to precisely envision it, but always shrinking back from the prospect! She had fled them—had injured them—had rejected them, in her heart: because they had failed to love her sufficiently: the which adolescent fancy struck her now as merely absurd, for why, in truth, should anyone have loved the orphan Deirdre *at all?*

Only twenty years had passed since the afternoon of the black silken balloon, no extraordinary span of time, perhaps, yet, to Deirdre's shocked eye, Mr. and Mrs. Zinn were so alarmingly agèd, they seemed rather of the sculptor's fancy of Matriarch and Patriarch, of another generation entirely. Finely creased skin—dry reproachful eyes—Mrs. Zinn's mouth so grim it would seem a stoic chore to smile—Mr. Zinn's gaze fixed and impersonal and, alas!—unloving.

Forced murmured greetings were exchanged, and stinging salt-tears so invaded Deirdre's vision, she could scarce continue to discern the unresponsive countenances of her adoptive mother and father. Yet she bravely spoke: "Dear Mother, and dear Father, I know you cannot—indeed, you *should* not—forgive me, and I have not come to ask your forgiveness, at this unhappy time. I assure you, I will not further upset you, by remaining any longer in Bloodsmoor than is absolutely required, for I suspect that the mere sight of me, the *ingrate orphan,* is repulsive. Nay, do not mind," she said, seeing that Mrs. Zinn felt compelled to issue a faint protest, "for you are entirely in the right, and God has judged me harshly, these past twenty years."

This speech having been most spiritedly uttered, the gathering received it in hushed quiet; and it was a long moment before Mrs. Zinn bestirred herself to reply, with but a weak stretching of her lips, and a markedly cool gray gaze. "Our Lord judges not harshly," she said, "but justly. As our family has always known."

And Mr. Zinn—John Quincy Zinn—the acclaimed inventor-genius

J.Q.Z. of Bloodsmoor—that very gentleman, so tall! so handsome! so robust! so kindly! who had, in another lifetime, it seemed, merrily stooped from his great height, that he might befriend a scampering fairy-child, a naughty little miss who had run into the woods above the gorge, and quite frightened her parents, with the possibility of her being *lost:* this gentleman, now so mysteriously aged beyond his seventy-one years, raised his eyes to sternly regard his renegade "daughter," and plucked absently at his beard, and opened his mouth to speak, and—and spoke not at all: but remained silent, and immobile, save for the scarce-perceptible trembling of his frame.

74

"May I escort you, Miss Zinn, to a comfortable chair?" murmured the solicitous Basil Miller, gauging the depth of Deirdre's distraction; and wishing to remove the young woman from her stepparents' propinquity, out of consideration for all three personages.

Thus Basil palliated, by his adroit action, the stridency of emotion of the scene; and the others, still somewhat flurried, and wiping tears from out their eyes, regained their seats.

Ah!—the morn was fast elapsing! And where was Constance Philippa?

Even before the audacious entrance of the problematic "Philippe Fox," it must be said that the atmosphere of the Golden Oak room, despite the elegance of its decor and furnishings, and the pleasing eurythmy of its high windows, pilasters, and stained-glass inserts, was exceedingly strange; and taxes my limited verbal resources, in seeking to describe it. An agitated quiet: a paralyzed tension: an air in which dread, and euphoric anticipation, and resentment, and even some small bitterness, were wildly commingled!—the very constraint of the principals, in their formal attire, and seated in such wise as to face the front of the room (where Basil Miller had arranged a graceful escritoire, of rosewood and gilt, for his own use), contributing to this strained sensation.

For, only consider: there were those present who, by dint of their age, and station, had every right to resent the theatricality of the scene: and the whimsy by which, from out the marbl'd mausoleum in which her corporeal being now slept, old Edwina manipulated the living, as if they were mere puppets, for her diversion. Many a time Mrs. Zinn had burst into tears of helpless fury, both before her sympathetic spouse, and in the

549

privacy of her locked room, that, by all the laws of God and the Devil (these being her angry words, I should explain, and hardly my own), it was *monstrously unfair* that, in his dotage, her father should decide to leave his fortune to his elderly, and notoriously eccentric, sister, rather than to his devoted daughter and son-in-law!—and cruel beyond measurement, that the tyrannical old man should state, in his official will and testament, that the mere *erasing of debt* should prove, in their case, an unlook'd-for boon. "That Father disapproved of our marriage, out of a cynical rejection of all that is pure, and spontaneous, and romantic," poor Prudence stormed, pressing both hands against her heaving bosom, "I have never doubted. That he had failed to forgive me, all these many years, and had, moreover, failed to measure the exceptional worth of my husband, I find remarkable—nay, insupportable. And then, and then—!" she raged, her ruddy cheeks pulsing crimson; "—and then, that Aunt Edwina should so wantonly refuse to correct the injustice, the effrontery of which she well knew, and restore the lost fortune to *me*, the rightful heiress!"

"And yet," J.Q.Z. observed, upon more than one occasion, in a voice somewhat hollow, and chilled, "and yet, my dear, we must not be small-minded. It does not do us proud, at our ages."

"Uncle Vaughan dies, and leaves Father an incalculable fortune. Why, consider his shipbuilding business alone; or his properties in Philadelphia. Mother having died earlier, and a substantial portion of the old Whitton-Steuben fortune being hers, it resides all untouched with Father: who surely knew that Mother would have wished, nay, would have *commanded*, that a goodly proportion fall to *me*, her sole offspring, and her devoted daughter. Now, consider, Uncle Vaughan's fortune; and Mother's; and the great Kiddemaster fortune here in Bloodsmoor; and, added to *this*, old Edwina's cache, the details of which she was fierce to keep secret: and do you grasp, Mr. Zinn, the monumental nature of what is at stake? Yet you bid me not to be *small-minded*," Prudence all but wept, in scornful frenzy, "as if one could succeed in being *small-minded*, about a fortune of such celestial proportions!" She paused, to draw a labored breath; and to steady her quivering bulk. And then proceeded, in a calmer, and lower, voice: "Why, if we heaped Rockefeller, and Vanderbilt, and Hanna, and one or two others, together, and assessed their collective worth, do you think it would be greatly *in excess* of this fortune, the which my greedy aunt accepted as her due? Not many years ago our national wealth was boasted of as sixty-five billion dollars: and, I daresay, we Kiddemasters have, of that, some five or ten billion at the very least!"

"You exaggerate, Prudence," Mr. Zinn said shakily. "Why, I cannot quite grasp such a notion: five or ten billion *dollars*, you are saying?"

"Enough to fill a pedlar's sack many times over, you will agree," Mrs. Zinn said curtly.

Thus the elder Zinns, with whom it would be difficult, indeed, not to be in sympathy.

And there were present, too, at the gathering, some personages not yet mentioned: the kindly old Miss Narcissa Gilpin, who had told intimates, in her unassuming manner, that Edwina had promised a high percentage of the fortune to *her,* in return for her lifetime of friendship, and critical suggestions; and Miss Flora Kale, a cousin of Edwina's, and a girlhood friend, upon whom Mrs. Zinn looked with especial resentment, and some apprehension; and some Philadelphia Kiddemasters, of advanced years; and the Reverend Silas Hewett and his wife, also greatly agèd, but in full possession of their faculties, and serenely confident as to *their* figuring handsomely in the will—for, according to their somewhat promiscuous testimony, old Edwina, on her very deathbed, had so promised them. And the zealous Dr. Moffet too was in attendance, no matter that he was badly wanted at another household in the village, where a troublesome young woman lay in labor for upward of twelve hours, with no end in sight. (Dr. Moffet had quite offended Prudence Zinn, by his reiterated boasts, that his "most esteemed patient" Edwina, had broadly hinted that he was to be remembered bountifully in her will, in proportion to the medical skill he possessed.)

As for the sisters, of them all only Malvinia harbored some small hope that Edwina might have remembered her; but Malvinia was, at the same time, too skeptical, both of her great-aunt's generosity, and her own deserts, to seriously expect any inheritance. Octavia had sighed, and dabbed at her tear-streaked face, and flatly declared to Mr. McInnes (with whom she spoke almost daily, on matters of financial and legal significance), that she expected not a penny: for the vindictive old lady had never forgiven *her,* that Little Godfrey had crawled beneath Edwina's skirts so long ago, as a mere prank. Samantha had so little expectation, she and her husband had worried betwixt themselves, as to whether they might dare ask Mr. Miller for some recompense, for their journey by rail from Guilford to Bloodsmoor: a mere $28 for both tickets, round-trip, but a dismayingly high price in their eyes. (They decided they must *not* ask. "I would not want anyone in my family," Samantha declared, "to know how poor we are: and to pity us.") As for Deirdre—she was too o'ercome with mortification, at the coldness with which the elder Zinns had greeted her, to give any clear thought to the purpose of the meeting: nor might her tear-beclouded eye have discerned the weighty parchments on the escritoire, at Basil Miller's elbow, which contained the Last Will and Testament of Miss Edwina Kiddemaster. *I must leave this accursèd place,* she silently wept, *for it is not my home, and never was; and Dr. Stoughton did me a singular disservice, to direct me here.*

Still the gold-and-ebony French Empire clock on the mantel continued its solemn ticking; and the minute hand advanced, now moving upward to noon; and the missing sister failed to appear.

Exhibiting some disappointment, in which vexation was mixed, Basil Miller at last cleared his throat to speak, and was rather petulantly declaring that the meeting might require postponement, for, according to Miss Kiddemaster's express wishes, *all* the sisters must be present, when, of a sudden, the door was opened, and a gentleman strode in, unannounced—a stranger with dark hair, graying at the temples; and fierce heavy brows; and a brisk, impertinent manner, enhanced by the tight-fitting frock coat he wore, and the broad-brimmed white Western hat he carried rakishly in his hand, and the strident hammering of his high-heeled leather boots!

Doubtless this strange gentleman felt some natural anxiety, to intrude upon a private gathering; yet he took care, to exhibit little apprehension; and maintained a practic'd poker face, as, curtly bowing to the amazed assemblage, he spoke: "I believe you are expecting Miss Constance Philippa Zinn, who, unfortunately, cannot be here today. She has designated me her sole agent in this matter, and has given me power of attorney: I am Philippe Fox, of the Rock Bluff Mining and Milling Company, of San Pedro, Arizona; I am, as well, a former Assistant Deputy to the United States Marshal, for Southeast Arizona. Please accept my heartfelt apologies for my tardiness—but I have come a very long way."

As you may well imagine, everyone stared at this impudent stranger; and even Basil Miller, ordinarily so composed, was taken aback.

For here was the very extravagance, the very audacity, of the West! —quite o'erwhelming, in this decorous Eastern drawing room.

All stared; several of the ladies gasped; and the interloper boldly stood his ground, his dark gaze moving agilely from face to face. He was brazen, and yet, was there not a certain quavering to his voice?—a nasal, or, it may have been, an *effeminate* note?

"I see you are struck mute," this personage said, his lips twisting in a delicate, and ironic, smile, "and so I have no choice but to repeat myself: your kinswoman Miss Constance Philippa Zinn has bade me come here, in her place, as her designated agent: Philippe Fox, of Arizona, and, more lately, of San Francisco."

Thus speaking, he bowed; and with a flamboyant gesture brandished his white hat before him.

Then, of a sudden, Octavia heaved herself from her seat, so distraught, her fan clattered to the floor, and her ample bosom rose, in passionate inhalation. She gasped aloud, and cried: "Dear God! I cannot believe it! What do I see! This person is—this gentleman—this stranger —*this*—" Sean McInnes quickly rose to his feet, to give her aid, for fear that she might sink into a swoon; but she forced herself free of his restraining arm, and half turned, reeling, to exclaim to the assemblage:

"It is Constance Philippa! It is our sister, Constance Philippa! It—he—this—in disguise—in masculine attire—ah, do you not see!—or am I mad! She stands before us, in obscene array: *our belovèd Constance Philippa!"*

Now all stared at the intruder, and saw: the face roughly tanned by exposure to the elements, and the figure consciously lean and erect, as a man's: yet, the very eyes, the very nose, the very set of the lips, of Constance Philippa, of old!

(And yet, as a number of the observers privately queried themselves, Was this not a man, indeed? A twin of Constance Philippa's who was—who was unmistakably—a member of the *masculine gender?*)

Thus, I hope to convey to you, some small measure of the disruption that ensued, upon the brazen entrance of "Philippe Fox"—yet it is exceedingly difficult, for the minutes jarringly passed, and the words that sprang to Mr. Fox's lips so readily, and so rudely, were of a blatant Western distortion, devilishly problematic, for one of my background to correctly transcribe.

Mr. Basil Miller, cloaking himself in the mantle of civil and legal responsibility, sought to interrogate Mr. Fox, who, flushing an angry brick-red, was suspiciously reluctant to be interrogated; or even to display documents pertaining to his identity, and to his relationship with Constance Philippa, tho', as he loudly reiterated, he *had* such documents on his person. It may well have crossed Mr. Miller's mind (that gentleman not lacking in instinctive acumen) to ask this personage if, in fact, *he was Constance Philippa, in disguise as a man:* yet such was his gentility, and so highly developed his sense of what might, and what might not, be spoken aloud, in a company mixed of gentlemen and ladies, that he naturally held his tongue; and the question went unasked.

The minutes passed, and now the first strokes of noon were sounded, and yet the contention persisted, primarily between Mr. Miller and Mr. Fox, tho' Mr. McInnes, being a fellow attorney, offered, after some hesitation, to give *his* opinion; and the doctor of medicine in the gathering, Dr. Moffet, emphatically delivered his judgment—that, as no lady would wish, or dare, or know how to, wear the garments of the opposite sex, this personage could not, under any circumstances, be Constance Philippa, whom he had known very well, he asserted, in her girlhood. "And a quiet, reposed, devout young miss she was," the elderly physician asserted. So distraught did Dr. Moffet become, as he spoke, that he ended by shaking his palsied fist at Mr. Fox, and crying: "What have you done with our young lady, you cad?"

Confusion and dismay! And grave concern, as to Constance Philippa's fate: for it spread through many minds, as the discussion raged on, that if, indeed, Philippe Fox *were* the renegade Constance Philippa, in male attire, might this not, in its obscene defiance of all the laws of nature, be a more heinous fate than nearly any other, which might be imagin'd by her kinsfolk? Octavia, having flushed an unhealthy crimson, was seated almost haphazardly in her chair, and vigorously fanning herself; so distressed, she bade the solicitous Mr. McInnes to let her be, and would not hear of it, that a servant be enjoined, to bring her a glass of ether and water, or Miss Emmeline's Remedy, to revive her spirits. Under her breath this distraught sister murmured: "It is *she*—it is *she*—but so horribly attired—so hideously changed—in masculine raiment—dear Constance Philippa—our lost sister—ah, *it is she,* after twenty years: *and yet not she, but a devil in her place!*"

Thus that sister, who, I hope I do not speak too explicitly in affirming, surely possessed, in her heart, the most bounteous sisterly affection; yet Malvinia, too, expressed great dismay, staring, and so struck by the horror of "Philippe Fox," that she could not open her fan, but held it before her, in her gloved hand, in an attitude of mesmeriz'd bewilderment. Constance Philippa?—and yet not Constance Philippa? Might this gentleman be a long-lost cousin, or even a twin? How familiar he looked! And his stance, and his manner, and his flashing dark eyes, and the impudence of his noble brow! Ah, how tantalizingly familiar! And yet—who was he?

Deirdre lifted her veil, to observe more closely, and satisfied herself, that the intruder was no one other than her eldest sister, in convincing disguise: for, being naturally narrow-hipped, and lean, and deep of voice, she could have no great difficulty in playing the part of a man, so long as no one examined too closely. Deirdre did not recall Constance Philippa with much clarity, or, indeed, much affection, but she believed she would recognize that inimitable expression of hers anywhere—a curious, and not uncharming, admixture of the satiric, and the outraged, and the amused, and the childishly *hopeful.* She had, in all, become a very attractive man: tho' rather too abrasive, and rough in his gestures, for Kiddemaster Hall.

The impetuous Samantha then arose, and advanced upon Mr. Fox, to extend her hand, and to say: "You do not know me, for I very much doubt that my eldest sister troubled, to speak of *me:* but I am Samantha, her youngest sister, now Mrs. Nahum Hareton, and very pleased to make your acquaintance."

It was the effect of this bold gesture, to disconcert Mr. Fox, rather than to console him (or her) in the folly being perpetrated; tho' that had been furthest from Samantha's intention. (She had divined a certain fixedness of notion, and a very real, if latent, ferocity, on the part of Philippe Fox, and had reasoned, it would seem admirably, that the wisest strategy might simply be, to acquiesce to the duplicity; there being the worry, too, that Mr. Fox carried, hidden inside his handsome cream-colored jacket, a handgun.) After a moment's hesitation, Mr. Fox did shake her hand, the while muttering, gruffly, that of course he knew her —he knew them all—Constance Philippa had told him *all*—and it was no use, their hoping that he was a mere *stranger,* to be lied to, and humored, and defrauded, of any inheritance that might be Constance Philippa's.

Whereupon the patriarchal John Quincy Zinn, rising unsteadily to his full height, and peering at the vulgarian interloper over his half-moon spectacles, declared, in a voice quivering with noble revulsion, and incredulity: "Would that the Twentieth Century never arrives, if it brings us such obscenities!"—and, leaning heavily on a servant's arm, insisted upon being led away, that he might purify his soul, in a place of solitude. "It is not possible," he murmured, shaking his grizzl'd head, "that I have seen, what I have seen."

This kingly exit had the effect of subduing the others, and even the brash Philippe Fox appeared somewhat crestfallen, turning on his heel to stare, with sombre blinking eyes, at the retreating back of the old gentleman. His lips moved, as if he might speak: but naturally he *dared not* speak, to further contaminate the sensibility, of that man who was, or had been, Constance Philippa's respected sire.

Now in the hushed silence that ensued, Basil Miller being, for the moment, stymied, as to how best to proceed, the assemblage was startl'd, to see Mrs. Zinn rise from her chair: the general thought being that, as Mr. Zinn's devoted wife, she would wish to follow him, and provide such succor and solace, as only the wifely consort can provide, in such predicaments. But Mrs. Zinn, stout-bodied in her purple drapery, her enormous leg-o'-mutton sleeves giving her a regal—nay, a *kingly*—aspect, made her way with no assistance to Mr. Fox, who, with great unease, and visible nervousness, bowed low before her: and this imperial lady, summoning forth all the steely graciousness of her Kiddemaster blood, spoke unsmilingly, yet not sternly: "I know not, Mr. Fox, if you are more aptly to be called my *long-lost daughter,* or, indeed, that benighted *emissary* of hers, which you make claim to be: and, as I am not accustomed to amusing myself, in charades, deceptions, and histrionic displays, I cannot further perplex myself, as to the true nature of the situation, if, indeed, any *true nature* there be." At this, Mrs. Zinn paused to draw breath, and the clock's ticking solemnly sounded, and Mr. Fox, his tann'd countenance darkening still further, bowed again, in mute and respectful submission. Mrs. Zinn then continued, extending a lace-glov'd hand, for him to kiss: "As, it is assumed, my dear departed Aunt Edwina watches o'er this assemblage, from her heavenly abode, we must acquiesce to her wishes: which, I cannot doubt, would involve a resumption of the proceedings, and a reading of the Last Will and Testament. I propose that Mr. Miller admit you to this private chamber, and, indeed, welcome you, as if both, or any, or all, possibilities were enmesh'd: my long-lost daughter Constance Philippa; or her designated agent Mr. Fox; or any combination thereof, which, tho' offensive to the civilized mentality, may yet prove acceptable, and pragmatic, so far as the *law* is concerned."

This excellent compromise being heartily accepted by all, and even pleasing to Philippe Fox, to some extent, the proceedings were resumed: with such unlook'd-for results, I am scarce able to continue.

75

In adjudging the revelations that were subsequently made, upon this extraordinary day in the lives of the Zinns—indeed, in the accumulative history of the great House of Kiddemaster itself—I am, after many years of consideration, tempted to state that, for the assemblage, and for myself as well, the disclosure that Miss Edwina Kiddemaster had had *a private life,* was very nearly of equal weight, in terms of the incredulous consternation unleash'd, as to the precise *nature of that life.*

That she had known tempestuous passion; that she had known the heart's frenzied tripping, and the outlaw euphoria of the racing pulse; that she had known—alas, and paid dearly for her knowledge!—even the gratified contentment (however temporary, however false) of *believing herself loved,* by a man: all this, so quickly and roughly disclos'd, and coupled with a most astounding disclosure, precipitated such chaos in the hearts of her kinsmen, and in their embarrassed companions, that it is exceedingly difficult, to this day, to comprehend the gravity of all that transpired!

On the one hand, we are presented with Miss Edwina Kiddemaster, the esteem'd authoress, from whose pen there flowed, with a most tireless and skilled facility, upward of fifty volumes addressing themselves to certain of the most knotty problems of etiquette and behavior, of our time: a lady correct in every detail, gracious, benign, condescending, and fully at ease in the most distinguished company, of both this continent, and England. On the other, we are confronted with a headstrong creature, who, tho' by no means young at the time of her folly, nonetheless plunged into the most sordid of liaisons, the most sordid, that is, short of actual immorality. (For Edwina and her seducer *were* married; and their

557

sole child was born, if we are to trust the official documents, some days past nine months, of the wedding morn.)

Alas, how piteous the irony, that, in the very same week of October, 1861, that one of Miss Edwina Kiddemaster's most influential prose pieces, "Thy Will Be Done: Woman's Ministration, as Mother, Sister, and Daughter," appeared in *The Ladies' Wreath*, she met, quite by accident, or the cruelest fate, the blackguard gentleman who was to prove the author of her undoing—how piteous, and how tragical! That Captain Burlingame was the scion of an historic English house, and, indeed, the eventual cause of Edwina's inheriting even more riches than, in her frenzied fancy, poor Prudence suspected, does, perhaps, somewhat mitigate the situation, as to its barbarism: yet it is difficult to comprehend, let alone forgive, such behavior, in a Kiddemaster of her generation. . . .

But I am sorry: I speak in such haste, and with such artless passion, that, in violation of all the rules of narrative discourse, I have o'erleapt my story once again; and must restrain myself. That I have, as the historian of this family, suffered not a few shocks to my constitution, in the course of transcribing *all the truth,* and *censoring naught a whit,* is a fact that must be borne in silence: nor should the reader be deprived of those reputed pleasures, of discovering, for himself, in faithful chronological sequence, precisely what has happened.

Thus it is most instructive, to return to the Golden Oak room of Kiddemaster Hall, where Mr. Basil Miller, his healthsome cheeks grown ruddy from the recent contretemps, and, doubtless, in anticipation of the gravity of the scene now to unfold, under his professional direction, casts his solemn gaze out amongst the assemblage, and declares the hour arrived: for all the requirements of Miss Kiddemaster's Last Will and Testament have been met, in spirit if not precisely in letter. And now the great waxen seal must be broke, and the contents of the massive document revealed, in compliance with the law of the Commonwealth of Pennsylvania, and with the custom of the land.

The reader will sympathize, I hope, with those divers persons—including, I am bound to say, Miss Deirdre Zinn and Mrs. Samantha Hareton—who, tho' far beyond hoping, or expecting, that any monetary or other reward might come to them, nonetheless found themselves, ah! so very like children! *halfway* surrendered to the wish: *Pray do not let me be forgotten.* Possessed of enough worldly sagacity, to know themselves thoroughly undeserving, and, in fact, to know the fantastical absurdity of their wish, these young ladies yet trembled inwardly, in anticipation of Basil Miller's pronouncements, with near as much dread and euphoric apprehension as Mrs. Zinn, whom both tradition and common sense—nay, and justice above all—would choose as the heiress, of the greater share of the fortune. It would be indeed a cruel sport, indulged in, doubtless, by many novelists, in their fictive fancies, to visit the secret hearts of each of the principals, in turn, to divulge their prayers, their fears, their wild baseless yearnings, whilst they retain masks of sombre decorum: or offer, even at this advanced date, countenances still sickl'd over, with mourning for the deceased woman. How the pale, drawn, subdued Malvinia, now but the wraith of her old beauteous self, clenched her gloved hands in secret, in her lap, the while staring at her cousin Basil (for whom, it should be said, she felt no rancor, or elemental dislike, for the part he had so whimsically played in her fall) as he opened the document, with elaborate ceremony; how poor Octavia, tho' giving every semblance of calm, and no longer breathing so laboriously, stared at her cousin with glassy eyes, praying *O Dear Aunt, please do not forget me: do not scorn me, and my child, another time!—for I fear my heart shall break.* And it would be remiss, to peer into Mr. Fox's heart, where, in all defiance of his impudent external form, and the bemused stoicism of his countenance, a child's blunt wish defined itself thusly: *Please!—and I will be good, forevermore.*

The atmosphere having grown most unpleasantly strained, Basil Miller cleared his throat, somewhat nervously, and, adjusting his spectacles, began to read, weakly at first, and then gaining strength, as, it would seem, the spirit of Edwina Kiddemaster was evoked, and certain of her voice rhythms observed. " 'Now that you are all, at last, assembled together, in our great ancestral home, as God has intended you to be—by ties of blood, as well as sentiment and loyalty—I will resist chiding you, my dear nieces, for your divers acts of ingratitude' "—thus read Mr. Miller, glancing up, of a sudden, at the drawn faces of the principals, and all the rest, who stared at him most blankly, " 'resist chiding you, and come directly to the point: I have passed many a month in torment, communing daily—nay, hourly—with Almighty God, Whose will, in every particular, I am bound to confess I did not always scrupulously observe, in my long life: I have humbled myself upon my knees, in the privacy and sanctity of my bedchamber; I have made many a surreptitious visit to churches, as the bells of midnight lugubriously tolled; I have sought the wise pastoral counsel of divers gentlemen of the cloth, ofttimes veiled, and under an assumed name. I have, in short, plumbed the depths of my own heart, to discover there not a malevolent, nor even a wicked, demon, but ah! how more humiliating! a *crabbèd and penurious creature,* not unlike a humped dwarf, luridly ugly of visage, and of an odor redolent of Dr. Eupep's Black Draught and Rhubarb Compound, left o'erlong in the bottle.' " At this point Basil Miller paused, to draw breath, and, doubtless, to steady himself, for, tho' we must remember that, as Edwina Kiddemaster's attorney and confidant, *he knew all,* he was, nonetheless, greatly affected by the arduous tension in the room, which seemed to be increasing minute by minute; nor was his refined sensibility oblivious, to the poignancy of the words he was reading aloud.

So he drew breath, and dabbed at his warm forehead with a handkerchief, and resumed: " 'And it was also the case that Almighty God, in His infinite compassion and mercy, allowed me to realize certain Truths, the which, in my worldly vanity and frippery of prose, I had oft *presented*, with but a modicum of inward conviction: alas, oft with very little conviction at all, but much secret jesting, and mockery! These are the sacred and fundamental Truths of our abode here on earth, and must not be sported with, else God's wrath is a terrible thing, as it rains upon our incredulous heads. Had I time, my dear nieces, I would instruct you with greater wisdom, and greater patience, than I did, in my lifetime: but this can be neither the time, nor the place, and I am obliged to insist upon brevity, in the matter of *penury*, and *generosity;* and *Christian charity;* and the *sacred obligations of the nobility* (by which, I hasten to explain, I mean a nobility of the spirit, as well as one of the blood); and the riddling question with which I have wrestled, both as an authoress, and a woman, upward of seven decades, *What constitutes a lady?* Ah, the fool responds with alacrity, to declare that a lady is no less, and no more, than what we have been taught from the cradle onward: a Lady is this, a Lady is that!—she *is* not this, nor does she *do* that! Jabber, jabber, jabber like monkeys in liveried vests, their furry tails atwist about their heads! Chatter, and gibber, and prattle, and rattle, and babble, repeating by rote all we have been instructed! A Lady embodies all that is high, holy, and pure in strength of intellect, clarity of heart, uprightness of moral principle; and that winning grace which makes every word and action seem "wisest, virtuousest, discreetest, and best" (to quote the Bard), to the beholder. All this, freely granted. We cannot subscribe to the vulgar *arriviste* notion, so promiscuously held, by those barbarian millionaires in our midst (whose names, do not fear, shall not appear in this sacred document, to sully it), that wealth, ostentation of dress, abode, and manner of living, and station (of a coarse political and financial type), make the Lady: or even, I insist, make her *possible.* Nay, this is repulsive. This is blatant ignorance. This cannot be allowed. . . .' "

The pretty French clock now striking the half-hour, Basil Miller again paused, tho' halfway dreading to glance up, to see the rigid countenances of his kinsfolk, and those others, who, seated immobile in their chairs, continued to stare with unblinking eyes, in whose glazed depths a curious commingling of *fatigue*, and *anxiety*, might be beheld.

Nevertheless, this sensitive gentleman did feel obliged to pause, and to inquire of a servant, whether he might have a glass of iced water —nay, perhaps a small glass of sherry, the hour now being well past noon —and again he wiped decorously at his dampening brow, and at his handsome curled mustache, before resuming his professional duty: all the while, I should make clear, standing proudly erect, behind the es-

critoire, in a fashionable but by no means gaudy black dress suit possessed of four cloth-covered buttons, and admirably wide lapels, the
which crossed over very high on his chest, to hide, unfortunately, the
black silken waistcoat he wore, and to reveal little of the plaster-of-starch
stiffened shirt, which announced to the eye, at collar, and cuff, a most
remarkable dazzling whiteness.

The servant bringing him his glass of sherry, he sipped lightly from
it, and, again adjusting his spectacles, drew breath, to resume: " 'This
cannot be allowed. Nay, is not a Lady one who, tho' being of the female
persuasion, ne'ertheless feels, in her pulsing veins, the *moral strength* (if
not the physical), of the male? Nay, and is not a Lady one who, tho'
dwelling in a humble rustic cottage, or in a marbl'd palace, ne'ertheless
submits to Our Saviour's enjoinders, as to charity, and love, and compassion, and giving alms to the poor—"alms," it may be, of the *heart,* and
not merely of the pocketbook? Does not a Lady exhibit symmetry of
character? nobility of purpose? refinement of taste? generosity to all?
virtue in its broadest respects? Is not a Lady one who, tho' perhaps
lacking a splendid equipage, and showy finery, and all the idle pretensions of wealth, ne'ertheless displays to the world a *richness* of sentiment?
I believe it is not an exaggeration to say that *personal merit alone,* should
be the sole test by which to try the pretensions of all "Ladies," and water
will not more certainly find its own level, than will the numerous classes
of society, when subjected to so searching a test! (By which bold utterance, I am not pleading for a leveling system, of that invidious sort known
as "socialism," or "communism," which shall break down all necessary
distinctions in society; and reduce them to a common mass of insipidity,
and vulgarity. Nay—the Bible itself recognizes these distinctions; and
they are as essential to the order and harmony of the Body Politic, as are
the divers members of the human frame, to form one perfect whole.)
Personal merit alone then being our measurement—' "

Poor Basil Miller was interrupted, of a sudden, by a fit of coughing:
and was able to calm himself only after some troubled minutes, during
which Narcissa Gilpin, and one or two other of the elder ladies, hovered
about him, greatly concerned for his well-being. It was feared that his
throat was being scraped raw, by both the protracted speech, and the
profound import of the words, which could not fail to instill apprehension
in the speaker. But, the coughing spell abating, and another glass of
sherry quietly supplied, Basil regained his attentive posture, and continued, in a voice only slightly enfeebl'd.

" '*Personal merit alone* then being our measurement, I believe it is
not remiss to state that a Lady is one who, in defiance of the opinions of
conformist society, and even in defiance of the wishes of her own family,
is courageous enough—nay, Christian enough—not only to acknowledge
her sinful failings, but to make redress for them, to the best of her ability.

That I have been guilty for upward of three decades of a lamentable *penuriousness* of spirit, is my secret sin: the which, I have reason to know, Almighty God will forgive me, if I truly repent; and if, as He has bade, I offer a public confession, posthumous if needs be (for, I feel, I am not altogether strong enough, to step forward with the Truth, in my own lifetime). Thus—' " Basil Miller read, his voice breaking suddenly, so that he was forced to clear his throat, and drain his glass of sherry, and, now alarmingly red-faced, plunge forward, to the heinous part: " 'thus I declare this document to be my sole Will and Testament, executed by me, with no coercion, in the seventy-eighth year of my life, and, being of sound mind and body, and animated throughout these proceedings with a bounteous love for Our Lord and His Only Begotten Son, and all His creation, excepting of necessity the villains, blackguards, communists, reprobates, anarchists, gamblers, immoralists, Free Thinkers, unnatural Suffragettes, divers members of the Popish Church, and, indeed, all manifestations of the Antichrist, in our time—I do hereby, on this 23rd day of September 1898, declare that I wish to divide my estate, including all its moneys, properties, and investments, in this wise: to my niece Mrs. Prudence Zinn, and her husband John Quincy Zinn, I shall *erase* the debt owed to me, of some several thousands of dollars, lent by me, from my estate, over a period of years: this *erasure* to constitute an outright gift, bearing with it no obligations or responsibilities, on the part of the heirs.' " (Basil Miller hurried onward, not daring to draw breath, and certainly not daring to glance up at his kinswoman Prudence Zinn—nor could anyone else look her way, out of very shock and mortification. Poor Prudence! It is not for me to say, the consternation that flooded her heart at this moment; it is not for me even to hint, the mingled rage, shame, bafflement, nausea, incredulity, benumbedness, and simple animal desire for violence, that churned within her upright figure, even as Basil Miller made haste to proceed!—save only to remark that, *from this instant forward,* she was to be a changed woman.) " 'To my four nieces, Constance Philippa, Malvinia, Octavia, and Samantha—' " and here, tho' Basil did not pause, a decided ripple ensued, throughout the room, and one might have observed the stiffening of Deirdre's slender frame—poor Deirdre realizing, in such wise, that her great-aunt by adoption had not, evidently, considered her a niece: nor even—for so her shamed, fluttering thoughts ran—a rightful member of the Zinn family! " '—to my four belovèd nieces, I hereby leave, to be divided equally among them, all my personal possessions of a literary and bibliographical nature: by which is meant, *original manuscripts* of my books; *drafts; revisions; note-cards; galleys;* and other valuable matter, the which has been, over the decades, meticulously filed and indexed, and stored against harm, by humidity, heat, solar rays, the incursions of insects and other natural phenomena, in a vault adjacent to my bedchamber, and kept under strict lock and key—' "

It was an involuntary intake of breath, a sharp hissing sound, from one of the sisters, that, for a moment, disconcerted Basil Miller: coupled with, but a scant moment later, the muttered words: "The deuce! The *hell!*"—which, no one wishing to acknowledge, was passed by in silence; nor did these unfortunate eruptions repeat themselves. (It may have been the case, judging from Octavia's stunned and slack expression, and Samantha's quizzical green stare, that these two sisters failed entirely to absorb the import of the words, which Basil Miller had read.)

" 'The remainder of my estate—the remainder of my estate—' " the agitated attorney read, in a voice sadly faltering, even as the document in his hands betrayed a nervous trembling, " '—I wish to leave to' " —and here again he paused, to clumsily swallow, " '—to leave to my *daughter:* that blameless child so cruelly abandoned by her mother, in a paroxysm of moral cowardice, and unspeakable penury of spirit: abandoned, unacknowledged, near-forgotten, but *legitimate!—LEGITIMATE*, I say, in the eyes of God, and of the Law.' " Basil Miller now paused, to drain his glass of sherry, and, not wishing to look out at his audience, plunged at once back into the document atremble in his hands: " '—and of the Law. After many troubl'd years, ah! so gaily clothed in *outward material success,* and the *high regard of my peers,* during which the ignoble action of my youth continued to gnaw at my soul (tho' proudly unrepentant even to myself); and after some months, this past year, of especial spiritual anguish, in which Almighty God oft conferred with me, in the privacy of my bedchamber,—I am moved to reconsider not only all previous existing *wills,* pertaining to my estate, but my previous *life* as well, in which the sacred role of *MOTHER* was forsworn. But Almighty God, in his wisdom, mercy, compassion, and ceaseless diligence, regarding my sulli'd soul, has seen fit to allow me this small act of penitence, and reparation: that I must leave the remainder of my estate, whole and unencumbered, to this long-despisèd daughter—*unacknowledged,* but *legitimate*—the personage known firstly to the world as *Deirdre Bonner;* and, latterly, *Deirdre Zinn.*' "

I cannot convey the effect of this declaration, as it fell through the air: save that, as Basil Miller could not, for the moment, bring himself to continue, the beauteous Golden Oak room was plunged into a silence so preternatural, you would think all the human figures had turned to stone! —nor could a breath be heard.

In fact, after some stunned moments, when a single expletive "Deirdre—!" sounded, to shatter the stillness, it would have been most difficult to say, who, precisely, had made the utterance: whether it had erupted from one of the beings in the room, or from out some unfathomable occult realm, the abode of bodiless spirits!

76

It were best, I believe, to follow the guiding aesthetic principle of this history, pertaining as to brevity, and thus to o'erlap the scene at hand, in the Golden Oak room—one whose startling disorder involved some fainting, on the part of the ladies (not excluding Deirdre herself, who slumped forward insensible, to sink to the floor in a helpless swoon, not many seconds after Basil Miller concluded); and much murmured, and muttered, stupefaction; and several unthinking expressions of ill-will, blurted out, as it were, involuntarily.

Instead, we will concentrate upon the reading of Edwina Kiddemaster's "secret priz'd shameful & glorious document" (for so the elderly lady called it, in her many conferences with Basil Miller, and in the privacy of her heart), the which transpired but some ninety minutes after the preceding scene, and in the selfsame place; all the principals in attendance, save the Reverend Hewett and his wife, who, tho' courteously saying very little, gave it out that they were so grievously offended by the disclosures, by the "once-esteem'd" Edwina Kiddemaster, that they felt it obligatory, out of consideration for Mr. Hewett's ministerial status, to remove themselves at once from the premises. But no one else chose to depart, not even the pouting Philippe Fox, who presented a somewhat stormy countenance to all who chanced to gaze upon him; nor the crimson-faced Dr. Moffet, who was heard to murmur beneath his breath, with an alarming persistence of repetition; "—betrayal—treachery—quackery at the spas—female senility—hysteria—wantonness—no shame—" Indeed, the principals evinced a most energetic interest in what Basil Miller offered as a "nobly forthright explanation, to be read, in submission to the deceased's dictates, by himself, in the presence of all concerned"—

564

and I am relieved to report that, summoned by his wife, John Quincy Zinn himself deigned to reappear, pallid of complexion, and now more visibly tremulous: but dignified nonetheless, and refusing to give vent to those haphazard expressions of emotion, of divers sorts, to which most of the others surrendered, the while Miss Deirdre Zinn remained isolated, now more clearly excluded than before.

Herewith, "The Confession of a Penurious Sinner":

What is that melody, vile in its very beauty, & tempting, across e'en the span of 38 years!—what is that loathsome song, which nightly assails my ears, & will not give me rest? Ah, to hear it; and again hear it; to thrill to it; & sink upon my bed, in mute despair; to hear it, & *to suffer it*—the while, with all the outward display of majestic calm, the years pass!

That my heart, so long ossified in other respects, might be, yet, prick'd to a secret frenzy, by this simple melody— this most haunting of immortal songs, by the German composer of uncontested genius Franz Schubert!—ah, what sorrow, what grave irony, and yet, I am compelled to say, what *justice:* for, tho' much confus'd at the time, I was not blameless, and take pen in hand, upon this wind-tormented midnight, to *confess:* to confess to the world, as Almighty God has gently bade me, both the gravity and penury of my sins, in the hope that, God having promis'd forgiveness, and restitution to His bosom, in that other realm we know not of, *the world* might pity me, and forgive me: and my long-lost daughter might comprehend the motives of my sin—tho' I scarcely expect *forgiveness,* let alone *daughterly love,* after my crime.

Adieu! Adieu, indeed! And yet, was it not a salutation as well, upon that momentous eve, in the great house of the Buffs, of Mt. Buff, Annandale-on-Hudson, not six months after the rebel assault upon Ft. Sumter?

For there—in the larger of the drawing rooms, of Mrs. Buff, the while a ball gaily ensued, in a near wing of the house, there I first heard Elisha's robust baritone voice, and thrilled to its manly prowess, all unknowing in my virgin simplicity (tho' advanced in years, as the coarse world would adjudge: being in my forty-first year, & much accustomed to sophisticated society, as well as flatterers & sycophants of every hue, as a consequence of my Kiddemaster blood, & my renown as an authoress)—all unknowing, I say, in my *innocence* & *ignorance,* who had imagin'd herself immune, to both male fortune-hunters, and to the tumultuous contingencies, of her own heart.

Cruel, & insufferable!—that so much pain should ensue, & such folly, from a haphazard visitation to the Buffs, at their elegant ancestral abode (Mrs. Amanda Buff being an old friend, from careless girlhood days, in the Philadelphia Seminary for Young Ladies, some years before); nay, from a haphazard visitation to that very drawing room, so tastefully decorated by Amanda Buff's discerning hand, in rococo-style carved pieces, of pleasing grace, and luxurious velvet drapes of that hue later to be known as Sebastapol blue, and a craved marble mantel, from out a pagan Turkish palace, inherited from Amanda's family! For there, in that elegant retreat from the merry but o'erexuberant sounds of musical revelry, in the ballroom, there it was my fate to o'erhear Captain Elisha Burlingame of the Union Forces (then on furlough, to visit his invalided mother, in Albany) zealously, yet with a conscious sensitive touch, singing the Schubert melody, whilst one of Amanda's elder sisters played the piano.

Alas, to *hear;* and to feel my heart *pierced;* and to know almost *beforehand,* what pain would ensue. . . .

For here was the dashing Captain Burlingame, well over six feet of heighth, with his thick manly torso, and his powerful neck & countenance, that earned for him the fond appellation of his men, *The Bull,* for both his vigorous appearance, and his bold behavior under fire. Captain Burlingame was then in his early thirties, tho', for purposes of courtship, so far as the foolish Edwina Kiddemaster was concerned, he gave out his age as being somewhat older—not wishing to appear an inappropriate choice, for her husband. He wore a Union costume that had been, by special permission, modified, that it cut a showier figure, with a smart crimson necktie, and fuller sleeves; and his hair—ah, the very Devil himself could not have conspired, to create a more winning picture of *masculinity, & angelic charm!*—his hair fell in red-burnished curls & ringlets, to his muscular shoulders. Was there ever a warrior—not even excluding the comely Boy General, George Armstrong Custer—who cut a more compelling figure on the raging battlefield, or in Society's bastions?

I know not whether my frame shudders, even now, with *revulsion* for the recollect'd song, or (may God forgive me!) ignoble hapless *sentiment:* but this was the seductive verse, of the song's numerous verses, that most enthralled me—

Adieu! 'tis love's last greeting,
  The parting hour is come!
Yet dare I mourn when Heaven—
  Has bid thy Soul be free?
A fresher life has given
  For all ETERNITY.

Adieu! Adieu! Adieu! to self-respect, & rational discourse, & all pretensions as to sanity, let alone the *moral fibre* of a lady's being.

Thus—the lamentable meeting occur'd & the confirmed spinster Edwina Kiddemaster, tho' on the brink of that age, at which *romance*, let alone *childbearing*, is commonly deemed hazardous, fell prey—I know not to what. A poignant & haunting melody, or a skilled blackguard, of such charm, & acumen, & practice, as to make an outright thespian blanch in envy. . . .

It is true, it is too true, that Amanda Buff, & certain of her concern'd relatives, sought to warn me; & to dissuade me, & I did in fact doubt the Captain's seriousness, at the very first. (Well knowing myself of an age, & of a reputation, that must take especial care, not to be deceiv'd.) Yet—I know not how, or why, or the precise steps—yet I fell: *fell*, I state openly, with as much stormy ignorance, & ludicrous hope, as the lowest servant girl, her ears gratefully blushing to hear all the prevarications, of which the masculine gender is capable!

I do not—indeed, *cannot*, in acquiescence to God's will—stint my words on this matter: I heard, & saw, & was in a matter of days enthralled, & secretly betrothed, & FELL.

FELL: in such humiliating wise, as I cannot bring myself to recount, reasoning that very little of a fructifying nature can come of it, save as a warning to the young ladies amongst us, who would, in defiance of their elders' warnings, & deeming it but a lightsome escapade, *slip away from a chaperon.* For thus I did: submitting to Captain Burlingame's blandishments, that I accompany him, alone, by phaeton, to the races at Saratoga Springs, some distance to the North . . . during the course of which wild journey, securely lock'd in the handsome canary-yellow vehicle, the impetuous Union Officer seized my defenseless hand in his great-sized hand, &, bringing it violently to his lips, bestowed so vehement a kiss upon it, that—

(Alas, I cannot continue: save to state, with as much frankness as decorum allows, that, upon that paralyz'd instant, I FELL, & ne'er was a virgin again.)

This unspeakable episode having transpired, it was swiftly succeeded by a secret *betrothal* (for I knew full well, the rage of my brother Godfrey should he learn), &, on the very eve of Elisha's departure for the War, a secret & shameful *wedding*.

All of which—I am greatly reliev'd now to confess—tho' witnessed by only two of Elisha's comrades, was nonetheless in compliance with the Law of the Land; & duly recorded, in the books of the Justice of the Peace, for Saratoga Springs, one darksome day in the autumn of 1862. I shall not pose Our Saviour's question, as to who, in our midst, is so blameless of sin, as to "cast the first stone": for I am beyond all such strategies, in seeking to alleviate my guilt. Yet—I cannot resist querying, who, in our midst, is so hardened of heart, as to be *immune* to Romance, in its numerous masks & costumes?

So it was, I went to dwell with my bridegroom in a "honeymoon cottage" of sorts, having given out the false information—for which lie, may God forgive me—that I had sailed away to the British Isles, to live for some time in solitude, for authorly purposes.

Alas, very soon afterward, e'en the foolish bride had no choice but to be disabused, of her airy notions: for her dashing Captain exhibited scant patience, for feminine decorum, or recalcitrance; & made bold to request—nay, to *demand*—cash for his insatiable vices, in which he freely indulged himself, the while the very War was waging!

Tear-dimm'd as those days & months have become, I yet recall the boisterous shouts of my husband, & the trembling cords that stood out, in his powerful neck, as, in great scorn of my *condition*, he did not shrink from corporeal abuse; & the spouting of such words, as to make my elderly ears burn crimson, at the mere recollection. For, tho' the descendant of a noble house, in Warwickshire, & indeed the grandson of the much-loved Sir Reginald Burlingame, Elisha was *yet no gentleman;* & it was not difficult to comprehend, why, at the age of seventeen, he had been encouraged to leave his native land, & seek his "fortune" in the New World, eager to become a citizen of the States, & to give free rein to his barbaric lusts, in those ranks of the Army that dealt with the question of the Indians, in the territories of Kansas & Nebraska, & elsewhere. (These heathenish natives, amongst them "Cheyennes" & "Sioux," yet evoking in my heart some measure of pity, for the great losses they sustained, & the persistent butchery, on the part of such patriotic warriors as Captain Burlingame!)

The War itself continuing, my villainous husband, now assisting General Sheridan, led vengeful cavalry charges upon the thinn'd ranks of rebel units, in the Shenandoah; & boasted that he "had no pity to spare," for the Confederate traitors, nor e'en for those civilians, whose misfortune it was to cross his path. When, on leave from these sanctioned slaughters, *The Bull* betook himself to Washington (in shameless disregard of his ignor'd bride, at this time sequestered, with a very small household staff, in a small village on the Hudson—the while her deceiv'd family thought her to be touring Europe), it was yet to indulge himself in his vices, with as much angered frenzy, as he expended in the heat of battle. (Must Vice have a name?—a specific title? Drinking—gambling, at poker & at the racetrack—consorting with females, of the most rank & promiscuous station—drunken brawling with his own comrades: such were the absorptions of my *husband,* & the *father-to-be,* of an innocent baby girl!)

That Almighty God did *not* forsake me, in my time of deepest despair, is evident in the fact that my confinement, tho' prolonged for some fifteen agoniz'd hours, & hideously interrupted by the *emergence of the blackguard* into the downstairs of the dwelling place (where, for some unfathom'd reason, he rode his neighing & snorting & stamping stallion into the foyer, thus injuring the old parquetry—the action of a drunken brute!), this confinement, with its extreme suffering, both of the spirit and the flesh, ne'ertheless resulted in the birth of a perfectly-form'd INFANT GIRL.

AN INFANT GIRL SUBSEQUENTLY CAST ASIDE, BY HER DESPAIRING MOTHER.

Adieu!—adieu: an innocent babe, & its rampaging father!

Elisha Burlingame, a captain of cavalry never advanced, save for a few weeks, when, due to the exigencies of the War, he was given the brevet rank of Lieutenant-Colonel—then, to his shame, promptly demoted, as a consequence of carousing & brawling; a self-proclaimed *patriot* of his adopted country, who so mistreated the soldiers in his regiment, he ordered deserters shot without trial, & wounded men, who, for some incalculable reason, had earned his displeasure, forbidden medical treatment (& how the vain-

glorious Captain had boasted of his soldierly skills, one day
to earn him the rank of General!)

Adieu!—Captain Elisha Burlingame, with your coarse yet
handsome face; your flaring nostrils; your tumbling red-
brown curls; your bristling whiskers! Adieu, treacherous
husband, mounted so arrogantly upon your thoroughbred
stallion, your broad-brimmed gray hat rakish upon your
head, your crimson scarf astir in the breeze, your laughter
loud, zestful, & pitiless!

"Ugly as sin! All a wager! Go away! Allow me to wake
up!"—thus the drunkard husband stormed, scarce knowing
what he said, upon returning to his home, very late one
night, from an officers' club, an Indian scalp (cured &
tanned, he afterward claimed) askew on his head, beneath
his captain's hat. "Allow us to wake," the bulging-eyed villain shouted, "from this gangrenous nightmare!"

Adieu, husband; adieu, baby; adieu—*love.*

For it was not long after the birth of the despised child,
that the father died: in a quarrel, it was said, in a camp near
Stafford, Virginia, where cavalry & infantry were stationed,
prior to that great battle of the War to be fought at Gettysburg—the which Captain Burlingame never saw. A quarrel
over cards—or over the favors of a female camp-follower,
of teenage years—or out of surly drunkenness: culminating
in a duel of sorts, tho', by all accounts, hardly more than a
murderous assault, in which two well-matched bullies, my
husband & a twenty-eight-year-old Brigadier-General, so
grievously wounded each other, both died within hours.

Adieu!—*'tis love's last greeting.*

The infant daughter, tho' blameless, was cast aside by her
betrayed mother; & given out to secret adoption, by a childless couple, who were said by all who knew them, to be
God-fearing, frugal, & industrious—yet, such was my delirium, & my zeal for revenge against Elisha, that I cannot
claim to have greatly *cared,* as to the fate of the child. Nay,
I cannot claim to have *contemplated* it at any length, save as
an affliction, a badge of shame, to be eradicated with as
much dispatch as possible, thus freeing me to leave the
scene of my ignominy behind, & sail for England. (It is not
altogether accurate, to say that my status as *Mrs. Elisha
Burlingame* remained secret: for, at the extreme of my distress, I had need of the counsel & support of my elder
brother Godfrey, who, surprising in his anger'd sympathy,
once seeing that *revenge* against a dead man was pointless,

gave me invaluable advice as to the future; &, tho' keeping free himself of the particulars, saw to it that a worthy & close-mouthed lawyer was retained, to aid me in the legal technicalities my unfortunate predicament had engendered. It was this lawyer—now long deceased, alas—who made careful inquiry, as to the very best home for my baby; and this lawyer, who arranged for Mr. Herman Bonner to be employed, on a clerical or managerial level, at one of my brother Vaughan's most prosperous factories. And—such are the glorious omnipotencies, of the Law!—it was this well-practic'd lawyer who arranged for so thorough an eradication of my status as *Mrs. Elisha Burlingame,* that I was able to resume, with all propriety, my maiden name, *as if the unspeakable marriage had never taken place.*)

And so it seemed!—and so I deluded myself, for upward of thirty years!

The while, I absorbed myself in my *worldly career,* & acquired a reputation of some strength, & sufficient monetary reward, to make the sustained effort more than an idle lady's amusement. An authoress whose works are, I am told, read & enjoyed by one out of every four Americans; precious for their close instruction, in the difficulties of social intercourse, & in moral comport, in these troubl'd times. (I know not whether proper etiquette be an *art,* or only a *craft:* that it is *difficult,* there is no doubt. And, as it cannot be acquired by instinct, it must be *learned.*)

Thus I deluded myself; & was not, in truth, unhappy. For I enjoy'd the company of the most worthy members of Society; I took pleasure in my travels, & speeches before divers assemblies, & literary friendships, with such persons as Mrs. Sigourney, and Mrs. Ann Stephens, and the Reverend Hargreave Tupper (author of the excellent *Proverbial Philosophy*), and many another star in our firmament. Such was my self-esteem, & contentment in my work, that the uncanny coincidence that my very own daughter should be adopted by my niece and her husband, & brought to dwell within a mile of my own home, *did not impress me at the time as more than a minor vexation.* For, tho' I knew that "Deirdre Bonner" was in fact my own child, sent away nameless from my side, to be baptiz'd by strangers, & tho' I believed it to be a mistake of judgment (alas, a not atypical lapse, in the Zinns' household), that she be adopted into our family, I did not feel any deep or tumultuous stirring, of emotion. That the adoption was a *mistake,* seemed to many of us patently clear: not because of the identity of the orphan, but because of the grave & chronic financial uncertainties, of that household calling itself, with some small smugness, the Octagonal House—tho' known amongst the Kiddemasters, & I believe in the village as well, by such less flattering appellations as "Dog-Hutch," "Crank-Cottage," & "Zinn's Folly." (My canny-minded brother Godfrey, tho' rarely lacking in generosity, oft stated that making loans to his son-in-law was but "throwing good cash down a rat hole—the rat hole, & the rats within, possessing a *perpetual* appetite"—this acerbic jest being lost, to those unfamiliar with the heroic toil, of many years, of our Bloodsmoor inventor, in his pursuit of the chimerical *perpetual-motion machine.*)

It is amazing to me now, in my enlighten'd state, that I could not perceive the hand of Almighty God, in that autumn of 1873, when my niece and her son-in-law brought home *my very own daughter!*—to dwell in their midst, amongst their own four girls, as *Deirdre Zinn,* late a pathetic orphan, cast upon the waters of Fate, by her adoptive parents' deaths. Nay, was I blind?—was I mad?—was I so puff'd up with the false splendors of my station in Society, & with my e'er-increasing literary fame, that *I could not discern Our Lord's intention?*

A mystery to me now—& one that does not, perhaps, repay too close a scrutiny, if I am to be left with any shred of self-respect, & belief in my own ratiocinative powers.

Yet I cannot truly think that I was blind; or mad; or even greatly absorbed by the public reputation of "Miss Edwina Kiddemaster," or by her increasing wealth—the which, as I had no need for it, was simply channeled into the family's investments, there to healthfully grow, in both times of boom & recession. Nay, I believe I was naught but deficient in feeling: hollow of heart: sterile of soul: *penurious in spirit.*

For which, I pray my once-despised daughter will forgive me: as God has only recently indicated, *He* has forgiven me.

Thus, by this Last Will & Testament, I, Edwina Kiddemaster, once the fool bride of Elisha Burlingame, do seek to make amends: as, Mr. Basil Miller will presently indicate, that great gentleman Sir Reginald Burlingame, the grandfather of Elisha, & consequently the great-grandfather of that child known as *Deirdre Zinn,* sought to make amends for his grandson's villainy, by bequeathing, on his deathbed, a substantial portion of his English properties, including partnerships in divers London, Birmingham, & Liverpool businesses, & some modest share of stock in an India-trade shipping line, & his ancestral home Burlingame Hall, in Warwickshire—all to the lost child, by way of a clause entrusting the fortune to *me,* for safekeeping. (That unparallel'd gentleman comprehending how, during my lifetime, I should be greatly distressed, by any disclosure of my shameful past, the which would surely have been uncovered, by gossipers, backbiters, & rabid journalists, should he have left this fortune directly to my daughter.)

These various bequeaths are made in full cognizance, I must make clear, of the unhappy fact that past sorrows cannot be erased, by present actions, however generous: & that the spirited bitterness of the spurned child, who guessed, in her heart, something of the *loss* she had endured, was, in the eyes of God & man, *entirely justified.* And yet—it is my fervent prayer, as, I believe, it was Sir Reginald Burlingame's, that the penury of soul exhibited by myself, and, perhaps, others amongst Kiddemasters & Zinns, *can yet be forgiven,* by an action of Christian charity, springing forth from within the heart of the lost child.

Thus, this Last Will & Testament, & this trifling literary attempt, not for publication, but only for private perusal, "The Confession of a Penurious Sinner," are offered as both legal *documents,* & heartfelt *prayers,* that, her faith in familial love having been so sorely tested, my daughter, *Deirdre Zinn,* shall yet (for it is not too late) experience that awakening of emotion, in the human breast, that is known by the wise as *love*—& too quickly cast aside, by the ignorant, reckless, & vainglorious, as mere *weakness,* to which the female sex is in particular prone.

Tho' the hour is late—alas, the proud old bells of Trinity have chimed *four!*—& I sense myself sadly enfeebl'd, I cannot bid farewell to those whom I love so dearly, without copying, in this document, a poem of singular inspiration, that flowed from my pen one morn some years ago, as I sat myself down, for my customary six-hour stint, before the midday repast, & to my astonishment felt not a whit of interest, in the subject at hand (tho' a most intricate problem, of grave social consequence, pertaining to the employment of *stuffed,* & of *imitation,* furred creatures—amongst them martens, minks, squirrels, small rabbits, and even, upon occasion, the handsomer breed of cat, and the comelier members of the ouistitis family—in the hats, bodices,

and sleeves, of ladies of fashion, in the Eighties): I sat myself
down, as I said, &, most astonish'd, pushed aside the manuscript upon which I was working, & drew out a fresh sheet
of paper, & felt my pen quiver with the giddy energies of the
Muse, so rarely allowed me in my lifetime: & penned, within
the space of a transcendent hour, this poem—later,to appear, under a pseudonym, in *The Ladies' Wreath:*

FAME

O tell me not that lofty minds may bow
In reverential homage, to a thought of *mine*—
That laurels yet may greenly deck this brow,
Or that my silent grave may be a shrine
In after-years, where men may rudely crowd,
To mark how low my once-great dust is bow'd.

O Fame is not for Woman: she must yield
The very essence of her being up;
Bare her full heart, fling off its golden shield,
And drain its very life to fill the cup!—
Which, like a brimming goblet rich with wine,
She poureth out upon the world's broad shrine.
Upon its golden rim they grave her name,
Fling back the empty bowl—and this is Fame!

And yet—methinks if sometimes lingered one
Whose noble presence unto me hath been
As music to the harp, around the home
Which death hath given me, though all unseen,
The sweet, mysterious sympathies which drew
My love to his, as blossoms drink the dew,
Would once again arouse a spirit strife,
And wake my marble heart once more to life.
Ask me not then to toil for wealth, and fame,
But touch my heart with sweet affection's name!

Thus, Mr. Basil Miller concluded his poignant reading of
that remarkable document, "The Confession of a Penurious
Sinner," from the pen of Miss Edwina Kiddemaster, deceased: and I am not able to convey, in the frail apparatus
of words, the atmosphere of tearful release, that reigned
supreme in the Golden Oak room!—save to say that not an
individual remained *unmov'd;* and there were one or two,
whose lives were permanently alter'd.

77

Before proceeding with my story, and leaping ahead to that hour, but a few days later, when, beneath that very same roof, the magnanimous Deirdre made her pronouncement (as to the *equal distribution* of her new-gained wealth, amongst her family), there is a small correction that should be made, for the benefit of the scholarly reader.

A minor, and, I think, a not very significant fact: that that song known to thousands of music-loving Americans, as Schubert's "Adieu! 'Tis Love's Last Greeting," was not from the pen of that composer at all —but from that of one *August Heinrich von Weyrauch,* of whom, I am afraid, very few of us have heard; tho' doubtless, considering his name, we should judge him a compatriot of Herr Schubert.

This error, I should hasten to explain, was not Edwina Kiddemaster's alone, but a general error, amongst the publishers of sheet music, and the enthusiastic but untutor'd public. *Schubert* being famous, and *von Weyrauch* sadly unknown, it seems a comprehensible error, and one of no great import: so I hope that those readers of skeptical persuasion, of whom, I suppose, there are some, will not consider it an ironical note, in the midst of the deceased Edwina's noble pathos. For it is the *sentiment* of romance, and not the *precisian's exactitude,* that moves our hearts.

78

It was on a balmy April Sunday, but a week past Easter, that, at tea time, Deirdre rose to make her historic pronouncement, her once-pallid cheeks now flushed with warmth, and her darksome eyes shining with a pleasure almost girlish: she rose, and lifted her lovely proud head, and all in the room grew silent at once, in anticipation of her words.

Yet she was shy!—*she*, the new mistress of Kiddemaster Hall, and the inheritrix of such incalculable wealth!—so that, at the very first, her voice quavered, and she was obliged to grip quite tightly her crimson silk-and-sandalwood fan.

"It is my wish"— Deirdre spoke—"of which a few individuals have already been informed, that my unlook'd-to good fortune not reside with me alone: for such, I cannot think, would have been the ultimate wish, of my deceased mother"—and here the greatly moved young lady paused, her eyes visibly moistening, and it was some seconds before she could continue —"my deceased mother, whose words, and whose model, have so powerfully impressed upon us all, the merit of Christian charity, and Christian love. That I might once, in my ignorance and self-absorption, have *imagin'd* injustice, and prejudice, and cruelty, and ill-will, and despair, and the minor sorts of failings—a niggardliness of spirit, an inappropriate jealousy, simple mockery—in the very midst of my adopted home, and, indeed, in the world in general, is a measure of my own blindness, of which I am now asham'd. Spite!—envy!—jeering glances, and curled lips!—revulsion for one's very *being*, on this earth: all this is not very flattering to me, when, at the present time, I cast my thoughts back, and realize that *my own* penury of spirit gave substance to these fancies, or, it may be, too energetically seized upon some small provocation, in the world, that, to feed my bitter heart, might then be exaggerated. For this troublesome imperfection in myself, *I* must beg *your* forgiveness: and pray that the past's negligible shadows might be forgot, in order that the greater share, which resided in sunshine, may, in memory, the more vividly define itself."

Deirdre then paused but a moment, her lovely bright eyes moving about the room, to rest upon the sympathetic and enthused countenances, that, in nearly every instance, were turned to her, as blooms to the April sun: and, taking heart from these encouraging expressions, and from some slow-gathering sense of her rightful significance (and, it may have been, from a modest—nay, reluctant—admission of her own healthsome beauty, the which had been skillfully enhanced, at her morning toilette, by Malvinia, whose practic'd and affectionate fingers had, once again, fashioned a most becoming hair style: a French chignon, its severity prettified by tight curls and loose, even languid, ringlets): taking heart too, we may assume, by her increasing sense that her mother *would certainly* have concurred, *did in fact concur,* as if her spirit dwelt in this very room!—she drew breath, and spoke more firmly, the while a girlish smile played about her finely sculpted lips: "It is my wish, then, which I have been encouraged to think, by Cousin Basil, is not only *just,* but, even more significant, to the law!—*practicable,* that I assign to him, and to his associates, the considerable responsibility of assessing my inheritance, that it might, as soon as is reasonably possible, be *divided equally* amongst myself, and those six persons closest to me: my dear parents, and my sisters, Mr. and Mrs. Zinn to constitute, as is only proper, *two* persons; and Mr. Philippe Fox, in his role as agent for Constance Philippa, to be allowed such share, as, were she present in the East, my eldest sister would then receive."

Tho', as Deirdre had indicated, one or two persons—amongst them Malvinia—knew beforehand, of the substance of this announcement, and tho' it would not have required an intelligence of great acumen, to anticipate, from various smiles and hints of Cousin Basil, that some very magnanimous—nay, queenly—disclosure was to be made, this little speech of Deirdre's was greeted with so stunned, and so gladsome, a general response, as to make the representation of it, in the chill rigors of prose, quite impossible! Imagine instead, if you will, a Bloodsmoor spring sickl'd over with the pale remnants of winter's snow, beneath a sombre and oppressive sky, ponderous with clouds: imagine, then, the first peepings of those lovely flowers known as *snowdrops,* forcing their valiant way through the cruel-crust'd earth: and then, of a sudden, the sun!—the sun!—bursting wide, and scattering the ill-visagèd clouds, to transform with his manly virility the very world itself, from horizon to horizon: but shining most significantly upon those selfsame *snowdrops,* that had, perhaps, registered some doubt, as to whether they had proceeded into the world with unwise precipitousness, and might have been preordained for a snowy death, and a snowy burial! But now my own words are inadequate; and I must give over, to one of the masters of our native poesy, Mr. Longfellow, who, in "The Lily and the Rose," illumines a scene not unlike the one I have painted, and concludes, in regard to the flowers with their "light and soullike wings"—

> And with childlike, credulous affection,
> We behold their tender buds expand;
> Emblems of our own great resurrection,
> Emblems of the bright and better land!

—and thus indeed it was, upon that momentous occasion in the history of the Kiddemasters, when all eyes without exception flooded with tears, and, at the last, the breathless young inheritrix *was* so moved, she turned aside weeping, to be crushed in an embrace by Octavia, and passionately admonished: "Oh, you are too good!—too good!—it is not deserved!— it is too generous!—our hearts will break!"

79

.

Ah, how passionately I should like to conclude *A Bloodsmoor Romance* upon this gladsome note, our heroine's Kiddemaster blood belatedly, but trenchantly, triumphing over her plebeian inclinations!—with, in fact, a sisterly embrace, all the more emotional, in that Deirdre and Octavia are not *sisters,* but *cousins:* the which relationship, as we have seen, is, in this particular context, a very special one indeed.

(Nor was the tearful Octavia the only sister to rush to Deirdre, to fold her in an embrace: the pale-lipped and trembling Malvinia also approached, as did the flushing, o'erjoyed Samantha; and, tho' he held himself at the periphery of the circle, for some minutes, Mr. Philippe Fox finally approached Deirdre as well, to offer her a vigorous, and very warm, handshake, and to thank her vehemently, in Constance Philippa's place, "for her Christian—nay, preternatural—munificence.")

Or, if it would strike the reader's sensibility as too abrupt, to consummate my history at this point, teatime of April 26, 1899, what a pleasure it would be, to do nothing more taxing than to leap sunnily ahead, and transcribe merely the felicitous events that lie in wait: the vast contentment enjoy'd by Samantha, and her devoted Nahum, and their several children, as a consequence of Deirdre's generosity; the flower-bedecked wedding of Malvinia and her faithful Malcolm Kennicott, in late September, in our historic old Trinity Church; the surprise betrothal of Octavia and the genial Sean McInnes, that tall, craggy-featur'd, red-haired Irishman, of whom it was said, by Octavia's family, that he behaved with as much natural dignity, as if he were an Anglo-Saxon. (It quite won their hearts, that Sean should so clearly adore his young stepson Lucius Quincy: a subdued, slender-framed, but gay-spirited child, whose infant's

579

blond hair was gradually darkening to a fine burnished red-brown: so that, one day, well before his teens, the *step*son might possess certain of the attributes of a *son,* quite by happenstance!)

Nor should I shrink from delineating certain of the remarkable changes undergone by Mrs. Zinn: the most defiant, perhaps, being her employment, as Mrs. Abba Goold Woolson's sponsor and aide, in the Ladies' Dress Reform Movement, of her *maiden name!*—as if she were but *Prudence Kiddemaster,* after so many fruitful decades, and never *Mrs. John Quincy Zinn.* Yet her stubbornness, and her perversity, were such that, despite her station, she insisted upon being known as *Miss Kiddemaster,* or even *Prudence!* (To her shame, Prudence was to be one of some seventy-five Dress Reform and Suffragette persons, arrested on Boston Common, for illicit marching, picketing, and demonstrating, in support of the futile "candidacy for President of the United States," of one of their number —this campaign undertaken despite the fact that the female sex *had not the privilege of the vote!* Was there ever a more foolish, and a more vainglorious, occupation? Prudence was seventy-six years old at the time of her arrest, in November of 1899, yet, when the examining magistrate sought to dismiss charges against her, that she might return home safely to her *husband,* her *children,* and her *grandchildren,* she vociferously protested, saying that her "home" was with her comrades in the movement: and if that meant jail, why then, jail it must be. "We are prepared," Prudence declared, "for all you can exact from us.")

Nor would I find it o'erly distasteful, tho' certainly it would be a sorrowful undertaking, to provide the reader with some small sense, of the mingled bitterness, and triumph, and frustration, and worry, and turmoil, and gratification, and puzzlement, to be endur'd by John Quincy Zinn: in part, because of his belovèd wife's defection; but more as a consequence of his still-deepening obsession with his work. (For the poor man took little pleasure, in his adopted daughter's generosity, feeling it, perhaps, no more than his due; and he seemed to know by instinct that he had but an abbreviated time to live—and to perfect, for future generations of Americans, the elusive principle of the *perpetual-motion machine.*)

Nor, I suppose, would it be entirely repugnant to me, to address myself to the predicament of the young heiress Deirdre Zinn: for, after several weeks, when the flurried excitement of the bequest had somewhat abated, she could not blind herself to the great paradox of her existence, *which suitor to accept.* (That other eligible bachelors were beginning to present themselves, not excluding certain Kiddemaster cousins, and Basil Miller himself!—does not concern us here, since it did not concern our heroine. Indeed, she cast a gaily sardonic eye upon these gentlemen, inquiring as to whether they sought *her,* or her *mother's daughter,* for a bride.) "Your newfound wealth, and your newfound station in society, do, I confess, gravely intimidate me," the noble-brow'd Dr. Stoughton said, bending a resolute gaze upon Deirdre, "yet, I am bound to say, no more than your beauty, and grace of person, of old." Thus Dr. Lionel Stoughton: and now hear the swarthy-skinned Hassan Agha, in *his* petition!

"In these wondrously-alter'd circumstances of yours, my dear Deirdre, you will require, more than ever, a *husband,*" Mr. Agha declared, in a low importunate voice, his eyes slyly shining. "A *husband,* moreover, who is not so lily-livered, as to be uxorious; nor so much of the rank and privilege of old society, as to commandeer your fortune, and you. Come, then, let us make an agreement at once: *will* you be my bride? My headstrong Lolo!"

Was there ever so bold, so vain, so impetuous a creature?

Possessed of the Indian cobra's eerie stealth, and the tiger's hot-gleaming eyes, with small even teeth, white as ivory, bared in a sensual smile: a complexion of amazing smoothness, yet olive-dark, and oft tinted by a fine film of damp, or oil: his date-black eyes thickly lashed, and outrageous in their presumed intimacy!—*this* is the suitor Deirdre could not bring herself to reject, tho' her heart, I am certain, resided with the Christian Dr. Stoughton. There may have been, from time to time, some subtle upsurging, in Mr. Agha's dark blood, of his mother's lineage—there may even have been, in the planes and angles of his face, some scarce-perceptible outline, of an Anglo-Saxon ancestor, the which drew Deirdre to him, against her wishes.

Once, there being no servant close by, Hassan Agha made so bold as to seize Deirdre's hand, and would have brought it to his o'erwarm lips, had she not snatched it away at once, and rose to her feet, her bosom heaving in visible distress. "You must leave!" the agitated young lady fiercely said. "I cannot be so insulted!"

As if uncoiling from his snake's posture, Hassan Agha rose languidly to his full height, and bowed, Deirdre knew not mockingly, or no, and murmured: "You are hardly insulted, my dear Deirdre, unless to be *loved,* and *desired,* is an *insult.*" These coarse words uttered, I am constrained to say, with all the elegance, and chill dignity, of which the son of a heathen prince might sometimes be capable.

These brief vignettes, constituting, as it were, a look into the future subsequent to that historic April Sunday, would not, I assume, greatly offend either the reader, or the authoress, were they more fully developed: yet my duty lies elsewhere; and I cannot any longer, in all conscience, forestall it.

That I, as the narrator, am not to *blame* for the sordidness of this particular enterprise, and that the sophisticated reader well comprehends this fact, does very little, I confess, to alleviate my sense of both *revulsion,* and *guilt.* Nor does the fact that, in seeking to illumine the duplicitous ways by which the eldest Zinn girl, Constance Philippa, alter'd herself, or was alter'd, into the outlaw Philippe Fox, I freely— nay, proudly—confess myself *I am ignorant of all detail, and wish to remain so.* For is not the artist, as I have argued earlier, obliged to serve the higher moral truths, in his or her craft? Is he not obliged to *better* the world, and not merely *transcribe* it?

Hard truths! A taxing mission! Yet, following the meritorious ex- ample of Our Saviour Himself, do we inhabit this vale of tears merely out of happenstance; or for a decided purpose?

Thus, I am wildly agitated, and have been so for many hours: indeed, when my thoughts veer to *this subject,* I am half tempted to aban- don my chronicle, even as it nears its consummation, after so many hundreds of meticulously wrought pages, and so many "serene sweet- nesses alternating with the Tempest's pranks"—to quote Mrs. Martyn. On the one hand, I have determined to record the truth, and naught but the truth; on the other, I shrink from appearing to offer, to the reader of refined sensibility, an *obscene document.* (And, too, I am heartsick, at the distinct possibility, that, amidst my readership, there may well be, here and there, those persons of the masculine gender, who, lacking an intrin- sic purity of character, may, by laborious effort, and much unseemly exercise of the lower ranges of the imagination, *summon forth a prurient gratification,* from these hapless pages!)

Yet, I cannot any longer procrastinate, but must, in a single outcry, publish my unspeakable truth: the which no one amongst the Zinns and the Kiddemasters was ever to know (God having determined to spare them!), and no one in this narrative, indeed, saving Mrs. Delphine Or- mond (whose sentiments on the subject will remain unknown), was ever to guess: that the mysterious Philippe Fox was not, as all quietly believed, the womanly Constance Philippa, in disguise, but, in incontrovertible fact, *a man.*

That he was once the Constance Philippa we have known, and, as such, was consequently female, I do not deny: for during the first two and a half decades of his life he, or rather she, was indeed female. Yet—this does not gainsay the fact that, from approximately 1887 forward, and certainly during the period at hand, Philippe Fox was a man in every particular: that is, no matter the happier life he, or she, had led before, in our belovèd Bloodsmoor, he was a male being in 1899: which is to say, a creature, in our species, *of the masculine persuasion!*

80

Our scene rudely shifts to a setting not far distance from the regally proportion'd Kiddemaster Hall, to one we have not before visited, the smaller, yet still gracious, Mt. Espérance, the ancestral abode of the Ormonds: and to that hellish night, in late October, when, against all the constraints of common decency, an adulterous elopement ensued—*the stealing-away of the former Delphine Martineau, by our blackguard Philippe Fox.*

Well may you recoil in disbelief, and in intrinsic disgust: yet it was so: and I cannot but think, greatly as it grieves my heart, that Miss Deirdre Zinn did irreparable, tho' unintention'd damage, by allowing the Fox creature *one-seventh* of Edwina Kiddemaster's massive fortune. (How much, dear reader, would *one-seventh* of that inheritance be?—granting even the woeful incursions of death taxes? As the precise calculations of the estate's worth were to involve some five years of labor, on the part of Basil Miller and a small, but keenly dedicated, staff of assistants, there being innumerable complications, not excluding the vicious contesting of Sir Reginald Burlingame's will, by certain of his spiteful English scions, and as the final settlement—ah, after *so much* costly labor!—lies well beyond the scope I have determined for myself, of this history, that is, into the Twentieth Century, I believe I shall confine myself to speculation, of the sort rampant, in 1899, amongst the inhabitants of Bloodsmoor, Philadelphia, and the East more generally, as to the final worth of the estate—which is to say (so Basil Miller thoughtfully hazarded), *some eighteen billion dollars,* albeit in the inflated currency of the time, which would divide into more than *two and a half billion dollars,* for each of the sharers! And whilst this staggering sum was by no means accessible, at present, to the Fox creature, he was nonetheless able to borrow from

Philadelphia sources such sums as he calculated might be necessary, to aid him in his immoral scheme—indeed, it was nothing short of scandalous, how gentlemen of divers rank and station, and, one might have thought, of principle, jostled with one another, in shameless eagerness to lend Philippe Fox money!

Our scene having been most reluctantly established, at the sombre Mt. Espérance, so close by Kiddemaster Hall that, upon that gusty October night, the depraved "lover" of Mrs. Ormond could in fact hear the bells of Trinity Church tolling the hour, I suppose there is no recourse but to continue: and to illumine, with as little graphic detail as possible, how the illicit lovers in loathsome stealth fashioned their plan, to circumnavigate the numerous obstacles Mr. Ormond had devised, to keep his wife captive; and how Fox made bold entrance into the very citadel of Mr. Ormond's sanctified marriage, his ancestral home; and how, brandishing a pistol, of o'erlarge proportions, he freed Mrs. Ormond from her turret "sickroom," and, before the astonish'd eyes of her husband, *bore her away into the storm-toss'd night,* in a carriage hired for that very purpose.

Mt. Espérance, erected at about the same time as Kiddemaster Hall, tho' in a less scenic part of the Bloodsmoor Valley, owed much to the Greek Revival style of architecture, then in fashion, yet possessed, withal, a gloomy and even fanciful air, as a consequence of old General Ormond's preoccupation with Rhenish castles of the fifteenth and sixteenth centuries. To the solid, foursquare, and, in my opinion, incomparably eurythmic, Greek Revival structure, the General had caused to be added upward of a half-dozen turrets, in handcut stone; as well as ornamental walls, ramparts, and bastions.

It was in one of the larger turrets, at the northeast corner of the house, that Mrs. Ormond, now a mature woman in her late thirties, and the mother of two children (an angelic girl of seventeen, very pretty, and small for her age; and a somewhat dull-minded, tho' husky, boy of fifteen), was ensconced, by Mr. Ormond's solemn decree. For it was the case, and evidently had been so, for upward of six years, that, inclining as she did toward alternating periods of melancholy and hysteria, and frenzied accusations of divers sorts, made against her husband, Mrs. Ormond was most prudently kept in an invalid's bower: so that the unhappy woman could not cause harm to herself, or, by spreading scandal amongst the household, contaminate others, whom, before her enforced convalescence, she had sought to enlist on her side. (The accusations Mrs. Ormond had made against her lawfully wedded spouse, having to do with his habits of gambling, alcoholic imbibing, and consorting with females of a certain rank, are not the sort I care to enumerate, in a chapter in which there will be, I fear, far too much deference made to vice, as it is. That there may have been some small kernel of truth, to Mrs. Ormond's proposals, cannot be seriously doubted; yet, withal, it was given out by many of Mr. Ormond's gentlemen friends, and business associates, that the hysterical woman exaggerated—an inclination, I am sorry to say, rampant in our sex. In any case, given the sanctity of the marriage vows, and the promise made by the bride, to *love, honor,* and *obey,* as well as the law of the Commonwealth of Pennsylvania, regarding property, the rights of married women, and of women in general, I cannot see but that it was an act of grievous error, on Mrs. Ormond's part, to so noisily protest against her husband's real or imagin'd vices.)

Thus—the once-vivacious *Delphine Martineau,* now the invalided *Mrs. Justin Ormond,* held, by order of her physician Dr. Popock, to a regimen of quiet, bedrest, and medicines of sufficient efficacy, to still her raised voice, and calm her tempestuous spirit.

It was with uncanny alacrity that Philippe Fox, not two days after his arrival in Bloodsmoor, came to know of Delphine Ormond's fate: *how* he made the discovery, and *who* was so reckless as to speak openly with him, I cannot guess.

Brashly he confronted Octavia, and interrogated her: What did she know of Delphine Ormond? Was it true, that the woman was *imprison'd* at Mt. Espérance, under her husband's lock and key? And why did no one, in her family, or elsewhere, spring forth to her aid?

Octavia, flush-cheeked, found it most difficult, simply to meet the Fox personage's eye (for, like the others, she fancied "he" was but Constance Philippa, in grotesque disguise); to be involved with him, in a heated discussion, was exceedingly unpleasant. "I cannot say," Octavia murmured, vigorously fanning herself; and stooping to plant a kiss, on the forehead of her little boy, Lucius Quincy, that winsome child who was, with the passage of time, called more and more frequently simply Quincy, as he expressed an adamant dislike to the name Lucius, for childish, and, it may be, inexplicable reasons. "I cannot say; I do not know; pray, excuse me, Mr. Fox."

Yet he rudely detained her, and, scowling most ferociously, said: "But, Mrs. Rumford, have you no sympathy for the poor woman? No sense of horror, and shock, and concern, at her distress? Have you," and here the abrupt-manner'd individual paused, giving Octavia a most withering look of contempt, "no gossipmonger's *interest?*"

His querying of Malvinia was of course to no avail: for Malvinia knew less than he did, of the lost Delphine Martineau. In a speculative voice Malvinia spoke of Delphine's marriage, many years back: how she, Malvinia, had thought the match a fairly good one, by Bloodsmoor standards, so far as the groom's wealth, family background, and social graces were concerned. "That the marriage has turned out tragically, as you seem to have learned, Mr. Fox, is perhaps less a matter for surprise, or concern, here in Bloodsmoor, than it might be elsewhere," Malvinia said.

And then, with no alteration in expression, she continued: "Our eldest sister Constance Philippa—with whom, of course, you are intimately acquainted—has surely told you of *her* tragic marriage?—the which was not, I believe, lacking in its comedic aspects, tho' the insulted Baron von Mainz was, I daresay, but slenderly amused. *You* have not, by any chance, ever had the pleasure of making the Baron's acquaintance—?"

Mr. Fox's hesitation was scarce perceptible, and his response, tho' hurried, altogether admirable: "I have not, Miss Zinn, had the *pleasure* of making the acquaintance of any European nobleman, in my entire lifetime: that is not precisely the word one might choose."

Samantha was naturally of little aid: she seemed most perplex'd, to be asked to recall Miss Delphine Martineau, from girlhood days; and had no awareness of, or evident interest in, Delphine's fate in subsequent years. "Have you inquired of our mother, Mr. Fox? It is unlikely that she will be helpful, no matter how great the extent of her knowledge: but, of us all, Mother can be relied upon, to *know* the very worst there is to be known, of Bloodsmoor scandals."

Mr. Fox's gaze visibly darkened, and his creased brow grew yet more furrowed. In a low breathless voice he spake: "Of all of you—that woman—*that* lady—of all of Bloodsmoor—*she* cannot be approached!—or, at any rate," he said with a mirthless laugh, the while dabbing at his damp mouth and throat with a handkerchief, "*I* am not the one, to dare it."

Nonetheless, this resourceful stranger was able, within a scant week, to discover a great deal about Mrs. Ormond, by means of the *bribery* of treacherous servants, in Mr. Ormond's employ at Mt. Espérance.

The comely and vivacious young mistress of the household, belovèd by all the staff, had learned, to her horror, that her husband enjoyed a kind of secret, or double, existence, in the "low haunts" and "houses of ill repute," of Philadelphia and elsewhere: this shocking discovery being made whilst Mrs. Ormond was with child, and so dumbfounding her, she sank into a swoon, and suffered a miscarriage, and would perhaps have bled to death, had it not been for the midwifery skills of one of the servants.

Mr. Ormond, made known of his wife's discovery, surprised all the staff by his *fury.* So far was he from repenting, and begging Mrs. Ormond's forgiveness, that he strode violently into the bedchamber, and slammed the door behind him, and locked it, there to confront his wife, in her pallid and weakened condition—the precise words of their dialogue naturally being not known, even to the most inquisitive of servants.

Whereupon there followed many weeks, and months, of turbulence: for, once recovered, Mrs. Ormond would not allow the matter to rest, but oft returned to it, to confront her wayward husband, against all the dictates of prudence. (For Delphine Ormond, née Martineau, remained a *most* spirited woman: at one time a near-match for the lively Malvinia, in wit, and gaiety, and beauteousness of countenance: nor was her intrinsic intelligence dull'd, by numerous pregnancies, miscarriages, births, and female maladies, of a commonplace nature; or by upward of a decade as Mrs. Justin Ormond.) She made her tearful accusations—she ordered the servants to pack her clothes, and those of her children—she threatened "public disgrace," and even, in her recklessness, "legal intervention": whereupon the florid-faced Mr. Ormond naturally opposed her, and shouted at her, and laid hands upon her, until, in one most unfortunate episode—*Mrs. Ormond physically fighting back, with fists and nails* —he rendered her unconscious with a blow!—and afterward carried her bodily to the master bedchamber, snarling at the terrified servants, that they should be gone, and forget about the matter entirely, for it was but a trivial episode.

Some days passed, during which Delphine Ormond did not stir from her bed: only one servant being allowed admittance, to bring her food. Dr. Popock was summoned by Mr. Ormond, to prescribe proper medicines, that Mrs. Ormond might be calmed, and her hysteria dealt with; and it was most unfortunate, that the imprudent wife should seize this opportunity, to recommence her accusations, and threats, and scornful weeping, so that the startl'd Dr. Popock was forced to deal with this agitation. (And I cannot think it to have been a pretty sight: a wife and mother in her early thirties, no longer a naïve bride, ranting against her husband to a third party, and displaying such vehemence, and unsanctioned knowledge, as to make one wonder at her breeding.)

In time, a sickroom was established, in the largest of the turrets of the mansion, and the invalid forcibly brought to it, by Mr. Ormond, Dr. Popock, and two of the more muscular menservants: this chamber declared to be ideal, from the standpoint of salubrity, in that it was freely ventilated, with fresh breezes from the countryside; and its distance from the rest of the house beneficial as well, as Mr. Ormond aptly noted. (For, despite certain failings, of temperament rather than of character, Mr. Ormond was a devoted father to his son and daughter: and trembled to think that, as a consequence of the "madwoman's" ravings, they might form distorted views, of either their sick mother, or himself.)

"And she has been imprisoned, like that, for years?" Philippe Fox exclaimed. "For *years,* Delphine Martineau has been kept under lock and key, and no one has protested, and no one has thought to come to her aid?" Thus the o'erwrought man queried, his eyes dilated, and his voice rising to an unnatural pitch.

The bribed servant did not know how to respond, save to offer, feebly, the explanation that the Martineau family, having suffered other disappointments in recent years, including grave financial losses of an undetermined sort, had not the energy, or the will, or the interest, to intervene; and that the Reverend Hewett, who visited the invalid at least once a fortnight, and dined with Mr. Ormond, did not offer any strong opinion, as to whether the mistress of Mt. Espérance was being *forcibly* detained, or *therapeutically.*

"By God, then—by God, *I* shall act!" Philippe Fox declared, bringing a small but manly fist down, on a tabletop, with such passion that the servant flinched in alarm. "*I* shall act—*I* shall rescue her—and *you* shall help me—and it will be accomplished—it *will* be consummated—I swear, before another week transpires!"

(Tho' in his braggart's impetuosity, Mr. Fox was wildly mistaken, about the *length of time* the abduction would take, he was correct in other particulars; and must be granted some small respect, for the alacrity with which he formed his plan.)

The last glimpse we were afforded of Constance Philippa Zinn, that desperate young woman was, in fact, the bride of Baron von Mainz: tho' she was never to be his—or any man's—*wife.*

Heavily veiled, clad in dark-hued clothes of such unfashionable shapelessness they might have belonged to an elderly woman, or to a nun, Constance Philippa departed from the Hotel de la Paix as stealthily as possible, by night; and, in the morn, might have been observed in one of the small private compartments of the Baltimore & Ohio, headed out of Philadelphia, bound for the West.

She had purchased a ticket for Cleveland, scarce knowing what she did, or even where, precisely, Cleveland was: being so distraught at the time, and so terrified that the Baron might pursue her, that she behaved in a most eccentric manner, not wishing to meet anyone's eye. It is important, I suppose, for us to recall that, in 1880, Constance Philippa had never ventured out of Bloodsmoor *by herself*—it was rare even that she was allowed a solitary walk, in the benign woods and meadows belonging to the Kiddemasters!

Thus, her criminal recklessness, to board a train unescorted, and to plunge into she knew not what!—adventure, or folly, or catastrophe, or serendipitous circumstance. It did not seem to her altogether real, that she was *alone* in a private compartment, on a train hurtling noisily westward: she half fancied, with a lifting heart, that, when she turned, she would see her mother; or her kindly smiling father; or Great-Aunt Edwina, fixing her with an earnest, contemplative gaze; or Narcissa Gilpin; or any of her other chaperons.

Her bosom heaved with a tumult of warring emotions: a gloating *joy* at having escaped the Baron, whom she detested; a paralyzing *terror* at the irreparable nature of her act; a childlike *giddiness,* and *befuddlement,* at the prospect of freedom.

"Freedom!"—so her benumbed lips shaped the alien word, which could not have sounded more strangely to her ear, were it an utterance of *Russian,* or *Turkish. "Is* this freedom!" she murmured, frightened and exhilarated, as the disorderly suburbs of the city fell back, and away; and the lumbering train, gathering speed the while, moved at last into the hilly countryside, so very like the idyllic landscape of Bloodsmoor, yet so very different: unfixed, vigorous, bold, fluid of motion, to her staring eye. *This,* at last, was freedom: the pastoral wooded hills—the deep-shaded ravines—the sun shining with yolklike splendor in the eastern sky—the noise of the train, yet the privileged secrecy of the compartment—the exuberant anonymity of speed—the o'ercoming of Constance Philippa Zinn!

"I shall never go back," the reckless young woman spoke, flinging back her veil, and unpinning her heavy hat, that she might toss it down on the seat beside her. "I shall never be *that person* again."

She then drew forth, from one of her several bags, a pretty miniature case in kidskin, decorated with purple velvet trim, and a scattering of tiny golden roses around an engraving of "The Crystal Palace": this case being from the workshop of the renowned Mathew B. Brady, and a birthday gift from one of her sisters, not a year before. Inside, on the right, Constance Philippa had inserted a likeness of Deputy U.S. Marshal Wild Bill Hickok, taken from a newspaper (this photograph showing the notorious scoundrel when he was in his early thirties, with hair parted in the center of his broad thug's head, and falling limply to his shoulders: its most striking aspect, apart from the grim-brow'd resoluteness of Hickok's expression, and his stance of virile authority, being the weapons he had thrust conspicuously into his belt—two white-handled pistols, and an unsheathed knife, of that wicked variety known as the "bowie"); on the left, she had inserted a somewhat indistinct daguerreotype of Mr. Zinn, seated in a rigid, yet noble, posture, against a backdrop of dark velvet curtains. His posture was no less manly than that of the blackguard ruffian Hickok, but his strong-boned countenance radiated intelligence, and kindliness, and mental ingenuity; and his gaze bespoke paternal love. Yet such was Constance Philippa's callousness, that, with but a moment's hesitation, she removed Mr. Zinn's likeness from the case!—and hid it beneath the discarded hat.

"I shall not—I shall *never*—" she whispered. "Never in this lifetime!"

She recalled, of a sudden, with vertiginous clarity, jumbled scenes of the previous day: the settled, gratified countenance of Mrs. Zinn, beneath a flower-trimmed hat made especially for the occasion, of her eldest daughter's wedding; the somewhat distracted, but smiling, and wondrously handsome, countenance of Mr. Zinn; Reverend Hewett in his ministerial robes, solemnly intoning the words of the sacred rite; the veil of Brussels lace, and the sprig of fragrant orange blossom in the bride-groom's lapel; the innumerable pink tea roses—ah, so lovely!—strewn with gay generosity, in the dining room at Kiddemaster Hall. And the frosted bride's loaf, and Cousin Basil's rollicking song, and Malvinia's proffered bouquet, of wilted tea roses and ugly white weed flowers: "For you, dear Constance Philippa, in celebration of your having been the *first* of the renowned Zinn girls, to surrender your maiden name!"—thus the merry, tho' perhaps o'erwrought, Malvinia, whom Constance Philippa had ached to slap: but, in her new position as the Baroness von Mainz, she had little recourse, but to accept the cruel prank as if 'twere but a jest, and to lay it wordless beside her plate at the table.

Now these images flooded her o'ertaxed brain, and she muttered aloud, *"Never in this lifetime!"* and her palpitating heart so tumultuously responded, she was in terror, for some minutes, that she might suffocate, or faint; and felt the panicked necessity, *tho' in the hurtling public vehicle,* to tear at her tight-buttoned bodice, and at her silken chemise, and, most desperately, at her armorlike corset, that she might loosen it, and forestall collapse.

All this, the while gasping, and whimpering, and murmuring peti-tions to that Creator, Whom in other respects she affected to scorn, the bold young woman did not stint from accomplishing: until her handsome traveling suit was in shocking disarray, and her white *crêpe de chine* blouse ripped, and her chemise trampled on the floor beneath her feet, and her whalebone corset injur'd—the which had cost her parents a substantial sum, having been ordered specially from London, by way of Madame Blanchet: numerous of the resilient laces broke, and the metal eyelets distended, and upward of a dozen bone stays twisted hideously out of shape.

(This rude act, I am moved to declare, was the true emblem of Constance Philippa's *fall from grace,* even more, perhaps, than her virgin flight from the marital bed—the one being *excusable,* or, at the very least, comprehensible, if viewed with necessary respect for the maiden sensibil-ity; the other being *inexcusable,* adjusted from any sane perspective, of Christian humanity and common decency.)

It had been my impression, that Constance Philippa—or, as she soon baptized her disguis'd self, "Philippe Fox"—journeyed with very little delay, to that rough and unseemly, yet, withal, picturesque, part of our great country, known as the Southwest: but, upon closer inspection, this was not the case. She took the Baltimore & Ohio westward to Cleve-land; and, some months later, the Chicago, Burlington & Quincy, west-ward to Chicago (now in her costume, as a gentleman: her waistlong hair tightly bound, and hidden beneath her hat); and, an indeterminate period of time later—perhaps as much as a year—the Illinois Central, westward to Kansas City. Should we wish to scrutinize Miss Zinn's odyssey, with the stern and unblushing eye of the moralist, until, at some indeterminate point, on the map of our states, Mr. Fox is born, in physiological veracity, as well as the fever'd fantasy of a renegade Bloodsmoor girl, it would necessitate the deliberate acquisition of far more intimate material than I wish to pursue: yet I believe it is accurate to say that, in turbulent and unlettered Kansas City, in the early Eighties, Mr. Fox was still naught but Miss Zinn, in ingenious disguise.

What class of individuals Mr. Fox chose to mingle with; how, despite his natural delicacy of manner, and slender physical frame, and soft-pitched voice, he managed not only to deceive *gentlemen,* but *men;* how, brashly o'ercoming the genteel upbringing of his childhood and youth, he had set himself the task of learning shopkeeping, and accounting, and rudimentary law, and horseback riding *with the employment of a man's saddle,* and sharpshooting, and stud poker and monte, and, in general, the agile exercise of his wits (where, as Constance Philippa, he had been forced to spend an inordinate amount of time learning, by rote, certain verses of Shakespeare, Milton, and Longfellow; and the intricacies of crocheting, and fancywork of every sort; and which of the four corners of a calling card to turn down; and how to navigate, with seeming artlessness, the great number of glass goblets, wine and champagne glasses, forks, knives, spoons, and majolica plates, with which one would be confronted, at a formal dinner); how he succeeded, in his vainglorious boast, of *o'ercoming Constance Philippa*—I cannot say: I am quite bewilder'd, and simply cannot say: save to observe that Constance Philippa was not only the sole Zinn sister who would have been capable of such a perverse transformation, but the sole female personage, of all of the Bloodsmoor Valley.

Next we observe Mr. Fox boarding the brand-new Pullman coach of the Kansas Pacific, attired in dandyish costume, his hair now fashionably shorn, and his voice effortlessly low-pitched, tho' possessing a singularly agreeable modulation, in sharp contrast to the plebeian twang and drawl o'erhcard on all sides: Mr. Fox with several items of handsome leatherbound luggage, and fine-tooled calfskin boots, and the poker player's squint of disingenuous friendliness; and the effrontery required, to introduce himself to strangers, in the diner, and in the smoking car *for gentlemen only,* and even in the solemn corridors of the Pullman coach.

He disembarks in Wichita; many months later, accompanied by another gentleman, he somewhat hurriedly boards the Union Pacific, with but a single item of luggage, to disembark in—was it Abilene, or Newton, or Hays City, or Dodge City?—where, as his partner freely promised, there was a great deal of money to be made, not only in poker, but in investments of various sorts, pertaining to the great cattle market, and to the appetite of the "cattle kings," for litigation against one another.

Alone, and again hurriedly, Mr. Fox, some months later, boards another coach of the Union Pacific, a wide-brimmed hat pulled low over his forehead, and his manner lithe and unobtrusive; he would push forward some thousands of miles, to the promis'd Elysium San Francisco, but, alas, his ticket can take him no farther than Grand Junction, Colorado: and it is a ticket obliging him to travel, not in the elegant *Pullman coach,* but in the common *chair car.*

In muddy Grand Junction Philippe Fox surprises us, by allowing himself to be seen, in public, in his shirt sleeves, as a somewhat abash'd clerk in Kearny's Dry Goods Store: then surprises us still further, by his rapid ascent to managerial status in that selfsame establishment (this position allowing him to wear daily a gray broadcloth suit, and to sport a black four-in-hand tie, and even, at selected times, a carnation in his lapel): then surprises us even further, by an abrupt alteration of fortune, which has him a mere "hand" on the great Pitzer ranch, attired in the rudest workclothes, a scant twelve-month later!

Next we glimpse Mr. Fox, or a slender, dark-complexion'd man very closely resembling him, on horseback, in the convivial company of two unshaven, feral-faced, yet, it is to be supposed, trustworthy comrades, headed westward across scrub country—into an uncharted vast region ceded to us by Mexico, in 1848, and not to be admitted to the Union, until 1896, that wilderness now called *Utah:* where, in the cattle market towns of Trickham, and Welcome, he emerges as a "Philadelphia attorney of good family," and a "specialist in railroad law."

Thus Utah: and then south and west to Las Vegas, a booming cattle town: and to Kingman, Arizona: and to the famous South Spring Ranch in Roswell, New Mexico (a kingdom stretching from horizon to horizon, owned by the great John Chisum, then in his late fifties, and rapidly aging). Mr. Fox is by turns a freelance journalist, writing for the Las Vegas *Herald* and the San Francisco *Chronicle;* an itinerate gambler, at poker and monte and horse-racing; again, a shopkeeper; an accountant; an attorney specializing in "cattle trade law." For Mr. Chisum, a millionaire greatly troubled in his mind, as a consequence of unspeakable losses in the Lincoln County War, Mr. Fox is an invaluable solace, proffering his services as a legal advisor, a secretary, and a confidant, assuring the rancher that posterity will sift through the evidence, to determine that *his side* possessed all the moral right: and that the cruel saga of "McSween" and "Murphy" and "Tunstall" and "Pat Garrett" and "Billy the Kid" and "John Chisum" himself will one day be perfectly understood; and the personages justly *condemned,* or *acquitted,* by history.

Of the numerous participants in the bloody dispute, known locally as the "Lincoln County War," only Pat Garrett, the lawman, and Mr. Chisum himself still lived: the colorful Billy the Kid having been shot to death, in nearby Fort Sumner, some years before, at a very young age. "It is a pity, Mr. Fox," old John Chisum solemnly observed, "that you come too late in our narrative, to be acquainted with my boy: for, I am sure, the two of you would have warmly taken to each other. *My boy* I call Billy, tho' of course he was no offspring of my own, save in temperament. Alas, that you have come too late!" To which heartfelt exclamation the discreet "man of law" made no clear rejoinder, save a vague murmur of assent; tho' I do not believe I o'erstep authorial propriety, in stating that Fox was not so entirely lost to all vestiges of good breeding, as to have wished, however fancifully, to "rub elbows"—as the saying goes—with such riffraff as "Billy the Kid"!

Sometime later, after Chisum's death, Philippe Fox appears one day in Silver City, riding a high-shouldered chestnut mare: he gets himself hired as a schoolmaster, until the schoolhouse is burned down. Hired by Mr. Plummer of the Bosque Grande Ranch, several hundred miles to the south, he is again a legal advisor and confidant and something of a bodyguard (his prowess with a six-gun and rifle having improved considerably). There are disagreements; or the Bosque Grande goes bankrupt, as a consequence of falling beef prices; or Philippe Fox too earnestly obeys Mr. Plummer's irascible will, and there are unfortunate casualties amongst the rancher's enemies, and, a sheriff and several deputies hoping to serve a warrant on Mr. Fox, he betakes himself away in the night, across the arid scrubland, and disappears: his horse's hooves, in the dust, visible for some miles and then lifting!—"into thin air," as his pursuers exclaim.

Yet, not long afterward, in the comfortable smokers' lounge of a coach on the Union Pacific, en route to Tucson, Philippe Fox, zestful, smooth-skinned, and conspicuously "well-bred," makes the felicitous acquaintance of both the U.S. Deputy for Southeastern Arizona, Reb Kingston, and his close friend Senator Hank Willis: Mr. Willis even at that late date—1888, 1889—enjoying a relatively healthsome reputation, despite his burgeoning wealth, and questionable methods, for dealing with political enemies, and Papago Indians, and luckless homesteaders "squatting" on his grazing land.

Thus, the years; and the hundreds, and thousands, of miles; and if Philippe Fox ever allows his restive mind to drift eastward, to the Bloodsmoor of old, it is only because his imagination has been spurred by an account, lurid in its particulars, of the first successful execution by means of the remarkable new invention, the electric chair ("the brainchild of the Pennsylvania genius John Quincy Zinn"); or by a much-battered copy of *The Christian House & Home,* by Miss Edwina Kiddemaster, found in the smoldering rubble of a sodhouse, unwisely erected on Mr. Willis's vast property—or on the open grazing lands, the "free lands," contiguous to that property; or by the lightsome spectacle of children shrieking as they play hide-and-seek . . . evoking a memory of four little girls playing together, or five little girls, or, at times, six, when the ringleted and shining-eyed Delphine Martineau was brought to the Octagonal House for an afternoon, to play Puss-in-the-Corner, or whist, or checkers, or casino. And what a little demon Delphine had been, at these games! Not even the quick-witted Malvinia could keep pace with her, save by cheating; and poor Constance Philippa lost every round, her fingers suddenly numb, and clumsy, and her face burning with mortification.

Four hearts in one I do behold, Mr. Fox hummed to himself, as he rode his new-purchased gelding along the main street of Tombstone, "They in each other do infold," he murmured aloud, scarce knowing what he sang, or why, or why it caused his tight fist of a heart to lurch with sudden pain, "I cut them out on such a night/And send them to my heart's delight./I choose you, D., for my Valentine,/I choose you out from all the rest,/The reason is, I LIKE YOU BEST."

And to the San Pedro Valley, and the Rock Bluff Mining & Milling Company, and an ill-considered partnership with "China" Bowdrie, and much confusion pertaining to bank loans, and forged signatures, and bankruptcy procedures; and a kerosene blaze at the Wheel of Fortune Hotel; and several dead men (including "China" Bowdrie); and another alacritous nocturnal flight, this time across the desert toward Naco, over the border—but this time less successful, as Philippe Fox, known locally as "The Fox," is apprehended a few miles west of Bisbee, and hauled back to Tombstone to be hanged.

Yet emerging, not long afterward, in a straw hat trimmed in red, and a coyote-skin vest, and leather boots with hand-tooled silver spurs: the most handsome, and the most "cultivated," of all the U.S. deputy marshals, or their assistants, in the Southwest. Mr. Fox is thus observed at Governor Willis's mansion, dancing with his eldest daughter; and at Governor Willis's great ranch, Casa Grande; dining in the Cattleman's Club, of Phoenix, with the good-hearted, but oft hot-tempered, Reb Kingston; playing poker in Mesa; horseracing in San Luis; leading a posse of some thirty newly deputized "assistants" against strikers at the Painted Rock Mining & Milling Company, which Mr. Willis happens to own.

Kingston is murdered, in a "gambling paradise" in Ajo; Willis is assassinated, whilst dining in his plush-lined private car, on the Union Pacific, en route to the coast; Fox disappears, with $40 cash, and six ounces of gold dust, and his second-best pistol, and the clothes on his back. Even his panic subsides, and refines itself to a cool dull dim ache, and that ache to a rhythm, private as his pulsing blood: *A fox went out on a starlight night, And he pray'd to the moon to give him some light, For he'd many miles to go that night, Before he could reach his den O!*

A maiden lady of advanced years, I count myself necessarily ignorant of the particulars of masculine biology—as, indeed, I am unapologetically ignorant of the particulars of the biology pertaining to my own sex: and to the corporeal life in general. Thus, I shall refrain from commenting, as to whether the gross alterations in Philippe Fox's physical being were a result of relentless masculine *attire,* including close-fitting trousers; masculine *activity* of divers sorts; or rough-hew'd masculine *companionship,* over a period of many years; or, it may be, an unwholesome amalgam of all. Nor can I comment as to whether this obsence transformation, undergone involuntarily, yet not unwillingly, by Mr. Fox (that is, the former Constance Philippa Zinn), was naught but a normal phenomenon, of the sort that might, and does, commonly occur, should any young woman be so brash as to behave, over a protracted period of time, in like wise: or whether there was, from the very first, something *especial* about the Zinn's eldest daughter—not unlike that repugnant manifestation of The Beast, in the otherwise lovely Malvinia. (Should the latter hold, I suppose the Fox case might be of interest to medical science; as cases of Siamese twins, virgin birth, hermaphrodites, giants, midgets, dwarfs, "snake-scalèd" personages, and other sad prodigies of nature, are of interest. Yet, lacking the original *Constance Philippa,* it would not seem to me that *Philippe Fox,* in himself, could be fruitfully examined: for he is but a man: that is, a member of the masculine gender, complete in all physiological requirements as to genitalia, tho' very lightly bearded, and possessing little or no chest hair.)

It is possible that excessive alcoholic imbibing of beer, ale, gin, tequila (a vile Mexican spirit), and whisky, in morbid conjunction with the above (tight-fitting trousers, including leather leggings; high-heeled boots; horseback riding in all weathers; card playing; tobacco; spicy foods of a Mexican and Spanish taint; profanity; hasty and rough toilettes; and the camaraderie of the unlettered), and stimulated throughout by a *coarse, uncivil,* and *primitive frame of mind,* might have been sufficient to cause the hideous transformation, with no blame cast upon inheritance, or congenital disposition. Constance Philippa herself, in her disguise as a man, naturally had no apprehension of what might happen; it should be remembered that, like any "outlaw" (for such the unhappy woman became, with the very act of placing her dressmaker's dummy in the sacred marital bed), she was far more concerned with the present, and with living by her wits, than with any clear sense of what lay before her, or behind. Indeed, this very preoccupation with the *present moment,* and with *action,* so characteristic of our Western frontier, lies so close to masculine habitude of behavior, as to be, perhaps, one and the same inclination!— hence, any thoughtless young woman who subscribes to this habitude, is in danger of being transform'd, late or early, into a *man.*

As early as Wichita, it might have been noted that Philippe Fox's voice was becoming more naturally guttural; by the time he reached Grand Junction, his eyebrows, always heavy, dark, and brooding, had become more prominent still; drifting into the Utah territory, on horseback, in the company of two desperadoes (later discovered to be wanted for murder, in Hays City), he had acquired considerable musculature, particularly in shoulders, upper arms, thighs, and calves. During the months he spent at the South Spring Ranch, it may have been the case that the practic'd eye of old John Chisum "smelled a rat," as it were— this being the result of Mr. Fox's initial dislike of chewing tobacco: but, if so, no taunts or accusations were ever made. "Your Mr. Fox is a true gentleman," little Sallie Chisum told her uncle, sighing mightily. "Ah, would there were more like him!" Whereupon the grizzled cattleman observed, with a droll twinkle of his eye: "Why, my dear, would you wish the world *depopulated,* in a single generation?" Yet, as I have said, there were no taunts, or accusations, nor even ribald hints, pertaining to Mr. Fox's virility, or lack thereof.

With the years, however, Philippe Fox grew e'er-more lean, and hard, and wiry, and stealthy, and resilient. He could sleep in the open, in the raw winds of March; he could sleep on horseback, or standing up; or in jail, wrapped in a filth-encrusted blanket. His gun hand grew uncannily steady, whether he was shooting at slow-circling hawks, or fence posts, or another man, who happened to be shooting at *him:* and his chill dark eyes grew steady as well, and appeared, at times, to have no human need for blinking. His fine dark hair began to gray at the temples, but was otherwise untouched by age. His brow crinkled; and faint white lines appeared about his eyes, and bracketing his mouth; yet, withal, his skin possessed an unusual smoothness, and took very well to the sun. By the time of the tyrannical Mr. Plummer, at the Bosque Grande ranch, Mr. Fox was assuredly a male, in every particular: the growth, and expansion, and forcible protuberance, of the inner female organ, being now nearly complete, and having attained a length of some five or six inches, in repose. (This tubelike structure, of solid flesh, boneless, thickly veined, and evidently lacking in sinew, could attain a remarkable length when flushed with blood, and heat—some nine or ten inches.) That the transformation of the *interior* to the *outer* was so gradual, surely accounts for the fact that Philippe Fox himself scarcely took note of the curious phenomenon, and felt very little intrinsic disgust, as, certainly, he would have done, as Constance Philippa Zinn. Concomitant with the extraordinary protuberance, there was a reversal of growth, in the torso: what had once been the bosom of Constance Philippa, now had flattened, or had, at the very most, a sinewy muscular curve, by no means of a feminine aspect. It must have been the case that, in solitude, Philippe Fox did contemplate the nether stretches of his body, perhaps with amaz'd chagrin, or a morbid brooding, or simple wonderment: but, as Constance Philippa Zinn, he had known so very little about his own body, and had, in truth, never inspected it, or dared touch it, that it is even possible he did not know, with any exactitude, whether a true change had occurred or not; or whether this forcible expansion, of the secret female organ, outward, was perhaps an altogether normal feature, analogous to certain female problems, or conditions, he had heard whisper'd, in Bloodsmoor. Even then, I am pleased to say, a natural gentility reigned, and Mr. Fox shrank from *touching himself,* save in the most pragmatic of ways; and if it occurred to him that this hideous, yet formidable, genital apparatus might be put to some use, in regard to the opposite sex (which, by this time, would pertain to the *female sex*), he happily did not act upon that notion; and was not to indulge his thoughts in such wise, until after his return to Bloodsmoor, when his heart was flooded with hope for the rescue of Delphine Martineau, and his mind with feverish schemes.

And yet—how accidental, his happening upon the notice of Great-Aunt Edwina's death, in a newspaper discarded at his elbow! "The Fox" at that time having beat a very hasty, and graceless, retreat, from Arizona: not many minutes ahead of certain vengeful ruffians, who had already "settled scores," in their words, with the Deputy Marshal Kingston, and Governor Willis. Thus he found himself in the Baldwin Hotel, with but $40 in his pocket, and some gold dust, and a single gun, and the somewhat rumpled clothes on his back; and, but look!—he picked up a newspaper, and leafed idly through it, and came upon the old woman's obituary, and a statement that *bade him return*—with the promise of an inheritance.

Near-penniless tho' he was, and without a friend in the entire West, he stood erect, and flung back his proud head, and exclaimed: *"Never!"*

81

Would that Philippe Fox had held true to his word, and refused to return to Bloodsmoor: but such, unfortunately, was not to be the case.

Tho' "The Fox" had once been counted "as good as dead," by former associates and acquaintances in Arizona, it was with an extraordinary burst of life, and malodorous energy, that he began to appear in the vicinity of sombre old Mt. Espérance; upon several bold occasions, Mr. Ormond being absent, he gained entrance to the house itself, by way of the suggestible kitchen staff. It was his strategy to make contact with the deranged woman by means of *secret missives,* carried to her bower, by a treacherous servant, in which he initially introduced himself, as a companion of Miss Constance Philippa Zinn (now in permanent residence on the West Coast), from whom he had heard a great deal about her: the memory of sweet Delphine Martineau, of the laughing brown eyes and sly dimpled cheeks, being sacrosanct in Constance Philippa's heart.

Thus the bizarre and immoral "courtship" was undertaken; and if we might applaud Delphine's early resistance—the unhappy but loyal wife did not reply to Philippe Fox's first three letters—we cannot but sigh with resignation, as, Fox's entreaties ever growing more emboldened, and more resourceful, the invalid *did* succumb: at the first, stoutly asserting that she was, for better and worse, in sickness and in health, *married* to Justin Ormond, and that, being a Christian woman, she could not take her vows casually; and then, as the weeks progressed, and Fox declared himself by no means a *temporary* presence in Bloodsmoor, but, as her "devoted courtier," as *permanent* a presence as she might wish, the disloyal wife and mother began to waver, and, in her scribbled missives, hint that—perhaps—she *might* respond to his plea, and *study him,* as best she could, on the lawn beneath her window, at an appoint'd time.

Well! I trust I am not being o'erly cynical, in observing that, as Jesus in His wisdom bade us not to gaze upon one another, with lust, lest we commit adultery in our hearts, so it was inevitable, should Mrs. Ormond comply with Mr. Fox's petition, to gaze upon *him,* in outlaw circumstances, lust would be experienced: and adultery committed, in the heart.

And thus it was.

And thus there was initiated one of the ugliest of Bloodsmoor scandals of recent decades: the more intolerable, in that Philippe Fox was not only intimately associated with Kiddemaster Hall, but was amongst Bloodsmoor persons of consequence, *believed to be Constance Philippa in disguise.* So that the criminal elopement, which took place on a rain-lash'd, gusty All Hallows Eve, was widely talked of, as not merely *adulterous,* but *unnatural.*

Alas! I cannot but deem it an act of God's great mercy, that John Quincy Zinn had become, with the darkening skies of autumn, increasingly indifferent to the vanities of the world: so mesmerized with his task of achieving the formula for a synthesis of the *perpetual-motion engine,* and the government's request for unfailing *detonations at a distance,* that he had not the energy to be wounded by his wife's eccentric behavior, in the New England states (where she had joined forces with the hellish pair, Mrs. Abba Goold Woolson, and the "Presidential candidate" Miss Elaine Cottler, in their muckraking activities in the Dress Reform Movement); and had not, of course, the ability to *care greatly,* about his youngest daughter's conversion to Christian standards of charity, love, and peaceableness of spirit, no more than he could, about the sinister Philippe Fox, and his carnal appetites. True, J.Q.Z. was a dying man, and may well have known it: but he directed his limited strength into those channels that transcended the domestic, and the merely finite, with no less zeal than ever, and daily vowed, that *he would achieve his human mission on earth*—before God called him thither.

So it came about, albeit after numerous petitions, that the suggestible Mrs. Ormond consented to peer out the single small window of her room, at her courtier some distance below on the grass: that interloper who did not, of course, dare to appear in wholesome daylight; but only by the stealthy light of the moon. It may have been that the faithless wife and mother imagined her Christian fortitude to be of sufficient quality, to allow her to withstand temptation; but, as she gazed through the window (a small, but quaint, orifice, oval in shape, dimmed by cobwebs, and perhaps twenty inches in circumference), at the comely figure of

Philippe Fox on the lawn below, something wicked evidently transpired in her heart, and the tragedy was conceived.

With self-conscious dignity Philippe Fox emerged from the shadows, to stand boldly in the moonlight, and to lift his handsome face toward the window. Tho' he could not see the object of his illicit regard, the expression of rapt—nay, mesmerized—passion, that radiated across his strong-boned countenance, was unmistakable.

"Delphine!" So he recklessly spoke, lifting one gloved hand: with such compelling force that Mrs. Ormond acted at once in like manner, raising and pressing her hand against the window pane, *that the white palm expose itself,* to the hungry eye of the man below.

The rescue—which was, in truth, no more than a sordid elopement—took place some weeks later, when, by prearrangement, Philippe Fox gained entrance to Mr. Espérance, and informed the astonish'd Mr. Ormond that he had been sent "to fetch his wife back home: for her mother was gravely ill."

Mr. Ormond, a flaccid-faced gentleman in his fifties, with a veined nose, muttonchop whiskers closely trimmed, and a small high rotund belly, grew visibly pale at the sight of this intruder; and shrank slightly from him, tho' Fox's pistol was well hidden inside his coat.

"Sir, I fail to understand," Mr. Ormond said, steadying himself against a chair; "you say you have been sent, *to fetch my wife back home?* But she is *my wife,* sir; and Mt. Espérance is her home."

Philippe Fox advanced upon him, smiling, and, as Mr. Ormond cowered, strode past, to the broad spiral staircase, saying the while: "You are wise, Mr. Ormond, to raise no objections, since Mrs. Ormond is greatly wanted, at home, and I have been instructed, not to return without her. And so I must act quickly; and beg your pardon, that I have no time for idle persiflage." Whereupon the arrogant interloper ascended the stairs, taking them two or three at a time, whilst Mr. Ormond, greatly agitated, could not think, whether to follow him upstairs, or run back down, to seek aid from the servants. (In truth, Mr. Ormond was suffering at this time from an undiagnosed ailment of the nerves, bowels, and spleen, which severely exacerbated his gout, and his temperamental inclination toward the morbid: so that, staring aghast at the lithe, sinuous figure of Philippe Fox, he could not have sworn, whether this creature was a *mortal man,* or a *phantom.*)

While the distraught husband stood paralyzed on the stair, Philippe Fox made his way with great alacrity to the third floor of the mansion, and to the turret: and, commanding Mrs. Ormond to stand back from the door, as much as she was capable, he drew out his gun, and fired once, twice, and a third time, that he might destroy the lock and swing the heavy door open, with no difficulty.

Thus it happened, that rude gunshots shattered the majestic calm of Mt. Espérance, one of the great old homes of Bloodsmoor!—and, to their shame be it recorded, every servant in Mr. Ormond's employ remained in hiding, out of quavering cowardice, or prearrangement with the seducer.

Poor Mr. Ormond screamed in terror for help, that he might be saved from being murdered "by the fiend," but no help was forthcoming.

"It cannot be—I will not allow it—I am master here—I am not to be shot down, in my own house—" the slack-faced husband babbled, the while grasping at the stairway railing, as if he had turned to stone.

Yet, upstairs, Philippe Fox heard not a word, and seemed to have no care, that he might be apprehended and thrown into prison, for this intolerable trespass. "Come, Delphine," he said, his deep voice but lightly trembling, "we have a considerable distance to travel, and the hour is late." He strode into the dim-lit bower, which smelled, alas, of time, and dust, and sickness, and neglect; and with great gallantry extended his arm, that Mrs. Ormond might grasp it. "Come, come! Too many years have passed," Fox murmured.

After but a moment's hesitation, the faithless wife took the proffered arm; and leaned heavily onto it, with a sob; and allowed herself to be led out into the corridor.

Was there ever so crass, so emphatic, so *public* a fall!

Ah, but *was* this woman Delphine Martineau, the pretty, vivacious, brown-eyed miss of so many years ago? A dead-white, drawn, somewhat ravaged beauty, the which one might have had to examine closely, to see it *were* beauty; eyes puffed and red-rimmed, from crying; a mouth that appeared distended, in a smile of fear, or an indecipherable grimace; and, most alarming of all, the once-lustrous mahogany hair now liberally threaded with gray, and *falling in a disheveled tumble to her waist.*

Philippe Fox gazed upon this apparition, and stared, and, inexplicably, felt his heart as wondrously pierced, as if this woman of mature years, and desperate straits, were but a high-spirited girl of seventeen: and no time at all had passed!

"My Delphine!" he murmured, agape, grasping both her cold hands in his. "My girl! It is you! But come, come: the hour is late: our carriage awaits, and the remainder of our lives."

And so, this infamous couple descended the stair, upon which, near the first-floor landing, the betrayed husband now sat, his face gone piteously slack, and his eyes bulging with terror. Unhappy Mr. Ormond! —the wretched scion of a once-great Pennsylvania house! Never was he to recover from the dismayed horror of this All Hallows Eve, on which, as he would babble and mutter to all, a phantom murderer gained entrance to his house, and fired bullets at his head, and made off with his protesting wife—whom he was never to see again.

And so Philippe Fox and his belovèd Delphine vanished from Bloodsmoor: to the Alaskan gold mines, it was said: or to Old Mexico, or Argentina, where they lived like royalty. In any case they never returned to our historic Bloodsmoor, and sent no communications, tho', in time, I scarce know *how,* the sinister Fox managed to collect his share, after taxes and attorneys' fees, of the great Kiddemaster inheritance.

82

It was upon the occasion of the reading of her aunt's eccentric will, that Mrs. Prudence Zinn, knowing herself again disinherited, experienced a most queer, and pleasantly lightsome, release in her heart. So I am free —I am *freed,* the astonish'd woman thought, all the while maintaining her posture of rigidity, and her expression of stolid, and, as it were, regal disdain. Tho' these words pierced her consciousness with an uncanny authority, and tho' she scarce comprehended their import, she knew them to be incontestable; and prophetic.

"I am freed—*of them.*"

Alas, how shall we describe the trajectory of Romance? How shall we, obliged to toil in mere words, seek to illume the fleet, fluttering, gossamer sensations, elusive as the hummingbird, that course along the veins, and swell the captive heart, of the credulous? It may have been, that, seated in the Golden Oak room of her father's great house, hearing with but a detached interest the lurid tale (which did not, in truth, surprise Prudence as much as it surprised the others: tho' she would not have guessed the *rejected infant* to have been Deirdre), whereby Edwina Kiddemaster made public her *disgrace,* yet, withal, her vainglorious *nobility,* Prudence cast her mind back, and back, and back, to a fateful meeting in Frothingham Square, in the study of her godfather Mr. Bayard. (Alas, long dead!—long dead.) It may have been that the now-agèd woman half closed her eyes, not in pious reverence, in regard to her deceased aunt, but in recollection of the moment in which her amaz'd eyes fell upon the manly form, and handsome countenance, of young John Quincy Zinn—then a mere boy of twenty-six: so tall! so vigorous! so animated! so *unknown!*

And, it may have been, as Basil Miller's sonorous voice unfolded the remarkable confession, of that other doomed romantic heart, Prudence Zinn enjoyed, with distant amusement, the recollection of one or two stanzas of verse, composed by a woman now long deceased—ah, how *very* long, it would not do to consider!—gay, tinkling, blithe, convivial, feverish, frantic: *I am immortal! I know it! I feel it! Hope floods my heart with delight! Running on air, mad with life, dizzy, reeling, Upward I mount—faith is sight, life is feeling, Hope is the day-star of night*— And on and on the happy words tumbled, a girl's voice, a girl's shouting exuberant voice, gradually dimming, and fading, to be replaced by young Miller's words, which seemed to Prudence both pitiless, and pitiable.

I am freed of *them,* Prudence inwardly declared, and of *it.*

One day, not many months before, whilst sipping her morning coffee, and perusing the pages of the Philadelphia *Inquirer* (a newspaper she read half secretly, in obedience, still, to the dictates of her deceased father, who had entered into a bitter feud, as a consequence of political differences, with the paper's owner, and expressly forbade it on "Kiddemaster soil"), Prudence came by chance upon an article, and a photograph, of such offensiveness, that she nearly spilt—nay, she *did* spill—her coffee, and heard herself laugh angrily aloud.

For here, exposed to the public's condemning gaze, and, doubtless, to its merry scorn, were some half-dozen *women*—not wishing to be termed *ladies*—who declared themselves campaigners for Dress Reform, and Woman Suffrage, and Equal Rights, and something most baffling, to Prudence's mind, a *Single Moral Standard.* Egregious enough, such a blatant display of folly—and, in their midst, none other than *Parthenope Brownrrigg,* of old!

Inwardly quaking, Prudence adjusted her reading glasses, and hurried to a window, that she might, with the aid of daylight, the better to read the extraordinary article: only to be the more gravely shaken, yet moved to childish jeering laughter, by the discovery that one of Parthenope Brownrrigg's younger companions, a woman by the name of Miss Elaine Cottler, had stepped forth publicly, with the support of the others, *to place herself as a candidate, for the Presidency of the United States!*

Prudence closely studied the countenances of the women, and was disturbed, in the case of old Miss Brownrrigg in particular, to find them not greatly differing from her own—from her own, that is, and those of her numerous female relatives. One or two of the women were most aggressively plain; one was erect of carriage, and remarkably attractive—this being, Prudence gathered, the bold Miss Cottler; all were smiling—brash and arrogant smiles, indeed, considering the circumstances of their being photographed: for, to their collective shame, these women were *under arrest as common offenders, in Hartford, Connecticut.*

"It should not—it must not—it cannot be allowed!" Prudence declared, thrusting the page of offensive newsprint from her, and feeling herself so o'ercome (for she was now in her seventy-sixth year, and frequently short of breath), she had need to be seated, and to calm herself in repose, for upward of ten minutes.

"It will be the end," Prudence murmured, scarce knowing what her words meant, "the end, of *everything*."

Yet, as her aunt's lengthy confession drew to its close, Prudence saw again that coarse photograph, and, far from being inclined to join with the others, who were now freely weeping (old Narcissa Gilpin sobbing loudest of all), she was struck with a curious wonderment, that she could recall not merely the outline of the picture, but the actual faces of the women: she could recall, with amazing clarity, certain of the statements of the Dress Reform Movement, and those of the National Women's Suffrage Association, and Mrs. Abba Goold Woolson, and Miss Elaine Cottler, and one or two more.

This extraordinary recollection flooded upon her, and for a very long time she ceased to hear her nephew's strained voice; or, indeed, the voice of old Edwina, straining through it. How many minutes passed, I cannot say, nor could Prudence have said: but, as Basil concluded the document, and the assemblage in the room murmured aloud, and the more liberally wept, Prudence Zinn spoke to herself in a startl'd voice, in which some reproach sounded: "But, I suppose, I am too old now, to run for President!"

83

Tho' it is but an accident of Fate, and of time, I am inclined to think it emblematic, that my chronicle draws to a close on the night of January 31, 1899: and that it concludes, not in the Octagonal House, nor in the austere splendor of old Kiddemaster Hall, but in the homely and cluttered cabin above the gorge, the famed workshop of J.Q.Z.!

For here, as a snow-driven midnight approaches, we find a solitary figure; and witness the caprices of her shadow, alternately shrinking and looming against the walls, in the eerie light cast by a kerosene lamp.

A thief, an intruder, a spy of Edison's? An idolatrous disciple?

Or one of Mr. Zinn's helpmeets?

Not Samantha, who once loved her father so dearly, and so gratefully subordinated her will to his—for Samantha, alas, is a loyal wife, and a doting mother, many times over, who is, at this very moment, keeping a merry vigil with her husband, by the fireside, in their home in Guilford, Delaware: kissing, and laughing, and holding hands, and preparing to drink *an alcoholic* toast, to the New Year.

Nor Mrs. Zinn, who has, by this date, virtually abandoned her household, to take up residence, with her girlhood companion Miss Brownrrigg, in a ladies' hotel on Beacon Hill, but a block from the brownstone headquarters for the Dress Reform Movement: so brutally severing herself from her former life, that the telegram, containing the news of Mr. Zinn's rapid decline, will go astray, having been addressed to *Mrs. John Quincy Zinn,* and not to *Miss Prudence Kiddemaster!* (Indeed, the callous woman will barely return to Bloodsmoor in time for the funeral.)

Nor does the lone figure belong to a simple servant girl, commanded by the weakening Mr. Zinn, to rummage through the great disorder of papers on his workbench, and locate the sheet of paper containing his most recent calculations, and bring it to him; that, on his sickbed (in truth, his deathbed), he might feverishly complete the formula, of the invention *to save the world!*

Nay, it is none of these personages, but Deirdre herself: our brave and beauteous heroine of old, Deirdre Kiddemaster (for such she is now called—with a sentimental, if not a legal, authority), the new mistress of Kiddemaster Hall!

That our sensitive young lady has yet to resolve the veritable tempest in her heart (as to whether she will accept the honorable proposal of Dr. Lionel Stoughton, or the coarse entreaty of Hassan Agha), and that, indeed, much remains unresolved, in her soul, cannot concern us here: for our concern is solely with her mission, in Mr. Zinn's service, and with its puzzling outcome. (Tho' this brief chapter, of tenebrous shadows, and a kerosene lamp's feeble glow, surely contains the clue, as to which man she will marry.)

The waxen-skinned John Quincy Zinn, lying abed with the chill dignity of a tomb effigy, and wondrously alert, in his quick-darting thoughts and suspicions, had, not an hour ago, summoned his adopted daughter to the Octagonal House, and to his side: that, in a low, hoarse, methodical voice, he might bid her go at once to his workshop, despite the late hour, and the growing blizzard, to seek out a certain sheet of paper, covered in scrawled calculations, *and bring it to him:* for, he feared, he would not live out the night, and, in any case, he would not be strong enough, upon the morn, to journey out there, and complete his great work.

"I shall never finish it," he said, in his reproachful voice, gazing at the frightened Deirdre from out his sepulchral eyes, "I shall never finish it *there.* But, perhaps, in the comfort and sanctity of my bed, and with *your* assistance—"

Deirdre acquiesced at once, giving no thought to the howling wind, or to her own premonition, that *something tragic* would occur, before dawn: on the contrary, the young heiress stooped to kiss her father on his gaunt, fevered brow, and to prop up the goose-feather pillows behind him, that he might be more comfortable. (Alas, J.Q.Z. rarely slept any longer!—but spent the interminable nights sitting, rather than lying, abed, entertaining dreams with his eyes open, the which, in his own words, proved paltry and disappointing, set beside the work that awaited him in the cabin: the final calculations pertaining to the *perpetual-motion machine,* and its principle, as applied to the phenomenon of *atom-expansion,* or *detonation*—a concept so foreign to my feeble woman's brain, I cannot pretend to describe it.)

"The victory is close at hand, and will be so sweet!—ah, so very sweet, I halfway think it might prolong my life!" the poor man murmured, for the moment so agitated, he grasped Deirdre's slender wrist in his chill fingers, and smiled upward at her. "For, do you see, it is an invention to save the world—to save our world—from all harm—from wickedness—from the Devil's camp—which will have no defense against *us*, once the explosive mechanism is perfected. My dear daughter—do you see?"

"I am not certain, Father, that I *see*," Deirdre said, covertly wiping a tear from out her eye, "for your inventions, like your genius, have long been beyond my ability to grasp. But perhaps it is not necessary for me, as your daughter, and, should you wish, your loving nurse, to *see*, or to *comprehend*: perhaps it is only necessary for me to obey."

"The device, once triggered, will explode effortlessly—and endlessly—and cannot, in fact, *be halted*," Mr. Zinn said dreamily, "and that is its beauty, that neither we, nor our diabolical enemies, might halt it. I fully realize, how the ignorant scoffers joke—how they prattle of crude sorcery, and black magic, and mere wishes!—for it is incomprehensible to them, that the invisible air cushioning the earth is, in fact, a dense element, and that its unique molecular constitution may be known to us, and, by our wizardry, unlocked—unlocked, I say, in *perpetual motion*, once the device be tripped. The spectacle is so vast, it cannot be contemplated: *an endless series of detonations*. And, once begun, not to be halted; for tho' our enemies see their predicament, and the tragedy of their lot, tho' they beg for mercy, tho' we should even wish to extend them mercy—it will not be possible: nay, it will not! it *will not!* And now, my dear daughter, do you see?"

Deirdre stooped to kiss the old gentleman's fever'd brow, not shying away from the dagger-shaped birthmark, which, in sharp contrast to his waxen skin, glowed a fiery red, and appeared to throb, with an especial vehemence, at this juncture in time: the dutiful daughter stooped, and kissed his brow, and whispered consolingly: "I begin to see, dear Father."

Alas, how strangely *brooding* J.Q.Z. has become, in recent years; how given to long silences, and secretive ruminations, and sudden outbursts of savage, mirthless laughter! The gratifying success of certain of his inventions (submarines, missiles, and e'er-more powerful bombs, of inestimable value in the war against the Spanish enemy), seems to have made very little impression upon him: a matter for pride, and gloating, rather more on the part of his manufacturer associates and investors, than on his own. (For, having been gifted with one-seventh of the famed Kiddemaster fortune, what possible need has this elderly gentleman for additional wealth? What energy, even, to calculate it?)

Most surprising of all, in his family's eyes, and, I am bound to say, in my own, was his irritable rejection of membership to the *American*

Philosophical Society!—those gentlemen having thought, in their igno-rance, that this long-delayed honor would be eagerly seized, by the Bloodsmoor genius. Mr. Zinn's relatives, not excluding his daughters, had supposed that the announcement of his election, at long last, would cheer him, in the midst of his preoccupations: but, quite the contrary, he had deemed the news, in his own words, *contemptible!*—and would not have had the elementary courtesy, to trouble to reply to the telegram, had not the new mistress of Kiddemaster Hall, conscious of the obligations rank and station confer, insisted. "I am deeply saddened, Father, that you take this pleasant news so indifferently," Deirdre said, daring to lightly chide the old man, who had torn the offending yellow paper in two, "but I must beg you, to at least allow *me,* to decline the honor as courteously as possible."

Whereupon Mr. Zinn paused, and, his skeletal face for a moment illuminated with a rare smile, said: "Ask them—demand of them—the fools!—ask them how they fancy, *they have the right,* to confer honors upon *me!*"

"Why, Father," Deirdre exclaimed, in genuine surprise, "you must know, the gentlemen mean only well—they mean only to please. If they have been somewhat tardy in their action, if, being but human, they have not until now adequately grasped the magnitude of your genius—"

"If, if! If, indeed!" Mr. Zinn laughed softly. "My dear daughter, I know not *if,* and have no interest in *if*—not my own, and certainly not another's."

So, her cheeks blushing, Deirdre left the bedchamber, to compose a message for the Society, declining the great honor, with regret—"with infinite regret," as her telegram read, "as a consequence of my extreme and continued immersion in my work," and signed it with her father's name.

Other honors were flung at J.Q.Z.—a "permanent" place in the Hall of Distinction, in Washington; an election to the Royal Society, and to the International Association of Scientists and Humanists—but Deirdre was prudent enough, not to trouble her irascible father: for his energies were swiftly waning, and he oft voiced the doubt, that he would be allowed to live long enough, to perfect his *atom-expansion* device.

In a mournful yet dignified voice Mr. Zinn spoke thusly: "I would not be so troubled, Deirdre, if I believed that another inventor, or man of science, might follow, to peruse my scribbled calculations: but, alas, I am obliged to be realistic. I am in my seventy-second year, and have labored in the service of my country, and of humankind, for upward of five decades; as Mr. Emerson solemnly bade us, to live not in ourselves, but in the greater World-Soul, which toils to perfect itself through us. Yet I have no disciple to follow me; nor even an apprentice. And my belovèd wife— But, no: I shall not speak of her, at this time." And the agèd man sighed, and closed his tear-dimmed eyes, his long thin fingers interlocked in a gesture suggestive of prayer.

"So far as I might help you, Father," Deirdre said hesitantly, "tho' I am painfully aware of my lack of scientific and mechanical knowledge—"

"Ah, to be so close, so very close!" Mr. Zinn interrupted. "So *very* close, to consummation!—and yet, so far. For it is all the difference between the Hell of our uncompleted labors, and the Heaven of our perfected discoveries—a mere scribbled formula, on a piece of foolscap!"

"I do not think you will fail, Father," Deirdre said softly. "You must have hope. Our Lord would not have drawn you hither, do you think, only to allow you to fail, so near triumph?"

Mr. Zinn opened his eyes, and blinked, and stared at his soft-featur'd daughter. "You speak of Our Lord? But do you, in truth, believe?"

Deirdre's cheeks heated, and, turning aside, she preoccupied herself, with an ordering of the bottles and vials on the bedside table, that took some minutes. "I believe," Deirdre murmured, "what it is, that I am obliged to believe."

"*My* belief," Mr. Zinn said, in a bemused voice, as he lifted his hands to contemplate—the knuckles so enlarged, the fingers hooked like talons!—"has naught to do with Our Lord, and only to do with myself: and, I fear, it is *myself* that weakens, not the Lord. For could He grasp a pen? Could He calculate a formula? Is it His wish, to detonate the atom, and release its miraculous powers of destruction? I have seen no evidence, my dear!—and, meaning no blasphemy, I do not think that the sovereign government of these United States, in its militant vigil against evil, can have o'ermuch faith in *Him*—or in that benevolent World-Spirit, of which Mr. Emerson so warmly spoke."

"It is unlike you, Father," Deirdre said slowly, "to speak in such a way. Indeed, it is *very* unlike you."

Mr. Zinn turned his pale gaze upon her, and stretched his lips, in a thin forgiving smile. His once-luxuriant hair had sadly thinned; and his once-bountiful beard now consisted of but a few silvery wisps, straggling to his bony chest. The ravaging disease had so greatly aged him, it would not have seemed unlikely, to be told that he was upward of ninety years of age, or nearing one hundred: alas, how tragically alter'd, from that husky young giant, who had strode with such bucolic confidence, in the drawing rooms of fashionable Philadelphia, so very long ago!

Yet the intrinsic wisdom of the *soul* remained, and spoke its own language, from out the dying man's eyes; and the gentle smile remained, forgiving Deirdre her ignorance, or her impertinence. When, at last, Mr. Zinn did deign to speak, it was in a voice subdued by melancholy, and by paternal disapprobation: *"Unlike* me! You fancy that it is *unlike* me! But, my girl, you do not *know* me; and cannot presume to speak."

Yet, lacking a true disciple, or an apprentice familiar with his work, or, it may be, even a genuine *scion,* born of his own blood, Mr. Zinn in his extremity was forced to summon Deirdre, late on the eve of the New Year, of 1900, and to bid her seek out, for him, certain sheets of foolscap in the cabin; and, you will be pleased to learn, the young heiress obeyed with alacrity, not minding the hour, or the freezing winds that swept up from the river, or the sickly man's importunate manner.

Alone, ah! alone!—thus Deirdre thought herself, with some bemusement, and, I am afraid, some self-pity, as, in the disorder'd workshop, she sought Mr. Zinn's papers with increasing desperation; the while the flame of the kerosene lamp flickered, and her distended shadow leapt and frolicked on the walls, as antic as Pip of old; and she could not prevent herself from shivering most convulsively.

She snatched up one sheet of paper, to examine it, and let it fall; and another; and yet another. It would be, Mr. Zinn had patiently explained, but an ordinary sheet of foolscap, with some nervous doodlings in the margin: simple and childlike representations of suns, and moons, and exploding planets, and perhaps multipetal'd flowers, and molecular structures freely imagined, and he knew not what else!—for his pen was oft playful, even as his brain feverishly worked. "Ah, here!—here it is," Deirdre murmured aloud, only to examine the paper closer to the flame, and find herself mistaken. "Or here!—but no—no—again I am wrong."

Even by the uncertain light of a kerosene lamp, the famed cabin bore mute but eloquent witness to the heterogeneity of mind, of its presiding genius: what a miscellany was displayed, of coils of metal, and wire, and glass tubing; and part-completed machines, both small and large; and scatter'd sheets of paper, aswirl on the workbench and floor both, in veritable waves! There was the domestic still J.Q.Z. had invented, but had never troubled to patent, for the desalinating of water; there was the modestly proportioned steam engine, which had not worked for years; there, on all sides, the numerous "automatic" devices J.Q.Z. had tinkered with, in the years before Congress bestowed such grants, and such prestige, upon him—what a welter of springs, knobs, cranks, pipes, chains, weights, and pulleys!

Doubtless Deirdre would have greatly enjoyed perusing her father's laboratory, had she more leisure, and were the circumstances more congenial: but, at the moment, as the minutes pitilessly sped past, and the hours of the old century waned, she continued to shiver despite the warmth of her fur-lined scarlet cloak, and felt the weight, and the great variety, of the *things* surrounding her, to be somewhat disorienting. Alas, that she could not locate the wretched scrap of paper, and bring it triumphantly back!—and betake herself to bed, and to some semblance of tranquillity! But she could not seem to find the desired item, and it struck her as an ironical note, that, as her father's helpmeet, she was at once his *favorite,* now; and, indeed, *the last of the Zinn daughters.*

For Malvinia now was married, and living with her much-devoted Mr. Kennicott, a sufficient distance away, in Rhode Island: to which the happy couple had retired, that they might escape the flurried publicity surrounding Mr. Kennicott's fame, as "The Young Longfellow," and that Malvinia might, all modestly, resume her thespian activities—now on a much reduced and agreeably *amateur* scale, with no pressure put upon her to excel, or to reap commercial gain; and Octavia was so immersed in her duties as mother, and mistress of Rumford Hall (which hallowed interior she was having completely renovated and refurbished, by the most skilled carpenters, artisans, and decorators, in the East), and *wife-to-be,* that, of late, she had but scant time for her ailing father, and, I am distressed to say, but a perfunctory interest, in her old household and its vicissitudes.

And, to no one's regret, Constance Philippa had, now, *quite* disappeared.

As for Samantha, it seems that, of late, she had resumed her activities in the workshop, alongside her belovèd Nahum, and was now dabbling with so divers an assortment of gadgets, mechanisms, and contraptions, I am reluctant to dignify them with the title *inventions.* After an interregnum of some years, this impulsive young woman was in the midst of constructing models for a *baby-mobile* (an apparatus not very different from a *baby-stroller,* albeit that the baby's, or toddler's, feet were free to touch the ground, and a railing encircled the seat, so that the enterprising tot could, if he wished, propel himself by the action of his legs: "In this way," Samantha argued, "both *self-locomotion* and *self-reliance* will be practiced, in a single gesture"); and a *self-filling pen* (wherein ink came somehow from within the stem, and, by a gravitational urging I cannot pretend to understand, flowed ingeniously to the point, with no need of replenishment, for periods of as long as *six weeks!*); and a *bicycle-umbrella* (this somewhat awkward object being portable, and made of near-translucent rainproofed cloth, to be fitted in place over the rider, to protect him or her from the vicissitudes of the weather). In addition, Samantha was experimenting with a *substitute for glue,* to consist of fine-ground pebbles, pitch, flour, and water; and a *timed kitchen,* wherein an ingenious network of wires, strings, wheels, and pulleys, attached to a clock, would allow the housewife to govern her kitchen by remote control, as it were—for what earthly purpose, I cannot fathom! Her notion of *pulp-paper napkins, bandages,* and *diapers,* to be used but a single time and then freely tossed away, was prized by her husband as an excellent idea indeed: yet he feared, rightfully enough, that no decent womenfolk should wish to be so visibly spendthrift, as to discard that which might be laundered, and ironed, and used again—and again.

Thus, Samantha was once again absorbed in her own life, some distance away in Delaware: and responded but vaguely, to overtures made to her by Deirdre, that she visit Bloodsmoor more frequently.

Alone!—alone of all the Zinn girls!—and, alas, on this night of pitiless howling winds! Yet—am I not grateful at last to be so? the shivering young woman bethought herself, as, to little avail, she continued her search; made increasingly difficult as the minutes passed, and her gloved fingers grew stiff from the cold. For whilst I might delight in the companionship of so cheery a sister as Octavia, or so enterprising a sister as Samantha, I should not, in any case, wish my malevolent spirits back; and I am not prepared—indeed, I am most decidedly *not prepared*—to leap, with unseemly haste, into the condition of *wifehood.*

(That Deirdre was beleaguered, even at this crucial moment, by recollections of Dr. Stoughton's earnest countenance, and Hassan Agha's smold'ring black eyes, should not, I think, discredit her, in the reader's stern judgment: for she was, despite the relative maturity of her age, and the elevation of her rank, but a *woman* in her sensibility, to be forgiven romantic excesses, inappropriate otherwise. And tho', at this time, she sensed a certain ineluctable *swaying* of her heart, in the direction of one gentleman, she surely did not, and could not, know, with any certitude —this being a grave decision to be made some months later, well into the spring of 1900; and in that temporal realm into which I have forsworn peering, for purposes of historical and structural symmetry, and in the interests of discretion.)

Thus, it is difficult to determine, whether the accident with the kerosene lamp was a consequence of Deirdre's *distracted thoughts,* or her *stiffened fingers,* or, as she herself adamantly believed, *a sudden intrusion from Spirit World* (the which, alas, she had believed o'ercome, forever!): or whether, in some solemn wise, as I shall not dare to inquire into, it was an *Act of God,* merely employing Deirdre as an instrument. (For I cannot think that Our Heavenly Father was greatly pleas'd, as to the recent surprising statement of J.Q.Z., relative to His, and J.Q.Z.'s, contrasting prowesses, in the making of explosives.)

In any case, the confus'd episode transpired in this way: Deirdre believed she had, at last, located the crucial sheet of foolscap; in her zeal to ascertain whether this was so, she brought it very close to the singed globe of the lamp; whereupon, by her own testimony, *a spirit hand of near-miniature proportions, possessing prehensile fingers, and o'erlong nails not unlike claws, grasped hold of her wrist, and forced the paper down inside the glass, and into the flame!*—with the immediate consequence, that it burst into greedy licking flames, and so terrified the young woman, that she dropped the lamp, and caused a larger conflagration to ensue, amidst the swirls and eddies of J.Q.Z.'s valuable debris!

Yet, such was Deirdre's courage, and moral fibre, that, after her initial panic, she summoned the rational strength—I know not from whence!—*to stamp out the spreading flames,* with her pretty kidskin boots: and so to save the greater part of the workshop, encompassing most of the machines, from destruction.

This she did, panting the while, and sobbing aloud, with fright, and, doubtless, with consternation, for the outrage that had transpired: and, it may have been, she felt some healthsome anger as well, that any spirit—even that, she guessed, of a furry, mischievous little imp!—should dare to touch *her,* in her new position as mistress of Kiddemaster Hall.

So the fire was extinguished; and the laboratory saved, for posterity; but, unfortunately, the critical sheet of foolscap was destroyed—a heartrending loss which, I hope I am not intrusive in saying, did not affect J.Q.Z.'s fate, or hasten the speed of his demise, since, it is estimated, the unhappy man expired, *at the very moment of the conflagration.*

But Deirdre did not know that, of course, as, shaken, and rueful, and strangely exhilarated (whether as a result of the drunkard pumping of her blood, or the bracing midnight air), she contemplated the smoking disorder about her, and racked her imagination, as to how she might hope to explain the loss to her invalid father. That it was *irreparable,* and *tragic,* she could not doubt; that it would not do for her to say, that another inventor might one day duplicate the formula, she certainly knew.

"And, should it *not* be duplicated," the excited young woman declared, "—will I not then have *saved the world?* Spared us, from the madman's dream?"—tho' in the next breath she chided herself, and bit her lip, for having uttered so blasphemous a statement.

84

The history of the remarkable Zinn family thus closes, upon the very stroke of midnight, of an eve long past: the death of Bloodsmoor's most eminent personage sadly upon us, and the unseemly *exhilaration*, in the very heart of *blasphemy*, of our heroine Deirdre.

Beyond this I cannot—indeed, I do not wish—to venture, for the Twentieth Century is not my concern. That thankless task I leave to the young, and to those yet unborn!—for whom, it grieves me to say, these immortal lines of Mr. Longfellow may constitute more a *riddle*, than a gladsome *certitude*—

> Tell me not, in mournful numbers,
>   Life is but an empty dream!
> For the soul is dead that slumbers,
>   And things are not what they seem.
> Life is real! Life is earnest!
>   And the grave is not its goal;
> Dust thou art, to dust returnest,
>   Was not spoken of the soul.

ABOUT THE AUTHOR

Joyce Carol Oates is the author of fourteen novels and many volumes of short stories, poems, and essays, as well as plays. She has been honored by awards from the Guggenheim Foundation, the National Institute of Arts and Letters, and the Lotos Club, and by a National Book Award in 1970 for her novel *them*. For many years her short stories have been included in the O. Henry Prize Stories collection, and she has received the O. Henry Special Award for Continuing Achievement. She is a member of the American Academy and Institute of Arts and Letters, and currently teaches at Princeton University.

A NOTE ABOUT THE TYPE

The text of this book was set by a cathode-ray-tube system in a facsimile of the Linotype face called Baskerville. This face is a reproduction of type cast for the English printer and designer John Baskerville (1706–1775).

Baskerville began his work in 1757 and became printer to Cambridge University. He introduced faces that we now call modern, with level serifs and emphasis on the contrast between thick and thin lines. His style influenced the Didot family in France and Bodoni in Italy. The revived Linotype Baskerville was cut under the supervision of the English printer George W. Jones.

This book was composed by Haddon Craftsmen, Allentown, Pennsylvania, and printed and bound by R. R. Donnelley & Sons Company, Harrisonburg, Virginia.